And Less Than Kind

And Less Than Kind

Mercedes Lackey
Roberta Gellis

AND LESS THAN KIND

Copyright © 2008 by Mercedes Lackey & Roberta Gellis

A Baen Books Original

Baen Publishing Enterprises
P.O. Box 1403
Riverdale, NY 10471
www.baen.com

ISBN-10: 1-4165-5533-1
ISBN-13: 978-1-4165-5533-9

Cover art by Larry Dixon

First printing, April 2008

Distributed by Simon & Schuster
1230 Avenue of the Americas
New York, NY 10020

Library of Congress Cataloging-in-Publication Data

Lackey, Mercedes.
    And less than kind / Mercedes Lackey & Roberta Gellis.
        p. cm.
    ISBN 1-4165-5533-1
    1. Great Britain—Kings and rulers—Succession—Fiction. 2. Great Britain—History—Tudors, 1485-1603—Fiction. I. Gellis, Roberta. II. Title.

    PS3562.A246A85 2008
    813'.54—dc22

                                                                    2007051442

10   9   8   7   6   5   4   3   2   1

Pages by Joy Freeman (www.pagesbyjoy.com)
Printed in the United States of America

And Less Than Kind

Prologue

The Underhill sky had no sun, no moon, no stars and yet a shining twilight gave light enough to see. No direct light means no shadows. Still a small crouching shadow slipped along the broad road, smoothly paved with glistening blocks of deep red marble. In the silver light, the road looked like a river of blood, but it was firm enough ... except in a few spots where it was suddenly glutinously liquid.

In other ways it was a dangerous road to travel. From time to time monsters leapt from between the dark bushes that bordered the road. Most were stopped short by a magical tether so that they fell back into the darkness, choking; one or two were free and leapt onto a traveler made unwary by previous protection.

Nor was that the only hazard. Slender stalks slid upward from between the stones and caught at a traveler's legs. They had sharp edges, those stalks, like sharp little teeth, and their bite drew blood—but only a little. The bite was not dangerous, but if the walker tripped and fell, a myriad more stalks would emerge and suck the victim dry.

Only the hazards did not affect the crouching shadow, which slipped along the road hardly darkening the blood red surface. If any had noticed it and watched, a slight hesitation would have been noted when the huge black bulk of Caer Mordwyn palace

1

rose to block further passage. However, there was no way around, and no way back either.

Behind was a wall of force. On either side of the open gates—the gates were always open—were two enormous heads with gaping mouths. Any who turned aside from the road, who sought to escape the entry into Caer Mordwyn palace, were swallowed.

Having hesitated once, the crouching shadow did not hesitate again. Crouching even smaller, the shadow went forward, up the black marble steps veined in red, past cackling witches and grunting ogres, slipping around boggles and banshees, who moved upward on the wide stairway and crowded the entryway into Prince Vidal Dhu's throne room.

The walls were polished black marble, adding to the oppressive darkness but yet able to reflect light; they were veined with red chalcedony that gave forth a sullen glow. The ceiling was gold, not bright enough to relieve the oppression but well able to distribute the red glare from the candelabra suspended from the ceiling.

Like the road to the palace, the center aisle was paved in red blocks that had a wet, bloodlike shine. At the end of the aisle was a dais, three steps high, on which were two thrones; one centered, huge, built of human bones, the grinning skulls facing Vidal's subjects. The other was smaller, almost delicate and pretty until one was close enough to see that it was made completely of hands, small hands, those of women and mostly children.

On that smaller throne was a woman with golden hair, cut low on her forehead in a thick fringe; her eyes were bright green, but strangely without depth, and there was something odd about the white skin and brilliant red lips—a porcelain perfection that made one think her skin would be hard and cold to touch. The man on the greater throne was as dark as she was blond, his skin nut-brown, his hair sleek as black silk, his eyes as dark as his hair. Those eyes were impenetrable and hard as the onyx they resembled.

Among the creatures crowding into the throne room, but each surrounded by an empty space that rejected association with the recognized symbols of evil, were the Dark Sidhe—-tall, beautiful, only with empty eyes and cruel mouths. They passed the other creatures that made up Vidal's Dark Court and took their places at the very front of the assembly.

In their wake came the shadow, no longer crouching to be smaller but still unnoticed. Somehow it seemed to flit from one black section of wall to another, avoiding the glowing chalcedony. It did not take a place on the seats claimed by the Dark Sidhe but melted into near invisibility quite near the edge of the dais.

The business of the Court went forward. A boggle that had refused an order by Vidal Dhu was brought forward by the hounds that had hunted it down. It was given over to its own kind, who tore off pieces and ate it alive. A witch accused another of stealing a human captive from her. The second witch, purpling and writhing as she tried to evade Aurilia's truth spell, finally confessed, complaining bitterly that the first witch would not share the human's blood with her when she needed it. She was condemned to bring Underhill two humans to pay for her crime.

Other cases were heard, a few settled as brutally as the first—one ogre putting up so spirited a defense that two other fatal injuries occurred before he was subdued and consumed—but most with reasonable verdicts. The shadow shifted slightly and close attention, which no one gave it, would have shown that it nodded, recognizing that Vidal's mood was unusually benign, but still it wavered, trembling.

At last no one new came forward. Vidal raised a hand, preparing to order that all the clotted blood and bits of broken bone, signs of the executions he had ordered, be removed. The shadow slipped around the dais, slid past the rows of seated Dark Sidhe and came before Vidal's and Aurilia's thrones, where it resolved itself into a short, slender Sidhe shaking with fear but visible.

"My lord," the barely noticeable Sidhe murmured, bowing low.

Vidal frowned and squinted slightly, as if he were having some difficulty fixing his eyes on the speaker. "Who?" he asked.

"Dakari, lord," the little Sidhe answered.

His voice was so low that Vidal's long, pointed ears twitched forward with his attempt to hear. An expression of disgust and impatience appeared on his face and one hand began to rise, but Aurilia put a hand on his arm.

"Something so indefinite, so indeterminate, might be useful," she said softly. Then she frowned as her erratic memory matched what she was seeing with a previous image. "Wait. It's been here before . . . I think."

The frown cleared from Vidal's face, and he smiled at Aurilia. "So he has." He turned his attention to the little Sidhe, remembering perfectly, now it had been called to his attention, place and time and what had been said. "Have you determined whether Alhambra would be suitable for my lady's pleasure?"

In the lengthening silence, the trembling Sidhe before Vidal almost drifted away into shadow. But the change in the pattern of light drew Vidal from his memories.

"Dakari," he said, "I have waited but you have not answered me. If you are expecting the reward I promised to the one who could discover whether Alhambra was fit to be taken for my lady's pleasure, you have not yet won the prize."

"Lord, I do not know the answer to your question," Dakari whispered. "The mortal and the elder Sidhe have removed all the small curses and nuisances, the biting things and the miasmas that brought illness. But at the heart of Alhambra is an Evil that they cannot touch. They have hurt It and troubled It, but It cannot directly touch them either and—"

Vidal's eyes narrowed. "An Evil. Did *you* touch it?"

"Oh, no, my lord!" Dakari backed away in fear, shaking so hard he almost lost his footing and fell.

Vidal laughed softly. He lifted his hand and pointed. What had been fading away into shadow firmed suddenly into a trembling, sobbing, very thin Sidhe. His hair, yellow-white, limp and with no body, clung to his long, thin head; his eyes were almost colorless, his skin pasty, his lips pallid. His ears looked wilted and his clothing sagged around him.

"But now you *will* touch that Evil," Vidal said; his voice was not loud but it reverberated with dominance.

Beside him Aurilia smiled watching the geas strike home. That would ensure the little Sidhe's obedience, no matter how fearful. But more important to her was the evidence of Vidal's strength.

"You will go to Alhambra," Vidal continued, "and approach the Evil with due submission. You will tell It how we admire It, how we would protect It from further nuisance by the mortal and his ancient Sidhe friends. You will offer yourself as servant, then ask It if It would welcome us if we came to Alhambra. If It has doubts, you will convince It. Then you will return here to me."

Dakari said nothing, eyes wide and staring.

Aurilia straightened in her seat, frowning as the force of the projected geas began to fade, seemingly becoming as diffuse as the Sidhe himself had been. Well aware of her own weaknesses since the second mind-scouring by Cold Iron, Aurilia needed a partner strong enough to provide for her the rank and power she needed. When Vidal showed signs of weakness, she had considered making Pasgen her partner. But she really preferred Vidal; Pasgen was so rigid in his concept of duty and honor.

"Do you hear me? Will you obey me?" Vidal's voice—sharp, hard, brittle—brought the wilting Sidhe upright, rigid.

"I hear," Dakari whimpered. "I will obey."

For the briefest instant Dakari seemed outlined in a thin dark red cloud. Then the color was gone, dissipated . . . or perhaps sucked within. For another brief instant Dakari's form seemed more solid, features firmer, body substantial. Then Vidal's arm dropped and only a vaporous shadow slightly darkened the area before the thrones. Aurilia leaned back again, smiling.

Chapter 1

Elizabeth Tudor, still asleep, stretched languorously and Denoriel Siencyn Macreth Silverhair looked down at his treasure and his burden from his pillow-propped position in the wide bed. The FarSeers had been right, he thought; she would be a red-haired queen. Her hair had barely darkened a shade from its childhood's golden-red glory.

He thought back to when his twin sister Aleneil, a FarSeer herself, had summoned him and he had first seen Elizabeth in the great lens that showed the future—a red-haired babe, scowling in her father's arms. And then the other Visions, of young Edward and his dour reign, of Mary and the screaming as what she called heretics burned, and then of the red-haired queen, Elizabeth, in a reign of glory of music of art of great poetry.

Denoriel sighed softly, careful to make no sound that would disturb Elizabeth's sleep. She would be queen if he could keep her alive long enough. So far he had managed to protect her for nearly twenty years, but the worst was yet to come. He shifted slightly and looked away.

They had been coupled only a little while ago, yet he felt his blood stir anew when he looked at her. Even asleep what she was seized and held him. Not a great beauty, although her body, spare and slightly boyish, was charming. Elsewise... No, she was no beauty. Elizabeth was, as she had always been, very pale, her face a long oval, her nose straight and fine, her lips thin and only faintly rosy. Her brows and lashes, more gold than red, were hardly marked. Compared with the women of the Sidhe, Elizabeth was plain. But the life in her, the purpose in her, could inspire desire in a granite boulder among the Sidhe.

Silence and stillness had not been enough. His attention had disturbed her and her eyes opened slowly, showing dark irises. She did not smile at him or reach to touch him as she often did after making love, but looked away and sighed.

"Denno, should we be disporting ourselves like this when it is all too likely that my poor brother lies dying?"

He should not have been staring at her, Denoriel thought.

"Should I not be with Edward?" she continued, not waiting for an answer. "I love him. Surely I would be of some comfort to him?"

Denoriel shrugged. "You would indeed be a comfort to Edward, if you were allowed to reach him. But I am quite certain some reason would be found to turn you away."

"Why?" Elizabeth lifted herself, and the pillows rearranged themselves to support her in comfort. "Northumberland has been very kind to me, always showed me favor. Remember he traded Hatfield for another property when I wanted Hatfield. And he is kind to Edward, too. Why should he want to keep me from him?"

"I am not certain," Denoriel admitted. "Cecil has sent no news, and I do not know enough about the twists of policy and politics. I know—well, anyone not a nodcock knows—that Northumberland wants to keep the power he has held during Edward's reign."

Elizabeth stared at him, shaking her head. "But that is not possible. If . . ."

Her voice trembled on the word and she swallowed. What she was about to say was treason in England—even whispered in a locked room. She could only say the words Underhill. In fact they had come Underhill because it was the only safe place to discuss what Elizabeth should do if her brother died. Then when she was weeping over Edward's illness—she really did love him dearly—Denoriel had taken her into his arms to comfort her. Somehow the caresses changed from comforting to sensual and they found themselves abed.

Steadying her voice, Elizabeth continued, "If Edward dies, Mary will come to the throne, and Mary will not need a regent, as Northumberland knows quite well; she does not trust him, and he is the enemy to her religion. As likely hold back the tide as change Mary's faith. Even my father could not fully accomplish that."

Denoriel nodded agreement. "So Northumberland must seek a way to bypass Mary. Which is what made me beg you to come Underhill and speak to Harry. He knows from Rhoslyn what Mary thinks—as well as it is possible for any of her women to know her mind. And I wanted to ask you . . . since you, too, favor the reformed religion, what will you do, Elizabeth, if Northumberland approaches you and offers you the throne over Mary's head?"

She was suddenly rigid against the pillows. Her mouth opened, closed. Her eyes, which had been dark, lightened until they almost glowed like gold. Desire, raw and naked, flashed across her face. Then it was all gone.

"Ridiculous," Elizabeth said quietly. "My claim to the throne is through my father's will and the Act of Succession of 1544. The will and the Act both state clearly, Edward, Mary if Edward dies without heirs, and only if Mary dies without heirs, Elizabeth. To set Mary aside would make the whole succession invalid—and likely would start a civil war. No, if he offers me the throne, I will tell him that I have no right at all while Edward and Mary live."

Denoriel breathed out a long sigh. He had guarded two heirs to the throne. Harry FitzRoy, Henry VIII's natural son, wanted no part of being king. Elizabeth desired ardently to rule. It was as if God had given each the perfect nature. Harry would have made a terrible king; he was clever enough and interested in the intricacies of political maneuvering but he was too honest, too good, too gentle to rule. Elizabeth . . . Elizabeth was born to be a queen, brilliant and devious with a streak of cruelty that would keep her high lords inclined away from angering her. What a Sidhe she would have made!

Denoriel nodded satisfaction with Elizabeth's answer, but suddenly her face changed again, flushing in distress. "Da!" she said. "Da is supposed to meet us." And she hopped out of bed and turned on Denoriel. "Dress me, by God's Grace. Do you think I want Da to find me abed with you while poor Edward . . ."

She raised her hands to cover her face, hardly noticing that rich blue velvet sleeves lined with silver brocaded satin covered her arms. With a gesture, Denoriel had clothed her, complete with shift and personals, in an underskirt of silver on silver brocade and an overgown of blue velvet. The undersleeve was tight from the elbow to the wrist and exposed by the wide uppersleeve, which was turned back on itself. It was a mark of how overset

Elizabeth was, she who passionately loved clothes, that she did not examine and comment on the dress but uttered a single sob and stepped forward into Denoriel's open arms.

"Oh, Merciful Mary, how horrible it is to be talking about what will happen when my little brother is dead. Should I not be praying for him to recover?"

"Have you not prayed for him to recover?"

Denoriel was not really asking the question but using it to remind Elizabeth that her desire for the throne, a desire she could not completely suppress, was not unnatural or unloving.

Tears made Elizabeth's darkened eyes shine. "You know I have. I even made you bring Mwynwen to him. Why could she not heal him?"

"I have told you that many times. It is through no fault of yours. Mywnwen cannot heal mortal illnesses, nor can any other Sidhe healer. She can heal a cut or a bruise, even a broken bone, but mortal illnesses like consumption or plague she cannot heal."

"She healed my Da."

"Only because Harry had been touched by elfshot, not mortal wasting sickness. She could draw out the poison of the elfshot and bring him back to health. Elizabeth, you know this. Why are you making me say the same words over and over?"

The tears ran over her lower lids and made shining streaks on her cheeks. "Because I want to be assured that Edward's illness is not my fault. I do not forget I failed to protect him well enough when that Dark Sidhe struck at him with a poisoned thorn."

"The Dark Sidhe struck at *you*," Denoriel snapped. "In any case, Edward would have been dead long since if that poison had touched him."

That last was not true, he thought. Likely the poison had touched Edward and weakened him so that the mortal illness more quickly and easily took hold. But it was the mortal illness that was killing the boy and no sense in Elizabeth feeling guilty.

"Then there is nothing left but a miracle from God." Elizabeth shivered slightly and Denoriel tightened his grip on her. "And I do not believe in miracles," she whispered. "But I have tried to believe, Denno, I have. I have prayed and promised that if God will only make Edward well I would strive to be a better person, to be meek and obedient to him always no matter what he bade me do, even marry. I have made offerings to all the churches in my domains for prayers for his health."

Denoriel's fine gold brows drew together and his arms stiffened around her. "Not I hope for relief of his sickness!" he said sharply. "You could be hanged for implying the king is sick."

Elizabeth sighed and shook her head. "I am not that much a fool. No. Only for his good health. For his continued good health. That was safe, wasn't it, Denno?"

She drew back a little so she could look up into his face. He was heartstoppingly beautiful, his eyes deep pools of emerald green, his hair a golden glory with soft curls at his temples and glowing waves to his shoulders. His skin was smooth and soft as the finest loomed silk, and he had a perfect nose and a full rosy mouth. Except for the touch of humor that curved his mobile lips, he looked like every other male Sidhe. Most often when he brought her Underhill and always when they made love, Denno wore an illusion of youth.

It was sweet of him to wish to be beautiful for her, so Elizabeth had not yet found the courage or the right moment to tell him not to bother, that what held her heart and roused a fever of desire in her body was his true appearance. That bespoke Denno's love and sacrifice—behavior not natural to the Sidhe.

All the years he had spent in the mortal world, enduring mortal weather as he cared first for her Da and then for her, had tanned and roughened his skin. All the worry he had suffered over his charges had drawn lines between his brows and around his eyes and mouth. The battles he had fought for them, both physical and magical, the wounds he had suffered, had turned his hair from gold to white and marred the smooth perfection of the uncaring Sidhe. Without illusion Denno looked like a rather harried, elderly mortal who had seen much trouble and endured great pain. Elizabeth loved him best that way.

He was frowning over her question and then he sighed. "I hope so, but it would have been wiser not to—"

His voice checked as there was a stirring in the air near him and the gentle voice of one of his invisible servants said, "Lord Harry has entered Llachar Lle."

Elizabeth squeaked in dismay and ran out of the room and down the stairs. She was seated, albeit a trifle breathless, in Denoriel's elegant parlor when Harry came through the door into the entrance hall. Elizabeth took a steadying breath. She was not trying to conceal the fact that Denoriel was her lover, she told herself. It was only that in some way Da regarded her as a daughter and Denno as a father.

Henry FitzRoy, natural son of King Henry VIII, dead and buried in the mortal world to the great relief of the English government, looked uneasily to the left at the door to the parlor. He felt a fool scratching to announce himself in the house in which he lived, but he hated to intrude upon Bess and Denno unexpectedly. They were usually embraced to some degree when they were Underhill because in the mortal world they could only acknowledge each other distantly.

It wasn't that he disapproved, Harry told himself, just that Bess . . . Bess was only a baby. As the words came into his mind he laughed aloud. Bess was twenty years old, a normal, healthy young woman who, had she not been Henry VIII's daughter, would by now have been married and had children.

The laugh was acknowledged by Denno's voice, saying, "Harry" from the landing at the top of the stairs.

Harry looked up and smiled. "Denno. Where's Bessie?"

"If you call her that, she'll murder you," Denno said, coming down the stairs. "She's waiting for you in the parlor. She's been crying over Edward, wanting to go to him to comfort him."

"Perhaps she should," Harry said slowly. "Mary went to visit him in February and knew." He shook his head. "It might be easier for Bess to believe he is dying and stop hoping if she saw him."

As he spoke, Harry took in Denoriel's appearance. He had not noticed it particularly at first, mostly because that was how Denno had looked when he first came to Harry and that was how Harry thought of him. But it wasn't how Denno looked now, Harry realized, and he blushed, knowing Denno had cast the illusion of youth over himself to please Elizabeth.

One part of Harry, the sensible, adult part, approved highly of the love affair between Denno and Elizabeth. It was just that another part cringed when he thought of the body of the child he loved entwined with that of the man who had protected him when he was a child. Nonsense, Harry told himself. For a young woman who could not afford another scandal without suffering serious political retribution, a Sidhe was the only safe lover.

Denoriel could come to Elizabeth in ways no mortal lover could, without anyone ever seeing him enter or leave the palace in which she lived. If by some ill chance they should be surprised by some unexpected intruder, Denno could disappear. And despite being Sidhe, Denno would not be unfaithful or abandon dearling Bess. Had he not proved his steadfastness over all of Harry's life?

Harry stepped forward and slid his arm into Denno's, pressing the arm affectionately to his side. "You don't agree that Bess should visit Edward?"

"I don't think she will be allowed to visit."

"Why not?"

"That I don't know. In truth, I cannot think of any reason. Northumberland knows she would not speak ill of him. But she wrote to Northumberland more than a week ago asking permission to come to London, soon after she heard that Mary had been to see Edward, and she has had no answer, not even a private word from Cecil."

Frowning, Harry opened the door and stepped into the parlor. The soft greens and blues accented in dull silver were very soothing and peaceful, but Elizabeth was sitting rigidly erect, looking out of the huge window over a scene that seemed to be a wide meadow surrounding a handsome manor house backed by a dark, dense wood. Now there was a garden near the house with a bright stream running through it.

He went and knelt on one knee beside Elizabeth and took her hand in his. "Love, I am so sorry. I know you care for Edward deeply, but you must let yourself believe that he cannot survive."

"How do *you* know?"

"From Mary though Rhoslyn."

"Mary spoke of Edward's . . . death . . . to Rhoslyn?" Elizabeth's eyes opened wide.

"No, of course not, not even to Susan Clarencieux or Jane Dormer, but Mary prays and often offers her fears and hopes to God. She whispers low, but—" Harry smiled "—Rhoslyn, like most Sidhe, has long ears."

That drew a small smile from Elizabeth because it was true literally as well as being a reference to their keen hearing. When he saw the sign of relaxation, Harry patted the hand he held, let go of it, and rose to sit on the sofa near Elizabeth's chair. Silently, Denno sat opposite. Unobtrusively, he lifted a hand and looked pointedly at the faint disturbance that appeared in the air.

"Mary has been praying for the strength and wisdom to rule." Harry was watching Elizabeth and noticed the faintest thinning of her lips.

"Not for Edward's cure or salvation?"

"Likely Mary, having seen him and spoken to him, believes him beyond even miracles, but Rhoslyn is careful to tell me only what she hears, not what she thinks. Rhoslyn is very fond of Mary and is torn between her desire for Mary's happiness and her knowledge of the misery Mary's happiness will bring to the realm at large."

Elizabeth sighed. "Mary intends to root out the reformed religion." A shrug followed. "Well, I knew it would be so. It could not be otherwise. But that means Northumberland must go, and I fear he will not go willingly or easily. I do not know what he can do, however. Denno thought he might offer me the throne, bypassing Mary."

Was there a quiver of hope in her voice? That was dangerous. Elizabeth must not yet betray her ambition. Harry suppressed a shudder. He had never wanted to rule himself, but, raised as the center of much political maneuvering, he had perforce learned a great deal. That knowledge and the need to protect himself from those who would use him as a pawn had sparked a deep interest in how England was governed, and being "dead and buried" had not abated that interest a bit. Harry FitzRoy had the means to keep himself well informed and did so.

"He will not succeed in that," Harry said, a note of warning in his voice. "Mary is too much beloved, even by those whose faith she will attack. She may not succeed in becoming queen—but that will be only because she is dead or prisoner by Northumberland's—"

"No!" Denoriel exclaimed with quiet violence. "Elizabeth could not take the throne after Mary's murder. She would be reviled by all and unable to rule no matter that she had nothing to do with the crime or did not even know of it. There is no way she could prove herself innocent, except to be dead first."

"I do not think I wish to go quite that far to prove myself innocent," Elizabeth said dryly.

Denoriel smiled at her, just as a low table appeared before Elizabeth's chair. On it was an exquisite tea service, the porcelain as delicate as an eggshell glowing with iridescent green and

blue, bluebells in a forest glade. Two tall stemmed glasses stood
before a bottle of wine, and two thick, crystal mugs sat next to
a sweating pitcher of ale. There was also a large plate, one side
holding slices of bread and slices of cheese and the other piled
with a variety of sweet pastries; cups of honey and a variety of
jams stood near the bread.

Absently Harry picked up a piece of bread and slapped a slice
of cheese on it, while Denoriel poured out two mugs of ale. "Yet
equal or greater danger may come from Mary alive." Harry's voice
was slightly muffled as he chewed and swallowed. "I do not want
to frighten you, Bess, but Mary . . . does not love you. You must
do nothing that can wake a suspicion in her that you desire to
unseat her and take the throne."

Elizabeth spread jam on a slice of bread and looked hard at her
cup, in which tea promptly appeared. "I would not if I could," she
said; she paused and sipped. "As I said earlier to Denno, I will
not contest Mary for the throne. My right is from my father's will
and the Act of Succession. Mary must rule before I can."

Harry nodded approval. "Rhoslyn is doing all she can to prevent
Mary from wishing to harm you. She is limited in how much
influence she can exert, but she assures me that she constantly
offers the image of you as a small child, running with cries of
joy to greet your kind sister."

"You must be wary and patient," Denoriel urged, "but it will not be
forever. Mary is many years older than you and sickly besides."

"And her desire to restore the old religion may cause unrest
and dissatisfaction," Harry said, "particularly as she wishes to go
further than bringing back the settlement devised by your father.
She intends to reconcile with the pope. Rhoslyn heard her praying that the papal father would forgive her for her weakness in
yielding to King Henry's demand she reject papal authority."

"She will not rule long if she tries to restore to the Church
what my father seized." Elizabeth's voice was carefully neutral.
"So many profited greatly from the closure of the abbeys. They
will not relinquish what they gained—even those who themselves
practice the old religion."

The voice was neutral, but something in the carriage of the
head, in the set of the shoulders, said there would be no prayers
for Mary's health and possibly even subtle encouragement of those
who resisted her policies. Harry cast a rather anxious glance at

Elizabeth, guessed that further warnings would only make her stubborn, and decided to change the subject. Mary was not yet on the throne; he would have time for sharper warnings.

"Atop all this, I have more bad news," he said. "At least, I am not sure it is bad, but I suspect so. Gaenor tells me that she and Hafwen and Pasgen can no longer detect Vidal in the mist that acts on its own."

"Vidal is loose?" Elizabeth asked.

Her voice was calm, curious rather than frightened. It was Denoriel who sat up straight and stared at Harry, setting down the mug of ale he had raised to his mouth.

"What do you mean the elder Sidhe 'cannot detect' Vidal?" Denoriel asked.

"I don't know what I mean," Harry replied with a touch of impatience. "The mist could have killed him . . . In which case, whether you like it or not, Elizabeth, we need to go to Oberon and tell him about it. Or Vidal could have escaped the mist . . . And I like that idea almost less than that the mist decided to kill. Vidal is dangerous to you, love."

"He has tried some four or five times to seize me or kill me, and failed each time," Elizabeth said complacently.

"He only needs to succeed once," Denoriel snapped, "and you will be dead or prisoner of the Dark Court and suffering terrible torments."

"I will be freed soon enough if you tell Titania that I was taken. And Oberon will help her. Not because he cares for me," Elizabeth said realistically, "but because he ordered Vidal to leave me alone."

"Do not be so silly, Bessie," Harry said, frowning, his voice sharper than usual when he spoke to her. "Titania and Oberon are not always available to us. Who knows what would be done to you before we could arrange a rescue! And do you think Denno would be content to wait until we found Oberon—or I would? We would seek for you at once, and could be hurt or killed trying to reach you."

Elizabeth had a sudden, vivid memory of one of Vidal's attacks that almost succeeded, a vision of Denno being blasted by fire and lightning, his shields shredding. And Da had been beset by ogres. He had survived only because she had bespelled one ogre's feet to stick to the ground so it could not reach him. What if she had not been able to cast the spell?

"I will be careful," Elizabeth said repentantly. "I will not ride hunting unless Deno is with me or even walk in the garden without my guard." But then she shook her head. "Only . . . only I *must* try to see Edward." Tears rose in her eyes again. "Likely it is foolish. Possibly he will not even know I have come, but . . . but *I* will know I tried, that I was not so lily-livered as to coddle my own safety and comfort without regard to him. Perhaps he is in pain or afraid. Perhaps I *would* be allowed to comfort him if I were there."

Some months before Elizabeth's visit Underhill, Vidal Dhu, once Prince of the Dark Court, lay still and thought of a Gate. He had thought of nothing else for a very, very long time. If there was still rage and hate in him, it was buried so deep that even he could not find it.

When he had first been wrapped in the bands of mist made smooth and strong as tight-woven silk, he had screamed and struggled. That had won him only more and tighter bonds, as the ribbons of mist wrapped his head and filled his mouth so that he could not even scream. Then, too late, he tried magic, spells of dissolution, spells of fire; but he could not even move his lips enough to form the spells and his hands, finger by finger, were bound so he could not gesture.

At some time, he had fallen and lain utterly helpless on whatever floored the Unformed lands. Rage and hatred tore him and lashed him. He thrashed, rolled about, struggled to bend his legs, to free his arms—and the bands of mist only tightened.

Eventually Vidal slipped into the state of rest that served the Sidhe for sleep. He was at first too totally enraged to notice, but the bands that swaddled him loosened somewhat while he rested, while he did not fight against his imprisonment, while the rage and hatred were dulled. Of course, each time he became alert and found himself still a prisoner, his wrath was renewed and the bonds tightened again.

It happened many times before Vidal's fury, diminished minimally by exhaustion, allowed him to sense the slight relaxation of his bindings. Unwisely he fought to free himself, with the usual result of greater helplessness. That, too, happened many times before he lay still after he became fully aware. He did not struggle, but he still hated, and the mist would not let him go.

A mortal would have died. Vidal could not even do that. The immense power that flooded this Unformed land seeped into him and satisfied the needs of his body. And as time passed, weeks, months, years in mortal time, Vidal learned. He lay quiet, almost peacefully, and thought of a Gate. The ribbons loosened.

Vidal still lay quiet. He did not think of revenge—what revenge could be taken on an insubstantial mist?—he did not think of the cause of his entrapment, of Elizabeth, who had escaped him again. He thought peacefully and quietly of a Gate. And the bands of mist grew flimsy, like silk worn gossamer thin over many years of use and many washings. Vidal did not press against them. Even when they were only mist again, he did not move, did not try to rise. He thought of a Gate.

Finally, thinking only of a Gate, he moved an arm. No band of mist formed to restrain it. He moved a leg ... and thought only of a Gate. And in the end, he rose and the Gate was there. Vidal stepped up on the low platform and patterned Caer Mordwyn. He did not even rejoice over his escape until he had stepped out of the Gate and into his own domain.

There not rejoicing but horror struck him. The road between the Gate and the palace was a dissolving ruin. Paving lay in uneven heaps; pit traps were exposed; predatory foliage was encroaching in some places, dying in others; and in some places the road had disappeared completely, vanishing into the mist from which it had been created.

Deep, deep within rage flickered, and with an ability most painfully learned, was instantly suppressed. A moment more and Vidal realized there was no cause for rage, that no power but his had touched the domain—this part at least. The ruin was a result of failure to renew the power ... and of hasty, shoddy work.

Quietly Vidal looked down the road and remade it. Then came rejoicing. Within him was an immense well of power, strength he had feared to assess while a prisoner of the mist. The remaking of the road was no effort, was so small a withdrawal compared with the power he now held that it was as if he had done nothing.

Vidal began to walk down the road toward his palace. He was smiling. By the end of a mortal week, he told himself, he would rid himself—permanently—of whoever thought to hold Caer Mordwyn and then he would rid the mortal world of the threat of Elizabeth as queen.

In the end he did neither. When he reached the palace, to his intense surprise, Aurilia was there to greet him—and with every evidence of joy. She was the one who had reined in the exuberance of the Dark Court and saved it from angering Oberon.

She had known of his entrapment from Albertus, she admitted. The mortal had Gated back to Caer Mordwyn with his amulet after the mist had made Vidal a prisoner.

"But I looked for you," Aurilia told him most earnestly. "You know how I hate to leave Caer Mordwyn. Still, I looked and looked but I could never find that Unformed land."

"Perhaps that is just as well," Vidal said mildly. "If you tried to help me, it might have taken you prisoner as well."

Aurilia looked at him and shuddered, even as her breasts flushed and heat washed across her loins. Vidal was changed, more powerful than ever, less careless, in far better control of himself. Perhaps he was the best partner for her after all. So long as he would still move in the direction she set for him.

She was brighter and more beautiful, Vidal thought, allowing his appreciation of her golden hair, green eyes, delicately formed ears, and lush body with its faint scent of decay to show. He did not hide the eagerness he felt to use that body.

Aurilia saw. She turned away swiftly and began to mount the black marble stair, smiling back at him over her shoulder. In the black depths of his soul, far too deeply hidden to give any sign, Vidal marked another reason to distrust his partner.

For all the outward gentleness, he was no less brutal in his coupling. He hurt her—well, she could have had no pleasure if he did not—but he did not cast her aside and leave when he was done. When they were at rest, Vidal lay back on the blood-red pillows of her bed and returned to the conversation lust had interrupted. Still softly but with adamant purpose he asked what she had done with Albertus. Aurilia took note, suppressing the chill that passed through her. She would need to be much more careful with this new Vidal.

"He is back in the mortal world, making himself agreeable to the king's doctors," Aurilia said with a bright smile. "He has even suggested this and that remedy which has been helpful to the dying king. So I have quicker and better news of the Court than anyone."

"Ah," Vidal said, one part of his mind pleased, but buried beneath that pleasure was resentment because Albertus had deserted him and not been punished. "That is good. I will be eager to hear how near Mary is to the throne. But before we come to that, do tell me how you managed the Court? I am very glad that Pasgen did not attempt to seize the domain again. I would hate to waste the power I have absorbed in destroying him."

Aurilia shrugged contemptuously. "The power would be wasted, indeed, and destroying him without purpose. He never wanted to rule Caer Mordwyn. Oberon threatened to destroy everything if the beings of the Dark Court were not restrained." She smiled slyly. "But managing your subjects was not really difficult. One does not need great power for that. One only needs to be cleverer than they, and that is easy enough. Most of them, even the Dark Sidhe, are self-centered fools. It is easy to trick them into obedience."

Anger flickered, was swallowed. "If it was so easy to deal with the Court, why did you leave the domain to rot!"

Aurilia sighed. "The palace is strong and sound." She shrugged. "I had not the power to do more." She met his eyes but then let hers slide away.

Vidal was not sure he believed that. He threw back the sheets and rose, aware of the admiration with which Aurilia examined his magnificent nakedness. Vidal was well aware of his striking perfection. He had worn the illusion of that perfection for so long that it was as instinctive as breathing. Aurilia stretched a hand to him and he was half tempted, despite being so newly sated, to respond. But he only smiled. Was cleverness managing him?

"You have done very well," he said, showing his teeth in almost a smile. "Perhaps you would wish to continue to manage the Court while I make sure of Mary's accession and Elizabeth's demise?"

"No!" Aurilia sat bolt upright and shuddered. Then she laughed. "No," she repeated more calmly. "I did not wish to lose Caer Mordwyn—" her eyes flicked around the luxurious room, the velvets and the silks, fur-rug strewn floor, the gold and diamond inlaid toiletries on the gleaming lapis lazuli counter, the flasks of priceless scents, the half-open door of the garderobe which exposed unbelievably rich garments "—so I contrived. But I want no part of ruling here."

Vidal cocked his head and gestured clothing over himself. He was surprised to feel a certainty that she was sincere. She did not want to rule the Dark Court. What did she want? The answer came at once. She wished to rule *him*. Vidal actually smiled. That made sense. Aurilia had many skills and had studied magic, but she was no maker. For her, it was a great effort even to clothe herself, as he had just done almost without thought; he had made this room and its furnishings. She needed servants to dress her.

He laughed and shook his head. "Lazy, that is what you are, Aurilia." It was perfectly true and he could now accept the fact that Aurilia was happy to pass to him the duties of ruling. What she wanted was status and the groveling of those to whom she gave orders.

"I have better things to do with my time than spend every moment planning how to outwit your stupid subjects," she said, simpering at him.

That was to make him believe she would occupy herself with devices to seduce him, Vidal thought, and in a way that was true too. But she would also study magic, strong magic that took little power. She *was* clever. Then if Elizabeth came to rule and little power came to the Dark Court, Aurilia would be the strongest worker of magic among them.

Vidal smiled one last time at Aurilia and left her chamber for his own. There he stood, staring unseeingly at the throne chair on which he usually sat. If Elizabeth came to rule . . . For a long moment the deep well in which Vidal had buried his emotions roiled and the hard layer upon layer of blank nothingness that he had built up over four long years of imprisonment threatened to shatter.

Unreasoning terror froze Vidal. He could feel the bonds of silken mist ribbons tighten around him. Elizabeth had caused his entrapment. If he had not tried to kill her and struck down that red-haired, doll-like creature which had contained the ribbons of mist, he would never have been caught. But he had learned from the experience. Rage and hatred were contained. He must not again leap at the first chance to destroy Elizabeth. He must think and plan.

At first Vidal kept busy repairing his realm, suppressing any thoughts of Elizabeth. He was more careful in his making, fixing the landscape and the subtle traps in the landscape and near the Gates to sources of power that renewed themselves. However as the work grew more complex, he worried about that.

Now there was an abundance of misery-generated power. With the young king steadily failing and the persecution of those who worshiped in the old faith increasing, anxiety and foreboding dripped more and more bitter-tainted power Underhill. But if something gave the realm hope, if the English welcomed Mary and were happy to return to the old faith, power might grow thin and what he had fixed to his landscape might deprive the living creatures and make them rebellious.

That concern brought Elizabeth to the forefront of Vidal's mind again. Near the edges of the domain he became less meticulous; he was growing bored. The desire for active evil against the mortal world grew with the need to ensure his power. But Elizabeth was still beyond his reach. She was watched so closely among the spies from the Court, from her sister, and from the Bright Sidhe, that it was a miracle the girl could breathe.

Worse, she was still able to look through illusion in the mortal world so he could not simply replace one of her servants or companions with an assassin. How would he reach her? The question nagged at him.

Annoyed at finding no answer that satisfied him, Vidal posed the question to Aurilia some mortal months after his return. They were dining in his private chamber, the flesh hacked from a still living faun almost quivering on Vidal's plate. Aurilia looked up from her somewhat better cooked portion, with surprise in her large, green eyes.

"Whatever would you bother about her for? She is making no preparations to usurp the throne from Mary—and if she started a civil war, it would be soon enough to act against her. Otherwise, when Mary comes to the throne, Elizabeth is as good as dead. Mary hates her for her mother's sake and envies her for her own charms—of which Mary has none. I would guess that within weeks of being settled into her power, Mary will have Elizabeth's head off."

"No." The flat negative surprised Vidal as much as it surprised Aurilia. "I do not want Elizabeth to be honorably executed. I want her shamed, humiliated." Vidal swallowed as his mouth watered with a hunger that had nothing to do with the food on the table. "I want her to die slowly in my hands—"

"No you do not!" Aurilia exclaimed, looking frightened. "Do you also want Caer Mordwyn invaded by Denoriel leading an army of Bright Sidhe, who all desire Elizabeth to be queen? He will no doubt bring that dung-spawned mortal with his gun and likely enough Titania and possibly even Oberon—"

"Oberon cares nothing for Elizabeth."

"Of course not, but he will care that he bade you let her be and you did not obey him. Let Elizabeth die at the hands of her sister, and leave the humiliation to Mary. No one will blame you for what Mary does. How she feels about Elizabeth is well known."

What Aurilia said was all too true. Mary would come to the throne when Edward died and might well dispose of Elizabeth, and there would be no danger of reprisal from Oberon and the Bright Court. Vidal grimaced. That would ensure that the Dark Court would not be starved for power but would give him no satisfaction at all. No, not at all. Elizabeth must die by his doing.

Vidal swallowed and sliced a tasty tidbit from the bloody portion on his plate. Recalling the fear on Aurilia's face when he spoke of disposing of Elizabeth, he decided it would be a mistake to confide too deeply in her. To save herself, she was quite capable of betraying him to Oberon.

"I suppose you are right about that," Vidal said, "but I have been long away from affairs in the mortal world and I wish to be certain that Mary will do what we need done."

"Ah. Yes. I said to let Mary do the deed. I did not say you should not help her along to make the decision. I know what is going on in the Court, but I have no influence there. You must sink hooks into those whom Mary trusts and they must advise her with one voice that to keep her throne, Elizabeth must die."

Vidal frowned. "To sink hooks, I need to be more aware of what is going forward in the mortal world. On the other hand, I do not wish to use the Otstargi persona simply to gather news. That would betray to Otstargi's clients that he is not all-knowing and would reduce his influence and power."

Aurilia shrugged. "You mean *you* wish to use Albertus?"

"Yes."

The slight hesitation before she replied showed she was unwilling, but what she said was "You are too rough with the minds of mortals. I do not want Albertus turned into an unthinking idiot. You can talk to him, but I do not want his mind stripped."

"Very well."

Vidal did not try to hide his dissatisfaction with the curb on his use of her servant. He hoped that would convince her that he would not meddle with Albertus's mind. But he did resolve to be careful in how he meddled. Aurilia was as skilled—no, to be honest, more skilled—in such matters as he. He would need to be very careful indeed, or she might armor her servant against him.

Chapter 2

On the very next mortal day, Vidal Gated to Otstargi's house. The nearly mindless servant was still there. The house was clean, the bedchambers ready; Otstargi's receiving room was the only chamber that had the feeling of long vacancy. The rest of the house, the parlor and dining room, were obviously in use and Vidal found evidence, clothes in a wardrobe, toilet articles on a dressing table in one of the bedrooms that Albertus lived there.

He looked in the servant's mind, somewhat more carefully than in the past, remembering that he had almost killed the creature and that if he did so he would have to rework another mortal. But he did not need to delve deep to discover Albertus's habits of coming and going. Generally Albertus was absent all day and returned to the house shortly before dark. Vidal told the servant to bid Albertus wait for "his master" and went back up the stairs.

He was about to Gate Underhill when it occurred to him that he was totally ignorant of current events in the mortal world, except for what Aurilia had told him and what Albertus might say. Since he did not trust either of them, he decided to have dinner out at a popular inn and see what news he could gather.

Standing before the cheval glass in what was called Otstargi's bedchamber, although he never slept in it, Vidal took on the guise of a prosperous merchant. He did not want to be recognized as Otstargi so he was careful to make his round pupiled eyes blue and his hair a nondescript brown. A bland expression completed a friendly and harmless appearance.

Fortunately, staid merchant garb did not change the way the garments of lordlings who followed fashion did. Vidal felt safe garbing himself in the same kind of clothes Otstargi had last worn. He uttered an obscenity as the suit formed on him; he had forgotten how much the effort to dress himself here in the mortal world would drain his well of power. Nonetheless, he sacrificed more power to ken coins for his purse.

He would not forget again, Vidal told himself, that he could not renew his power in the mortal world. For now, however, he did not expect to need to do any more magic, and since he had already made the effort, he went out.

Eating in the mortal world was never a pleasure. Beef and mutton, always overcooked, could not compare with human flesh, well tenderized by beating and terror; however, the information he gathered, swiveling his long ears this way and that under their human illusion, was worth the effort he had made. Picking such information directly out of one man's mind was never safe; it was too colored by that one person's interpretation. General conversation provided far more reliable news.

Aside from the general state of the realm and of trade, Vidal heard of the young king's mortal illness (in whispers with anxious glances around to note who might hear) and of the attempts of the Court to conceal it. He had known Edward was dying but not about Northumberland's cronies and servants who made the rounds of inns and drinking houses to insist to anyone who would listen that the king was recovering, was almost well.

Just when he felt he could linger no longer over his dinner and ale, his attention was drawn to a hissing whisper. A well-dressed man, whose jacquette gaped open to expose a crucifix as he bent toward a companion, confided that the Lady Mary had been seen to weep after she had visited her brother as long ago as February.

This was nothing new to Vidal, but the companion shook his head and, not whispering now, said he wondered why the Lady Elizabeth had not also come to visit the king. Was she not said to be dearer to her brother than Lady Mary? A third man snorted contempt and said she would come, was just waiting . . . he paused significantly and finished . . . for the time to be ripe.

Vidal ordered another pot of ale and listened intently, both ears pointed at the group who, he now detected all wore crosses in one form or another. But though a few more vague hints of distaste for Elizabeth passed, no one even guessed when she might leave Hatfield. He gave up after he got rid of the ale. Several other inns brought him no new information, except the unwelcome fact that the first group he had heard speak of Elizabeth were the only ones who had any ill to say of her.

He discovered by questioning the landlord, who never recalled the question nor who asked it, that the men who wore crucifixes and crosses were very likely those who worshiped in the old faith. He had hoped that no one would rise to Elizabeth's defense if he arranged that she be attacked, but apparently those he first overheard were a rabid minority. Elizabeth was much loved. There was no chance a mob could be incited against her. But he could use a rabid minority.

As the light faded, Vidal made his way back to Otstargi's house. He dropped the illusion he had worn as soon as the servant had closed the door behind him, indifferent to the fear in the dull eyes when "Otstargi's" appearance was revealed.

"Go tell Master Albertus to come to the parlor," he ordered, understanding when the servant at once went up the stairs that Albertus was in the house.

Vidal himself stepped into the parlor, where he flicked a hand at the kindling and logs in the hearth. Although the day had been warm, the evenings had a chill even at the end of May. He stood watching the fire for a few moments, then frowned with impatience, but before he could act, Albertus arrived.

"My lord?" Albertus bowed nervously. "I hope you do not think I can do more for King Edward. Nothing I can do will prolong the king's life even so much as a few weeks more. By the end of June or the beginning of July, he will be dead."

"That will be long enough," Vidal said, nodding. "However, you are to continue to attend him. Whether you offer hope or tell the truth I do not care, so long as you remain free of the Court. I want you there because I have an important 'gift' which must be bestowed a week or so before Edward dies. This is a ruby ring for the new ambassador from the Empire, Simon Renard. Also you are to make sure that Baron Rich still wears the yellow diamond ring he had from Otstargi." Vidal smiled thinly. "I will know that the gift was received because Renard will come or write to Otstargi soon after he receives it."

"I am not such a fool as to think of stealing from you, lord prince—" Albertus's voice cut off abruptly and his hand flashed up to pull on the gold chain around his neck. "What must I call you here, master?" he gasped.

So Aurilia's curb on Albertus's tongue was still working well, Vidal thought approvingly. That handsome gold chain Albertus wore tightened a warning at any reference to Underhill and would strangle the man if he did not take the warning. Since there was no man who could be called "lord prince" in this house and Vidal was a prince only Underhill, the chain had tightened.

"Master Otstargi would be safest," Vidal said, adding contemptuously, "That way you will not need to remember anything complicated."

He smiled slightly again when rage flickered in Albertus's eyes, but then he lost interest in the mortal and stared past Albertus's right shoulder until the man began to twitch with discomfort. Vidal smiled more broadly at the sign of uneasiness.

"Another task, equally important," Vidal said, "is that I want you to form a private fighting force for me."

Albertus looked alarmed. "That will not be easy, m— Master Otstargi. The fate of the last men I hired to kill Lord Denno and Lady Alana is not unknown. I doubt I would be able to convince—"

Vidal gestured and Albertus fell instantly silent. "No, I don't want criminals this time. I want men who cleave to the old Catholic rite, men with a hatred for the reformed religion, or men with a grudge against the present government. The single binding factor is that all must wish to fight to see Lady Mary as queen and Catholicism reestablished."

Albertus had lowered his eyes; Vidal thought he was considering what had been said, then realized his gesture had gagged the man. He twitched a finger. Albertus expelled a long breath, drew another. He had not lifted his eyes and the hate in them was hidden from Vidal who, mindful of Aurilia's warning, did not wish to invade the mortal's mind except for a significant purpose. Vidal knew that Albertus would report everything to Aurilia, but he had nothing yet to hide from her; he was sure she would agree with what he was doing.

"That gives me a wide range of choice," Albertus said finally, looking up with a thoughtful frown.

Vidal shrugged. "Not so wide as you think," he warned. "I will need at least fifty men and one or two leaders who can think out for themselves how to accomplish a purpose set for them."

"You will not direct them closely, my lord? I could not. As God knows, I am no fighting man."

"No, you certainly are not." Contemptuous again, Vidal shook his head. "Beside that, I do not want any of them to know that Master Otstargi pays their wages."

Albertus lowered his head again for a moment, then lifted it. "Then I must not be known to pay the wages either, my lord. I am sorry I did not forsee this eventuality when the Lady sent me here to help attend the king. I needed a direction at which I could be reached, and gave them the tale that I was Master Otstargi's house-watcher while he was journeying. I thought I was saving the Lady the labor of ken—" His voice checked and his hand flew up to the gold chain. "—of finding money for my lodging."

"Stupid clot," Vidal muttered, then shrugged again. "Well, you have just cost your Lady the trouble of making an amulet that will disguise you when you deal with the troop you are going to hire. Do you at least have any idea where to look for such men? I am aware you have friends in the muck at the bottom, but it would be well if these were respectable men."

For a moment Albertus did not answer. Then he swallowed, cleared his throat, and said, "Oh, yes, my lord. I know of one man who would be perfect. He is a by-blow in the duke of Norfolk's family."

"Norfolk's by-blow?"

"I am not certain of that. He was not recognized by the duke, although he used the name Howard during the old king's reign. After Surrey was executed he began to call himself Mowbray, but if the Lady Mary becomes queen, I am sure he will be Howard again."

Vidal frowned. "He does not sound the kind to hold hard by a purpose. I need men who are willing to die for a cause."

"Possibly not, but he is a clever fellow, quite devious enough to accomplish a set purpose without any previous plan. And I think he knows others of his ilk—base-born sons of the nobility. Among them, it is possible I will find a devoted Catholic who will be able to recruit others."

"How long will it take to buy these men?"

"I could have Howard-Mowbray in two days, three at the longest, but fifty men . . . That will take time."

"Speak to this Howard-Mowbray then and discover whether he can assemble a troop large enough to attack Lady Elizabeth's cortege when she comes to visit her brother."

"Is she coming to London? I heard a rumor at Court that she had written for permission to visit and it had been denied."

"Mary visited. Elizabeth cannot do less than her sister. She must show herself no less loving. I will arrange for listeners in the inns and drinking houses around Hatfield so I will know at least a day before she leaves. Your man will need to be able to call up his troop within that day to accost her on the road."

Albertus was clasping his hands together so hard that the fingers whitened. Slowly, hunching his shoulders against his fear of punishment, he shook his head. "I do not believe Mowbray is the right man for such a purpose. He is brave enough and likes to fight, but he would not attack if the odds are not in his favor."

"That will suit me well enough," Vidal said calmly. "If her cortege is too large, he should not attack. Elizabeth and her guardians will remain ignorant of any danger and will not be warned for the future. Then Mowbray will be able to gather more men to take her on the way back to Hatfield."

Vidal was pleased to notice a slight gleam, almost of enthusiasm, in the mortal's eyes, but all Albertus said was, "Very well, my lord. I will seek out Mowbray as soon as possible. How can I let you know what he says?"

It seemed to Vidal that Albertus was also eager to be rid of Elizabeth. Perhaps he was attached to the old faith. So much the better if he was. Vidal felt almost pleased with the mortal, but he decided quickly not to tell him to Gate back to Caer Mordwyn. It would be best to keep Albertus away from Aurilia while he was using the man. Aurilia had a more delicate touch with minds and Vidal knew he would not be able to tell if she had set some ideas into Albertus that would forward Aurilia's purposes instead of his own. He preferred she have no chance to touch Albertus's thoughts.

"I will return tomorrow and give you the ruby ring, perhaps some other trifles. Do not give them out until the king is almost dead. You can tell me tomorrow what Mowbray said."

✧   ✧   ✧

Denoriel, Aleneil, Rhoslyn, and Harry were seated at a table
in the Inn of Kindly Laughter, talking desultorily. Each looked
impatiently at the doorway and then looked aside. Rhoslyn had a
very faint flush on her cheeks that might have indicated embar-
rassment. Harry reached over and patted her hand. She started to
speak, then turned her head abruptly to the door. Pasgen walked
in, smiling faintly. Denoriel shifted closer to Aleneil so there was
a space for Pasgen beside his sister.

"Why are you always late?" Rhoslyn asked sharply as Pasgen
sat down beside her.

"Mostly because I am working and I forget it is mortal Tues-
day," Pasgen replied with an amused grin. "But today I was with
Hafwen and Gaenor in the Unformed land that makes by itself.
We have been watching it closely since Vidal escaped."

"I hope it was not angry," Denoriel said. "Elizabeth has a real
fondness for that place and would be heartbroken if it became
dangerous and we needed to appeal to Oberon to . . . I am not
sure what he could do, but take away its initiative."

Pasgen's brows rose. "And how would I be supposed to know
if an unformed mist was angry?"

"Somehow," Denoriel said without any humor in his voice, "I
think it would make its temper clear to you."

"Then, no." Pasgen's response was dry. "It is not angry." He
sighed and shook his head. "But it is doing *something*."

Everyone looked appalled, but before anyone could speak one
of the very odd servitors of the Inn of Kindly Laughter—odd even
for Underhill—slithered up to the table. Now everyone looked at
the thick, snakelike body, furred in alternating stripes of yellow
and green. The fur was a short, soft-looking plush, and did not
cover the completely human head and face. That had no hair at
all, being bald and without eyebrows and eyelashes. Regardless
of its appearance, the creature radiated good humor.

"Your party is complete," it said. "How may I serve you?"

"Beefsteak," Harry said, "with lots of onions and mushrooms.
And a pot of ale."

Rhoslyn sighed softly, then smiled. "Fruits," she ordered, "with
a light, sweet sauce. Wine . . . muscatel." However she did not look
at the server but kept her gaze on her brother.

Aleneil and Denoriel repeated Rhoslyn's order, except that

Denoriel asked for a dry red wine, and Pasgen wanted stew, any kind, and aqua vitae. Everyone turned to look at Pasgen, who was more likely to ask for fowl's breast or ham in paper thin slices than stew. No one even noticed as the servitor slithered away.

"Don't you *dare* go into that mist to find out what it is doing," Rhoslyn said anxiously.

Pasgen laughed aloud. "You think I am fortifying myself for some hard endeavor? No, love, but I am afraid I forgot to eat last . . . Hmmm. I don't know when, but I am hungry."

"Rhoslyn is right," Harry said. "That Unformed land is dangerous."

"Not by intent," Pasgen insisted, and raised a hand to still Rhoslyn's half-uttered protest. "You should come and meet it."

"The Chaos Lands can do great harm without evil intent," Denoriel said.

Pasgen sighed. "I promise I will not leave the Gate platform—at least not yet." He frowned around the table at the troubled faces. "There is no need to be bringing Oberon into what the Unformed land is doing. Hafwen has a fine nose for detecting evil—she nearly fainted when the elder Sidhe and I took her to Alhambra—and she has scented no ill in that Unformed land. And Gaenor is trying to explain to it that we would like to know what it is making, not to interfere but to admire."

"I do not think you should lie to it," Aleneil said, her eyes wide, her voice anxious.

"Nor I," Rhoslyn agreed.

Pasgen looked from one to the other and then at Denoriel who nodded agreement. "Very well. I will speak to Gaenor. It does learn. It no longer reaches for us when we are on the Gate because we used to Gate away when it sent tendrils toward us. And Hafwen believes she detects a kind of pleasure when we are there, as if it likes company but has learned it must not touch us." He sighed deeply. "Fascinating. Utterly fascinating."

His head turned as if he could look through the mad mysteries of Underhill to that place.

"Pasgen!" Rhoslyn laid a hand on his arm and shook it. "I wish you would put aside playing with that Unformed land. I am worried about Mary."

"No one in the Bright Court is threatening Mary, no matter how little we look forward to her as queen," Aleneil said quickly.

"No, no, I know that," Rhoslyn agreed. "But there was a nasty accident yesterday. A servingman tripped and bumped into her as she was going down that wide stone staircase at Hunsdon. Fortunately I was near and quick enough to catch her."

"You think he did it apurpose?" Harry asked, looking worried.

"Servants do stumble," Denoriel said. "But if you have reason to doubt the intentions of this one, have him dismissed."

"That is not so easy with the lady Mary. She is very softhearted and very reluctant to dismiss any servant. I even went so far as to remind her that the same man had not long ago dropped a fur at her feet so that she nearly fell into a rock-rimmed pond. If she had hit her head and drawn water into her lungs . . . She would not hear of dismissing him. She said all the more reason not to send him away, since he was clumsy and likely could not find another position."

"Then make sure that that servingman never again has occasion to come near Mary," Harry said.

Rhoslyn's dark eyes glittered hard. "I would have done more than that. He would have had a serious accident himself, which would surprise no one . . . clumsy as he had shown himself to be. But he disappeared."

"Disappeared?" Denoriel exclaimed. "As in used magic to become invisible? But Vidal would not send anyone to harm Mary. He *wants* Mary to come to the throne. He thinks she will bring in the Inquisition."

"No, I did not mean disappeared in that way. I do not believe Vidal had anything to do with this. I mean the servingman ran away." Rhoslyn tapped her fingers on the table uneasily. "No one else thought it was strange. Everyone thought he was just frightened of being punished for nearly pushing the Lady Mary down the stairs, but now I do not know who to watch."

"I do not understand," Aleniel said. "I swear it is no doing of the Bright Court and I also agree with Rhoslyn that the Dark Court would offer no harm to Mary. And she has always been a kind and thoughtful person. Who—"

"Northumberland," Harry said grimly.

Denoriel opened his mouth but did not speak. The servitor had returned. It now had arms almost as long and thick as its body on which rested a variety of dishes. These slid along the arm as if each dish had little feet until the dish came to the edge of the table where the person who had ordered the food sat. Harry, still fascinated by the wonders Underhill, seized his plate of steak and lifted it up so he could look underneath.

To his mild disappointment, there were no feet. Despite her concern over Mary, Rhoslyn smiled at him.

"It's the arm," she said, and Harry looked at the arm as she lifted her bowl of fruit off it. Under the bowl were little flat fingers that withdrew as Rhoslyn placed the bowl and her cup of wine on the table.

There were some moments of silence while everyone began to eat, Pasgen with considerable eagerness. After a while, however, Denoriel, who had been frowning, repeated, "Northumberland?"

"Would he dare?" Aleneil asked.

"He faces ruin if Mary comes to the throne," Harry said a little thickly as he swallowed steak, onion, and mushroom, and then more clearly, "Why should he not dare to try to be rid of my sister Mary, especially if it can seem to be an accident."

"Would he really be ruined?" Aleneil asked. "I know he would lose his power and not be able to add to his wealth when Mary is queen, but ruin?"

"Ruin," Harry said firmly. "Do you think Mary will forget how he plagued her to accept the reformed religion? Will she not press him as hard to renounce reform and profess himself Catholic?"

"From what I heard of Northumberland from Lady Denny," Denoriel said, "Northumberland cares very little about which rite he worships by. So why not become Catholic?"

"I suspect Mary will require some more substantial evidence of his conversion than his simple word," Harry said dryly, "like the return to the Church of any lands he received in the dissolution of the monasteries."

"Oh, my," Aleneil breathed.

Harry nodded. "And he would be watched very keenly, indeed, for any slip for which he could be accused of treason. Oh, yes, for Mary to come to the throne would be ruin for Northumberland."

"Nor is he such a man as Norfolk," Denoriel remarked, with a wry twist to his mouth. "Norfolk served Henry devotedly all his life—never mind that he profited greatly while he served—but only said when that ungrateful king condemned him to death that if his master wanted his life, that, too, he would give."

"So what you are all saying is that Mary's life likely *is* being threatened." Rhoslyn sighed. "I will warn Susan Clarencieux and Jane Dormer. Among us we can make sure that no servant approaches her. And I can just touch the mind of any visitor, but what if I detect danger to her? I know well enough how to kill a man and one I can be rid of but not more."

"No, indeed!" Harry exclaimed, pushing away his near empty plate. "If one man's heart gives out and he dies in Mary's presence, that is a tragic accident. If two or three suffer the same ending, *someone* will be called a witch."

"Let us see what happens before we act," Pasgen said. "If worse comes to worst, Rhoslyn has a way to call me to her and I can take on the seeming of one of the guards. For a guard to kill any man who attacks Mary is an act of duty and heroism, and will not arouse suspicion or merit punishment."

Denoriel had signaled for another glass of wine and the server came with refills for all the drinking vessels. He sipped and put down the cup. "Do you think *Elizabeth* is safe from Northumberland?" he asked Harry.

Harry pursed his lips. "I wish I could be sure. On the one hand, he and Elizabeth have always got along well, and he has gone out of his way to please her—so much so that if you remember, there were rumors he intended to put his wife aside and marry Elizabeth."

"I remember all too well," Denoriel said dryly.

"That was never meant seriously," Rhoslyn said. "Well . . . if the idea had met an enthusiastic reception it might have become more serious. But Lady Catherine, who is Mary's woman at the Court, has heard him call Elizabeth a willful bitch."

Denoriel uttered a brief snort of laughter. "And so she is."

"Yes, but—" Harry's gesture cut off what Rhoslyn was about to say, "—that is why I am not certain of Northumberland's good will toward Elizabeth. With her advent he would not be ruined, but he would soon be powerless. He is devious and long-sighted and I am afraid he sees too clearly what Elizabeth is. Northumberland would not rule as he does now if Elizabeth were on the throne."

"But there is no one else," Aleneil protested.

"The duchess of Suffolk, Frances Brandon that was, is named in Henry's will and in the Act of Succession," Harry said. "She and her husband are both stupid beyond belief so Northumberland could twist them any way he liked."

Pasgen slowly shook his head. "I know nothing about mortal

affairs," he said, "but stupid people, even Sidhe, are often stubborn and even more often prideful. If your Northumberland is as clever as you say, he would not put on the throne stupid adults. A stupid child is something different; a child could be trained up in the pattern he wanted it to follow."

Denoriel sighed heavily. "I hope you are right, Pasgen. Then I would have one less threat to Elizabeth to watch for." He grimaced. "And you are all sure that Vidal is not only free of the thinking Unformed land but again ruling Caer Mordwyn?"

"Yes. And more than ruling it, rebuilding it." Pasgen's lips thinned. "He is also ruling much better than before he was made prisoner. His punishments are just as cruel and public, but they are much more rational. The Dark Court is quieter, but Vidal has found sufficient mischief for them to do that they are satisfied."

"I do not like that, not at all," Aleneil said.

"I cannot say I like it myself," Pasgen agreed. "I am sorry to say it, but I believe that Vidal is more in control of himself than he has been since he was damaged by Harry's metal shot."

"I could attend a Dark Court and try to discover whether he has made plans against Elizabeth," Roslyn offered, but she did not look happy.

"No!" Harry exclaimed. "That could be dangerous if Vidal suspects why you are there."

Rhoslyn smiled at him and a faint flush colored her cheeks. "It would not be dangerous. I could say with perfect truth that Elizabeth is a danger to Mary—"

"No!" Now it was Denoriel who protested. "Vidal hates Elizabeth enough. Let us not give him any real reason to urge him to do away with her."

"And he might try to hold you Rhoslyn," Pasgen said with a worried frown. "I prefer not to come to an open confrontation with him. I was stronger than he when he fell into the mist's embrace, but from the work he has done on his domain, I am not so sure I am still the stronger."

"Then let him be, Brother," Aleneil said. "For you to confront Vidal is a total loss to you, no matter who turns out to be stronger. If you lose . . ."

"Likely I would be dead."

"And Rhoslyn with you," Harry said bitterly, taking Rhoslyn's hand into his own.

Aleneil nodded grimly. Neither she nor anyone else doubted that in any fatal confrontation Rhoslyn would be right beside her twin, supporting him to her last breath.

"And if you win, you would be prince of Caer Mordwyn." Suddenly she laughed. "Which, from the expression on your face is to you a fate worse than death. It would be best, I think, if both you and Rhoslyn avoided Vidal as much as possible. I will speak to the other FarSeers and see if the great lens will tell us anything new."

Chapter 3

Elizabeth's visit Underhill at the end of February had had a pacifying effect on her, but not for very long. All through March she struggled with her fears, and in the first week in April she wrote again to Northumberland. This time she had a reply—from William Cecil but over Northumberland's signature—saying the roads were too dangerous, the weather too unsettled, her brother's health, although improving, still too uncertain, for a visit at this time. As soon as the situation improved, she would receive an invitation.

She did not believe Edward's health was improving or in the forthcoming invitation, but the hope of one, of a sanctioned visit, held her quiet until the middle of May. Then Elizabeth became aware of the lovely spring England was enjoying. The weather was perfect, the roads in as good condition as one could desire. As for Edward's health, that was what she wished to establish.

In the beginning of June, she told Denno flatly that she would set off for London in three days. If she was established at Somerset House, rumor of her residence would surely come to Edward; perhaps he would ask to see her. Even if he did not, she would know she had made the effort and he would know she had tried to come to him.

Denoriel was not happy with her decision, but he knew when arguing was hopeless and only begged her to come Underhill again so Harry could give her the latest news. Harry was no happier with her decision. The rumor in Mary's household was that Edward was failing rapidly and Mary was clearly fearful that some attack would be made upon her.

"It is foolish, Bess, to go to London. There is no way to secure Somerset house in the same way Hatfield can be secured. There Denno and your men know every person who lives in and around the neighborhood and strangers can be carefully watched."

Elizabeth wrung her hands. "I know it. I know it, but I must go. I must try. I have nightmares that Edward is asking for me and being told that I do not care enough for him to see him in his time of need."

Harry and Denoriel consulted each other in speaking glances but neither voiced any more reservations. For Elizabeth, her moods always strung so tightly, it was sometimes better to dare physical danger than to court safety at the price of guilt.

"Then how should she go?" Denoriel asked Harry. "For a trip to London, Elizabeth could call in the country gentlemen from Ashridge and Enfield as well as Hatfield and have a small army to protect her. You remember that Pasgen told us Vidal is ruling Caer Mordwyn again. And the Dark Court is reveling in snatched humans, but so cleverly snatched by Vidal's planning that Oberon does not disapprove. A small army would be proof against any attack by Vidal."

"No," Harry said, immediately. "Such a show of strength, and for no reason anyone in the mortal world would know, would be very provocative. God alone knows how Northumberland would react to Elizabeth appearing with hundreds of armed gentlemen. And it might not be wise to flaunt such strength in Mary's face either."

Elizabeth bit her lip. "I am not so afraid of Vidal. I think he would not dare attack me or use monsters openly lest Oberon hear of his disobedience, but I am worried about Northumberland. I cannot understand why he opposes my coming to London. And if my appearance there would thwart some plan of his, how far would he go to stop me?"

"If I knew the plan, I could answer better," Harry said, his mouth a thin line of dissatisfaction.

"That we have no hint of it from Cecil worries me also," Elizabeth said. "He has always warned me of anything important."

"I can only think he does not know," Denoriel said. "That he does not write at all, even common news, is a warning in itself. He knows that Northumberland is planning something, but he does not know what and does not want to hint lest he hint the wrong thing."

Harry looked thoughtful. "Bess's question—how far would Northumberland go to stop her—is significant. If he is merely trying to keep her away from Edward, either because he does not want her to influence the king or because he wants to conceal how ill Edward truly is, he will not go too far. Likely you will have another message soon discouraging you from traveling."

Elizabeth's jaw firmed. "I will not be discouraged. I will go to London." Then she bit her lip again. "Nonetheless, although I agree with Da that I dare not call up my tenants. I do not think I can travel with just Gerrit, Shaylor, Dickson, and Nyle."

She cast a guilty glance at Denoriel. He had been urging her to pension off her old guardsmen, but she could not bring herself to cast them aside, to make them feel old and useless. And for such duties as guarding her doors in a residence they were perfect, knowing from long experience whom she would welcome, whom she would need warning was come, and whom she would not wish to see at all.

"They are brave and steady and would die for me, I know, but," she admitted with a sigh, "they *are* growing old. They have all seen more than forty winters."

"That is true enough," Denoriel agreed, smiling; he was well aware of Elizabeth's fierce loyalty to those who served her. "But you need not go with them alone. If they are well supported by younger guards they will do very well." He uttered a soft laugh. "And just in case the attack *should* come from Vidal, those four would not be surprised by anything from mouse-sized trolls to green giants. They have seen it all and fought it all already. And so have Ladbroke and Tolliver and Sandy Dunstan."

"Of course," Elizabeth said, also smiling. "I had forgot them."

Ladbroke and Dunstan, she thought, must be at least as old as the guardsmen, but they showed little sign of it. Elizabeth knew they had been snatched Underhill as children and returned to the mortal world when Denoriel needed servants with special skills to help protect Harry as a child. They had only dim memories of the world of the Sidhe and, in addition, like Elizabeth were bespelled to be incapable of speaking of the Sidhe or Underhill or magic or enchantment while in the mortal world. However the years spent Underhill had not added to their age, so they looked ten years younger than the guardsmen—and Tolliver, rescued as a young boy from abandonment in a churchyard, was actually more than ten years younger than the other men.

"That makes seven who will be steady no matter what happens," Harry said. "I think with them as a strong core, a force of twenty all told would be large enough. I do not think Northumberland can possibly be desperate enough to order his men to fight yours and I agree that Vidal will chance no monsters in the mortal world, at least not yet. So another ten or thirteen who are young and strong and—" he grinned broadly "—already hard smitten by our Elizabeth's enchantment, and only a whole army will be able to endanger her."

Elizabeth had taken warning from Harry's remark that she might receive another message from Northumberland forbidding her to come to London. Because she did not want to seem to defy him openly, she hurried along her preparations for leaving Hatfield. The servants, harried to make ready all that would be needed for a protracted stay at Somerset House and thinned in ranks because some had already been sent off to London, had neither time nor energy to walk down to the inn for gossip (and complaint) and an ale or two.

If Vidal had had Sidhe spies in Hatfield town, they would have noticed the sudden absence of Elizabeth's servants from their usual haunts. However, he knew none of the Dark Sidhe would be willing to spend so much time in the mortal world, particularly at an inn where the cauldrons and spits for cooking and the frequent presence of Elizabeth's guardsmen in their armor and carrying weapons of steel, caused them constant pain. And the few werewolves and witches who could pass for human were too unstable. The presence of so many tasty and helpless mortals might draw them to attack. Therefore only imps watched and listened.

The imps did not like the presence of so much iron either, but they had compensation in being allowed to pinch and trip and pull the hair of the inn's patrons and drink the spurts of power generated by the pain—at least now and again. Though they were invisible, too much mischief caused comment, and comment brought punishment from their master. To the imps, who were not too clever and only interested in mortals as objects of torment, the absence of Elizabeth's servants had no significance. It was only the very night before she left that several tired servants came to the inn and remarked on their hope for a good rest now that their mistress would actually take to the road the next morning.

Vidal was angry, but he dared not punish the imps lest they try to disappear to avoid further duty. If they did that, he would have to destroy them as a lesson to the other imps, and Vidal had become chary of destroying his subjects since his return. His own tendency to destroy and his conflict with Pasgen had decimated his Court. As he could, he was creating more ogres and trolls and the witches and boggles, and some others were reproducing on their own, but he wanted more subjects not fewer.

He Gated at once to London and some of his ill humor was dissipated when he found Albertus still awake, just returned from an evening entertainment. Albertus was startled and alarmed at the shortness of Vidal's notice, but he picked up the brooch that disguised him and went out again at once to the small set of rooms he rented on the respectable border of a dangerous slum. There beggar children were always available for carrying messages and for mischief too. He sent one boy with a summons to Francis Howard-Mowbray's lodging and another to his favorite inn.

The first boy came back with the note undelivered; Francis was not at home, but the other found him at the inn and actually brought him back to Albertus's lodging. Francis was not drunk; Albertus made a mental note that although Francis spent a lot of time in inns, he did not drink to excess. He was glad of that, partly because it made his hireling more reliable and partly because a drunken man was more prone to violence than a sober one—and Francis was enough prone to violence without drink.

Francis was not pleased when Albertus told him to gather his men and get onto the road to Hatfield. But at least he did not need instructions and long explanations. Francis already knew what he was supposed to do and had actually scouted the road to find suitable spots to ambush Elizabeth's party.

"You said I would have a day's notice," he growled. "I cannot possibly gather the full troop at this time of night."

"Take who you can," Albertus replied, through gritted teeth. "I only learned a quarter candlemark before I sent the boy for you.

You know I am only a go-between, and I do not even know for whom. I am given orders, just as you are. And I doubt the man who transmits the orders is the one who gives them. He is not rich or important enough. But I believe that whoever the orders come from knows that the notice was too short. He or she will be satisfied if you take the lady on her return."

"When will that be? How long will I have?"

"I cannot even guess, but I believe she will be staying some time in London. I have been told that she wishes to visit her brother. You can set your own spies on her to give warning when she makes ready to leave."

Francis only nodded to that. He had made his protest and by it prepared an excuse for failure to seize or destroy his target. Now he was free to do what seemed best to him. He nodded again as Albertus stepped forward and handed him a purse that clinked softly.

Fortunately it was not very late, Francis thought, as he left Albertus's rooms. Some, at least, of the young men committed to support him would still be drinking if he went back to the inn and they would summon their fellows when he told them their work would begin before dawn on the morrow. As he went down the dimly lit, empty stairway, he tossed the purse into the air once, grinning, then caught it and concealed it in a deep pocket of his doublet.

No one need know that he was being paid. So far all those committed to support him believed he was planning to abduct Lady Elizabeth because he was determined to see Lady Mary on the throne. To those hot-heads who simply admired Mary for her courage in the face of so much persecution and the fact that she was King Henry's eldest daughter, he spoke of the Act of Succession and her father's will, which named her heir after Edward. Those who were Catholic, either secretly or openly, he reminded that the duke of Northumberland was dedicated to the reformed religion and must be intending to bypass Lady Mary, who would surely bring back the old rite. If they were not prevented, Northumberland and his supporters would force the dying king to call Parliament and make Lady Elizabeth his heir.

Francis pointed out that if they removed Lady Elizabeth, Lady Mary would be the only heir remaining and even Northumberland would have to accept her. To those who nervously asked what he meant by "remove," he said he hoped they would be able to carry Elizabeth off to France. Perhaps they could make it seem she wished to enlist the French to put her on the throne in defiance of Mary's right. Surely then she would be removed by Parliament from the succession and no longer be a danger to Lady Mary.

In any case, the men he had recruited thus far were all volunteers and would not expect to be paid, except perhaps in drinks or a dinner or two. Francis did not mind that; he would enjoy it himself and the conviviality would bind the men to him. He patted the bulge, well hidden by his clothing, and stepped out quickly for the inn.

After a few moments his steps slowed. He was not sure why the swarthy and stocky Master John Smith—Francis's lips twisted in disdain at the notion he would believe the man's name was John Smith—wanted him to gather as many as fifty men. Francis frowned over that, then shrugged. With the king on his deathbed there was bound to be some disorder. Either for protection or attack those who could afford to pay in good silver might want a fighting force.

Francis frowned again. The near twenty younger sons he had recruited were likely all he could get for "honor." And after he had lost the excuse of Lady Mary's right to be queen, he might lose them and need to hire men—although one could never tell. Some of the hot-heads who had sworn to him might develop a taste for the kind of work he was offering. Whoever was John Smith's master likely would have more exciting projects for them than snatching or, at worst, killing one young woman.

When Elizabeth's cortege came slowly over the low hill on the road from Hatfield to London, Francis Howard-Mowbray drew a harsh breath. He had not expected so many to be with her. And then he realized that most of those in the train that followed the armed men who surrounded her were servants. He smiled and softly called his men to make ready. The train of servants was more a danger to Lady Elizabeth than to his men. They would panic and run away as soon as his troop rode out shouting and brandishing weapons.

His men were moderately well concealed in a patch of woods in the narrow valley between two hills. The stream that had worn the land into a valley had diminished, but it still flowed shallowly over the road, which made the bottom of the valley pebbly and muddy.

Francis signaled for the men to wait and himself moved forward, keeping to the far side and the shade of a large oak. Two men rode well ahead of the main group, one somewhat stout in well-worn armor, the other in a newer breastplate that fit well but had seen less service. Francis glanced at them and dismissed them; when the main group was attacked, they would probably flee down the road toward London. He gave no signal, waiting for the main group to reach the treacherous muddy portion of the road.

Another cautious glance told him his prey was there, following another two men-at-arms. He smiled to himself; she was making everything very easy for him. On one side she was accompanied by an elegant but ancient gentleman, his white hair showing under his bonnet. He was armed with a sword, but if he had drawn it in twenty years, Francis would be much surprised. On the other side was what must be an upper servant with a fine lady riding pillion behind him. The servant also carried a sword—much good it would do him with the woman behind him blocking every movement.

Down the hill they came, Lady Elizabeth and her companions talking animatedly. The two advance guards passed the muddy stretch of road. Francis raised his hand; he heard the horses behind him move. The old gentleman suddenly turned his head toward the wood in which Francis's men were concealed. Francis opened his mouth to shout and then swallowed back the word "Go!"

Over the other hill, the one to the south, a horse appeared suddenly, pounding along at a gallop. As he came down the hill, it was clear the horseman was wearing the king's livery. Francis shrank back to where the oak's broad trunk and deep shadow would better conceal him. Elizabeth stopped her horse just before its forehooves touched the muddy area, watching the rider approach. Francis clearly heard her say "Shit!"

The old man said "Elizabeth!"

Francis felt mildly shocked by the gentleman's familiarity in addressing the king's daughter without any title, but that was only the surface of his mind. Underneath he was rapidly reviewing the advantages and disadvantages of going ahead with the attack. The greatest disadvantage was that his party would be seen by the king's messenger, but second thought said that was a minor matter. His party wore no identifying colors or tokens and with any luck the messenger would be among the dead.

The greatest advantage was that their quarry was now a sitting target, totally concentrated on the arriving messenger. Francis again raised his arm as a signal and looked around to make sure his troop was still in place and ready. At that moment the messenger slowed to pass through the pebbly mud, came between the two men-at-arms immediately preceding Elizabeth, making her more vulnerable, and pulled his horse to a stop.

"From the king, my lady," he said, fumbling in a saddlebag.

"Go!" Francis bellowed.

"Shield!" the old gentleman cried.

That seemed a very strange thing to yell when an attacker plunged out of the trees, but Francis had little time to consider it. The old gentleman had whipped out his sword and the horse he was riding was suddenly, incredibly, athwart Francis's own mount, which shied violently sideways. Since Francis's sword was in his hand, he was able to parry the old gentleman's thrust, but his whole arm felt numb from the power of the blow.

Meanwhile the rest of his party was pouring out of the wood, shouting threats. Francis had just a moment to notice that his hope that Elizabeth would panic and lose control, allowing her horse to bolt, had not been fulfilled. Then the monster the old gentleman was riding bit his poor horse so fiercely that the animal screamed and bolted away with blood streaming from its neck.

Francis fought his frightened beast to a standstill and then turned it back to the fray, which in that short time had taken on an entirely different aspect from what he expected. Before he could force his reluctant horse back into the action, he saw that Elizabeth had backed her mount away from the messenger, as if she believed he were part of the attacking party.

Although the two guardsmen who had preceded her had wrenched their horses around to come between her and the attackers, both of them were engaged as were four other guardsmen who were fighting their way in her direction. For one moment she was alone. Henry Clinton broke through the fighting and reached out to grasp her, to pull her from her horse. Francis shouted encouragement, but Henry's hand never touched her; it seemed to strike an invisible but very solid wall about two inches away from her shoulder and slide away.

Then Francis shouted again, for a knife had sprouted from the side of Henry's throat. And the old gentleman and his monster horse were suddenly beside Elizabeth, his sword flashing with shocking speed to ward away another who had forced his way through the fighting. Again the monster the old man rode struck and the other horse screamed and bolted, driving away two more of Francis's party. And then the two men-at-arms that Francis was sure would gallop away to safety were back, plunging into the melee and striking right and left from behind to throw his party into even greater disarray.

They did not need more disarray. The guardsmen who had been following behind Lady Elizabeth had drawn weapons and driven their horses forward, forming a wall that most of his own men could not breach. Francis stopped trying to force his horse back into the battle and took time for a look around.

Immediately he saw that another of his expectations had been dead wrong. Far from panicking, the male servants had hopped down from the carts in which they rode carrying long, stout cudgels and, following two men dressed as grooms but with drawn swords, were running toward the few men who were trying to flank Elizabeth's men-at-arms.

One man's cudgel struck the rear of an attacker's horse a solid whack while another man's cudgel struck the rider so that when the horse bolted away, the rider fumbled helplessly with the reins. Another of the servants dodged under a blow launched at him and thudded his cudgel against George Coleg's thigh. The blow was so violent that Coleg screamed and dropped his reins to clutch at his leg. A second cudgel rapped the injured man's horse alongside the tail and that animal too bolted. Meanwhile the armed grooms had wounded and driven back two more of Francis's men.

Near Lady Elizabeth another man died. Francis watched with starting eyes as the upper servant he thought would be immobilized by the lady riding pillion pulled a knife from his boot top and sent it into the eye of a second man who was reaching for their quarry while the old gentleman was engaged.

Francis's whirling thoughts brought up the image of Henry Clinton who had first tried to seize Elizabeth and died with a knife in his throat. And then William Pausey fell as the old gentleman's sword drove William's blade aside, slid under it, and whipped forward with terrifying accuracy to stab above the breastplate collar right into the throat.

No coward, but no fool either, Francis bellowed, "Withdraw! Retire! Enough! We are done here! Withdraw! Withdraw!"

Two more men slumped in their saddles, holding themselves ahorse with a desperate clutch on the pommel. Francis rode forward to try to distract the guardsmen who were attacking them, but the retreat of most of his men gave the wounded space to turn their horses. The guardsmen surged forward after the retreating men and Francis cursed luridly. The woodland in which they had set the ambush was too small to hide them for long or give them room to escape. However he was spared being hunted.

"Stand!" a stentorian voice bellowed.

The guardsmen pulled up their horses, muttering their dissatisfaction. And the servants swinging their cudgels were just as angry and eager for revenge on those who attacked their lady.

Now Francis understood why John Smith wanted him to have a troop of fifty. He took the chance of stopping where he had initially watched Elizabeth come, as he thought, into his trap. He saw the guardsmen, specially four older men, move restlessly, obviously wanting to pursue their attackers, and he was surprised himself to realize that the powerful voice had come from the younger man who had been riding ahead of the party.

"I agree. Sir Edward is quite correct. We dare not spread our strength. The retreat might be a device to separate us and make us vulnerable, thus making our lady an easier prize."

It was the old gentleman speaking and it was of considerable interest to Francis that the guardsmen instantly quieted. The old man was someone important. He was visibly trembling after his exertions, but the voice was strong and very beautiful. Francis thought he was not likely to forget it. Cautiously he eased his horse away from the shelter of the great oak and moved deeper into the wood, where a charcoal burner's track led to a farmer's lane that would eventually take him to the road to London at some distance from where they were. The last thing he heard was a girl's voice, high with anxiety.

"You weren't touched, were you, Denno?"

"No." Denoriel smiled at Elizabeth. "I'm just getting too old for so much excitement."

He could not say that the pain of close contact with steel transmitted through his silver sword was still rolling through him, but he knew Elizabeth understood that and only wished to assure her that the death metal had not touched him and that he had no need immediately to go Underhill. If he had been poisoned, she would have sent him off on some errand so that Miralys could transport him to Mwynwyn to be healed.

"Thank God," Elizabeth murmured and then, raising her voice, "Is anyone else hurt?"

She looked around at the guards and servants who had fought for her. Two of the servants sat down on the ground rather suddenly, only then realizing they were hurt. And some of the guardsmen started to dismount, groaning now that the furious action was over and they felt their injuries.

Sir Edward Paulet was enchanted anew. Most women he knew would have been screaming or fainting with fear. Lady Elizabeth was concerned only for her entourage. The only fear he had heard in her voice was when she asked Lord Denno if he had been touched.

Sir Edward wrenched his mind away from Lord Denno and Lady Elizabeth to the current situation. "Tom Woolman and Roger Heartwell," he called, "watch the wood. Henry Coldhand ride down the road to the top of the next rise and watch there. Benjamin Carpenter ride back and watch the road behind. All of you give warning if you see so much as a dog on the road."

"There are bandages and salves in the baggage cart," Kat Ashley said.

Her voice was trembling and her whole body shook, but Sir Edward noticed that she had herself well in hand; Lady Elizabeth set the example and her whole household tried to live up to her. Mistress Ashley looked around sharply.

"Gerrit, come help me down," she said. "We must see to the wounded before we decide what else to do."

The old man-at-arms who had been riding point with Sir Edward before the attack—and had been as quick as Sir Edward himself was to ride back to the fighting—swung off his horse and came to lift Mistress Ashley off the pillion.

"Very nice," Gerrit said to Dunstan, as he set Kat on her feet. "Very nice indeed. Didn't know you could do that. Neat trick when you can't get hand-to-hand."

Sandy Dunstan watched Gerrit steady Mistress Ashley, saw her straighten herself up, draw away from Gerrit and walk toward the injured. He shrugged, pushing away a long-ago memory of himself throwing silver knives with jeweled hilts into a target he could see clearly though the silver sky had neither sun nor moon. That life had been easier and less dangerous, but he had almost died of boredom and his service was often mindless and humiliating.

"Takes a lot of practice," Dunstan said, smiling, "but considering how my lady is getting nearer and nearer . . ." He did not say 'the throne' but Gerrit nodded understanding. "For safety, in house and on the road, I keep a few knives around my person and keep up my practice."

Tight as blood-kin that group, Sir Edward thought. Of course they'd all been with Lady Elizabeth since she was about three years old and he had only been given the place of captain of her guard a month ago. For all that closeness, they had welcomed him pleasantly enough but were clearly withholding judgment until he should prove himself one way or another.

He covered a smile with his hand, thinking that he had been very annoyed when the place had been offered because he thought he would be bored. He had expected interest and variety when he applied for a place in the king's guard, and had been disappointed when he was recommended instead for this position with Lady Elizabeth. But just living in the same household with her provided excitement and as for journeys—he wondered if every one would be as dangerous as this one.

He thanked God now he had been unable to refuse because the distant cousin who had offered the place was high in Court circles. Sir Edward had thought at the time that his mother, who invariably lectured him on being too daring, had urged her relative to find a sinecure for him. He should have known better. His cousin, William Paulet, now marquis of Winchester, was a wily old dog.

Doubtless, although he said nothing except that Edward was likely to do better with his offer, Winchester had known the king was very sick and his guard might well be disbanded if he died. Also his cousin did hint that Lady Mary would require Catholic observance from him. Thus, service with Lady Elizabeth was best.

Of course, Sir Edward knew that Winchester expected him to provide information about Lady Elizabeth and her household. And so he would. Sir Edward smiled behind his hand again. Although it was true that Winchester liked Lady Elizabeth and wished her well, Sir Edward was not going to trust his cousin's good will. He might well pass information; there was plenty to be said about his lady's studies, how carefully she managed her household, and how she behaved when ambassadors were sent to visit her. But Sir Edward would tell no tales that could harm his enchanting lady.

The women servants had now descended from the carts in which they had been sheltering and begun to root through the baggage to find the medical supplies everyone carried on a journey. The roads were rough so that broken axles or wheels could tip wagons and cause injuries to the passengers. Worse, because of the bad times there were outlaws who attacked travelers.

After a single glance to be sure that the wounded were being attended, Sir Edward took stock of the men who were unhurt, ordered the baggage wagon and the cart that had carried the servants drawn closer, and set his diminished troop—enlarged by the armed grooms—into defensive positions. He would have liked to tell Lady Elizabeth to sit in the cart where she would be stationary, surrounded by fighters, and safer, but he suspected that if he made the suggestion he would get his ears burned off—and might lose his place, too.

Another glance showed him that Lady Elizabeth had drawn her horse as close as possible to that of Lord Denno, and they had their heads together . . . as usual. A real puzzle was Lord Denno. Rich as Croesus and indulgent to Lady Elizabeth as a doting father. Old enough to be her grandfather, too, but . . . Sir Edward looked away, around the busy site. He did not want be caught staring. But . . . there was something between those two that had nothing to do with the rich presents Lord Denno brought or Lady Elizabeth's need for a father-like friend, as Mistress Ashley would have it.

In the next moment Sir Edward had good reason to join them.

"Those weren't outlaws." Elizabeth's voice was indignant.

She had pulled her horse close to Miralys, and nodded to Sir Edward as he joined her and Denoriel.

"No, I do not believe they were," Lord Denno replied, with the faint accent that Sir Edward could not place no matter how hard he tried.

All of them turned to look at the messenger in royal livery, who had done nothing to help them when they were attacked.

The man was quivering like aspic in a nervous servant's hands and for a moment Elizabeth could not imagine why he had not fled. Then she saw that Nyle, bared sword in hand, was right behind him, and one of the young men-at-arms, whose name Elizabeth did not know, was to the side, holding of the messenger's reins. The young man had a bloody sleeve.

"Are you hurt, Nyle?" Elizabeth asked anxiously.

"No, m'lady."

"Good." She smiled at him, her gladness warm and open. "Then let your partner go and get his wound dressed." She looked directly at the younger man. "I am sorry you were hurt . . . ah . . . Robert—" She had not known the name but caught it from Nyle's mouthing.

"It's naught but a scratch, m'lady," the young man muttered, his eyes worshipful.

"I hope so." Elizabeth smiled at him. "But let us be sure rather than sorry. Let it be cleaned and bound so it will not fester. Among Nyle, Sir Edward, and Lord Denno, whoever this is will do me no harm. I will be safe."

"Yes, m'lady," Robert whispered and reached the reins toward Denoriel who had come to his side.

Denoriel smothered a grin. Apparently the young man would sit bleeding rather than be salved if he could watch Elizabeth. The messenger reached forward as if to intercept the reins before Denoriel took them and found the "old man's" rapier an inch from his neck. He cried out and sat back.

"I am a royal messenger!"

"Are you indeed?" Elizabeth's voice could have cooled a drink on a day far hotter than this one.

"I am. I am. I can show you my patent. And here is a letter to your ladyship from the king."

Elizabeth's face suddenly lit with hope. "Edward was well enough to write me a letter?" she said, reaching out eagerly.

The messenger found the letter in his saddlebag and handed it to Elizabeth. As she breathlessly broke the seal, he showed the order for him to use post horses to Denoriel. The order was under Northumberland's seal. The sword at his throat did not waver.

"It is not from Edward," Elizabeth cried. "It is not even his signature!" Hope of her dearly loved little brother's recovery destroyed, fury took its place. She turned on the messenger. "Who are you? Who sent you? Who paid you to lead that armed band of assassins to attack me?"

"No, my lady! No! I *am* a royal messenger. I knew nothing about those men. Nothing!"

Elizabeth's pale cheeks flushed slightly with rage. Denoriel's arm drew back in readiness to stab at her word. And Kat Ashley came and plucked at her riding skirt.

"Elizabeth, we can go no farther just now, and I think we should go back to Hatfield, which is much closer than London. Two of the men have serious wounds. I do not understand how men can keep fighting with great holes in them—"

Worry dampened rage. "Not any of my four," Elizabeth said softly.

"No, no. Dickson has a cut, but it is truly no more than a scratch. The others are all well. But Dunstan says it would be better if we could pull off the road. Dunstan will decide whether we could make horse litters for the wounded or whether we should make a suitable place for them in the wagons."

"We should certainly remove ourselves as soon as we can from this place," Sir Edward said.

"Yes, and I think we should read that message carefully and try to discover from whom it came. And since the reason for your setting out from Hatfield so swiftly no longer exists—" Denoriel eyed the messenger with disfavor "—we might as well go back to Hatfield. We can set out anew . . . if you decide to do so, any time at all."

"I agree," Elizabeth said, her thin lips becoming even thinner. "And Hatfield would be a better place to get answers from this 'royal messenger.'"

Chapter 4

William Cecil, chief secretary to John Dudley, duke of Northumberland, cast one flashing glance at his master before lowering his eyes to the sheet on which he was making notes. Inside he was cold with horror. He could hardly believe what he was hearing. He had known that his master was growing more and more desperate as the young king's health worsened and he had guessed that Northumberland was making plans to protect himself, but it had not occurred to him that the duke would try to solve his problem by changing the succession.

All of England had accepted the succession as defined in the Will of Henry VIII and the Act of Succession voted by the Parliament. England had been satisfied with their paragon of a young king; some it is true had not been happy with his weak economic policy and strong leaning toward the reformed religion or his increasing intolerance for any hint of Catholic practice. Most of the commons, the merchants, and the minor nobility blamed those who governed for him. They hoped by the time he came of age he would better understand the political and religious realities so that when he took the management of the kingdom into his own hands the wrongs would be righted.

When rumors began to ooze through the country of Edward's illness, no one was happy. Still, no one was in a panic either. The country would not fall into anarchy. The succession was established.

There were two recognized heirs—or, rather, heiresses—the royal line of England was singularly without males. That was most unfortunate; no one really looked forward to a queen regnant. But the entire country dearly loved Lady Mary, who was known for her kindness and her steady courage.

What William Cecil was hearing was treason. Yet how could it be treason when the device he was recording was said to come from the king himself? Cecil did not believe it. Edward was inclined to reverence his father and not to wish to change what Henry VIII had decreed—except in matters of religion.

Cecil's lips tightened and he took the lower between his teeth, concealing the mark of anxiety with his bent head. Religion. That was the crux of the matter. Edward was a violent bigot. He abhorred all things Catholic, and Mary, his heir, was devotedly Catholic. No pressure placed on her, not even Edward's own pleading and remonstrance had induced her to put aside her Masses. So it could be that Edward *had* worked out this "devise."

Only this arrangement excluded Elizabeth as well as Mary and Cecil knew Edward was fond of Elizabeth and knew her to prefer the reformed religion. Cecil himself had not been looking forward to Mary coming to the throne. He was convinced that the Catholic religion and, in particular, the Catholic papacy and priests were corrupt and greedy, and his wife was strongly of his opinion. Cecil was perfectly willing to keep his lips sealed over his religious preference, but he was quite sure that the Lady Mary would not be satisfied with quiet nonobservance. If he wished to serve and, more especially, rise in her government, open conformity would be required . . . Mass, confession, tithing to the Church . . .

"Let me see what you have written—and you yourself need to write this matter. No secretaries. No hint of the king's devise should go farther than your chamber."

"No, Your Grace, of course not. But . . . but I cannot understand why the king has . . . has disinherited Lady Elizabeth. I understand that to have a strong Catholic on the throne, who would be inclined to marry only another Catholic, would be a disaster for this realm. Lady Elizabeth, however, believes as the king does. I remember that he called her his Sweet Sister Temperance and always took great joy in her company."

Northumberland stared down, his face expressionless except

for a twitch on the left side of his mouth. "Ah, yes. You are in high favor with Lady Elizabeth. You hold a position as surveyor of her estates, do you not?"

"Yes, Your Grace, I do."

"And you looked to rise higher still if she became queen."

Cecil shrugged. "That possibility was far in the future if it were ever to come about. I—"

"Well, it will not!" Northumberland's jaw clenched. "The king himself saw that it was impossible to disinherit one sister because she was declared illegitimate and not the other, when she, too, was declared illegitimate and is, moreover, a very headstrong young woman, disinclined to take advice." He paused, then said, "I want that document in my hands before dinner. Do not make any copy and destroy the notes you have made. And if there is any hint of a rumor about this disposition . . ."

Northumberland turned and walked out of the room. For a moment Cecil sat staring down at his notes. No, this time he dared not send even a distant hint to Elizabeth. And what good would a hint do? Unless he was totally explicit, no one would understand what he was hinting about. The idea was incredible! To change the succession to heirs male of Frances Brandon or of her daughters. Why the girls were just barely married. Who knew if there would be heirs male . . . or any heirs at all . . . The poor little king was fading fast.

To exclude Mary and Elizabeth . . . Could Northumberland carry enough of the Council? Cecil sighed. They were all so much afraid of him. The shock to Elizabeth would be dreadful, but . . . Wait! What did Northumberland intend to do with Mary and Elizabeth? To ignore them was an open invitation to rebellion. That Mary should rule and Elizabeth follow if Mary had no heir was a settled fact in the public mind. Whatever the Council was forced to agree to, the gentry and the people would be shocked and angry. The first event anyone disapproved would bring an army of supporters to one princess or the other.

Cold coursed down Cecil's spine. Northumberland was far too good a soldier to leave an armed and unbeaten enemy free in his rear. He fumbled in the drawer of his writing table for a sheet of parchment. Northumberland would try to seize both ladies. And God alone knew what would happen to them once they were in his hand.

Then Cecil breathed a soft sigh of relief. He had only the day before sent an order under the king's seal telling Elizabeth that she should not come to London, that Edward would not be able to receive her. Cecil bit his lip again. Would she obey it? Elizabeth was just the kind to confine the messenger until after she had reached London and claim she had not received the message in time to turn back. Despite his anxiety Cecil could not restrain a chuckle. Biddable? No, Lady Elizabeth was not biddable. Northumberland would be much happier with an infant heir from one of Frances Brandon's daughters.

Cecil flattened the sheet of parchment on the table and dipped his quill into the ink. Without glancing at the notes he had made, he began to write out the king's "devise." If the king survived until a boy child was born to one of the girls named in the "devise," Cecil knew he would have time enough to provide some warning to Elizabeth against falling into Northumberland's hands.

By then, too, news of the altered succession might well be abroad from other sources so Northumberland would not blame his secretary for tattling. And surely Lord Denno would warn Elizabeth that she was in danger from Northumberland if even a hint of the change of succession came to his ears. Also, Cecil's long silence would ring an alarm bell for Elizabeth. She would know he had been forbidden to communicate with her by the duke. Neither of them ever mentioned the future, but . . .

Despite her original insistence on going to see her brother, Elizabeth was actually glad to be back in Hatfield. The messenger had been hurried away between Gerrit and Shaylor to be questioned, and Sir Edward had ordered the gates be closed and a watch be set to warn of any large party approaching.

Now that she was safe, Elizabeth found she was cold with shock. She had been attacked before, but that had been Underhill, where everything was somewhat unreal to her.

She remembered now that Denno had told her an attempt to abduct her had been made when she was only three, but apparently she had slept peacefully through that desperate battle and knew nothing about it. Had this been another attempt to abduct her? Gerrit and Shaylor would wrench that out of the messenger—if he knew. The man who had reached for her and been unable to seize her because of her shield had not threatened her with any weapon. But he had a weapon in his other hand. Who knew what he might have done if he could have dragged her away from her defenders.

The entrance doors had shut behind them and Elizabeth started down the corridor toward her apartment, Kat and the maids of honor trailing behind.

"Lady Elizabeth?"

She turned quickly. "Lord Denno?"

He stood a little apart from the women and Elizabeth could see the lines of pain around his mouth were graven deeper than usual. "I think, perhaps, I should leave you now—"

"No!"

Regardless of the fact that her maids of honor were following and that she and Denno were careful never to show any sign of intimacy, Elizabeth took a long step toward him and seized his arm.

"No," she said somewhat more softly, but still clutching his arm. Tears stood in her eyes. "At least . . . at least . . . You said you were not hurt. Do you really *need* to go?"

Because of the geas put upon her by Queen Titania when she was allowed to come Underhill and return to the mortal world with her memories of the kingdom of the Sidhe intact, Elizabeth could not speak of that place. She could not ask Denoriel if he needed healing or to go Underhill to restore his power.

Denoriel covered Elizabeth's hand with his own and looked over her shoulder at Mistress Ashley, who was nearly the color of her name. There was no censure in her expression. Of course, Mistress Ashley was not the finest and most severe judge of propriety. Her affection for Elizabeth often outweighed her good sense—as it had when she encouraged the idea that Thomas Seymour would be allowed to marry Elizabeth. Still, in the aftermath of an armed attack, allowances might be made.

"For myself, no. I do not need to go," he said. "I thought that you would wish to change your clothes and rest . . ."

Elizabeth tightened her grip on his arm. "I can change in my dressing room. Please, Denno, do not leave me. You saved me twice when my men could not win near. Stay, at least until we are sure there will be no further attack. I am all shaking inside."

The last was only a murmur that her women could not hear, but Denoriel felt her hand strike cold through the silk of his sleeve. He did not need the added pain that her iron cross was sending from her grip to his arm, but she really was shaken. Without saying anything, he led her toward her own apartment, where two young guards bowed respectfully, stepped aside, and opened the door to her reception room. Elizabeth's hand closed harder on his arm.

"Where are my men?" she whispered.

"Gerrit and Shaylor have taken the messenger off to question him, my lady," Denoriel said. "And you sent Dickson off with Nyle who had been slightly wounded. I am sure the men Sir Edward has chosen to guard you are both skilled and devoted."

"Oh, of course," she said, trying to lighten and steady her voice. "I am just so accustomed to seeing my four . . ." Her voice faded and she looked around the large, empty reception room. "I . . . I do not want to receive anyone," she said, sounding strained and defensive. "Let us all go into my bedchamber. There are seats enough and we can be closer together."

"Oh, my lady," Kat Ashley began, but her eyes fixed on Elizabeth's hand, gripping Lord Denno's sleeve so tightly that the cloth was ridged. And she added weakly, "So long as we all go together, I suppose it will be safe enough."

Denoriel opened the inner door and hesitated on the sill, looking around as if he had never seen the chamber before—which was far from true. He often spent the night with Elizabeth when for some reason she did not want to go Underhill. It was safe enough with the maid of honor who slept in her chamber spelled not to wake. However, he did not want to slip and speak as if he knew the room. A good long look now would cover his familiarity.

Elizabeth had finally released his arm, because the door to her dressing room had opened and Blanche Parry was coming toward her, arms outstretched. Elizabeth rushed toward those sheltering and protective arms, but Blanche stopped as soon as she saw Kat and the other ladies come in. Elizabeth continued toward her maid, but more slowly.

There was some jealousy between Kat and Blanche since Kat had foolishly tried to urge Elizabeth to encourage Thomas Seymour's suit. Kat had never noticed Blanche much before, as the maid was only a maid and by her lowly status could not, to Kat's mind, engage Elizabeth's affections. But Blanche had been Elizabeth's only support and confidant when Kat had been in prison and all Elizabeth's maids of honor sent away and replaced with Lady

Tyrwhitt's dependents. Elizabeth had noticed Kat's slight anxiety and was careful not to increase it.

"Are you well, Blanche? You were not hurt, were you?"

"Not at all, m'lady," Blanche said calmly. "The fighting never came anywhere near us. You will want to change out of your riding dress."

Elizabeth was whisked away into the dressing room and Kat, reminded of her duties by Blanche's concentration on her own, set about making the chamber comfortable. Like all bedchambers, it was used for many purposes. At the foot of the great bed was a sofa, deep-cushioned in red velvet; facing the sofa were chairs cushioned in a silvery gray fabric picked out in red to match the sofa. A tall candelabra stood behind the sofa to shed light if the studious Elizabeth wished to read. Between the sofa and one of the chairs was a table for drinks or comfits.

One of the maids who assisted Blanche came timidly to the dressing-room door and Kat sent her to summon the maids of the girls who had accompanied Elizabeth and then to fetch wine and sweet cakes. Denoriel stood back, half hidden by the bedcurtains. Technically he could not go until Elizabeth dismissed him, since she had bade him stay, but Kat could dismiss him too, and he did not want to go. He needed to make sure that Elizabeth understood what the attack meant.

She spent much longer in the dressing room than it usually took her to change clothing, unless she was preparing for some formal occasion. By the time she emerged, there were cakes and wine on the table near the sofa as well as on a table drawn forward from the wall about which several seats were clustered, two small benches, two stools, and a single chair. And the ladies' maids had come, bringing their mistresses' current needlework projects.

At first while the women settled themselves on the benches and stools with Kat in the chair, all talking about the attack, Denoriel had just stood with closed eyes, trying to bring calm to himself. He was worried about Elizabeth, fearing she was weeping and terrified. In a way he would have done better to go to the lodge he rented about a mile from Hatfield; Blanche could have sent an air spirit for him and he could have Gated into Blanche's bedchamber, behind the dressing room, and calmed Elizabeth.

Now Denoriel was afraid when Elizabeth came out she would send him away immediately because she was ashamed of showing her weakness. Instead, she hurried from the dressing room and rushed to him where he stood by the bed. She looked as if she were about to throw herself into his arms, but he could not embrace her; all the women had turned to look. Denoriel could only bow low and offer his arm. She took the warning but seized his arm and drew him toward the sofa and chairs, shaking her head at Kat who had started to rise to come to her.

"Can you—" she began, and there was a scratch on the door to the reception room.

Denoriel's hand went to his sword hilt and he heard several of the maids of honor draw gasping breaths. How had anyone passed the two guards at the reception room door to scratch at the door to Elizabeth's bedchamber? Kat Ashley, however, looked relieved, and called, "Who is it?"

"Gerrit, Mistress Ashley."

Everyone breathed a sigh of relief. Gerrit's heavy baritone was well known to all, and of course the guards at the door would have let Gerrit pass without asking permission.

"Come," Elizabeth said.

The man-at-arms entered, looked around, hesitated when he saw Kat but then spotted Elizabeth, and came to where she stood by the sofa at once. He bowed, then shook his head. "There's nothin' to be learned from that messenger, m'lady. He really is a messenger . . . knows all the roads, knows all the royal post houses. But he don't come from the king."

"From whom then?"

"I don't know and he don't know. I swear he don't. There's dozens a'clerks in Whitehall and one on 'em—good family or good money he guessed; well dressed the clerk was—handed him the message and bade him deliver it to you wherever he found you. To follow if you had left Hatfield but on all accounts to deliver the message." Gerrit shrugged. "I'd say he was picked to carry the message 'cause he can stick on a horse come fire or flood. He sure wasn't picked for brains."

"Or maybe he was picked because he had none," Denoriel said. Gerrit's mouth opened slightly and then he nodded.

"Whitehall," Elizabeth said softly. "I thought Edward had removed to Greenwich."

"And so he has, m'lady," Gerrit said. "Asked for the king. Messenger said he was at Greenwich. Asked why if king were at

Greenwich he was getting royal messages at Whitehall. Just stared at me, like how was he to know and then started cryin' again." Gerrit sighed. "Weren't picked for courage neither."

"What did he say? Everything, Gerrit."

Denoriel handed Elizabeth to the sofa and she sat down while Gerrit reported how he and Shaylor had interrogated the man. No pressure, and the messenger was indeed a weak reed unable to withstand pressure, was able to force from him any admission concerning the attackers. Neither trick nor threat had produced a slip in his story that he knew nothing about them and had been so utterly terrified when they rushed from the wood that he had not even presence of mind enough to run away.

"It is true that he could easily have run away," Elizabeth said softly in response to Denoriel's remark that a paralysis of terror was the only reason he could see for the messenger remaining with them.

She gestured him to the chair at right angles to the sofa, and he poured wine from the bottle standing on the small square table into a cup for her. Kat Ashley started to rise again as Denoriel seated himself, but then she sighed and resumed her place with Lady Alana, Agnes Fitzalan, and Dorothy Stafford All the ladies had their needlework in their hands, which were idle. All were listening intently to Gerrit's tale.

Elizabeth glanced at the group and then back at Denoriel. The younger ladies were rather pale and Dorothy Stafford's hands trembled. Now and again Dorothy cast a glance at Lord Denno and seemed to take comfort from his thoughtful but calm expression.

"The road back to Hatfield was clear," Elizabeth pointed out. "He could even have escaped any blame for not delivering the message. He could have said that we were not on the road and he assumed we had not left Hatfield so he went there."

Denoriel cocked his head. "But how was it the attack came just as the messenger distracted us all? Was that not planned?"

"It may have been, but not by him," Elizabeth said. "Would you rest the planning and timing of an attack on that man?"

"No." Denoriel shook his head and chuckled, glancing at Gerrit, who also shook his head firmly. After a moment Denoriel added, "Let the man go, Lady Elizabeth."

She frowned. "He will run back to his master and tell him what happened."

"Yes, but I am not at all sure he understands what happened. He will certainly tell his master we were attacked, drove off the attackers, and returned to Hatfield. Do not give him time to consider just who and what the attackers were."

That drew a chuckle from Elizabeth. "Perhaps he does not even know who it is who wanted answers from him." She nodded and looked up at Gerrit. "Send him back to Whitehall. Send one of the men-at-arms with him to make sure that is where he goes and tell your man to try to stay with him and see to whom he delivers his report and, if possible, hear what he says."

"Mayhap I should—"

"No." Elizabeth smiled at her man-at-arms. "Not you or Dickson or Shaylor. You are all too well known as my trusted men."

Gerrit's brow creased for a moment and then he looked relieved. "I know just who to send, m'lady. Sir Edward will agree with me, I'm sure."

He bowed and strode out. Elizabeth lifted her cup and took a sip of wine then said, "Pour some for yourself, Denno." And when he had and also sipped, she asked, "Then who were they? Could they have been outlaws?"

"No, Lady Elizabeth," Lady Alana said, "they were not brigands."

"Because you think brigands would not attack so large and well armed a group?" Kat asked uncertainly.

"No, not that," Lady Alana said, her cooing voice carried a smile. "You will all think I am quite mad for thinking about such a thing when we were like to be robbed or slain or worse, but those who attacked us were all too well dressed to be brigands."

"Well dressed?" Dorothy uttered a slightly hysterical giggle. "Really, Lady Alana, do you think of nothing but clothes?"

"However Lady Alana thinks," Elizabeth said thoughtfully, "what she thinks has told us something of great importance. If those were not common brigands, who or what were they?"

To Elizabeth's surprise, Lady Alana shook her head in a slightly exaggerated way. Clearly it was a signal. And then Lady Alana said, "There was nothing . . . ah . . . strange about them. If they had not fought so hard, I would have said they were a naughty bunch of too idle young gentlemen out to make mischief."

Denoriel nodded emphatically, confirming Lady Alana's hint that the attack was not by Underhill creatures disguised as human.

"Not . . ." Agnes Fitzalan's voice trembled and hardly could be heard by Elizabeth. "Not sent by . . . by Lady Mary?"

"Oh, no!" Elizabeth exclaimed. "Why should you say such a thing, Agnes?"

"Because you are of the . . . the right belief and there are so many who love you and hope you will keep them on the straight path to heaven . . ."

"Agnes," Elizabeth said reprovingly, "Lady Mary is a good, kind person. She is my sister. I am sure she wishes me no harm."

Agnes and Dorothy both looked down at their needlework and began to ply their needles. After a moment Lady Alana commented on the design Dorothy was creating. Kat also leaned forward to look at the pattern. No one said any more about the attack, but the same thought was in all minds. Mary or her supporters, who were desperate to bring back Catholicism, might well wish to remove Elizabeth, who might offer the nation a choice.

"Whitehall," Elizabeth said softly to Denoriel, repeating what she had said earlier. "Northumberland most often works out of Whitehall. That is where the messenger came from. I cannot believe that she—" Elizabeth did not wish to say Mary's name in any context that could be warped into treason "—had any part in this."

"Likely not, from what Rhoslyn says of her. But that Northumberland would use such a man as that messenger . . . No. He is too good a soldier to be unable to judge a servant's courage."

"But the messenger may well not have known that there was a troop following him. He was only a point dog, to show who I was."

For a moment Denoriel was silent and then he slowly wrinkled his nose. "Well, Northumberland will understand that you ordered the questioning of the messenger. I can only hope he does not realize how deeply I was involved. It would be a nuisance if Northumberland forbade you to see me."

"Unfortunately he will hear about how you fought to protect me. The captain of the group will report that."

Denoriel shook his head again. "No, that is meaningless. I was of the party and would naturally fight to save myself."

There was silence for a moment and then Elizabeth asked, "But why? Why was it so important that I not try to see Edward?" She hesitated and tears came to her eyes. "Can he be dead already and Northumberland keeping it secret? But why send men to attack me?"

Denoriel did not reply at first. He hated to frighten Elizabeth but the attack proved to him that Northumberland was desperate enough to hold his power to want her dead as well as Mary. Elizabeth had to understand that she was in active danger from the duke, that she must be very careful to keep free of him no matter what blandishment he offered to bring her to his hand.

"Because you are not a child nor are you the kind to content yourself with toys and gewgaws and let him continue to govern the country—"

"And rape it also!" Her voice was louder.

Agnes Fitzalan looked around at her. Elizabeth smiled and shook her head, indicating she had not meant to ask for service. Denoriel shrugged.

"Because you are clever and charming and would soon have the Council listening to you, obeying you," Denoriel continued, his voice lower, soothing. The tone had its effect; the ladies looked back at their needlework. "Northumberland cannot afford to have you come to the throne," Denoriel said even more softly, "even though you also favor the reformed religion."

Elizabeth's eyes widened. She leaned forward to take her wine in hand, which brought her closer to Denoriel and permitted her to speak even more softly. "Are you saying he wants me . . . dead?"

"Or in his power where no one can use you as the figurehead for a rebellion. Perhaps he will try to force you into marriage with some obscure German princeling."

She took that in, sipping at the wine, knowing that "try" was the significant word. Her Denno would have her safe away before she could be shipped abroad. And any man who had a contract with the British government to marry her would certainly not survive. Then she leaned forward to set the cup on the table again. Denoriel noted that she was no paler than usual and did not seem shocked only sadder.

"Does that mean Edward is dead? And what of Mary?"

"I do not think Edward is dead yet." This time Denoriel leaned forward to fill Elizabeth's wine cup. "And Mary . . . has her own protector."

Elizabeth nodded, glanced again at the women, but Alana, bless her, had begun an animated conversation about clothing.

Without ever saying anything about the king's failing health she had begun to speak about how mourning colors might be made more attractive. It was a subject that held the ladies' attention. Elizabeth kept her voice low but no longer needed to worry about ears straining to catch a word from her conversation.

"I am very glad she is protected." Elizabeth deliberately did not say Mary's name. "I do not look forward to her rule. But she must come to the throne before me or—" her eyebrows lifted "—as you pointed out I will be accused of ordering or taking part in whatever evil befalls her, which will make it almost impossible for me to rule." She sighed. "The whole country believes me to be Northumberland's favorite. Many would say he committed a crime against her to benefit me."

"Another device to keep you powerless?" Denoriel frowned. "That is not impossible. I will pass the word about the attack on you and make sure that Rhoslyn is extra alert to protect Mary. Meanwhile you had better take to your bed, the shock of the attack having disturbed your health. That way, Mistress Ashley can forbid all visitors and we will wait to see what happens next."

Chapter 5

On the last Tuesday of June it was more than guesses that Denoriel brought to the Inn of Kindly Laughter. Elizabeth, who usually did not come because she still avoided Pasgen when she could, had received so peculiar a visit from Chancellor Rich that she accompanied her lover. For once Pasgen was waiting for them, standing close to Rhoslyn with a hand on her shoulder. Both wore expressions of concern and Harry held Rhoslyn's hand.

The whole party went toward their favorite corner and the table, which was for four, obligingly enlarged itself and sprouted two more chairs. They all sat down together. The server glanced in their direction and then ignored them as if it knew they were not ready to order.

"I am beginning to think that Northumberland has gone mad," Elizabeth said, looking around at her companions. "He—it must be he because he controls the Council, but to do something so stupid . . . He is not a stupid man . . ."

"I am not so sure of that," Pasgen said in a hard voice. "What did he do to you?"

"He sent Chancellor Rich to me to propose that if I would come to London and there give up my claim to the throne he would reward me with rich lands and heaps of gold. The Chancellor brought two brooches and a tiara as earnests of the treasure that would be mine."

"You did not touch them did you?" Pasgen asked sharply.

"No, you may be sure she did not," Denoriel replied; Pasgen had once set a spell into a jewel that nearly killed Elizabeth. "Nor was Rich himself allowed to approach her, although he tried. He asked the honor of kissing her hand, which she could not allow because she was shielded. She said she was afraid to transmit her illness to him. Elizabeth has used the excuse of that attack I told Harry of to take to her bed."

"How can you give up a claim you do not yet have?" Harry asked, frowning. He had been thinking about the political implications of Rich's visit.

"That is the answer I gave to Rich," Elizabeth replied. "I told him that they must first make their agreement with Lady Mary since during her lifetime I had no claim or title to resign."

"Oh, Holy Mother," Rhoslyn sighed, "nothing will make Mary resign her right to the throne. That much Northumberland clearly understands. He is taking another tack with Mary." She looked around the table. "He is trying to kill her."

"I warned you," Denoriel said.

"Oh, keep good watch," Elizabeth cried. "If anything happens to Mary . . ."

Rhoslyn nodded. "Your warning was just in time, Denoriel. If I had not been made so anxious, likely I would not have watched the food. After all, Mary's servants have long been in her employ and all of them love her. But there was poison." Rhoslyn shivered. "I upset the platter on which it was served so no one could eat from it, but one of Mary's little dogs licked the stuff from the floor . . . and it died."

Elizabeth's eyes had grown large. "But you said her servants love her. Surely they would not—"

"No, not Mary's servants, but when they were hard pressed to answer for the dog's death, we discovered there were very loose practices in hiring casually acquired helpers. And one of them had disappeared soon after the dog died." Rhoslyn's lips thinned to a hard line. "That practice is now ended."

"You need not worry, Elizabeth," Aleneil said. "Since the attack no one is allowed into Hatfield except those who are your own servants. Produce and other supplies are delivered to the gate and our servants carry it in."

"Very wise," Rhoslyn said. "I wish we could convince Lady

Mary to take such precautions. On Sunday there came to Hunsdon an elderly man. Susan Clarienceaux admitted him and when
I objected because I did not like the way his eyes glittered, she
said he was old and weak and wished to talk to Mary of God.
Susan thought such a discussion would be a good distraction
for our lady."

"What happened?" Harry asked.

"I felt a long knife with ill substance on it concealed in his
clothes, so . . . so I stopped his heart before he ever came into
Mary's presence."

"Good!" Elizabeth said emphatically, "But you should have
made the threat clear."

"Oh, I did. I made sure that the knife fell out of his doublet
so everyone recognized the threat. Mary then agreed to be careful about whom she permitted to petition her." Rhoslyn sighed
and shook her head. "She *is* afraid, but she has never allowed
her fears to interfere with what she felt was her duty. She has
the courage of a martyr."

"Well, watch her close," Denoriel urged irritably. "I do not
want her to drag Elizabeth into martyrdom with her. She will be
a terrible queen, but she must rule before Elizabeth."

"But what am I to do?" Rhoslyn asked anxiously. "That one
elderly man, clearly intense and excited, should die is nothing to
raise any comment, but if another and then another die, surely
Northumberland will use that, call Mary a witch or say she used
her faith to curse those who came to remonstrate with her."

Harry said, "We spoke of this before. The next attack, if there
is one, must be ended by ordinary means. I assume you must be
with the attacker to . . . ah . . . terminate him. If you are always
there, you might be tied to the deaths. Can you not put in one
of the guards' minds a compulsion to kill anyone who is a danger, Rhoslyn?"

Rhoslyn shook her head vehemently. "Not unless I take the
man over completely, and then he could never succeed in stopping a determined attacker. To use someone else's body . . . that
is very difficult. If I just made him want to kill a petitioner, he
would wonder why he felt that way and try to reason himself
into doing the deed—but by then, likely the attack would have
succeeded."

Pasgen sighed heavily. "I suppose it is now time for me to do my part. I will go to the mortal world with Rhoslyn so she can point out the guard most commonly closest to Lady Mary. At need I will take on his appearance and do the killing and Rhoslyn will make the man's memories match what I have done."

Harry laughed. "I wish I had Rhoslyn's persuasive powers when I was in the mortal world. Heaven knows no one seemed willing to believe the reasons for my most innocent excursions."

"Were they innocent?" Rhoslyn looked up at him through her long black lashes.

"More innocent than I wished," Harry said, blushing and returning her teasing glance with one combining pleading and admiration.

"Do you want me to bind an air spirit to you Rhoslyn, so you can let Pasgen know when you need him?" Aleneil asked.

For a fleeting moment Pasgen's expression darkened with regret as he remembered how he had killed one of those innocent sprites when he was still serving Vidal, but all he said was, "No air spirit will come to me. It does not matter, Rhoslyn and I have a way of knowing when we need each other."

His hand rose and touched the small furry snakelike creature that nestled under the collar of his shirt. He knew that a similar construction was concealed somewhere on Rhoslyn. If either of them were alarmed or in danger the little construct would tremble as would its counterpart. The greater the danger, the more violent the quaking.

That had been sufficient until the time Rhoslyn had lost the Gate and been temporarily trapped in an Unformed land. Pasgen had nearly gone mad because he knew Rhoslyn was afraid and in danger—and he did not know where she was to come to her rescue. Later, when she had extricated herself from her difficulties, he bespelled the constructs so that he would also know where Rhoslyn was when she was in trouble.

Pasgen had not told Rhoslyn at first because he did not want her to come to face danger with him; later he realized how foolish that was. If she knew he was threatened from the convulsing of the furry snake and she could not reach him and he died . . . No, he could not inflict the grief and horror that would cause on his twin. Not after how she had suffered because of Llanelli's death. He was all she had. Better they be dead together, he thought, and bespelled her construct so she would know where he was.

Denoriel noticed the movement of Pasgen's hand, but he asked no questions. Pasgen was strong in magic, possibly strong enough to be considered a Magus Major, but he kept his abilities to himself. Denoriel understood. For a Sidhe raised in the Unseleighe Court everyone, including his blood relations if he had any, was an enemy. If Pasgen revealed his secrets to anyone, he would be sure that person would use the secrets against him. In fact, his mind might well know that was not true, that his half-sister and half-brother would not want or try to hurt him, but suspicion was trained into him.

He also noticed Harry's concern for Rhoslyn. There was something brewing there, Denoriel thought, absently replying to a question from Elizabeth. Harry had been living with him since Mwynwen had taken a new lover. Denoriel was pleased and relieved that Harry and the healer had parted so amicably, that Harry was not mortally wounded by the loss of his Sidhe lover as so many humans were.

Harry had never been much of a student, but he was clever about people. He had come to understand that what Mwynwen sought in him was the child she had called Richie, Harry's simulacrum. And while Harry was still very sick with elfshot poisoning, he had been dependent, like a child. But as the years passed, Harry was cured—and grown into an adult in his mind, no matter how young Underhill kept his body. Thinking and acting like a man had reduced Harry's appeal and made Mwynwen indifferent.

Luckily Harry had been growing indifferent too, tired of being regarded as a child. He had made friends among the elder Sidhe and engaged in some very risky enterprises that absorbed him completely—until he met Rhoslyn. Denoriel thought she might have attracted Harry at first because she was dark like Mwynwen and also very beautiful. But what drew Harry most was that Rhoslyn was a lonely, vulnerable creature, who had rejected the Unseleighe Court but was not acceptable to the Seleighe.

For a moment Pasgen thought that Denoriel would ask about the means he and Rhoslyn had for communication, but his half-brother did not ask, just looked from Harry to Rhoslyn. And then the server approached the table and everyone's attention was riveted. This time it looked like a besom broom stood on its handle. Two sturdy twigs extended from the pole to make arms and hands and the pole had somehow been split to form two legs. That was odd enough, but the besom itself seemed to be brightly on fire.

"What will the patrons have?" The words hissed and crackled.

"Does it occur to anyone," Pasgen said, "that we have never had the same server twice. Can working here be so fraught that new servers are hired every week?"

"It's the same one," Rhoslyn said after studying it for a moment. "I mean, whatever it looks like, it's the same construct."

"Don't you know it is not polite to make personal remarks, even about a lowly server?"

There were two black places in the burning besom that stood for eyes, an upright slit between them for a nose, and a larger, round black place for a mouth. Burning strands around the top and bottom of that round place moved up and down and in and out when the besom spoke.

"I would like to meet your maker," Rhoslyn said, her voice full of concern. "Clearly you are self-aware."

"Of course I am self-aware. I am my maker, and I am not a construct," the besom snapped.

"I beg your pardon," Rhoslyn exclaimed, flushing painfully.

"Your forms are extreme," Harry said quickly, with a touch of anger. "I must admit it did not occur to me that you were alive."

"Are you going to have steak with mushrooms and onions again?" the server asked.

"It certainly is the same being," Harry said, dryly, "and one with a very good memory. I had that to eat some time ago."

"And the blond one had stew that same day."

"Yes, I did," Pasgen agreed. "From what are you hiding that you alter your form so drastically and so often?"

The besom turned its hollow black eye-spots on Pasgen. "Unseleighe," it said. "Only Unseleighe think that way." The burning head shook back and forth and turned to Denoriel. "Do you think that way?"

"I, too, wonder why you do it," Denoriel replied.

The besom sighed heavily, causing flames to gyrate wildly and a burning sliver fell from its mouth to the table. Elizabeth put out a cautious finger to feel the heat, but there was no heat, and the flame winked out when her finger touched the burning thing.

"You have been too long among mortals," the besom said. "I

do it because it amuses me. Any Bright Court Sidhe should know that. Think of the things you do for amusement. Now what do you all want to eat and drink. I do have other patrons to serve."

Aleneil suddenly laughed. "It would amuse Ilar too." She shook her head. "What is your normal form? None at all, I guess, but you have a perfect memory. How strange. I will have a clear soup and a cold collation."

Elizabeth, who had been very quiet, looking at the scrap of . . . something . . . that had been burning, gave her order, for roast venison, new peas, and baked turnips last. When the server had stalked away, she said, "Things are often not at all what they appear, not only here but in the mortal world too."

"Whatever do you mean, my love?" Denoriel asked.

"Have you not heard what Rhoslyn said about Mary? That there were actual attempts on Mary's life?"

Denoriel lifted his brows. "So? What is your problem? Do you envy Mary the attention?"

"Denno!" Elizabeth protested, laughing because he often said she craved attention, then sobered. "Do you not realize that if Rhoslyn was not there with her special abilities, either of those attempts might well have succeeded? Both were well planned and almost impossible, I suspect, to be traced to their initiator."

"That's true, Bess, but what is so significant . . ." Harry frowned and then added, "Oh, I see. You think the attempts on you were not so well planned."

Elizabeth nodded. "Not that Denno did not protect me better than anyone else, but even if he had not been there, my guardsmen would have routed the men who attacked us. There were not enough of them and they were not trained soldiers. And there is another thing, even more significant. If Northumberland wanted to take me prisoner, why did he send the messenger at all? Why did he simply not send a troop of guards in Royal livery? To fight them would be treason."

"Likely he did not want anyone to see you taken by Royal guards." Harry said.

"Why not, Da? It would not be strange for the king to send a Royal guard to escort his sister. Who would know I was being taken unwilling?"

"That is a very reasonable question," Pasgen said, "and when coupled with the gift of jewels . . . Are you sure Prince Denoriel that it was Northumberland who sent the troop to attack and sent Rich with such a stupid proposition and . . . hmmm . . . jewels?"

"That is a question I have been asking myself," Elizabeth said, nodding at Pasgen; it was the first recognition she had given him and considering they were talking about bespelled jewels significant. "I think we have two threads tangled. The messenger was, indeed, from Northumberland, but the attackers and those stones . . ."

"Vidal is a great one for using amulets," Pasgen said. Then he looked fully at Elizabeth. "I am not trying to excuse myself for what I did. I should have refused. It was a terrible thing to do to a child . . . and I am sorry for it. I wished to say that."

Rhoslyn briefly touched her brother's cheek and Elizabeth again nodded. "He was your lord. It was your duty to obey him. It is a very hard thing when your lord orders something you know is wrong. I saw that in my father's Court more than once."

It was not the same thing at all, Pasgen knew, but he was glad of the raprochement with Elizabeth and felt no inclination to make himself less in her opinion. But it was not duty but fear and self-interest that had made him obedient to Vidal. And then he shrugged mentally. Was it not, except for a few noble souls, the same in the mortal world, that fear and self-interest made men obedient to their king?

Before Pasgen needed to decide what to say, the server was again approaching their table. Remembering the little hands on the broad arms which had delivered plates the previous week, Harry craned his neck to see the server, but the burning besom was wheeling a service cart in the most ordinary way. The only extraordinary happening was that the server did not need to ask which dish went to which person. Each was delivered correctly and when Rhoslyn, guiltily, said "Thank you," the server nodded its burning head and said, "Accepted. Enjoy," and went away.

"I am free of Vidal now," Pasgen said when the creature was gone, then he smiled at Elizabeth. "How did you resist those jewels? Aleneil has told us how you love them."

Elizabeth shivered slightly but cut and lifted a slice of the venison without any diminution in her appetite. "I assure you they did not tempt me. Even wrapped in silk there was . . . something ugly about them. And the ring on Chancellor Rich's hand, the beautiful yellow diamond, that too had . . . I do not know how to explain it, but it was like seeing though an illusion, only it was not with my eyes that I saw. Something is in that diamond. But how could Chancellor Rich get a diamond bespelled by Vidal Dhu?"

"Too easily." Pasgen swallowed his mouthful, and his lips thinned. "While I was still Vidal's servant, I established a human 'sorceror' called Fagildo Otstargi and made him quite fashionable at Court. Otstargi predicted the future and gave advice to King Henry's courtiers. I suppose when I decided to leave Vidal's service, I should have 'killed' Otstargi in some very public way, but truthfully I had lost interest and forgot about him. Now Vidal is using that character—I think for the same purpose I used it."

"But how could Vidal hire a troop of humans to attack Elizabeth?" Harry asked. "No. If one of them should have been taken prisoner, Otstargi would have been exposed."

"Vidal might have done that before the mist trapped him," Pasgen said. "He acted then as if the whole world was blind, deaf, and stupid. But he is much more cautious now. There is also a human healer who lives in Otstargi's house. Currently he is attending on the little king—"

"Not harming him!" Elizabeth exclaimed.

"No, no. I think he is doing all that he can to keep King Edward alive. Vidal wants Mary on the throne, but the uncertainty about Edward's health and the succession is providing the Unseleighe Court with plenty of power."

"Not 'us with plenty of power'?" Elizabeth asked, but there was curiosity not animosity in her voice.

"Elizabeth!" Denoriel protested. "One does not ask about another's source of power."

"I beg your pardon," Elizabeth said easily, "but since it is impossible for me to encroach on Pasgen's source . . ." And she addressed herself to her plate.

"That is true," Pasgen said complacently, spearing a last few remnants on the point of his knife. "But I doubt anyone could encroach. I have my own sources of power and owe nothing to the mortal world."

Aleneil looked interested; Denoriel indifferent. With the power-gathering spell that Mwynwen had given him, the ambient strength of Underhill filled him quickly and completely. Then he cocked his head.

"You haven't found a way to take power from the mortal world, have you?" Denoriel asked, also cleaning the last bits from his plate with some of the Inn of Kindly Laughter's very good bread.

"No. And I thank you for your warning about that white lightning. I barely touched it and was well scorched for my temerity. I am thinking about it, though. I promise if I find a way, I will tell you."

"I will be very grateful," Denoriel said. "I try not to do magic in the mortal world, but circumstances can build a trap that makes magic necessary."

"Which brings me back to Albertus—that is the mortal healer who lives in Otstargi's house. I brought him Underhill to see if he could cure Aurilia's headaches. I found him in the basest slum of the city, tending on the whores and criminals. He has an acquaintance that could make the hiring of thugs easy."

"But I am sure the men who attacked me were not brigands," Elizabeth pointed out.

"No," Aleneil agreed. "I thought then and think now that they were idle young gentlemen, possibly men recruited to fight for a cause."

"Cause?" Rhoslyn asked.

"Reestablishment of the Catholic Church," Harry said. "Mary will subject England to the pope again."

"No!" Rhoslyn exclaimed, then added, "Oh, yes, Mary will bring back the Catholic Church as fully as she can, but Mary would never hire men to attack Elizabeth." She flushed slightly. "She does not . . . love Elizabeth, but—"

"That was not what I meant," Harry said quickly. "I doubt, if the men were hired for the Catholic cause, that Mary knew anything about it. God knows, there are enough men who follow the old religion in their hearts, some of them right beside Northumberland. Any one of them could have made up a plan to take Elizabeth prisoner."

"For what purpose?" Elizabeth asked, tensing.

Harry shook his head at her. "Only so that Mary could come to the throne without any challenge. Most of those men fear that the country will rise to keep their new ways and freedom from Peter's pence and push you onto the throne instead of Mary."

Elizabeth shook her head. "That would render the Act of Succession invalid and that Act is what my own claim to the throne rests on."

"Possession is nine-tenths of the law," Harry remarked cynically. And then said, "No, don't think about it. Stay safe. Stay quiet. If Mary and Northumberland fight over the crown, just lie still at Hatfield. If Mary is hurt, I think the country will rise to overthrow Northumberland. Also remember that Mary is many years older than you."

"And she is not strong," Rhoslyn said with tears in her eyes.

"I am sorry Rhoslyn," Harry said, pushing away his plate. "I know you are fond of her—"

"Because she is a good, sweet, kind person."

"Perhaps. But she will make a wretched queen and do great hurt to the country."

Rhoslyn sighed. "I know."

Harry looked at her sadly, then turned back to Elizabeth. "The elder Sidhe and I are going to make another assault on the evil that is lodged in Alhambra and I must go. Is there anything you need from me Bess?"

"No, except your promise to be very, very careful. Da, you have no magic. I do not like to think of you struggling with evil without any defenses."

Harry leaned over and kissed Elizabeth's forehead. "What a silly child you are. I am ringed about with defenders, all rich and tried in magic. And I have my gun loaded with Cold Iron and my silver sword. Do not waste any fear on my account." He rose to his feet.

Pasgen also stood up. "I will Gate to Elfhame Elder-Elf with you. I need to let Gaenor and Hafwen know that I will not be available to them for a few weeks. That mist is doing something, but without going into it we cannot tell what, and none of us is desperate enough to go in after what happened to Vidal." He turned to Rhoslyn. "Making sure Mary is not hurt is not likely to take longer than a few mortal weeks, is it, Rhoslyn?"

"No," Rhoslyn said. "Although Northumberland keeps speaking of improvement, no one believes the poor little king can survive much longer. Lady Catherine tells Mary that the real physicians have given up and that Northumberland has called in any charlatan who promises a cure. Poor boy. He is in such pain they keep him drugged almost all the time."

On that somber note they parted, Elizabeth clinging to Denoriel with tears in her eyes and saying, "No, I don't want to go to the market now. Take me home, please, Denno."

Later, Elizabeth acknowledged that she would have done better to go to the market and try to distract herself. Having taken to her bed as a defensive measure against Northumberland, once she was in the mortal world she had little to keep her occupied beyond the wild fluctuations of her hopes and fears. One moment her throat tightened with tears for her little brother; the next a thrill swept her when she realized she would be heir presumptive to the throne when Edward died.

That thrill of eagerness and excitement, however, was always followed by a thrill of fear. Mary did not want her as heir. Mary was rumored to deny that Elizabeth was her father's daughter. Mary was one of the few who had actually believed Elizabeth's mother was a promiscuous whore and that Elizabeth was Mark Smeaton's child—in spite of Elizabeth's resemblance to Henry VIII.

Then her thoughts would skip back to Edward and she would hope a little that the rumors of his mortal illness, which came mostly from Mary's supporters at Court, were only traps to make her seem to desire his death. William Cecil, her own main source of information, so faithful and infallible in the past, had been strangely silent. So maybe Edward was not so desperately ill; perhaps he would recover. A flicker of hope, mixed, to Elizabeth's inner shame, with a hollow regret. Was she a monster after all to desire a chance at the throne at the cost of Edward's life?

Had the enforced idleness lasted long, Elizabeth would likely have made herself truly ill. Within the week, however, warning came from the closed gate of Hatfield that there was come a messenger, not wearing royal colors but openly from Northumberland. Sir Edward came to the gate himself and put out his hand for the packet. The messenger—not the dolt who had carried the order for Elizabeth to turn back from her intended visit to Edward, but a wiry gentleman of middle height with crisp, dark hair and sharp features—did not deliver.

He dismounted from his saddle as the gate was closed behind him and asked, "What is the meaning of locked gates and the guards? Are you arming for war?"

"Not war, defense. My lady was attacked on the road only last week," Sir Edward replied as they started for the house. "I am Sir Edward Paulet, captain of the guard here and taking no chances that the attack was no accident. You may give me the message."

"No, I may not," the messenger replied. "I was sent by the

duke of Northumberland himself. My name is Richard Verney and I am enjoined to place this message into Lady Elizabeth's hand and no other."

"Lady Elizabeth is ill and lies abed. She was sadly shocked by the attack, which brought on an inability to eat. She is very weak."

"I have my orders from His Grace," Verney said stubbornly.

"Well, you may come and speak to Mistress Ashley, but I doubt she will give you news other than what you have had from me."

The messenger said nothing more until Sir Edward saw him into the reception room and gave his name to Kat, who rose to greet him, holding out her hand for the message. However, he clutched it tight against his breast and repeated that his orders were to put it into Elizabeth's hand alone.

"Then you are likely not to deliver it at all, Master Verney," Kat said calmly. "Lady Elizabeth is most unwell. She has not risen from her bed since we were attacked on the road."

"I am sorry to hear of the lady's illness," Verney said, "but I am commanded by His Grace of Northumberland to give this message into her hand, and I assure you that it will be the worse for her if she does not have it."

Kat looked at him for a long moment, but he did not offer the packet and she sighed and said, "I will tell her you are here and see if I can get her to attend to me."

"I will come—"

Verney stopped as the guard at the inner door made an ugly sound in his throat and stepped forward, his hand on his sword hilt. Kat raised a hand and shook her head at Shaylor.

"Very well," she said, "come then."

First Verney felt a fool because he clearly detected a note of satisfaction in Mistress Ashley's voice. She had wanted him to insist, to act as if he thought they were hiding something. But then he swallowed hard. Sir Edward was pacing him behind Mistress Ashley to the door and he had drawn his long knife from its scabbard on his belt. Perhaps they were hiding something and if he detected it he would never leave that inner chamber.

"You will not approach the bed closer than Mistress Ashley leads you," Sir Edward said.

It was not Lady Elizabeth in the bed, Verney thought, that is what they are trying to hide. But it was Lady Elizabeth! She lay still and white under a thin coverlet. And Mistress Ashley only stopped him about a foot from the bed. The curtains were drawn back all the way. He could see her plainly.

Verney's glance flickered down the outline of her body under the coverlet. It was nearly as flat as the bed itself. Not the smallest rounding of the belly to hint at the sin she might have inherited from her mother.

"Lady Elizabeth," Kat crooned. "My dear. Open your eyes, do."

A long moment passed. Mistress Ashley repeated herself. The thin lids twitched, twitched again and opened over dark eyes, almost as black as those of Ann Boleyn.

"Here is a messenger from the duke of Northumberland, Lady Elizabeth, and he says he must give his message only directly into your hand."

"His Grace," Lady Elizabeth breathed.

Verney saw her right arm move a fraction, as if she were trying to brace it to lift herself on her elbow. She did get the elbow bent under her, but slipped back to lie flat at once. Finally, very slowly and with great effort, she raised her hand.

"Give me the message," she whispered.

Sir Edward moved forward with Verney, the point of his knife now pressing hard into Verney's side. Verney hesitated and the knife passed through his clothing and pricked his flesh, a warning and an impatient prod. He withdrew the packet from the satchel in which he had carried it. Elizabeth's hand had fallen to the bed, but it lay palm up to receive the message. And then, to Verney's surprise, a glowering maid took a quick step forward and laid a heavy silk kerchief over Lady Elizabeth's hand, as if contact with the message would in some way contaminate her.

Now Sir Edward laid a heavy hand on Verney's shoulder; as he drew him away from the bed, he sheathed his knife again. "You have delivered your message into Lady Elizabeth's hand," he said. "Your duty is done. Come and refresh yourself."

But his duty was not done. Verney had been told to report on the lady's reaction. "Will not the lady wish to read the message?" he protested. "I am very willing to answer any questions."

Sir Edward uttered a low, indeterminate sound and his lips twisted as he shepherded Verney out. "Does she look as if she could read it or ask a question? If you had given it to me or to Mistress Ashley, you might have had an answer to take back. Now she will insist on reading it herself and that will have to wait until she gathers strength."

"Why did the maid cover Lady Elizabeth's hand? And why did you nearly stab me when I was about to give her the message?"

Sir Edward shrugged. "How did I know that you would not whip out a poisoned pin or even a knife and stab my lady? Nor will you be offered lodging in this house. No strangers are permitted within, lest they do harm. You can have a cup of wine while I watch you, but I will not leave you until you are outside our gate. Someone hired a whole troop of men to take Lady Elizabeth or even kill her. Likely it is fear that has made her so ill. When she is sure she is safe, I hope she will recover."

Verney drank his wine and was escorted out, the gates closed and were barred behind him. No one short of an entire army would be able to reach Lady Elizabeth and do her harm, Verney thought. He himself had no such instructions—and would not have accepted such an order, even from his good friend Robert Dudley's father. But something was brewing connected with the young king's death. Verney rode at a moderate pace, sparing his horse. He would not be sorry to emphasize how well Lady Elizabeth was guarded.

Kat had followed Verney and Sir Edward to the door and watched them through a crack until the outer door of the reception room had closed behind them. Then she closed the bedroom door and said, "He's gone."

Elizabeth popped upright and watched Blanche as she carefully wiped the outside of the message packet with the silk kerchief. "Do you think it is poisoned, Blanche? Do you . . . ah . . . see or smell something? I did not."

She had been about to say "sense something" but the geas Queen Titania had put on her when she was given leave to visit Underhill with her memory intact would not permit her to say anything that would hint of magic or the supernatural. Thus she had to find words natural to the mortal world.

"No, m'lady," Blanche lifted the packet and sniffed at it through the silk. "Don't smell nothing up close either, but the messenger was wearing gloves. No sense in not being careful."

"For the Grace of God, Blanche," Kat said, sounding shocked. "Are you implying that the duke of Northumberland is trying to poison Elizabeth?"

"Don't know, Mistress Ashley. But the men who attacked us wasn't really friendly. Don't know what the men would have done if they'd taken Lady Elizabeth. Maybe, like Lord Denno said, they would've only held her till Northumberland's plans were worked out, but maybe . . . What hurt can it do to be safe?"

"None," Kat murmured. "None. . . . Oh dear."

Elizabeth stared hard at the packet too but could see and sense nothing. She reached toward it, but Blanche told her to wait and hurried off to the dressing room, from where she came back with a pair of gloves. When they were on, Elizabeth broke the seal, turning her head aside so as not to breathe in anything. Then she unfolded the message and read it, crying out softly as if she had been caught by a small pain.

"What is it, love?" Kat asked.

"I am ordered to come to Court to say fare well to Edward. He is dying, Northumberland says. Oh, poor Edward. Should I go?"

"Lord Denno would skin us all alive," Blanche said.

"He would have to be here to skin us, so we are safe enough," Elizabeth said with a spiteful hiss.

"Oh, no, my dear," Kat added, deliberately not hearing what Elizabeth said about Lord Denno and answering the question about going to Edward.

It was true that Lord Denno had left Hatfield as soon as he was sure Elizabeth was calm and Sir Edward had deployed his men and locked the gates so Hatfield was safe. It was also true that Lord Denno had not returned, but by now Kat knew Lord Denno well enough to be certain he was on Elizabeth's business, likely trying to find out who had hired the attackers and/or why the attack had been made.

"There cannot be any question of going to London," Kat went on. "Not after you were so clever at convincing the messenger you were too ill to travel. And . . . and the truth is, my love, that it is more likely the king is already dead than that you will be allowed to see him. I do not think Northumberland would have admitted his key to the royal power was gone until King Edward truly drew his last breath. So why does he want you now, when he did all in his power to keep you away from Court for so long?"

Chapter 6

Not long before Richard Verney passed through the gate at Hatfield, Denoriel learned the answer to Kat's question. He had returned from a third fruitless attempt to see William Cecil or his wife—but Mildred had gone to be with her father in the country—in a sour temper. It did not improve his mood to find a stranger seated in the entry hall with Cropper standing watchfully near the entrance to the kitchen.

"Yes, what is it?" Denoriel asked impatiently. "It was useless to wait for me. If my man of business cannot or will not accommodate you, neither can or will I."

Denoriel was badly out of temper and his voice was hard, but the man simply jumped to his feet with a pleased expression and bowed.

"I must speak to you, my lord, and alone."

"I just told you that I do little or no business and—"

"My name, my lord, is Henry Carey." The man paused as if he expected Denoriel to react; when he did not, he continued, "And I know you will want to hear the proposition I will make. Come, my lord, in private I will say two names to you. If you are not interested after hearing them, I will leave and trouble you no more."

Henry Carey. The name was familiar to Denoriel, something he had heard a long time ago, but he could recall nothing significant about it. He stared for a moment at the man's face. There was something there that was familiar too, possibly the shape of the large, dark eyes. No, it would not come to him.

"Very well," he said, "this way."

Cropper turned toward them and reached for his cudgel.

"I don't think that will be necessary," Denoriel said.

"He's armed, m'lord," Cropper pointed out, "and that sword looks like he knows how to use one."

So it did. There was a handsome jewel pommel at the top of the sword hilt, but the hilt itself was wrapped in worn, oiled leather that would not slip in a man's hand if he sweated . . . or bled. Before Denoriel could speak, Carey undid his sword belt and handed it to Cropper. Denoriel began to say, "That isn't necessary"; instead he only shook his head. It wasn't necessary, but it made it far more likely that what Carey had to say *was* important.

Without speaking again and signing Cropper to stay behind, Denoriel led the way into the private parlor beyond Clayborne's office. He left the door open as he entered, but Carey closed it carefully behind him.

"My mother was Mary Boleyn, Anne's elder sister," Carey said. "I am Lady Elizabeth's first cousin."

"Carey," Denoriel said, shaking his head over his faulty memory. "I knew the name was familiar, but—"

"I am not asking Lady Elizabeth to recognize me," Carey said hastily.

Denoriel shook his head again. "While her father was alive, she dared not remind him of her mother, but if you care to visit her, I am sure she would be most happy to receive you. I will take you to Hatfield myself. No one cares about Ann Boleyn now."

"The Lady Mary cares," Carey said stiffly. "She told the king I was a whore's son when I applied for a place at Court and saw that I did not get it."

"That is not at all like Lady Mary." Denoriel said, surprised then frowning, but then he sighed. "But if she still holds such a bitter grudge, it will make the path for Elizabeth even harder."

"We will have much ado to keep Lady Elizabeth's head on her shoulders."

"We?" Denoriel repeated.

Carey blushed. "I do not mean to enlarge myself to such great importance, but I am acting for Master William Cecil, who heard of my disappointment and engaged me as an assistant."

Denoriel laughed. "Is there anything of which Master Cecil does not hear?"

"The thing I have come to tell you, he almost heard too late. Possibly it is already too late."

"Speak."

"The duke of Northumberland has extracted from the king—although he says it is the king's own device—a declaration that since both his sisters were illegitimate, they must be debarred from the throne. Instead he has named the male heirs of the daughters of Frances Brandon—at least that was the device that was shown to Master Cecil first. When it became clear that the king was in extremis and he could never live to see male heirs of either of the girls, who were hastily married a few weeks ago, the device was altered and Lady Jane Grey, Frances Brandon's eldest daughter, was named in particular."

For a long moment Denoriel simply stared at Carey. "That is mad," he said at last. "How can he hope..." He shook his head and then waved a hand at the chairs on either side of the hearth. "Sit, please. Would you like some wine?"

"Nothing, thank you," Carey said as he sat down. "How can Northumberland hope to put Lady Jane on the throne? By fear. He does command the armed troops in London and the entire Council has signed the device."

Denoriel took the other chair, still staring at Carey, then he took a deep breath and put a hand across his eyes "So that was why he was trying to have Mary killed. I thought he wanted to elevate Elizabeth but she could see only disaster from such a plan. It did puzzle me why he kept warning Lady Elizabeth away from London. I suppose he feared she would hear of his true plans. How come Cecil did not warn us?"

"Northumberland trusts him... but not with regard to Lady Elizabeth. Cecil's appointment as surveyor of her lands is known and he was instrumental in the exchange of Hatfield for the northern property. Any messenger Cecil sent would have been scrutinized—and he did not learn of this 'devise' himself until yesterday when it was brought to him to sign."

"He signed?"

"As witness only."

"Now I begin to wonder whether that attempt to take Elizabeth prisoner—"

"Did he seize Lady Elizabeth? We must save her at once!"

"No, the attempt did not succeed. She is safe in Hatfield." Denoriel had slumped back in his chair, but he abruptly sat hard upright. "You say it is known at Court that the king is dying? Merciful Mother, I *hope* Lady Elizabeth is safe! If someone sent her word . . . or if Northumberland himself sent word that her brother was dying . . ." He stood up. "She always cared deeply for King Edward. I hope she did not fall into any snare of Northumberland's and set off to see Edward before his death."

"She must not!" Carey exclaimed, also on his feet. "Cecil believes the duke wants to hold Elizabeth in case there is too much turmoil over enthroning Lady Jane. If there is, perhaps Jane will have an accident or some fault will be found in her heritage, and Lady Elizabeth can be produced. But if Lady Jane's rule is accepted, Elizabeth will die."

Denoriel nodded. "I am leaving for Hatfield at once. Do you want to come with me?"

The moment the words were out, Denoriel could have bit out his tongue. He could not spare the time to ride at a horse's pace to Hatfield and it would be impossible to conceal Miralys's rapid arrival there from a fellow rider. Fortunately, however, Carey shook his head.

"No, Master Cecil says the less I am known to be related to Lady Elizabeth the more use I will be to her. Carey is not an uncommon name. I will leave here carrying a basket of wine samples for my master to choose from. Everyone knows that business is done with Master Clayborne so there will be no particular reason to connect me with you and from that with Lady Elizabeth. I have also arranged for watchers to warn me if any large group of men sets out toward Hatfield."

"Good. Then I leave you to collect your wines. If you want to meet in a less well-known place, only leave the time and direction with Master Clayborne. I will try to see him every morning to receive your message or leave a message for you."

Miralys left the stable behind the house on Bucklersbury at a dangerously fast pace. Out of sight of the house, the elvensteed darted into a dark, narrow alley . . . and never came out. In less than a quarter candlemark, Denoriel was pounding on the gate of Hatfield with the hilt of his sword.

The lookout called that it was Lord Denno and he was alone.

The guards below opened the gate. By the time he was within, Denoriel realized that Hatfield was calm, there was no bustle of impending departure or the reorganization of a diminished household after a departure. He turned Miralys toward the stables, dismounting and handing his reins to Ladbroke who met him before he needed to turn off the path to the house.

"All peaceful?" Denoriel asked.

"There was a messenger from London, but Sir Edward didn't let the man out of his sight and put him out as soon as the message was delivered. Peaceful enough for us. Not sure, m'lord it will be so peaceful for you."

Denoriel sighed and started toward the house. He was not surprised when Kat came to lead him quickly from the reception room into Elizabeth's bedchamber. Elizabeth did not take well to enforced idleness. She would have been fretting over her virtual imprisonment, over not being able to ride out to divert herself, and over his absence. The message—Denoriel was virtually certain it was Northumberland's trap invitation to come to Court, which Elizabeth apparently did know she had to refuse since she had not prepared to leave for London—would have made her even more fretful. What he had to tell her, atop the other irritations, would throw her into a rage.

Only it did not. True, they had first to get past Elizabeth's angry accusations of being neglected. To those, Denoriel made so sharp a response that he surprised and shocked Kat. Denoriel was usually careful to keep a respectful and subservient manner when in the mortal world, but Kat's distress allowed Aleneil to offer a soothing reminder of Denno's long privilege and draw Kat away to the other end of the room. Most often Kat was blind to the true relationship between Elizabeth and Denno but that exchange had been revealingly intimate.

Slightly shamefaced over Denoriel's rebuke, Elizabeth told him about the message from Northumberland, shedding a few tears over the confirmation that Edward was beyond hope.

"Are you sure it would be so dangerous for me to go to him?" she asked piteously. "Even if he could not speak, I could hold his hand. He could feel there was someone with him who cared for him, not for his crown."

"More dangerous than you know," Denoriel responded, and told her everything Carey had told him, including the conclusion

that Northumberland wished to hold her a prisoner to be used
if needed and sacrificed otherwise.

Denoriel expected a burst of rage, but Elizabeth listened in silence,
all the while rubbing her hands over her arms as if to warm them,
though her bedchamber was almost too warm. Then she said, "How
badly does he want me? Is it safe to stay here? Should I remove to
Donnington, which is a truly defensible castle?"

"Not yet. You must seem to be innocent and ignorant and too
ill to leave your bed. We will have time enough to get you safe
to Donnington if any force is directed against you. Your cousin
Carey has watchers to warn us if armsmen march this way."

"My cousin Carey." Elizabeth smiled slightly and her eyes lightened. "I never met him but I look forward to it."

"Yes, yes, it is very nice to have a family ... well, sometimes
it is nice. If the family is not too greedy. But what do you think
we should do about Northumberland's attempt to establish Lady
Jane on the throne? Cecil seems helpless and since Denny died
I really do not have any influential friends ..."

Elizabeth shivered. "We should do nothing. Oh, poor Jane. It
is true I never liked her very much. She was always too meek
and colorless for my taste but this ..."

"Elizabeth! This poor Jane may soon be sitting on the throne
and calling for your execution!"

"No," Elizabeth whispered, "Mary will do that." She shivered
again, then shook her head briskly. "Jane ... no, the people will
never accept Jane. Northumberland does not understand. He can
force his Council to obey him and make them sign his decrees,
but the people, they *love* Mary and me too, a little. Even my
father had to change his path when the country people, the
squires and their tenants, were aroused. They will support Mary.
You will see. Northumberland cannot prevent Mary from coming
to the throne."

Denoriel opened his mouth, but no words came out. He had
come prepared to soothe Elizabeth's hysterical reaction to the
attempt to shunt Mary and herself aside, but she was calm, her
eyes narrowed somewhat in thought. Like her father, Elizabeth
seemed to know by instinct how the common people would
respond and to know, too, how to engage their sympathy.

"Mary will be dead and buried if Northumberland lays his
hands upon her!" he said at last.

Elizabeth started at the harsh tone. "Oh heaven! She might have been taken in by Northumberland's letter. She cared for Edward too, and would consider it her duty to attend his deathbed. She might even dream of saving him from hell in a last-minute conversion. No, Northumberland must not capture her. Cannot you get word to Rhoslyn (that name was common enough for her to say; she did not attempt Pasgen) of what Master Carey told you?"

"I will send a messenger," he said, looking up to where the air spirit flitted above, sometimes settling on a curtain or on a piece of furniture, sometimes engaging in dizzying gyrations.

The messenger to Rhoslyn, although its path through Underhill was far swifter than any bird's flight, would never have arrived in time. However, Lady Mary had a better informed partisan with far greater resources than the limited help Denoriel and Aleneil could look for from the Bright Court.

Vidal Dhu had learned of Northumberland's device two weeks before Carey brought the news to Denoriel. Chancellor Rich, greatly troubled when the scheme was first suggested to him, had stared down into the flickering light in his yellow diamond ring. He had no desire at all to resist the will of Northumberland, but he also had no desire to be caught in a treasonous plot and have Lady Mary calling for his execution. He needed to know the future and was suddenly sure who could read it for him.

Accordingly Rich dispatched a messenger to the house of Fagildo Otstargi demanding an urgent meeting. The message came to Albertus, who recognized the name at once and Gated to Caer Mordwyn. He told Vidal that the king's condition was unchanged, a week or two, if so long, remained of life. Even he did not pretend to Northumberland that Edward could live, and gave his reason for continuing to attend the dying king only to give Edward what ease could be found in drugged sleep.

"Good enough," Vidal said. "Be sure you are available to me after I have spoken with Chancellor Rich. I may need Howard-Mowbray and his men. And they had better be more successful in this second task than in the first."

But Vidal was only mildly annoyed at Howard-Mowbray's failure to capture or kill Elizabeth. She had been traveling before the full troop was assembled; Howard-Mowbray had warned Albertus that he did not yet have enough men. Vidal had learned patience from the self-aware mist; he had not exercised that patience in bidding Albertus set the ambush and had lost his prize.

Worse, the attack had given that prize warning. Vidal had heard how Hatfield was shut and guarded. Even deliveries of food stopped at the gate and were brought to the house by Elizabeth's own servants. Vidal remembered four years of fighting against bonds he could not loose . . . until he stopped fighting. Now he withdrew all but the imps that infested the alehouse. They would tell him if the vigilance around Elizabeth decreased or if she left her haven. Until then, he would make no attempts on her. Let her confidence return and make her careless.

Three days later Vidal Gated to Otstargi's house, assumed the charlatan's features, and was waiting for Rich with an intense frown on his face. The frown, he was sure, would be appropriate because Rich would not have been in a panic demanding a meeting for good news.

Rich stopped just inside the doorway and groaned, "Oh, I knew this scheme would never work."

"As you know it, it will not," Vidal replied, having no idea what the scheme was but assuming from his client's nervousness that it was elaborate and risky. "However, if you will tell me all the details, all the small things that are planned, perhaps I can see a solution . . . or a way out."

When Rich began with Northumberland's plan for Lady Mary to be taken and sent to her uncle, Emperor Charles, Vidal uttered a hard laugh. "You know and I know that cannot be true. To have Lady Mary in the Emperor's hand is to invite an invasion by Spain. Here it is safe to say what you know must be the truth, that Lady Mary must have a fatal accident."

Rich made a few gabbled protests but then shrugged and admitted so much, saying it could be blamed on Lady Elizabeth, who would also be taken prisoner. But she was to be held safely for a few months, until Queen Jane was accepted by all. "And then Queen Jane would find her guilty of some treason . . ."

For a moment Vidal looked interested and murmured "Ah . . ." but in the next he shook his head. Elizabeth's execution could come only after Mary's death, and that was a price Vidal was not willing to pay. Mary would be just as willing to execute Elizabeth as Jane. And the people—idiots that they were to care who they worshiped and how—would be far more miserable under Mary's rule, so that the Dark Court would wallow in the power of pain.

Vidal did not interrupt Rich again, simply keeping his head bent, his eyes on his hands and shaking his head until Rich faltered into silence. Then he looked up. "I will offer you a chance at a way out." he said. "There is no way to accomplish Northumberland's purpose. Mary will be the next queen."

"But Northumberland has an army at his command. And he is sure that the ladies will come willingly into his hand when he bids them come to say fare well to their dying brother. Both Lady Mary and Lady Elizabeth are very fond of King Edward."

"I think the duke has not taken into account the anxiety and suspicion of the ladies. And I cannot tell you why his plan will fail, only that Mary *will* reign as queen."

"How can you know that?"

Vidal laughed. "I have known that since Edward was crowned. When Great Harry died, I looked into the future. I saw that the young king's reign would be short—"

"To look into the future of the king, that was treason," Rich muttered and then, "Why did you not tell me?"

Vidal laughed again. "Because it *was* treason. And what you and Northumberland are doing is treason. Mary is her father's daughter. She will not forget your betrayal."

Rich turned an ugly shade of yellow. "You said there was a chance for me, a way out."

"Only if you make your peace with Lady Mary. Northumberland is lost—not that you will miss him. You will do much better without him. But Mary must be convinced that you truly favor her and that much of your reason for obeying Northumberland was that you saw it as the only way to be able to warn her of Northumberland's plans. You must send her a warning that the invitation to her brother's deathbed is a trap and that she should take herself to a defensible castle, declare herself queen, and call in her tenants to support her."

"How?" Rich gasped. "I cannot warn her without Northumberland knowing I have betrayed him."

Vidal looked speculatively at Rich, wondering if now was a good time to rid himself of this henchman. After a moment he decided that Rich could still be useful. Chancellor was a powerful position and Rich was very easy to manipulate.

"Surely there are others, others whom the duke will suspect

before he thinks of you. Are there not any who have been taken back into favor since the king fell ill? Those, I am sure, strive to discover any action Northumberland plans. One among them at least should be willing to believe you his friend or that you are more his friend than Northumberland. Send that man to Lady Mary to warn her in your name."

"And what if he goes to Northumberland instead?"

"Then you ride to Lady Mary yourself. I tell you, she will be queen. She will be queen no matter what you do or do not do. I am not telling you to go to her for her sake but because you asked me for a chance to save yourself when Northumberland's plans fail."

That was a flat lie. Vidal had no more certainty about the future than Rich did. The pale Sidhe in the tower could only tell him that the vision of Edward as king was gone, but three futures still showed in the dark pool—a thin, pale girl wearing a crown and weeping; Mary presiding over the burning of what she called heretics; and Elizabeth in the midst of joyous multitudes.

However, Vidal was a lot more certain of Mary coming to the throne since Rich had exposed Northumberland's secrets to him. When he finally rid himself of Rich, who had wasted another half a candlemark begging for a second or third way to escape ruin without betraying Northumberland—information Vidal would not have given him even if he had it—Vidal Gated back to Caer Mordwyn. From there he captured an imp to order Rhoslyn to come to him. He was taking no chances on Rich's wavering; he would warn Rhoslyn about the danger to Mary himself.

The creature squalled when Vidal drew it from a crowd of like creatures and squalled again as he pressed into its mind his memory of the essence of Rhoslyn. By the time he was finished impressing upon it where to find her in the mortal world and then his need for her to come to Caer Mordwyn as quickly as possible, the ugly little thing had no strength to squall. It could utter no more than a pathetic whimper when he released it.

Aurilia had come to watch Vidal work, and she enjoyed it heartily, but when Vidal was about to order the imp to go, she said, "If you send it out as it is, it will take a week to find Rhoslyn. Give it some power and a touch of reward."

"You are right," Vidal agreed easily.

She was, and he did as she suggested. He noticed with some pleasure that Aurilia glanced at him sidelong, made uneasy by his good humor. The imp, renewed, circled twice around Vidal's chamber and bedewed the carpet with excrement. Vidal's lips thinned; he hissed rage and raised his hand to extinguish the creature altogether, but Aurilia, more secure now that his temper showed, laid her hand over his.

"Do not waste the effort you made to catch it and imprint your message," she said, and gestured at the stain which disappeared. "What do you want with Rhoslyn? What she knows, Pasgen will soon know. Do not trust the break between them."

The warning annoyed Vidal, who knew Aurilia read people better than he did but did not like to be reminded. And despite her apparent satisfaction with handing his power back to him, he did not trust her. Also in the past she had known little and cared less about the mortal world. That, too, had changed during the years that he had been in the mad mist's thrall, and he was not certain why. For a moment he felt reluctant to tell Aurilia anything. Still, she said she had remembered that Mary must come to the throne, and she had tried to move toward that goal.

She had sent Albertus to "help" the physicians trying to save Edward so that he could bring her news of the Court and, in case Edward's doctors should happen on some treatment that would prolong the boy's life to circumvent them. Albertus could have finished the boy off if he lingered too long. That no longer seemed a problem, Edward was dying, but Vidal was glad Albertus was established at Court. He might yet have uses for him.

Better to tell her what she wanted to know, Vidal thought. What Aurilia had done thus far had been clever and was useful. If she were ignorant their purposes might cross.

"I do not care if Rhoslyn tells Pasgen this," Vidal said. "Pasgen could not care less what happens in the mortal world. I need to warn Rhoslyn that Mary is in grave danger," and then he unfolded the entire plot that Rich had described.

"So Jane Grey is the name of the pale girl with the crown that the FarSeers keep mentioning," Aurilia mused. "And Northumberland is trying to enthrone her instead of Mary. But if this is likely to cause civil war, why should we interfere?"

"Civil war would be welcome," Vidal said, grinning. "I am not trying to foil Northumberland's plan to crown Jane. I only want to keep Mary safe, for it is in her reign that the people's misery will furnish us in the Dark Court with a rich feast."

Chapter 7

Rhoslyn was fuming when she arrived in Caer Mordwyn. She had been startled by the urgency of the imp's message because she had not been summoned in four long years. Even after she remembered that Vidal had returned, she had not hurried to respond, bearing stoically the attempts of the imp to pinch and prod her into obeying. It was always Vidal's way, she thought, to make the response to any desire of his urgent.

In fact the imp could do her no harm. Her shields were more than enough to protect her from its malice. But it did mean she needed to keep shields in place; when she relaxed them, the nasty creature pulled her hair and pushed or pulled at her so that she seemed to trip. She was exasperated by the mindless harrassment. The imp could drink in the fear and pain of mortals it mistreated, but she did not exude pain and fear, and the creature should have abandoned its attempts to hurt her.

She was further irritated on her way from the Gate to the palace by the traps Vidal set to bedevil his less than clever subjects. Because she was distracted by the refurbishment of Caer Mordwyn, one of those traps had partly penetrated her shield and stung her. That reminded her Pasgen had warned her Vidal's sojurn in the mist land had changed him. But the reminder of Vidal's new strength only increased her vexation. How a being of such power could take pleasure in the fear and

pain of those so much less than him was beyond her willingness to understand.

Once she had simply accepted that Unseleighe life was like that,
but recently she had been spoiled. Her time Underhill had been
spent mostly with Harry in Elfhame Elder-Elf and twice she had
dined with him in Denoriel's luxurious chambers in Llachar Lle. It
was true that she could not travel alone in Logres (she had never
been to Avalon where the watchers at the Gate would likely have
destroyed her). Harry had to be with her and vouch for her—but
there were no traps and there was so much beauty.

She had been in Alhambra too; Rhoslyn stopped suddenly
and looked behind her, feeling as if she were followed. But the
road was empty. What in this ugly, gloomy place had brought
Alhambra to her mind? Alhambra, all white marble and delicate
lacy turrets . . . Shadows. Yes, shadows moved on the blood-red
path behind her. Shadows always seemed to move on their own
in Caer Mordwyn.

That was what brought Alhambra to mind, Rhoslyn realized.
Shadows had moved on the glistening pathways of Alhambra too.
She had felt what she felt now, watched . . . followed.

But Elidir had said she was not alone in feeling as if something trailed behind her in Alhambra. Mechain agreed and told
her they had searched both physically and by magic, only once
catching a glimpse of a shadow that seemed to move by itself and
disappeared as soon as their attention was fixed on it. Rhoslyn
recalled that Mechain's remark brought something ugly and half
forgotten to mind and she had shivered. Harry put a strong,
solid arm over her shoulder and the crawling sensation down
her back had stopped.

The memory of Harry's solid warmth, of the way most spells
bounced off him by Oberon's protection, made her smile and
she started toward the palace again, watching her way but still
thinking of Alhambra.

Beauty was no guarantee against evil. Long as Harry and his
friends had labored over Alhambra, it was still tainted. Rhoslyn
had been asked to make suitable harmless creatures to clean away
the detritus of long abandonment and the filth generated by the
cursed things the Inquisition had left. To her horror, although
the Evil in the elfhame had been so much diminished that even
Hafwen could hardly sense it, when she and the others returned,

the servants had been corrupted. They had attacked Mechain and Harry, and Rhoslyn had to unmake them.

Rhoslyn stopped again as a long arm snapped out of the brush that lined the road and tried to seize her. It slipped off her shield and she used a small spark of power to drive it back into hiding. Recalling the energy reminded her of the far more subtle trap the Evil in Alhambra had set. Hafwen had barely been in time to stop her from absorbing the power she had expended in making the servants, which was what she always did. This time, had she drawn the power in, the Evil would have come with it.

A split suddenly opened in the road. Rhoslyn cast a bridge of power over it and crossed, sighing. There was danger and evil in the Seleighe domains also, but it was not this kind of petty, senseless mischief simply designed to make stupid, weak beings more ridiculous. Even the mortal world was not so silly. There was logic and purpose to the threats against Mary.

The reminders that all of Underhill was dangerous and for her the mortal world hardly less so made Rhoslyn's mood black and crossgrained when she climbed the red-veined black marble steps into Vidal's palace. She wrenched her mind away from her mistress and the problems of the Bright Court to face current reality. But pushing Vidal to the back of her mind had produced no new insight on what to say to him or how to act.

Partly because she was uncertain about how to present herself to Vidal, she snarled at the Sidhe who blocked the way to the second set of stairs, which would take her to Vidal's apartment. The Sidhe was arrogant, but at least he was not near mindless from being drugged. Nor was he an idiot. When she said she was there because she had been summoned by Prince Vidal, he disappeared, presumably to carry her message.

Rhoslyn continued on her way, then laughed—and was annoyed at herself for doing so—when the messenger reappeared where she had been when she first spoke to him. Apparently he had assumed that, overawed by being summoned by Vidal, she would stay where she was until Vidal's permission was received. He had thus set his translocation spell to a place instead of fixing it on her.

The laugh had been unwise. The Sidhe rushed at her and tried to strike her. Rhoslyn struck back, drawing bitter/sour power from around her and spitting it back at him. She felled him, but the foul intake further exacerbated her temper and she was literally grinding her teeth when she arrived at Vidal's door.

Her mood was so foul that despite knowing she was the only remaining direct link to Vidal, the only way to know what he was planning, Rhoslyn would have turned and walked away if the door had not opened for her at once. But the door did open, and she drew a deep breath, doubled her shields, and walked in.

"You summoned me," she said, her voice cold, her tone almost contemptuous, almost inviting an assault.

Vidal looked up at once from a plaque he held in his lap. "Where is your brother?" he asked. "I wish to speak to Pasgen, and I am sure you have some way to summon him."

Rhoslyn blinked, silent for a moment because she was so astonished at the courtesy of his prompt attention and his lack of reaction to her tone. His voice was mild, only questioning and interested rather than aggressive. On the other hand, his question was part of an old story. Had Vidal lost bits of his memory again and forgotten that Pasgen had renounced his loyalty?

But Vidal did not look lost; he looked strong and calm, his eyes well focused, almost alight. And Aurilia was beside him. She, too, looked better than she had when Rhoslyn had seen her last. Pasgen's warning seemed all too accurate. Rhoslyn thought she had better swallow her bad temper and try to discover what they really wanted from her.

She shook her head and sighed, speaking quietly although her words were sharp. "You summoned me with such urgency to ask a question you know I cannot answer? As to summoning Pasgen, I would not if I could and you know why. I try not to annoy Pasgen."

"She is so heavily warded that my truth spell does not recognize her," Aurilia said, lifting a hand.

Rhoslyn poured more power into her shields and braced herself against an attack. She laid a hand over her lindys to prevent it from shaking. The last thing she wanted was for Pasgen to believe he had to come to her rescue. She did not think Vidal would permit Aurilia actually to harm her. And, indeed, Vidal put his hand over Aurilia's and bore it down although Aurilia was frowning blackly.

"My lord," Rhoslyn said pacifically, "I assure you it is not worth my effort to lie. You need no truth spell for me. Pasgen is in one or another Unformed land. I have no idea which and no way of finding out. I have no idea what he is doing there, except that likely it is something to do with power."

That was all perfectly true and if Aurilia was lying about the effectiveness of her truth spell it would report Rhoslyn *was* telling the truth. Still, there was something about the quiet, passive way Vidal was watching her that made Rhoslyn cold. She was not going to be able to fool this Vidal into believing her stupid and weak. So, though it was true she could not afford to break with Vidal, she did not need to act as if she did not know he and Aurilia were playing with her.

Rhoslyn shrugged. "If you want to speak to Pasgen, you can leave a message in the empty house. I can do no more than that myself, but I will gladly leave a message for you. Now, if that is all you want of me . . ."

She started to turn away, her irritation returning over this senseless cat and mouse game.

"Why are you in such a hurry to leave?" Vidal asked, but still without temper or threat, as was the reprimand that followed. "You knew my message was urgent, but still you did not hurry to respond to it. I have something of importance to tell you."

"Then I wish you would tell me quickly." Now Roslyn frowned. "As to why I am in haste to leave and did not come as soon as I had your message . . . This is a bad time for me to leave my lady. There have been several attempts on her life and I did not dare leave while anyone was still awake in Hunsdon."

"Already?" Vidal suddenly flushed with anger and bluish light flickered on his fingertips, but the threat was not directed at Rhoslyn and was quickly controlled. "I summoned you to warn you that I had learned Northumberland wished to be rid of Mary and to bid you take good care."

Rhoslyn sighed. "I am taking care, great care. We have had an attempt at poison and another two at causing an accident and I was forced to stop the heart of a man—fortunately old and greatly excited so his death did not cause any suspicion—who would have stabbed her."

"And you did not bother to tell me?" That question was not so mild. The old Vidal snarled past the barrier of calm.

"That was foolish, Rhoslyn," Aurilia said. "You know Vidal and I are deeply interested in Mary's well-doing."

"Of course I know, but what could you have done to help me?"

"I would have been sooner alert to examine the Court for plots and I could have provided more watchers," Vidal remarked, his calm restored.

"Watchers. Imps!" Rhoslyn wrinkled her nose. "The whole palace would soon have been in such disorder from their nasty tricks that I would never have been able to detect ill-wishing. No, I do not need such help."

"Nor can you watch day and night," Aurilia snapped. "Not without giving away what you are. That is why Prince Vidal wishes Pasgen to join you."

"I am not a fool," Rhoslyn riposted. "I have help enough. I have made the attempts on the Lady Mary clear to her ladies and guards—the servant who nearly caused the accidents fled, the poison killed a dog, the assassin's knife fell from his clothing. Jane Dormer and Susan Clarencieux, her other favorite ladies, allow only old, trusted friends to approach close."

"Do not trust even those 'old trusted friends' too much," Vidal warned.

Rhoslyn drew a quick breath. "Why not?"

"The Chancellor of England told me that as the king failed Northumberland began to make plans to be rid of Mary. He has somehow tricked the dying king to name Jane Grey as his heir and disqualified both Mary and the accursed red-haired bitch because they were declared illegitimate. And the whole Council has been coerced into signing agreement to this device."

For a long moment Rhoslyn was silent, then slowly she shook her head. "It does not matter. Mary will never accept it. The king is not yet of age; his will can have no validity, specially not reaching so far for an heir when one of the direct blood stands ready."

"Of course. Northumberland knows that and it is why he decided Mary must die. He cannot have her as queen bringing back the Catholic rite, and in that, according to Chancellor Rich, the whole Court agrees to some extent. They have all been following the reformed religion and some have pressed Mary hard to conform."

"Yes. I understand. I will be doubly careful and present what you tell me to the other ladies as a fearful speculation."

"No, you do *not* understand," Vidal said, his voice sharper. "If you and Mary's other servants contrive to keep her safe from secret attacks, Northumberland is so desperate that he is prepared to use force."

"Force?" Rhoslyn breathed. "What kind of force? Will he bring the army to attack Hunsdon? Oh, I think the whole country would rise if he did that."

"What Rich told me was that Northumberland will write to Mary and bid her come to Greenwich, or perhaps London, to say fare well to her dying brother. On the road a large detachment of royal guards will meet her. There would be nothing to arouse popular suspicion in an honor guard being sent out to greet Mary. Rich does not know where they would take her, but she will be a prisoner then and easy prey to an 'accident' or 'illness.'"

"I see." Rhoslyn stood biting her lip. "Oh, it will be very hard to dissuade her from going to Edward. She will hope for a last minute conversion that would save his soul."

"That is no problem. I have already directed Rich to arrange for a high nobleman, recently restored to favor, to ride secretly to Mary and tell her her brother is already dead and the message a mere ruse to bring her into Northumberland's power."

"What nobleman?" Roslyn asked. "I am not certain Mary will believe just anyone."

Vidal shook his head. "That I cannot tell you. Rich himself did not know which of the courtiers he would be able to convince to ride to Mary without betraying him to Northumberland. As for who Mary will believe, surely you can do that much to her mind without any hint of the meddling getting back to Oberon."

Rhoslyn sighed thinking that if an idea inserted into Mary's mind could take root, by now she would dearly love her sister Elizabeth. In fact, when Rhoslyn slipped thoughts of Elizabeth's fondness for Mary herself or of how clever and dignified Elizabeth had become into Mary's mind, they only seemed to make Mary distrust herself and cling more firmly to her past judgement that Elizabeth was a bastard who would drive out the old faith.

"It is not easy to influence Mary's mind on most things," she said slowly. "Oh, I could easily make her even more of a fanatic about her religion, but in most things she is so distrustful of herself that if I try to make her think this or that nobleman is trustworthy, she will immediately suspect herself of some weakness toward him and send him away."

"This is too important to leave in the hands of someone so

unsure of herself, so afraid to act," Aurilia sneered. "We need Mary safe, not a lot of excuses for her failure." She put a hand on Vidal's arm. "Is there not some Sidhe you could send to take Rhoslyn's place, my lord?"

Rhoslyn laughed. "After my being Mary's servant for nearly twenty years? Who could know how I act, what I am accustomed to say, who are my intimates. No, there is no one who could take my place and to send a new servant . . . She would not be allowed anywhere near Mary. I am what you have, but I do care for Lady Mary and I assure you I will do my very best to keep her safe. I thank you for the warning you have given."

Vidal patted Aurilia's hand. He knew she did not like Rhoslyn. Well, he was not too fond of Rhoslyn himself, but she was right about her position with Mary. And Vidal was certain Rhoslyn spoke the truth about her fondness for Mary and would protect her.

He would have liked Pasgen, who was considerably more powerful, to have joined with his sister in protecting Mary from Northumberland's plots. Vidal's eyes narrowed. He would indeed send a message to the empty house. He would send a message to Pasgen detailing the danger in which Mary was and Roslyn with her.

"We have a little time," Vidal said, "a few days at least, perhaps a week or two until the boy is dead." Something moved, a darker shadow in the shadow by the door. Vidal's eyes flicked to it and then fixed on Rhoslyn's face. "I will think about what help I can send that will cause no disturbance in Mary's household." He nodded. "And now you had better do as you suggested and go back to guard your lady."

Rhoslyn was surprised. She had been sure that Vidal was going to make some suggestion concerning the guarding of Mary before he had momentarily looked away. However, the movement of his eyes had been so swift before they came back to her face that she assumed a conflicting thought had changed his mind about speaking. In any case she had no intention of lingering when she had been given leave to go. Holding such strong shields was draining and she did not want to draw on the disgusting power of Caer Mordwyn.

The door opened and then closed behind Rhoslyn. Vidal waited, watching Aurilia's face. When the frown on her brow smoothed, which indicated that Rhoslyn was gone, he looked again at the shadows near the door and gestured.

A small, pallid Sidhe fell to his knees. Slowly, clearly unwillingly, at another gesture he crawled forward until he was near the dais on which Vidal's and Aurilia's almost-thrones sat.

"And have you bespoke the Evil in Alhambra?" Vidal asked. "And where have you been all this while?"

The small Sidhe, trembling, his form wavering slightly, did not reply directly to Vidal's questions. Instead, he said, "If Rhoslyn is your servant, lord prince, she is a traitor." His voice squeaked with fear.

"I said so, my lord," Aurilia remarked with satisfaction.

"I am not greatly surprised," Vidal said calmly, "but she serves a necessary purpose now. When I have no need of her, I will . . ." Actually he did not know what he would or could do. To deal with Rhoslyn meant a confrontation with Pasgen and he was not sure he was ready for that, but he was not going to expose that weakness. He let his voice fade and fixed his gaze on the shadow-Sidhe. "I will do what is necessary. But what makes you say she is a traitor, Dakari?"

"Because I know her. I have seen her in the company of two of the elder Sidhe and of that mortal marked with Oberon's star. They were all together in Alhambra. The mortal serves the Bright Court and the elder Sidhe—"

Vidal made an impatient gesture and Dakari fell silent. "The mortal is nothing. He has no magic at all. Only Oberon's protection keeps him alive."

As he said the words, Vidal remembered Harry's gun and the iron dart that had almost killed him. But that was in the mortal world and after a battle with Denoriel; here Underhill Vidal knew his power was far greater. Nonetheless he did not choose to think about Henry FitzRoy.

"And the elder Sidhe do not well know the difference between Dark Court and Bright," he continued hastily. "I would liefer they were not mixed into this matter, but when we hold Alhambra they will sink into Dreaming again. More important is my question, which you never answered. Have you approached and spoken with the Evil there? Can we move into Alhambra?"

"It would not listen to me," Dakari wept. "I did try to speak to It, to tell It of our admiration and desire to serve It, but It made no response other than sending a . . . a black glob that I am sure would have swallowed me if I remained. Later the elder Sidhe came again and destroyed the black thing of the Evil's making.

They did other things too; I have followed them many times. They have brought silver worked into mystical signs and placed it all over the elfhame. Then the mortal came with iron, also worked into signs which he placed throughout the palace. Now the Evil is diminishing. I can barely feel it."

"It seems they are trying to destroy the Evil," Aurilia said, frowning. "That is impossible but I do not like it. It is possible that the Evil will be driven out. I do not like it. Once It is gone, the Bright Court will send Sidhe to take up residence there and we will have to fight for the place."

"So? We have fought the Bright Court before and seized what we wanted."

Aurilia shook her head. "That was a very long time ago when the whole world was in turmoil and the Dark Court was very strong and as numerous as mortals. Your followers are increased since you were taken by the mist, but not to the point that they can overwhelm by numbers, and the knights of the Bright Court are not to be dismissed lightly."

Vidal glanced sidelong at her, not liking what he heard. It was the first mention she had made of the benefits to the Dark Court during the period in which she had ruled Caer Mordwyn. He remembered his unwise attack on the domain called the empty house to punish Pasgen and to bring him to heel. Deep inside something hot roiled and nearly burst. Vidal suppressed it with four years of practice at burying rage. The attack had cost half his subjects, and driven Pasgen openly to renounce his allegiance. Unwise, yes, but he did not like Aurilia's reminder.

Nonetheless he said calmly, "You are the one who wanted Alhambra and I so much wish to please you that I am willing to fight for it if I must. It was a great making, as great as any of Oberon's better works. However, I agree that to take it by agreement with the Evil is better than battle with the Bright Court." He turned from Aurilia to look at Dakari. "Now is the best time, while the Evil is under attack, to offer assistance. Tell It we will remove the iron and the silver and welcome among us any of Its creatures that do not attack us."

Dakari collapsed on the floor, weeping. "I cannot," he wailed. "How can I remove iron? To go near it racks me with pain. To touch it would kill me."

"Fool." Vidal sighed, but he did not release a punishing bolt or his little needles of agony. "Take a witch or a werewolf with you. They can gather up the iron. You can pave the way for them by removing the silver. And do not tell me passing the iron will hurt you. So long as you do not touch it or remain long near it you will come to no harm."

There was hardly more than a shadow on the floor near the dais now, only a wavering, flickering outline of a Sidhe. "They will not obey me," the shadow thing sobbed.

That was true enough, Vidal realized; this Sidhe was too weak to command obedience from anything. Vidal grimaced. He would need to give Dakari an amulet that would force a werewolf or witch to obey, but Vidal hated the thought of allowing any of his Dark Sidhe, even so weak a creature as Dakari, to command the creatures that served him. Aurilia put a hand on his arm.

"There are Wahib and Wahiba," she said, smiling broadly so that all her sharp pointed teeth showed. "They were insolent the last time I bade them bring me a child and brought so scrawny a creature that I could get almost no blood from it. And Wahib had bitten it so the blood was foul. They need a lesson."

"So they do." Vidal smiled back at her. And it was Aurilia the witch and werewolf would blame for their degradation. "Will you make the amulet then to bind them to service with Dakari?"

Aurilia laughed. "Yes. Yes I will." She looked down at the grey-ish mist leaking away from the dais. "Come back in a mortal day, and I will give you an amulet that will make one witch, the witch Wahiba and her son Wahib, the werewolf, obedient to you."

The mist firmed and ceased moving. The shadow of a Sidhe looked up at Aurilia and the thin voice whined,. "But if the iron and silver that the Sidhe of the Bright Court set in Alhambra are removed, they will know someone has been there. They will search for me . . ."

"Then you had better work swiftly both to remove the silver and iron sigils and to convince the Evil to receive us," Aurilia said sharply without sympathy and waved at the shadow to be gone.

When they were alone she said to Vidal, "That is a weak reed on which to fix our hope of taking Alhambra."

Vidal nodded indifferently. "And we may not get it, but there is still El Dorado for you, and to tell the truth I am much more concerned about Mary's safety than taking possession of either of those domains. When Mary is queen, so much power from pain and misery will flood down upon us that I will be able to make a domain for you if Alhambra and El Dorado are taken by the Bright Court."

Aurilia's lower lip protruded in an ugly pout. "I do not want your making. You are strong, but no artist. Besides, I want Alhambra *because* the Bright Court desires it."

"Then we will take it from them. I tell you, Mary must be queen. When Mary is queen we will have power to spare to drive the liosalfar out of any domain we desire. We will be fat and rich, but Mary must come to the throne, and now she is in great danger."

The pout became less pronounced. "I agree that Mary must be queen, but if you do not think Rhoslyn is enough to protect her—"

"To keep Mary safe from personal attack, Rhoslyn is enough," Vidal interrupted. "She always pretends to be weaker than she is. But according to Rich, Northumberland is truly desperate. I think he will decide to send a troop to take Mary prisoner, possibly to arrange that she have an 'accident,' and Rhoslyn can do nothing about that."

"Then what will you do?"

Vidal stared out across the room for a moment. "First I will tell Albertus to call up the men he hired to capture Elizabeth. They failed at that but there are more of them now and many dedicated to serving Mary and bringing back the old rite. They will gladly fight or distract Northumberland's men, which will give Mary time to find a haven. Second, I will leave a message for Pasgen that Rhoslyn might be destroyed in Northumberland's attempt on Mary. Rhoslyn will not go with Pasgen leaving Mary to her fate. Thus Pasgen will have to save them both."

"How?"

Vidal laughed aloud. "I have no idea but Pasgen may well be strong enough to build a Gate and drag the women through. Mary will know something strange happened but let her cry aloud of magic if she wishes. Either Rhoslyn will be able to wipe what happened from Mary's mind or Mary will only be able to describe Pasgen as the magic maker. And if the tale comes back to Oberon and invites His Majesty's displeasure in Pasgen . . . *tant pis* as they say in Melusine."

Chapter 8

Rhoslyn hurried away from the palace in Caer Mordwyn so worried about what Vidal had told her of Northumberland's plans that she nearly fell into one of the slimy pools that dotted the red marble road to the nearest Gate. She drew back in time, but her shoes were ruined, the glutinous, foul smelling stuff that filled the pool clinging to anything it touched. However, Rhoslyn noted with some interest that, disgusting as it was, the liquid did no real harm.

That was new. In the past, Vidal's traps if not fatal caused agonizing pain so that he could enjoy listening to the shrieks and bellows as the trapped creature escaped or died. The realization that Vidal had seemingly stopped destroying his own subjects did not wake any hope that Vidal's essential nature had changed. It only reinforced Pasgen's warning that the Prince of Caer Mordwyn had somehow learned self-control, which made him all the more dangerous.

The idea of Vidal as a reasoning and calculating being only made Rhoslyn hurry faster. One thing Vidal now saw clearly was where his own benefit existed, which made his warning about the threat to Mary all the more urgent.

Achieving the Gate, Rhoslyn transferred to the Goblin Market and from there to the empty house. Her favorite in the past was the Elves' Faire, but she avoided it now because that was where she used to meet Llanelli when her mother was alive. To her surprise and relief, Pasgen was sitting in the atrium with several closely written sheets spread out in front of him.

"Thank the Mother that you are here," she said.

"I stop in often now to see if you need me," he said, turning to face Rhoslyn. "Hafwen reminds me, but today I wanted to talk to you in particular as you are a maker. Hafwen says the self-willed mist wants to know what a house is."

"That seems to be a singularly pointless inquiry for something like a mist," Rhoslyn said absently, still thinking about what Vidal had told her. And then, really hearing what Pasgen had said, she asked, "How can Hafwen know what a mist wants to know?"

"She has no idea," Pasgen admitted, "and is rather shaken by the communication. She—"

"Never mind the mist," Rhoslyn interrupted, putting a hand to her head. "We will get to the mist when we can. I've just been with Vidal—and you are quite right, Pasgen, he is much changed. Not once did I need my shields . . . Well, Aurilia threatened me but not Vidal. And Caer Mordwyn is no longer rotting away." She grimaced. "But it is still full of stupid traps." Then she shuddered. "That does not matter. Vidal told me that those attempts on Mary's life were not just random lunatics who hate and fear Catholicism but likely directed attempts to kill her by Northumberland."

Pasgen thought for a moment. "I am not surprised. He is tied too close to the reformed religion and has himself pressed Mary too hard to conform to his rite. He cannot hope that his experience in ruling could recommend him to her. If she comes to the throne, she will dismiss him at once and might be likely to put him in the Tower." He glanced down at the closely written sheets he had been studying and sighed. "I suppose you want me to come help you protect Mary."

"It will not be for long," Rhoslyn said apologetically. "Vidal says the boy cannot live beyond two mortal weeks longer, and Mary's fate will be decided within a mortal week or at the most two after that. If she is not taken prisoner and killed at once, many in England will rally to her. Once that happens she will be guarded like a queen."

Pasgen sighed again. "Very well. I must tell Hafwen that I will be mostly in the mortal world for one of their months. Then I will come through your Gate. Draw aside the man you want me to imitate. I think it will be much easier if I simply take his place and put him in stasis. I will extract from his mind what his duties are and who are his intimates, and I will feed to his mind the happenings of each day, so I can free him to his own devices each night. That way, his body will take no harm and when the crisis is over, he can take up his life again."

"Oh, Pasgen, that would be wonderful. Can you do it?"

"Yes, of course. It is distasteful to me and a dreadful waste of my time when I should be attending to the mist Underhill, but I can do it."

It seemed over the last two weeks in June that Pasgen's distasteful task was also useless. He daily took the guardsman's place, but Mary's household ran in its usual placid course. The few persons who came to Hunsdon with pleas for help or works dedicated to Lady Mary were mindscanned by Rhoslyn or Pasgen or both and were innocent of any ulterior purpose.

The only sign that life was not as placid and ordinary as it seemed, was the extra Masses that Mary requested with an anxiety that made her voice shake and her ladies' inability to settle easily to ordinary tasks. Also unusual was the eagerness with which Mary seized on the usual twice-a-week letters from Lady Catherine, who had resumed her place with the duchess of Northumberland.

The news in the letters was scarcely startling, the only unusual items were personal and seemingly had nothing to do with the Court. Lady Catherine was planning a series of visits for later in the year, certain dates were noted as being likely times for Lady Catherine's departure. There was some uncertainty about the dates, but they seemed to become firmer as the fact that one of Lady Catherine's daughters-by-marriage was with child became more certain.

On the fourth of July, the outwardly placid tenor of life in Hunsdon was broken. Midday there came a letter from the duke of Northumberland. Anxious to know what Northumberland had to say, Mary did not wait for the priest she had summoned but withdrew into her bedchamber with only a few of her trusted ladies. The news was bad. His Majesty Edward VI had taken a serious turn for the worse in his illness. In fact, Northumberland wrote, the king was on his deathbed and was asking for his sister Mary.

Rhoslyn sent a thrust of thought into Susan Clarencieux's mind. Not a new thought; Susan had had it before, but Rhoslyn needed Susan to speak it. Susan wavered on the stool she sat on near Mary's chair and put a hand to her head. A sharp pain had pierced her temple. Then her lips thinned with determination.

"I do not think you should go, my lady," she said. "I fear . . . I am not sure what I fear, but the duke of Northumberland has London in a grip of iron. Oh, my lady, remember Lord Arundel's warning. If you enter the city you will be totally in his power."

"But Edward has asked for me."

The slight uncertain apprehension in Mary's deep, strong voice betrayed that she knew all too well the truth of Susan's warning. A martyr's courage would not permit her to accept it.

"Perhaps, now that Edward knows he must face God he sees that he has strayed from the true path. If he repents . . . if he desires to confess and hear Mass, he can still be saved."

"Unless what he desires is to make you swear to keep his rite as the price of being named his heir," Rhoslyn said, and cast another spear of thought, this time at Jane Dormer.

"Surely not, Rosamund," Mary said. "Surely by God's sweet mercy Edward has been vouchsafed a last chance at salvation."

She believed it; Mary truly believed in miracles. She was convinced it was by God's direct intervention that she had always narrowly escaped being forced to conform to the new rite. Rhoslyn barely swallowed a hiss of irritation. She dared not insert more fear, more suspicion of Northumberland's purposes, into Mary's mind. Rhoslyn suspected that the greater Mary's fear, the more sure she would become that her brother's last chance at salvation rested in her hands. Desperately, but with more care, Rhoslyn changed the thought she was pressing on Jane.

"I do not believe Northumberland would have sent you this message if there were any chance that King Edward would convert," Jane Dormer said slowly. "I greatly fear, my lady, that the king is already dead and this summons is no more than a trap."

"There is good sense in that," Rhoslyn said, keeping her hands folded in her lap. "Only think of the dates in Lady Catherine's letters. The last one surely implied that the king would live only until today, and it is most likely that he would slip away sooner considering how weak he was rumored to be."

"And no mention was made of sending for Elizabeth," Susan put in. "Surely both sisters should be summoned . . . unless the duke only needs to trap *you*. Elizabeth is of his persuasion, after all, and she is said by many, if wrongly, to be King Henry's daughter."

Rhoslyn had a brief image of cramming a large, soft roll into Susan's mouth to gag her, but it was too late. Mary bit her lip.

"But it is also possible that no mention was made of Elizabeth because Edward did name me," Mary said. "And because he knew it was Edward's dying wish, Northumberland feared to deny it."

"There is very little Northumberland fears," Rhoslyn said. "Certainly not violating an inconvenient dying wish. I am sorry to dampen your hope, madam, but I cannot believe the duke would invite you to see Edward unless all hope of your actually seeing him were extinguished. Like Jane, I fear the king is dead."

Mary rose to her feet, gesturing at her ladies to remain seated, and began to pace, wringing her hands. "I do not know what to do. If there is the smallest hope that I might be the means of saving my brother's soul, my own danger should count for nothing."

"No, madam," Jane said. "Although he is the king and your brother, Edward is only one soul. If Northumberland succeeds in keeping you from taking the throne, which is your right and your duty, every soul in England would be lost."

There was a dead silence. Mary stood absolutely still, her hands pressed together but no longer twisting with indecision. Rhoslyn drew a deep breath as she felt Mary's exaltation mingled with iron-hard purpose conquer doubt and fear. And behind her eyes Rhoslyn saw the dark pool in the FarSeers' tower where flames leapt over twisting bodies and burning children screamed.

She had blanked that Vision from her mind for a very long time, concentrating on the fact that Mary was a sweet, kind woman and did not deserve to be sacrificed to Northumberland's ambition. She had almost forgotten that Mary was determined to bring England back not to her father's religious practice but her mother's. She would reconcile with the pope and reinstate the full catholic rite, believing she would thus save every soul in the country. And she would not count the cost.

Momentarily Rhoslyn was tempted to reverse her effort to save Mary and send her into Northumberland's hands. Then she recalled Denoriel's guess that the lens of the Bright Court and the black pool of Vidal Dhu's tower were showing a sequence of events rather than three different possibilities. That might be true.

Edward had come to the throne, but the Visions of Mary and Elizabeth had not faded—although there was the puzzling new Vision of the pale, weeping girl, which one moment was clear and in the next wavered. Still, now that Edward was dying or dead, the Vision of his rule was gone, and Mary and Elizabeth came in that order. If the Visions were of what would be—and Aleneil said her fellow FarSeers all knew of such Visions—then if Elizabeth were to rule, Mary must come safe to the throne first.

"Well," Mary said, breaking into Rhoslyn's troubled thoughts, "although I am still not sure exactly what to do, I know we must move from this house. Hunsdon is not defensible. If we leave tomorrow morning and take the road to Hoddesdon, we will be going toward Greenwich—"

"My lady—" Susan began to protest, but the guard by the door opened it and Susan stopped speaking.

"My lady," he said, "you sent for Francis Mallet, but he is laid upon his bed with an uneasiness of the belly and sent another priest in his stead. Will you see him?"

Mary sighed. "Only to ask about Father Mallet. A stranger can give me no advice. Yes, let him in." She then turned toward Susan and said, "We will not go too far south, but I wish to be on a good road, so if we go to Hoddesdon—"

Mary stopped speaking as she became aware that a young man in priest's dress, but clutching around him a thigh-length cloak as if he were chilled, had come through the door and was approaching, bowing repeatedly. Rhoslyn stood up abruptly as a wave of hatred and desperation flooded out from the black-clad form, but she was on the far side of the group of women. Why did Pasgen not act?

"Madam," she cried.

It was the worst thing she could have done. Mary looked away from the man advancing on her toward Rhoslyn, who gasped "Beware!"

That was also a mistake because Mary looked wildly around the room and, nearsighted as she was, saw little beyond a blur. The only thing that was moving was the dark-clothed priest and Mary had no fear of a priest who was connected to Father Mallet. But the priest had let go of his cloak and leapt forward, a long knife now gleaming in his hand.

Mary did not see clearly enough to notice the knife, but Jane

Dormer, who was closest, screamed and jumped to her feet. She started forward, but she was not close enough to throw herself between Mary and the attacker. And then the guard who had admitted the man was there, sword in hand.

Only the attacker did not back away from the threatening guard. Instead he tried to dart around the sword, and the guard leapt ahead a long pace and thrust at the priest. But the priest still did not retreat; his eyes fixed and staring, he shrieked, "Papist bitch!" raised the knife and, as if he could see nothing but Mary, threw himself forward to strike at her.

Everyone was in motion now. Mary backed a few steps away from the struggling men. Jane reached Mary and flung her body before her mistress, her arms outstretched to ward any attack from the side. Susan was only a few steps behind Jane, the two providing a living wall of protection. Rhoslyn, who could not reach Mary except by going around the men seized the back of the attacker's cloak, ostensibly to pull him away, but actually to push him forward sharply.

The guard cried out, but his warning was too late. The attacker had spitted himself on the sword. The guard gasped and stepped back as the knife fell from the priest's hand almost striking his foot, and now Rhoslyn did pull on the cloak and the man slid off the guard's sword and fell to the ground.

"Are you safe, my lady?" he cried, turning to Mary.

"Yes." Mary's voice was loud and steady. She sounded more indignant than frightened. "I am perfectly well, but you had better hurry to Father Mallet's chamber and discover whether this madman did him any harm."

"But—" The guard gestured at the body on the floor, which was beginning to twitch and moan.

"Let me call another guard, madam," Rhoslyn said. "Susan, pick up that knife and put it out of that lunatic's reach."

As she spoke, Rhoslyn went toward the door on the heels of the guard. She saw Jane run to the hearth and picked up the poker, holding it so the heavy knob on the end could be used as a weapon. In fact, Rhoslyn did not need to call a guard. Apparently Jane's and Susan's screams had been heard. One guard was reaching for the door and another was no more than two steps behind.

"A madman attacked Lady Mary," Rhoslyn said.

Both men exclaimed in horror and rushed into Mary's chamber while all the other attendants cried out and hurried in the same direction. That permitted Rhoslyn to catch hold of the guard's sleeve and say, low-voiced, "Holy Mother, Pasgen, you cut that close. He was so full of hate and fear and rage that he almost stunned me. I could not move fast enough to get between him and Mary. Did you not sense his intention?"

"Of course I did, but what did you want me to do, run him through before he made any threat?"

"But what if you had not reached him in time?"

"Oh, he would have stumbled or, at need, forgotten what he intended to do." Pasgen shrugged, irritated. "Besides I think so close an escape will be a salutary lesson for Mary. She will take more care now and perhaps be a little less trusting of priests, and I will be able to go back to my own affairs."

"Not yet," Rhoslyn begged. "When we get to some place that can be defended—it will only be a few days more—you can go. Oh, by God's Grace, I forgot all about Father Mallet. You had better go and see if he is all right."

"I will go, but there is nothing wrong with Mallet. That false priest was going to hit him on the head, but I checked the blow and cast a sleep spell on Mallet." Pasgen paused, pretended to make a huge sigh and added, "Could we not leave the man asleep and pretend he was struck. It would keep him quiet for a while. I could do without another Mass."

Rhoslyn giggled. "I also, but unfortunately Mary has three more chaplains. If Father Mallet does not say Mass, one of the others will, and Mary says she thinks better after prayers." Then Rhoslyn looked slightly indignant. "What have you to complain about? I have to be in the room with her and at least look as if I am paying strict attention."

They parted then, Pasgen going toward Father Mallet's room and Rhoslyn hurrying back to Mary. She found that the guards had bound and removed the attacker but that an argument was going on about what to do with him. Sir Robert Rochester, Mary's Comptroller, was demanding that the man be straitly questioned and Sir Francis Waldgrave agreed with him. Master Edmund Englefield was asking, "Question how? He is a priest. Surely you do not intend to lay hands upon a priest?"

"Who, beside he himself, says he is a priest?" Rhoslyn asked.

Everyone turned to look at her with expressions varying from scorn to shocked realization.

"He said he was Father Mallet's . . ." Mary began and then said, "Oh no, of course he could not have been in Father Mallet's service. Did he harm Father Mallet? Where is the guard?"

"He should be back any moment, my lady," Rhoslyn said. "But it is too easy to gain admittance to your lodging by claiming to be in holy orders. This is the second so-called priest who has come with a knife instead of prayers."

Susan Clarencieux gasped, recalling the old man with the wild eyes who had suddenly grasped at his chest and fallen and the long knife with a discolored blade that had slipped from his clothing. "Madam, we must be more cautious. You must give orders that no one even one in holy orders should be admitted."

"Or at least anyone not known to us must be accompanied by a guard," Jane Dormer said.

"And what true priest would harm another priest in order to attack an unarmed woman?" Rochester put in. "If this man is in holy orders at all, it must be in this reformed rite that does not demand of its priests true holiness. And if he did attack Father Mallet, as we know he attacked you, he has forfeited the protection of Mother Church. He must be straitly questioned so we discover who instructed him to kill you, madam."

There was another silence as the horrified members of Mary's household faced the truth, finally stated bluntly, that someone desired their lady's death. Before anyone could think of what to say, the door opened and the guard stepped in.

"Where is Father Mallet?" Mary asked. "Was he hurt?"

"Not severely, madam," Pasgen said, looking around the crowded room. "He is safe, but laid upon his bed. I called his servant to him. The intruder struck him on the head, but he is awake now and seems to be recovering, except for the pain in his head."

"How did Father Mallet know this man?" Rochester asked, his voice sharp and suspicious, his eyes traveling from face to face.

The question was not addressed to the guard, who could not be expected to have questioned Father Mallet or to know who among Mary's people had introduced the man. The guard bowed slightly and turned to leave, half drawing his sword as the door opened and then stepping aside as Father Barkley entered.

"I have been with Father Mallet," he said, bowing to Lady Mary.

"His servant sent a boy to tell me he had been attacked and to warn the household."

"You are a little late," Rochester said. "This guard was fortunately in time to save Lady Mary from being stabbed. How did it come about that Father Mallet invited this murderer among us."

"God have mercy," Father Barkley breathed. "Father Mallet was in haste to send me to warn you all. He only told me that he did not know the priest at all. He came, he said to Father Mallet, to beg asylum. He said he had been expelled from his parish by Bishop Ridley for using the rite King Henry had established. And when Father Mallet began to warn him that Lady Mary was not likely to be able to help him, the times being so uncertain . . . he suddenly did not remember any more but he thought the young man had jumped forward and struck him on the head, since his head ached fiercely."

"It is time now," Waldgrave said, "to shut the gates against all comers, no matter their garb or what sad tale they tell. My lady," he turned to Mary and bowed, "you are not safe, and each hour makes you less safe."

"Yes, I see that," Mary said.

She seemed about to say more, but Rochester interrupted her. "And I think I will now go and discover who sent that pretend priest. Then we will be able to plan further what to do. I will leave you now to rest and recover, madam. But if you will forgive the boldness, my advice is that you keep with you only a few of your ladies, those who will not trouble you with much talk."

"Yes." Mary smiled wanly. "I give you all leave to go."

The room emptied quickly, but Mary signed for the three ladies who had been with her and had all defended her against the attacker to remain behind. She then went to kneel at her *prie-dieu* to thank God for her escape, her ladies kneeling behind her. Rhoslyn strangled a sigh but bowed her head, seeming also to pray. What she thought was that Denoriel might know what was going on at Court and whether Edward was dead already. Eventually Mary rose to her feet.

"We will leave tomorrow, as early as possible and go to Hoddesdon," she said, casting a glance over her shoulder at the crucifix hanging on the wall. "That is a safer house and it is on a good road that goes south to London." She hesitated, then went on with a twist to her lips. "Let whoever passes news to Northumberland

and must tell him that the attacker failed also tell him that I seem
to be moving toward Greenwich. But the road from Hoddesdon
also goes north to Newmarket and Thetford toward Norfolk."

A letter carrying the same news and order as that delivered to
Mary was also delivered to Elizabeth on the fourth of July, but in
Hatfield it elicited no more than a sigh from Elizabeth. She had
long since given up any hope of seeing her brother ever again.
She showed Kat and Sir Edward the letter. Neither one raised
the question of obeying Northumberland's order or discussed
the possibility of going to London or Greenwich. She did not
tell her ladies what the message said. Perhaps they guessed. If
so, none spoke of it.

The messenger had not been allowed to see Elizabeth and was
hustled out before the letter could possibly have been read. When
he was gone, the household went about its business much as if
no message had been received. The state of the king's health was
not mentioned. No spy from Court or Council could report any
reaction at all to the announcement that Edward was dying.

Only when all were asleep—Dorothy Stafford in the truckle bed
bespelled not to wake—Elizabeth crept from her bedchamber to
that of Blanche and sat on her maid's bed, waiting for her Denno.
When Denoriel stepped through the Gate, she ran to him to seek
shelter in his arms.

"Is poor Edward already dead?" she whispered, her voice catching on a sob.

"I do not know," Denoriel replied. "I think it likely but no
announcement has been made, and I still have no safe friend
at Court. More than one among the Councilors wear bespelled
gems, which means that Vidal has his talons well into them. I
dare not inquire too openly lest light gossip carry my interest
where I do not want it to go."

"Still nothing from Cecil?"

Denoriel shook his head. "Northumberland is planning something desperate and he has always known that Cecil is your friend.
I sent Cropper on an errand to Canon Row—not to Cecil's house
but to another who does business with the mercer Adjoran—and
Cropper reported that at least one man was watching Cecil's door to
see who called or whether any footmen or other messengers came.
He could not see any other watcher, but said he was sure the back

door was also watched. In fact, I do not believe Cecil is at home and I know Matilda is not. She went to stay with her father some time in May."

"Can we get no news?"

"I can think of no way until Tuesday. Perhaps Rhoslyn and Pasgen will come to the Inn of Kindly Laughter. Rhoslyn will at least know what is happening in Mary's household and it is possible that Pasgen can discover what, if anything, Vidal is doing."

"Vidal? The illness that has killed Edward is his fault, or perhaps mine for not protecting my brother well enough."

"Elizabeth you were a child and what happened was no fault of yours."

She blinked away tears and asked angrily, "What more has Vidal to do with Edward's death?"

"With that, nothing, I believe. There was enough conflict and misery in Edward's reign to keep the Dark Court well supplied with power. But Vidal has always wanted Mary to reign. He thinks she will summon the Inquisition and so much trouble will be caused, perhaps even civil war will be raised in your name to free the people from that scourge, that the Dark Court will gain enough power to overwhelm the Bright. It has happened in the past."

Elizabeth closed her eyes for a moment. "Civil war . . . No. Even if it is successful and I am so raised to the throne, it will be endless as long as Mary lives." She closed her eyes again. "I could not . . . I could not order her killed."

"Let us hope she feels the same about you," Denoriel said, his voice harsh. "For I fear there will be rebellion against her attempts to force England back under the pope's rule and that rebellion will be blamed upon you. You must have nothing to do with any attempt to overthrow Mary—not by word or look and most certainly never in writing."

Chapter 9

King Edward was not yet dead when Northumberland sent his letters to Mary and Elizabeth on July 4th—in that much he told the truth. Had they hurried to Greenwich, they might just have been in time to see Edward breathe his last, and perhaps to see guns carried up into the Tower and men hired to fight.

On Tuesday, July 6 1533, Edward Tudor was at last released from his lingering agony. Northumberland forbade any person, on pain of death, to spread news of the king's demise, and made clear to his Council that his preparations to ensure the ascendency of Queen Jane—to which they had all agreed—were not yet complete. The greatest problem was that Lady Mary had not responded to his letter. She was still free, and he needed to secure her to prevent any rising against Jane in Mary's name.

Privately, Northumberland ordered his son Robert to ready three hundred men and ride to Hunsdon to take Mary prisoner. If she tried to escape, the duke said, she was to be taken by force, even killed, for in the hands of her cousin, the Emperor, she would be a knife poised at England's throat. Undoubtedly Emperor Charles V would use the change in succession as an excuse to invade England and with Mary in his hand could claim he was not invading but restoring the natural order.

Robert Dudley was brave and clever but, partly owing to having been the indulged son of the most powerful man in the kingdom for years, not much given to acting in secret. Moreover, he soon realized it was impossible to gather and arm three hundred men very quickly or completely in secret. Robert was not ready to ride to take Mary until midday on July 7th.

Long before then, in fact as soon as Lord Richard Rich heard of the king's death and the need to keep it quiet, the yellow diamond on his finger began to flash and glitter. Rich was not completely happy with Northumberland's attempt to set Mary aside, although he had voiced no protest. Deep in his heart he believed in the old rite. As he admired his ring, he remembered his interview with the sorcerer Otstargi who had told him that Mary *would* be queen, that all plans against her would fail.

Rich knew that the trap Northumberland had laid for Mary and Elizabeth had already failed. That further shook his confidence in Northumberland's arrangements. And when he soon caught wind of Robert Dudley's collecting men and arms he was even less happy. Otstargi had said that whatever expedients were used, Mary would be queen and Rich could save himself only by betraying Northumberland's plans to Mary. Was there no way, Rich thought desperately, in which he could show himself Mary's friend without exposing what he had done to Northumberland?

He would not risk himself by trying to send a message, but before the king's body had grown cold, Rich bethought him of Sir Nicholas Throckmorton. Sir Nicholas was a man of no importance a hanger on at Court but one who had barely escaped punishment for his strong leaning toward the catholic rite. Throckmorton, never trusted, had not been near Edward, had no close cronies among Northumberlands's few confidants, and thus was unlikely to have heard of the king's death or other dangerous secrets. No one would think it significant if Sir Nicholas left the palace.

Rich drew Throckmorton aside and told him of Northumberland's plan to replace Mary and take her prisoner. The man's eyes lit, first with rage and then with enthusiasm. When Throckmorton left the palace, he did so quietly; he did not take his horse—and indeed, no one noticed him. He walked into town and to the shop of a goldsmith with whom he had done business and in whose house it was sometimes possible to hear Mass.

Throckmorton passed along his information; the goldsmith, who had reason to trust his visitor was horrified. When Throckmorton explained he did not dare leave Greenwich lest his purpose be suspected, the goldsmith agreed and pressed his hand. He would go, he said, eyes bright with a fervent hope. He saw Throckmorton out and for a few moments watched as he walked back to Greenwich Palace. Then he turned to his journeyman and said he had to run an urgent errand.

The goldsmith left his shop by the back door. Unremarked, he made his way to a livery stable—he did not own a horse although he had been raised in the country and rode very well—and thence to the gate to the London road. At the first crossing out of the sight of the guards, the goldsmith turned north.

He rode hard, changing horses as necessary, sustained by the hope that, as queen, Lady Mary would restore the true religion. He was riding for Hunsdon, but when, in the late afternoon, he came to Hoddesdon he saw a concourse of folk around the manor house and the guardsmen were wearing Lady Mary's colors. The goldsmith made his way through the crowd, asking for the Comptroller or the captain of Lady Mary's guard.

As she came down from her own horse, Rhoslyn felt the goldsmith's anxiety. She did not know whether he was another assassin, but Pasgen was no great distance. Together they went to where the goldsmith was now surrounded by suspicious guards.

"Why do you want to see Lady Mary?" Pasgen asked.

The other guards, knowing it was he who had saved their lady's life only a day since, stepped back so he could ask his questions.

The goldsmith, clinging to his horse for support, shook his head. "I do not demand that honor," he said, "only to speak to someone who has her ear."

Rhoslyn stepped around Pasgen. "I am Mistress Rosamund Scot, maid of honor to Lady Mary." She looked at the man trembling with weariness, at the lathered horse. "What news do you carry?"

"Desperate news. The king is dead, and Northumberland has sent his son with a large troop of men to take Lady Mary prisoner. He has a 'device' signed by every Councilor and almost every man of note in the Court to declare Lady Mary and Lady Elizabeth bastard and of no condition to take the throne. He will make Lady Jane Grey queen."

"God help us," Rhoslyn breathed, and then, "How do we know this is true?"

"I have no proof," the goldsmith admitted, and went on to identify himself and mention Throckmorton who brought him the news of the device to set Jane Grey on the throne in Mary's place and to take Mary prisoner to prevent her from contesting his plans. "But," he finished, "I have no purpose beyond bringing this warning. I have no suggestions for Lady Mary. She can ignore my news or she can go in any direction. You have no cause to trust me, but you have no need to trust me. I can tell no one anything, except that I found you at Hoddesdon. If I go now, I will not even be able to say whether you left or stayed."

"I will go to Lady Mary now," Rhoslyn said. "You—" she looked at Pasgen, fumbled in the purse that hung from her belt for some coins, which she pressed into Pasgen's hand "—take this good man into the town and to a good inn and buy him drink and supper. When he is thoroughly rested, let him go his way."

"I will tell the captain where you are," another guard said.

Pasgen thanked him, took the tired horse's rein from the goldsmith so that he could not mount and ride away, and drew him out of the milling crowd of arriving carts and servants toward the town. He could feel his lindys stiff and slightly quivering and knew the little creature was reflecting Rhoslyn's tension and anxiety. He did not expect that to change very soon.

Rhoslyn hurried into the house and pushed through the bustle in the reception room to the bedchamber where Mary had just sunk into a chair. Brushing by the other maids of honor so roughly that Mary's attention was drawn, Rhoslyn curtsied deeply and then simply sat down on the ground beside Mary's left hand. Straining upward, she muttered "Northumberland intends to set a usurper, Lady Jane Grey, on the throne and has sent a large troop of men with his son to take you prisoner. Likely they are on their way to Hunsdon, but they may pass here and stop to enquire because of your retinue. What shall we do, my lady?"

Mary paled, then flushed. "No one will usurp my throne," she said through her teeth, and then, "Are you certain of this news?"

"Not at all, madam. A man says he has ridden from Greenwich. He claims to be a goldsmith of that town and a true believer, that Sir Nicholas Throckmorton, also a true believer, told him the news and bade him ride to warn you."

"Throckmorton," Mary murmured. "I do not know Nicholas, but I remember Sir George Throckmorton, who was trusted by my father." She blinked. "Sir George had a passel of sons. Sir

Nicholas may have been one of them. But that does not tell me whether to believe this warning."

Rhoslyn had sensed the goldsmith's sincerity. It was possible that Throckmorton had lied to the goldsmith; Rhoslyn could not sense that, but Mary had not meant to stay at Hoddesdon and certainly had not meant to go on to Greenwich. To take the man's warning, then, could do no harm.

"My lady," she said softly, "even if the news is false—indeed, more particularly if the news is false—I believe it is not safe to stay here where we are known to be. Even if he means well, who knows to whom the goldsmith will carry word of your lodging."

Mary turned her head to look at the crucifix hung over the *prie-dieu*. Her lips moved silently for a moment, then were briefly bitten together, until she said, "Rosamund, find Rochester, Waldgrave, and Englefield and bring them here, also Jane. Bid Susan to rid this chamber of the other ladies and arrange they prepare to settle in for the night."

As Rhoslyn left, she saw Mary rise and walk toward the *prie-dieu*. She was still praying when Rhoslyn returned with the men of the household. Jane, who Rhoslyn had met just outside the door, was kneeling behind Mary. The men genuflected. One of them drew a sharp breath. Rhoslyn did not know which, but she sympathized with him. Mary could spend an inordinate amount of time on her knees.

This time she did not. She rounded out her prayer with a Ave Maria, rose, and went back to her chair, gesturing to Jane to close the door of the chamber. "Now, Rosamund, repeat what you told me."

Gasps and mumbled curses met Rhoslyn's news and Englefield asked sharp questions about the likelihood of it being true. Rhoslyn started to admit there was no proof of it, but Rochester made a sharp gesture.

"I fear the news is all too true. I knew something ugly was brewing. A few friends wrote that they were uneasy but had no sure word, only men who would no longer meet their eyes."

"Rosamund thinks we should leave here." Mary said.

"But we are all weary and the horses are tired," Waldgrave protested.

"I do not think it wise to move the whole cortege," Rhoslyn put in hastily, thrusting the thought of a secret escape into the men's minds. "Surely we can find a dozen fresh horses in the stable here."

The thought, diluted by the need to impress three minds at once, was somewhat less effective than usual. Frowns wrinkled foreheads.

Nonetheless Englefield, the least strong-minded of the three nodded. "If the goldsmith betrays our position—or even if he does not, my lady, you made no secret of our coming to Hoddesdon. Say that those seeking you are told by a servant left in Hunsdon or someone from the village that you planned to come here. If they follow and see all your people settled in and you are denied to them because of the hour or for any other reason, I am sure they will wait some time on your convenience."

"Yes," Waldgrave agreed. "And in the meanwhile, we can be gone in any direction. If we have fresh horses . . . I will go and see about that right now on the pretext of seeing how our own horses traveled."

"Yes." Now Rochester also nodded. "Have something to eat, my lady, and then say you are weary and wish to lie down on your bed and rest. Then, quietly, we can saddle up and be gone, no one to know any better than that you are here, asleep."

"Why not?" Rhoslyn said, projecting a feeling of relief. "We can send a messenger back here. If no one has come seeking you, my lady the cortege can join us all the better for a few day's rest."

Albertus had slipped out of Edward's chamber some hours before Edward drew his last breath. He was a good enough physician to know that the boy would not live out the day. While Northumberland was still insisting to the ambassadors from Charles V that Edward was somewhat improved, Albertus went down to the river and hired a boat. From Otstargi's house in London, he Gated to the only place his amulet would take him, the palace of Caer Mordwyn.

As always he reported first to Aurilia, but she wasted no time bringing him and his news to Vidal. Vidal instantly launched a probe to strip Albertus of everything he knew, but his probe met a block. He snarled at Aurilia but she did not release the shield.

"I told you before," she snapped, "I value Albertus's mind. I do not want it damaged. You are too rough when you are excited. Albertus will gladly tell you anything you want to know."

"You are too tender of him," Vidal snapped back. "I do not wish to waste the time with speech."

Aurilia shrugged indifferently. "Then when you send him back to London, you need only twist time so that he arrives only a few moments after he left."

That was true enough, Vidal thought, his teeth set hard; his glance at Aurilia was angry. He remembered better, absorbed all the details better, when he stripped information from a mind. Aurilia, he thought, was all too fond of this human. When Mary was on the throne and power was pouring into the Unseleighe, he would truly strip Albertus. Then he would have the secret of that cloudy blue potion Aurilia loved so well, and he would have a much tighter rein on her behavior.

"Well?" he said to Albertus.

"What I know for fact is that the king will be dead in a few hours. What I have gathered from a word here and a word there and put together with guesses is that Northumberland has forced the Council and the Court in general to agree to set Mary aside. The reason he gave to Edward was that Mary was declared a bastard when Henry's marriage to her mother was declared invalid."

"Then Elizabeth must die in the next few hours!" Vidal exclaimed.

"How?" Aurilia asked, smiling with lifted brows. "Hatfield is not a great keep, but it is a strong house and Elizabeth has a large troop of defenders guarding the place. No one is allowed admittance so there can be no human assassin. A whole army would be needed to break Hatfield, which would scarcely go unnoticed. And you cannot send any from Underhill to kill her. So open a defiance of Oberon and Titania will not go without reprisal."

"But she will be dead!" Vidal's calm had cracked and blue flickered over his fingers.

Albertus's knees gave way and he sank down on the floor, sobbing.

"Will she?" Aurilia asked, ignoring her henchman's terror. "Where are the mages you called to do away with Denoriel in that unformed land? One Elizabeth caved in like an eggshell and translocated to the Void; the other lost both his legs when she melded them with what he stood upon. Sufficiently aroused, Elizabeth can protect herself all too well."

Vidal snarled and Aurilia lifted a hand.

"No, no," Albertus whimpered; if Aurilia lost the confrontation, he would have no protection against Vidal. "Northumberland does not intend to put Elizabeth on the throne. He knows he cannot declare one daughter bastard and the other legitimate. Elizabeth is also named bastard and unfit to rule. Northumberland has another candidate for the throne and, I have heard it whispered, has forced nearly the entire Court to sign the device naming Lady Jane Grey queen."

"Ah." Aurilia nodded. "The pale weeping girl the FarSeers see come and go in the black pool. But the image is so unstable. If she rules, it will not be for long."

"Oh." Vidal's ill humor eased. "Well a civil war will be good for us." Then his expression darkened. "But Mary has no common sense. Unlike Elizabeth she has taken few precautions to protect herself. She has only twenty or so guardsmen, and the gentlemen of her household are not so young and were never soldiers."

"You cannot send Underhill creatures to protect her," Aurilia exclaimed, sounding really horrified. "As it is half of England believes Catholics are allied with the devil and the pope is his vicar on earth. You cannot surround Mary with such forces or she will not be able to rule."

"Of course not." Vidal laughed. "Albertus has hired for me a force of humans who have no connection with the devil aside from preferring the Catholic rite. They will all fight for Mary." He turned to look at Albertus who had, trembling, climbed to his feet. "That is correct, is it not?"

"Yes, my lord." Albertus nodded eagerly. "As you bid me, I told Howard-Mowbray not to dismiss the men and I supplied him with the coin you provided to pay them. I believe that most of the men he hired are of the Catholic persuasion and will be eager to protect Lady Mary and be faithful to her."

"That is excellent," Vidal said, calm again. "You told me that this Howard-Mowbray is able to use his head, so your orders to him will be simply to protect Mary in any and every way he can, not only fight for her but try to enlist others in her cause. Gold will be forthcoming if it is needed. But he is not to try to prevent a civil war. Let them fight, so long as Mary is safe and can rule when the fighting is over."

Aurilia nodded. "Very clever, my lord, just what we need." She looked toward Albertus. "And to help matters along, you will go with them, Albertus. Keep a watching over this Howard-Mowbray. If he disobeys, slip away and let me or Prince Vidal know."

"It might not be easy for me to get away if Howard-Mowbray plans to violate his trust," Albertus said weakly.

"I will give you several amulets," Aurilia said. "When you invoke one, no one will notice you. You will not be invisible. If you touch someone they will feel it and be able to see you. But if you are clever, no one's eyes will fix on you so you will be able to escape to London, from where you can Gate here."

By Tuesday, July 11th, Elizabeth was nearly hysterical with anxiety. Since Northumberland's letter had arrived on the 4th, her fate had been more and more in doubt. On July 6th there had been several small parties that rode by and even around the estate. Sir Edward believed they were scouting parties to examine the defenses of Hatfield. Sir Edward had suggested a retreat to Donnington, which was well fortified and safer, but Elizabeth was afraid to move and when Harry met her in Llachar Lle the night of the 7th, he advised against it. It was important, he felt, that Elizabeth seem less cautious than she and her advisors were. If Hatfield were attacked, Harry pointed out, Denno would Gate her to Donnington. Once she was gone, her household would be safe and could follow.

In the inn in Hatfield town on the 8th, Sir Edward heard that the king was dead—the news was all over London and was freely talked of in the tap room. And Elizabeth had a letter from a lady at the Court which she read aloud, pale-faced and thin lipped, describing how, on Sunday, July 9th, Bishop Ridley had preached against both her and Mary, calling them bastards and unworthy of the throne. The same letter mentioned a meeting of the Council that very day, not in Greenwich or Whitehall but in Syon House, Northumberland's residence.

On July 10th a hastily and ill-written letter came to the house on Bucklersbury from Cecil. It exposed the device that disinherited both Mary and Elizabeth and named Jane Grey as Edward's heir; Cecil also reported he had heard rumors an armed troop had been sent to take Mary prisoner. He was free at last to send news, he explained, because Jane had been brought into the Tower, the traditional place for a monarch to wait coronation. She had been proclaimed queen in London—which had greeted the proclamation with sullen silence.

With considerable effort Elizabeth neither screamed nor threw anything. How would Mary react? Elizabeth could do nothing. While Mary lived—as she herself had told Northumberland when he wanted her to sign away her right to the throne—she had no right at all. She could not protest against Northumberland's attempt to wrest the throne out of the direct line. The right to act was Mary's.

Elizabeth did not doubt Mary's courage to fight for what she wanted. She had seen her sister stand up against Henry himself, against Edward, and against the whole Council for the sake of her religion. But Elizabeth also knew Mary had never desired the throne, never wanted to rule. Poor Mary, she had desperately wanted to marry, to be her husband's comfort and helpmeet, to have children . . . most of all to have children. Would Mary fight for the throne, or would she accept a marriage to a suitable prince that would take her out of England?

On Tuesday July 11th, Elizabeth was so waspish that all her ladies, stung once too often, found good reason to seek employment out of her sight. Seemingly annoyed, she begged Kat to sleep in her chamber instead of one of the girls. That was not Kat's duty, but Elizabeth merely said she wanted her.

The truth was that Kat was the only one who might come in the middle of the night with tinctures or possets to calm Elizabeth, who wanted her governess in a sound bespelled sleep. With Kat asleep Elizabeth would not need to worry that Kat would get by Blanche and discover her absence. And Elizabeth intended to attend the meeting regularly held in the Inn of Kindly Laughter on mortal Tuesday nights.

Jaws clamped together on hasty words, Elizabeth allowed Blanche to array her in a night rail, allowed herself to be tucked into bed and kissed on the forehead by Kat, waited, hardly grinding her teeth together, for Kat to settle herself into the truckle bed . . . and then at last muttered the *bod cyfgadur* spell. Barely had Kat's eyes closed when Elizabeth sprang out of bed and ran into Blanche's room where she twitched, mouthed imprecations, and pulled her night rail this way and that until Denoriel appeared in the Gate.

"Let us go. Let us go," she urged, rushing at him. "I must hear what Rhoslyn has to say. I should have made you take me to the Inn of Kindly Laughter last Tuesday, but—"

"It would have done no good," Denoriel said soothingly. "Last

Tuesday Rhoslyn knew no more than you. Mary also had a letter from Northumberland summoning her to Edward's deathbed.
Last Tuesday Mary had not yet decided whether she should go
and try to save Edward's soul or take refuge."

Elizabeth made some wordless sound of impatience and Denoriel
took her hand and stepped back into the Gate. As they arrived
at the Gate of Logres, Miralys appeared.

"What would you like to wear?" Denoriel asked as he turned
to the elvensteed to mount.

"Oh, can we not go directly to the Inn of Kindly Laughter?"
Elizabeth begged. "I do not care what I wear. Just anything that
you can make on me. I could even stay in the night rail. No one
Underhill is likely to know it is a night rail—"

"You are absolutely right about that," Denoriel said, laughing.
"But I would have a dozen offers for you every third step we
take. That gown is a little revealing."

Elizabeth looked down at herself, saw her dark rose nipples
pressing forward against the nearly transparent lawn, saw the
shadow of bright red curls on her mount of Venus. Color rose
in her cheeks, but before she could turn beet red or speak, she
was dressed in black boots over long black hosen, a white shirt,
open at the neck and with wide sleeves buckled at the wrists, a
light blue tunic that almost reached her knees belted in soft black
leather, and a little hat with a feather. Absently Denno had made
indentations in the brim of the hat for long Sidhe ears, which
called attention to Elizabeth's human ears, but before Elizabeth
could mention it, they were back on the Gate and at the Bazaar
of the Bizarre.

In spite of Denoriel being far taller than Elizabeth with much
longer legs, she was ahead of him past the first cautionary sign:
NO SPELLS, NO DRAWN WEAPONS, NO VIOLENCE . . . ON PAIN OF
PERMANENT REMOVAL and then past the second, which to her read
CAVEAT EMPTOR and to Denno YMOGELYD PRYNWR. He caught
up with her as she stepped through the market gates and turned
to look for the sign of the inn.

He was just in time, as a long-legged creature with a head
remarkably like a grasshopper and burnished golden scales reached
for her arm, saying, "Whither away pretty mortal?"

"Not for sale," Denoriel said, interposing his body before the
clawed hand could fasten on Elizabeth's sleeve.

"I assure you the mortal would be with her own kind and well treated," the creature said earnestly.

"Not for sale because she is a free person with all rights owing to any person in the Bazaar of the Bizarre."

"Ah. Then I must address myself to the person herself."

"Good sir or madam," Elizabeth said with a brief curtsey, "do forgive me for being less than polite, but I am in great haste."

"But I can offer you such delights as will make haste unnecessary forever."

Elizabeth shivered. "I am mortal. My life is short. Haste is natural to us and gives us pleasure. Forever is difficult even to believe in. Do pardon us and let us go on our way."

At which moment a flying creature trailing a cloth emblazoned with "Tafarn Caredig Chewerthin" came to a hover before them. Although there was no breeze, the emblazoned cloth streamed away from the flyer.

"That is the inn we want," Denoriel said.

"For what do you need an inn?" the golden-scaled creature asked irritably. "I can furnish—"

But before any more words were spoken, the entrance to the inn was no more than a few steps away, down an opening in the stalls that Elizabeth had not seen before. Ordinarily she would have asked—not how the inn could appear where it had not been moments earlier, but what would happen if two different parties wished to find the place at the same time. In this case, Elizabeth was so intent on seeing Rhoslyn and learning what Mary's decision was, if Mary had come to a decision, that she simply shook her head at the golden-scaled creature and rushed in the entrance.

There was a corridor, a feature Elizabeth did not recall but to which she paid no attention, and a faint sense of disorientation, which was common enough anywhere Underhill that it made no special impression. Then she and Denoriel were in the common room. Elizabeth looked to the left and back against the wall. Aleneil and Harry were already seated opposite each other at the table for four, which would have room for more if more arrived.

"Da, have you had any news?" Elizabeth asked, rushing to the table.

"No more than what Aleneil has already told you," Harry said, getting to his feet and embracing Elizabeth. He kissed her on the forehead and pressed her into a chair now next to his. "Jane is lodged in the Tower and Northumberland has sent out heralds and trumpeters to proclaim her queen."

Elizabeth did not react to that. Denno had already told her how the crowds in London had stared in silence, not one person aside from the archers sent to save the heralds from being torn apart had cried "God save Queen Jane." Elizabeth was not surprised. She had a sure instinct for how the people of England would react to what those who governed them did. She knew that her sister Mary was dearly beloved, her kindness and generosity to the humble folk widely known.

"His men have not taken Mary, have they?" Elizabeth looked up at him anxiously.

"That I cannot answer, my love," Harry said, sitting down again. "My eyes and ears are the servants in the Court and in a number of households—including that of Northumberland. I would think they would have picked up on the excitement if Mary were taken prisoner, but—

"No, she is still free. But I do not know for how long."

Chapter 10

Rhoslyn's voice was high and strained. Harry jumped to his feet and drew her to the table, where another chair had appeared.

"You look so tired, Rhoslyn," he said, urging her wordlessly to be seated.

"I am tired," Rhoslyn admitted with a sigh. "I have been riding with Mary since she had warning on the evening of July sixth that Robert Dudley and three hundred men were preparing to take her prisoner."

"Who?" Elizabeth asked eagerly. "Who sent warning? We had no word and you know Cecil is usually faithful. Denno and I agree that he must have known spies were set on him to prevent him from telling me of Northumberland's plans."

"I think Cecil was 'discouraged' from leaving the palace for his own home," Denoriel said. "I tried once to see him and sent my man by his house to other places on Canon Row. Cropper said he thought Cecil's house was watched."

"The man who came with the warning was a goldsmith from Greenwich," Rhoslyn said, replying to Elizabeth's question. "He said he had the warning from Sir Nicholas Throckmorton and made no secret of the fact that Throckmorton and he were Catholics."

Elizabeth shook her head. "I do not remember him from my time at Court."

"I imagine he would stay clear of you, sweeting," Harry said. "Dear sweet Sister Temperance was not likely to look on him with favor."

"Even Mary does not remember Sir Nicholas, but she did remember his father, Sir George, and that her father had trusted him. The men of her household, thank the Mother, were already fearful for her safety and among us we convinced her to leave her household at Hoddesdon, take the few fresh horses we could find, and steal away." Rhoslyn closed her eyes. "But we have been riding ever since."

"And on mortal horses too."

Pasgen's sour comment drew everyone's eyes. He had just come from the entrance to stand behind his sister's chair. He put a hand on her shoulder and gave it a gentle squeeze. Opposite her place at the table, a chair appeared to Aleniel's left. Pasgen patted Rhoslyn's back and went by to seat himself.

"But I will say," he continued "that Lady Mary has a far more iron will than I had ever suspected. She is not well or strong, and yet she rode with us without faltering."

Rhoslyn sighed again. "We did over twenty miles that night, riding until we could not see at all and then resting until the moon rose and riding again. We stayed with Master John Huddleston—also of Mary's faith; they look to her to bring back the Catholic Church in its entirety and are truly devoted. He found us fresh horses and we heard Mass at first light—Huddleston has a Catholic chaplain—and rode on again."

"But Mary is safe now?"

Rhoslyn raised her brows as she looked at Elizabeth, who had asked the question. "You seem very concerned. I must warn you that Lady Mary is . . . is not at all certain what she feels about you."

Elizabeth shrugged. "I know that. Mostly she dislikes me. That is nothing to do with my concern. If anything ill befalls Mary, I will be blamed, no matter that I had nothing to do with it. I am worried about my own reputation." She hesitated, then went on. "And a little for Mary. I remember that she brought me gifts of toys and clothing when she had next to nothing herself."

Everyone at the table was now looking quizzically at Elizabeth, Denoriel in particular with a slightly cynical smile. Elizabeth sighed. "Oh, very well, and because I am so sure that Mary will make a right shambles of ruling. She is convinced that the realm will joyfully follow her back under the pope's authority and will so welcome the return to the old rite that they will gladly restore the Church to what it was."

Harry groaned. "She cannot believe that, can she?"

"*She* will do it." Elizabeth said.

"The Council will not, nor will the Parliament permit it," Harry remarked, shaking his head. "All the gentry will resist violently if she tries to take from them the Church lands my father distributed, and the common folk will resist paying Peter's Pence to the pope. Nor will they willingly accept again the summoners and pardoners who so befouled Catholic practices."

Elizabeth nodded, a small smile just lifting the corners of her mouth. "Before Mary is done, the people will eagerly be looking toward me to be queen as to a bright salvation."

She could say Underhill what would have her executed in the mortal world, and she did say it, looking challengingly around. Pasgen shrugged, indifferent. Rhoslyn bit her lip; she was very fond of Mary but suspected Elizabeth saw more clearly how the people of England would react than Mary did or ever would. It was Harry who frowned and shook his head.

"That may be so," he said. "But do not make the same mistake as our sister. I agree that Mary has not the disposition nor the understanding to rule—neither did I have it. But there will be many who benefit from her mistakes, and they will *not* look to you. And worse, Bess, the more you become a focus of the discontent against Mary, the greater will be your danger."

That silenced Elizabeth, who bit her lip and shuddered. Denoriel leaned across the table and took her hand. Harry put an arm around her shoulders and hugged her, but turned his head to gesture at a server, a very ordinary kitsune, whose dark eyes were very bright in her fox face.

"Wine," Harry said. "Human rumney or white malmsey. Or, if you have both, a bottle of each."

"That will do for us also," Denoriel said, then looked at Aleneil. "Unless you want mead or nectar, Aleneil?"

She shook her head. "We are all being corrupted by living so much in the mortal world. White malmsey will do well for me. Which is your preference, Rhoslyn? Pasgen?"

"I want nectar," Pasgen said. "I need something to wash away the sour taste of restoring the memory of the guardsman whose place I have been taking." He grimaced. "I must feed the memories slowly so that they seem the man's own."

The server nodded and strode away, her handsome red-fox tail swaying behind her. For the next few minutes everyone concentrated on what they wanted to eat and by the time the server returned with the wine and nectar they all had made selections. When the kitsune was headed toward the kitchen, Elizabeth remembered what she had asked Rhoslyn and not been answered.

"If Mary is free, why did you say you do not know for how long?" Elizabeth asked, and then, with widening eyes, "Is she being attacked?"

"Again I must say not yet, but she has cast her gauntlet in Northumberland's face and he must do something, and that soon."

"Cast her gauntlet . . ." Elizabeth's eyes blazed golden. "She has declared for the throne!"

"Yes." Rhoslyn sighed. "Two days ago, when we reached Kenninghall we had news of Ridley's sermon declaring you and Mary bastard and unfit to rule. She sat down at once and wrote a letter to the Council, rating them harshly for not sending her immediate notice of her brother's death and not proclaiming her queen as set by law in the Act of Succession. She stated clearly her right to the throne and her intent to take it."

"Thank God for that," Elizabeth breathed. "If she had yielded her right, my own would be worthless."

"Oh no. Yielding was never considered," Rhoslyn assured her. "Mary might have fallen into Northumberland's trap, but that was because she wished so much to save Edward's soul. She was so sure once he knew he was dying that he would turn to the 'true' faith."

Elizabeth shook her head. "How was she turned from that good work?" she asked rather tartly.

Rhoslyn spoke just as dryly. "Jane Dormer pointed out that if she fell into Northumberland's hands in the attempt to save her brother's soul, she would surely lose the chance to save the souls of all the English people."

"Mine, too, no doubt." Elizabeth sighed and closed her eyes.

Denoriel squeezed Elizabeth's hand and spoke hastily to distract her; there was no sense in Elizabeth worrying about how to deflect Mary's desire to make her accept Catholicism until she knew how intense Mary's attempt would be.

"So, how did you escape Northumberland's troop?" he asked.

"That was rather strange," Rhoslyn said. "We were riding hard for Kenninghall disguised as John Huddleston's servants when a troop burst out of a wood behind us. We thought we were lost as our horses were weary and they were many more than we, but they never tried to overtake us merely riding along behind, matching their pace to ours. And when we arrived at Kenninghall they stopped a quarter mile or so from the gate. One man alone rode to the gate, naming himself Mary's devoted servant, Francis Howard."

"Francis Howard?" Harry said. "I don't remember any *Francis* Howard. I remember far too many Howards, but no Francis."

"Mary did not remember any Francis Howard either," Rhoslyn continued. "Fortunately he did not ask to be admitted. We would have been in a quandary if he had asked. He said he and his troop would do their best to divert Northumberland's men and to bring to Lady Mary those who would support her, and then he rode away."

The kitsune returned with the food on a tray that floated in the air. When it had to consult a tablet on the tray to see which dish went to which person, Pasgen said, "Where is the other server who is usually here on mortal Tuesdays?"

"You don't like my service?" the kitsune asked, the fox tail beginning to lift.

"Your service is fine," Aleneil said quickly. "We are just curious about what form the other server would take, since it has been different each time we came."

The kitsune wiggled her shiny black nose. "It is aestivating or undertaking some other kind of renewal." The tail lowered and wagged slowly from side to side. "I will tell it you were asking for it."

When the kitsune had moved away, Pasgen sighed. "There is one single thing I like about the mortal world. When you eat or drink at an inn or an alehouse, the servers just serve. They do not make clever remarks nor take offense at whatever you say."

Denoriel laughed aloud. "You must tell me where you eat and drink. I've never found the servers in the places near Bucklersbury to be backward about coming forward, specially the women."

Elizabeth sat up straighter, her eyes growing bright. "Denno! For what do you need—"

"What I need," Denoriel said hastily, "and that most urgently is to know more about Francis Howard and his troop."

"I cannot help you," Rhoslyn said. "I assure you we would like to know more also, but by the time we had settled Lady Mary in bed—we had ridden altogether near sixty miles—and explained to the master in charge of Kenninghall what we wanted, the troop was long gone. I suppose if he has something to say, this Francis Howard will come again or send a messenger."

"Or send a larger troop to take Kenninghall," Harry said slowly. "Oh, it is not very likely, since you say they could have overtaken you on the road and did not, but there may be some reason for that. Perhaps this Francis Howard wishes to ingratiate himself with the Dudleys and is not certain just how far he could go to take Mary prisoner. Now that her presence in Kenninghall is known, I just do not think it is safe for Mary to stay there. Kenninghall is moated; it is somewhat defensible, but not really a castle. An embattled queen should be in a castle."

Rhoslyn closed her eyes and her shoulders slumped. "I do not want to believe you, but I do. Only Mary is exhausted. I do not think she can go farther right now. She needs a few days of rest."

Pasgen frowned. "If we are attacked, she must and she will go on. But while there is no threat, I agree she can be allowed to rest. I will see that the captain sends out scouts to warn us of any body of armed men approaching." He grimaced. "I have some influence since I killed that assassin."

"And I will suggest to Mary that her consequence will be greater if she takes residence in a place of importance, like Framlingham. It is not far away and is almost as strong as a royal castle."

By July 18 Albertus was quite at ease when he activated the amulet that would take him from Otstargi's house in London to Caer Mordwyn. He was confident that his master and mistress would be pleased with his report, for Francis Howard—he had dropped the Mowbray from his name as soon as Edward died—had done very well indeed. Far more than Albertus had known enough to advise.

Francis must have personal reasons to want Mary to be queen, Albertus thought as he followed the Sidhe who often greeted visitors to the palace toward Aurilia's apartment. Albertus suppressed a smile; that Sidhe had several times teased and once physically tormented him, when he arrived, but would do so no more. Aurilia had "instructed" that cruel, beautiful monster that she and she alone had rights over Albertus's person. His thoughts returned to Francis's personal commitment to Mary. There was no need to admit that he had not known of it when he chose Francis to lead the troop.

Aurilia was seated at her dressing table rather than stretched out on her long-seated chair. She turned her head when Albertus entered and watched him bow low.

"So you have good news," she said.

"Yes, my lady, very good, very good indeed. The mortal arms-man hired performed better than I expected."

"Very well." Aurila gestured and a chair appeared near Albertus's leg. "Sit and tell me." Aurelia said.

Although he was flattered by being offered a chair, Albertus was disappointed when Aurilia turned her back on him and returned her attention to her mirror. He was annoyed that she would not look at him and he could not see her expressions. Usually he was terrified and had all he could do to hide his fear and all he saw on her beautiful face were scowls and scorn. Now when he could expect praise and pleasure, she looked only in the mirror.

In that Albertus had misjudged Aurilia. Her mirror showed not her face but his. When he was reporting failure or disappointment, she did not need to look for nuances in his expression. Today when he said he had good news and his carriage and movements also showed his confidence, she needed to catch any unguarded look of doubt or private satisfaction.

"So?" Aurilia urged when Albertus did not speak at once.

"You know, of course, about Ridley's sermon calling Lady Mary a bastard and you know that I learned by listening to those who attended on King Edward's deathbed that Northumberland intended to set Lady Jane Grey on the throne. I wished to warn Lady Mary, but there had been attempts on her life—I have no proof but I think by Northumberland's direction—and there was no way I or any messenger from me could have approached her."

"It was a good thought, but unnecessary. Prince Vidal had a warning arranged from high in the Court."

"I wish I had known," Albertus said mildly. "I was so alarmed by the plot that I felt it worth the risk to try to reach Mary, say I was a physician and I had come to tell her of her brother's death. I all but compromised myself by trying to get a horse and leave the palace as soon as Edward was dead."

For all the mildness of the voice, Aurilia saw a flicker of expression, swiftly suppressed, shade Albertus's look of satisfaction. Clearly Albertus did not love Vidal. Aurilia's lips twitched toward a smile; that Albertus should hate Vidal was all to the good. If she wanted something Vidal did not approve, Albertus would not deny her.

"As it was, however," Albertus continued, "the attempt was fortunate. While I was hiding myself in the stable, I heard Robert Dudley, who is Northumberland's fifth son, speaking to the head groom about the need for three hundred horses on the next day for a troop to ride north. I guessed that Dudley had been instructed by his father to take Lady Mary prisoner, so I returned to the outer chambers of the king's apartments and sent my little page, the boy who fetched medications for me, out with instructions for Francis Howard to gather up his men and ride to Hunsdon."

Aurilia turned on the cushioned stool before her dressing table to frown at him. "This was the day the king died? I am not certain of mortal time, but surely that was many days ago in their terms."

"Yes, my lady, but when the king died I had nothing to report to you, so I did not come. I know Prince Vidal bade me go with Howard but I was forbidden to leave the palace and I did not think it wise to hold back Howard and what protection he could give Lady Mary until I was free to go."

"No. You are right about that. Sometimes Prince Vidal does not foresee all the conditions surrounding an order. Was your man successful in protecting Lady Mary? Surely he did not have as many men at his command as did Northumberland's son."

"No, but he has more years and more brains than young Dudley. He set out a full half day earlier but he and his men did not ride into Hunsdon. He set the troop to rest and wait just outside the town and himself rode into the manor alone, claiming to be a messenger with an urgent letter for Lady Mary. What he would have done if she was still there, aside from warning her about Dudley and the three hundred men, I do not know, but she had left already. Those few left behind to care for the house made no trouble in telling him that Lady Mary had ridden south toward Greenwich, according to a summons from Northumberland, and intended to stop in Hoddesdon."

"So they rode to Hoddesdon?" Aurilia frowned and turned back toward her mirror, her nails clicking impatiently on the table top. "Am I going to need to listen to every single hoofbeat along the road? What is this news of yours that is so good?"

For one moment fury surged up in Albertus, but then he bowed his head, swallowing a laugh at himself. He had been relishing the notion of telling Aurilia of Howard's cleverness and the fact that Howard had responded so brilliantly and achieved far more than he himself had expected or, truly, intended. But there was no need for him to lose the credit of how Howard had tricked Dudley into camping before Hoddesdon and negotiating terms with Engelfield for Lady Mary's surrender while she made good her escape or how Howard had fooled Dudley into believing that many more men had come to support Mary in Kenninghall than actually had come.

"No, of course not, my lady."

"You still have not given me this good news."

"The first part of the good news is that Lady Mary is safe in Framlingham castle and that a number of gentlemen—I know for certain of the earl of Bath, the earl of Sussex, Sir Thomas Wharton, Sir John Mordant and Sir Henry Bedingfield—are already with her, together with a host of common folk."

Aurilia's eyes brightened with pleasure. "Are there enough men supporting her to have a battle against Northumberland's forces? That will provide a tasty supping for me and my lord."

"About the battle, I do not know. Northumberland intends to try to take her prisoner or kill her, but the matter still could be settled without fighting. I heard that the people of Norwich were on their way to Mary and just before I left I learned there was a muster in Tothill fields in London, but the number who replied to the summons, despite a promise of ten pence a day payment, was disappointing."

"No battle?" Aurilia sniffed and turned around again, showing her lower lip protruding in a dissatisfied pout.

"I do not think so," Albertus replied, "but the second part of my good news likely means Mary will be queen. Is that not what you and Prince Vidal desire, my lady?"

"Oh, yes," Aurilia replied with no enthusiasm, "but a battle with lots of killing and looting... So what is the second part of the good news?"

"That the six ships of the navy Northumberland sent to prevent Lady Mary from fleeing the country to her uncle, the emperor, are now Lady Mary's. I was riding north to meet Howard as soon as I was allowed to leave Greenwich palace, and I fell in around Colchester with a Sir Harry Jerningham, who was riding south. He urged me to bring my services to Lady Mary and told me how the sailors mutinied against their captains unless the captains would turn the ships to Lady Mary's service."

"Oh well." Aurila stood up. "I suppose you had better come with me to give this news to Vidal. But I am disappointed that this clever Howard of yours could not arrange a battle."

Aurilia's dissatisfaction made Albertus uneasy, but Vidal received the information, which Aurilia transferred in a long, thoughtful look, with greater enthusiasm than Aurilia had.

"Very good," he said to her, smiling. "The creature is more useful than I thought he would be."

"His man should have arranged a battle," Aurilia complained, seating herself in the chair that had appeared near Vidal.

"No, not unless he was certain he could win. Once Mary is on the throne, we will be well fed on misery." Vidal smiled at Aurilia again, thinking that her childish greed was a weakness he could use and forgetting that before his imprisonment he was as greedy and short sighted.

When he turned to Albertus, however, the smile was gone. His dark eyes ran over Albertus as if he were a piece of offal left in the middle of the floor. Briefly Albertus closed his eyes. Creature was he? Somehow, someday, he promised himself, he would get his revenge.

"Your work is incomplete," Vidal snapped. "Even the surrender of the ships does not ensure Mary's accession."

"That is true, my lord, but now that the king is dead, I have no more excuse to be at Court. No simple physician would be listened to if he gave advice on political matters. One higher than I must spread the news of the mass defections in Mary's favor, must describe the fate of all those who continue to support Northumberland, and must hint of Lady Mary's compassion toward those who escaped Northumberland's influence and brought the Council to proclaim her queen in London."

There was an infinitesmal pause while Vidal realized he had not thought of the need to induce Northumberland's supporters to desert him. He had been thinking of using the men Albertus had hired to attack Northumberland himself. But that would likely waste the force this Howard commanded, which according to what was in Albertus's mind was far fewer than Northumberland's. It would be much easier to have Rich convince the council to proclaim Mary.

His hesitation was brief enough that Albertus would not have noticed and Vidal said smoothly, "No, of course not. I have those bound to me at Court. I was thinking that now that they are free of needing to protect Mary, this Howard of yours can busy himself with removing Elizabeth."

Albertus frowned. "I doubt it, my lord. The last time Howard examined Hatfield, he reported that it was closed so tight he wondered the air could get through. No one is allowed in—"

"They must eat and drink, I suppose," Vidal snapped.

"Victuals and drink are left by the gate. The victualers must draw off as far as the town before the guards open the gates and the servants bring in what they left. This much Howard told me the month before the king died, when you bade me order him to take Lady Elizabeth. He said it would take an army to break into Hatfield."

"My lord," Aurilia said, "why would you bother with Elizabeth now? She is not setting herself up as a rival to Mary, and once Mary is on the throne, *she* will remove Elizabeth. All her advisors will agree that she can never rule in safety while Elizabeth lives."

"Whatever she herself does, there are others who will contest Mary's rule over their idiotic differences in religion."

Aurilia's eyes opened wide. "So much the better. I have been hoping all along for a civil war. Let Mary and Elizabeth fight over the throne."

Vidal sighed heavily. "Were we assured of Mary's victory—as I said before—I would agree. But we are not so assured." He turned away from Aurilia to look at Albertus again. "Send Howard to test Hatfield's defenses. They may be relaxed now that Elizabeth knows Northumberland's attention is fixed on Mary."

That same night Elizabeth was Underhill at the Inn of Kindly Laughter. A great deal of her anxiety had been dispelled by the news she had from Denno already. London was abuzz with talk, and the merchant community, whose well-doing depended on peace and a steady government, was gathering every scrap of news.

They knew already that the Council that Northumberland had left in London to protect his interests and Queen Jane was rapidly tearing apart. Some had secretly hoped Northumberland would restore Catholic practice when they first supported him, but he had become radically reformist. Now with the temptation Mary's accession held out to them, only fear had bound them to Northumberland. When he left London to oppose the forces gathering to Mary, the grip of fear loosened.

Others truly indifferent to what rite was observed grew more and more uncertain about the highly questionable device Northumberland had used to set Queen Jane on the throne. They knew, the whole realm knew, the succession had been long established and the realm, according to the news of those flocking to support Mary, was rejecting Northumberland's devise.

There was no longer a great secret to hide. Queen Jane had been proclaimed. The tight control of the servants was loosened and interesting tales trickled out to those who did business with the Council.

The Lord Warden of the Cinque Ports—from where the ships that had declared for Mary had sailed—and the earl of Pembroke were making ready to slip out of the Tower where the Council was supposed to remain all together. The lord treasurer, the old, clever marquess of Winchester, had escaped; his fellow councilors sent a force to bring him back, but Sir Edward Peckham, Treasurer of the Mint, had gone beyond recall and taken with him all the money from the king's privy purse to make over to Mary.

Cropper, sent to deliver wines to the Tower in the late afternoon of July sixteen, only two days after Northumberland had left, did not return to the house on Bucklersbury until after dark. He told Master Clayborne that the clerks coming and going from the chamber in which the Council had gathered whispered that there was already argument about saving themselves by declaring Northumberland a traitor.

On the afternoon of July 18 Denoriel heard the outcome of that argument from a grim-faced Cecil, who stopped by the house on Bucklersbury. Cecil had resigned his office as secretary of state in protest when Northumberland had Jane proclaimed queen, but he still had eyes and ears inside the Tower. Master Clayborne showed him at once into Denoriel's parlor.

"This may be the last news you will have from me," Cecil said, shaking his head at the offer of a chair and a cup of wine. "I kept hoping Northumberland would come to his senses. If he had publicly demanded that Mary accept the reformed religion and she refused, he could have declared her a papist unfit to rule, and presented Elizabeth as the proper heir."

Denoriel shrugged. "He knew that Elizabeth would be rid of him as soon as she could manage to call a parliament. Her will is as strong as that of Lady Mary, and Elizabeth has her father's ability to judge the possible and make others obey her."

"It will take all the skill she can muster to stay alive when her sister is on the throne," Cecil said, "and I will not be able to help in any way." He uttered a dry, mirthless chuckle. "Likely I will not survive Queen Mary's crowning."

"Now that is an appeal for unnecessary sympathy." Denoriel snorted gently. "You are not even in office and signed the devise only as witness, not supporter. You will be in no danger from Queen Mary who, I have heard from very reliable sources, is gentle and compassionate, not naturally vengeful. What irks you is that you may not be employed by the Catholic queen. Just be quiet, do not openly parade your reformist inclination. There are those who will return to power under Mary, like Norfolk, with whom I have some influence, which you may be sure I will exert on your behalf. You will soon have a place."

Cecil nodded. "It is not only for myself that I am concerned. Lady Elizabeth will need all the help she can find. She is, I am sure, too wise to involve herself in any intrigues against the crown, but there will be those who use her name without permission and, unfortunately, those who Lady Mary trusts far more than she should will make such use known to the queen."

"I know. I have warned her, but I am no more than a rich merchant." That was a bald lie, but even Cecil could not be allowed to know the truth. Denoriel went on without a blink. "If the warning comes from someone deeply involved in the government, it will stick more firmly in her mind. But we are talking as if Mary had the throne already."

"She has," Cecil said. "I have heard that the Council has written a proclamation offering a reward for the arrest of Northumberland for treason. That was not long after word came from Framling-ham that Mary's army has swelled to near twenty thousand. The Council, or at least those not fanatic reformers, will have her proclaimed Queen tomorrow."

The increase in Mary's army and the likelihood that it could stand successfully against Northumberland, who was England's best soldier, was the news being discussed in the Inn of Kindly Laughter. That Mary would fight if she must was promptly confirmed by Rhoslyn, who had the further information that the forces Northumberland had brought with him from London were deserting. He was arro-gant and still unable to recognize the nation's antipathy to him. His eldest son quarreled with Lord George Howard, who promptly rode off to join Mary at Framlingham. And when Lord Grey opposed Northumberland's orders to burn and loot the property of Mary's supporters, Northumberland shouted Lord Grey down. It was unwise; the burning and looting took place, but Lord Grey and the force he had brought with him were riding north to join Mary.

"I am glad to hear it," Elizabeth said although she sounded rather uncertain. She was glad Mary would be queen because that increased the likelihood that she, herself, would reign, but she foresaw the problems she would face. With a sigh she added, "But as you all know, Mary does not love me." Her eyes went to Harry FitzRoy. "What should I do now, Da?"

"Summon every gentleman who owes you allegiance, love," Harry said, his eyes gleaming. "They will have, I think, about two to three weeks to make ready and gather at Hatfield or Enfield. Bid them all be arrayed in Tudor colors, the green and white of your father and grandfather, and be sure that each message you send says in plain words that you ride in *support* of your sister, Queen Mary, and to do her honor and service."

Elizabeth frowned. Ever since her faith in Parry's ability as controller had been shaken, she checked on her accounts and, seeing the cost of her household, had become quite frugal. Deno-riel could ken gold for her, more than enough to help with the expenses of a young girl living retired in the country, but there was no chance at all that he could provide gold enough to sup-port a queen. Elizabeth was well aware that she must find the lion's share of her expenses out of her own income.

"That will be expensive, Da, and will not Mary feel threatened if I come with a great concourse of followers to London?"

"I do not think Mary will notice your followers. In the rosy glow that will surround her from hearing herself proclaimed queen and hearing and seeing the joy with which she is welcomed, I think your people would need to fire an arquebus at her to cause her alarm. However, many others will notice—her people and the foreign envoys will note you have support and are not defenseless."

"Is that not a double-edged sword?" Denoriel asked. "Those who desire Mary be followed by another Catholic may not like a show of Elizabeth's strength."

"Poor Mary," Rhoslyn sighed. "She has not even come to rule and you are talking of her successor."

"She is near twenty years older than Elizabeth and has never been strong," Pasgen said.

Elizabeth shook herself briskly. "You are right, Rhoslyn. It is unwise to talk this way. I must consider how to live while Mary rules, not even think of a most unknowable future. And Denno, you are right about the double-edged sword, but I think I know how to deal with that. I will discover how many attend Mary, and if my attendants are more numerous, I will dismiss some so that our numbers are near equal. That will also reduce the cost to me."

Harry nodded. "Some you will have to supply with suitable garments, but many will provide their own finery. And sending away some of your followers is a wise thought." He hesitated and looked from Rhoslyn to Denoriel. "Will one or both of you be able to tell us when Mary will arrive so that Elizabeth will be perhaps a day earlier and able to adjust her numbers?"

"I hope we are all not dreaming a future to our liking," Aleneil said. She had been very quiet, and now everyone looked at her with worried frowns. "When last I looked into it, the great lens still showed an image of Jane. And Northumberland is not yet taken. He has fought before against forces larger than his own and triumphed, and most of Mary's army are untrained peasants."

Chapter 11

Aurilia spent far more time than she had expected in making the amulets she had promised Dakari. She was surprised by the unexpected difficulties; dominance amulets had long been a specialty for her. The trouble came about because most of the amulets had been created during Vidal's absence so that she could rule the Dark Court. The dominance they generated was general. Any being who came within their emanation would be forced to obey. Aurilia had no intention at all of giving so powerful an amulet to Dakari. Who knew what so weak a creature given power would do, certainly not confine his commands to Wahib and Wahiba.

No, the power of the amulet must be directed only to the witch and werewolf who had offended her. For that she needed something of the essence of each. The imps she dispatched on that errand either did not return at all or returned to say that the witch and her werewolf son were guarded against such attempts. Aurilia bestirred herself; she had bested those two before and in time she had samples of hair and even a scraping of skin from the ear of the werewolf.

More time was expended in molding the spells to the subjects, and then testing them. It was the end of June before Aurilia was ready to send for the witch, the werewolf, and Dakari.

When the imp Aurilia sent as messenger found Dakari, he was

clearly visible, a short Sidhe with mud-colored hair and mud-colored eyes, scrawny, and wearing a rumpled tunic and hosen with holes here and there. He was, for once, completely at ease, lying on a slightly worn but elegant sofa. The chamber was bright with elf-light and had a glowing fire (in which Dakari sometimes burnt small creatures so he could hear them squeak); it was low-ceilinged . . . but Dakari was not tall, and most important of all, the chamber was forgotten, down in the bowels of Caer Mordwyn.

Dakari had made the chamber his own many, many mortal years before. Weak as he was and constantly the target of the cruel games the Dark Sidhe played, he had sought a safehold and found it. For centuries no one had discovered his place, and he had furnished it to his taste by stealing this and that or picking up furniture discarded by Sidhe better skilled in making.

The imp attacked without explanation, pulling Dakari's hair and biting the tips of his ears, catching at his clothing and pulling so that if he did not come, the imp's claws would have made more holes. Imps were imps and took great pleasure in tormenting those they were sent to summon, but there was just that shade of extra insolence that told Dakari that it must be either Vidal or Aurilia who had sent for him.

First Dakari was frozen with horror, fearing that his masters had discovered his one safe place in the world, but after a moment he remembered that imps did not need doors or windows, corridors or stairs. An imp could always find him, but it could not betray his hiding place. In a second moment, he had swatted at the annoying creature and risen to obey the message it finally communicated. Aurilia wanted him.

Dakari began to fade even as he moved toward the door of his room. He knew Aurilia would be angry before he even reached her. Unlike an imp, he could not ooze through walls and he was not strong enough to make a Gate. He would have to thread his way through the mazelike corridors under Caer Mordwyn and climb the stairs, and it would take time.

As he hurried along, Dakari did not wonder why Vidal had constructed the complicated understructure of Caer Mordwyn. He had done so in the past, but it had never occurred to him that Vidal had simply copied his keep from some great mortal structure. The mortals had used the lower chambers for storage (or for keeping prisoners) and the corridors had been useful for their servants and armsmen to get from place to place without contacting and "contaminating" their betters.

The curses and howls Dakari heard when he approached Aurilia's apartment only made him more insecure. The witch and the werewolf were already infuriated. They would be more difficult to force into obedience. His instinct was to flee, to hide himself. Possibly he could catch and kill the next imp sent after him, but what good would it do? Aurilia would just send a horde of the things to catch him and she would be much, much angrier.

Dakari slid along the wall of the corridor and eased around the door frame into the room. He saw Aurelia gesture, and the noise the witch and werewolf were making shut off as if she had slit their throats. But she did not look at them.

"What took you so long?" she snapped at Dakari.

He bowed double, shadow shifting around him. "I beg your pardon, madam. The Gate is a long way from my humble dwelling."

It was a lie; Dakari could only hope Aurilia had not set a truth spell, but he was unwilling to admit that he lived in Caer Mordwyn itself; she might set herself to discover his only safe place if he did.

"Oh, well, come up here." She gestured to the raised dais on which her magnificent chair was set.

Trembling, Dakari approached, stopping at a respectful distance, but Aurilia gestured him closer. Then, squinting as if to enhance her vision, she suddenly stabbed a finger at him. A small jolt of power ran over him and he knew she had overwhelmed his little magic of fading to shadow so that he was completely visible.

Laughing, Aurilia reached out and caught his ear. Dakari shrieked as pain, like a red-hot needle lanced through one earlobe and then, when he turned to run and was caught, through the other.

"Be quiet you ninny," Aurelia said contemptuously. "I have just placed the amulets that will give you power over Wahib and Wahiba where you cannot carelessly lose them and they cannot steal them." She smiled, showing her sharp pointed teeth. "They look quite decorative."

"Oh, are you sure they will work for me?" Dakari faltered.

Aurilia's lip curled in disdain. "Give them an order—" she smiled again this time at the furious pair bound by her will to stillness and silence near the door "—an order they will not like, and see whether you are obeyed. Perhaps when you are through with them, they will have learned that it is unwise to be insolent to and careless about obeying my commands."

Dakari looked at the tall dignified looking witch whose face was twisted with rage and hate. "Dance," he commanded, touching the amulet in his right ear.

He judged doing a dance to be what the witch would least like to do and the most mortifying to her dignity. He could see her throat working with curses, but she could not make a sound, and dance she did. So did the werewolf when he was so ordered, though he was less graceful. Dakari laughed. Aurilia laughed too.

"Good for you, my little Dakari," she said. "You have a sense of humor, which I never would have expected."

The approval bolstered Dakari's courage. He bowed, almost with panache, to Aurilia, and she laughed again and gestured him to leave.

"Come with me," he said to the witch and the werewolf.

They would have followed dancing despite the expressions of horror on their faces, but the habit of centuries drove Dakari not to draw attention and he ordered them to walk. Then relief mingled with venom, with the silent threat of future harm, glared from their eyes. Dakari grew cold as they came to the stair down to the outer doors. What if this were all a cruel trick of Aurilia's? What if they were less in his control than he believed and would turn on him? Throw him down the stairs, then fall upon him?

"Go down the stair ahead of me and wait at the door," he ordered.

That command, too, they obeyed and Dakari grew a little more confident as he bade them leave the palace and go to the nearest Gate. He remembered that placing Wahib and Wahiba in his power was not a whim of Aurilia's. She had done it because Prince Vidal wanted him to clear the sigils of iron and silver from Alhambra to make that palace available to the the Dark Court. It was unlikely that Aurilia would play a trick on him until that task was completed.

Dakari Gated from Caer Mordwyn to the Goblin Market, changed Gates, Wahib and Wahiba now trailing obediently behind him, and then Gated to Alhambra. He had always used that path, fearing that some taint of the Caer Mordwyn Gate might linger in the Gate at Alhambra and warn those of the Bright Court of his visits.

Usually he was far more cautious, trying to sense whether the
Gate had been recently used, but today he did not care. If the
accursed FitzRoy and his puling ancients were there, he would
set Wahib and Wahiba on them. He would have plenty of time
to escape and if they killed Wahib and Wahiba, Aurilia would
simply have to find him another pair to clear the iron and silver
from Alhambra.

The breathtaking palace was empty, however. Dakari glanced
at it indifferently; he was accustomed to the gleaming, delicate
minarets which rose into what seemed a clear, blue, sunny sky,
to the lacework of stone that adorned the many balconies and
doorways, to the gardens, once rotting and now restored with
myriad flowers that bloomed in intricate patterns and scented
the softly moving air.

The stunned expressions on the faces of the witch and the
werewolf made him look at the palace again, but he still could
not understand at what they were staring with such admiration.
The place was too bright; it hurt his eyes. A little black slime
running down like tears from the many windows would improve
the view.

Dakari could not fathom why Aurilia had set her heart on living here; that was not important. Possibly the whole Dark Court
would leave Caer Mordwyn and settle here... Now that was a
fine idea; he would have the Caer Mordwyn palace to himself.

With a little effort, Dakari shook off that pleasant dream and
reminded himself that it would be typical of Aurilia to time her
amulets to fail as soon as the silver and iron were removed. Then
Wahib and Wahiba could tear him apart and Prince Vidal would
not need to give him any reward for bringing the Evil to agree
to the Dark Court coming.

For once it seemed that Aurilia had outsmarted herself. In a
firm voice, he ordered the witch and her werewolf son to search
Alhambra thoroughly and remove from it every trace of Cold Iron
or anything that contained iron. They were to wrap everything they
found in silk hangings removed from the palace, bring all the iron
carefully wrapped to the Gate, and to take the iron to... Dakari
hesitated for a moment and then started to laugh.

"Take it all to Wormgay Hold," he said. "You hear me? Nod
your heads if you hear me. To Wormgay Hold."

Fear and hate distorted both faces, but each nodded and set

off for the palace. Dakari first sat down on the edge of the Gate platform until he reminded himself that the accursed Bright Sidhe might come through at any time. Then he removed himself to a bench in the garden where a rose arbor would conceal him. It took a long time for Wahib and Wahiba to remove the iron but at last they did not return from the Gate. Yes, they were gone and all the bundles of silk-wrapped iron too. And the Gate looked all right.

Dakari giggled. He wondered if the witch and the werewolf had been trapped in Wormgay. That hold sucked power out of anyone who had the misfortune to come there by accident or evil intent. The Gate that brought one in would not take anyone out, and the Gate out was not self-powered as most Gates were either. To make the Gate work, the being wishing to use it had to supply the power. He did not know whether Wahib and Wahiba knew about that. Dakari giggled again; he did not care if they died there.

However, he had better get about his part of the business while they were gone and he did not need to watch them. He walked into the palace by the great main doors. Unlike the usual shining twilight that suffused most of the Bright Court domains, the whole of Alhambra seemed flooded with golden light. Dakari squinted.

When his vision cleared, he saw how the pointed arches on open doorways to each side of the entrance hall seemed to lift the whole structure. He felt as if he might rise through the air to the top of the huge dome that covered the entryway, and he shuddered and lowered his eyes.

Ahead were two tall doors of worked silver. They were closed, but Dakari had crept in here after the Sidhe and the Oberon-marked mortal had departed. He knew that behind the doors was a room where the golden light was not pure but dark and reddish and in that room was a great block of stone. Perhaps it had been white and gleaming once, like all the stone in Alhambra, but it was black now, veined with a dull, slightly pulsing red. There, near the block of stone that once, perhaps, was an altar, the feeling of Evil was strongest.

The open space, the golden light pulled at him. Dakari hated the feeling that if he let himself fly limitless joy would be bestowed upon him. Who wanted the endless sound of laughter, the murmurs of love?

Shuddering, Dakari hurried to the silver-worked doors and pulled them open. Then he stopped, staring in suprise. The altar stone, which had been black and pulsing with red life, was now a pallid grey. What had been thick arteries of red were shrunken to dull bluish threads. The Evil was indeed much diminished.

Dakari paused and thought over the possibilities. With the Evil so much weakened, he could simply go back to Caer Mordwyn and tell Prince Vidal that the Evil no longer had enough power to do them harm. They could take possession without asking permission.

A sound from the great entryway behind him made Dakari whirl around, but no one was there. Only a light breeze had flapped a hanging that had been pulled loose. But it was stupid to leave the doors open. It was possible that Wahib and Wahiba would escape, even possible that Aurilia had not put a limit on the amulets and they would return.

As he reached to shut the doors, Dakari hesitated. If he was to return and tell Vidal the way was open, he could just go now. But second thoughts brought him to close the doors. Instead of being grateful and rewarding him for news, Vidal likely would be angry. He wanted the Evil as an ally from whom he could ask, and get, favors. Dakari began slowly to walk toward the altar. Should he simply do as Vidal had bid him? Make an agreement with It for the Dark Court?

Just before he reached the altar Dakari stopped. Before he decided what to do, should he not make sure the Evil would listen to him? The last time he spoke to it, either it would not or could not answer him.

"Great Evil," Dakari said "Will you speak to me?"

No answer. Dakari bit his lip and ground his teeth. *Stupid thing, you are almost gone; what right have you to ignore me?*

Sneering, not realizing himself how much he had been emboldened by the power Aurilia had fed into the amulets in his ears, Dakari stepped forward and slapped a hand down on the sickly grey stone.

"Listen to me!" he ordered, in the voice he had been using to direct Wahib and Wahiba. "You will soon be nothing, leached away by the spells and metals of those who hate you. Make me your vessel, and—"

Dakari's voice stopped. His eyes opened so wide that the whites showed all around the muddy iris. His mouth also opened wide, wider. His arms sprang away from his body and stiffened. He was rigid, even his hair standing out around his head like an aureole.

The grey of the altar paled, the ugly bluish veins took on a silvery sheen that, as the stone turned glittering white, grew richer in tone, richer, then became glowing gold. As it was before the mad priest of the Inquisition had carried in the evil in his heart and brain, now it was again. Alhambra the beautiful, the enchanted in loveliness.

With the king dead, Albertus was no longer welcome in the Court, but he had been careful while he was there to spread *pour boire* coins among the servants. At first he only urged them to come to him at Otstargi's house to tell him if the king needed his calming potions; later he added a coin or two for news of any importance whether or not he was needed by the king.

Thus any anxiety he had felt about Mary's accession was soon laid to rest. On July eighteenth one of the grooms of the chamber came, grinning, to tell him that the Council had escaped the Tower. Albertus passed a golden guinea for that piece of news—why not? Either Aurilia or Vidal could ken as many as he needed. Likely news of that guinea was what brought a second groom after dark to tell him that the Council had met in Baynard's Castle, the earl of Pembroke's house. The Lord Mayor of London had been invited there by the earl of Shrewsbury and Sir John Mason and between five and six in the evening the meeting had borne fruit; Mary had been proclaimed queen.

There was considerable difference from how the proclamation of Queen Jane had been greeted. Albertus himself had gone out into the city to see whether this news would be spread and how it would be received. He found there was a huge crowd milling around the Cross in the Cheap. The Lord Mayor and some aldermen with several trumpeters had a hard time winning through, but at last they reached the Cross where the trumpeters sounded their horns. Even more people rushed into the area. Albertus accosted a merchant whose house was near the Cross and offered good coin for a place at his second story window. There were so many people that he could not see a thing.

Hearing, however, was different. The crowd was frighteningly silent after the fanfare and the sense of threat and hostility had grown steadily while the Garter King of Arms read out his proclamation until he spoke the name of the proclaimed . . . Queen Mary. Then the dam of silence burst and the crowd roared with joy, throwing their caps into the air and shouting "God save Queen Mary." The rest of the proclamation could not be heard, but it hardly mattered. Mary was queen.

Albertus brought this news Underhill. Just before he touched the amulet that opened the Gate in Otstargi's house for him, he paused to consider whether to go first as usual to Aurilia or for once to present himself directly to Vidal. He had no doubt that the information he brought would please the prince. Did he want to share the satisfaction Vidal would feel with Aurilia?

Share? Nonsense. For this news the likelihood was that Aurilia would not even bring him with her into Vidal's presence. She would get all the credit. Was that important? Did he want Vidal to think of him as clever and efficient? He hated the Dark Sidhe's open contempt and he was determined some day to make Vidal suffer for it, but that did not answer the question. Was he better off if Vidal believed him slow and stupid? And how would Aurilia react if he bypassed her to speak to Vidal?

That thought gave Albertus pause. He had spent so much time recently in the mortal world that he had pushed to the back of his mind Aurilia's cruelty when he had displeased her. And he could not count on Vidal to protect him. Far from it. He was essentially of no value to Vidal; Aurilia actually needed him to make the potion that soothed her headaches. So in the end Albertus did go first to Aurilia with word that Mary had been proclaimed in London, that the rest of the country was following that lead, and that Northumberland was taken prisoner.

"Hmmm," Aurilia said, lifting her upper lip to show her sharpened teeth. "I intended to recall you from the mortal world. My supply of the headache potion is nearly exhausted. How quickly can you renew that?"

"If I have assistants to grind and boil and filter, only a few days."

"No, that will not do. If Vidal hears from anyone sooner than he hears from you . . . or, rather, from me . . ." She thought for a moment, then rose and left the chamber without another word to Albertus.

He stood—Aurilia had not given him permission to sit—trying to keep all expression from his face. The chances were' that she had left a watcher and was just waiting for him to show what she would call impudence (sitting down without permission) or resentment. In fact, having been reminded of Aurilia's less appealing characteristics he was less sure than ever whether or not he wanted Vidal's notice.

He did not need to decide what he felt; whether or not he spoke to Vidal was not a matter or his choice. In another few moments an imp pulled his hair and pinched him, driving him out of Aurilia's chambers and toward Vidal's. The door opened as Albertus approached it and he bowed as he entered. Aurilia, who was seated to Vidal's left, did not acknowledge him. She was frowning abstractedly into the distance.

"So it is certain that Mary is to be queen," Vidal said. "Very good. Aurilia's potion will have to wait until you complete some minor tasks for me."

"Yes, my lord," Albertus said, but he glanced nervously at Aurilia and to his relief she nodded curtly.

"The first is simple enough. Now that Mary is secure and Northumberland has lost his power, Elizabeth may feel less threatened. Perhaps she will start riding out again. Tell Howard that he and his men are to return to Hatfield. They are to watch for an opening to take Elizabeth prisoner or kill her."

"I will tell him, my lord," Albertus said, cringing a little as he prepared to say something Vidal would not like. "But Howard does not simply take orders. I know that Lady Elizabeth is calling in her dependents. I doubt he will agree to risk himself and his men trying to get at her." He saw Vidal's mouth twist into a snarl and dropped to his knees. "I have a suggestion. Perhaps Howard and some of his men can try to make friends among Elizabeth's guard so we will know what she is doing."

The ferocious scowl eased from Vidal's face and Albertus breathed again. He had managed to divert Vidal from punishing him because he could not exert the same power over Howard as Vidal could over his servants. Vidal was growing less accepting of Howard's inability to attack Elizabeth than he had been at first. His master's fixed desire to remove Elizabeth from any chance at ruling was one obsession that his imprisonment by the self-willed mist had only driven deep, not affected.

Then Vidal sneered at him and Albertus had to bow his head to hide his anger. To have Howard's men mix with Elizabeth's was a good idea; it actually might allow them to find a way into Hatfield. Albertus did not want to suggest that because if the plan failed Vidal would be furious with him. In fact the bowed head hid more than Albertus's resentment. It hid his sudden realization that the one hope he had of really hurting Vidal was to see Elizabeth mount the throne of England.

"That is of some value, or may be," Vidal said grudgingly. "Very well, let Howard try his luck at ferreting out Elizabeth's plans. But there is something more important you must do at once. I want to hear no excuses. I gave you a ruby ring you were supposed to have Chancellor Rich pass to the Imperial Ambassador Renard."

"Yes, my lord," Albertus said, bowing low from his kneeling position so that his nose nearly touched the floor. "But I must remind you that Baron Rich is no longer the chancellor—"

"Remind me!" Vidal roared, glaring at Albertus as if Albertus himself had deprived Rich of his position. "Why did you not tell me of this?"

"I thought you knew, my lord," Albertus whispered. "Goodrich was made chancellor before you sent me to the mortal world, but by then Baron Rich was back on the Council and active at Court—so I thought you knew and gave him the title for respect." Albertus forced his trembling voice to continue. "And Rich did give Renard the ring. I saw it on the ambassador's finger two days after the king died."

Vidal's hand had twitched, shimmering blue gathering at his fingertips. Aurilia laid a hand on his arm keeping him from lifting his hand. Albertus stared at the bluish light like a bird fixed by a serpent's gaze.

"Your purpose is accomplished," Aurilia said. "Renard has the bespelled ruby. Do not deprive me of a useful servant. Now what?"

Vidal opened his mouth to say that Albertus was of no use to *him*, that Albertus must have done something wrong to the ring. Renard should have tried to contact Ostargi a few days after he had been given the ring—that was its first compulsion. Then Vidal remembered that Renard might have written to or visited Otstargi but Vidal had not been back to the house recently. And the servant was so brain-damaged that he would not have thought to mention to Albertus that there was a message for Otstargi. Moreover he had no idea how long it was since Renard had been given the ring.

"Now," Vidal replied to Aurilia's question, "I must imprint indelibly on Renard's mind that to keep Mary on the throne and ensure her alliance with the Empire, Elizabeth must die. But for that purpose I myself must meet the man." He looked from Aurilia to Albertus and asked, "How many mortal days have passed since you saw Renard with the ring?"

"Near a fortnight," Albertus replied.

"A little too long." Vidal again sounded as if it were Albertus's fault, but he did not make any move to hurt him and turned his head to Aurilia. "That first compulsion might be wearing thin and I must recharge the ring with other spells. It is time for Master Otstargi to return to his business for a little while."

"Then Albertus can make my potion," Aurilia said.

Albertus's heart sank. Once he was immured in the laboratory Aurilia had devised for him, he would be forgotten except for receiving messages from imps for this or that potion. He would have no chance at all to interfere with Vidal's plans for Lady Elizabeth. But in the next moment Vidal shook his head.

"Never mind your potion," he snapped. "You have enough for now. Albertus must set Howard onto testing Elizabeth's defenses and finding a way to penetrate them. Mary is queen, but she is only a weak mortal. She is not young and is often sick. We must be rid of Elizabeth. Perhaps that will bring civil war."

Vidal's words intensified Albertus's new purpose in life, to frustrate Prince Vidal Dhu. He bowed yet again, looking from Vidal to Aurilia whose eyes had brightened at the mention of civil war. Finally she made a hissing sound and nodded and Vidal gestured. Albertus found himself outside the door of Vidal's apartment.

He wasted no time in hurrying to his laboratory; if there really was no reserve of potion, he would need to fudge something. However, there were two generous flasks of the cloudy blue potion. It gave Albertus some satisfaction that if he did help Elizabeth to rule, Aurilia as well as Vidal would suffer some deprivation.

He was able to get to the Gate that would take him to the mortal world without encountering either of his masters. He did not linger at Otstargi's house, only took up the brooch that disguised his appearance. Both to show his diligence and to avoid Vidal, who would be Gating to Otstargi's house very soon to arrange a meeting with Renard, Albertus sent a message to Howard's lodging and himself set out for the inn at which they met.

As often was the case, Howard was there already with several of the troop. They waved cheerfully to Albertus to join them, all of them in the best of spirits at the success of their endeavors and because Mary would bring back the true faith to England.

Albertus went over and took the stool one of the men pulled from an adjoining table. He looked up and around, but knew it still was not possible for him to find any of the spies that Vidal or Aurilia were able to send into the mortal world. He had heard Aurilia curse Elizabeth's ability to detect Underhill creatures, but he could not. He would need to be very careful about what he told Howard and his men.

"You have more work for us?" Howard asked cheerfully.

"Yes, I do, and work you will enjoy," Albertus said. "Not for the whole troop, only for you, Francis, and for a few of the men who are not too much Queen Mary's partisans."

"What the devil does that mean?" One of the men down the table asked hotly.

"It means my master wishes to find a way to reach Lady Elizabeth, and prating to her servants about the true faith will not endear you to them."

"Reach Lady Elizabeth to do what?" Francis Howard pushed his wine cup aside and sat straighter.

"I have not been told that," Albertus said with a sigh. "You know I am no more than a message boy. Now that the attempt to take the lady failed and made her cautious beyond hope of another attempt, it may be that my master only wishes to have a safe way to communicate with her. It may be that he wishes to know what her intentions toward the queen are. It may be that he wishes to know where and when she will come to Court or if she will come at all."

"And how are we to accomplish that?" Howard asked.

"I have heard—there is gossip from the servants at the Imperial embassy—that Lady Elizabeth is calling in all her tenants and supporters. It is my notion that you and a few others who will not too violently urge religious obedience to the queen should go to Hatfield and mingle with Elizabeth's own guardsmen and with her liegemen and servants. Listen to what they say, what they hope, to any plans if there are plans. You, Francis, should feel out the possibility of joining her forces."

Francis Howard laughed. "And if I succeed, do I get to keep all the pay?"

"If your attempts to reach Lady Elizabeth are as successful as your efforts on behalf of Queen Mary were, there may be more than pay as a reward." Most of the men leaned forward eagerly, but Albertus shook his head. "I am only making guesses. I have found it best to do what I am told without looking too far ahead."

So far every word Albertus had said would cast no shadow on him if Vidal chose to look into the mind of any of the men. He knew that neither Vidal nor Aurilia would bother with his thoughts while they were together, which was why he then had dared think about frustrating Vidal's plans for Elizabeth at that time. Neither Vidal nor Aurilia dared be distracted lest the other take some advantage.

Now, as Albertus left Howard and his men, he began to worry about how he would conceal this delightful hope that had come to him. He could do nothing more toward his purpose until Howard and his men had time to get to Hatfield, to become familiar with the guards and servants . . . That thought was safe, but the other, forbidden one, flickered under it. Now Albertus was frightened. Somehow he must bury that idea so deep it would not show when Aurilia looked into his mind.

He walked very slowly, which did not draw attention because the weather was hot and most people were moving slowly. But Albertus's dragging steps were because he had nowhere to go. Soon, if he were not there already, Vidal would be in Otstargi's house. Albertus was afraid his treachery would broadcast itself; he could not live in Otstargi's house when Vidal would be there often. And he did not want to live in the mean rooms he had near the slum.

Wait, he did have a haven where Vidal would not look for him. He took a deep breath and began to hurry. The laboratory. He would have to use the Gate in Otstargi's house, but perhaps Vidal would not be there yet. In the laboratory he could fix his mind on lotions and potions and his thoughts would be safe behind those recipes.

Chapter 12

The proclamation of Mary as queen that Albertus had witnessed in London was very soon duplicated in town after town throughout England. By the twenty-second of July, Elizabeth had written to her sister congratulating her on her accession and naming herself Mary's very humble and loving servant.

Elizabeth did not ask whether she should come to meet Mary—boldly assuming that Mary's accession meant that Henry VIII's will and the Act of Succession were in force and she was heir presumptive. What she asked was whether she should wear mourning because Edward was dead or colors for the joy of her sister becoming queen.

Elizabeth had also sent out summonses to her dependents, tenants, and supporters to accompany her to meet the queen, and all that week they rode in haste to gather at Hatfield. They came arrayed in the Tudor colors—green guarded with white, in fabrics graded by their rank: velvet for the lords, satin for the knights, and taffeta for the simpler gentlemen. By the twenty-eighth of July, all who would come had gathered and were making ready to leave for London early the next day.

Denoriel did not accompany Elizabeth when she went out into the camp to greet her supporters. Some of them knew of the "old" merchant who had long been a favorite in Elizabeth's household; all the more did Elizabeth and Denoriel feel it unwise for him to appear with her, possibly to be thought to have influence, when Elizabeth was about to establish herself as her sister's heir. It made Elizabeth very nervous to go into the crowd of men without her Denno beside her, but it was necessary and she straightened her back and lifted her head and went, smiling.

She did not go unguarded, of course. Sir Edward walked to her right, Shaylor to her left. Gerrit walked ahead opening a path and scanning the crowd, Nyle and Dickson behind to guard her back. Elizabeth smiled and nodded to all impartially, stopping to offer a few personal words and thanks to those she actually knew and to ask the names of their companions. One man, stepping back out of the way, caught her eye. There was something familiar about his spare body shape and black hair.

She cocked her head and smiled her enchanting smile, holding out her beautiful, long-fingered hand. Sir Edward closed in on one side of him and Gerrit on the other.

"I feel I know you, sir," Elizabeth said, "but to my shame I cannot bring your name to mind."

Francis Howard swallowed hard as he bowed to kiss her hand. When Sir Edward stepped to one side and Gerrit to the other, he was sure he had been recognized as leading the attack against her. He expected to be taken prisoner. Lady Elizabeth's words were a temporary reprieve, but he had to give her a reason to find him familiar that was *not* the glimpses she had had of him on the road to London.

"No fault to you, madam," Francis said, releasing her hand and bowing low. "We have never met, but my name is Francis Howard. It is a large family so you may have met some relation of mine."

"Howard?" Elizabeth repeated. When her father was king, she would have turned her back on the man and walked away. Now she did not need to do that, and she had certainly met Howards in plenty. Her uncle, the duke of Norfolk was a Howard; he too was spare of body and when young had black hair. Elizabeth smiled again. "Then perhaps I may call you cousin. My grandmother was a Howard."

Her eyes were bright, her face alive with interest. Interest in *him*. Not as a man, as a person. Francis Howard was enchanted. But that was no safe feeling. He had no idea what "John Smith," he of the message-boy status who nonetheless handed out purses

filled with gold, wanted him to do about Elizabeth. His first order
had been to take her prisoner; his next might be worse. He must
not be tempted into liking. He bowed again.

"My lady, I wish it were so, with all my heart I wish it could
be so, but I . . . I have no legal right to that name."

Elizabeth had been called bastard since her father declared her
illegitimate at the age of three. She understood what his honesty
had cost Francis Howard. Her smile disappeared.

"That does not change the blood, Francis Howard," she said, her
voice firm, her nostrils pinched with distaste—but not distaste for
him, "or make you less a cousin." She reached out and touched
Francis gently on the shoulder before she walked on.

He looked after her with a sense of despair and then smiled at
the men who now approached him with much warmer welcomes
than he had first received. Some may have heard her call him
cousin; they would trust him now. He had better get on with
his work.

"A wonder, is she not?" Francis said.

"You do not know the half of it," an older man replied. "I can
only wish that it was she who had been proclaimed."

"Shush!" another man urged sharply. "The law is the law and
the Act of Succession names Queen Mary. We were called together
to honor and do service for Queen Mary. Our lady is her loyal
subject, and so are we."

Elizabeth was exhausted by the time she managed to greet,
individually and en masse, those who had responded to her summons. She hoped she had made clear that not all would actually
go with her to meet the queen, that she did not dare bring with
her a force of armed men larger than that accompanying Mary.
Men of her household, Thomas Parry, Sir Edward, Master Dunstan,
and others would pass through those assembled and ask whether
they would rather endure the expense of lodging in London
until Queen Mary arrived—because Elizabeth confessed frankly,
she simply did not have the money to defray their expenses—or
return home.

Perhaps she should have waited to talk over with Parry and
Sir Edward what she should do if not enough wished to stay or
to go, but Elizabeth's nerves were in tatters. It was not so much
dealing with her supporters that had shaken her—although the

enthusiasm of some of those supporters was very dangerous—as the continual reminder of what she would have to face once she had joined Mary's Court. Now it all ran through her head again as she sat and waited for Denoriel to come for her.

"Denno," she cried and jumped up from Blanche's bed as he came through the Gate. "Why are you so late?"

He took her into his arms and kissed her hair before he looked at Blanche. "Am I late?"

"No, m'lord," Blanche said. "Just she was tired with talkin' to all the men who are here and she went to bed early. Then a'course she couldn' sleep so it seems she was waitin' forever."

"I sent the messenger," Elizabeth said plaintively.

She referred to the air spirit that was bound to her, Denoriel understood, not a human messenger. But air spirits were happy and simple minded; they did not understand crises of nerves. Danger had to be more direct or at least caused by some immediate threat before the air spirit would become alarmed. So when Elizabeth sent it, it looked for Denoriel, but not frantically; and when it found him, it communicated that Elizabeth wanted him but not any sense of urgency.

Elizabeth knew that, but she was cold and shivering so Denoriel did not bother to explain it to her again. He nodded to Blanche and steered Elizabeth into the Gate and when they arrived in Logres, only said, "I am sorry, love. It took it a while to find me. I went with Harry to Alhambra. Something very strange has happened there. No one knows what to make of it."

"You never took me to Alhambra," she said accusingly, as he pulled her up into the rear saddle on Miralys, who had been waiting for them.

"I didn't dare." He twisted around to look at her since there was no need for him to direct Miralys. "There is . . . was . . . an Evil there that reached out to any who came to Alhambra. It offered . . . whatever was your innermost desire. The temptation is . . . dangerous."

"But Harry goes all the time, and Mechain and Elidir and some of the other elder Sidhe."

Denoriel shook his head. "Harry cannot be tempted by Evil. I have no idea why. He was a perfectly ordinary little boy and got into ordinary little-boy mischief. And when he was a young man, he sinned his sins in a perfectly ordinary way. Well, perhaps with less enthusiasm than others of his age with his wealth and power, but that was because he'd been Underhill and found our vices more to his taste than mortal vices. The elder Sidhe only go there shielded to within an inch of being able to breathe."

"I have good shields," Elizabeth said pettishly.

"Elizabeth," Denoriel said softly, "you are too precious to be risked. If you should be touched with that Evil . . . it makes me sick to think of the ill you could visit on your whole realm, perhaps even on all of Europe. No, there is enough nastiness in you just as you are. You do not need to be stained with Evil."

She laughed when he said there was enough nastiness in her; she had spent much of her youth deliberately bedeviling her Denno. Then they were at the foot of the white marble steps leading up to the portico surrounding Llachar Lle. Elizabeth was silent while they climbed the stairs and went through the person-sized door alongside the huge brass doors, large enough for the Cerne Abbas Giant to pass through. A few steps through the broad corridor and a short walk down the more normal-sized passageway to the right took them to Denoriel's door. Elizabeth, still smiling faintly, looked at the scene beyond the doorway.

"It changes all the time now. Are there people on the terrace of the manor house?" she asked, peering intently at the scene.

"Only a table and chairs, no people." Denoriel smiled too. "A stranger who does not know me would think the people are real. People on the terrace might frighten away anyone who wants to enter without letting me know they are here. And I would not want any who wish me ill—who else would try to enter without touching the knocker that would signal they had come?—to go away before my doorway lessons them."

Elizabeth turned suddenly and clutched at him. "Who wishes you ill Denno? Is it because of me?"

"No, love, of course not," he soothed, prodded her gently to go through the doorway, and then stood in the square entryway with his arms around her so she was sheltered against his body.

Elizabeth closed her eyes and leaned against him. She knew she should talk over what she had learned from and about the men who responded to her summons. She also knew she should ask Denno to send for her Da who could best interpret what the men said. But she was achingly conscious that this was likely the last time she could be with her lover until Mary released her from attendance at Court. He bent over her, his breath warm on her ear, and when she turned her head toward him he kissed her.

Still, conscience warred with the need of her body, with the tautness of her breasts which brought her upstanding nipples into suggestive contact with her night rail, with the unmistakable sensation that her nether mouth was hot and wet. Her arms dropped down Denno's back, pressed on his buttocks so that his hips were driven forward. Unfortunately he was too tall and the pressure came against her belly. She rose on tiptoe to rub against him.

At the same time, conscience won enough for her to say, "I think I need to talk to Da about those who answered my summons."

Denoriel laughed softly. "And so you shall, beloved, when you can give more than a small part of your attention to what he will have to say. We are Underhill, love. I shall spread the hours so that we have all the time we need." And he picked her up and carried her up the stairs to the wide, soft bed that—because Sidhe did not sleep—was only used for making love.

The bed was well used that mortal night. With all the time Elizabeth and Denoriel had for love, it was nearly not enough. Each time they were done loving and resting and made to rise, one or the other would remember this would be the last time for love for neither knew how long.

Fear drove Elizabeth as much as passion. She had no real idea of how Mary would greet her, whether she was going to be acknowledged as her sister's heir or seized to be executed as a danger to the peace of the realm. Oddly the fear did not diminish her lust; it lent so special a savor to her Denno's caresses that, even sated, just dozing in his arms woke her appetite for more.

Denoriel was storing in his body, in his memory, every sigh, every breath, every murmur of her need and her desire. He had always hated when she went to Court because she loved it so. She said she missed him and that she thought of him . . . but that was after she had left the Court. The glories and wonders of Underhill had never drawn her as they had drawn Harry. The English Court might be coarse and crude and dirty by comparison, but to Elizabeth it was real and important.

Although he was no FarSeer, Denoriel knew that some day Elizabeth herself would be the Court and he only a small part of her life, a distant, pleasant dream of the past. And each time he thought of losing her, he made love to her again, determined that no human would ever rival his skill at bringing her pleasure.

It was fortunate that a cheerful whistling from below and a shout for wine roused them from a brief rest and warned them that Harry had come home. Elizabeth was ashamed to linger longer abed. She laughed, gave Denoriel a large smacking kiss on the cheek, and slid from under the light cover. Denoriel laughed too, curbing the desire to pull her back. He knew it was necessary to return to the mortal world very soon or the twist he would need to give time might have unfortunate side effects.

Thus Denoriel quickly gestured them both into clothing, and they hurried out onto the stair landing to see Harry, still in the square entrance hall talking to the air.

"Nectar too," he said, then hearing some sound looked up and saw them. "Drinks?"

"I'll have whatever wine you are drinking," Denoriel said, smiling. "It's all very good. I know. I import it."

Harry laughed.

"Ale for me," Elizabeth said. "I'm thirsty but I want to keep a clear head." She saw the gun holstered at Harry's waist and the silver sword too. "Whatever have you been doing?" she asked.

Harry gestured toward the parlor and Elizabeth went in. Elidir and Mechain were standing near the fireplace where multicolored flames danced over crystal logs. Elizabeth smiled at the fire, remembering that it had once irritated her to have a fire Underhill where the temperature suited itself to each person and the clothing that person wore. Now it was a familiar thing, designed only to be beautiful—as so much of Underhill was—and dear to her as everything related to her Denno was dear.

Elidir and Mechain greeted her with cries of joy, commenting on how long it had been since they saw her. Elizabeth sighed.

"Life has been very fraught. My poor brother is dead—"

The two elder Sidhe nodded sadly but without surprise.

"And the duke of Northumberland tried to set aside my sister and myself and put Jane Gray on the throne."

Elizabeth shivered and both the Sidhe came to her. Mechain stroked her hair and Elidir put an arm around her shoulders. "You can always come here," Mechain said.

"No, she cannot," Elidir snapped. "She has a great purpose to fulfill."

His hand dropped as if to touch his sword hilt and Elizabeth suddenly noticed that he carried not only his sword but a strange looking whip with a thick handle and a lash that was more like a coiled ribbon than a punishing strip of leather. Mechain was also armed. Elizabeth looked more closely at the Sidhe, but they did not have the fragile transparency that spoke of much use of magic.

"It appears that your lives as well as mine have been busy and dangerous," Elizabeth said.

There was a wavering in the air and suddenly a small table stood beside the elder Sidhe with flasks and cups for the nectar and the wine and a substantial mug with ale. Mechain, Elidir, and Elizabeth helped themselves to drink and to a few of the tiny sweets from a gold plate.

"Busy, yes. Dangerous, no," Harry said, coming in and taking a cup of wine before settling down on the short sofa that faced the fireplace. "Denno is going down to his workroom to bespell some amulets. Didn't he tell you that something very, very strange has happened in Alhambra?"

"What does he want the amulets to do?" Mechain asked.

"Locators for opening Gates into the mortal world," Harry said. "It is possible that Elizabeth will be away from her own houses for a time and Denno wants to be sure that he can reach her if there is a need."

"Oh, we know a trick or two to make the Gates open easily," Elidir said. "Will Denoriel mind if we go to his workroom?"

"I'm sure not," Harry said. "He left the stair open. Likely he would welcome any help. He's only started to study magic seriously in the last few mortal years."

The elder Sidhe took themselves out of the parlor carrying their nectar to where a stairway going down now yawned in the middle of the entrance hall. Elizabeth sat down beside Harry and raised her brows.

"All right, Da, what is it about Alhambra that Mechain and Elidir don't want to talk about?"

"I'm not sure I want to talk about it either. It makes me damned uncomfortable. I'm surprised Denno... No, it's true that I've hardly seen him since..." He put an arm around Elizabeth. "I'm sorry, love, I know you cared for Edward."

Tears suddenly filled Elizabeth's eyes. "I should have guarded him better. I tried, but my shield wasn't enough. I should have covered him instead of myself—"

"No! Absolutely not! And you are not at fault. It is Vidal Dhu who sent an assassin to kill *you* my love. That an accident caused him to touch Edward instead is *not* your fault."

"I suppose so," Elizabeth sighed, "but I miss Edward. Even though we did not see each other often, we wrote to each other. I miss his letters. He was always interested in what I was studying . . ." She sniffed and wiped her eyes. "The gun and your sword . . . and you are trying to divert me from Alhambra. What has happened there?"

"The Evil is gone! The iron sigils we placed to control Its creatures are missing. But there is not a sniff of them or of It. Now we must search more carefully."

"Oh, Da, be careful," Elizabeth said, clinging to him for a moment.

He kissed her again and freed himself, smiling. "Now, now, there is nothing to worry about. You know that the Evil has never tried to force me—It only offers silly temptations—and Elidir and Mechain are ready with shielding if It should change Its mind."

"It has pretended to be gone before, and then sent out a new plague when you were less prepared."

Harry shook his head. "I think It is really gone this time, and that is what troubles me. We thought, since It did not flee when we destroyed Its minions, that It was somehow fixed in Alhambra. We hoped to bind It with a spell . . . but Sawel has not yet perfected a binding strong enough. We hoped to send It to the Void. And now It is gone." He sighed. "There are so many places It could go and when we are not watching grow strong again."

"How can you find It? Oh Da, I don't like the idea of you hunting for that Evil." Elizabeth clutched at him again.

He stroked her hair. "It was my idea to drive It out of Alhambra, so it is my responsibility to see It does no harm. The elder Sidhe and I will search. If we have any suspicion of where It is—Its creatures will surely try to attack us—Hafwen will be able to sense It. The last time she came to Alhambra, none of us could feel It much, but Hafwen showed us where it laired before she nearly fainted and Pasgen had to carry her to the Gate."

"Can you not wait until matters are settled in England, please?" Elizabeth begged. "If I am afraid for you as well as for myself, I will go mad."

"What?" Harry sat upright, hands going to the weapons he bore, but even as he touched them he realized that weapons would be of no help and he embraced Elizabeth again. "Why should you be afraid for yourself?" He leaned back to look into her face.

"Because to Mary I am Ann Boleyn's daughter."

"That is true," Harry said, "but Mary has mixed feeling about you. She wants to have a sister to love. No, Mary would not harm you for that. And Rhoslyn is with her. Rhoslyn will warn us if the queen threatens to turn on you. But why should she?"

"Because she will try to make this realm Catholic again and subject to the pope. I am not only my mother's daughter but also known to favor the reformist rite. Those of that persuasion might prefer to see me on the throne. Thus Mary or her advisors might decide I am a danger to her and to the stability of her reign."

Harry made an exasperated noise. "This business of Alhambra distracted me. Once Mary was proclaimed on the strength of being our father's daughter and the Act of Succession, I put England temporarily out of my mind, thinking Mary would reign as long as she lasted and then you would be crowned. There was no Protestant faction in my time. Hmmm. No. No, it will not be so easy."

"Mary is now on her way to London."

Harry sat silent for a long moment, obviously considering alternatives. Finally he said, "Yes, and you must meet her."

"You do not think she is likely simply to seize me?"

"No." He frowned then added slowly, thinking as he spoke, "I do not believe there is any reason to be afraid. From what Rhoslyn has said, Mary is too happy just now to do anyone any harm. After all, she has not even condemned Northumberland and she has freed Courtenay. True, he is not named in the Act of Succession, but he is male and has a good claim to the throne. Still," his frown deepened, "be careful, my love. Be very careful that you give no sign of planning any act against her."

"I almost wish I could stay on my own lands."

"No, you must not do that. When the glow of being chosen queen fades, Mary will remember that you could be a danger to her. Others may speak against you and Mary will be quick to believe that you are hiding so that you may foment plots against her. You must show Mary and the Court that you are a dutiful subject and a loving sister."

"She will press me to convert to Catholicism."

Harry was silent, biting his lower lip gently. "I think you will need to agree to that and go to Mass. Just do it as privately as possible or in the presence of those who are already Catholics—and I do not mean those who have converted to keep their offices. I mean those closest to Mary and those who you are sure clung to the old rite even while they attended reformist churches."

Elizabeth shuddered and tears glittered in her eyes. "I always loved being at Court. Even when Somerset glared at me and tried to make me unwelcome, Edward and I would manage to exchange a few words and laugh with our eyes. Now, I dread it. There will be no one to laugh with."

"No, love, I fear there will not. At least, not anyone safe. And if Mary is determined to make England Catholic again, I greatly fear there will be nothing to laugh about."

"I am frightened," Elizabeth whispered.

Harry shook his head. "Do not let yourself be frightened. Fear will drive you into making mistakes, into hiding yourself when you should be standing boldly beside the queen so the Court and the people see you as her heir. Think of the fact that Mary's nature was always gentle and kind, and she remembers how much you loved her when you were a child."

"Let me at least know you are safe, Da, not chasing Evil."

"No, no. Do not trouble your head about me. And remember that you are never really alone. Aleneil will bind an air spirit to you that can summon us if you face any real threat. Denno is making amulets so that we can come to you, wherever you are." Harry touched the gun and the sword, his good-natured face suddenly hard and grim. "You have nothing to fear. Da will protect you."

Chapter 13

Albertus's fears that Vidal or Aurilia would detect his desire to see Elizabeth on the throne were wasted. It was not until August that Vidal arrived at Otstargi's house prepared to interest himself in the affairs of England. A strange eruption of trouble, of domains damaged and deaths Vidal would not have ordered, had kept him busy Underhill.

To Vidal's intense surprise, the perpetrator was Dakari, hardly more than a shadow before the cataclysmic event that had changed him. Nor was Vidal pleased to learn that *he* was the indirect cause of Dakari's new power. Vidal understood from Dakari's description of the symbols scribed on the stone in the inner chamber of Alhambra and later defaced that the large stone had been an altar.

"Oh it was a wonderful thing," Dakari said, licking his loose lips and staring boldly at Vidal. "I had sent Wahib and Wahiba away and at first I was afraid, but later there was a scent to it as sweet as putrid meat. The stone had turned pale, as if it were weak." He laughed. "I suppose then I was more afraid of you than of what was under the stone or in it. I went close and spoke to It, telling It what we had done and what we wished to do for It, but It would not answer. So I got angry, and I slapped the stone. It struck back like a thousand bolts of earthly lightning."

A wild laugh rang out and Dakari's hand, suddenly elongated

and tipped with three-inch-long claws, swiped at Vidal. The master of Caer Mordwyn did not even flinch, only lashed out with a rope of force and caught the arm above the wrist and above the elbow. Vidal had eons of practice in dealing with inimical creatures.

He remembered how he himself had been captured by the mist. It was not because the mist was so strong and he was so weak but because he had been so surprised that for just that crucial moment he had not resisted. Vidal was not sure just how strong the Evil that possessed Dakari was, but he could see no point in an open confrontation with an enemy of unknown strength. While the Evil within Dakari was shocked by the failure of Its attempt to harm him, he sealed It into a self-reflecting shield. Now whatever force the Evil projected would reflect back upon Itself.

In fact, Vidal had been considerably amused by the various shocks and wounds It inflicted on Dakari—he had *not* been amused by Dakari's new found power and insolence when he first caught him. But the punishment soon stopped; apparently the Evil was Itself subject to the pain inflicted on Its host. When It was quiet Vidal thought it might be useful to learn how the Evil had moved itself.

"So you laid your hand on the altar. What happened then?"

"The world ended!" Dakari breathed. "Then It was born anew in lightnings and thunders—and I too was born anew. I had such power! I threw away Aurilia's stupid amulets. I dealt with Wahib and Wahiba and others, too. I will deal with you when I get loose."

To that Vidal made no reply. Apparently the Evil was as stupid as Dakari. But Vidal knew he needed time to consider the best use for the Evil, and he had time enough now that the once-shadowy Sidhe was under unbreakable bonds. A fine resource, but not to be used in haste, without thought, lest it be wasted.

While Vidal hunted Dakari, he had become aware that the emanations of anguish and anger from the mortal world were sadly reduced. He had barely been able to draw enough power to fix the spell on Dakari. Vidal had forgotten that for a while after Mary's accession, everyone would be joyous and the power coming from fear and misery would diminish. It was time and more than time to visit the mortal world and make trouble.

Once he turned his mind to mortal affairs, Vidal remembered Albertus bringing news of Mary's victory; he was amused all over again by how possessive Aurilia was of her silly mortal. But as he stepped from the Gate in Otstargi's house, he frowned. That mortal bore a sense of ill will. Vidal grinned; imagine that helpless creature daring to feel resentment. When he was ready—and Aurilia had annoyed him enough—he would squash her pet like a bug.

The good mood that thought engendered was reinforced when he went to the table in Otstargi's office and found half a dozen messages from Rich and one from Ambassador Renard. At first Vidal considered ignoring the messages from Rich, but the man was active among Mary's Council. He might still be useful. It was from Rich he had learned of Mary's dependence on the Imperial ambassador. Rich might have lost much of his power, but he still knew what was going on at Court and could pass that informa-tion on. Vidal sent a message with a civil apology, saying he had been abroad unexpectedly, and making an appointment with Rich for that evening.

After a little thought, Vidal picked up the note from Renard and studied it. He then checked to make sure his Otstargi disguise was perfect and set off for the Imperial residence. This once, he would need to forget he was a prince Underhill and act humble in order to catch and bind the man.

The seal on the message from Renard gained him entry into the embassy. Vidal was even prepared to bow and say he would come again if Renard was not present, but he was fortunate. Renard was in the embassy. However, Jacques de Marnix, Sieur de Thoulouse, Renard's superior in birth if not in understanding, had Vidal brought to the embassy office to ask sharp questions.

Alone as they were, Vidal easily solved the problem with one sharp thrust into Marnix's mind. Vidal then knew exactly what Marnix thought the situation was, and Marnix himself went off to fetch Renard. Having done so, he bowed himself out.

Renard was no fool. He knew Marnix, knew that what Marnix had done was totally unnatural. Renard lowered his eyes to hide his thoughts and the ruby ring, glowing now like a hot coal, caught his gaze; his eyes widened and his mouth opened. Vidal struck.

"Sit down in your usual place," Vidal said softly, and began to rummage through Renard's mind.

He was gentle in his seeking. As time distanced him from his years of imprisonment, his natural imperiousness was coming back. However, he still remembered that force could not always get what he wanted. When he took control of Marnix, Vidal had seen Marnix's blended contempt and envy of Renard and understood that Marnix would damage Renard if he could. Thus, if Renard behaved in any way strangely or lost an iota of his sharpness, Marnix would send word of his failing to the emperor and have Renard recalled.

Gently, then, Vidal wiped all suspicion of Otstargi from Renard's mind and replaced it with a measured respect for the sorcerer's good will and astuteness. He reached across the table, touched the ruby ring, and reinforced and altered the spell of compulsion. Now the ring would compel Renard to seek Otstargi only when Vidal wanted to talk to Renard; unless Vidal activated it with a thought it would be no more than a beautiful ruby ring.

Now Vidal needed to decide whether he should implant the idea that Elizabeth must die into Renard's mind as a fixed, unbreakable conviction or tell him that Otstargi had foreseen many futures, in all of which by varying means and most often by doing nothing at all, Elizabeth caused Mary's reign to be overthown.

Vidal would have preferred to fix Elizabeth's necessary death into Renard's mind, but he dared not do it. Renard needed to be able to convince Mary to have Elizabeth executed and to convince her he needed to be flexible, to argue the pros and cons of letting Elizabeth survive. Once a compulsion to cause Elizabeth's death was fixed into Renard's mind, his ability to reason on the subject would be gone. Vidal grimaced. Otstargi would need to convince Renard rather than tamper with the ambassador's mind.

Having released his hold on Renard's mind, Vidal nodded, and as if Renard had asked why he had come, said, "I am glad you were willing to see me, Ambassador. Perhaps you do not believe in foreseeing or think it a sin, but without any asking on my part, indeed, when I was thinking about matters of trade and weather, for that is what most of my clients desire to know about, again and again I have seen . . . what I would rather not have seen."

For a long moment Renard was quite still. Vidal felt a faint anxiety that he had damaged something in the man's mind, but then the ambassador's lips thinned and he cleared his throat.

"You have seen something pertaining to a realm? To mine?"

Vidal shook his head. "This one, England. For several weeks I have kept silent, but I admire Queen Mary and desire her to have a long and fruitful reign."

"You have seen some threat to the queen? But I know you have contacts in the Court. Why did you not go to them?"

"Because I dare not speak of this to any Englishman, most particularly any officer of the Court. What I have seen is treason to see, treason to speak of."

Renard blinked and drew a breath. Vidal saw his mind take in the word treason, saw his thought that only foreseeing anything concerning the royal family was treason, but . . . Softly, gently, Vidal inserted a tendril to nudge Renard's half-formed thought into certainty; what the sorcerer had seen was about Elizabeth.

"Ah," Renard said, "but if what you have seen concerns England, to speak of it would not be treason in my land. And, in this house, you are on Imperial soil."

"Yes, my lord, that is true," Vidal agreed, forcing an expression of deep anxiety onto Otstargi's features. "But if you leave this house and mention my name when you speak of the matter, I am like to be hung, drawn, and quartered. I am afraid I am a fool for coming here, but with Queen Mary's reign so new and facing so many dangers and my great desire to make that reign sound and lasting, I have taken my life in my hands and come."

Renard shrugged. "But if I cannot use what you tell me, what good does your coming to me do?"

"Oh, no, my lord," Vidal said, shaking his head vigorously. "Of course you must use what I have seen in any way that will help the queen. I only beg you not to use my name, if any should ask why you advise what you advise."

"Ah." Vidal could see Renard struggle against a smile, as if he found amusing the idea of admitting he was using information from a charlatan crystal gazer. "No," he continued when he had mastered his expression. "I can promise you sincerely, even give you my oath on my honor, never to use your name."

"Thank you!" Vidal said fervently while needing to struggle against laughter himself. "It is . . . I have seen a dozen, no more, premature ends to the queen's reign. I have seen this caused by rebellion, I have seen this caused by the queen's illness owing to anguish, I have seen this caused by assassination . . . There is no need for me to detail the causes but only . . ." Vidal took a deep breath as if he were nerving himself to continue against his fear, and blurted, "Every disaster was caused by Lady Elizabeth."

To Vidal's great pleasure, Renard did not look shocked. He merely nodded his head. "I am not surprised," he said. "Even about the vision of assassination. And I will make you a rich man if you can tell me how she does it and how we can stop her."

"Alas, my lord—" Vidal shook his head again, but gently this time as with resignation "—most often the lady has done nothing at all. In one vision or another she has actually conspired with rebels, but most often she does *not* encourage them and sometimes does not even know what they are doing. It is her very existence that is a fatal danger to Queen Mary."

"Ah . . . so I have always thought, Master Otstargi. I cannot say that I believe in your visions, but common sense raises the same specters in my far from fantastical mind. If you wish to be truly useful, tell me what to do about this."

Vidal leaned forward earnestly. "The queen trusts you. She trusts you far more than she trusts any of her own ministers or courtiers. Do not mince your words about the danger to her that Lady Elizabeth's existence poses. You cannot repeat what you think often enough. And if she shrinks from kin-slaying, say that it is common knowledge that Elizabeth was not Henry's daughter but the product of some illicit contact."

Renard uttered an impatient snort. "You have nothing new."

"New? You need only tell her it is her uncle's will, that the Emperor Charles wants her freed from her sister's contamination."

Renard jerked back, away from Vidal. "I would not dare. The emperor of course hopes for a long reign for Mary and that she will soon marry and produce an heir, but Charles is a cautious man. Until there is an heir of the queen's body, if any ill befall Queen Mary, the emperor insists Elizabeth must inherit the throne."

"But she is a heretic!" Vidal protested. "She will bring back the heretical religion."

"In this case, England's faith must come second to a more important problem. The next heir after Elizabeth is Mary of Scots—she who is betrothed to the heir to the French throne. It would be a disaster for the Empire to have the King of France as consort to the Queen of England."

Vidal was not terribly interested in mortal affairs unless they pertained directly to eliminating Elizabeth. He had mentioned Elizabeth's preference for the reformist rite because in Mary's reign it would be anathema. He had not realized until that moment it might not be enough to counter the complication caused by enmities on the continent. What Renard had said meant that Emperor Charles might order Renard to *protect* Elizabeth.

Vidal now knew he would need more than reason to force Renard to continue insisting on Elizabeth's death when political disaster to the Empire might come of it. No matter. Vidal cared nothing about the Empire. Elizabeth must die. He froze Renard again, reversed his decision not to tamper with Renard's mind and impressed on it the substance of Otstargi's "visions": to ensure the stability of Mary's rule, Elizabeth must be dead.

Vidal had to strain for power to work the spell and he feared it might not be strong enough; worse, the power he used could not be restored in the mortal world. He was sick and empty by the time he had inserted into Renard's mind an end to their conversation and Renard's dismissal of Otstargi. Also Vidal was dissatisfied with the fact that he had needed to use magic on Renard. Setting a spell on the man would make it possible for Oberon or Titania to find the traces of his interference in Renard's mind.

Still, all in all, Vidal was well enough pleased with his morning's work. The likelihood of Oberon or Titania looking for traces of his influence on Renard was minimal, and anyhow what they would find was an image of Otstargi, a mortal sorcerer. Besides, there were many good reasons based in mortal politics for Queen Mary to be rid of her embarrassing sister. However disappointed Titania was over the loss of what she thought of as a golden age, she would have no reason to suspect Vidal had a hand in Elizabeth's death.

Vidal was even more pleased with his evening's interview with Rich. He had expected the man to demand a way to retrieve his position as Chancellor, and possibly need to use a spell to remove that desire. Fortunately Rich did not want that at all. He had been seriously ill at the end of 1550 and was content now with a lesser role. What he wanted was to be assured through Otstargi's visions that Mary would not continue her present policy of toleration. He wished to hear that the queen would restore Catholicism and that the old faith would remain the official religion.

Vidal was delighted. He did not need to use any more magic, which was at a low ebb in him, and he was able to direct another member of the Council to urge Mary to execute Elizabeth. He told Rich that Mary would restore the old faith but that if she died or was overthrown, Elizabeth would bring back the reformed religion. Rich would need to watch Elizabeth closely, expose her misdeeds, and be prepared to urge her execution.

Rich's enthusiastic agreement was very satisfying. After using magic on Renard, Vidal had Gated back Underhill to restore his strength, but the Gating had depleted him further and the flow of power in Caer Mordwyn was very thin. Vidal ground his teeth and swore by the Great Evil that he would be rid of Elizabeth. If she came to the throne the Dark Court would be starved, as he was now, throughout her reign.

After dealing with Rich, Vidal lingered in London long enough to witness the meeting of the sisters. He hoped that Elizabeth's coming accompanied by near two thousand armed horsemen, all decked out in Tudor colors of green and white, might elicit a preemptive strike from Mary to deal with the bold, threatening chit. However, Elizabeth dismissed more than half of her following when she heard that Mary was only accompanied by about eight hundred. "Clever," Vidal snarled when he heard. She must die.

Worse, when Mary and Elizabeth finally met, Vidal's hopes were further dashed. In her joy, in her firm belief that her ascension to the throne was the work of God, Mary feared nothing and loved the whole world. She embraced Elizabeth with tearful tenderness. What was more, she held her sister by the hand in all the processions and ceremonies, keeping Elizabeth beside her and marking Elizabeth's preeminence as heir. The crowd was enchanted. All along the route of the procession, over and over the people roared "God save Queen Mary."

One of Mary's first acts when she entered London was to free the political prisoners who had been held in the Tower by Northumberland. The duke of Norfolk, who had escaped beheading only because Henry VIII died before he could sign the order of execution and because neither Somerset nor Northumberland wanted to deal with the problem he raised, was scarcely surprised by another miracle. Mary, not only seemed to forgive him for sitting on the court that declared her mother's marriage incestuous, but favored his petition to Parliament to reverse his attainder. The petition was granted and he was restored as duke of Norfolk on August third.

He was also named to the Council, which was not surprising since few of Mary's household had any experience of national or foreign affairs. Norfolk was very willing to serve the new Queen but was disturbed by the large, unwieldy Council. Mary had not dismissed or even weeded out Edward's Council; most had been retained and she had added to them the members of her own household who had served her so long and so faithfully.

That was reasonable enough but instead of learning from the experienced members, Mary's faithful suspected those newly sworn to abhor Northumberland's plots and to have been Catholic in their hearts. Norfolk did not blame Mary's household members; he himself knew that most of Northumberland's men did not care a pin for the queen's policies or religion. Their main purpose was to retain their power and escape punishment, but many *were* experienced and efficient officials.

The confusion and growing animosity between the two parties wore on Norfolk. He was no longer young and had lived a hard life. Moreover, Norfolk's own temper was not mild and his preeminence owing to his "martyrdom" aroused envy. Often, having done what he could in the Court, he retired to his own house to find a little peace and quiet. That was why, about the middle of September, when Lord Denno called at Norfolk House only intending to leave notice of his good wishes with one of the duke's servants, he was told to wait while the servant determined whether Norfolk wished to see him.

Before Denoriel could decide on which chair in the entry hall to seat himself, the servant was back with an invitation to present his good wishes in person. Eyes a little widened with surprise, he followed the man up a set of stairs and into a chamber that was certainly a private parlor. Norfolk, seated in a cushioned chair near a hearth filled with handsome ferns rather than a fire at this season, spoke at once. First he told the servant to bring wine and cakes and then he addressed Denoriel directly.

"You will pardon me for not rising to greet you, Lord Denno. I am always tired these days."

Denoriel bowed and smiled. "Of course, Your Grace. You have been given a heavy burden by the queen, a wise act for there are few better able to help steer the ship of state. But I must say that, new burden or not, I am happy to see you looking so much better than the last time we met."

The last time they had met Norfolk had still been a prisoner in the Tower under sentence of death. An odd expression, one

Denoriel would have said was guilt—except that he had never seen much beside temper and pride on the face before—drew Norfolk's brows together and his lips down.

"I should have written at once when I was released to thank you for your many kindnesses to me when I was a prisoner," he said. "I hope now I will be able to do something to show my gratitude."

Denoriel was astonished. Apparently the years Norfolk had spent with the threat of the axe hanging over him had had an effect. Even as a prisoner, Norfolk had seemed to take any offer of service as his due, requiring no gratitude or thanks on his part. Now Denoriel realized that had only been the old man's pride, all he had to uphold him. Denoriel could not speak of that, however; he could do no more than bow and shake his head. Then his surprise increased because Norfolk gestured toward a chair opposite his own and bade him sit. And when the servant came in, he bade him pour wine for them both and give a goblet to Denoriel.

"I thank Your Grace from the bottom of my heart," Denoriel said, "but I have as little interest in politics now as I ever had. I did not expect to speak to Your Grace, only to leave a message of good wishes." He bowed his head in thanks as he took a sip of wine. Then he laughed, "And, of course, to remind Your Grace that I am still seeking your custom and that of any friend you wish to recommend—" Suddenly he stopped speaking and drew a sharp breath. "Your Grace, I have just bethought me that there might be something you can do, not necessarily for me but for the merchants of England in general—if you think it wise and proper, of course."

"Yes?"

Now Norfolk sounded as if he regretted admitting he owed Lord Denno a favor. Denoriel looked into his face, holding his eyes. "The queen is Catholic. That is her choice and her right and no one questions it, but there has been some feeling among the men of the Hanse that she is avoiding buying from them. I do not know if this is true, but they say she favors only Spanish merchants. You know, Your Grace, that it would be a mistake to offend the Hanse. I would guess that they will make up any insult they feel or profits they lose to the Spaniards by raising the price of what is essential and cannot be purchased from Catholic merchants—like salt."

"I said I owed you a favor, Lord Denno, not that you could threaten me."

"Your Grace—" Denoriel shook his head "—I do not intend any threat." He took another sip of wine. "I only wish you to know what I have heard when I have visited the Steelyard. This is nothing to do with *my* business; I do not buy or sell salt and if the Hanse does not sell furs and amber and goldwork to the Court, likely their prices to me will be lower. Nor, to speak the truth, do I care what rite is used to worship y—" Denoriel swallowed down the rest of the word "your" and simply added "—God. I leave that to the priest of my parish church. I am satisfied with whatever the government decrees."

Norfolk was as little interested in what rite was used as Denoriel. He gave the moments Denoriel took to explain to polish up rusty memories and realized that Lord Denno had not cast off the spots of a leopard for the stripes of a tiger. Denno was, as he always had been, eager only for peace and stability in the realm. Since he dealt mainly in luxuries and wine, upheaval of any kind was bad for his business. Even the rich did not buy Turkey carpets and jewelry in the midst of a civil war. And offending the powerful Hanse trading guild could be dangerous to a shaky reign.

"I beg your pardon, Lord Denno. I should have known better than to accuse you of threat. Fortunately I am sure that the queen does not mean to be prejudiced against the Hanse merchants because they are mostly Protestant. She just naturally inclines to those who speak her beloved mother's language and attend Mass with her. So, again I must thank you for a word in time. I will speak with the queen and explain why the Hanse must not be neglected."

"No need for pardon," Denoriel said, smiling and setting aside his now-empty goblet. "I understand that it might have seemed I was trying to interfere in a policy selected by the queen."

"Not at all. Not at all. Queen Mary hardly thinks in terms of policy yet, and certainly not about what she buys or from whom." Then Norfolk frowned and set aside his own goblet. "As I recall you were once a favorite with Lady Elizabeth. Do you still have the lady's ear?"

Denoriel laughed. "Not when she is at Court. Lady Elizabeth has no time for an old merchant when she is surrounded by courtiers. I am still somewhat welcome to her when she is in one of her country houses. Then anyone from London is welcome for the news they carry."

"Too bad." Norfolk frowned. "I thought you might drop a word in her ear. She has professed herself willing to take the queen's faith and become a Catholic, but she is so private in her devotions that few know her change of heart. It would please Queen Mary greatly if her sister would show more enthusiasm for religion."

Denoriel bit his lip. "I wish I could be of help, but the truth is that I have not seen or spoken with Lady Elizabeth since she left Hatfield on the twenty-eighth or twenty-ninth of July. I do not think, however, that Lady Elizabeth's outward lack of enthusiasm should be taken as a sign of any inner lack of conviction. She was never one to make a great show of her faith. More could be determined by what the lady reads than what she says."

"Ah. That is very helpful."

"I will try to get word to her that she should be more open about her new understanding and belief, but for a merchant to request and receive permission to visit the Lady Elizabeth . . . A friendship with me would not redound to her credit."

"Hmmm. I will see what I can do," Norfolk said. "I will have my secretary send you a note."

Chapter 14

The joy the people felt at having their country safe in the hands of Henry VIII's heir, was nothing compared with the joy Pasgen felt when he was able to restore Mary's guard to his life and position. Pasgen was careful to record into the man's mind all of the dangers and threats he had helped Mary survive. The guard was a much wiser, more alert, and more cautious man when Pasgen was done with him. In addition, he was filled with pride at his accomplishments and "knowing" what he had accomplished steadied his courage and gave him confidence that would stand him in good stead.

All but singing hosannas, Pasgen hugged Rhoslyn hard as he stood in front of the small Gate he had created, assured her he would be at the meeting on mortal Tuesday night, and fled Underhill. He had set the Gate for the empty house so that Rhoslyn could use it. Not that he would have minded having Rhoslyn Gate to his domain, but then she would have needed to thread the tortuous route that concealed his home from Vidal and his creatures to get anywhere.

As it turned out, Pasgen felt he had been rewarded for his consideration of his sister. At the empty house he found a message from Hafwen asking rather querulously where in the Empty Spaces he had been recently. Involuntarily, Pasgen smiled. Hafwen had more spice on her tongue than most Bright Court Sidhe.

He had been tired when he was finished with Mary's guardsman and had intended to Gate to his own domain from the empty house and do something calm and restful until the dull ache of the iron ubiquitous to the mortal world had leached from his bones. By the second time he read Hafwen's message and ascertained that the seal was truly hers and not some Dark Court trap, he found he wasn't tired and aching at all.

One of the least mindless servants of the empty house asked whether to transmit new messages to his domain or whether he was returning to the mortal world. For one moment Pasgen wondered at the question and then realized he was still dressed as Mary's guardsman. A gesture decked him out in soft black boots with a dagger down each, fitted black trews, a full-sleeved white silk shirt under a long, black, silver-brocaded vest cinched at the waist with a broad black leather belt which supported his silver rapier.

Pasgen looked at himself, assessed his inner strength, and then looked around at the house itself and the patiently waiting servant. Something was different. There was more power drifting around and the servant looked somehow more substantial, as if he were healthier and his clothing fit better and was brighter.

"Transmit, then," the servant said.

"No, hold them. I will stop here before I go home . . . if I go home, and Lady Rhoslyn will be stopping here too."

His reply reminded him that Rhoslyn still did not have a home. She had been staying at the empty house when she spent any extended time Underhill and he had been staying there with her so she should not be alone. As he walked from the empty house to one of the Gates nearby, he grinned and wondered whether he should stop doing that. He suspected if he assured Rhoslyn he had other business and could not give her his company that Harry FitzRoy would be only too glad to take his place.

A bit to his surprise, he found that a pleasant thought. He had always hated Rhoslyn's few associations with any of the Dark Court Sidhe and had wondered uncomfortably from time to time whether he had unnatural feelings about his sister. Now, having spent so much time in her company, he was convinced he had only feared for her. He could not imagine a Dark Sidhe who would not hurt her. Harry was something else altogether.

Pasgen hesitated before stepping into the Gate. What was

happening to him? Not long ago he would have found the company of Harry FitzRoy, who was of an exceptionally good and noble nature, boring and sickening. Now he looked forward to their meetings on mortal Tuesday. If it wasn't one kind of devilment Harry had in mind it was another, and his devilments hurt no one and usually left sweetness behind. Pasgen actually hoped Rhoslyn would find Harry's open admiration something she wished to return.

Shaking his head, Pasgen ordered himself to mind his own affairs and leave Rhoslyn's to her. His problem at the moment was how to respond to Hafwen's message. No air spirit would come near him or obey him; Pasgen lowered his eyes and suppressed a sigh. How foolish and cruel he had been to destroy that little one only for his momentary convenience.

He had regretted the bright little dancer's death even as he dealt it and he regretted it more bitterly now. But it was done and he had no way to send a message to anyone in the Bright Court. He would not be welcome in Avalon or Logres himself and he could not send an imp; it would not survive a moment—and he would not send an imp to Hafwen in any case. He stared at the low Gate platform, then stepped up on it smiling. He could go to Gaenor in Elfhame Elder-Elf. That elfhame cared nothing for Dark or Bright and Gaenor would know how to find Hafwen or send her a message.

As he stepped off the Gate platform onto the soft, white-flower starred moss of Elfhame Elder-Elf, Pasgen sighed. It was no small walk to the homes of the elder Sidhe. The last times he had come he had been with Gaenor and her beautiful elvensteed Nuin had been waiting to carry them to Gaenor's house. Pasgen drew a quick breath over a sharp pang of mingled joy and pain. Nuin had permitted him to ride; experiences he would always treasure. Then he laughed at himself, shrugged, and set out hoping he would find Gaenor at home.

Despite the apparent distance between the Gate and the dwellings of Elfhame Elder-Elf, Pasgen made almost as quick progress afoot as he would have astride Nuin. He realized as the ground flowed away under his feet that some spell must have been set to carry those afoot swiftly to the dwellings. He frowned slightly, wondering if that was safe. There were evil creatures Underhill that could and did attack the Sidhe.

But when he reached Gaenor's house, the door opened before he could call a greeting and the thought came to him that the spell of swift travel might have been keyed to him. Surprised, he stood in the doorway. In that moment Gaenor's voice, tart with disapproval, came out to him, and she followed in person.

"Well, where in the Empty Spaces *have* you been? Hafwen and I have sent messages all over Underhill."

Pasgen blinked. It was strange but oddly pleasant to have anyone but Rhoslyn care about him. "I have not been Underhill, except for a few hours to restore myself, and then I was in my own domain which is sealed against messages. I have been in the mortal world, helping Rhoslyn guard Lady Mary."

Gaenor snorted. "I suppose that was important. It is a long time since I bothered with mortal folk—except Harry, of course."

"I am no expert in mortal affairs," Pasgen admitted, "but Rhoslyn—well, she is fond of Lady Mary and wished to protect her. Also, she and all the rest of them are convinced that Lady Mary must reign as queen of Logres before Lady Elizabeth can come to the throne. The FarSeers all agree that Elizabeth's reign will bring a golden age of mortal achievement that will flow over us with untold riches."

Gaenor's lips parted, most likely to make another sharp remark, but then she closed her mouth and her face stilled as she looked back through time. "Yes," she sighed, "I remember such times. Once there was Atlantis and then those who worshiped the Bull God." She was silent for a moment, sighing again, then shaking herself. "Be that as it may, right now something very, very strange is taking place in the self-aware mist."

"More creations?" Pasgen tilted his head inquisitively and his eyes brightened with interest.

Before answering Gaenor looked up at a particularly tiny air spirit that was dancing among the beams that supported her roof. "Find Hafwen," she murmured to the little thing when it descended to dance on a finger she held out. It disappeared promptly, and she looked at Pasgen. "Yes . . . No . . . More creations but no living beings . . . Unless you count grass and trees and such."

"Grass and trees?" Pasgen looked away at the large window that showed a carefully cultivated garden, but he was not seeing that. "Could the mist be trying to fashion a true domain for . . . for whom? For itself? Can it wish to take living form?"

Slowly Gaenor shook her head. "I do not think so. The dolls it made did not seem to have that kind of life. We instinctively called them dolls. They did not have even so much life as the constructs Rhoslyn makes."

"Some of those have too much life," Pasgen said, grimacing. "They think. And Rhoslyn becomes fond of them and weeps as if they were Sidhe when they are damaged or destroyed."

"She is a great maker," Gaenor said. "Far greater than I. It is a pity she is so bound up with mortal affairs. I think that Rhoslyn might discover what that mist is seeking and likely could control it."

Pasgen had been smiling rather smugly at the compliment Gaenor gave his sister, but lost his smile and shook his head nervously at the idea of exposing Rhoslyn to the self-willed mist. He uttered an uneasy laugh.

"Rhoslyn is too softhearted. If she felt the mist's need, it is more likely that she would aid and abet the accursed thing."

"The mist is not accursed . . . yet."

Both Pasgen and Gaenor turned to see Hafwen in the doorway.

"Yet?" Pasgen echoed, and then more sharply, "Do you sense a growing evil in it?"

"No, but . . . Do not laugh. I think the mist is lonely."

"Lonely?" Pasgen felt a fool, constantly echoing Hafwen's last word, but she smiled at him and he found himself smiling back and protesting, "But it gets plenty of company. You and Gaenor visit it often, and until I was so taken up with protecting Lady Mary, I came also."

"Yes," Hafwen agreed, but her voice was doubtful. "Mayhap I should have said the mist is bored. All we do when we come is tell it to be quiet and rest."

"Ah." Pasgen almost sympathized. He hated to be told to give over a project and rest. He pursed his lips. "I think I understand why you said it is not accursed *yet*. Idle minds are easily trapped into doing mischief."

"Not itself doing mischief, but possibly it might be directed to do mischief," Gaenor said. "When I first said that something strange was taking place and told you about the grass and trees, you asked whether the mist was trying to build a domain and then asked for whom. That, I think is a key question. Who will direct the character of the domain the mist wishes to build? Who will live in it?"

As Gaenor asked those questions, a host of ideas swirled about in Pasgen's mind. His first thought, following from Gaenor's comment about Rhoslyn controlling the mist, was that Rhoslyn needed a domain. And it was true that Rhoslyn in her making did control the mists from which she made her constructs. Caution woke in him. His second thought was whether the "offer" of a domain was really a subtle trap. When one entered the "promised land" would the mist absorb the Sidhe who took the offer?

"I think before we talk any more about this," Pasgen said. "I had better go with you and see what the mist is doing."

To that, Gaenor and Hafwen agreed. Outside of Gaenor's house two elvensteeds waited. Pasgen blinked and looked away. He desired an elvensteed with a kind of desperate hunger, as if something within him was empty and needed to be filled, and then he thought of Torgen and felt disloyal. Oh, Torgen was vicious, but not really to Pasgen although he snapped and snarled. Pasgen knew that if the not-horse had really desired to hurt him, it could likely have disemboweled him before he or Rhoslyn could have destroyed it. And Torgen *was* strong and beautiful . . .

"Will the seven-league boot spell take me back to the Gate?" Pasgen asked Gaenor.

"No, no. Nuin will carry you."

"Or Talfan," Hafwen said, smiling. "You are on Bright Court business, after all."

As she spoke, the double saddle formed on Talfan's back. Pasgen bowed and thanked the elvensteed as Hafwen mounted. Talfan's eyes, the same blue as Hafwen's were today, fixed on Pasgen and studied him intently. Nervously, Pasgen bowed again.

"Don't make such a ceremony of it," Hafwen said. "Since the saddle is there, she intends for you to ride."

She extended a hand, and he came up, swinging his right leg over Talfan's back. Joy suffused Pasgen. He swallowed. Torgen had no joy, no emotion. It was not the poor not-horse's fault. When Rhoslyn made the not-horses, joy was no part of her life, and in any case she would not have thought to instill emotion into her making. Not until she made a simulacrum to replace Harry and had needed something close enough to real life to fool the child's nurses and other attendants . . . Thank the Great Mother that that had gone wrong!

"Thinking hard, are you?" Hafwen asked.

Pasgen realized that they had been mounted far longer than an elvensteed usually took to reach the Gate. "No," he said, then laughed. "Yes, I was thinking hard, but not about the self-willed mist . . . or maybe in a way I was thinking of that too. I was thinking of my sister and her makings."

"I met Richey once," Hafwen said, a faint frown creasing the skin of her brow. "That . . . that was marvelous . . . but dangerous."

"Very dangerous," Pasgen agreed. "Although she now knows that Richey lived much longer than she expected and died happy, I do not believe she will ever recover from that making." He shrugged. "She might as well have borne a child and had it die. In a way she still mourns him, but she will make no more like that."

On that last word they arrived at the Gate. Talfan stepped up on the platform. A moment of blackness and falling and they were on the platform of the Gate in the self-willed mist's domain. Pasgen's eyes widened and he slid off Talfan's back, looking out and then around.

Just beyond the Gate platform was grass . . . mortal-world grass. Pasgen stared down at it. There was no grass Underhill, except in a few domains like the Shepherd's Paradise, which Harry and Denoriel spoke of, where grass had been created specially. Underhill was carpeted by the white-flowered moss. How had the mist heard of grass? From whose mind had it come?

Pasgen started to step off the Gate platform, and two hands grasped at him. Hafwen had him on one side; Gaenor on the other.

"Is that really grass?" he asked.

"How would I know?" Gaenor said. "It must be some five thousand years since I last visited the mortal world."

"And I have never gone," Hafwen said.

"I need to know," Pasgen said. "Keep watch and ready a strong shield to hold back the mist if necessary." He stood still a moment, looking out into the mist. "I do not think any defense will be necessary."

"Why do you need to know?" Gaenor asked suspiciously. She had been warned repeatedly by Rhoslyn about Pasgen's insatiable curiosity, which regularly drove him into dangerous situations.

"There is no grass Underhill," Pasgen said, "so from where did the mist learn of grass? And why is it here?"

Almost as if in answer to Pasgen's question, both elvensteeds stepped off the platform onto the grass and began to graze. Pasgen looked from Hafwen to Gaenor and back again. "Could it have learned from the elvensteeds?

Both women shook their heads in unison. "Who knows what the elvensteeds can do? In all the years Nuin and I have been together, I have found no reason, no pattern in what she can do . . . or, perhaps, will do, and what she will not."

"That is true for me also," Hafwen said. "I am sure that they are capable of speaking to us, yet I have never heard of any Sidhe who has had direct communication with an elvensteed."

"Pictures," Pasgen offered. "I think Denoriel said he had once received a picture from Miralys."

"I would be grateful for so much," Gaenor said rather dryly, but she was looking out toward the mist, which was, as it had been for some while, well withdrawn from the Gate platform.

Pasgen laughed. "Then I don't need to waste any more thought on that solution to the problem. Still, I want to go down and see for myself. I don't think there's any danger, but do ready a shield."

Again Pasgen looked from Gaenor to Hafwen. For a moment he got no response, then Gaenor sighed and Hafwen nodded. Pasgen smiled at them. Another moment and both women nodded; each had a shield ready.

The shields seemed a work of supererogation. As soon as Pasgen stepped off the Gate platform, the mist rolled farther back as if in invitation.

"Don't go, Pasgen," Hafwen called. "Come back. It is aware of you."

Pasgen started to turn back toward the Gate platform but stopped abruptly. The retreat of the mist had revealed a house . . . well, what was meant Pasgen was sure to be a dwelling of some sort. It was a weird mixture of cottage, manor-house, and palace. Oddly, the manor house and palace portions seemed to be better defined than the frontmost part, which had a thatched roof and small windows with diamond-shaped panes of glass. Behind that rose the two story height of a brick-wrought manor. Suddenly Pasgen knew where he had seen that manor before; it was Elizabeth's manor of Hatfield. And behind that were the fanciful turrets that Pasgen knew could exist only Underhill and which he had last seen on the palace in Rhoslyn's domain.

At the front of the cottage was an area of grass broken by

a graveled path, to each side of which was what must be what
the mist thought were beds of flowers. Those, however, were not
individual plants but simply masses of color atop a mass of green.
The colors were familiar as, now that he looked more carefully,
was the cottage. Yes, Pasgen knew it. It was Gaenor's cottage in
Elfhame Elder-Elf.

The whole making was pathetic, as the gold- and red-haired
dolls had been pathetic. Pasgen took a step in the direction of
the "garden."

"Pasgen!" Hafwen's voice was high and urgent.

He turned at once, fearing that while his attention had been
on the "house" the mist was attempting to attack Hafwen and
Gaenor. However, there was not even a small wisp near the Gate
platform, and from the way Hafwen was stretching her hands
toward him, it was he she feared for.

"No, it's all right," Pasgen called back. "It's just . . . I really must
see what is inside that house thing."

"Pasgen, do not be a fool," Gaenor said. "It has set some kind
of trap to attract you. Come back here."

"The other creations, the gold-haired and red-haired dolls, were
no trap," Pasgen protested.

"No? What do you call what happened to Vidal Dhu?"

Pasgen laughed and shook his head. "I call it Vidal's fault. He
attacked the red-haired doll. I was near both those dolls several
times, once when a lion had disemboweled the gold-haired creature, and no ill befell me."

"Your sister will chop us both up into small pieces if you are
trapped here," Hafwen said.

He smiled at Hafwen, but shook his head. "I . . . it is trying so
hard," he said.

His voice was not quite steady as bitter memories washed over
him, bitter memories of the cold indifference and frequent cruelty
of his teachers of magic in the Dark Court. When he thought
back, it was not the cruelty, the punishments for failure or for
spells the teachers did not approve, that hurt him. It was the total
lack of interest in his successes and experiments.

If it had not been for his mother and Rhoslyn, he would have
turned to the Dark in truth, taking his only pleasure from the
pain and misery of others. But Llanelli had marveled over his
spell-casting, making him feel proud, and Rhoslyn had matched

him spell for spell—or if she could not do that, excelled in her own way by making.

Hafwen started to come down off the platform and Pasgen shouted for her to stop. "I don't think we should offer it two of us," he said. "You and Gaenor try to get across to it that if it does not let me go no one will ever come here again."

"He's right," Gaenor said. "I don't feel anything from it except . . . maybe . . . hope? But I don't think we should offer too much temptation."

"I've got shields up too," Pasgen said. "Believe me, I'm very good at shields. Living in the Dark Court tends to teach you that. If it tries to wrap me, I think I'd be able to wriggle free under the shield. And I'll be very careful not to damage anything. I promise I won't trample the flower beds or take anything from the house."

"Very well," Hafwen agreed reluctantly, "but don't stay too long." Then she sighed. "I know what is long to us may seem like ten breaths to you, but if you don't come out when I call, I'm going straight to Oberon and tell him about this."

Pasgen lifted a hand in salute and turned eagerly toward the graveled path, which obligingly extended itself in his direction. He drew a deep breath as he stepped onto it, but nothing happened, except that the gravel was soft and sort of flattened when he stepped on it.

"Ah," he said, "the look is right—did you take that from Elizabeth's mind?" He made an image of Elizabeth in his head. "But gravel is hard and sharp-edged."

There was a moment of disorientation as the path dissolved under him. Plainly the mist had no idea what hard and sharp-edged meant.

"Pasgen!"

He heard Gaenor's voice, tight with anxiety and turned around toward the Gate. "No, it's all right," he called. "I told it the path wasn't right, and it is correcting it."

But it couldn't correct without knowing how. Pasgen took another deep breath and kenned a handful of gravel. He had a moment of panic as he put the gravel on the . . . whatever he was standing on, hoping he wouldn't be buried in gravel in the next moment.

That did not happen. Ahead of him and behind him, but not where his feet were planted, gravel spread on a remade path. Pasgen let out the breath he had been holding and walked forward. He passed the blurred areas of color and green, keeping his mind carefully neutral. He simply did not know enough about flowers to try to image a bed of them or ken even one and he was afraid to criticize what he could not suggest a way to mend.

Then he was at the house. He reached for the doorknob, but it, like the gravel, was soft and deformed in his hand. There was no way it could be used to open the door.

"In?" he said.

The door melted away.

"Pasgen!" That was Hafwen. He turned toward the Gate again. "Don't you dare!" she called. "Don't you dare go in that house where we can't see you."

He might have tried to argue, but from the open doorway he could see that there was not much sense in going into the house. There did not seem to be any walls or any furniture. On the floor near one of the small windows was a patch of brightness, as if sunlight were shining through it. That must be an image the mist took from Gaenor's mind.

He looked into the empty space. "I can't help you any more now," he said. "I am not a maker. I have a sister who is a maker. I cannot bring her here to you now. She is doing something very important to the Sidhe. Oh, I am Sidhe as are those others on the Gate. As soon as I can, I will ask my sister to come here."

And suddenly, before him hung the image of Elizabeth he had offered when he asked about the gravel. For a moment he was frightened, but as soon as he reacted, the image disappeared and he was not bound; his shields felt no assault. Then he understood. He had been talking about bringing Rhoslyn and he had identified himself and Hafwen and Gaenor as Sidhe. The mist was asking about Elizabeth.

"Pasgen!" Hafwen called again.

"Wait. I'm quite free and I'll come in just a moment. I think I am communicating with the mist."

"I will count one hundred. Then you start back," Gaenor said.

Elizabeth. It was Elizabeth who had asked the mist to make a lion. That lion was not soft and easily deformed. It was so real a lion that it had killed two men and disemboweled the blond-haired doll. The kitten she wanted had also been real, real enough to trade for something in one of the markets.

"Elizabeth. You want Elizabeth?" The image of Elizabeth flashed briefly. "Elizabeth is mortal. She does not live with us Underhill. However, if she is allowed to visit again, I will try to bring her. I do not promise . . . as if you know what a promise is . . . but I will try. I must go now or my escort will do something very bad."

He turned and then gasped. There was a sudden resistance to his movement, a pressure on his shield. Before he could call up a counterspell or cry "Let me go," the pressure was gone. Pasgen completed his turn and began to walk toward the Gate. Nothing touched him.

When he stepped up onto the Gate platform, Gaenor said, "What happened? You started to turn toward us and suddenly stopped."

Pasgen hesitated. "You will believe I am quite mad," he said slowly, "but I think . . . I think the mist embraced me."

There was an absolute silence. Gaenor and Hafwen looked at each other, then both looked at Pasgen. He shrugged. The elvensteeds stopped grazing. Both mounted the Gate platform, but Talfan watched Pasgen again as she made the second saddle. Gaenor activated the Gate.

Elizabeth was growing more and more uneasy as the weeks passed. Several times since her "conversion" in September she believed attempts had been made on her life and neither she nor Lady Alana had any idea of who was guilty. Nonetheless, it was not fear of assassination that made her shiver in the December chill of the chapel. She ignored the all-too-familiar sounds of still another Mass and reviewed the steady disintegration of her relationship with her sister.

At the beginning of August Elizabeth had some hope that Mary would not insist on her conversion to Catholicism. Mary herself had been so tormented over her faith that Elizabeth thought she might have sympathy for another's conviction. This delusion lasted a little while, largely because the Emperor Charles, through Renard, advised Mary to move slowly in religious matters.

Mary was willing to take that advice because she was still convinced that all of England had suffered as she had. She truly believed that the moment they were released from forced acceptance of Protestantism the people would flock back to the Catholic rite with tears of joy. Even two weeks later when priests who tried to say Mass were assaulted, Mary issued a proclamation stating her intention to practice openly the faith she had held all her life but offering not to compel or constrain the consciences of others. She believed the people only needed a little time to consider before they embraced Catholicism once more.

At that time, buoyed up by the relief generated by Mary's warm welcome, Elizabeth hoped that if she made no show of her reformist tendencies and was sufficiently inconspicuous, Mary would ignore their differences. She really knew better but did not want to face the fact that it was impossible for the queen and her heir to worship by different rites. For a few days her false hopes were supported because the Imperial ambassadors convinced Mary that to give King Edward a Catholic funeral would result in riots.

Grudgingly Mary agreed that Archbishop Cranmer should be permitted to bury Edward in Westminster Abbey using the English funeral service, but she would not attend. To satisfy her conscience, Mary and her household would listen to a High Requiem Mass in the chapel of the White Tower on the day Edward was buried. Then, openly, in full Court, in her deep, loud voice, Mary invited Elizabeth to the Requiem Mass.

Elizabeth remembered her surprise, remembered staring, eyes and mouth open. She knew that Mary must at some time invite her to worship at a Mass and had all kinds of clever evasions worked out, but she had not expected Mary to try to make her commit herself so soon or so publicly or to use Edward's funeral as a trap. At least the shock had not frozen her mind and she made the shock work to her advantage. Elizabeth closed her mouth, swallowed, and allowed tears to flood her widened eyes.

"I cannot," Elizabeth choked out.

"Why *can* you not?" Mary asked, her voice louder and deeper than ever.

One could almost see the ears of the courtiers perk up as they heard Mary's emphasis; she was implying Elizabeth would not rather than could not.

"Because I loved him so," Elizabeth said, allowing her tears to overflow and her voice to catch on a sob, but making sure it carried clearly. "And because *Edward* would have hated a Mass."

Still weeping freely Elizabeth went down on her knees to show her submission. She was surprised at how hard it was. She had bowed to Edward without the smallest reservation, with a warm satisfaction. Now she was trembling with angry resistance—but no one realized that. Everyone thought she was shaking with grief.

Around her the Court sighed and murmured sympathy. Elizabeth's deep affection for her brother was well known; many of the Court had seen them together when Elizabeth visited, had heard their young king utter a rare laugh when his sister was with him.

"Your Majesty," Elizabeth cried, "wrong or right, Edward believed in the reformist rite. I could not . . . I could not pay homage to his memory with prayers he would have hated."

"So you will go to Westminster to see him buried with unhallowed prayers in an heretical rite?" Mary challenged.

Elizabeth would no more take up that challenge than try to fly. She would have liked to say a last fare well to her dear little brother but he was dead and could not be hurt, whereas *she* could be called traitor or heretic for defending Protestant belief to her fanatically Catholic sister.

"No, madam," she murmured. "I have no need to make a show of my loss. I did not see my father buried. I will mourn King Edward as I mourned King Henry, quietly, in my own chamber."

"Very well." Mary's voice was somewhat softer and she stretched out a hand to sign for Elizabeth to rise. But she did not touch her sister in sympathy or consolation, just walked away.

"That was very clever, indeed."

A man's voice just behind Elizabeth's shoulder. She started and turned her head. Kat and Lady Alana closed on her to help her to her feet. Over her shoulder she saw Stephen Gardiner, bishop of Winchester, smiling at her. It was not a pleasant smile.

Elizabeth's teeth snapped together. She did not need Bishop Gardiner explaining aloud in the hearing of those courtiers who were near them how skillfully she had avoided attendance at Mass without implying she herself objected to it. For the moment she had the Court's sympathy and she intended to keep it. The bishop was already urging Mary to depress Elizabeth's consequence. She owed him neither truth nor more courtesy than he offered her.

"Clever?" Elizabeth repeated in a shaken, puzzled voice.

She took a half step fully to face the bishop and stopped dead in her tracks. Perforce Gardiner had to stop too unless he wanted to push her aside, and that he dared not do; she was the queen's sister and the next highest lady in the land. The distance between them and Mary widened. The space was quickly filled by courtiers more desirous of being close to the queen than hearing the exchange between Gardiner and Elizabeth.

The movement of the courtiers kept Gardiner from making any comment to the queen on the plausibility of Elizabeth's remarks. She knew it would give him considerable satisfaction to spoil the small sympathy she had created between herself and Mary. Mary had been fond of Edward too, and seeing Elizabeth weep for him had moved her. Finally, the widening space between them decreased any danger of Mary again pressing Elizabeth to attend the Mass or asking any further questions.

Before the bishop could step around her or speak again, Elizabeth found a tone of quiet outrage, stiffening and drawing herself even more erect to say, "You think I am using my brother's death to be clever, my lord bishop? That I do not mourn him? I loved my brother."

"More than you love your sister," Gardiner said, but he spoke softly enough that only those closest could hear.

"I—" Elizabeth began, but Lady Alana put a hand on her arm.

Two members of the Council, Lord William Howard and Lord William Paulet had been following on Gardiner's heels and been forced to stop when he did. They had heard Gardiner's remark.

Howard, in his loud seaman's voice, said, "King Edward loved you too, m'lady." He looked at Paulet. "Remember how he used to say he'd save this or that book or picture or tune 'until Elizabeth comes.' He looked forward to Lady Elizabeth's visits."

"And I came as often as I was allowed." Elizabeth flicked a glance at Gardiner. She decided to make a bold statement of her detachment from politics to the courtiers around them and raised her voice. "I do not know why Lord Somerset and Lord Northumberland very often rejected my appeals to come to Court. The king never spoke to me of governing or politics and I did not wish for it. It is not my place to be political. We talked of our studies."

"True enough," Paulet agreed and laughed heartily. "I was standing near one time. Didn't understand above one word or two. You were talking in Latin with now and again a sentence in Greek. All stuff you had both read in those texts your tutors set you."

"Yes, because we studied together for years when our father still lived." She blinked away bright tears. "Edward was not king then, only my little brother. I could take him in my arms and give him a kiss . . ."

Gardiner made an odd noise. Elizabeth did not acknowledge it but she knew she had won that round when he bowed and pushed past those in the group around her. Lord William Howard made an exaggerated wink in her direction just before he and Paulet took off after Gardiner.

Elizabeth barely restrained a shudder. Perhaps she had not won after all. She had gained a little more sympathy, but at the cost of annoying Gardiner further. He had Mary's ear and the more favor. Elizabeth won with the courtiers, the less he liked her. She knew that he had already advised Mary that it was unwise to acknowledge her sister, to hold her by the hand and show her favor.

Chapter 15

Elizabeth stiffened slightly as someone brushed her arm. She had been so deep into her memories of her first weeks at Court last summer that she had almost felt warm. Drawn from those memories into the present chill December, she began to shiver again. Lady Alana, herself looking pinched and pale said, "Mass is over," and helped Elizabeth to her feet.

They were the first out of the chapel, but they paused no great distance from it and drew back against the corridor wall. Elizabeth stepped forward to greet several of the worshipers who left after she did with a smile and a small bow. As Mary passed, she curtsied deeply, gritting her teeth as her stubborn knees had to be forced to bend. Mary did not deign to look at her.

The duke of Norfolk, however, paused and said, "Did you attend the Mass, Lady Elizabeth? I did not see you."

"It is very beautiful," Elizabeth said. "Very uplifting. Unfortunately I came late and was at the back. I woke with a chill this morning." She smiled. "You can see I am shivering still."

The duke frowned. "You should put yourself more forward. I know the queen would be glad to have you closer during Mass."

"The queen is very gracious." Elizabeth forced a smile.

Norfolk did not bother to pursue the subject. He asked, "Have you spoken to Lord Denno again? I arranged for him to have permission to visit you, but I have not seen him recently."

Elizabeth shivered again. Her brief meeting with Denno had been acutely painful, exposing her passionate need for him and the impossibility of satisfying it while she was at Court.

"He was very grateful for your kindness, Your Grace," Elizabeth said. "And so am I. As for Lord Denno, I believe he is on a trading voyage. He told me he would need to set out at the beginning of October. He expected to return before now, but the weather has been frightful. It is possible that he has been delayed by the heavy rain and contrary winds."

"Hmmm. He had a wine I liked—a sweet rumney."

"Your Grace, I will gladly write Lord Denno's man of business. Master Clayborne will see that you receive—"

"Come along, Norfolk," Bishop Gardiner interrupted without apology, grabbing Norfolk's arm and drawing him away. "Rumney wine will get you in trouble. Now we will be buying only Spanish wines."

Elizabeth stepped back against the corridor wall, ostensibly to get out of the men's way. Her face was mostly hidden, her head bent, her eyes lowered, her hands clasped lightly at her waist. Gardiner's voice was hard and sarcastic. He was her enemy, but in his opposition to Mary's choice of husband, Elizabeth was in total agreement . . . and she had to be very sure her expression did not display that agreement. Spanish wines indeed. Spanish everything. How could Mary be such a fool as to have chosen Prince Philip of Spain, the Emperor Charles's son, to be her spouse?

Shocked anew at the thought, although the choice was a *fait accompli* and the Council was already working with envoys from Emperor Charles on the marriage contract, Elizabeth turned her back on those following the queen. She could not join the Court . . . she could not! She was cold with fear and her throat was tight with tears, aching for the comfort of Denno's arms, for the wise counsel of her Da.

But Mary would not release her from attendance at Court and she dared not call Denno to come and take her Underhill. She dared not be missing from her bed or lock her doors. The new ladies in her household were spies. They found excuses to peep into her chamber at all hours and her guards could not keep them out, not ladies assigned by the queen. Elizabeth could bespell her own attendant lady to sleep, but not more than one. That all the ladies should sleep like the dead would be suspicious in itself. Mary had already called her "witch" in the past. If the *queen* called her witch . . . she would burn.

Calling her witch was not impossible, Elizabeth thought, wrapping her arms around herself and shivering more convulsively. She had worked magic in the past few months . . . and Mary might have seen her do it. But she could not help it. It was use spells or die. She might die anyway. Why would Mary not let her go?

In September, shortly after Elizabeth had attended Mass for the first time, she had been warned of danger by Alana's silent shout of "'Ware!" Ahead of her, Elizabeth saw a man roughly pushing his way into the front rank of those who were waiting to see the queen. As his hand lifted, Elizabeth caught the glint of steel and cried "No!" She knew the protest was useless, but to don a shield and let the whole court see a knife bounce off her was disaster; in desperation she had gestured and whispered, "*Cilgwthio*."

The queen barely flinched at Elizabeth's shout but looked around at the sound. She was the only one, Elizabeth believed, who might have noticed her pushing gesture. Everyone else was staring at the disturbance as the attacker staggered back and then at the knife which thudded into the wall.

Aim ruined, the knife had flown beyond Elizabeth, passing between her and Mary who was a few steps ahead. When it hit the wall by the queen's head, her attendants and the crowd erupted into chaos, shouting and grabbing at each other, seeking the attacker. Naturally enough in the confusion he escaped.

Elizabeth was so terrified by Mary's seeing her cast a spell she almost fainted. Alana and Eleanor Gage supported her while she gasped and trembled. Some courtiers murmured contemptuously about Elizabeth's cowardice. They believed the attack had been directed at the queen, but Elizabeth knew she had been the target.

Did Mary know? She was so shortsighted she might have missed Elizabeth's gesture. But Mary had looked at her so oddly when the knife hit the wall. Still she said nothing and remained completely calm as she made her way to the chapel where she had been headed.

Elizabeth's blood ran cold, expecting that after Mary thanked God for her deliverance from danger she would accuse Elizabeth of spellcasting. But she did not, merely looking puzzled and troubled every time her eye fell on Elizabeth. Elizabeth began to hope that the queen was not sure of what she had seen and then, later, began to wonder whether it could be Mary who had hired the assassin. What other reason could there be for Mary's calm, except that she knew the knife had not been aimed at her?

No. Such an act was completely out of Mary's nature. And a second attack, soon after the coronation in the beginning of October, convinced Elizabeth that Mary was not directly involved. The second attack failed because Elizabeth now wore a shield when she was taking part in any large assembly. She thought that safer than needing to use a spell like Stickfoot or *Cilgwthio*, which required a word and a gesture that someone might notice. The shield was invisible and could be assumed or dismissed by a mental command, and she had practiced how to throw up her arms to seem to deflect any missile cast at her.

Of course, if she were dancing or any gentleman tried to take her hand to kiss it, she had to dismiss the shield. But when the second attack came, Elizabeth had just come up to Mary and bowed. As she rose, a finely dressed man passed behind her. Suddenly he struck her so hard that her slight body fell forward . . . and Mary saw the knife slide across her back without penetrating.

Elizabeth did not see Mary's reaction. Alana caught Elizabeth's arm (shocked as she was, Elizabeth had dismissed the shield) and cried out about the cut across the back of her lady's dress, thanking God the knife had been deflected by Elizabeth's stays. Lady Alana's explanation was reasonable, but Mary's long glance at Elizabeth was again both puzzled and doubtful.

This assassin was captured, but without result. Mary told Elizabeth the next day—still looking at her strangely—that the assassin could not betray who had hired him; his tongue had been cut out in the past. Nor was the clothing, suitable for Court, suitable for the person who wore it. His body was marked by scars of whipping, his hands callused by hard labor. Moreover he had died a few hours later for no apparent reason, although the physicians sent to examine him suspected a delayed poison.

That Mary should be involved in her own servant's death and in such a manner was ridiculous. *But* someone *is trying to kill me,* Elizabeth thought.

Two attempts on her life were enough. Elizabeth asked for permission to leave Court . . . and discovered Mary still believed the attacks had been aimed at her. Convinced she was the target and Elizabeth the intended beneficiary of her death, Mary refused Elizabeth permission to retire from Court. Mary said, with mingled doubt and suspicion, that she wished to keep her sister close by.

Later Rhoslyn reported to Alana that Mary was greatly disturbed by what had happened. Deep in the back of her mind she feared Elizabeth had used witchcraft to save her life—once by bespelling the knife thrower and again by getting in the way of the knife wielder. But Mary knew she could not prove witchcraft, and besides, if Elizabeth had used spells to save her, was not she also guilty? She could not destroy Elizabeth for saving her, no matter God's law, which said you must not suffer a witch to live.

Rhoslyn had not meddled with the thought, not being able to reinforce the belief that Elizabeth had saved Mary without adding to Mary's conviction that Elizabeth was a witch. And on mortal Tuesday night in the Inn of Kindly Laughter, Rhoslyn warned Alana that Renard had changed Mary's near gratitude to Elizabeth into more doubt by saying that it was likely Elizabeth had hired the assassins herself. Mary did not, for once, completely believe the ambassador but her gratitude to Elizabeth was now tainted.

The chancellor, to whom Mary mentioned the matter, did not believe Elizabeth had any connection with the assassins—Rhoslyn made sure he remembered a thorough investigation that did not uncover the smallest hint of evidence of Elizabeth being involved. But Elizabeth's desire to leave Court was very suspicious to him. The only reason he could see for that was to free her to plot rebellion. And there was nothing Rhoslyn could insert into his mind that would shake that conviction.

Elizabeth walked almost blindly along the corridor in the direction of her own apartments. She knew should be following Mary, meek and bowing no matter what insult the queen visited on her, but she also knew it was useless. All of her skill in dealing with people, all her cleverness about what she said, seemed to desert her as soon as Mary was involved.

As far back as August, before the worst of the pressure to convert to Catholicism was applied to her and misled by Mary's delight in music and dancing, which was so akin to her own, Elizabeth had misread her sister badly. She had taken far too much pleasure in one evening's entertainment. Stupidly, forgetting she was nearly twenty years younger than her sister and far more attractive, she gaily welcomed the young bloods who flocked around her, replying to their playful challenges with swift repartee.

Robin Dudley was not among the young men, of course; he was in the Tower and might well be executed for his part in his father's scheme to deny Mary the throne. Elizabeth felt a mild prickle of regret. He was lusty and amusing, full of outrageous jests and warm glances, but although still wanting to believe she and Mary could be comfortable together, Elizabeth was not stupid enough to speak in his favor.

Thought of Robin Dudley passed easily from her mind as she made lively conversation with the young courtiers and somewhat later danced until the queen ended the evening by retiring to bed. A few times Elizabeth was aware that Mary was watching her; it never occurred to her that Mary watched with envy. Elizabeth always tried to smile at her sister as she danced by. She had meant the smiles to show her gratitude and appreciation; later she learned Mary had taken them as smiles of contemptuous triumph.

Tonight came a whisper in her mind. Elizabeth did not stop dancing, did not associate her pleasure with trouble even though she felt her heart sink. Lady Alana never used magic unless she had an urgent reason. Thus, when Elizabeth was undressed and her maid of honor deep in a spelled sleep, she was not surprised to see Lady Alana come softly into the room through the dressing room in which Blanche Parry slept. To make Elizabeth even more apprehensive, Alana got into the bed with her so their voices could be kept to a murmur.

"You need to be less popular," Lady Alana said without any introduction; Elizabeth drew a shocked breath and Lady Alana went on, "She watches you. Perhaps she tells herself that she is not asked to dance because she is the queen, but she sees the way the young men look at you, the eagerness with which they contest with each other to be your partner, and the way few of them look for any other partner when you rest from the dancing."

Elizabeth had been silent for a long moment and then said bitterly, "That too? I thought at least dancing and light talk of art and music were safe."

Lady Alana shook her head and said, "Nothing is safe. Everything you do and are grates on the queen. She is envious of your appearance too. I have word from Rhoslyn that Mary asks her ladies if you do not use paint on your complexion and use potions to make your hair so light and bright a red. Perhaps you should ask permission to leave the Court."

"No!" Elizabeth exclaimed, her voice still too low to be heard a foot away but carrying passionate conviction. "I cannot do that. I must be here at least until the coronation. I must follow in the procession directly behind Mary to be seen by all as the heir presumptive. I must be fixed in that place in the minds of the Court and the people. So far Mary has not dared to displace me. Northumberland's devise to change the succession is too clear in everyone's memory."

"You cannot count on that for long."

"I know." Elizabeth shuddered. "Gardiner is already telling her I am a danger to her rule. But there is still time for me to make my mark. Mary is better at defense than attack. She will want to think and pray, ask Emperor Charles's advice, convince herself it is God's will, before she tries to put me aside. Perhaps she does not realize that every time I walk directly behind her or follow her in procession, the people and the Court are more fixed in the idea that I am her heir."

That much she had accomplished, Elizabeth thought. She was recognized by everyone except the most passionate Catholics as her sister's successor. Now she was ready to leave, ready to flee to safety and freedom . . . and Mary would not let her go and would not believe she was in danger. As she reached her apartment and made her way toward her chair, Elizabeth set her teeth.

She would not display how tired and frightened she was to all the watching eyes. That she had fixed in the minds of the people and some of the Court her place as heir presumptive was all but useless now. Another chill ran icy fingers along her spine. She was heir presumptive until Mary married and bore a child.

Marriage was now certain and, Elizabeth knew, probably the worst marriage Mary could make, in a political sense. Elizabeth sank into her chair and watched as her ladies—her own loyal friends and those pressed on her by the queen—took their places around her. Which of them, she wondered, had hastened to carry to Mary's ears the most recent colossal blunder she had made?

Only last month when she first heard that Mary would choose Philip of Spain as spouse, her political shock opened her mouth before her brain fully accepted what she had been told. Half believing the news was a jest, Elizabeth had denied that Mary had decided on Philip of Spain; even as a jest such a rumor about the queen was a political disaster.

"No! No," Elizabeth remembered herself crying, half laughing. "The queen could not think of sharing the English throne with the future king of Spain."

Eleanor Gage's hand had caught at her arm and pressed hard. Eleanor was the queen's lady, sent to serve (and spy on) Elizabeth, but Elizabeth thought Eleanor had come to like her new mistress better than her old. She often did her best to save Elizabeth from doing anything that would offend or annoy Mary. Elizabeth glanced at Eleanor, carefully smoothing a piece of embroidery over her knee and felt a flick of gratitude.

Likely it was not Eleanor who had told the queen what she said. Elizabeth felt her lips twist wryly. Or if it had been she would certainly have also told Mary what Elizabeth said next, in an attempt to retrieve her blunder. "Oh, how silly I am. It is no business of mine so long as Queen Mary marries to please herself and get us an heir."

That, too, had been a mistake. In her eagerness to make clear that she would not oppose the queen's choice, no matter what it was, Elizabeth had forgotten Mary's sexual jealousy of her. Her last words, if they were repeated, would only make matters worse. Likely Mary would take them as a sly sexual taunt.

Yet if that child survives, the acute danger in which I now live will mostly be over. With a clear heir to the throne borne by the queen and raised in the Catholic faith, I will no longer be a threat. Elizabeth's lips quirked again. Far from lifting her spirits, the idea of safety through Mary's child inheriting the throne made her sick and hollow within.

Elizabeth reached down to the elaborate work basket beside her chair. Marriage, yes, that was certain now. But the growing public disapproval of the marriage was another danger to her. The chance of a child resulting from the marriage was not great. Mary was thirty-seven and frequently ill. If only, Elizabeth thought, she could herself stay alive until her sister's natural demise . . . but her constant presence continually irritated Mary. Between the attacks on her and her own awkward stupidities, to remain with the Court was increasingly dangerous.

Yet she had so far failed to discover a reason to leave that Mary would find compelling. Elizabeth sighed. It was very strange. There could be no doubt that Mary did not really want her at Court. Someone was influencing Mary to keep her at Court. Who?

Elizabeth wore away the rest of the morning in blameless occupation, embroidering a book cover for Mary. It was replete with Catholic symbols and Elizabeth did the needlework openly, often showing off her accomplishment to her maids of honor, specially Mary's spies. Embroidery, even for her sister, was calming. Then Elizabeth had to blink hard to clear a mist from her eyes. She had been reminded of how much she enjoyed embroidering for Edward and how much pleasure he had taken in her handiwork.

The calm brought Elizabeth by setting stitches did not last long. When those invited to dinner were assembled, Mary, as she had done repeatedly in the last weeks, gestured for Margaret Douglas, countess of Lennox, and Frances Brandon, duchess of Suffolk, to precede Elizabeth. And while Elizabeth was swallowing that bitter pill, Renard walked past her, without a bow, and with such a glance that her indignation was swallowed up by shock.

Elizabeth had not spoken to, in fact had seldom seen the Imperial ambassador recently. Now that he had come so close, she realized he must have been avoiding her. She could remember seeing him near Mary but then seeming to disappear if she approached her sister. Not that she had often approached Mary for the last few weeks; she was too likely to be waved away or insulted in some other manner.

As was her practice when she had been so slighted, Elizabeth made no protest, bowing meekly as Mary passed. But she never remained in the queen's presence to be further slighted. Erect as a sword, she withdrew to her own apartment, knowing all the young and lively courtiers would soon follow. Elizabeth chuckled bitterly as she sent Mary's spies to fetch refreshments and musicians. Let the queen know that she was not alone and trembling with fear. And let the queen hear that the ladies she had sent to watch Elizabeth had joined her in laughing and dancing and singing with the gallants of the Court.

But when the dancing and singing was done and the young men departed, Elizabeth made ready for bed silent and withdrawn. She could not rid herself of the memory of Renard's look of hatred, and she was very glad when the door to Blanche's chamber opened softly. Elizabeth saw but gave no sign, sliding under the covers Alice Finch, held up for her. Alice, not too clever and unaware of her lady's tension, smiled, wished her lady a good night and sweet sleep, and drew the heavy winter bedcurtains closed.

"*Parachoro drimuz,*" Elizabeth whispered, and suddenly the sound of the brocade bedcurtains sliding out of their folds was as loud as a rushing river.

Elizabeth bit her lip. She had asked to learn a spell for keen hearing and Mechain had warned her it would be of little use unless she learned to direct and fix the spell. That was beyond Elizabeth's ability, but ever-indulgent Elidir had taught it to her anyway.

Elizabeth had soon learned that Mechain was right; the spell was useless. She had intended to use it to eavesdrop on conversations in the Court, but when she invoked it, the uproar had almost battered her brain numb. She did not only hear those conversations in which she was interested but every sound in the audience chamber—footsteps, the rustling of clothing, everyone's breathing, all mingled in a mind-rattling roar.

Since she and Alice were alone in the bedchamber, the results of the spell were not as catastrophic. Elizabeth had quickly recognized the sound of the curtains moving and now she identified a series of loud thuds as Alice walking to the truckle bed. The leather straps twanged and groaned; there were crackling sounds and a rustling as loud as a boar running through brush which Elizabeth reasoned must be Alice settling herself in bed. And at long last, the steady roaring that must be the maid of honor's breathing.

"*Bod cyfgadur,*" Elizabeth whispered, pointing toward Alice.

The roaring of Alice's breathing became louder and deeper.

"*Metakino parachoro drimuz,*" Elizabeth said hastily, quite aloud and beginning to breathe rather hard with nervousness.

The words were like cracks of thunder. How long could she endure such noise in her head? Tears of fear sprang to her eyes. Usually when she worked a spell the first few times she was Underhill where Mechain or Elidir could save her if she did something wrong. This time she had been too impatient to wait until she was sure Alice was asleep naturally before she added the sleep spell; she wanted to hear when the girl got into bed and started to doze and she had used a spell tried only once before.

However before Elizabeth's tears could gather the room fell silent. She breathed a long sigh of relief . . . which she barely heard. She had cast and removed the keen hearing spell successfully.

"Come," she called softly toward Blanche's door, holding back the bedcurtains.

Lady Alana slipped through the barely open door and hurried across to the bed. Elizabeth breathed another sigh of relief as Alana climbed into the bed. Once she was behind the curtains, none of Mary's spies could see her and if someone came to the bed, Alana could use the Don't-see-me spell.

"The 'messenger,'" Lady Alana said, looking up toward the ceiling to indicate she meant the air spirit, "told me you were very upset. I am sorry, my love. The queen is a silly woman. Not even her own courtiers take Lennox and Suffolk seriously. And all such spitefulness does is wake more sympathy for you and admiration for your dignity and restraint."

Elizabeth shook her head. "I wasn't upset by Mary's putting Lennox and Suffolk before me. It was Renard." Her breath came a little faster when she remembered the Imperial ambassador's eyes. "Mary does not like me, but I have never seen such hate as looked out of Renard's eyes." Elizabeth shivered. "It was terrible."

Aleneil sighed. "Yes, I saw. Elizabeth, I have no idea what to do about Renard. Perhaps—" now *she* shivered "—I should stop his heart, but—"

"Stop his heart," Elizabeth repeated in a horrified voice. "That would be murder. No. Why should you even think of such a thing? Killing Renard would not change Charles's mind about me."

"Emperor Charles has nothing to do with why Renard hates you."

"That is ridiculous. The feeling cannot be anything to do with him and me. I have done my very best never to offend Renard. Why should he hate me? His dislike can only be by order of his master, but Emperor Charles should have no objections to me—not compared with having Mary of Scots as heir."

Aleneil only looked even more worried. "This has nothing to do with Emperor Charles. I fear that Renard is not only the emperor's servant."

"I cannot believe that!" Elizabeth exclaimed.

Aleneil sighed. "Not of his own will or for gold or favor. Rhoslyn sees a great deal of him. He is forever with the queen. Rhoslyn believes Renard is bespelled and stinks of Vidal Dhu."

"God's Grace support me," Elizabeth breathed. "Could those attacks on me be Renard's doing?"

"It is possible." Aleneil said, nodding as if she had the same idea herself. "When I told Denoriel about the man who died, he said the lack of a tongue, the scarring on his back, and the calluses on his hands sound like what might have happened to a Spanish slave. If he had been promised his freedom, he might even have taken so desperate a chance as an attack on you in full Court. And the poisoning . . . that is not unknown in the Spanish Court too. What is more, if you twice thwarted Renard's attempts to kill you, he could be growing quite exasperated."

Elizabeth began to tremble. "Mary thinks of Renard as the Mouth for Emperor Charles. And Mary is absolutely and utterly convinced Charles's is the only advice worth taking." She rubbed her arms as if she were cold. "If Renard tells Mary Charles wants me dead . . ."

"I do not think Renard dares go so far as that," Aleneil said offering comfort. "He is still too aware that Charles does *not* want you dead."

Elizabeth drew a deep breath. If Vidal's influence could not make Renard tell Mary Charles wanted her dead, she was in less danger of being executed. Although she had been repeatedly warned against overconfidence, she had so often bested Vidal's attempts on her that knowing he was behind Renard made the ambassador's hatred less frightening.

"No, Charles would not want me dead. The next heir—setting aside Mary's silly notice of Lennox and Suffolk, which the country would not abide—is Mary of Scotland, who will soon be the wife of the French dauphin. Compared to Mary of Scotland and her French husband on the English throne, Charles would think of me as an angel of deliverance."

Aleneil nodded. "So far Vidal's influence has not gone beyond making Renard constantly tell Mary that you are a danger to her rule. Unfortunately I think Mary believes him, but he suggests things that would throw the Court into an even greater uproar when added to this Spanish marriage. If he should begin to hint that *Charles* wants you gone, Rhoslyn would let me know at once. Then between us—" Aleneil shivered again "—we will stop him." She sighed. "Is there not some way to make Mary less enamored of Renard's advice?"

"I do not think so," Elizabeth said slowly, considering; then shook her head. "I cannot blame Mary for being so dependent on the emperor. He has been the only support she has had since her mother was set aside. Charles has always counseled her, and even went so far as to threaten war if she were deprived of her Mass."

"Harry says Charles is no real problem for now," Aleneil said. "The emperor is very cautious and has been preaching the greatest moderation in everything since marriage to Philip has been proposed. Harry thinks Charles does not care how long it takes to make England Catholic or even if it ever becomes Catholic. His concern is to make England an ally against France."

"Likely Da is right. He usually is about Court politics. And I know that Charles often writes to Mary himself. That should be some protection for me. Renard would not dare go farther than the advice Charles himself gives to Mary."

Suddenly Elizabeth fell silent. She wanted to ask how Vidal had managed to bespell Renard, but no sound passed her lips. By Titania's geas she could not speak of spells or magic while in the mortal world. The frustration added to her fear, and misery overwhelmed her. Her eyes filled with tears.

"I miss Denno," she whispered. "Thank God that you can be with me, but I miss my Denno." She swallowed, sniffed.

"You have the amulets he gave you, have you not?" Aleneil asked. "So call him."

Elizabeth shook her head. "I dare not. We thought I would be able to put a token in a safe place." Two tears ran down her cheeks. "But there is no safe place, nor even in the dead of night a safe time. It is barely safe to whisper to you because you are my lady. Strong efforts will be made to discover what we said. Someone will have seen you coming to me and tell the queen. But if Denno appeared in my chamber or I was absent from it . . . Nothing can be kept secret in this palace. Nothing."

Aleneil sighed and nodded. Perhaps she should have used the Don't-see-me spell to come to Elizabeth, but she hated to use any magic in the mortal world. Even the tiny spell that made her look so plain drained her. And in the mortal world there was no way to restore her power. All she could do was to lean over and pat Elizabeth's shoulder.

"You need not worry over curiosity about what we were saying to each other. I have an excellent story about why I came secretly to see you. A surprise you are planning as a gift to the queen."

Elizabeth smiled faintly. That was a good excuse and Lady Alana would surely come up with some elegant trifle that she could present to her sister. But it did not solve her basic problem or suggest a way for her to spend an hour or two in Denno's arms.

The smile disappeared and two more tears ran over. "I must ask again for permission to leave the Court. I cannot think of why Mary will not let me go home. Can Rhoslyn help?"

"I don't know, but I will ask," Aleneil replied, then more grimly, "Renard tells her that the moment you are out from under her eye you will conspire with the rebels who are writing broadsheets and rousing fear of Spanish domination among the people. You will put yourself forward as a 'mere English,' Protestant queen to save them from the Spaniards and the pope."

"That is ridiculous. I would do nothing of the kind. I am not an idiot. Aside from that, which Mary may not believe, I will have to take home with me the new servants with whom Mary presented me. She will doubtless know how often I turn in my bed, not to mention whether I conspire with rebels."

Aleneil laughed. "She does not trust her spies. She fears you have lured their devotion away from her And Renard keeps talking about your enchantment of spirit. Would it not help if you simply converted to Mary's faith? Are you as set against being Catholic as she was against the reformed rite?"

"No, of course not," Elizabeth said, wiping away her tears and smiling slightly again. "I *do* believe in God and in Christ who died to redeem us all. But I *cannot* believe that our Merciful Redeemer cares a jot by which rite we worship Him, whether we have candles and incense or bare walls and a simple table as an altar. My faith is in Christ. All the rest is details."

"Then give Mary her candles and incense."

"I actually like the candles and incense," Elizabeth said rather sadly. "But they are an offense to those who took to heart the reformist rite. I need to hold out some hope for the reformists. Besides, it does not matter how sincere I am or am not in Catholicism. Mary will never believe I have changed. She could not and she does not want to believe I could."

Aleneil nodded and sighed. "She is a fanatic."

Elizabeth shrugged. "I show myself to have yielded. I attend

Mass regularly. There was no other choice for me but the axe. I have no emperor uncle to threaten war to save me. But as long as I do not *flaunt* my attendance at Mass or other Catholic observances, the reformists will have hope. There are many in the realm who cheered Mary's accession because she was the heir assigned by my father but who do not want the Catholic rite. They look to me in hope that if I come to the throne I will bring back the practices of Edward's reign. I must sustain that hope."

"Elizabeth," Aleneil said warningly, looking troubled, "Mary is . . . is not quite sane on the subject of her faith. Rhoslyn cannot touch her mind on that subject at all. She has tried. That is something burned so deep into Mary's soul that only complete mindlessness or death can change it."

"I know that." Elizabeth shivered and rubbed her arms again although the room was warm enough. The cold came from inside her. "I will be walking the edge of a sword between martyrdom and rejection. I must be Catholic enough that Mary does not call me traitor or heretic and have an excuse to kill me, but I must do it in such a way that those who think of me as the upholder of Protestantism will not abandon me."

Aleneil wrinkled her nose. "Since most of the courtiers have shifted their faith several times already for the sake of their skins and their purses, they should understand."

"I hope so," Elizabeth sighed. "I hope I can balance on this bridge of swords."

Chapter 16

"Whatever am I to do about Elizabeth?" Mary said, her brows drawn together in a worried frown and her lips downturned.

It was now after midnight a week after Parliament had been prorogued, but the queen's days were so full that she had no other time for a private word with the ladies who had been her support and companions through good and ill to her final triumph. They were forgathered in the queen's bedchamber, Susan Clarencieux, Jane Dormer, Rosamund Scot, and Mistress Shirley, one of Mary's personal maids. Jane Russell, the other maid, had carried in a flask of sweet wine and a plate of cakes and then taken herself into one of the queen's tiring chambers to sort out the queen's dresses for the morrow.

The group sat on stools around Mary's great chair, Mistress Shirley a little to the side and farther back than the high-born ladies. Behind, on the wall to the left of the bed, was a *prie-dieu* facing a large crucifix. Rhoslyn pulled her eyes from the crucifix and fixed her gaze on the queen. The image of Christ, twisted in agony on the cross, brought back too vividly to her many scenes from her life in the Dark Court.

The exasperated question Mary had asked was no surprise to her ladies. Ever since Mary's coronation on October first Elizabeth had been a growing irritant. Not that Mary had been happy with her close association with Elizabeth since the passing of the first surge of tenderness when Elizabeth had come to greet her on her arrival in London. Within weeks, Renard's and Gardiner's warnings about the threat posed by Elizabeth and Elizabeth's own actions, flaunting herself before the young men of the Court, had removed the rosy haze of affection and cleared Mary's vision.

Through the end of July and August, Mary came to see and increasingly resent Elizabeth's hypocrisy. Elizabeth professed affection but, Mary reasoned, would she not love Mary's faith, the central focus of her sister's life, if she truly loved her sister? Elizabeth seemed to cling to her, always ready to stand hand in hand or follow close behind . . . except when it was time to attend Mass. Then Elizabeth was nowhere to be seen.

When Mary taxed her with her resistance to the true faith, Elizabeth pled ignorance, asked for teachers. Yes, Elizabeth had finally attended a Mass, groaning and complaining that she was sick; her stomach knotted with cramps so it was hard for her to breathe. If Elizabeth had truly believed what she now swore she believed, would she not have been light and happy, assured of Christ's forgiveness and the hope of heaven? And even now she crept into the chapel for Mass, always late, and as if going to some bitter punishment.

Yet in every public celebration since Mary had been proclaimed queen, Elizabeth was first in precedence. And the people and the whole Court were satisfied it should be so. More than satisfied; there was indignation, angry looks, and defection from the queen's company if Elizabeth was slighted and retired. Now even Renard and Gardiner insisted that Elizabeth must be treated with respect and seeming affection if Mary would not send her to the Tower and find some reason to have her executed.

Mary choked and pressed her handkerchief to her lips as bile rose in her throat at the same time as it constricted. She could not breathe. Mistress Shirley jumped from her seat and rushed to hold a glass of wine to Mary's lips. At first she could not drink, not until she swore silently she never would order her sister's death; then she was able to take a sip and gesture at her ladies, who had exclaimed and started to rise, to remain seated.

The thought of execution, the reaction she could not control, confirmed again to Mary that to order Elizabeth's death was to bring on her own. But how else was she to prevent Elizabeth from inheriting the throne?

Not through any action of Parliament, Mary thought bitterly. On most matters, Parliament had been most cooperative. The members repealed laws that raised minor offenses into treason and reversed the decree that had divorced Catherine of Aragon from Henry VIII.

The repeal was embarrassing to Elizabeth as it declared her illegitimate anew, but not one member followed the logic of that ruling and raised his voice to contest the Act of Succession. Gardiner made private efforts to raise that point with a few Catholic members, but he soon desisted. There was not the smallest hint that the Parliament would consider removing Elizabeth from the succession. Elizabeth was as firmly heir presumptive when Parliament rose as the day Mary was proclaimed queen.

"Be rid of her," Rhoslyn said in answer to Mary's question about what to do about Elizabeth. Aleneil had told Rhoslyn that Elizabeth needed to get away from Court.

There were gasps all around, and Mary, pressing her handkerchief to her lips, said breathlessly, "No, I cannot."

"Oh, no!" Rhoslyn exclaimed, painting an expression of horror on her face while inwardly congratulating herself on the efficacy of her working on Mary's mind. "I did not mean any harm to Lady Elizabeth. Indeed, madam, any harm to her would bring more evil upon you than her. Whatever ill befell her would be blamed on you no matter how innocent you were. And there is so much unrest already about your proposed marriage."

"Everyone is so . . . so . . . *stupid*." Susan Clarencieux said. "Why can they not see how much better ruled the country will be with Prince Philip's help and one strong faith?"

"The English have a powerful dislike and suspicion of foreign rulers," Jane Dormer said softly. "You must be patient, madam. When Prince Philip is your consort and they see no ill follows, they will grow more accepting. And Elizabeth has been very careful not to show any disapproval."

"But she does disapprove!" Mary said, her hands trembling slightly with anger and frustration. "In the hearing of the whole Court, she said no queen of England should think of marrying the future king of Spain."

"But she then said she had been silly and all that was important was that you marry to please yourself and get an heir." Jane Dormer frowned as she spoke, not exactly sure of why she said what she did. But she agreed with Rosamund that harm or even further insult to Elizabeth would bring trouble on the queen, who was in trouble enough for proposing to marry Philip of Spain.

Susan Clarencieux snorted gently. "Oh, Elizabeth would say that. She is clever enough never to give any open cause for Your Majesty's disfavor. To the eye and ear of the Court and of the people, she has been as meek and obedient as a slaveling."

"She is a liar and a hypocrite," Mistress Shirley said, not mincing words.

Mary's frown deepened, but it was Susan Clarencieux who said, "I think she is, but she is equally clever about that. She does attend Mass, but only those in Your Majesty's private chapel. Somehow she always has an excuse to avoid Mass at St. Paul's or any other public place."

Jane Dormer looked worried; she was young and she had a little corner in her mind that liked and admired Elizabeth. "But is that hypocrisy or only her pride, which shrinks from a public admission of her earlier foolishness?" Still Jane dearly loved Mary and was a good Catholic. She sighed. "Perhaps it is for pride that she avoids public display of her conversion, but she must abate that pride and show the reformers that she has recognized the true faith."

Rhoslyn sat up straighter on her stool. She did not like the direction Jane Dormer was now leading the conversation. She said rather sharply, "She is an irritant, madam. To press her harder to display her conversion will doubtless bring her to take to her bed and claim illness and the Court will blame you. What I meant when I said be rid of her is that you should send her away."

Mary sighed. She would have liked nothing better than to be rid of Elizabeth who was more and more a favorite in the Court. After the coronation she had tried to depress Elizabeth's prominence by giving precedence over her to Lady Margaret Douglas, a granddaughter of Henry VII. Furious—Elizabeth did not make the smallest effort to hide her affront—but nonetheless quietly obedient, Elizabeth had curtsied to Margaret and followed after her in entering the room.

Mary bit her lip. Sneaky and sly and accursed clever, that was what Elizabeth was. Instead of insisting on her right, as Mary herself had tried to do with disastrous results when her father had reduced her rank, Elizabeth simply withdrew from Court and kept to her chamber. That had the most unwelcome effect of causing about two-thirds of the young men, and a number of the young women, too, to abandon the Court festivities. Mary knew from the ladies she had sent to serve Elizabeth that the young ladies and gentlemen had all gone to play, sing, and dance in Elizabeth's apartment—and Mary's spies with them.

"Your advice is decidedly attractive, Rosamund," Mary said, "but Ambassador Renard says I must keep her under my eye. My uncle, the emperor, fears she will plot the overthrow of my rule if she is left free of supervision. Perhaps I should have taken Renard's advice when he spoke against her following me in the coronation procession."

"No, madam, you could not do that," Rhoslyn said, looking shocked. "Not yet. It is far too soon to try to thrust her aside. You did what was exactly right about the coronation procession in inviting Lady Anne of Cleves to sit in the litter and at table with her. That shows Elizabeth followed you by precedence only. Send her away and keep her away and she will soon be forgotten."

As she spoke Rhoslyn could not help wondering by whose advice Anne of Cleves was seated with Elizabeth. Whoever it was had done Mary no favor. Strong Catholics may have seen it as a grouping of heretics but Rhoslyn thought that the proximity of the ageing Anne of Cleves emphasized Elizabeth's youthful charm and bright abundance of energy. And that was a sharp contrast to Mary's dogged endurance throughout the procession and the coronation ceremony, during which the weight of the crown sometimes forced poor Mary to support her head with her hand.

"That could be the right choice," Mistress Shirley put in, having gone back to her seat a little behind the others. "Mayhap out of sight will be out of mind. With her here, half the Council is complaining that Lady Margaret is not in King Henry's will and should not have precedence over Lady Elizabeth. Stubborn, King Henry was. Not willing to admit she weren't his."

"It is very unfortunate that King Henry always recognized her," Susan Clarencieux said, a slight warning in her tone; she knew there was indignation among some over Mary's attempt to say Mark Smeaton was Elizabeth's father. "And her hair, just like the king's, and the hands she so proudly displays—one can see them in the portraits of Henry VII."

"I do not see that at all," Mary snapped coldly.

Susan Clarencieux sighed and frowned. She did not like to

contradict her beloved mistress, but Mary only harmed herself with senseless attacks on Elizabeth that nearly everyone put down to spite. Susan was also eager to get Elizabeth out of the Court. Anger grew on Elizabeth's behalf each time Lady Margaret was given precedence. Renard was wrong to insist that Elizabeth stay.

Susan believed that he hoped Elizabeth would act defiant, perhaps challenge the queen's right to displace her. But Susan knew Elizabeth was too clever and too pliable—unlike her own dear lady who lived by her honor—to be openly defiant. The clever minx would make everyone sorry for her while behaving meek as a nun.

In any case, Susan thought impatiently, Elizabeth was not important. The queen spent too much time worrying about her when all her attention should be given to convincing England to accept Philip. The growing uproar over the Spanish marriage, the vicious pamphlets, the crude broadsides . . . why, a dead dog with its head shaved like a priest's tonsure had been cast into the queen's audience chamber just the other day.

The queen must deal with that; Elizabeth was nothing. Yes, Rosamund was right. It would be best to get Elizabeth out of the way. The last thing they needed was to have Elizabeth using her mobile face to display horror and disgust of the Spanish marriage while she bent her head and bowed her knee in seeming obedience.

"Your Majesty," Susan said, "Elizabeth is not important. For now you cannot change the Act of Succession. I agree with Rosamund that it is too soon to seem to thrust Elizabeth aside—specially when you are planning a marriage that, with God's help, will set her aside in a most natural and joyful way. Thus I also think with Mistress Shirley that sending her out of the Court might be best."

"Bishop Gardiner wants me to put her in the Tower," Mary said, and closed her eyes as if in pain.

She was in pain. Rhoslyn sent out a punishing pang, like a sharp blade in Mary's skull, whenever Mary thought of acting against Elizabeth. Rhoslyn no longer attempted to change Mary's mind about Elizabeth; she had long ago accepted that Mary's conflicts went too deep for surface interference. What she had done was to arrange a kind of self-punishment, physical discomfort and mental guilt, for thinking of harming her sister.

Susan Clarencieux shook her head nervously although the idea Rhoslyn sent seemed her own. "To send Lady Elizabeth to the Tower when she has done nothing . . . oh, madam, think of the fear and suspicion it would cause among all those who supported Northumberland. The bishop's assurances to them that Your Majesty means them no harm would not convince the lords of the Council. They would only see Elizabeth, who has obeyed you in everything and has not spoken a single word against your will, who has even gone to Mass as you entreated her . . . they would see her sent to the Tower. Their trust would be terribly shaken."

"Susan has the right of that," Rhoslyn said, also shaking her head. "And I cannot see the danger Renard complains of. You can have Elizabeth watched most carefully. If she communicates with the French or any other suspicious persons, you will be warned. And then you will have *cause* to arrest her."

"Very well." Mary looked around and saw agreement on all the faces; she sighed with relief. "I will give Elizabeth permission to retire. At least I will not need to see her every day."

The ladies were by no means sure the matter was settled. Mary was notorious for making up her mind and then having it changed by the next persuasive person to speak to her, except that no argument could alter her decision to marry Prince Philip. It was Mary's heart that was set on being Philip's wife . . . and Mary's heart was not changeable.

However Mary was not totally unaware of her weakness. Thus she was careful not to mention her decision to give her sister permission to depart from Court to either the Imperial ambassador or the chancellor. She did not want to chance being swayed by their objections or sickened by their urgings to send Elizabeth to the Tower.

Besides, Mary was looking forward to telling Elizabeth she was free to go, expecting that Elizabeth would be overjoyed and show it. If she did, Mary would be able to point out how ungrateful her sister was to the courtiers who favored her. But as usual in any dealings with Elizabeth, to add to Mary's anger, nothing went as Mary planned.

She called Elizabeth to her after dinner, when the Court was assembled in the great audience chamber, and said, "You have asked several times for permission to leave my company. And I see that you are not happy here when you are not the first in importance. So you have my leave to depart when you will."

Instead of thanking her coldly and sweeping out of the room, Elizabeth, who had been warned by Alana through Rhoslyn and had planned what to do, fell on her knees and cried, "Madam, how have I offended you? It is true that I have asked permission to depart, but that was only because I felt you did not want me here. I have always been happy when you said I could stay. And I have tried most earnestly to obey you in all things."

The words came out choked, as if with sobs, and indeed Elizabeth did feel as if she would strangle saying them. She had rarely spoken words so very much against her true feelings. If she were unlucky, Mary would believe her and say she had no intention of driving her away.

Folding her hands prayerfully and gazing up into the queen's face, Elizabeth did pray. She begged Christ to forgive her her trespasses in lying and offered to do penance (mingling without regard the reformist notion of trespass and the Catholic idea of penance) if only Mary would order her gone.

She did not quite get what she wanted. Glancing around, Mary saw several accusing gazes fixed on her. The High Admiral, Lord William Howard, the secretary of state, William Paget, and the controller of her household, William Paulet were all looking from her to Elizabeth with concern. Renard was coming toward her, his face furious. Gardiner, the chancellor, seemed disgusted.

"You have not offended me," Mary said, her deep voice harsh. "As you say, you are obedient . . . to a fault. We will speak of this further anon."

Elizabeth grew so pale that her great-uncle Lord William Howard moved forward to support her. Her eyes were enormous yet seemed blind; she was seeing her freedom snatched away by her own too-great cleverness in trying to make Mary appear harsh and unreasonable, seeing her reunion with her Denno lost, seeing lost also the joy of wandering the great markets, of visiting fabled Alhambra. Her great uncle helped her to her feet and would have drawn her away, but though she trembled in every limb, she insisted on remaining near the queen, head bent, wiping away occasional tears.

Mary had all she could do to keep from screaming at her sister. Elizabeth was making her out a monster when she was just doing what the girl had plagued her about. She was so proper, so well-behaved that Mary felt sick with hate. And as the hatred roiled in her, her heart felt as if daggers were piercing it. She must not hate Elizabeth or her own heart would fail!

She must free herself of Elizabeth's presence, Mary thought, no matter what the result. How could she help but hate the base-born bastard? Sly as her mother, who had ensorcelled and trapped a previously virtuous king, Elizabeth worked without words. She did not make herself prominent; she stood aside and back from Mary's chair, but Mary could feel her there, pale and trembling so that every person who came to speak to the queen had "poor, mistreated" Elizabeth in the corner of his eye.

Then she could bear it no longer; Mary turned so she could see her sister and address her directly. "You are too much moved," she said, trying to make her voice kind but hearing its loud, deep timbre spread through the room like a threat. "Go now and calm yourself. I promise you will have what you truly desire."

Elizabeth curtsied right down to the ground. She had not intended that lest it seem overdone and subtly mocking, but once she got her knees to bend at all, they collapsed. Kat and Eleanor Gage hurried forward and helped her up. She left the audience chamber without even a glance right or left. It seemed to her that her awkwardness and stupidity in dealing with Mary had reached a new peak. She could not even seek comfort from Kat or Alana, not with Mary's ladies all offering her handkerchiefs soaked in lavender water or wine and cakes.

No summons came that day. If Rhoslyn had known Elizabeth was truly afraid Mary would not release her, she could have sent comfort. Mary had spent a good part of the afternoon refusing to listen to Renard's arguments in favor of "giving Lady Elizabeth what she said she desired" and keeping her at Court. But to Mary's surprise, when he found her immovable on sending Elizabeth away, he opposed Gardiner's urging to sequester her in the Tower.

That way, Gardiner pointed out, Mary would not have to see or deal with her sister. The instinctive leap of Mary's heart in agreement turned into a pang so fierce that she caught her breath.

"No," she said.

And Renard echoed, "No."

With Elizabeth in the Tower he felt it would be even more difficult for an assassin to reach her. And he was all too aware of the rising opposition to Mary's marriage to Philip. To allow any threat to Elizabeth that could be attributed to the queen or her Spanish advisors would cause the swelling boil of hatred to burst and spew poison throughout the country. Charles would have him killed! That fear, more real and too possible, completely overwhelmed the insidious prompting of the glowing ruby ring.

The emperor had made plain that Renard was supposed to encourage a good relationship between Elizabeth and Mary. He was to encourage Elizabeth to hope she would be named Mary's heir. That, Charles was sure, would keep Elizabeth quiet, would prevent her from conspiring against her sister . . . at least until after Philip and Mary were married. After Philip had control of his wife, they could decide what to do with Elizabeth.

Renard made a curt bow to Gardiner and a deeper one to Mary. "You know I agree with you my Lord Chancellor that Lady Elizabeth is dangerous," Renard said. "But she would be more dangerous as a martyr. Let her go to Ashridge, her estate nearest London. Your Majesty can seed the town and neighborhood with spies and your women are already in her household. If she looks in the direction of a rebel, you will have evidence against her. *Then* she can be sent to the Tower and there will be no rising in her favor."

Little as Gardiner liked allowing Elizabeth out of the strict control of life in the palace, he was aware of the practical sense in what Renard said. To imprison Elizabeth now, when there had never been any indication she was not heir apparent, even though Mary had shown favor to others, would doubtless generate riots and ten times the blizzard of broadsides they now endured.

What Gardiner feared was that, surrounded by her own guards and servants rather than those controlled by the government, Elizabeth would be "abducted" from her manor house (he believed with her heartfelt connivance) and then used as a figurehead for a civil war. Considering the growing animosity of the English populace to both the restoration of Catholicism and the Spanish marriage, Gardiner was not sure the queen would triumph.

For a few heartbeats Gardiner contemplated the effects of a civil war after which Mary retained her throne. That would be the end of the Spanish marriage. No matter how much Emperor Charles desired the alliance with England, he would not risk his precious, only, son. Prince Philip would be delighted to withdraw; he obviously had no enthusiasm for this marriage. Then Gardiner drew a long breath. It was far too likely that Mary would lose and Elizabeth would reign. No, far better to let Elizabeth go. Surely she would hang herself, given enough rope.

"As Your Majesty wishes," Gardiner said at last.

And then, although he feared it would be useless, he thought he should make clear to Elizabeth that she was already suspect and watched, that if she joined any conspiracy against Mary, her treachery would be immediately known. Perhaps if one man she knew to be her friend and another who was neutral warned her, she would think twice about making trouble. Gardiner suppressed a sigh. They had trouble enough without adding Elizabeth to the pot.

"Perhaps," he said, "Your Majesty might wish me to dispatch Lord Paget and the earl of Arundel to warn Lady Elizabeth of the need for circumspection?"

Chapter 17

Chancellor Gardiner's dispatch of Lord Paget and the earl of Arundel with warnings and strictures about her behavior, was a source of unintentional happiness to Elizabeth. The advent of Paget and the earl of Arundel, who gravely lectured her about the necessity of keeping absolutely free from any and all political action when she was on her own lands, was the first hint she had been given that Mary did intend to let her go.

To Lord Privy Seal and the earl of Arundel she insisted with a gravity (and an honesty) equal to theirs that she had no interest in politics; that she was only Queen Mary's loyal subject and loving sister. However, with Paget and Arundel she took no chances; she made no plea to remain at Court, saying that her first object was always to do what would best please and comfort the queen. She believed she convinced Paget, who had always liked her and considered her clever and cautious; Arundel gave no sign of his opinion and she could only hope.

The very next day, Elizabeth was summoned to the queen, who met her in a private parlor. Mary came forward alone; her ladies grouped at some distance, too far away to hear what was said. Elizabeth had entered the parlor alone to be seen to be without support. She knelt at once, trembling with hope, with anxiety, with fear that her chains would not be unlocked.

"There is no need to be so fearful," Mary said, recalling that both Renard and Gardiner had insisted that if she let Elizabeth escape the Court, she must make her sister sure of her goodwill. But she could not help adding, "Although I think you will be happier where your tender pride will not be so easily affronted. Still, I wish you to know I love you well."

With some considerable effort, Elizabeth kept her head bent so the blazing fury that had, she knew, turned her eyes a burning gold could not be seen. What she wanted to do was remind Mary of how *she* had felt when their father had given Elizabeth precedence over her elder sister. Of course, Elizabeth had been totally unaware of that, being an infant in arms at the time. Suddenly, Elizabeth remembered how clumsy Mary was politically and wondered if her inept sister had been taking a petty revenge in giving Margaret Stuart precedence rather than making a political point.

"Your affection is my greatest treasure," Elizabeth murmured; if she was only sure Margaret Stuart's precedence was not politics but revenge, she would gladly grant Mary her little triumph. "That I may carry your assurance of love with me warms my heart."

Elizabeth did not see Mary's sudden frown or her quick angry glance at the ladies clustered out of hearing range behind her. To assure Elizabeth of her affection, Mary had selected a valuable sable hood and two strings of pearls as a parting gift. That remark about warming her heart sounded as if Elizabeth knew about the hood. Mary wondered if one of her ladies was passing news. No, it could not be.

"To remind you of that love, I will arrange that your head as well as your heart be warm," Mary said, trying to smile and not succeeding. "Here, take this as a parting gift."

Elizabeth looked up, allowing the hope she had felt to show in her face. Mary nodded and gestured for her sister to rise, then turned and beckoned to Jane Dormer, who came forward carrying the hood in one hand and the pearls in the other. Mary's expression became less dour, a slight smile touching her lips as she saw surprise changing to delight on Elizabeth's face.

"Oh, madam," Elizabeth said. "How very kind of you. How very generous. I thank you. These will be precious to me indeed, not for their value but as a mark of your good will."

But the slight smile disappeared. Mary did not respond to the real warmth in Elizabeth's voice. She only nodded again and said, "You may go."

Release! Until Mary said those words, Elizabeth had expected every moment that Mary would change her mind, would laugh and say it was all a jest and Elizabeth must stay at Court. The fear was ridiculous, not a real expectation, just a mark of how desperately Elizabeth wanted to get away.

With that fear still driving her, Elizabeth barely managed to retain her dignity, backing slowly away from the queen and bowing again just before the guard stationed at the door opened it for her. In the corridor her women joined her, all smiling when they saw the parting gifts clutched to Elizabeth's bosom. She said nothing, swallowing and swallowing nervously until they were out of sight of Mary's guards. Then she cast dignity to the wind and fled to her apartment where she bade her household make ready to leave. *At once.*

There were a few moments of panic while the maids of honor asked shrilly what was wrong? Why had the queen been so generous if Elizabeth was in disgrace? Were they trying to escaping arrest?

"No, no, of course not," Elizabeth assured them, and holding out the hood and the pearls, told them they were parting gifts from the queen, marks of her sister's affection. "Just . . . just I have this crazy fear that she . . . she loves me too much to let me go. And I am so tired of the formalities of Court, so tired of all the talk about Prince Philip and the emperor, may they both live forever and the queen also. I need the peace of the country. Let us go *now.*"

Fortunately a great deal of packing had been done after the visit of the earl of Arundel and Lord Privy Seal had provided Elizabeth with the expectation that Mary would release her. Still there was a little more than an hour of chaos while messages were sent to the stables, wagons to carry Elizabeth's goods were made ready, and the household was organized to leave.

Still in irrational terror of pursuit, Elizabeth insisted on riding. Being mounted gave her the feeling that she was free, that she could gallop away if pursuit came. Despite the cold and the fine rain drifting from the sky, she could not bear the thought of being closed into a litter. That might protect her from the weather, but it could not move faster than a walk.

The ladies foisted on her by the queen stood by the litter that Elizabeth ignored and expostulated with her until she was actually mounted and riding away. Lady Alana sighed softly and gestured for Ladbroke, the head groom, to bring forward her own horse.

Ystwyth was already saddled, and Ladbroke only seemed to lead her, knowing the bridle would fall away from her head at a touch. Lady Alana mounted and rode after Elizabeth.

"Oh, surely Lady Elizabeth does not expect us to ride in this weather," Elizabeth Marberry said, her voice high with protest.

"No, no," Kat assured them calmly, moving toward the luxuriously cushioned travel wagon. "Truthfully, none of you rides well enough to keep up with our lady. Lady Alana will be with her. The travel wagon is for us. Ladbroke and Tolliver will ride with us until Sir Edward's men are sent to watch over us and the baggage."

Elizabeth Marberry and Eleanor Gage exchanged worried glances. The previous day, the chancellor had sent for them and told them again that they must watch everything Elizabeth did, to whom she spoke, who were her favorites specially now that she was on her own. There was some danger, Gardiner explained, that Lady Elizabeth might be led astray by her distaste for the Spanish marriage into consorting with rebels. She must be saved from the dangers inherent in such an association. And now, in the first hour of her freedom, Elizabeth might well escape them.

She did not, however, try to escape while they passed through the city, curbing her horse to respond with smiles and waves to the increasing number of people to who came out into the rain to see her pass. Beyond the city, not half a mile along the road, Lady Elizabeth's four elderly guardsmen were joined by a dozen armsmen dressed in Tudor colors. As soon as their wagon came into view, six of the men offered Lady Elizabeth brief bows and rode back to meet the travel wagon and baggage. Ladbroke and Tolliver rode ahead to join Elizabeth, who waved and gestured to the road.

But then Lady Elizabeth did escape their watchful eyes. Sir Edward himself and four of his men, Master Dunstan, now armed with a sword and two pistols, the four elderly guardsmen who always watched Elizabeth's apartment, and Ladbroke and Tolliver, also well armed, set out at a fast trot with Lady Elizabeth and Lady Alana in the center of the group.

Eleanor Gage looked alarmed. How could they watch Lady Elizabeth if she were so far ahead? They should have insisted on riding too. But Marberry smiled and leaned closer to Eleanor Gage.

"We don't have to ride with her," she murmured. "I'll find out from the armsmen who she spoke to and where she stopped."

The trot escalated into a canter and the entire party disappeared. Marberry and Eleanor Gage looked at Kat Ashley, but she did not look after Lady Elizabeth's party. Her attention seemed totally absorbed by arranging the cushions to ease the jolting of the wagon. Blanche Parry, who had been Elizabeth's nurse and was now her personal maid, laughed. Despite her low birth, she always traveled with the maids of honor, which was shocking; but Lady Elizabeth was much attached to her.

"Don't worry about her ladyship," Blanche said. "She sticks on a horse like a burr." She looked knowingly at Marberry and Gage and added, her lips slightly twisted, "She's truly eager to get to Ashridge. Won't stop to talk to nobody until the horses need a rest."

About halfway to Ashridge that prediction proved accurate. The rain had ended and Kat rolled up one of the leather curtains to look ahead. A turn in the road disclosed a crowd of horses being led through the gates of a large inn. Sir Edward stepped out and signaled them to stop. The jolted and bruised travelers in the wagon all smiled with relief. Sometimes the slow vehicles were sent on ahead instead of being allowed to rest with the riders.

Queen Mary's women hurried into the inn and saw that Elizabeth and Alana were alone at a table with cups of what smelled like mulled cider in their hands. There was no one in the inn except the armsmen, sitting at a large table, but Marberry knew that any number of conspirators could have come and gone before they arrived. Then she told herself not to be foolish. The armsmen were too relaxed to have been watching Lady Elizabeth conferring with strangers.

Nonetheless when she had approached Lady Elizabeth and dropped a curtsey, she asked innocently why the inn was so empty.

Elizabeth laughed. "Because Sir Edward had his men drive out the poor folk who were warming themselves here. Well, not really. They are gone into the kitchen, I think . . . and are likely warmer than we."

"No doubt," Alana said, also smiling "because all we have is the one fireplace and the kitchen is also warmed by the baking ovens." She shook her head at Elizabeth. "You will have to tell Sir Edward to leave the innkeeper a few more shillings as I suspect the company now in the kitchen may have snatched some extra loaves of bread or slices of cheese."

"Lady Alana is a clever traveler," Elizabeth said, nodding at her women and gesturing for them to join her at the table. "The warm cider was a good thought." But when they were seated she looked around, sighed and said, "Very well, now who has remembered something left behind that must be fetched? We are just too far along in our journey to go back, but a servant can ride back to London and likely still reach Ashridge at the same time as the traveling wagon and baggage."

To the protests that they were not so careless, since she had warned them a day ahead, Elizabeth shrugged.

"Now how can you know you have forgotten anything before we are even unpacked?" Kat asked.

Elizabeth leaned closer to Kat, who had seated herself on Elizabeth's left. "Because it is something I never had," she said softly, although her voice was just loud enough for the ladies across the table to hear. "The queen was so kind to me, and her gifts so much surprised me, that every idea beyond that of her gentleness and generosity went out of my head." Elizabeth stared hard, warningly, into Kat's eyes. "I completely forgot that the chapel in Ashridge is not properly furnished."

Kat's eyes widened, but she only nodded and said, "True. I had not thought of that."

Most of the other ladies looked either surprised or dropped their eyes to hide their expressions.

Eleanor Gage smiled brightly. She had found that she liked Lady Elizabeth and enjoyed her company; she wanted to believe the best of her. "Of course, you are right," she said. "As I remember the king required chapels to be unadorned." She gave a little shiver of distaste. "So . . . plain. So . . . ugly. Nothing to lift the heart."

Elizabeth made no direct reply to Eleanor's remark. She said only. "I had intended to ask my sister what I should do, what I would need to fit the chapel for worship."

"Oh, my," Eleanor said. "It is really too bad that you did not ask. It would have given Her Majesty so much pleasure. I am quite sure that the queen would be willing to advise you. In fact, perhaps you could write to Her Majesty. Doubtless her reply would reach Ashridge before time for vespers so you could send out at once for proper furnishings."

"A most excellent idea," Elizabeth said and gestured at Dorothy Stafford.

Dorothy, her lips tight with distaste but her eyes full of understanding, nodded. She rose, went to the table where the armsmen sat, and sent one of the men to fetch a servant who could discover and bring to her Lady Elizabeth's writing desk with its paper and pens and stoppered ink flask.

Elizabeth was not sure how much effect her request for chapel furniture would have on Mary, but she hoped it would assure her sister that she intended to continue to worship by the Catholic rite. Likely the request would save her the cost of the chapel furniture too, Elizabeth, who kept a tight reign on expenditures, specially unnecessary ones, thought.

Likely Mary would send a priest as well as chapel furniture. Elizabeth repressed a sigh. At least her request had been private. Those who clung to the reform rite might never know, and she had not been burdened with a black-garbed priest riding with her for all the people who had come out to cheer her to see.

One of the servants was sent off with Elizabeth's letter. Warm drinks were served to the latest come ladies. They had barely finished when Sir Edward came to tell them the horses were sufficiently rested. Elizabeth rose at once. Kat groaned, but also got to her feet. A party of guards went out first, then two of Elizabeth's guards, then the ladies, the other two guards and the rest of the armsmen.

By now the folk who had been sent to the kitchen had had time to spread the word in the village around the inn of who had come. The inn yard was full of folk, and the murmur "Elizabeth, the Lady Elizabeth" ran, until she appeared, when hearty cheers rang out. Elizabeth smiled and waved graciously and sharply ordered her men to be gentle when they pushed back the crowd so the horses could be brought.

When they were mounted, Elizabeth smiled all around again and said sweetly, "Thank you, good people," waving as the party rode out. She knew the signs of her popularity would be reported, both the crowds that had gathered in the London streets and this, but was uncertain of the result. It might be a danger or a protection, but one thing she was certain about: she was not going to have her armsmen use force to disperse any crowd cheering her.

Having worked out their fidgets and high spirits on the first lap of the journey, both horses and Elizabeth, who had at last shaken the fear she would be pursued and ordered back to the Court, were willing to go forward at a walk. The travel wagon was still easily in sight of her when a single horseman appeared riding toward them. He waved his cap, then pulled to the side of the road as if to wait until they passed.

Suddenly Elizabeth burst through the horses ahead of her, crying aloud, "Denno! Oh, my Denno how glad I am to see you."

Marberry and Gage gasped with shock, but Kat, Blanche Parry, and most of Elizabeth's long-time ladies were all laughing.

"Who wagered against his appearing?" Dorothy Stafford asked.

All of Elizabeth's ladies, except the queen's new additions, grinned and shook their heads, Agnes Fitzalan remarking, "I swear if we were magically carried to China and set off from one of their cities to come home, Lord Denno would be on the road somewhere, waiting for us."

"Who or what is this Denno?" Marberry asked, gazing with horror at Lady Elizabeth leaning precariously from her saddle to offer her hand to a white-haired old man, who kissed it . . . rather too lingeringly in Marberry's opinion.

"Lord Denno is a merchant, rich as Croesus, who, quite literally, I believe, dandled Lady Elizabeth on his lap when she was an infant," Kat said, smiling fondly at Denno and Elizabeth who were talking hard and fast. "I only became her governess when she was three so I did not see that myself. Lady Bryan told me—and mentioned his generosity."

"A merchant was given such access to a royal child?" Marberry's voice was contemptuous. "No doubt he was her mother's friend."

"Oh no." Kat flushed, knowing what kind of stories ladies in Mary's confidence would have heard about Ann Boleyn. "He was friend and companion to the duke of Richmond and came with him when Richmond visited. Until he died, the duke was mad for Lady Elizabeth. She called him Da, although we explained and explained that Richmond was not her father."

"But Richmond died years ago," Marberry remarked. "How come this merchant is still so much a favorite that Lady Elizabeth nearly falls off her horse to give him her hand."

Kat shook her head. "Lord Denno grieved terribly over Richmond when he returned from a long voyage and discovered the

young duke had died. He said Lady Elizabeth was his legacy
from his dear Harry, that to please her gave meaning to his life.
He has no one of his own at all . . . except Lady Alana is some
distant cousin." She smiled reminiscently. "When Lady Elizabeth
was a little girl, she was a veritable plague to him, always quarreling with him and demanding the most unsuitable things. But
he never lost patience and always gave her only what was right
and proper."

"And very rich and expensive," Alice Finch said, giggling.

"And he is most generous to us also," Dorothy Stafford added,
grinning again. "You should see the furs he brought us—all Lady
Elizabeth's ladies. A very nice man, clever and amusing."

"And what does he get in return?" Eleanor Gage asked, her
eyes round with distress.

Kat laughed. "A smile from Lady Elizabeth. Her hand to kiss.
The privilege of being soundly beaten at chess—although he usually beats her at tables. He adores her and is so rich that what he
gives is meaningless to him, except as it makes our lady smile."

"Surely she arranges lower taxes or easier passage for his goods
through customs," Marberry said.

"No," Kat answered sharply. "You are newly come to Lady
Elizabeth's service and do not understand Lord Denno's special
place. Though it may shock you, I must say it so you understand.
He is her friend, her true friend. He cares nothing for any favor.
It is as if she is all he has in the world to . . . love."

"Not in any wrong way," Dorothy Stafford said quickly. "You
can see he is too old to be interesting as a man, but she has a
very strong affection for him."

"And he is a *safe* friend," Kat put in, defending her indifference
to the relationship. "He never cared about political party. He is
so rich that the trading is a game to keep him busy. He pays his
taxes and if the way of his goods is eased through customs, it is
his man of business, Joseph Clayborne, who arranges it. In all the
years Lord Denno has come visiting Lady Elizabeth, I have never
heard him say a single word about his business, except sometimes
to make us laugh over his or Master Clayborne's experiences with
foolish or greedy clients."

"Does he cling strongly to the reformist rite?" Gage sounded
worried. "Many merchants do espouse that false rite."

"If he does, he has never spoken of it to us," Alice Finch

remarked; her brow furrowed in difficult thought. "And he never, that I can remember, came to any church service with us."

"He never talks about politics or religion." Dorothy Stafford offered a guileless smile.

"What does he talk about then? Gossip?" Marberry asked.

"No, Lord Denno doesn't gossip," Kat said, seriously. "He doesn't seem at all interested in the Court or the courtiers. He was friends with Sir Anthony Denny, but Sir Anthony died, and I know the duke of Norfolk is the one who got permission for him to visit Lady Elizabeth while she was at Court, so Norfolk must know him. Mostly he talks about the strange countries he has visited and his adventures as a trader."

Elizabeth Marberry made some inconsequential remark. It was clear that Dorothy Stafford knew she was Mary's spy and would say nothing that could cast a shadow on Lady Elizabeth. Likely Kat Ashley knew too, but Alice Finch did not; poor Alice though not totally simple was certainly a few bricks short of a full hod. It was significant that Alice innocently confirmed what Ashley and Stafford said. This Denno was no rebel and no contact for them.

While those thoughts passed through her mind, Marberry watched as Sir Edward rode over to join Lady Elizabeth and Lord Denno. It was interesting to see that Sir Edward, who was careful and punctilious about his place, accorded the older man a bow, and as the wagon drew nearer the small group, they could see that all three were smiling. In another moment the old man nodded; the women heard Elizabeth's joyous laugh and Sir Edward's hearty "Glad to have you, my lord."

Then Elizabeth rode back to the armsmen with Lord Denno by her side. Lady Alana fell back to give him room. Sir Edward again moved to the head of the cavalcade and they all set off. It did seem a little strange to Marberry that Lord Denno, who had come from the direction of Ashridge should ride back again, but when she remarked on it, Kat smiled again.

"Lord Denno must have ridden to Ashridge to see if Lady Elizabeth was yet in residence and been disappointed. So, when he found her on the road, it is not at all surprising that he should ride back to make the visit he had hoped for."

"But it will be dark if he stays to visit. Will he ride back to London in the dark?" Gage asked.

"No," Dorothy Stafford said, rolling her eyes. "He doubtless has a house or a lodge only a mile or two from the manor."

Alice Finch nodded. "Yes, it is very strange. Lord Denno seems to have a lodging very near all of Lady Elizabeth's manors."

Blanche Parry, who sat as far back in the wagon as she could so as to give the least offense with her presence to the high-born ladies, looked down at the jewel box safely cradled on her lap. She did not smile, but inside her head bubbles of mirth rose. She could easily imagine what had been said in the few moments of earnest talk before Sir Edward joined her Bessie and Lord Denno. "Where have you been?" Elizabeth would have snarled at her long-suffering lover, and he would have made some gentle rejoinder, reminding her of how terrible their meeting at Court had been.

Poor Bessie, she had wept so hard in Blanche's arms after her maid of honor was deep-spelled in sleep. Not seeing her Denno was terrible, she had sobbed, but seeing him where foul-minded and loose-tongued courtiers watched her every word and glance was far worse. She did not dare even seek a quiet corner to converse with one they would consider a common merchant so she was unable to truly speak to him or smile at him or touch him. Denno would remind her, Blanche thought, that Elizabeth herself had told him she could not bear such meetings and told him not to return.

In fact, for once Blanche was wrong about what had passed between Elizabeth and Denoriel. She had wasted no time in quarreling. Too aware of the armsmen who had seen her rush to him and aware that any with keen hearing would catch some of their exchange across the too-small width of the road, Elizabeth had said, "Denno! I did not know you were back. How long have you been in England?"

He, with his back to the armsmen, had asked softly, "Will you come Underhill tonight?"

His eyes were as bright a green as the finest emerald touched by sunlight. Elizabeth had a double vision—of her Denno in the mortal world worn by years of watching over her and of her lover Underhill, smooth-skinned and golden-haired. How she loved them both. She laughed aloud but ducked her head so her lips would be hidden from the watching men and her voice was only a murmur.

"I am so eager—" through gritted teeth "—that if you do not

come I swear I will build a Gate myself," and then, louder, she asked, "Will you not come back to Ashridge with us?"

"Yes, I will." And more softly, "I think your new ladies should see how much at ease I am in your household."

"Yes, they should. Even Gardiner cannot make *your* visit a crime. Everyone knows you have no interest in politics."

"Good. I have some pretty trinkets for you from the voyage also."

That was when Sir Edward rode up, and Denoriel explained that he had a rumor from the Court that Lady Elizabeth would be leaving to take up residence in Ashridge. Naturally, since he was just back from a trading voyage and had a bag-full of trinkets for his lady and her ladies, he had ridden out to Ashridge. He had been at his lodge for two days and then decided he had better return to London to discover if the rumor had changed.

"And so here I am. And Lady Elizabeth has just asked if I would ride back to Ashridge—to make my visit after all."

Elizabeth laughed aloud and Sir Edward smiled. He hoped there would be no attack on the road, but if there were, he was doubly happy to have Lord Denno's skilled sword in their party.

Sir Edward had been appalled when he was told of the attempts on the queen's life while Elizabeth was beside her. He had at once applied to the chancellor for the right to assign guards to Lady Elizabeth. His request had been refused angrily, the chancellor saying that Elizabeth was in no danger; it was Queen Mary who had been attacked. Sir Edward knew better, but he could not prove it.

Now Sir Edward joined Nyle at the head of the cavalcade. "Be wary," he warned.

Arriving at the Gate in Avalon, Harry swept his hair back from the blue star that blazed on his forehead. The four knights, armored and with their visors obscuring their faces, looked at his companions.

"You know us," Mechain said sharply.

"No, maybe they do not," Elidir suggested in a reasonable voice. "Likely they were not born when we still came regularly to Oberon's Court."

"Oh, very well. I am Mechain and he is Elidir. We are both of Elfhame Elder-Elf."

"You are recognized . . . And most welcome."

There was a definite note of surprise in the somewhat hollow voice that appeared to come from the air about the middle of the Gate platform. Often the Sidhe of Elfhame Elder-Elf had lived too long. Because there was nothing new for them, nothing to keep their minds alert, they drifted off into Dreaming and eventually ceased being. Harry had changed that for most of the older Sidhe. One way and another, between mortal curiosity and love of meddling, he had involved them in challenging and dangerous projects and they had come alive.

As Harry stepped off the Gate platform Lady Aeron, Phylyr, and Gogonedd appeared. All three mounted and set out across the white-starred mosslike ground cover toward Avalon.

"Welcome?" Elidir repeated. "Are we likely to be welcome?"

Mechain made a indeterminate noise that was not an answer, and Harry looked up at the palace, which changed frequently. Today it seemed to be made of slightly translucent mother-of-pearl. Light from within a myriad of lacy minarets stirred pale gleams of gold, of rose, of soft blue within the walls. From the tallest, central tower, Oberon's black and gold banner flew.

Harry sighed. "He *is* here. I sort of hoped . . . I don't know whether we will be welcome. I'm sure he would have been pleased to know we had cleared Alhambra of evil, but not knowing where it went?" He sighed again. "He isn't going to be pleased that we waited so long to tell him about it, that's for sure."

"Let's get it over with," Mechain said.

One stride after Mechain spoke, the elvensteeds were at the broad steps of the palace. Harry dismounted and then stood still, looking doubtfully down at what appeared to be mother-of-pearl steps and then at his sturdy boots. In the mortal world, mother-of-pearl was fragile. However, Elidir and Mechain had started up the stair without cracking anything; they were heavier than he, and their boots were as sturdy.

He followed them through the tall central doors and along a gracious corridor to another pair of wonderfully decorated golden doors, before which, quite suddenly, there was a tall, elegant Sidhe whose silver hair trailed down his back and over his shoulders in shining waves. He smiled at the elder Sidhe and bowed.

"Elidir. Mechain. What a pleasure it is to see you here."

"So, Lord Ffrancon, you are still serving Oberon," Elidir said.

"Yes indeed. You laughed at me once because I had no time for pleasure, but I have no time to grow bored either."

Mechain laughed. "And we have grown old enough, at last, to come to your way of thinking. But it took a mortal to teach us. Can you find time for us to speak to King Oberon? Harry has news."

"And it may not be welcome news," Elidir said flatly.

"A private meeting?" Lord Ffrancon suggested.

"Perhaps that would be best," Elidir agreed.

Harry said nothing. If a great Evil had been loosed Underhill it was his fault. He was the one who had suggested clearing the evil from Alhambra and El Dorado, not leaving those wonderful domains in the grip of the Bright Court's enemies. The elder Sidhe had risen to the challenge and helped him, but it was his idea, his fault.

The elder Sidhe might be reprimanded, but Oberon would do them no harm, except perhaps banish them to their lovely (and very boring) elfhame and tell them to stay there. But he . . . He could be sent back to the mortal world. The elfshot poison had been completely leached from his body. He had not felt ill or needed to ask Mwynwyn's help in a long time. If so, he could survive in the mortal world. But who would he be? What would he do?

The thought of being driven out of Underhill was terrible to him. From the first time he had come here with Denno, he had been enchanted by the place. He loved the silver twilight coming from the star-spangled sky that held no sun, no moon, the lawns of dark moss with their tiny white flowerlets, the faintly perfumed air. He even loved the swirling and dangerous mists of the Unformed lands and the ugly, inimical domains. And Lady Aeron . . . if he were banished, he would lose Lady Aeron!

A faint snort sounded in his mind, and his spirits lifted. Lady Aeron, like any other elvensteed, was her own law. If she wished to come to him in the mortal world, she would. Then Harry reminded himself that the duke of Richmond was dead, long enough dead that it was likely no one would recognize him.

He would not need to worry about money; he could trust Denno to provide for him. He could live in the house on Bucklersbury where the servants were Low Court Sidhe, who would speak Elven and bring him news. He could see Elizabeth . . . That thought cheered him enough that when Lord Ffrancon beckoned them along a corridor to a side door, Harry squared his shoulders and went in first.

The room was (for a palace Underhill) small. The wall that faced the door from which he and his friends had entered seemed to be one large sheet of glass that displayed rolling hills with silver water in the distance. It was impossible, of course; that wall should have either faced the corridor or been part of an equivalent wall in another room. Harry hardly gave it a glance or a thought. The apartment he lived in in Llachar Lle had a wall like that.

What Harry's eyes fixed on was the being who stood looking out of the window. Harry was a tall man, but considerably shorter than his Sidhe friends. This being—he was not really a man at all—stood head and shoulders above Elidir and Mechain. He turned slowly to face them.

His hair was thick and black, combed back in smooth waves from a deep widow's peak. His eyes were black too, so vibrantly alive that to Harry they seemed to flicker with golden lights. The nose was fine, the lips perfect, the chin firm without being aggressive. Altogether the face was so beautiful, it was unreal.

"So you have news, and since you request a private audience it must be bad news." A deep chuckle sounded. "I have never known a subject to want to give good news in private."

"My lord." Harry took half a step forward and bowed. "Some of the news is good. Alhambra is free of evil."

There was a moment of silence and then Oberon asked with some amusement, "Now how did you manage that?"

He could have sent his Thought into their minds and known everything at once, but the Thought caused pain and sometimes even damaged the minds it touched too directly, especially those of fragile humans. Besides he found it interesting, and amusing, to ask and be answered.

"That is the bad news." Harry sighed. "We have no idea. Can evil die?"

"No," Oberon said. "It can be diminished and then bound, but it will always exist."

"Yes, that is what we were trying to do, to diminish it. And one of the elder Sidhe who has long studied mortal Christianity was seeking a spell to bind the evil. Then we hoped to send it off into the Void."

Oberon cocked his head. "As good a plan as any. Even evil would find escape from the Void difficult. From the fact that you are here, clearly your plan did not work. What happened?"

"We were successful in diminishing the evil and confining it to one place in Alhambra, what had, we thought, been the place to which it was first drawn when the priests cursed the domain."

"How?"

"By attrition, my lord," the warrior Elidir said. "It created evil things and we killed them, draining its power."

"I sealed the domain against the dark power of sorrow and pain," Mechain said, "and drew to it the strength that comes from light and laughter. In that way the evil was not fed."

"That is powerful magic," Oberon said.

"I was once a sorcerer of power," Mechain replied, lifting her chin and smiling.

Oberon's curved brows rose. "And you are again, it seems."

Mechain's smile grew broader. "By Harry's mischief. You do not know the half of the spells I have uncovered from eons past and learned to use again to protect him . . . and us."

Oberon looked at Harry. "And your part?"

"I helped Elidir kill the little evil creatures, and as we cleared parts of the palace Elidir and Mechain placed silver sigils and when they were away I put down iron. Little by little we wore the evil down."

"And then?"

"We went away for a time, leaving behind some simple constructs. They were corrupted when we returned and we destroyed them. The evil was weaker after that; it had used much of its power to alter the constructs. I think it intended us to use the constructs so that they would have a chance to harm us."

"Likely enough. But you were not fooled?"

"A friend, who is very sensitive, warned us and told us that it was in the altar and we surrounded that with silver and iron. We intended to return quickly to discover if it was still contained, but Sewel had not yet completed his spell and . . . and we were distracted by another problem. When we did come back . . . in mortal July, the new constructs we had left were untouched and our sensitive told us the evil was entirely gone."

"Where?"

Harry, Elidir, and Mechain all swallowed. "We don't know."

"That was July. This is mortal December . . ." Oberon no longer sounded amused.

"We have been seeking it, my lord," Harry said. "We have been seeking news of what it can breed, what it can do. Of course, we cannot seek in the Dark Court's domains, but there is nothing unusual, not in any Unformed land we have visited and not even in such places as Wormgay Hold and Fur Hold."

There was a long silence into which Oberon loosed a heavy sigh; however, the amusement was back in his eyes.

After another moment, he shook his head. "Mortals," he said.

Chapter 18

In Caer Mordwyn Prince Vidal seethed. The journey so swiftly undertaken by Elizabeth had caught him entirely by surprise. He had no opportunity to send Francis Howard and his men to attack the party. Renard had not warned him that Elizabeth might be allowed to leave the Court. The last time he had spoken to the Imperial ambassador, Renard had been certain that Mary was convinced Elizabeth must remain at court where she could be watched.

It was awkward working with a mortal who could not be brain burned, who must believe that he was obeying his Imperial master when that Imperial master wanted the opposite of what Vidal wanted. Unfortunately Emperor Charles did *not* want Elizabeth dead—and Vidal had no way to reach Charles to change his mind. The Dark Court in Spain and the Low Countries was very weak. They would give him no help and absolutely refused to chance any confrontation with the Bright Court of Melusine.

There was enough misery generated by Charles's and his son Philip's attempts to wipe out Protestantism in the Low Countries to keep the Dark Court well fed. They would brook no interference with Charles. He was growing old. They wanted no pressures on him that could damage him in any way. So Vidal had no way to reassure Renard that arranging Elizabeth's death would please his master. He was forced to use compulsions that were in a separate place in Renard's mind.

Vidal arranged that Renard find a suitable man among the embassy staff and order him to kill Elizabeth. Renard had enough free will in that "hole" in his mind to make promises to his agent to see that he had a suitable weapon and suitable clothing. When the first attempt failed, the "hole" called Renard to Otstargi, who was waiting for news. Otstargi gave other instructions and a vial of clear liquid to be added to a glass of wine for the agent. When the second attempt on Elizabeth failed, the "hole" closed. Renard had no knowledge, no memory, of ever having thought of doing Lady Elizabeth any physical harm.

Now Elizabeth had escaped the Court with all the public appearances that made her vulnerable. She would be totally inaccessible to anyone except her trusted servants. A mortal messenger would not be allowed into her presence at all or so surrounded by her people that he could not touch her. A Dark Sidhe could possibly throw a knife accurately enough to reach her at such a distance, but no Dark Sidhe would endanger himself so much for Vidal, and besides that accursed Elizabeth would see through any disguise and expose the attacker.

Vidal shuddered. If the Dark Sidhe were recognized for what he was, Oberon would hear of it. There had been a Thought raking Underhill too recently. Something had disturbed Oberon and sent his Thought seeking. Not that Vidal was willing to touch that Thought to find an answer to the question of what it was seeking, but just in case . . . perhaps he would abandon attempts to rid the world of Elizabeth by mortal means.

Would that mean she would escape him? Vidal's hands, which had been lying peacefully on the arms of the cushioned chair even while unpleasant thoughts racked him, curled. His sharp, diamond-hard nails scraped along the polished Sidhe bones that made up the chair arms. With a faint screech one of the bones cracked and then shattered. Vidal was staring down at the fragments in his lap and on the floor when the door of the private parlor opened and Aurilia came in.

"I felt your unease, my lord," she said, "and your thought that Elizabeth is loose. Is that so much worse for us?"

Shocked at the loss of control that allowed his thoughts to be read, for once Vidal did not stop to consider the advantages and disadvantages of actually speaking the truth to Aurilia. "It is much worse," he said. "You remember how it was at Hatfield. She sees no one except the faithful. And she herself can see through any disguise so I cannot send one of our own enchanted into a form of her own familiar. I do not know how I can reach her as long as she is not forced into formal appearances."

Aurilia said nothing for a moment, only coming forward and seating herself in the chair, this one of scented precious woods not bones, beside his. Then, her voice uncertain she said, "There is a Thought roaming all through Underhill." Aurilia shivered. "It touched me." Her voice shook. "I had to drink Albertus's potion to calm myself. It is horrible to be touched by Oberon's Thought."

Vidal did not turn his head to look at her, but he nodded. The Thought had not touched him; he had learned from the mist's bindings to withdraw deep inside himself.

"I am aware."

"Was he seeking us?" Aurilia bit her lip and then said in a rush, "If Titania is prodding him about protecting Elizabeth, perhaps you should give over trying to be rid of her, my lord. Mary already hates her. We have never touched Mary. We should leave Elizabeth's fate in Mary's hands without trying to help."

"That is a wise thought, Aurilia." Vidal did not smile, but he was pleased at having maneuvered Aurilia into stating aloud and approving what he had been thinking. Then he added, "Rhoslyn is there, but she has never advocated physical harm to Elizabeth; she has only protected Mary. Oberon would not object to that."

Aurilia was silent for another moment, then said thoughtfully "I have noticed that power is again flowing into Caer Mordwyn. It seems that many are less and less happy with Mary's reign. Perhaps we should work in the other direction. Instead of removing Elizabeth, we should make sure she never comes to the throne by giving Mary a living heir."

Vidal turned not only his head but his body in Aurilia's direction. "That is another wise thought," he said, nodding. "I know through Renard that the queen is negotiating for a marriage to the son of Renard's master."

"So? That makes everything easier, although Mary is not young and may not conceive easily."

Now Vidal smiled. "We can help with that, I think. I must consult our sorcerers but it might be possible to arrange that one of the Dark Sidhe be disguised as her husband—as soon as we get a look at him—and get her with child."

"Sidhe cannot breed with mortal . . . not without spells that even make me think twice," Aurilia said, frowning.

Vidal laughed. "It need not be Sidhe substance that is placed within Mary."

Aurilia nodded at that but then her frown reappeared. "No suspicion must be aroused about the conception." Her brow cleared and she nodded again. "I think I will send Albertus back to the mortal world. Can you not arrange through Renard that he be taken on as one of the physicians who attends the queen?"

"Why not?" Vidal said slowly, brows lifted. "Indeed, why not? Many of the physicians at Court already know him because of his attendance on the dead king. And I doubt he made them dislike him. I must ask him about that. Yes, send an imp for him, Aurilia. You have had a very clever idea, but I want to be sure he understands his purpose."

Aurilia did not look happy. "I think Albertus *would* be useful to us as one of the queen's physicians, but only if his mind is his own. He is very clever, Vidal. Give him a purpose and let him know he will be rewarded and he can accomplish much. Remember it is likely he kept the little king alive for an extra week or two. But if you damage his mind he will fail."

"Oh very well, very well. I will not touch your pet's mind. Send an imp for him. No, don't bother. Let us together bring him from his laboratory. It will impress him with our power, remind him that we can seize him wherever he is and bring him to us. And it will not disturb the functioning of his—" Vidal sneered "—precious mind."

Aurilia was annoyed at Vidal's attitude. She felt he was backsliding. For a long time after he escaped the mist, he had been less self-important, more awake to the uses he could make of others. She hoped she would not need to circle around him to accomplish anything as she had in the past. However, actually it would do no harm at all to throw a fright into Albertus, so she merely imaged Albertus's laboratory for Vidal and let him snatch the physician from that chamber to this private parlor.

The sudden translocation seemed to have accomplished its purpose more thoroughly than Aurilia had expected. Albertus gave Vidal one wide-eyed glance and sank to the floor, head bent, hands folded prayerfully.

"What is your will, my lord, my lady?"

"My will is that you obey Prince Vidal," Aurilia said.

That would flatter Vidal and accomplish what was, after all her own purpose. It was *her* idea to produce an heir out of Mary. The woman was not young and had always been sickly. With any luck she would die while her child was an infant. That would mean a regency, which would make everyone unhappy and very likely cause Elizabeth and her partisans to rebel, which would mean civil war. Aurilia ran her tongue gently over her lower lip in anticipation of the rich harvest of pain and misery to be garnered. She paid no more attention to Albertus.

Vidal was flattered by Aurilia's all encompassing order to Albertus and satisfied, too, with the obvious terror the kneeling man felt. Clearly it would not be necessary to place any compulsion in Albertus's mind. He would obey implicitly out of fear.

"I have information that Mary's government is negotiating with the emperor Charles to marry Mary to his son, Philip. It would be best for the Dark Court if Mary had an heir. You are to go back to the mortal world where I will arrange to have you appointed as one of the queen's physicians. You will do everything in your power to keep Mary in good health until she is married. One way or another I will see that she conceives. Then you will make sure she bears a healthy babe."

Albertus could hardly believe his ears. When he had been snatched out of the laboratory and deposited before Aurilia and Vidal, he had been certain his rebellious intention of somehow foiling Vidal's plans to destroy Elizabeth had been detected. He had expected a punishment so terrible that he could not even imagine it. Instead, he was being given orders that would gain him praise and status in the mortal world as well as satisfying his masters Underhill.

Slowly his shaking stilled and he fixed his full attention on Vidal's words. He would think of Mary, of keeping Mary healthy, of increasing her fertility. If either Vidal or Aurilia looked into his mind, he would be thinking of potions to improve her health.

"I will do my very best, my lord," Albertus said, still kneeling. "I beg you to consider that I could only extend the little king's life for a week or two. Mary, of course, is only frail, not dying. I may be more successful with her, but she has long-trusted physicians. I may not be able to treat her or influence her."

"I will arrange that," Vidal said. "You will be welcome to Mary and trusted by her. You need only take care not to make the other physicians jealous."

"That I can do, my lord. Will I go as myself, as I did when I served the late king?"

Vidal reached out and lightly stroked Aurilia's arm. When she turned to him he passed Albertus's question to her. She looked at her servant and touched the very surface of his mind lightly. He was excited, thinking already of what herbs would best soothe and strengthen the queen. He was looking forward to being a Court physician again. He had enjoyed working for the late king, regretted he could not keep him alive longer, and knew just how to ingratiate himself with the other physicians. Aurilia smiled.

"Yes, let us send him as himself. The queen's physicians know of him but have no reason to be envious. Renard's recommendation will perhaps wake some animosity, but that cannot be helped, and allowing him to keep the same character will prevent any accidents that might be caused by his confusing his identities."

"Do you need anything from your laboratory here to take with you?" Vidal asked.

"No, lord. I dare not take anything from here. If you furnish gold, I can buy what I need in the mortal world."

"There will be gold in your chamber in Otstargi's house."

Ashridge was much closer to London than Hatfield, so even with necessary stops to rest the horses, they arrived well before sunset. A courier sent ahead as soon as Elizabeth had received Mary's congé had warned the servants who had remained to care for the house. Fires were lit, beds were made, dust sheets were removed from any furniture left when the house had last been occupied. A mad rush ensued to ready a meal for those arriving.

It was, of course, impossible to arrange everything perfectly on half a day's notice, particularly when the incoming servants considered themselves superior (because they had accompanied their employers) to those left behind. Fortunately Dunstan settled quarrels and assigned duties before open feuding that could affect the comfort of Elizabeth and her ladies could begin.

Sir Edward was also busy, sending trusted guards to inspect all the rooms, the stables, and the outbuildings. Several relatives of the resident servants were routed out and sent away. Ordinarily such hangers on were not disturbed—they were useful for errands

and odd jobs and only cost a penny when employed rather than
a regular salary—but Sir Edward was wary because of what he
still believed were attempts on Elizabeth, not Mary. Finally, he
set a guard and arranged for men to rotate on that duty.

Elizabeth did not trouble herself with the problems of arrival.
Warm from riding, she wrapped her fur-lined cloak tightly around
her, settled her new sable hood on her head, and announced that
she would walk in the garden with Lord Denno.

Mary's ladies gaped and groaned; everyone was sore and tired
from being shaken and banged in the travel wagon. No one wanted
to walk in a cold, dead garden, and Elizabeth's long-time maids
of honor made no move to follow her, merely dropping curtsies
before holding out their hands to the leaping fire. Kat spoke, but
she only warned Elizabeth to take care not to get chilled. Elizabeth
Marberry, looking around at the women clustered near the fire,
rose crookedly to her feet and reached for her cloak.

"Where are you going, Elizabeth?" Kat asked.

"Does not Lady Elizabeth need an attendant?"

Kat laughed. "Not in this weather, in her own house, with Sir
Edward's guards posted and . . . I think that was Gerrit who was
following her when she went out the door or perhaps it was
Shaylor. I assure you that either of the men would fling himself
between Lady Elizabeth and any danger—as would Lord Denno,
who is a skilled swordsman."

Elizabeth Marberry was equally sure of that; she was not worried about Lady Elizabeth's safety. "But . . . But . . ."

She stared around at the women, casually rubbing their bruises,
resetting their garments, and murmuring to each other. They
would not care if Lady Elizabeth met with rebels or planned to
overthrow her sister. They would be blind and deaf to her treason,
as would the guard. But Marberry had been tasked with preventing such acts. She did not dare even hint of her real purpose to
these women, who all seemed to think the sun rose and set at
the order of their lady and that was the way things should be.

"But why?" she finally got out. "Why should Lady Elizabeth go
walk in a freezing garden in the middle of the winter?"

Kat raised her eyebrows. "To quarrel with Lord Denno, of course.
She has been spoiling for a good fight with him for weeks."

Elizabeth Marberry shook her head in disbelief and angry
helplessness. Her one comfort was that because they had left

Court so suddenly it was unlikely Elizabeth could already have arranged to meet with any anti-Catholic faction.

"But do you not think that is a strange thing to do?" Eleanor Gage asked anxiously.

Kat laughed again. "Not for Lady Elizabeth. She and Lord Denno have been walking in winter gardens and arguing about what to plant where since Lady Elizabeth was eight years old."

"Aren't you cold?" Denoriel asked Elizabeth anxiously. "The sun is setting. We are sure to arouse suspicions coming out here alone like this."

"We won't stay long. Kat will tell them that we are arguing about what to plant. Lady Alana disappeared as soon as I had leave to go, and I didn't know whether she had spoken to you."

"No. She didn't even go home. I think she went off to Cymry."

"I'm sorry," Elizabeth sighed. "I knew she was longing to go, but I was so frightened I couldn't let her leave me. She was my one comfort."

"She understood."

"Oh, Denno, it was horrible." Elizabeth swayed closer so that her shoulder touched Denoriel's arm. She could feel the tension in him as he resisted the impulse to hug her. Gerrit, behind them, could not hear what they said, but he could see them. She sighed again. "Everything I did was wrong and made Mary angrier. And I know that Gardiner was urging Mary to send me to the Tower."

"I do not think he will be successful. Rhoslyn has convinced Mary that worse will befall her if she harms you. That, of course, is a double-edged sword, in that it increases Mary's fear of you, but there is a limit to what Rhoslyn can do."

"I know." Elizabeth's voice was thin and hard. "I am Ann Boleyn's daughter and a heretic, too, no matter how many Masses I attend."

Denoriel chuckled. "Well, you are."

"The worst kind," Elizabeth said, finding a small smile. "I do not care *what* rite is used to worship God, and I do not believe God cares either." She shook her head, dismissing that hopeless topic. "Really why I came out was to warn you that the whole household has been seeded with Mary's and Gardiner's spies. You will not be able to be at home as you were in Hatfield."

"That is not exactly a surprise. I will set my Gate in your

dressing room, behind your gowns and be ready with the Don't-see-me. Do you want me to listen and see if I can determine which of the women are spies?"

"No, no. Mary is not very subtle." Elizabeth laughed. "She simply presented me with two ladies as if I would not guess they were urged upon me to spy. I wonder if she expected me to reject them? Mary herself might have done so. She is devastatingly honest." She laughed softly again. "One I have already subverted, but the other, Elizabeth Marberry, does not like me at all."

"I could listen to the servants, I suppose, but there are so many of them."

Elizabeth winkled a hand out of her cloak and took Denoriel's for a moment. "No, that would take too much power. You would be drained. Anyway Sir Edward, Dunstan, and Blanche have mostly discovered which of the new servants and armsmen are spying."

"Dismiss them?"

"I daren't do that." Elizabeth shivered. "Da said I must seem ignorant. Then the spies will actually work to my benefit as they can testify I had no commerce with Mary's enemies."

"Unless they lie, but the accusation of servants without real proof, especially servants that can be proven spies, will not move the Council against you. Anyway with Roslyn beside her it is not Mary I fear. Harry says it is Gardiner and Renard who are the worst danger. You must write *nothing*, except letters to Mary if you like."

Suddenly Elizabeth's eyes filled with tears. "How I miss Edward! I did so enjoy writing to him and having his answers. Mary does not care about books or my lessons."

"I am sorry, my love, but we could not save him and I think he would not have been happy, where Harry is happy."

"That is true, and Edward had changed. He loved me, I know, but he was growing as rigid in his way as Mary is in hers. I am sure he signed that 'devise' of Northumberland's willingly because he felt a woman should not rule. Too bad we could not take him and show him your queen."

Denoriel laughed. "That would have cured him. Come, love, you are shivering. We have been out long enough. I will be careful when I come for you."

Elizabeth breathed a long sigh of relief and hoped for pleasure and caught Denoriel's hand again. "I cannot wait," she breathed and then as they turned to go back to the house and would pass

Gerrit, she said sharply, "I do not see why I should not have an arbor with milliflora roses near enough to be seen from the windows of the chamber in which we dine."

"Because," Denoriel replied, not loudly but clearly enough for Gerrit to hear, "the roses need sun, and if you place the arbor there, the house will throw a shadow over it for most of the day."

They passed the guardsman, who grinned and shook his head as he fell in behind them. He had heard similar arguments for at least twelve years. Soon the question rose about whether a rose arbor was suitable elsewhere in the garden. Denoriel spoke of the delicacy of roses, of their falling prey to all sorts of blights; Elizabeth shrugged the problem away. It was for her gardeners to worry about. She admired the flowers and the scent of roses.

The discussion had passed on to what mixture of flowers should be in the knot garden by the time Gerrit opened the doors and servants removed outerwear. Elizabeth and Denoriel reached the parlor where her ladies waited. Nyle opened the door and Elizabeth went in, her voice raised in defense of primroses. Denoriel spoke less loudly, but he stubbornly claimed primroses grew too tall and had a limited period of blossoming.

Eleanor Gage and Elizabeth Marberry drew sharp breaths of surprise over Lord Denno's tone, but as she rose to greet Lady Elizabeth, Dorothy Stafford, far from showing surprise, said her mother had developed a kind of primrose that grew low to the ground. Denoriel said he had heard of it, but also heard the flowers were small. Kat agreed that the flowers were small, but had been told that the colors were very intense. The discussion became quite general until Elizabeth seated herself and gestured for a stool to be brought for Lord Denno.

"Sit, sit," she said to him with a brilliant smile. "I will leave the flowers as they are this spring. Dorothy will bring me some of her mother's primroses when they come into bloom and then I will decide. You will stay and have an evening meal with us, will you not, Lord Denno?"

Gage and Marberry were surprised again, but a single glance around showed that none of the others regarded Elizabeth's invitation as in any way unusual. And when Gage repeated her question about Lord Denno riding back to London at night, he laughed and confirmed Dorothy Stafford's and Alice Finch's assumptions that he had a lodge close by.

Everything else said about Lord Denno also seemed true. Food was served and he made teasing conversation with Kat and the other women, who knew him well. He and Elizabeth had several short differences of opinion, during which he answered the high-born lady with complete freedom. He was not at all subservient yet there was nothing in his manner that anyone, even Elizabeth Marberry, could take as too familiar. So, indeed, would an old friend who had dandled a young lady on his knee speak.

They talked about everything. Elizabeth's progress in her lessons in mathematics and navigation produced some hearty laughter that neither Gage nor Marberry understood. Whether she would keep up her Greek—Lord Denno commented on the differences between the classical language and that of the traders in modern Greece with whom he dealt. And Alice Finch, who often tread innocently where others feared to go, asked if Lady Elizabeth was now considering learning Spanish, since she was already fluent in French and Italian.

Lord Denno prevented the awkward pause that would have followed Alice's question by nodding briskly. "Since you already know French and Italian, you will find Spanish very easy," he said, apparently ignorant of or indifferent to any special implication in Alice's remark. "They have most excellent wines and I have done some trading and visited the country."

"Have you?" Eleanor Gage asked eagerly. "Oh, Lord Denno, do tell us what it is like. The queen will likely marry Prince Philip of Spain. Do you know anything about him?"

"Only the most common talk of the country, that he is a most estimable person but rather grave and reserved. As to the country, there is a great deal to be told and perhaps I will save that for another day. If Lady Elizabeth will give me leave, I think I should go now and come back tomorrow? With all the trinkets I have gathered up for her and her ladies, which are lying in my lodge."

A burst of expectation and thanks and pleas to Lady Elizabeth to invite Lord Denno for the next day broke out. Kat silenced the maids of honor and Elizabeth held out her hand to Lord Denno who rose to his feet as she gave the requested invitation and he accepted it.

"Then I will see you again very soon, my lord," Elizabeth said, smiling brilliantly at him as he bowed over her hand.

"Very soon," he replied.

Chapter 19

It was Elizabeth Marberry that Elizabeth invited to sleep in her chamber that night. Marberry was the most suspicious, the most likely to intrude into Elizabeth's bedchamber in the middle of the night. Blanche could send Elizabeth's own ladies away, but she had been told not to interfere with Mary's spies. Thus, it was Marberry who was in a bespelled sleep when Elizabeth tumbled her bedclothes into a heap that might conceal a slender body to a glance from the dressing room door.

She was in a light and laughing humor when she huddled a night robe about her and came into her dressing room. Tonight there was no need for a greedy gobbling of love and freedom as there had been the night before she went to meet Mary, newly proclaimed queen. Elizabeth was looking forward with eagerness and joy to her coming pleasure, but without desperation. She was sure she would have months to enjoy her lover and her dream world where palace windows that could not exist showed living, changing landscapes that were not there. Invisible servants served food and cared for well-furnished rooms, colored flames leapt endlessly over crystal logs, and magnificent clothing grew with her so that favorite gowns fitted her year after year.

There was a cushioned stool waiting. Blanche had carried it in with the excuse that much of her work was done in the dressing room and it was more comfortable for her to sit. No one, not even Kat, criticized anything Blanche did; she had been nurse and maid and now was keeper of Lady Elizabeth's jewels.

"Don't wait up," Elizabeth said, kissing Blanche's cheek before she sat down. "Probably Lord Denno will bring me home very late."

"Just make sure it is not so late that Mistress Ashley comes looking for you or that you are so worn out the ladies will notice."

"No, I—"

There was a soft sound that Blanche obviously could not hear. Elizabeth spun around to see Denoriel coming past a group of gowns. With a soft cry, she rushed forward and threw herself into his arms. He embraced her so tightly that her ribs creaked and she was not aware at all of the steps he took backward or the falling in pitch blackness that usually marked a passage through a Gate.

Loud cheers together with the feeling of solid ground beneath her feet made Elizabeth aware that they had arrived, but clearly not at Logres Gate where she had expected to arrive.

"Damn," Denoriel said in her ear. "Fur Hold."

Elizabeth gasped. "Oh dear," she murmured. "It's my fault. I have been thinking of Fur Hold, wanting to make merry here all the while I was preparing for bed, but I didn't intend to arrive before I was dressed or we . . . I'm afraid the Gate must have taken us where I was thinking."

"A very nice entry," a creaky voice a little to the left and ahead of them said. "But you'll have to do more than simply embrace now that you're on the stage."

"Of course," Denoriel agreed, releasing Elizabeth and turning to face the speaker. "Lady Elizabeth will dance, but my lute got left behind. I must borrow one."

Dance? Elizabeth was frozen with panic for a moment. *In my night rail? With my hair flying loose?* But the binding fear did not hold her for more than a moment. Her eyes took in the bright blue sky with its painted white clouds, the round, petalled sun, which winked down at her and waved its petals, the audience of creatures that no one but the incurably insane could imagine; only these were not creatures of terror. They were all waving something or other in greeting—whatever would wave, arms, tentacles, wings, tails, fuzzy spots on their bellies, long hairs—and cheering with delight. Of course she would dance for them.

As panic receded an exuberant joy took its place. She was free to dance, free of stays and heavy brocades with stiff embroidery,

free of the angry stare of an ageing woman jealous of her youth
and lithe body, free of the fear of what the Spanish marriage would
do to her country, her people, while she was helpless to interfere.
For this night and for every coming night as long as the queen did
not recall her to Court, she was free to dance in Fur Hold, free to
bargain for ornaments with the skilled and clever crabs of Carcinus
Maenas, free to lie and make love in her Denno's big, soft bed.

Elizabeth waved back at her audience and swung around and
around, to try the feeling of her bare feet on the polished boards
of the stage; her hair made a gleaming, billowing red curtain
around her and the full skirt of the night rail flared up, showing her neat ankles and full calves. In the back row a gloriously
dressed Sidhe leaned forward to look more closely. In the front
row two adult kitsune grabbed with human hands to control the
enthusiasm of two young ones seated between them. The little ones
bounced in their seats, their fox tails waving violently and their
little black ears pointed eagerly forward over their small red fox
faces. Laughing, Elizabeth blew them a kiss, raised her bare arms
to pull back her hair, and turned around to look for Denno.

He was bending over a chest, watched by . . . a child's stick
figure? Elizabeth laughed again. How appropriate for that creaky
voice. But it was not really a stick figure. There was some depth
to the impossibly thin arms and legs, a shadowy rounding beyond
the sharp line that delineated a head. The round, seemingly lidless
eyes moved from Denoriel to her. The mouth opened and closed
as it accepted Denno's choice of a lute and invited him to sit on
the chest to play. Denno bowed to it gravely. It bowed to him
in return, then shifted to face Elizabeth, bowed again, and came
to the edge of the stage.

"Lady Elizabeth, human mortal, will dance the galliard, a dance
popular in the Court of Logres, to the music of the lute played
by Prince Denoriel Siencyn Macreth Silverhair, Sidhe of Elfhame
Logres. Attend for edification and pleasure."

Denoriel struck the lute, picked out the tune in simple notes.
Elizabeth began to circle the stage, lifting and pointing her toes
with stately dignity. She circled once deosil, whirled and repeated
the slow and stately walk widdershins. The audience waited in
wide-eyed silence. Now the music began to quicken. Elizabeth
took five quick steps forward, turned, and took five steps back
and bowed. Then five slow gliding steps, which were no part of

the ordinary dance but served in the absence of a partner to mark the completion of one measure and the start of another.

Again the music quickened. Elizabeth darted forward, darted back, leapt in the air to make her turn, her skirts and her bright red hair swinging around her. And Denno played faster and faster until each measure flung her body forward and back and each turn was a high jump, her feet beating together, twice, thrice before she came to earth. And then there was no time for the steps of the dance. Elizabeth whirled round and round and leapt upward while the audience cheered louder and louder, until Denoriel struck a single loud chord. On her last leap upward as the music ended, Elizabeth came down into a full curtsey.

She remained down, panting with her exertion, her bright hair spread around her like a cloak while the beings on the benches whistled and croaked and shrilled and shrieked and even called out in human words. Denno came and helped her to her feet, bowing and steadying Elizabeth as she curtsied again.

The stick-figure overseer of the entertainment came forward and bowed to them both, then said to Denoriel, "Can she dance again? You have made my audience very happy."

"No, I am afraid not," Denoriel said, putting his arm around Elizabeth and drawing her close. "You can see she is exhausted. Remember, she is mortal."

"Ah yes, too bad," the master of ceremonies said, putting out his hand to take Denoriel's lute. "Can she sing perhaps?"

"Not until I catch my breath," Elizabeth began, and suddenly she and Denoriel were off the stage and outside of the little performing place altogether.

Fortunately she was still in the safe circle of Denoriel's free arm; his other hand still held the lute. Both stood looking around in surprise, until their attention was drawn to the stage, which they could see through the gateway, on which a very confused looking gnome now stood surrounded by gardening implements.

"How efficient," Elizabeth said, giggling. "When a new performer appears those who have completed their acts are summarily removed. What if I had wanted to sing?"

"I don't know," Denoriel admitted, also laughing. "I don't think the performer's preference is consulted. From his expression I would say the current holder of the stage is not very eager to display his talents."

Elizabeth giggled again. "Poor thing. But I really enjoyed dancing even though it was so unexpected." She uttered a long sigh of satisfaction. "I haven't been able really to dance all the while I was at Court. Lady Alana warned me that Mary was jealous of my ability so I had to be extra stiff and decorous." She sighed again. "Still, I think you'd better put some clothes on me."

"What do you want to wear?" Denoriel asked.

Before Elizabeth could answer, a short, somewhat plump and very overdressed Sidhe came up behind them, caught a handful of Elizabeth's hair, and pulled her head toward him. She exclaimed and to ease the pull, stepped backward, out of Denoriel's grip.

"So, it's real," the plump Sidhe said. "Very well, I will take her. What do you want for her?"

Denoriel's lips lifted in what was not a smile. He shifted the lute to his other hand so he could drop his right to his sword hilt.

"Lady Elizabeth is not mine to keep or give." His voice could have frozen boiling water. "She is a free mortal, Underhill by the special permission of Queen Titania." Then his voice turned into a nasty snarl. "Let go of her hair."

The plump Sidhe, half a head shorter than Denoriel, paid no attention to the threat, as if no one dared threaten him. He looked shocked and offended.

"Free? What do you mean free? Mortals are all—"

His voice broke into a half astonished, half indignant squawk as Denoriel's sword flashed up, past Elizabeth's shoulder to come within a hair's-breadth of his throat.

"I said to let loose of her hair."

"How dare you—"

Again the words ended in an indignant squawk as the tip of Denoriel's sword just pricked his throat. Several things happened simultaneously: the stranger Sidhe released Elizabeth's hair and sent a levin bolt against Denoriel, who seemed to disappear, the edge of the bolt flickered into blue sparkles against Elizabeth's shield, Elizabeth shrieked "*Cilgwthio*" and made a hard Pushing gesture, and the stranger Sidhe flew backward as a giant Push sent him up into the air and down again into an urso's alfresco party.

"Oh!" Elizabeth cried and ran toward the bearlike creatures. "Oh, I am so sorry—"

"And so you should be, you unnatural abomination!" the plump Sidhe shouted, jumping to his feet with shocking agility, his rage

made somewhat ridiculous by the various portions of different
luncheon dishes that stuck to his clothing and dripped from his
hair. "I will see you skinned alive—"

"Oh, shut up!" Elizabeth shouted, turning away from the angry
Sidhe. "I wasn't apologizing to you, you pest."

What had happened to Denno? Where was he? She turned around,
terrified by Denno's disappearance, tears stinging her eyes. The
levin bolt could not have felled him! His shields were surely better
and quicker than hers, and she had had time to shield. Besides
that bolt should not have been strong enough to harm him. It
had not even buffeted her shields, just broken apart.

The overdressed Sidhe shrieked with rage and stepped forward,
trying to seize her hair again. He could not touch her because of
her shield. Nonetheless she felt his attempt and swung around to
snarl "*Cilgwthio*" and Push again. The male urso began to rise,
but the plump Sidhe shot backward, fortunately away from the
urso family. This time he did not fly as far, but his head hit the
ground with a thud and he lay still. The urso shrugged and sat
down again.

"Denno!" Elizabeth wailed.

She wanted to run and look for him, but she did not know
where to look and she was afraid the fat Sidhe might revive and
take out his anger on the ursos. They were strong, but as far as
she knew had no magic. *She would kill that fat Sidhe!*

But she knew no killing magic and she still wore nothing
more than her night rail so she had no weapon. Swallowing
down more tears she looked back to the last place she had seen
Denno, just outside the gateway to the performing place. And
there was Denno, trying to push his way through a crowd of
beings leaving their places in the audience. Elizabeth breathed a
long sigh of relief.

Denno had just got to the gateway of the performing place
when Elizabeth sensed a nasty humming behind her. She whirled
and saw the pestiferous Sidhe beginning to stir again, both hands
shining blue. That looked more dangerous than the levin bolt he
had originally used. She thought her shields would hold, but she
backed away, looking over her shoulder for Denoriel. He was still
trapped. He would never reach her in time.

And that fat pig would surely start flinging levin bolts around
and hurt the ursos or some other innocent bystander. Elizabeth

realized she would have to control that nuisance herself. Hastily she began to recite the *"Bod oer geulo"* spell. It only took a long moment, but by the time she was finished, as Mechain had promised, she was calm enough not to be in danger of wiping his brain empty. Quietly she murmured, *"Epikaloumai,"* and with a faint smile of satisfaction saw the blue on his twitching hands disappear and the hands grow still. Denno had almost reached her and she signed at him to take his time.

Then, with a sigh of relief, she turned her back on him and stepped forward to face the urso family again and said, "I am so sorry I spoiled your party. It was an accident. I didn't expect him to fly so far."

The young bears were laughing and clapping their hands—very human-looking hands although the backs were covered by fur and only the palms naked. "Do it again!" One of the young ones chortled. "Do it again."

"I don't know if I can," Elizabeth said, relieved that the small ursos had not been frightened. "I haven't had much practice with spells recently. Just . . . just when I'm frightened they work . . . ah . . . better than what I intend."

"He frightened you, missy?" the largest of the ursos said, his forehead and muzzle wrinkling. "I would have helped, but I saw you quiet him down quick enough. Not nice what was in his head. Not supposed to get nasty in Fur Hold. Fur Hold is for fun, for pleasuring little ones."

Elizabeth did not think it wise to mention the levin bolt. There was no more danger now. She just hoped that Denno would be able to think of a way to get the stranger to Gate back to wherever he came from and stay there.

"He wanted to buy me," she said to the urso, "and would not believe my escort when he said I was a free human, permitted by Queen Titania to visit Underhill."

Denoriel did not come directly to Elizabeth, but stopped beside the frozen Sidhe, sword in hand. When he saw what Elizabeth had done, he sheathed the sword, came to her side, and bowed to the urso.

"I apologize for the disruption of your holiday," he said. "My lady is not used to being seized and defended herself—" a wry smile twisted his lips "—with an excess of energy. Can I replace your alfresco? There is a vendor of food coming this way."

"Just the melted cheese tubers," the mid-sized urso said, holding up the dish that now had no more than a smear on the sides. "Most of it is on that silly Sidhe's backside. We were through with the salad and he didn't touch the meat when he landed."

Elizabeth felt eyes on her and looked automatically at the performing place. Lingering just outside of the seating area, she noticed a rather nondescript Sidhe, brown-haired, with light-brown green-flecked eyes and soft red lips. Dark Sidhe, she was sure, but *he* was not looking at her, and when he felt her gaze, he only glanced back briefly. Then his eyes moved to the Sidhe who lay frozen and then to Denno, who had summoned the tall, tiger-striped food vendor and was conversing with him in low tones.

Elizabeth looked away quickly suppressing a smile. *He's not interested in me. He thinks Denno froze that fat pig.* Nonetheless she continued to watch the Dark Sidhe in quick glances. Too many of them *were* interested in her. She saw him looking over the urso family and then past them back to Denno. *I'll have to warn Denno*, Elizabeth thought, but to her relief, the Dark Sidhe turned away and melted into a concourse of creatures playing a wild game.

That made her mildly uneasy, because she still felt as if she were being watched, but her attention was distracted by the food vendor. Drawing behind him a shiny wagon covered with colored doors, he came to the edge of the sitting cloth the urso family had spread and began to ask what they wanted. The small colored doors popped open as the vendor named dishes so the ursos could see what he was suggesting. The young ones crowed loudly when a long loaf, tiger-striped like the vendor, appeared; the mid-sized urso chose that and when she asked the price the food seller shook his head and said that the cost for whatever she chose had been covered.

Meanwhile Denoriel had come to Elizabeth's side and caught her to him. "I am sorry, love, so sorry for deserting you, but the spell took me utterly by surprise."

"The levin bolt took you by surprise? Oh, Denno, were you hurt?"

"What levin bolt? Did that . . ." Denno glared at the prone, food-spotted form. "You mean he loosed a levin bolt? In Fur Hold? In the midst of the alfresco ground?"

"He wasn't in the alfresco ground then. It was when we were

all outside of the performing place. You had your sword at his throat, and he . . . Denno, what happened? He cast the levin bolt at you and you disappeared. I was frightened half to death."

He pulled her tighter for a moment and bent his head to kiss her lips. "It was the lute, not the levin bolt. I didn't even know he had thrown one. Apparently the lute is enchanted to return to the stage if someone needs it. It seems the gnome thought he could sing and play. He wanted the lute. Since I was still holding the stupid thing, it just carried me with it back to the stage."

Elizabeth pulled back enough to be able to look at him; she shook her head and sighed. "This is a wonderful place." For a moment she closed her eyes. "Do you think there is someone I could take to law for having frightened me so much when the lute carried you away? I knew that fat Sidhe would never meet you honorably so I expected the levin bolt and called up my shields. But the bolt shattered on them and for a moment I could not see. When I could see again, you were gone. I almost died of fright."

"But Elizabeth, you dealt with him very well without my help. You had no need to be afraid. You *can* defend yourself."

"Of course I can defend myself," Elizabeth said crossly, wresting herself free of his grasp. "It was not me I was afraid for, you idiot. It was *you*."

Denoriel blinked, speechless for a moment, then said, smiling "You were afraid for me? I am supposed to be the protecting warrior. Why should you fear for me?"

"Because even protecting warriors can be felled by unexpected levin bolts, and you disappeared after his struck."

"Tsk, tsk," Denoriel said playfully. "Should I take offense at your lack of trust in my abilities do you think?"

But Elizabeth was not paying attention. She had been aware all the while they spoke that someone was watching her. Now she turned expecting to see the Dark Sidhe. What she saw, to her relief, was the kitsune family that had been in the front row of the performing place, standing politely out of earshot. She smiled at them, and the kits rushed forward.

"Stop, you naughty ones," one of the adults said. "Beg pardon, Lady Elizabeth. The children have never seen a mortal dancing before and they wanted to speak to you."

Elizabeth held out her hands. "Let them come to me. They are adorable." At one adult's nod, the kits bounced forward again, one taking each hand. "It is very nice of you to enjoy my dancing," Elizabeth said, bending down toward them.

"Where did you learn?" one squeaked.

"In the mortal world," Elizabeth said, "a very long time ago. But I can show you the steps. They are very simple. The trick is the music, which goes faster and faster."

She began to show them the five-step pattern and the difference having a partner made. Meanwhile the elder kitsune had approached Denoriel and looked down for a moment at the frozen Sidhe.

"We saw part of what happened," he said. "At least, I caught the sparkle of a disrupted levin bolt. I even started toward your lady, but the next thing I saw was that person flying through the air. It seemed my interference was not necessary, that the lady could manage on her own, but I did agree when the children wanted to speak to her because I thought perhaps I could help if needed."

"Thank you." Denoriel nodded. "She might have needed help. Her magic is very weak unless she is frightened or very angry, and she only knows a few spells."

The kitsune laughed heartily. "I will not pass on what you said."

Denoriel nodded gratefully. To advertise that Elizabeth's magic was weak was to invite attack.

"But she uses what she does know to great effect," the kitsune continued. Then he looked down. "What are you going to do with him?" he asked, gesturing toward the unconscious Sidhe. "He was working on something very nasty when your lady froze him. I saw the spell-light on his hands."

"If I had any idea where he comes from I would stick him in a Gate and tell it to take him home just as the spell was released. Unfortunately the spell she used wipes out the bespelled one's sense of time, so he'll wake up just as angry as when she froze him. She was afraid he'd start flinging levin bolts around. She is shielded and so am I, but most of these folk aren't."

The kitsune's black lips lifted away from his sharp white teeth. "I will help you get him to a Gate. You should set it for Gateways. He will have plenty of choices of Gates, but it is most unlikely that any of them will bring him back to Fur Hold. Let me just tell my mate where I am going."

Denoriel thought the kitsune's idea so good that he came along to try to convince his partner, in case it objected. It was watching the kits dancing the galliard with each other to Elizabeth's soft singing. Both children were thrilled and laughing, stepping forward and back and bowing to each other.

When they had explained what they intended to do with the frozen Sidhe, the second kitsune lifted its lip to show long, sharp teeth. "You are quite right. When he is released, he will try to do harm. His kind does not well accept being made to look foolish, but anyone in Gateways is likely to be wary of trouble already. Very well, I'll stay with the children. Will Lady Elizabeth need to go with you?"

All three looked at Elizabeth, who was laughing happily while the young kitsune were collapsed on the hardy moss gasping for breath. Then Elizabeth's head turned and she stiffened slightly, feeling watched again. But the explanation was near and pleasant. The young ursos were just behind her, looking at her and the young kitsune. In their hands, they held out portions of the striped delicacy the food vendor had sold.

The mid-sized urso stood behind her family. She bowed slightly to Elizabeth. "They want to learn too," she said, nodding at the young ones. "Is that possible?"

Elizabeth looked at the short thick legs of the urso young, at the solid, blocky bodies, at the heavy arms. "Why not?" she said, grinning. "The dance will look different, but that does not matter if the dancers are content." She looked down at the kitsune. "Will you dance with the ursos?"

"Surely," the very smallest said, "it will be more fun to have four dancing." And she dashed off to pull at the second kitsune's hand.

"All beings are good and the same for you," that kitsune said to Elizabeth in an approving tone when she came with her youngest.

Elizabeth laughed without much mirth. "All the same, but not all good. I have met more than a few who did not deserve the name 'being' and were in no way good."

The kitsune nodded. "My mate and yours are agreed to take the Sidhe you felled to Gateways where he can do no harm. Can you teach the young ones to dance first?"

Both glanced at the four children; the ursos had given part of their striped whatever it was to the kitsune, who were munching delightedly and seemingly describing the dance since the ursos were stumping forward and back. Then all four looked toward Elizabeth, sort of shuffling their feet. It was apparent that the not too great store of patience children held would soon be exhausted. Elizabeth smiled.

"Yes, I can. Denno can release the spell."

"He has control of your spells?"

The kitsune sounded utterly neutral, voice flat to conceal shock. Elizabeth laughed again.

"I know that is not usual, but I am mortal and with an uncertain Talent. The elder Sidhe who taught me magic deemed it safer if any mistake I made could be unlocked. And usually my spells are cast in the mortal world, where no one has the ability to undo what I have done. Underhill I am always accompanied by those far more skilled and have no occasion to use magic." She shook her head. "Today was an exception, but I am no longer the child Mechain and Elidir taught. I think perhaps the safeguards on my spells should be removed."

"Very wise." The kitsune's lips lifted.

Elizabeth went to join the children and the kitsune moved to stand by the mid-sized urso.

When Denoriel and the other kitsune realized the ursos would be peacefully included in the dancing lesson, they turned to the unconscious Sidhe. They had taken a single step in that direction but both stopped and stood staring. The plump Sidhe was gone. Some bits of the ursos' alfresco meal still lay on the ground, mute evidence that he had been there, but the being himself was gone.

"Could the spell have worn off and he simply walked away?" the kitsune said in a voice that showed his disbelief of his own words.

"Not worn off. Not in the time since it was cast," Denoriel said. "I looked at him when I arrived and it had him fast. But it is true that anyone who knows the spell could release it."

"Who here would be likely to know what spell was cast?"

Denoriel shook his head and they both advanced on the place where the Sidhe had lain.

"Invisible?" the kitsune said, cautiously probing the area with a toe.

But there was no resistance. The Sidhe had not by some mechanism of self-protection turned himself invisible. Denoriel stared at the ground marked by the bits of alfresco nuncheon. He felt something, a trace of effort, perhaps a trace of magic, a trace of magic that made him vaguely uneasy.

"Dark Sidhe," he said to the kitsune. "I cannot be sure, but I think that one of the Unseleighe took that nuisance away. May the Great Mother lay curses on him."

"Why?" the kitsune said, grinning. "I know the Bright Court does not love the Unseleighe, but this one did you a good turn. You are well rid of that levin-bolt casting stranger."

Chapter 20

Beyond the hardy moss, carefully maintained for those who wished to eat and play in what for Underhill was being outdoors under a sunny sky, were buildings. Some were shops where those who visited Fur Hold could buy the things they had forgotten—cloths to spread on the moss to lie on, on which the nuncheon dishes could be set; the dishes on which to place the food; the utensils with which to eat it; balls, hoops, various implements with which to strike balls (and each other). There were other shops, some of which sold clothing to those who had played too vigorously, and a few that displayed ornaments for those who wished to cement a new or old bond.

There were also places to supply food to those who had not intended to eat in the open. Those were largely blank doors behind which were various cook stations and food vendors congregated with their carts. Behind one of those doors, a typical Bright Court Sidhe raised the top of a food vendor's cart and lifted out a frozen Sidhe. The striped owner of the cart hissed disapprovingly.

"Why did you put him in all dirty like that? Now I need to clean out my whole cart."

The blond, green-eyed Sidhe gripped the body he had lifted in one arm and raised a hand in a way that boded no good for the speaker, who shrank back. The frightened gesture seemed to remind the Sidhe of something, and instead of striking, he smiled.

"I was in a hurry," he said. "I was afraid those who had stricken down my friend would return and strike us both." He felt in a pouch at his belt and tossed a wooden token to the striped food vendor. "That for your trouble."

And before the vendor could really examine the token, he clutched the frozen Sidhe to his side and carried him past the food-preparation stations to a rear door. The vendor did not watch him leave; all his attention was for the token he held. Bright Court Sidhe could often have strange and rich resources; he wondered for what the token could be exchanged.

Meanwhile the seemingly Bright Court Sidhe had not gone out the back door. He had turned right into a short passage that held a stairway up which he carried the frozen Sidhe to the second story of the building where there were rooms for hire. Some of the cook-folk lived in the building and some of the vendors also found it convenient, but most of those who sold to the visitors to Fur Hold had more permanent dwellings and there were always empty rooms.

Cretchar tried three doors before one opened. A swift glance showed that the room was untenanted. He laid the unmoving body on the narrow bed, the Sidhe's head at the foot so that when his eyes opened he would be looking at the wall, not out into the room. He closed the door and magicked the lock, then walked slowly to the one hard chair and sat down.

So far so good. When Cretchar had first seen Elizabeth on the performing place, he had remembered Vidal's offer of a whole domain to anyone who could rid the world of the red-haired menace. Cretchar also remembered that Oberon had forbidden any attacks on the girl. A domain was a fine thing. Cretchar would like to have one, but not if it cost Oberon's enmity. That surely meant nonexistence or such an existence as would make nonbeing a great good.

But after he had regretfully dismissed the thought of doing away with Elizabeth, Cretchar had noticed the great interest in her displayed by the plump, overdressed Sidhe on the other side of the audience. At first it was only a passing notice, but when Elizabeth left the stage and that Sidhe followed, an idea began to form in Cretchar's mind. That Sidhe was not from any elfhame under Oberon's dominion; what if *he* carried Elizabeth off to his domain? If Cretchar reported that to Vidal, he would be rewarded.

So Cretchar watched and discovered that Elizabeth was not easy prey. She was small and frail but with formidable shields and a really nasty stasis spell that felled her attacker. Cretchar had no interest in trying to take her himself, but the rage bottled up in the felled Sidhe . . . that might be put to use.

In moments Cretchar melted back into a wild game, slipped away, found a quiet nook, and changed his brown hair and hazel eyes to the normal appearance of a Bright Court Sidhe. Blond and green-eyed in tunic and trews of pale lavender and rose, he hurried back to where the ursos were still choosing treats.

When the food vendor finished serving the ursos, Cretchar intercepted him and made the arrangement to borrow his cart. He was given directions where to return the cart, watched as the striped creature went back to the food distribution center, and then moved slowly in a wide arc around where the unconscious Sidhe lay while Elizabeth's escort and the kitsune talked and where Elizabeth ludicrously taught kitsune kits to dance.

Cretchar had only thought to follow and discover where the escort and the kitsune would dump the Sidhe Elizabeth had frozen. Then if he could he would pick it up and see if he could reverse the stasis spell. He was pleasantly surprised when the Sidhe and the kitsune left the body all alone and went to talk to the other kitsune. Food vendors were everywhere and of every species; they often hurried to answer a signal from a customer. No one paid attention when Cretchar rushed across the field with his cart.

Cretchar was sure he would not be associated with the foreign Sidhe who abducted or killed Elizabeth. He did not think anyone had seen him pick up the body and the food vendor from whom he had borrowed the cart had only dealt with a nameless Bright Court Sidhe, one of which it probably could not tell from another. So far as the vendor knew the Sidhe who took the cart was the same Sidhe that paid for the food for the ursos.

Moreover the ursos were aware that the foreign Sidhe had wanted the red-haired girl. The Sidhe had said—Cretchar had very good hearing—that he would skin her alive. Whatever that Sidhe did to Elizabeth could not be blamed on the Dark Sidhe under Oberon's dominion nor in any way be traced to Prince Vidal. Cretchar glowered at the body on the bed. That meant he could not go to Vidal for help or advice; if Titania's fury over Elizabeth's fate drove Oberon to Seek for the guilty, Vidal must know nothing.

Sighing, Cretchar rose, leaned forward, and gently touched the forehead of the still figure. He knew magic, which was why he had conceived the idea of using the rage in this Sidhe to remove Elizabeth, but he hated to use it. Using magic drained him quickly and his power was slow to renew. It was why he left the Bright Court. Cretchar was not enamored of pain, but the absorption of life force was what best renewed him. In his own domain, he could catch and kill without restriction and always be full of power.

As he traced the intricacies of the stasis spell, his spirits fell. The enchantment was a masterwork, with so many interwoven spells that he feared even his knowledge of magic would be insufficient to break its grip. And then he saw something he could hardly believe. One hook? One single binding that, if undone, would release the whole spell? That was ridiculous! A spellmaster who created this would intend that the separate parts of the spell would hold even if one part was negated. Was there a trick? Would using the release cause a backlash?

Cretchar examined and reexamined but could find no sinister binding. Then he had to consider how to release the prisoner without being blasted or having the room blasted. Careful consideration convinced him that the only answer was shielding. That would protect him from any backlash from the spell and from the destructive magic that his almost-certainly ungrateful subject would release. To protect the room and control the furious Sidhe until he could explain the situation, he would have to place a shield on him, too.

Cursing softly, Cretchar pulled up shields and felt his power diminish; he was not yet empty and cold but he knew he would be after he released the spell. Cursing again, he prepared to undo the single binding. He had made the shield around the frozen Sidhe thin but somewhat reflective, enough to disperse a moderate magic blast and send it stinging back on the creator.

Pausing, he reconsidered the reflective innermost shield. If the offensive blast was strong enough, the reflective coating might incinerate the sender. Take it off? A moment later, Cretchar smiled. No, of course not. If the frozen Sidhe incinerated himself Cretchar would be right there to drink in the escaping life force.

Drawing a deep breath, Cretchar made a ritual gesture and spoke the words of dismissal, drawing back a little as he spoke.

And . . . nothing happened. There was no trap on the unbinding, no backlash. No magic result, except that the once-frozen Sidhe roared with rage, blue light glinting on his hands.

"Stop, you fool," Cretchar snarled, hoping the intensity of his tone would get through; he could not shout lest he be heard. "You will blast yourself. Do you not see that you are shielded?"

The last words were spoken because he had already planned them, but they were not necessary. Already the blue light was dying from the hands of the Sidhe on the bed. Presumably he had felt the tingle of the reflected power before he launched any magic blow. A remarkable stasis spell indeed; it did not even momentarily cloud the mind of its victim.

Another shield sprang up within the one Cretchar had set. An interesting act of self-preservation. It seemed that the once-frozen Sidhe had reason to protect himself.

"Where are you? Who are you? Where am I?" The Sidhe on the bed pushed up to a sitting position, looking wildly around until his gaze fell on Cretchar.

"Who are you?" he repeated.

"My name is Cretchar. And as to where you are. You are in a safe place."

"Safe place? Why do I need a safe place? How did I get here? I was standing in the meadow, about to teach that little red-haired bitch a lesson—"

Cretchar laughed. "More powerful Sidhe than you have tried to lesson Lady Elizabeth of Logres. Most are dead. The rest wish they were dead."

"Nonsense! She is nothing but a mortal. How could she contest against a Sidhe?"

"First because she has the favor of *very* powerful Sidhe. The queen of our whole realm, Titania, has made her an especial pet, has threatened dire consequences to any who harm her. Prince Denoriel and his sister Princess Aleneil are her heart-friends and her guardians. Even the king, Oberon—" Cretchar shuddered slightly "—has forbidden any direct attack on her."

"Your king and queen are nothing to me—"

Cretchar laughed again. "Until they catch you. Our Lady Titania thinks nothing of turning such as you into a pillar of flame and when you have felt King Oberon's Thought harrow your mind . . ." Cretchar's teeth snapped together and he shuddered. "Enough. Do not be more of a fool than you must. You must realize by now that you were overmastered in magic, either by Elizabeth herself or by her escort Prince Denoriel, and placed in stasis. I stole you from them and carried you to safety. You are a stranger here and do not know the perils of these realms. Now, who are *you*? And why did you come here?"

There was a moment of silence while the stranger Sidhe considered what Cretchar had said. Then he nodded. "My name is Paschenka and I come from Elfhame Novosk. I have come to your realm to collect mortals. Elizabeth—that is the red-haired girl?—seems eminently suitable for my purpose.

"You wish to take her back to Novosk?" Cretchar said slowly. "Hmmm. Let me think. It is possible that I will be able to aid you."

"Why should you?"

"That is no business of yours. Be satisfied that it would be of benefit to me that Elizabeth should be removed from this realm. I am not too particular what becomes of her afterward, so long as she is gone and my part in her departure remains secret."

"Then let us go look for her. I have her aura. I should be able to pick up her whereabouts."

Cretchar groaned. "Likely she will still be teaching the kits and the young ursos to dance. Why should she fear you, who were so easily vanquished? And do you think she will be less protected now that a threat to her has been made clear?"

"But now there are two of us," Paschenka pointed out.

"Not for attacking Lady Elizabeth," Cretchar snapped. "I told you that my assistance must be secret. And I am *not* a fool. I do not wish to be marked as her enemy. Be careful that when she sees you again she does not Push you so hard that she caves in your chest and hurls you into the Void. That is what she did to a well-practiced mage when she was no more than thirteen or fourteen years old."

"A mortal?" Paschenka said, shaking his head, but there was some doubt in his expression. And after a pause, his lips tight around slightly gritted teeth he said, "I *will* have her. I will teach her not to attack her betters."

"Yes. I hope so, but not now," Cretchar replied. "For now you will avoid her. I will help you to snatch a mortal here and there. I know a place where mortals are plentiful, or—" he hesitated because his inability to gather power was intensified in the mortal

world "—I could take you to the mortal world. I have a place
to keep your captives and to teach them to obey you. In a few
mortal weeks or months, we will lay a trap for Elizabeth. Then
you can take all your spoils back to Novosk. She being one of
several or many with you, her aura will be obscured from those
searching for her."

Paschenka stared expressionlessly at Cretchar for a little while,
then he dismissed the shield he had raised inside the one Cretchar
had made. Removing his protection wordlessly affirmed that
Paschenka had accepted Cretchar's offer. It did not surprise
Cretchar that Paschenka did not look happy. He was having to
take a lot on faith.

To give him some assurance, Cretchar relaxed the shield he had
created to control Paschenka's initial anger. As the power drained
away into the general ambience Underhill, Cretchar gritted his
teeth. A waste that it would take him a day and a night to replace.
He could only hope that Paschenka could spirit away Elizabeth
and that his reward would compensate for his weakness.

Elizabeth came away from the mismatched dancers laughing
happily. The urso female had come up with a small stringed
instrument on which she could play a dance tune so Elizabeth
did not need to sing any longer. She was just standing back, when
several other young creatures arrived and asked to be included.
Denoriel shook his head.

"I don't think she should stay here any longer," he said to the
kitsune. "If we had dealt with that Sidhe ... But the way he
disappeared makes me uneasy."

The kitsune nodded. "Take her and go. My young ones will be
able to teach the others and the ursos will keep the peace."

So Denoriel came up to Elizabeth, slid an arm around her
waist, and drew her away. She did not resist and he asked what
she wanted to do next.

"Sit down," Elizabeth said, laughing. "And perhaps get something
to eat." Then she sobered suddenly and looked around. "What did
you do with that nuisance who wanted to buy me?"

Denoriel glanced around but no one seemed to be close enough
to hear him and he said, "Nothing. When the kitsune and I went
to help him to a Gate, he was gone."

"Gone? Do you mean my stasis spell failed?"

"I don't believe so. I think if the spell had failed that stupid fool would have blasted us or someone else. I know that spell. The bespelled come out of it with no sense of time passed and simply complete any action they had started when they were frozen."

"Then how . . ." Elizabeth began as Denoriel pushed her gently up on a Gate platform, ". . . could he have left?" She finished as they stepped off near one of the four main entry roads into the Bazaar of the Bizarre.

Accustomed from years of visits, Elizabeth did not even look around the place where vehicles and riding creatures were left. The creatures were weird and wonderful—twenty-foot long caterpillars, jewel-bright dragons, silvery vehicles with no obvious methods of propulsion, cagelike boxes suspended under what looked like large pillows, horses of every describable and indescribable coat, saddle, number of legs, and occasionally wings.

"I am sure he did not leave on his own," Denoriel said, steering her past the first warning sign. "Someone must have helped him."

"Perhaps he came with a friend," Elizabeth said doubtfully as they passed the sign that she read as CAVEAT EMPTOR.

"A friend that did not set up an outcry when he found his companion frozen stiff?"

Elizabeth giggled. "Well, if he was as arrogant and stubborn with everyone as he was with us, perhaps the friend was used to dragging him away and was just glad he didn't have to apologize to anyone."

"That would be very nice," Denoriel said, but without any real hope, as they passed under the arched gateway into the Bazaar. He looked up into the air and said, "Food and drink."

A banner promptly appeared. On it a cow lay in a green meadow, her head resting on crossed front legs. "Lazy Cow/Tender Steak" Elizabeth read.

Another banner appeared to the right: "The Never-Empty Cauldron—Stews and Soups of Every Kind."

And a third banner forced itself in front of the Lazy Cow, proclaiming that the Rolling Pin had every variety of breads and cakes.

Denoriel held up a hand. "Enough," he said. "Well, Elizabeth, what will it be, stew, soup, steak, bread and cake?"

"What would you like, love?" she asked. "Right now I could

eat the whole cow, uncooked, and then go on to the soup and stew. I haven't had a meal that didn't sit in my throat and choke me since August."

"Steak, then," he said. "Lazy Cow."

The banner passed the other two, wriggled seductively, for a moment and then set off down the road. Denoriel and Elizabeth followed.

"So you don't think any friend of the fat Sidhe took him away," Elizabeth said, returning to the important subject of what had happened to the Sidhe who had been so insistent about buying her.

"No. I think it more likely to have been one of Vidal's Court who saw the interest that Sidhe had in you. The Dark Sidhe come often to Fur Hold; I am not sure why. But any Dark Sidhe who saw you would pay attention."

"I thought I saw one of the Dark Sidhe when we were just outside the performing place, but he barely glanced at me. It was you he was watching, and then he just walked away."

Denoriel sighed. "Vidal has become more sensible since he was the mist's prisoner. Possibly he is taking Oberon's threats more seriously and has told his Court to let you be. Possibly the Sidhe you saw wanted to know why the one you froze was so interested. In a way I wish Pasgen had not broken so completely with Vidal. If he still went to the Dark Court, he could have told us whether any of the Dark ones brought that Sidhe to Vidal."

"Vidal could break the stasis spell," Elizabeth said and stopped walking.

The banner was circling and then darting to the side. Denoriel looked around, saw the doorway, and drew Elizabeth inside.

"Yes, certainly," he agreed. "Any competent mage could break that spell. Mechain altered it so you could use it when you were little more than a child. One of the things we should do while we are here is to get her to put it back in its original form."

A tall, very thin being, not quite human but not quite Other either, had been waiting until Denoriel finished speaking. He bowed to them and led them to a table near an open window through which Elizabeth saw a mannered garden. A slight breeze came through the window, bringing the scent of flowers. Utterly impossible, as they had entered the eating place from the noisy, busy aisle of the market. Idly Elizabeth wondered whether the garden was an illusion or whether the entrance of the restaurant was actually a Gate that carried guests to a pocket domain that only contained the restaurant. Whichever, she was not curious enough to enquire. She was hungry.

When the server or major domo had pushed in her chair, Elizabeth looked up at him. "We would like steaks, if you please."

She was answered with another bow and a long list of cuts and methods of preparation, which made her look bewilderedly at Denoriel. He nodded and began an animated discussion with the server, who looked more pleased and interested by the moment. Here was someone who truly appreciated his calling. Elizabeth lost interest and looked around at the other patrons. She was rather relieved when she saw no other Sidhe; mostly the guests were chimeras of every kind of animal. A few had human faces or parts, but it was very odd indeed to see something with the head of a goat and the bony claws of a bird industriously cutting up and chewing a thick slab of meat.

"Do the other guests trouble you, mortal woman?" the server asked as Elizabeth looked back at him. "I can bring a screen to keep your table private."

"Oh no," Elizabeth assured him. "I was only rather surprised to see a goat eating a steak. In the mortal world goats, poor things, are more often steaks themselves."

"Stews, surely," the server said. "The flesh is too tough and . . . ah . . . rancid for steak. As to eating steak. A goat will eat anything."

He bowed and turned away. Elizabeth giggled. "That took long enough," she said to Denoriel. "I had no idea you knew one cut of meat from another or anything about cooking."

"In my misspent past," he said, smiling, "when I had no more pressing duty than to ride in Koronos's hunt, I filled my days with this and that pastime. Designing lavish meals was one of them."

"For all your elven lovers?" Elizabeth asked waspishly, her giggles gone. "Were the meals designed to tempt them into your bed or as payment after service?"

"Oh, ho." Denoriel's arched brows rose almost to touch a golden curl that had wandered down onto his forehead. "Jealous, are we? Well, I am not going to say I am sorry over what happened long, long before you were born. I did not know then that in the future I would find a lady who would care enough to be angry about whom I took to my bed."

"And if you had known, would it have changed what you did?" Elizabeth snapped.

"Not if I knew I would need to live without any pleasure of the body for a hundred and fifty mortal years," Denoriel snapped back.

"I'm sorry," Elizabeth said softly looking down at the table, reminded of how long her Denno had lived before even her father was born.

How stupid to be jealous of women he had loved a hundred years past. But they were not mortal women. They were still alive, still elven beautiful. She bit her lip.

Denoriel laughed and reached across to take her hand. "An elven lover would not care enough to be angry; cold-hearted they are. But I am a little hurt that you think I would need to prepare a special meal either to tempt a lady or to make up for my deficiencies as a lover. Am I so lacking in myself?"

The tone was light, but there was a kind of uncertainty about Denoriel that Elizabeth felt. "No, of course not," she said.

"Are mortal lovers more ... are they deeper? more intense?"

"How would I know?" Elizabeth asked, smiling ruefully. "The only mortal lover I had—if you can call Tom Somerset a lover—was only playing a game. He 'loved' for profit or ambition."

"Perhaps it is I who should be jealous, who should fear you will find someone who will satisfy you more. We ... perhaps we live too long. Nothing is ... desperate. There will be so many tomorrows to find anything we have missed ... but I know now that we ... we never find it."

"So you are still looking?" Elizabeth's voice was thin and sharp.

Denoriel shook his head. "No," he said softly. "I have found what I want, but I do not know how long I can hold it."

Now it was Elizabeth who leaned forward and took Denoriel's hand. "Mortals can be fickle also," she said, "but I will always love you, my Denno. Always. Even if I seem to waver, you are the first and the most precious, the deepest set into my heart."

There was a little silence and then he burst out suddenly, "Mary ... Mary wants you dead. My love, will you not come and live here with me as Harry has done?"

Elizabeth paled slightly when she realized that Denno had not been talking about losing her to a mortal lover but losing her to execution, to sickness, to death from old age. Almost no matter how long she lived, that would be a short time to him. She looked out at the pretty garden, drew a breath of the perfumed air, remembered how a palace stank if the Court remained in one place too long.

"I would live longer," she agreed, "but you would lose me anyway. I would not be the same person, Denno. This lovely place, this scented air, this ease of living, would soften me until I was nothing. I have come to love Underhill, but as a needed escape, a rest from struggle, a short, pretty dream. I need the hard reality of the mortal world. I need to outwit Mary and escape her ill will." The eyes Elizabeth fixed on him glittered. "Mary will not live long. I am only one person's heartbeat away from the throne. I *need* to rule England."

A wide smile bloomed on Denoriel's face. "So you do, my love. And so you must. Titania would find some very special way to make me sorry if I did not see you onto the throne." He turned his hand under hers so he could grip it. "But you do love me? You do not need an elaborate dinner to bribe you to my bed or pay you for your services?"

Elizabeth laughed aloud. "Oh, that stung, did it? Enough for you to imply I need to be paid, like a whore. No, indeed. You are bribe enough in yourself, with your long-fingered hands and sweet lips. What a fool I am to be jealous. I should bless those past lovers of yours for making you so skillful. If I were not so very, very hungry, I would drag you to the nearest Gate and prove it."

"My servants—" Denoriel began, half rising from his seat, intending to say that they could leave at once and his servants would feed them at home.

At that moment, however, the tall, thin major domo arrived at the head of a procession. Since Elizabeth had not seen anyone more than a single server delivering food to other tables, she wondered whether it was because Denno was clearly High Court, Bright Court Sidhe or whether it was the discussion about cooking and cuts of meat he had had that provided the special service. A moment later, odors from the serving dishes the procession carried reached her nose. She sniffed audibly and swallowed as her mouth watered.

First came a slab of meat, thick as the first knuckle of a finger. It was browned, but not scorched hard as a piece that thick would be in the mortal world. Then there were a half dozen smaller dishes set around the central platter. Elizabeth was not sure what any of them held, but she was accustomed to eating strange things Underhill. Only once or twice had she been disappointed in a peculiar-looking dish.

There was no disappointment this time. The meat cut easily, showing a pink and tender interior. Elizabeth put a piece between her lips and sighed with satisfaction. The bits she took from the surrounding plates were equally delicious and somehow the textures made her want to touch them, to touch something that she could smooth between her fingers. Still chewing, she reached out with her free hand and stroked Denno's hair.

"A masterpiece," Denno said to the major domo, and looked back at Elizabeth with half-closed eyes.

Elizabeth took another bite of her meat. As she chewed, she added to it small bits of what was in the side dishes. She sighed and swallowed. Lifted her eyes to Denoriel's face.

"You are a monster," she whispered. "I could not be worse tortured if I were being pulled apart on the rack. I must eat slowly and savor every bite. Equally, I must stuff the food down my gullet so I can rush you into your bedchamber."

She chewed the mouthful she had faster, but was lingeringly slow about cutting another slice from the meat and choosing which side dishes to mingle with it. The major domo and the servers, who had watched while their customers took their first bites had now disappeared. Denoriel cut a thin strip of a flesh paler than beef which he was eating.

"This is very good," he said, "but I was not sure it was robust enough for you."

He put an end of the slice he had cut in his mouth and then leaned forward. Elizabeth did not hesitate. She drew the other end of the slice into her own mouth. Their lips met and moved sensuously together as they chewed. Whatever it was Denoriel had ordered for himself seemed to melt away. Elizabeth pressed farther forward and caught Denoriel's lower lip between hers and sucked.

"Stop," Denoriel whispered, drawing back. "Do you want me to leave here with a wet codpiece."

"I want to leave, dry codpiece or wet," Elizabeth muttered, even as she cut another slice from her steak. "But I cannot bear to leave this food behind."

So they finished their meal, but when they rose to go, Denoriel unhooked his entire purse from his belt and left it on the table. Just how they came to Denoriel's big bed in his chambers in Logres, Elizabeth had no idea. Her whole body ached to be handled and she was grateful to her Denno when a gesture sent the clothes from her body and from his and they fell down on the bed, already fiercely embraced.

Chapter 21

Elizabeth slept very late the next day. She would have been in serious trouble if Blanche had not resisted her impulse to drop into her bed and sleep immediately instead of staying conscious long enough to release the sleep spell on Elizabeth Marberry. Never dreaming what kind of night—and several other days and nights—Elizabeth had had, Marberry tried to rouse Elizabeth (against Blanche's advice). To her intense horror, she was not only struck but reviled in language obviously culled from guardsmen in a temper. Never had Lady Mary done such things.

"You will miss Mass," Marberry said. It was a warning that certainly would have roused Lady Mary and she herself from bed.

"Bugger Mass and the priest that says it," Elizabeth snarled. "Go away!"

Marberry gasped and staggered back, away from Elizabeth's bed. Blanche chuckled softly.

"I doubt Lady Elizabeth is much concerned with her soul this morning," she said, and shepherded the shocked girl from the bedchamber. Then, more seriously, she added, "My lady has come all undone. She wished so much to please Queen Mary that she was all tied into knots inside. Now that she needs to please no one at all she will sleep more than she usually does."

But when Elizabeth finally crawled, yawning and stretching,

from the bed and Blanche had closed the door of the dressing chamber, she said, "Making merry, were you?"

A slow smile lifted Elizabeth's lips. "Very merry." She sighed. "In those dreams I have mentioned to you, we made love to repletion, went to balls and to see the queen's private garden. Such flowers as she has, such grassy hollows overhung with sweetness, perfect for lovers. They could be only in a dream."

Blanche frowned. "You do not regret waking from those dreams, I hope?"

Elizabeth shook her head. "Oh, no. Not at all. It was only that I found them too entrancing and overstayed my dreaming. That leaves me very tired." She sighed but smiled languorously again. "I do not think Lord Denno will come today."

He did not come, but it was just as well that no one else came to visit Ashridge that day or the next either. Elizabeth was sluggish, skipping the lessons she ordinarily did most faithfully even when she had no teacher and dozing over her embroidery. Denoriel did come to pay a call on the second day, but he looked pale and the lines in his face were graven deep.

They were both at fault to some degree. Elizabeth had been reveling in her freedom from tension and ordered behavior. She wanted to make love, to play, to go to balls, to see wonders of the elven world in which she had shown little interest. Denoriel knew he should have spread out their lovemaking and merrymaking over several weeks but he could not resist indulging her, having her all to himself; she did not even ask to see Harry.

Too much time passed. In order to bring her back to the mortal world on the morning after she had left it, Denoriel had to twist time far more than was safe or sensible. Elizabeth arrived in her bedchamber shortly before dawn, but she was badly disoriented and Denoriel was drained to the dregs.

Over the few days it took Elizabeth to recover completely, several messages had come from London, mostly from the young men who bemoaned the loss of her liveliness and wit. A middle-aged priest came too, together with beautifully rich furnishings for a chapel. Elizabeth turned a lackluster eye on them all, only when prodded by Kat troubling to read the message from Queen Mary and, with gritted teeth, to write a reply full of grace and gratitude. To the young men she made no reply at all, but she did attend Mass when Mary's priest said it.

Slowly as the week passed, Elizabeth's liveliness began to return. She went riding with Lord Denno on Thursday, read the piled up letters her secretary had kept for her on Friday and to Mary's ladies' shocked surprise discussed them with Lord Denno who came to dinner that day. Laughing, he advised her not to reply at all or, he said, she would soon have no time for anything but their nonsense.

Saturday was given over to estate business. Elizabeth having learned that her treasurer, no matter that she was very fond of him, was not overly accurate in his accounts, checked all Master Parry's figures, initialing the bottom of every page. Sunday she attended Mass, but to Gage's and Marberry's disappointment did not invite any gentry from the neighborhood to join her. She did, however, appear attentive to everything the priest said and did, and at dinner that day asked the priest, most civilly, what he thought best to do to celebrate Christmas, which was coming soon.

To no one's surprise but most of the household's dismay, he advised against appointing a Lord of Misrule and spoke against many of the season's typical excesses. Elizabeth listened gravely. That she was regretful of missing the celebration was plain; nonetheless, she took the advice.

Usually the entire neighborhood was invited to eat and make merry at the lord of the manor's expense. This year, Elizabeth quietly, and out of sight of the priest, put a fat purse into Sir Edward's hands and told him to arrange for the guards and servants to go into the town in shifts over the twelve days. There was no reason, she said, for those who preferred a merrier celebration of Our Lord's birth to be bound by Mary's priest's prejudices.

Sir Edward met her eyes for a long moment; then he bowed deeply and promised her that his men and her servants would drink her health in the town with all their hearts, although they would be sorry to miss her company.

It was the priest who was disconcerted when he realized that no one had been invited to join the religious celebration he planned. Ashridge had a very quiet Christmas, closed and silent, impervious to the curious glances of those who traveled past its gates. Elizabeth did attend a late Mass on Christmas Eve and two Masses on Christmas Day. Her ladies, perforce, attended also, but Elizabeth Marberry noted that they were sullen, that some simply ignored the kneelings of Catholic ritual and obviously paid little attention to the sermons.

Both Marberry and Gage noticed that the old merchant, who usually visited two or even three times a week, did not appear even once between Christmas Eve and the end of the year. His absence was so unusual that the priest asked Elizabeth if the so-called Lord Denno was a heretic, avoiding the Catholic Mass.

"I have no idea," Elizabeth replied, with wide-open eyes. "I do not believe so. Lord Denno and I do not talk about religion. The only thing I ever remember him saying on the subject was that it was too important for a common merchant like himself to decide, and that he was happy to follow the order of the ruler of the realm that had given him shelter. Now that Queen Mary had decreed it so, he attends the Catholic Mass at his neighborhood church."

Whatever doubts the priest and Marberry had concerning Lord Denno's absence were put to rest on New Year's day. Well after breakfast (and after Mass too) a loud summons from the gate brought the diminished guard to full alert. But alarms soon changed to cries of welcome and Sir Edward himself went to open the front gate. Not only had Lord Denno arrived, but he was at the head of a small caravan of sumpter mules.

With a crow of delight Elizabeth ran out into the courtyard to meet him, all solemnity cast to the winds. Her long-time maids followed giggling and crying out welcomes. Thereafter there was no need of a Lord of Misrule. Everyone fell upon the separate parcels Lord Denno had had prepared for each group of residents in Ashridge. There were gifts, male and female, for the lowest servants, the scullery maids and men who forked the manure from the stables, different gifts for the grooms, for the cooks and bakers, for the men-at-arms, the laundresses and upper maids.

Sir Edward saw to the distribution of those and then himself carried in what remained: one parcel for Nyle, Gerrit, Shaylor, and Dickson and another for the maids of honor. The guardsmen had gold, ten fine guineas each; for each maid of honor there was a package of the finest silk, worth double that sum. Kat had silk, too, enough for two gowns or a gown and a night rail. The priest had a heavy gilt cross. For Sir Edward a single narrow box with his name, which opened to show a beautiful poniard, the blade of Damascus steel, the hilt of chased gold set with semiprecious stones, small enough and close enough to make a slightly rough surface that would not slip even when wet with sweat or blood. Sir Edward was speechless, staring at it.

All were examining their own gifts. No one saw the expression on Denoriel's face as he knelt beside Elizabeth's chair and opened the box. In itself it was a treasure, smoothed of scented woods and inset with mother-of-pearl. A tray atop held a magnificent emerald necklace with armbands and a tiara to match. In the body of the box was a gown that Aleneil had created for Elizabeth Underhill and could not be matched with mortal-woven fabrics.

"How?" Elizabeth whispered, touching the shimmering folds; she still, and always would, believe that nothing made Underhill could persist in the mortal world.

"It was specially blessed by the queen," Denoriel whispered back.

So the new year of 1554 began more merrily than 1553 had ended. And prospects continued hopeful at first even though Mary had succeeded in forcing her Council to agree to the Spanish marriage and envoys had arrived to write a treaty. Unfortunately that was all Rhoslyn knew when she reported on the first mortal Tuesday night of the new year. Having secured a victory, the queen, as she so often did, became all gentle female. It would ill befit her, Mary said to Renard, to herself meddle in the treaty of marriage. Rhoslyn knew Renard wanted her to join the negotiations; he had known that she would yield anything and everything to have Philip with whom she was already deeply in love.

The first week in January, Elizabeth made Elizabeth Marberry and Eleanor Gage wonder why anyone was willing to serve her. Mary was often lachrymose and, even they felt, good Catholics as they were, spent too much time on her knees. But her tongue did not cut like a knife nor did her hand as often raise welts on her maids of honor's cheeks. Even Lord Denno made himself scarce.

"I will try to find out," was the last thing Marberry heard him say as she passed closer than necessary behind Elizabeth and her favorite when he last bowed in farewell.

He did not soon return—the ladies sighed but did not blame him; he took the brunt of Elizabeth's bad temper when he was present. But on the thirteenth of January he rode into Ashridge. Without cloak or shawl, Elizabeth ran down the steps and out into the courtyard. Elizabeth Marberry followed her, holding out a warm shawl. She was in time to see Lord Denno dismount and

Ladbroke, the head groom, lead Denno's mount away—not by taking hold of its bridle but with a hand on its shoulder.

"What news?" Elizabeth asked breathlessly.

Lord Denno smiled. "Good news. I have a letter from an old friend to show you, but I think you should read it where everyone can hear."

"Ahhh." Elizabeth drew out the word. "That is good news indeed."

As Marberry came up to her and placed the shawl over her shoulders, Elizabeth turned and smiled. "Thank you," she said graciously, but it was Lord Denno's arm she took and, Marberry noticed, pressed to her side.

When they reached the parlor, Elizabeth hurried to the fire, her ladies slipping to the sides to give her room. Without particular invitation, Lord Denno joined her, taking a folded letter from an inside pocket of his doublet.

"My lady." He bowed and handed her the papers.

She took them without acknowledgement, unfolded them, scattering some pieces of wax from the broken seal, and began to read. After a moment she laughed.

"A long enough salutation to be a whole letter itself, but I have come to the meat at last." She began to read aloud:

"As you must know, my lady, the queen convinced her Council that the most suitable husband for her would be the emperor's son, Philip of Spain. Once this was decided, Queen Mary most wisely withdrew herself from any negotiation concerning the articles of the marriage, leaving that wholly in her Council's hands. I heard that the Imperial ambassador feared no treaty would be written because of the animosity of the councilors against each other, but this did not prove to be true. Understanding the queen's will, they worked together nobly to a most excellent result.

"To wit: Although the prince of Spain will have the title of king and it is acknowledged that he will assist the queen in governing, he is to have no legal power in the government. All offices of government and the Church will be conferred only by the queen and must be held only by Englishmen."

Elizabeth heaved a great sigh. "That will save us from the horrors of oppression by foreign lords which drove rebellion after rebellion in the reign of King Stephen." She lowered her gaze to the letter again.

"Moreover, England was not to go to war against France whether or not the Empire made peace."

Elizabeth nodded, smiling now. "That will save us from being drained dry the way the Low Countries were, paying for a war from which only the Empire could profit.

"Furthermore, the laws and customs of England were to remain intact and not be overruled by the laws and customs of Spain or the Empire or any other realm in the Empire.

"Thank God and all the saints for that," Elizabeth breathed.

Eleanor Gage looked satisfied by Elizabeth's mention of the saints. Elizabeth Marberry frowned and asked why Elizabeth should be so pleased with that part of the agreement. Elizabeth raised her brows.

"The Spanish are reputed a cruel people. The tales that have come out of the Low Countries with merchants and what I have seen of their slaves gives some credit to that accusation. But whether it is true or not, the English common folk believe it. They envision themselves with their doors broken in—which you know is forbidden by Magna Carta—" (likely they did not know before, but Elizabeth made sure they now knew the value of English law) "—and their wives and daughters violated by Spanish soldiers."

"That is not true," Elizabeth Marberry cried. "Queen Mary would never permit it."

"I know she would certainly try to protect her people," Elizabeth said. "But if the law was Spanish law, she might no longer have the power to do so. However, we need not be concerned. The Council, wise men that they are, have secured our own laws to us." She sighed, frowning. "Now if only this can be explained to the people, all will be well."

Her eyes went back to the letter and she smiled again. "They have protected the queen also, as well as they could." She read: *"And Queen Mary was not to be taken abroad by the order of her husband or any other person without her consent."*

"That is, I suppose, a good provision to include," Kat remarked with a wry twist to her mouth, "but I question whether the queen is likely to refuse consent if her husband asks her to accompany him."

"If he plans ill, it would not do him any good," Lord Denno remarked. "Come to the provisions in case one or another dies."

Elizabeth's eyes skipped over several lines and then she said "Ah!" again, a smile like sunrise lighting her face and eyes.

"*If Queen Mary should die childless, Prince Philip is to have no further right or interest in England.*"

Safe! Her mind caroled in silence. *Safe! I will not need to fight him for my throne.*

"But if she should have a child?" Eleanor Gage urged.

Elizabeth looked back at the letter. "If Mary has a son, he will inherit Burgundy and the Low Countries as well as England and in the event of Don Carlos's death without children, Mary's son will inherit everything, the entire Empire."

"That is very generous, is it not?" Dorothy Dodd said, looking rather awed.

"I suppose it is," Elizabeth agreed, grinning, "but think of the troubles poor Emperor Charles has had ruling that empire." The grin broadened. "I wonder if it is a kind of revenge." She was no longer grinning. "I really would not envy that poor little boy."

"What 'poor little boy'?" Alice Finch asked, looking bewildered.

"The putative son of Queen Mary and Prince Philip who would outlive Philip's son Don Carlos," Elizabeth said. Alice clearly still did not understand and Dorothy was explaining softly. As Elizabeth listened, a decided gleam came into her eyes. "Oh my!" she breathed. "Think of trying to get advice and forge agreement in a Council where no more than two or three councilors spoke the same language. Heaven knows that although all of the queen's Council is supposed to speak English, they do not seem to be able to understand each other."

Dorothy Stafford uttered a strangled giggle. Lord Denno shook his head. Elizabeth cocked a brow.

"Who knows?" she said, looking raptly into the distance. "Perhaps if they could not think they spoke the same language they would quarrel less."

Lord Denno, frowning, stepped closer and touched her arm. Elizabeth started, looked at him, then suddenly smiled.

"I hope all the queen's children will be taught several languages," she said, with an expression of angelic innocence. "Think of the advantage a ruler would have if he was the only one who could understand each member of his Council."

"Lady Elizabeth!" Lord Denno protested. "I am not even interested in real political events. These flights of fancy are ridiculous."

"Yes, of course," Elizabeth said sobering. "But I must agree with

Dorothy. I cannot help but be surprised at the generosity of the agreement. Apparently the emperor so greatly desires this marriage that the Imperial envoys have been ordered to yield anything the British really insisted upon. Why is it so important to His Majesty Charles that Queen Mary should marry Philip?"

"I think it is partly because the emperor has not been very well recently," Eleanor Gage offered. "It is said he is tired of war. I think he did not wish to face the possibility of Noailles, the French ambassador, calling the Imperial negotiators greedy and convincing Queen Mary to unite with France against him."

"The queen is far too clever for that," Elizabeth said.

In fact, she thought her sister utterly stupid for choosing Prince Philip and arousing the whole country to rage against her. Elizabeth herself would have played France against Spain and not chosen to marry at all. Marriage . . . marriage was fatal. Her mother, her cousin . . . If a woman did not die by execution for the foolish act of marriage, then she died in childbed, like Jane Seymour and her poor stepmother Catherine Parr.

A general discussion broke out among the ladies about the effect of the Spanish marriage as limited by the Council's agreement. Elizabeth moved closer to Denno and started to fold the letter as if to return it to him. He shook his head and glanced toward a table. Elizabeth laid the letter there for all to see so no one could suspect her of concealing anything. Eventually no doubt someone would give it to her and she could pass it back to Denno. She would not want anyone who knew it, say in the Court, to recognize William Cecil's handwriting.

For the rest of the week, Elizabeth was in a much better humor. The horror of needing to wrest her realm out of the hands of the Imperials if it had been left to Philip on Mary's death no longer tormented her. There was, of course, the chance that Mary would have a child; then Philip would be Regent, but Mary was thirty-seven and Elizabeth did not think a child too great a danger. And, in that case, she would not be ruling anyway.

So it was in an easy, pleasant mood that Elizabeth accompanied Denno to the Inn of Kindly Laughter on mortal Tuesday night. It was Alice Finch who rested comfortably in an ensorcelled sleep in the truckle bed. Eleanor Gage and Elizabeth Marberry no longer intruded on Elizabeth in the middle of the night. No matter what had been whispered about her, Gage and Marberry knew she had no male favorite, except Lord Denno, who was never a guest at Ashridge after sundown and was old enough to be her grandfather.

Nor was there purpose in watching Elizabeth's religious practices. Elizabeth attended Mass regularly and gave the service lively attention, if not fervor. Certainly there was no one in the household who might conduct an heretical service in the middle of the night. Spying on her was not worth a night of broken sleep.

She was surprised then when Harry jumped to his feet as soon as she came into sight and said, "Bess, you've had no dealings with the rebels, have you?"

"Rebels?" Elizabeth echoed, stopping dead before she reached the table, which was busily rearranging chairs to accommodate the new arrivals. "What rebels?"

Harry came forward and led her to a seat next to his chair. Rhoslyn, large-eyed, nodded to her, and Denoriel, frowning, took a seat on her other side.

"There are whispers, specially in Courtenay's house, of a rising against the Spanish marriage," Harry said. "Has anyone visited or written to ask your approval of such an action?"

"No!" Elizabeth exclaimed. "Da, how can you ask such a question? I am not an idiot. The only visitors I have had are Denno and a few tenants, who came on estate business."

"What did they say to you?"

"Me? I never saw them. Master Parry deals with the estate."

Harry grimaced. "Parry! I remember all the trouble he got you into when he talked too freely to Tom Seymour. The man is a fool."

"Not such a fool that he would listen to talk of rebellion and not mention it to me. He did tell me what Tom Seymour wanted."

"Not clearly enough for you to realize he had put you in danger. What did he say the tenants wanted, Bess?"

"The tenants." She looked down, frowning. "I do not think he mentioned them at all." She raised her head to look at Harry. "That means it was a very ordinary matter—a tenant being late with his rent or wanting to change what he had intended to plant." She sniffed loudly. "It cannot have been anything like asking my permission to support a rebellion."

Denoriel laughed. "Yes, Harry, I imagine even Parry would not forget to mention a little thing like armed rebellion."

Harry did not laugh in return. Perfectly soberly he said, "He would not if he thought mentioning it would endanger Elizabeth. As I said, the man is a fool, but he does love his lady and intends to serve her well."

Elizabeth and Denoriel exchanged glances; he chewed his lower lip and she pressed both lips together until her mouth was no more than a thin line.

"I do not think he would be foolish enough to completely conceal treason. I am sure he would warn me if he heard anything of that kind, but . . . but I will make sure to question him tomorrow."

"Good, only be sure you do not sound as if *you* know anything about any rising. Parry means well, but do not forget how he spilled word of Seymour's advances when he was in the Tower. He is likely to confess to too much if you speak too freely to him."

Elizabeth sighed. "I will be careful. But he must have known what he said could really do me no harm. Katherine was alive then and present during Seymour's indiscretions."

Harry also sighed. He was accustomed to Elizabeth's loyalty to her old servants. "What about letters? You have not replied to any letter from one of those courtiers that hang about you, a letter that might have seemed to be wooing you, have you?"

"The only letters I have received and replied to have been from members of the Council—and I wrote to Mary to thank her again for the sable hood and for the chapel furnishings and the priest. Kat and I thought it would not be wise to have too much correspondence. I did receive some letters bewailing my absence from Court when we first arrived, but I did not answer any of those."

"You still have the letters?

"Yes, of course.

"Good. Keep every letter that arrives so it can be perused if there is an outbreak."

Elizabeth's eyes widened. She knew that Mary did not trust her. Indeed, the reason that most messengers were turned away at the gates of Ashridge was because she feared some innocent message might be misinterpreted. And that fear was when there was no rumor of rebellion to sharpen it.

"Surely no one will attempt rebellion," Elizabeth said plaintively, possibly proving the triumph of hope over foreboding. "There is nothing to rebel about. A little patience and reasonable discussion will surely smooth out the religious problems . . ."

"It is the Spanish marriage," Rhoslyn said, also sighing.

"But the terms the Council arranged protect England in every way—except if Mary has a child and dies in childbed."

"I am glad you see it." Rhoslyn's voice was sharp. "It seems as if you are one of the few. When Gardiner explained the terms to an assembly of nobles and gentlemen at Westminster on January fourteenth and to the mayor and a council of citizens of London on the fifteenth, they were sour as unripe apples. Mary was furious! Both the mayor of London and the lords at Westminster said flatly that they did not believe the Imperial promises."

"Oh my," Elizabeth said feebly.

"So, my love, you must be careful," Harry said. "You must be very, very careful."

Chapter 22

The household at Ashridge closed tighter around Elizabeth as two tense weeks passed. She had enemies at Court and knew it. But it was her friends who brought danger with them.

Sir James Croft was admitted to Ashridge when he came asking for an interview with Elizabeth "on a matter of importance," because William Saintlow, a long-time servant requested she speak to Sir James. Moreover Croft's father had been Mary's learned counsel before he died and Sir James himself had been knight of the shire for Hereford. The last Elizabeth had heard about him was that he was deputy constable of the Tower of London, one of Queen Mary's many officers.

Sir Edward asked about the Tower and Sir James replied that he had not been there in some time, having been on a mission to Wales. Because Elizabeth wanted her household to look normal for the spies she was sure were seeded in it, Sir Edward no longer hung over every new arrival. It seemed safe enough to receive Sir James, and Shaylor was summoned to escort him in and watch him.

Elizabeth suspected Sir James had been sent by some member of the Council to again warn her against making contact with the rebels. She was certainly willing to listen and agree with total sincerity to obey such a warning. Her first inkling that this was not an unofficial visit sanctioned by one of the queen's councilors was when Sir James, bowing over her hand, softly requested a private interview.

"I am very sorry, Sir James," she said, backing up a step and not lowering her voice. "I have been too often accused of taking lovers. I do not receive any man in private."

"But—" He shook his head, lowered his voice again. "I have news it is better for you to hear without witness."

Elizabeth did not like that at all. It sounded as if some action was to be taken against her and Croft had been sent to warn her of it. Her first panicked thought was that no councilor would risk his place to send her a secret messenger, but she really knew she did have friends on the Council. Sir William Howard was her great-uncle and was fond of her; the earls of Arundel and Sussex, although they lectured her against treasonous acts, had eyes that saw Mary was thirty-seven and frail and Elizabeth was next in line; even Paget who was his own friend first did not want her dead. If someone on the Council wished to deliver a warning he did not want Mary to know about, it would be unsafe to ignore it.

"My ladies can withdraw out of hearing," she offered without lowering her voice. "More privacy than that is not necessary and would do my reputation harm."

Croft frowned but then gave a brusque nod; he waited while Elizabeth gestured to her women to withdraw, then stepped closer. Elizabeth withdrew again and held up a hand to prevent Croft from coming closer. Plainly he wanted to whisper. Elizabeth did not care about hiding from her ladies the name of whoever had sent Croft; she wished only to keep Mary's spies from being able to say that she had a whispered conversation with a man who might be a messenger of treason. She remembered all too well her dangerous passage through accusations of a secret marriage to Tom Seymour. Then even so innocent a thing as a blush had been twisted against her.

"I wish to warn you that there may be some unrest around the country," he said.

Elizabeth drew a sharp breath. Her throat tightened and her heart leapt. Had Sir James been sent by Chancellor Gardiner to tempt her into admitting knowledge of the coming rebellion? When she spoke her voice was not hushed; it was high with shock.

"What are you talking about? I know of no unrest in this realm. There is no reason for any unrest."

Croft frowned again and shook his head. "I thought you would have received word . . ." Elizabeth's eyes widened and she stepped farther away from him. His expression puzzled, Croft added, "However you feel, my lady, much of the country is violently opposed to the Spanish marriage and to being driven again under the pope's yoke."

"My sister has a right to marry as she thinks best," Elizabeth retorted. "She said herself it is not the place of others to choose a husband for her. As to the pope, the queen has always been a devout Catholic and regretted the lack of the pope's guidance. That is a matter for the Council and the Parliament, not for you or me. I have heard and will hear nothing about unrest in the countryside."

"But it is dangerous, my lady. Remember there are two sides in any quarrel. It would be only simple caution for you to withdraw to a place of safety, like Donnington, where you can be properly defended."

Elizabeth shook her head. "Defended? Defended against whom? The queen bade me to go to Ashridge when she gave me leave from the Court. Do you carry an order from Her Majesty or from the Council that I move?"

Shaylor had come closer, his hand on his sword hilt. Croft looked nervously over his shoulder. "No!" he exclaimed. "But you would be safer in Donnington until the country is quiet."

Elizabeth was torn with indecision again. If there was a rebellion . . . What if the rebels tried to take her and then the rebellion failed? Surely Mary would take advantage of her being with the rebels, even against her will, to order her execution. Still, Da had said she must seem to be ignorant of the rebellion and in such matters he was always right.

"I know of no unquiet," Elizabeth insisted, "but I will think about your warning. It is kind of you, Sir James, to be concerned for my welfare. If it is true that there should be any disturbance, I will consider your advice."

A finger twitch brought Dunstan out of the quiet corner from which he had been, as always, watching Elizabeth. An inconspicuous movement sheathed the knife he had been ready to throw. He stepped around the cluster of ladies and somewhere along the way picked up a salver on which there was a bottle of wine and a glass.

"Let me offer you some refreshment," Dunstan said, bowing and offering the tray.

His arrival effectively prevented Croft from saying anything more to Elizabeth, who, Sir James found by the time he had refused the wine, had turned away and summoned her ladies. She frowned slightly as she held out her hand to him to kiss in farewell, but it was to the ladies she spoke.

She had no idea how much if anything they had heard of the conversation, but she had no intention of keeping it secret. "Sir James," she said, allowing her eyes to follow him as Shaylor escorted him out, "says there is unrest in the country because the people are unhappy with the queen's choice of a husband. I cannot believe how foolish that is. The Council has arranged that Spain will have no power over this country. Still, Sir James thinks that we would be safer in Donnington."

"Donnington?" Alice Finch repeated. "Where is Donnington?"

Elizabeth shook her head. "I would need to ask Master Cecil who has been my surveyor for some years. I have never been to Donnington in my life."

"Do you think there is real danger of a rebellion?" Elizabeth Marberry asked.

"I cannot believe it," Elizabeth replied. "The queen is so kind and works so hard for the good of the people—" *and cannot whittle down her Council so they could actually help her govern instead of fighting each other nor can she hold for an hour together to a plan . . . except to marry that pallid offspring of the accursed emperor.* "Who could be foolish enough to rebel?"

"Perhaps you should ask Sir Edward to send out scouts so we would have warning if any unrest should start," Dorothy Stafford said. "Until there is any real danger, I would think it wrong to move from the place the queen designated for us."

"I think so too," Elizabeth agreed.

But she really did not know what to think about being urged to move to Donnington, and later, quietly, when Sir Edward came to tell her that the scouts he had long since sent out had found no local unrest, she suggested that he should order in extra arms and supplies for Ashridge in case of trouble.

"Against whom must we guard?" Sir Edward asked.

Elizabeth could only shake her head helplessly. "I do not know. I would not move to Donnington without an order from the queen or the Council, yet Ashridge is so spread out. I do not wish to be taken by the rebels and put up as a mock queen, like poor Jane Grey."

"Rebels." Sir Edward snorted. "We can keep you safe from them. But what if there is an order from the queen?"

Elizabeth shivered. "That I must obey. To fight against queen or Council is treason. I am Queen Mary's faithful and loving subject."

Sir Edward bowed, but there was anger in his eyes. Elizabeth shivered again. She could only be grateful that it was Tuesday and that night Denno would come to take her to the Inn of Kindly Laughter where she could get reliable news and good advice.

Elizabeth entered the inn eagerly, looking left to see whether anyone had preceded them. She was shocked to see a half-sized table with a family of gnomes seated in the space their table usually occupied. There had been too many shocks that day; her eyes filled with tears.

"We will find them, Elizabeth," Denoriel assured her and began to look around for a server. "There," he said, nodding at a pole about six inches thick with red and white stripes constantly rising to a round white head. "The server will know."

Elizabeth blinked at the thick pole; the moving red and white stripes sliding up and around made her a little dizzy. Despite her disappointment and anxiety, she could not help smiling and the fear that had made her so tense eased. "Of course we will—"

Her voice checked when, suddenly, the small table with its family party of gnomes began to slide around the wall of the inn. None of the gnomes gave any sign of awareness of the motion. Elizabeth closed her mouth. As she and Denoriel stared, a human-sized table at which Rhoslyn and Harry were seated slid into place. They also showed no awareness that the table had moved and looked up to greet Elizabeth and Denoriel, who hurried over and sat down before the table got away from them.

Elizabeth kept a wary eye on the wall behind them but then shook her head infinitesimally recalling that she could not detect illusion Underhill.

"What's wrong?" Harry asked.

Denoriel opened his mouth but made no attempt to answer the question directly, only saying, "This is a very strange place . . . even

for one of the great markets of Underhill. Were you aware that
the table was not in its usual position?" Both Harry and Rhoslyn
gaped at him as if he were mad, and he shrugged, abandoning
the topic to ask, "Is Pasgen coming?"

Rhoslyn, looking pale and worried, said, "No. He came to
leave a message at the empty house and I was fortunate enough
to catch him before he left. It seems that he took Hafwen to a
favorite Unformed land where he often collected power from the
mist." She shrugged "I do not completely understand what Pasgen
does, but somehow he draws power out of the mists. Only when
he and Hafwen arrived he found what had been a rather gentle
Unformed land was now an ugly chaos with dead places that stank
of evil. The whole domain was stained and soiled. Hafwen, who
is very sensitive to any taint of evil, was struck unconscious."

"Is she recovered?" Elizabeth asked. She did not know Hafwen
well, but had liked the quiet Sidhe when she met her.

"Yes," Rhoslyn said. "It was only the shock. She begged him to
leave her and discover what had happened. As you know Pasgen
is clever with Gates. He was able to trace back from which Gate
the evil had come and he followed it back and discovered a whole
trail of cruel, brutal, and senseless crimes."

"That does not sound good." Denoriel frowned. "Has Vidal
burst out into—"

"I don't know," Rhoslyn said. "I spoke to Vidal myself not very
long ago and he was completely calm and self-contained. As he
was I cannot imagine him wreaking such havoc for no purpose.
And I cannot think of any purpose . . . But Pasgen is . . . is going
to report the trouble, and you know that Pasgen and Vidal never
get along. I offered to go instead, but—"

"No," Harry said. "That makes no sense. You did not see the
places. What could you really tell Vidal? Pasgen is no fool. If Vidal
is gone mad, he will not stay to confront him. If this is none of
Vidal's doing . . . the armed truce between them will hold."

"That is what Pasgen said," Rhoslyn admitted, "and the lindys
is quiet, but I cannot help worrying."

Denoriel shook his head. "Aleneil is not coming either. It seems
true enough that when one thing goes wrong, everything else does
too." He hesitated. "I wonder if the trouble Pasgen has found is
anything to do with Elfhame Cymry's problem."

"Cymry?" Elizabeth repeated. "I hope nothing serious is wrong there. I like visiting Cymry. Yes, Vidal tried to snatch me from there, but that was years ago and I enjoy the place. Mortals actually seem safe and happy there."

"Yes, well, that seems to be the problem," Denoriel said. "Cymry prides itself on the happiness and safety of their bound mortals. The Sidhe of that elfhame do not use magic for common tasks; they have mortals who farm and are servants so Cymry always has more power than they need. The Cymry Sidhe took a terrible vengeance on a Dark Sidhe who violated their rules, but recently several mortals have disappeared. Ilar came to fetch Aleneil to Cymry because sometimes she can See what has happened."

Elizabeth felt cold and alone, not because Alana was in Cymry but because she knew she would be deprived of her ladies if she were suspected of treason. She had been pleasantly distracted by the news about events Underhill. She was not worried about Pasgen, who could take care of himself, and she had complete faith that the Sidhe of Cymry would find and rescue their mortals. She did not want to be reminded of her danger. Soon she knew she would need to ask Da what he knew about the possibility of a rebellion, but not yet . . . not yet.

"So will you finally order something or are you all going to sit here all night talking?"

The pole of revolving stripes was standing beside the table. The white ball atop was not featureless all around. Apparently she had seen only the back of it when she and Denno had entered the inn. In the front, it had large eyes which seemed painted onto the surface; they had long, curling lashes. There was a line for the nose and two short curved lines to indicate nostrils. The painted mouth was formed into a slight smile. Elizabeth blinked. She could not decide whether or not she had seen the mouth move when the creature spoke.

"Oh, yes," Rhoslyn said. "I think I would like a light wine and some kind of fish."

"Broiled, baked, poached, breaded?"

Again, although she had been watching, Elizabeth could not decide whether the painted mouth moved. And she was sure it was the same server who had been the caterpillar and the besom broom. There did not seem to be any arms connected with the pole so it could not write down the orders as the kitsune who had taken its place wrote them down. And the way it had appeared when she did not want to talk about the coming rebellion. And the way the table she wanted had appeared when she was disappointed. It was all very strange.

Of course the Bazaar of the Bizarre was always strange, but Denno had remarked that the Inn of Kindly Laughter was peculiar, even by Sidhe standards. Elizabeth looked intently at the server, but it seemed as solid as any pole she had ever seen, except for the constantly rising stripes.

"Ah, broiled and medium spiced," Rhoslyn said.

The round, white ball nodded or, rather, rolled slightly forward and then back into position, since there was no neck to nod from.

"And you, little mortal?"

"Where do the stripes go?" Elizabeth asked.

A faint, chortling sound came from the interior of the pole. "That would be telling."

"So it would," Elizabeth said. "Please do tell. That is why I asked."

"What will you give for an answer?" the server asked.

Denoriel opened his mouth to protest, just as Harry said, "Elizabeth, be careful."

Elizabeth cast them both an irritated glance. "Fish," she said. "I will arrange for you to get a barrel of fresh-caught mortal fish if you will tell me where the stripes go."

The server emitted a gusty sigh. "I would like the fish," it admitted. "But I have no idea where the stripes go. I saw this barber pole and I liked it ... so I copied it."

"What is a barber pole?" Elizabeth asked. "I know what a barber is and what a pole is, but together ...

"This," the pole said, turning around so Elizabeth could see all sides of it, "is a barber pole." If a painted face could have a smug expression, the features on the round, white head certainly did. "Broiled fish medium spiced for one lady. What will the other have?"

Somewhat bemused, Elizabeth ordered baked goose and then Harry and Denoriel ordered. The server rolled its head toward Elizabeth again and tipped it forward.

"Respite has been granted," it said. "You must now gather your courage and grasp the nettle."

"What nettle?" Harry asked. "I swear that server gets stranger and stranger every time we come."

"I don't think it is a server," Elizabeth said softly. "I think it is one of the great mages who has made this place as a place of relief..." She let her voice fade and shrugged as the others looked at her. She knew that great mages were seldom altruistic. "So, let me grasp my nettle. Da, a man called Sir James Croft came to Ashridge today, and I am very much afraid he was sent by Gardiner to trap me into admitting I knew of the rebellion."

Denoriel took her hand and kissed it. "Elizabeth, you cannot be trapped. No one can really hurt you. I will come and take you away from any threat."

"I know that," Elizabeth whispered. "I know you can save me, but... that salvation would be hell to me. Oh, I love you my Denno, I love you with all my heart, but I cannot live Underhill. I cannot. Underhill is too easy. I... I want to be queen. I see what Mary does wrong and I burn to set all right..."

"And so you shall, my love," Harry said, and smiled. "In any case, you need not fear that James Croft came to trap you or was a spy for Gardiner or any member of the Council. He has no part in Mary's government. He is a strong and confirmed Protestant, and he is part of the brewing rebellion. In fact one of my informants tells me he has been talking to Courtenay about joining it."

"But his father was a counselor to Mary," Elizabeth said.

Harry shrugged. "That was many years ago. Counselor... hmmm... Sir Edward was no Catholic. Most likely he was trying to find a way to reconcile Mary with her father. Anyway Croft himself is so strongly attached to the reformist rite—and so unwilling to hide his convictions—that he was dismissed from his position as deputy constable of the Tower of London. He went off to Wales to raise men for the rebellion."

"Oh, God's merciful Grace!" Elizabeth exclaimed, her lips thinning. "He is a clever liar. He told Sir Edward that he went on a mission to Wales. Sir Edward thought he had been sent by the queen or the Council. We should never have let him into Ashridge."

Harry frowned. "What did he say? What did you say?"

Elizabeth repeated to the best of her ability, which was very good indeed, the conversation between her and Sir James. Halting at first, the tale flowed more smoothly as Harry nodded and the frown eased off his forehead. When she was done, he shrugged.

"It would have been better if you had not received him at all . . . no, perhaps not. No matter what you do, no one will believe that you had no knowledge at all of the rebellion. This way you can blame Croft for your knowledge if questions are asked."

"Questions?" Elizabeth's voice was not quite steady. "You mean the rebellion will fail and I will be suspect."

Denoriel took her hand again.

Harry sighed. "You must be prepared, my love. I am not Aleneil and cannot see the future, but I know men and their weakness. If the plans laid out for Courtenay by Croft are actually carried out . . ." He shook his head and sighed again. "No, I do not believe the rebellion can succeed, although there is much bad feeling over the introduction of the Catholic rite and Mary's plan to marry Philip has brought the anger to a boil. Some will rise."

"I do not care about that," Denoriel said grimly. "I want to know how to make Elizabeth safe."

"I do not know," Harry muttered, looking down at his own hands. "I would have begged her to forget the stupid mortal world, to come here and live with us, but you heard her answer to that already." He set his teeth for a moment, then said, "Elizabeth, you are much loved in the country. I do not believe Gardiner will dare harm you if there is no proof of treason." He reached out and touched Elizabeth's cheek. "You must remember and trust in your true innocence and never confess to supporting the rebels—"

"I never did support them," Elizabeth protested.

"That will be your defense."

"Why will the rebellion fail?" Rhoslyn asked. "If I can offer some comfort to the queen, she will be less inclined to give in to Gardiner's and Renard's demands to remove Elizabeth."

"Croft and Carew should never have approached Courtenay, who is loose-lipped and weak," Harry said. "I am certain he will betray them. They thought, because Courtenay took it very ill that Mary preferred Prince Philip, he would raise Devon for them. Courtenay believed the queen would marry him because Gardiner urged it. He thought he would be king."

Rhoslyn nodded. "Mary heard rumors that he had his servants bowing to him as if he were king already. She pretended she did not hear. I do not know why, but she likes Courtenay."

"Mary cannot hide what she feels and she does like him. I suppose that is what deceived Courtenay," Harry continued.

"And Croft is a clever liar—not in words but by implication. He and Carew never intended Mary to marry Courtenay; they are all of the reformed religion. Croft and Carew intend to remove Mary and her Catholicism from the throne and to have Bess and Courtenay marry."

"Marry Courtenay?" Elizabeth shrieked, fear completely routed by outrage. "No! Absolutely not! Not even to save my life and gain the throne would I consider marrying that . . . that boorish dolt."

Harry began to laugh. "Courtenay is no more enamored of the prospect than you are. He wants the rebellion to prevent Mary's marriage with Philip and force him on Mary as bridegroom."

"Yes, but it is nothing to laugh about," Rhoslyn said. "Mary *will* have Philip—at any price. She is actually in love with Philip. She keeps looking at his portrait. And the trouble is that Courtenay is not only a dolt but a weak one at that."

"You mean that Courtenay has betrayed the rebellion already?" Rhoslyn nodded. "He went weeping to Gardiner with the tale."

"What am I to do?" Elizabeth asked.

"Pray that there is no rising," Denoriel said flatly. "And if there is, do not lose your courage. You stood fast when Somerset wanted to use you to destroy his brother and you must do so again."

"I wish I could say that there is any likelihood Mary will accept your word and the evidence of her own people that you had no correspondence with the rebels," Rhoslyn said. "But there is no hope of that. If there is a rising, you and all your servants will be strictly examined."

"She will have me beheaded," Elizabeth cried.

"No she will not!" Denoriel snarled. "Always keep within reach a token that will permit me to open a Gate to you. Remember, I will not permit anyone to hurt you. Do not let yourself be overmastered by fear."

"No," Rhoslyn said. "There *is* danger, but I have made her fear any harm to you will somehow rebound on her, and I have reminded her constantly of how much you loved her as a child. Whatever she orders cannot be carried out in a moment, and as soon as she has time to think, she will refuse to order your death."

Elizabeth drew a deep breath. Not relief. Execution was an all too common reality in her life. Her mother, her cousin, her would-be lover, her meek and innocent school-mate had all died under the ax. That was one reality. That she *had* escaped similar threats by defending herself against her accusers was just as real.

The calming thought together with the determination to endure made Elizabeth long for a new subject. That seemed to conjure the barber pole, who suddenly appeared at the table with a serving cart. Rhoslyn, whose lips had parted to continue what she was saying, sniffed instead.

"That smells lovely," she said. "I am almost sorry I ordered just the fish."

"No need to be bound by your order," the server said, and a set of empty plates accompanied by knives and forks floated onto the table.

Then the dishes of food followed. Each dish was set closest to the person who had ordered it, beside the empty plate. Serving pieces appeared beside each platter.

"Help yourselves and pass it along," the barber pole said. "I have other clients to serve."

As it glided away Elizabeth made a small frustrated sound. "I cannot tell whether the mouth on that thing moves or not."

"We need Pasgen," Rhoslyn said, spooning fish and noodles garnished with sauce into her plate. "He is sensitive to spells."

"Mmmm," Elizabeth sighed as she took a mouthful of the goose and forked up some of the roasted, mixed vegetables. "This is as good as it smells." She pushed the plate to Rhoslyn. "Here, have some."

For some time the table was silent, except for the sound of the platters sliding over its surface and brief comments of satisfaction. The light wine Rhoslyn had ordered had come in a large flask and was also passed around. It did not cause any surprise that there was plenty of food and drink for all.

At some time during the meal, Denoriel was heard to mutter, "A great mage? But why?"

No one argued, but no one answered either. Elizabeth smiled to herself. It was true that she lost her power to see through illusion and feel magic when she left the mortal world, but she could still feel purposes no matter what the being. Eventually everyone pushed away plates empty but for a few scraps and bones.

Rhoslyn picked at a tiny shred of fish clinging to a bone and said thoughtfully, "The trouble is not with Mary. I can bend her opinion, but I cannot *bind* her to that opinion. Renard and

Gardiner both push her to be rid of you, Elizabeth. They both hiss into her ears that you are a snake in her grass and if she does not cut off your head, you will poison her and her faith."

"Why?" Elizabeth asked, her hands clenching. "Why do they hate me so?"

Rhoslyn shrugged. "For Gardiner it is not hate. Your death is good politics. The people love you, Elizabeth, and you can be used as a symbol to rouse them. There is no other heir to the throne that they would follow as they would follow you."

"But I have not tried to lead anyone!"

Harry snorted. "That has nothing to do with it. Remember the crowds that came out to watch you pass and cheer you when you moved to Ashridge? Also others use your name. Thank God these rebels have kept their cries to 'Stop the Spanish Marriage' rather than 'Crown Elizabeth.'"

"It is a matter of faith also," Rhoslyn said. "Gardiner is a devoted Catholic, more devoted because he weakened once and obeyed King Henry. As you know, he was imprisoned during Edward's reign because he would not conform to the reformed rite. And Gardiner knows that when Mary dies, if you rule you will not enforce the Catholic faith—not if it means subservience to the pope."

Elizabeth's lips thinned. She had never made any comment about Mary's plan to reconcile with the pope, but that was one aspect of Mary's return to Catholicism with which Elizabeth had no sympathy at all. She did not care a pin whether worship was carried out with gilt chalices and swinging censers of sweet incense or in an unadorned chapel, but to make England obey papal decrees was anathema to her.

"Well, he is right," Elizabeth said coldly. "I will break all relations with Rome as soon as I am empowered to do so . . . or let Rome break relations with me when I refuse to pay Peter's Pence. Perhaps Parliament will not wish openly to renounce Rome again, but I am quite sure they will agree to withhold papal taxes. I can keep my mouth shut as long as Mary is queen. I can go to Mass. But I will not promise to obey the pope."

"And there is no hope of Renard countering Gardiner?" Denoriel asked. "He has more influence on Mary than anyone else."

"No." Rhoslyn was flatly certain. "He wears a ring, a yellow diamond. It stinks of Vidal and glows with an inner light whenever

Elizabeth is mentioned. The one small hope with Renard is that he *does* know that Emperor Charles does *not* want Elizabeth dead."

"Vidal," Elizabeth said thoughtfully. "I had occasion to stop at the inn in the town of Ashridge the other day and there was not an imp to be seen or smelled. There were always imps in the inns in Hatfield. Could Vidal have lost interest in me?"

"I do not believe that for a moment," Rhoslyn said. "I think he does not wish to attack you for fear it will somehow spoil what he thinks is going his way. Likely he hopes Mary and Gardiner will take care of you. And I know he has not abandoned his interest in Logres. Mary has a new physician, introduced to her by Renard, and the man *stinks* of the Dark Court."

"Renard urged a Sidhe physician on Mary?" Elizabeth asked, wide-eyed.

"Not a Sidhe physician. The man is entirely human. He is a good physician too; he attended King Edward and did what he could for the poor boy, but he carries an amulet devised by Aurilia to carry him back to Caer Mordwyn and I can read the touch of Vidal on his mind." Rhoslyn frowned. "Vidal's touch is light, Aurilia's more marked."

"But surely Aurilia and Vidal do not wish any harm to Mary," Denoriel said.

"No, not at all." Rhoslyn smiled. "I think for once Vidal has no ulterior motive. The physician is just a physician and will do his best for Mary. Vidal wants Mary to live, to marry Philip, to try to force Catholicism on Logres. The greater the unhappiness in the realm, the more power of hate and misery leak down to enrich the Dark Court.

Chapter 23

An ogre and two trolls had fallen out over a trembling mortal, too frightened even to scream—but not too frightened to scurry on hands and knees under the benches and between the legs of the other creatures watching the fight. Vidal and Aurilia, seated in their great chairs of bone on the black marble dais veined with red, also watched with amused smiles.

The mortal was not worth fighting over; diseased and emaciated, it would not have lived much longer if the foraging party from the Dark Court had not taken it. There was not enough life in it to make it worth a Dark Sidhe claiming it, but the fear that was draining what remained of its life force tainted the air of the Court and Vidal sucked it in.

It did not get far. Two rows down a goblin felt its passing, seized it and twisted its neck. Usually the goblin would have eaten what it could while the mortal was alive, to enjoy its screaming, but if it screamed here everyone would know it was caught and want a piece. The goblin picked out and ate both eyes and then bit off the flesh of one cheek. It only bled a little, but the goblin's neighbors smelled the blood and fell upon their fellow to tear away what they could.

The flurry of activity alerted the neighbors of the ogre and the trolls, and they rushed to seize what was left from the goblins. Aurilia and Vidal laughed at the antics, and laughed harder as the more fragile but cleverer members of the court, the witches, lamias, succubi, and incubi sneaked away bloody gobbets from the duller but more powerful creatures in the struggling mass.

One or two of the Dark Sidhe, the weakest and least favored, began to look interested in the remains, but although Cretchar had not been offered any share in the spoils of the foraging party, he only laughed. He and Paschenka had collected a whole family only two days before, and there had been a nice, plump three-year-old that Paschenka did not want. Delicious. He watched the spreading chaos with an indulgent smile.

The uproar was terrific and more and more of the Court was getting involved. A goblin was thrown and struck one of the Dark Sidhe. He rose from his seat, blue light flickering on one hand. Aurilia laid a hand on Vidal's arm. She was no longer laughing. When levin bolts were loosed serious accidents could happen.

"Stop!" Vidal roared, and a mist of flickering bright motes drifted from the chair on the dais over the struggling throng.

The Dark Sidhe who could build shields stood and sat untouched, laughing harder as most of the Court jumped about and slapped at the motes that stung and burned. At the same time, the command Vidal had issued rolled through the room, gaining rather than losing volume. The fighting died down; quiet came faster as they realized there was nothing to fight over any longer—a cracked bone or two, a small patch of straggling hair.

Vidal gestured and the stinging flickers of light rushed back to him, slipping between the bones of his chair and blinking malevolently out at the battered and torn creatures of the Court.

"I can see," he said, "that the last hunt was insufficient."

"The mortals are not so stupid as we hoped," a boabham sith whined. "Once there were many on the doorsteps and drunk or wounded in the alleys. Now they all find places within, and the metal in those places hurts us and makes us weak."

"So." Vidal looked over the Court. "Why did no one tell me that game was growing scarce?"

Mutters and murmurs moved through the Court, but no one answered.

Vidal sighed. "Fools. It is time to move to another town. When my messengers go out to gather you again, I will have decided on a new place to glean. This Court is finished. The mortal was the last prize. Get you gone until the summons goes forth."

He watched as the creatures straggled out, some limping, some bleeding but none so weak they could not glare around and dare the others to attack. The Dark Sidhe were the last to leave; each bowed to him before turning away toward the door. Vidal watched with satisfaction. There was no mockery in those bows as there had been sometimes in the past. On the other hand, none of them backed out of the chamber so he could watch Vidal all the time. They were becoming trusting. Vidal uttered a brief laugh. So much the better if any became too bold and he had to remove a few. But for now—

A gesture brought a dead gray mist; another gesture caused the mist to swirl vigorously around the benches and floor that had been soiled with blood and skin and some scales. A few muttered words and the mist gathered itself together and flowed out through the still-open doors. The red floors shone again, glistening almost like freshly spilled blood; the benches, also deep red, grew out of the floors, which was all that kept them from being torn up and used as weapons. The doors closed.

Aurilia looked around the high, dim chamber; it was dark and threatening but still rich and luxurious. "You used to use cleaning up as a punishment," she said. "I kind of liked that. I was able to add this or that surprise to the cleaning and enjoy the shrieks."

"The screaming was amusing, but they never did clean the place thoroughly. It was always grimy and greasy. It's true that it smelled of blood and bad meat, and that was rather appetizing, but the smell distracted the simple-minded creatures too much."

Aurilia laughed suddenly. "Yes, I remember that. The ogres and trolls would try to gnaw on the benches. The grating noise was a nuisance. And I am sure you have no trouble thinking of punishments when you need them."

"True enough."

Vidal smiled, rose, and held out a hand. Aurilia placed her hand on his and also rose to her feet. Vidal said a single word and a miniGate took them to his private chamber. Graciously Vidal handed Aurilia to her velvet-cushioned chair; he bowed slightly to her and seated himself in his own chair. A raised finger brought a cringing servant.

"Do you want more than wine?" Vidal asked.

"Some sweet cakes would be good."

Vidal nodded and the servant disappeared. "I do not know

why I bothered to summon the servant. There is so much power ready to hand that I could have brought the wine and cakes without him."

"But he scents the air with fear, which is pleasant."

Aurilia paused as the servant reappeared pushing a small silver cart; the top opened to display decanters of wine, glasses, and a golden plate piled with glazed cakes. Trembling, the servant backed away from the cart toward the door. Aurilia giggled and snapped her fingers. He flew up into the air and turned a somersault. Before he could hit the floor, Vidal signaled the door to open and flicked his fingers. Wailing softly, the servant flew out of the door. Both laughed at the thud when he hit the floor and laughed harder when a shriek and a series of thuds indicated that the unfortunate creature had fallen down the stairs as well.

The door closed and Vidal and Aurilia faced each other smiling. "It is a real pleasure to have so much power to play with," Aurilia said as she reached into the cart and poured a glass of wine.

She offered it to Vidal; he took it, his smile broadening. "And it is even a greater pleasure to know that the flow will only increase, since it does not depend as it mostly does in Scotland on shifting political alliances." He breathed a large sigh of satisfaction. "Queen Mary is all and more than I expected of her. She does not see and does not care that she is making the people hate her. She will continue to enrage them and power thrown off by their hate and fear will flow as nectar to us."

Aurilia frowned as she poured another glass, from which she sipped before she spoke. "That she is feeding us with power and more power is good, but Mary's stupidity is also dangerous. She nearly lost her throne. Albertus was really frightened. He thought Mary was mad because she would not flee as most of her Councilors advised her when the army of rebels advanced on London."

"She has courage and this idiot faith that her God will protect her." He laughed aloud. "She would regard me as the Devil incarnate, yet it was I who was her shield."

"Then you knew of the rebellion," Aurilia said in a tone of admiration, which for once was not all pretense.

The flood of power from the raging passions in the mortal world was making everything in the Dark Court easy. Because there was enough power for all, the constant struggle to absorb a little more, to steal a little from another was in abeyance. The back of Aurilia's mind was no longer full of the temptation to do away with Vidal so he would not seize the lion's share of power that came to the Dark Court. She was more than usually pleased with her position, which gave her luxury and freedom to torment without labor or responsibility.

"To a certain extent I made it," Vidal replied. "Otstargi's advice enflamed some, assured others, who will never trust Otstargi again—but since they will doubtless be hung or beheaded, that will not matter." He laughed. "And it was I who ensured that the rebellion could not succeed."

"Well, it came all too close to succeeding."

Vidal sighed. "Mortals are always a nuisance. Unfortunately I was unable to reach Wyatt himself and he has more courage and less good sense than I hoped. He held that ragtag army together."

"And the hatred the people have for the Spanish and their fear of the Spanish marriage turned into a double-edged sword."

"Yes." Vidal's expression darkened. "Imagine the stupidity of sending that old man Norfolk out to stop Wyatt. I had hoped there would be a decent battle with a great many deaths and more lovely bitter pain and dying life force for us. Instead, most of Norfolk's force simply deserted and joined Wyatt."

"That was when Albertus fled back here and told me that Mary was about to be taken prisoner and perhaps killed."

"It was not quite as desperate as it seemed," Vidal said and smiled. "The plan for the rebellion had already been ruined. What arrived in London with Wyatt was no longer a real army. It was only a quarter of the intended force."

"Ah." Aurilia smiled back.

Vidal shrugged. "I made sure that two of the conspirators, Croft and Carew, were convinced that the earl of Devonshire would raise Devon for them. Courtenay agreed to do so, because he was angry with the queen. He was about to set out for Devonshire when his valet suggested that he had better go to Otstargi to ask about the future. Otstargi suggested that he had better give a warning of the overthrow of the government to his good friend Chancellor Gardiner."

Aurilia set down her glass because she was laughing so hard she would have spilled the wine. "And he listened to you? He gave a warning to the queen's chancellor?"

Vidal laughed also. "Courtenay is ultimately stupid." A moment later his eyes narrowed. "Maybe he is not so stupid. He has probably saved his neck by betraying the rebellion. Gardiner 'forgave' him for thinking of rebellion after he extracted all the information from Courtenay. Carew was somehow warned—I was not interested enough in Carew to discover all the details—and fled. Croft also fled, but he is one of those idiots of 'principle.' He did not abandon the rebellion; he rushed off to the fourth conspirator, Wyatt to tell him all was known."

"But Wyatt did not flee."

"Another cursed mortal of principle. However in this case it worked just as I had planned. Wyatt had already raised an army and decided to use it, even though he had to strike too soon and without the forces promised by others. I wanted a battle after all. War always brings us the richest flow of life force. But you are right, Aurilia. It came too close. If Mary had not been able to arouse the people of London, and considering how opposed they are to restoring Catholicism and the Spanish marriage she might well have failed—" Vidal ground his teeth. "—Wyatt would have put Elizabeth on the throne. I must be rid of Elizabeth."

"No!" Aurelia gasped.

The roiling power that surrounded Aurilia, warmed by flickers of rage and stabs of pain, made rich by the flood of fear and desperation that came with imminent death, suddenly stilled and chilled. Oberon had forbidden Vidal to act against Elizabeth. To do so now, when Oberon must be watching the Dark Court more carefully than usual because of the amount of power it had, would certainly call forth swift and possibly dreadful punishment.

Aurilia did not care about Vidal, but she enjoyed what he provided for her. He had fulfilled his promise of unlimited power once Mary came to the throne. He had a plan to ensure that Mary would bear a child deeply tainted with Evil so that the power of the Dark Court would not only continue but increase. But if he flouted Oberon now and was destroyed... No. She must somehow convince him to leave Elizabeth alone—and not by reminding him of Oberon's threat, which would only incite him to stupid action.

"I tell you we came within a hairbreadth of having Elizabeth on the throne." Vidal snarled.

"Oh, no." Aurilia shook her head firmly. "According to Albertus,

Wyatt claims he never intended more than to prevent Mary from marrying Prince Philip."

"Wyatt was defeated and taken prisoner. Of course he would say that. I do not believe it."

Aurilia giggled. "No one else does either, so for you to act against Elizabeth now would be useless and dangerous. Wyatt will lose his head . . . and so will Elizabeth. Albertus says that Renard, the Imperial ambassador, and Gardiner have both been urging Mary to have Elizabeth executed since Mary first came to the throne."

Vidal nodded impatiently. Renard's efforts were largely his own doing; he did not need Aurilia's reminder, but it calmed him.

"So see what will happen of its own," Aurilia continued, "Mary already hates Elizabeth, but she could not order her death because the Council and the Parliament would never have agreed. The whole country would have been enraged. Now Mary can prove her sister has committed treason and everyone will agree that Elizabeth should die. Dear Vidal, let nature take its course."

It was fortunate, Denoriel thought as he came hurriedly down the stairs of the house on Bucklersbury, that Sidhe did not sleep. If they needed sleep, he would be dead instead of just merely exhausted. Now that Wyatt's rebellion was out in the open, Mary's ladies were watching Elizabeth close enough to count each breath she took. Denoriel knew; his exhaustion was largely owing to their watchfulness.

He could not take Elizabeth Underhill where they could talk and plan in peace. Elizabeth did not dare be absent from her bedchamber and could only cast the sleep spell if she was there to dismiss it so the lady who slept in her chamber could be wakened. The need to be there and alert was no figment of her frightened imagination.

It seemed Mary's spies had been warned that no communication between Elizabeth and the rebels must go unmarked and the likelihood was that such secret communications would come in the middle of the night. Thus either Eleanor Gage or Elizabeth Marberry had found excuses to come into Elizabeth's bedchamber several times each night and had roused poor Alice Finch, Dorothy Stafford, and Agnes Fitzalan to answer stupid questions—to be sure they would miss nothing and were not beglamored or drugged.

After some days of this, Elizabeth was so despairing and frightened—not so much of dying; she knew her Denno would not let her be killed—but of being wasted, of being denied her chance at ruling, that Denoriel had Gated to Blanche's bedchamber in Ashridge and stayed with Elizabeth for most of the next three nights. By the end of that time, he would cheerfully have slain both Gage and Marberry, if he had not known that killing Mary's spies would probably sign Elizabeth's death warrant.

Denoriel was drained out not only by needing to wear the Don't-see-me spell every time those damned women came creeping in but because he could not ask Aleneil to help him. Matters in Cymry had taken an ugly turn and she was needed there. Thus Denoriel had to find an air spirit to bind to Elizabeth and do the binding himself. He could only be grateful that Lord Denno would not be expected to visit Lady Elizabeth while London was under threat of attack.

However, he would be expected by his now numerous business acquaintances to be in London, so instead of Gating Underhill, Denoriel came up from the wine cellar in the house on Bucklersbury. He had just set his foot on the first step to the upper floor, when the door of Joseph Clayborne's study flew open and Joseph popped out.

"Thank God you are come," Joseph said. "I must go down to the warehouse. I do not want our guards and porters to go haring off to join . . . whichever side they favor. They are all men I can trust to carry expensive goods and I do not want them involved in any fighting unless the warehouse is attacked. I hope you will be here today. I do not want to leave the house empty."

"Cropper?" Denoriel asked.

"Down at the warehouse too."

"Very well," Denoriel said, "but do not become desperate in defense of the warehouse. Goods can be replaced. Even the warehouse can be replaced. You, Joseph, cannot. And remember that Mistress Standish will have me skinned if harm comes to you over my property."

Clayborne colored slightly and smiled. "I am more concerned with keeping the men out of trouble than of real danger. There are a few, I fear, who would rush off to join Wyatt's force if they came near. No matter what I say to them, they insist that the Spanish will arrive in force and overwhelm us."

"Thank God you have more sense," Denoriel said. "I will be here, at least until after dark."

Joseph pointedly did not ask where Denoriel might be after dark. He went out the door; Denoriel locked it and struggled wearily up the stairs. The room was cold and he remembered that he had not used it for nearly a week. Mumbling epithets he turned to the fireplace and gestured. The laid fire burst into dancing flames, but Denoriel sat down suddenly on the bed, dizzy and empty.

He sat for a moment, looking down at his boots, wondering if he had the energy to take them off or enough power left to magic them off when the knocker on the door was plied so violently that Denoriel jumped.

"Hold!" he shouted, the sound of his voice nearly drowned by the renewed thudding of the knocker.

Denoriel realized that whoever was at the door probably could not hear him—or might not want to hear him. He pushed himself off the bed and went to the window, which he flung open. He was about to order the person away, to the warehouse if he had urgent business, when he recognized the man. Not a London merchant wanting to do business but the guildmaster for Maidstone in Kent.

About to call him by name, Denoriel bit his tongue. Mortal eyes could not have seen his face in the predawn dark. *And besides,* Denoriel admonished himself, *do not be more of an idiot than you need to be.* What merchant would have urgent business to conduct before dawn with an honest man like Joseph?

"Just a moment," he shouted. "I am coming down."

When he opened the door, however, he was startled to see the guildmaster pale visibly. "It is true then," the man said. "The Spanish are about to take London!"

Denoriel shook his head. "What Spanish? There are no Spanish in London, except a few merchants."

"Then why are you dressed at this hour, if you are not making ready to leave?"

Laughing, Denoriel said, "Come in out of the cold, Guildmaster. I am dressed because I have not yet undressed. I was in my bedchamber about to go to bed when you knocked."

He drew the man in and shut the door behind him, pausing to throw the bolts and hook the chain. Watching him, the guildmaster asked nervously, "Where were you, that you came home near dawn?"

Denoriel laughed again. "That is not a question one should ask of an unmarried man, but I see you are sadly overset so I will tell you. I was visiting a lady. Wherever did you hear that the Spanish were about to take London?"

Now the guildmaster looked uncertain and in the light of the candelabra in the entryway, he could see that Denoriel's clothing was elegant visiting attire, not at all suitable for riding. He drew a deep breath and shook his head.

"It is all abroad in Maidstone that the Spanish have been coming in small groups, in harness, carrying harquebussea and morions. Lord Denno, you have friends at Court and connections abroad, will you not tell me the truth? There is a proclamation from Thomas Wyatt nailed up on the Maidstone Market Cross saying that the English must rise to ensure that the queen gets better counsel and counselors who will protect us from the Spanish."

Wyatt had been cleverer than Denoriel expected. Instead of trying to rouse those of the reformed religion against the queen's Catholicism—which would set Englishman against Englishman—he had appealed to the hatred both Catholic and Protestant alike felt for foreigners.

"My news from abroad is no later than two days old," Denoriel said, "and I can tell you that rumor and Wyatt are wrong. No Imperial army or Spanish army is moving. No ships are gathered in the ports of the Low Countries to carry invaders across the narrow sea, and the 'Spanish' you have heard about are Flemings come to negotiate the queen's marriage to Prince Philip."

"But that marriage is an abomination. What am I to do? Is Wyatt strong enough to drive off the Spaniards?"

"Guildmaster, there *are* no Spaniards. *None.* And while I could wish that the queen's Council was more unified, they have not done so ill in the marriage treaty. They have secured England against any interference in the government by Prince Philip. What are you to do? Go home. Tell the merchants of your guild to call in their apprentices and journeymen and lock their doors until this madness passes. That is where my own people are, at my warehouse lest this lunatic fear of nonexistent Spaniards sets off mobs that desire only loot."

"Are you sure?"

"I am sure there are no Spanish threatening to overrun England. Like you, I do not like this marriage, but if it is the queen's will and if it will get us an heir to the throne, I will say and do nothing against it. Now, if you have ridden from Maidstone, you must be cold and tired. Come sit in my parlor. As soon as my servants arrive, they will ready a room for you."

The guildmaster took a deep breath. "I thank you, but no. I have bespoke a room in the Fox and Geese."

"I hope you did not 'warn' them about any Spaniards," Denoriel said, his voice tense.

"No." The guildmaster looked a little shamefaced. "I saw that all was quiet. My fears of any immediate threat were almost put to rest, until you answered the door yourself all dressed instead of a servant opening the door to me." He uttered a slight laugh. "I have given over visiting ladies and am somewhat younger than you, my lord, so I never thought you would be out late for that."

"You have a good wife and have no need to be out and abroad in the night," Denoriel replied, smiling as he unlocked the door and let the guildmaster out.

He went back up to his bedchamber, but only to sit by the fire and think. What he had said to the guildmaster about the Spaniards had been the truth. There was no threat from the Empire, not when Charles no doubt had reports of Mary's infatuation with his son and the idea of marriage. England would be in the emperor's hands through Philip's influence; Charles did not need any army.

Wyatt was a different problem altogether. The rumors spread abroad by his orders and proclamations might indeed rouse the countryside. Denoriel frowned. If Wyatt won . . . Likely like many young enthusiasts he believed in the reformed rite. That meant, surely, that he would try to put Elizabeth on the throne to end the threat of reestablished Catholicism. If Mary were dead . . .

Denoriel shook his head sharply. Wyatt would not kill her and Elizabeth could not, not if she wished to rule England. The people would never support her if she had Mary murdered or executed. And it would not be possible to rule England in peace if Mary were alive. No, this revolt must be put down. Denoriel cast around in his mind for anything he could do to impede Wyatt's progress but realized that he truly did not know what was happening. Tomorrow, he thought, letting his eyes glaze over and his mind grow empty.

❖　　❖　　❖

After early Mass on January twenty-eighth Denoriel went down to the warehouse. Joseph was wearily finishing his records of what he had the men sort and store. Most of the furor over the Spanish threat had died down and there had been no further rumors about the rebels. The men were all on notice to be back in the warehouse early on Monday.

Joseph had sent Cropper home and readily agreed to come back to Bucklersbury to sleep so Denoriel could ride out and learn what was actually happening in Kent. Joseph made it sound as if he expected Lord Denno to ask for news among his acquaintances at Court and possibly at the Hanse, but he knew there was something very strange about Lord Denno's horse? horses?

Although Denoriel felt slightly sick to his stomach and once or twice found difficulty focusing his eyes, Miralys made nothing of the distance to Maidstone. There Denoriel joined at church a merchant group with whom he had done business. He heard that Wyatt had taken Rochester and also that the Londoners sent out to put down the rebellion had instead joined it. There was much speculation but no real knowledge, and after he had made clear that there was no Spanish threat, he rode off to Rochester.

There Denoriel sought and found the Rochester guildmaster in an inn across from the church he attended. Lord Denno, well known as a rich and successful factor, was eagerly asked for news. He repeated what he had told the guildmaster from Maidstone—that there was no threat from Imperial or Spanish forces, that any threat of disruption was from Wyatt and his followers.

"I told those young fools from our guild who were hot to join Wyatt," the guildmaster said, "that no merchant had seen or heard of any foreigners armed for war in small groups or large. They would not listen. They were all afire to save the queen from her counselors' bad advice and when the London white-coats who had come with the duke of Norfolk deserted to join Wyatt, it was quickly decided that London would not resist but welcome them."

"That is ill news indeed," Denoriel said. "Not that London will welcome them, for it will not. But the loss of Norfolk's force leaves the road to London completely open. And I do not look forward to fighting in the streets of London."

"Warn them in London to watch the river as well as the road," the guildmaster said.

"The river?" Denoriel repeated.

The guildmaster nodded, his lips bent sourly. "Wyatt stopped at Gravesend where Queen Mary had ordered a fleet be assembled to escort Prince Philip when he arrived. The sailors were not much enamored of their duty and half the seamen deserted to join Wyatt's army. It is said they even took guns from the ships."

Denoriel sighed heavily and stood up. "That too is bad news, and so I must say my fare wells quickly. If I change horses along the road, I will surely outdistance an army and carry this warning to London in good time."

"God watch over your going," the guildmaster said, and no one else in the group tried to delay him.

Not, of course, that Denoriel was worried about arriving in London before Wyatt's army. If he only could muster the energy to mount Miralys, he could be there in a quarter of an hour. But he really had no idea what to do with the information. Bringing it to the Court would be like carrying coals to Newcastle; he was sure there had been messengers in plenty. But the purpose of coming here had been to find a way to frustrate Wyatt—and he still could think of nothing.

Before he could cudgel his whirling brain into deciding on his next move, Miralys was coming to a halt at the portico of Llachar Lle. Denoriel found himself on his own feet, facing the Sidhe-sized portal.

"Wait—" Denoriel said, turning to face Miralys.

But Miralys was gone. Denoriel stood there for a moment wide-eyed with surprise. Damned elvensteed. Since when did it think it could tell him what to do. He could reach the Gate on foot . . .

And then he started to laugh. He could, when his knees stopped shaking and his body felt less like a hollowed-out, overcooked gourd that was going to collapse.

Slowly Denoriel entered the palace and walked toward his apartment. *I am spending far too much time among mortals,* he thought. *How ridiculous to drive myself to exhaustion. I can't believe I simply forgot I could go Underhill, restore myself, and twist time so that I was back almost at the time I left.*

Of course it was not quite as simple as that. Twisting time took power, a lot of power, so he would come back to the mortal world only a little stronger than when he left it, but he would have had time to consider what would be best to do. If he could think of a way to demoralize Wyatt's force, he might even find help to do it among those who had ridden in the Wild Hunt with him.

He walked through the door to his apartment, through the entryway and into the parlor. He was already feeling slightly better as Mwynwyn's spell for absorbing power began to fill him. In the parlor, he dropped onto the sofa and stretched out. What a shame that William Cecil was not part of the Court any longer. Before he decided what kind of trouble he could make for Wyatt's army, he had to know what the Council was planning. And his best informant was not even in the city.

Or was he? After Edward died and Northumberland's scheme had fallen apart, Cecil had withdrawn to the country, where he had been very busy building anew and extending existing buildings on his property. But now? In the depths of winter? There had been no persecutions of Northumberland's officers; in fact, many of them were now Mary's officials. And there had been no overt persecution of the followers of the reformed faith. How strong were Cecil's religious feelings? Could he put them aside to be engaged again in the work and world he loved?

What a shame, Denoriel thought, as he lay quiet, resting, watching the colored flames flicker over the crystal logs in his hearth, that he could not set Miralys to sniffing out Cecil as huntsmen set their dogs to sniffing out game. He was smiling as the unmarked time slipped by, but he was distantly aware that the sweet flow of power from laughter and story and song was thinner than in the past, that it was taking longer than usual to restore his strength.

Chapter 24

Although Denoriel had no definite plan for delaying and disorganizing Wyatt's army when he left Underhill, he had found two strongly mischievous friends from the Wild Hunt who could endure the ambiance of iron and steel for short periods and liked nothing better than making trouble in the mortal world. They agreed enthusiastically to join Wyatt's party and encourage in it mutiny, disorder, and pandemonium. Denoriel had worn his young aspect when he spoke to them, although he showed them his present appearance so they would recognize him if they encountered him in the mortal world.

Miralys had been waiting when Denoriel left Llachar Lle. "I am not a small child who needs to be told to be still and rest," he said severely to the elvensteed as he mounted.

There was no sound in his mind; there was no physical reaction to his reproof that Denoriel could detect. Nonetheless he knew Miralys was laughing at him.

Denoriel sighed. He had never yet won any point contested with the elvensteed. He should know better than to try. What he had to decide before they reached the Gate was whether he should twist time to the mortal night after he had been with Elizabeth or skip a night. To twist time an extra day would cost him power, and staying with Elizabeth, with the frequent need to use the Don't-see-me spell, would cost him more. And he had nothing, really, to tell her—only that Wyatt was coming. He did not even know what preparations, if any, the Council would take to protect the city.

The last thought decided him. The Gate brought him to London in the late afternoon of the day after he left. It would cost him no more than an hour or so to learn what Joseph knew and to pass by Cecil's house on Cannon Row. He could explain his reasoning to Elizabeth; she was not a child and not quite so unreasonable.

Denoriel did not forget that if Cecil had won a position with the new government, it would do him harm to be known as consorting with Lady Elizabeth's favorite Lord Denno. Therefore, while they were still Underhill and the illusion would not cost so much, Denoriel put on the aspect of Charles Paget, third son of Lord Paget, a respected member of Mary's Council.

When he dismounted from Miralys, he was delighted to see the knocker affixed to the door of Cecil's house; that meant that Cecil was in London, although he might not actually be in the house at the moment. That did not matter. As Charles Paget, Denoriel plied the knocker. When the door opened, the servant bowed and stepped back to allow entrance to Lord Denno.

"If your master is not within," Denoriel said, "may I leave a note for him?"

"He is within, m'lord," the footman said, "but I know he is busy and may not be able to—"

At which point the rest of the sentence became unnecessary because William Cecil had appeared in the open doorway of the parlor and said, "Lord Denno. A surprise and yet not a surprise. That's all, Perry, but bring some wine and some of those sweet cakes cook prepared." And he turned to Denoriel. "If you would join me in the parlor . . ."

There Cecil closed the door carefully and said in a very low voice. "I cannot tell you how glad I am to see you, but I hope no one took note of your coming here."

"No. I made very sure of that," Denoriel assured him in an equally low voice. "I thought if you had renewed your connections to the Court that it would do you no good, specially in these times, to be seen having private meetings with a favorite of Lady Elizabeth."

Cecil smiled broadly. "I should have known you would consider that." He sighed, then gestured to chairs well away from the table piled with papers. "I tried to think of some way to let you know I was back, and that Lord Paget finds me very useful, but...ah... you know Lord Paget. I am very much afraid that I am watched and any letters I dispatch might be carefully examined.

I am almost ready to believe in the mortal God, Denoriel thought, *and that He, like Titania, wishes to see Elizabeth on the throne of England. It is Paget who is employing Cecil and quite by chance I picked Paget's son to be Cecil's visitor.*

Denoriel shrugged. "I know you enjoy politics and there has been no persecution of Northumberland's followers nor any great pressure yet on individuals to worship with the Catholic rite. I thought you might have taken the chance to offer your services to those who knew you. As you can imagine, Lady Elizabeth is strung tighter than any fiddle."

Cecil shook his head. "I knew it must be so, and if I had any news that would help, I *would* have found some way or other to send it, but I have nothing...except that she still has friends. Rochester, who you know the queen loves and trusts as few other men, speaks well of Lady Elizabeth always, and assures Queen Mary that her sister does love her and is loyal. Paget does what he can, although never openly before the queen. I wish there was more, but Gardiner and the Imperial ambassador continue to use every device to turn the queen against her sister."

"I wonder if it would help if Renard had an accident," Denoriel said softly.

Cecil shuddered. "Truthfully I do not think any 'accident' would not be put down to murder. Mary is convinced the Imperial envoys are in danger. I think the death of the Imperial ambassador by any means would convince the emperor that England was too dangerous for his only, precious son. And if Mary is deprived of Prince Philip—whose portrait she goes ten times a day to see...She will kill Elizabeth in revenge and to be sure that Elizabeth cannot inherit, since Mary will feel it was for Elizabeth's sake she was deprived of the possibility of having a child."

Denoriel swallowed hard but did not need to reply because the door opened to show Perry with a tray. Both men stared silently at each other, until the tray was set on a table and wine poured into each of the two goblets. Cecil nodded at Perry and thanked him and the servant withdrew, shutting the door carefully behind him.

"I see," Denoriel sighed as soon as he was sure Perry was gone. "I am glad to hear that Rochester is still Elizabeth's friend. That may help. But to tell the truth, I did not come to hear about Elizabeth but to discover, if you can tell me, what the Council is planning to do about Wyatt. I assume you know that most of the troops sent with Norfolk joined Wyatt instead of fighting him and that the sailors of the ships anchored at Gravesend did the same. There is now nothing to prevent Wyatt from marching straight into London."

"I did not know about the sailors," Cecil said, shaking his head, his lips pressed into a thin line. "Not that it matters. The Council appointed Pembroke and Clinton to command the queen's forces and Lord William Howard to see to the defense of the city."

"Clinton and Lord Howard know what they are doing," Denoriel said, "but why Pembroke? He is barely twenty years old."

"Yes, but he is very hot to protect the queen, and will shame the others if they do not resist with all their strength." Cecil's lips twisted. "Who knows why they do anything. It is not as if one strong will drives them. They are too taken up with blaming each other for this disaster to even propose a proclamation to call the city to arms. Most blame Paget for supporting the Spanish marriage and many blame Gardiner for pressing forward with the change to the Catholic rite. There are all kinds of rumors about Lady Elizabeth also."

Denoriel put down the glass he was holding and sat forward tensely. "Rumors? What rumors?"

"That she is moving away from London to a great castle. That she is gathering troops to join Wyatt—"

"That is utter nonsense!" Denoriel interrupted furiously.

Cecil stared at him for a long moment, then said, "You have seen her. Yes. She would have no part in an open rebellion. I said to Paget that Lady Elizabeth was not such a fool, but he merely shrugged. Paget is too busy defending himself to take a chance of annoying Renard by speaking well of Elizabeth. And the treasurer insists there is proof of the gathering of troops and Elizabeth's household now eats in a week what usually lasted them a month."

Denoriel laughed bitterly. "If Elizabeth hears of any increase in expenses, she will skin Parry alive." Then he sighed and added, "Elizabeth will be able to prove the extra cost is a lie. She insists that Parry keep very exact records of every penny spent, since the Seymour business when she discovered he was lax. She is loyal to her servants so she would not dismiss him, but she made note of his weaknesses and now reads over his accounts and initials them."

"I fear she will need whatever proof of innocence she can get if Wyatt does not succeed."

"I cannot believe he will," Denoriel said, wondering if he should try to gather the merchants and rouse them to defense.

Cecil shook his head. "The Council all fear the worst and are running about like hysterical chickens. They are all urging Mary to flee London because they wish to run themselves but do not dare to leave while she stays." He shrugged. "I am packed and ready to go myself, and will follow if the queen leaves."

Denoriel sighed again. "Let me know if you can if the queen decides to abandon the city."

"I will do my best," Cecil replied as Denoriel rose to his feet, "and for Lady Elizabeth also. But there are hard times coming for her whatever the outcome of this rebellion."

"She is as earnest as I in wishing it had never happened," Denoriel said, as Cecil accompanied him to the door.

"I am certain of it."

Lord Denno stepped through the opened door of William Cecil's house, but Charles Paget, after a slight pause with a hand against the door jamb to steady himself, went down the stairs to untie Miralys's rein and to mount. It was already growing dark. Days were short in February.

Although he did not expect to be seen, Charles Paget rode a little way along Watling Street, then turned his chestnut mount into a quiet alley. After a little while Lord Denno on a black horse rode out of the alley and proceeded sedately to his warehouse near the river.

Joseph was glad to see him. He had news from the east. Wyatt was moving toward London along the south shore of the Thames, nearing Deptford. Lord Denno gathered the men and told them he had news from a newly arrived fellow merchant. Over the narrow sea there is great surprise over the foolishness of the English. No Imperial army is moving anywhere. No ships are being gathered in any port. The Spanish are *not* planning on an invasion of England.

The men seemed somewhat disappointed rather than relieved, but they all had a very high opinion of Lord Denno and readily agreed not to join any force that claimed to be against the Spaniards but would probably be used to raid the rich shops and houses of London.

Later, privately, he said to Joseph, "Indeed, why should the Spaniards invade England? Once Queen Mary is married to Prince Philip they will have more influence than a conquering army would. The last thing Emperor Charles desires is any unrest in England."

They left the warehouse with only its normal night guards and returned to Bucklersbury where he and Joseph ate dinner, after which Joseph went out to visit his betrothed and give her family the latest news. Denoriel read for a while, but soon after Joseph returned he went up to his bedchamber, slipped behind the cheval mirror that replaced the one Pasgen had shattered, and Gated to Ashridge.

"Where have you been?" Elizabeth whispered, holding out her arms as he stepped into her chamber from Blanche's. "I am so frightened I can hardly breathe."

"I am sorry, my love," Denoriel replied, his cheek against her hair. "Miralys took me Underhill after I went to Maidstone and Rochester for news of the rebellion. I—" he hesitated and then spoke the truth "—I was . . . tired."

For a moment longer Elizabeth held him tight, then she shivered slightly, released him, and said, "Tell me the news."

Rhoslyn was as exhausted as Denoriel. Usually it was safe for her to retreat Underhill to restore herself almost every night, but not since Gardiner brought word to the queen of Courtenay's confession. The chancellor had followed his news of the planned rebellion with an urgent request that he be allowed to arrest Lady Elizabeth and place her in the Tower for safekeeping. He did not mention eventual execution, but Rhoslyn read it in his mind and sent a sharp reminder of disaster to Mary.

As she always did when urged to deal with Elizabeth, Mary hesitated, raising a hand to her temple. The she shook her head at Gardiner and said he could not expect her to make so momentous a decision without serious thought. Gardiner's mouth opened and his face flushed, but he bit back whatever angry words he had been about to say. Mary looked after him, a faint frown wrinkling her brow.

When Gardiner was gone, Rhoslyn eased the thrust that made Mary touch her temple. More gently she renewed in Mary's mind all the fears she had set there about doing harm to Elizabeth. She knew the mental doubts were no longer enough, however. The real threat of rebellion was making the imagined fears pale. But before she could spare any mental effort to influence one of Mary's ladies, she was supported by Jane Dormer, who asked with wide eyes what Elizabeth had done to deserve arrest.

"That will be determined when she is held safe," Mary said.

Rhoslyn drew a shocked breath. Mary sounded as if she were breaking free of the instilled fears, but she did not give an order to recall Gardiner. She was looking at Susan Clarencieux, who was frowning and shaking her head.

Without any pressure from Rhoslyn, Susan said slowly, "I do not like Lady Elizabeth. I think her insincere both in her profession of the Catholic faith and in her affection for you, Your Majesty. Nonetheless I must protest against Bishop Gardiner's advice."

"Why?" Rhoslyn asked, playing devil's advocate to get Susan to state her reasons aloud.

"To arrest Lady Elizabeth without proven cause would, I fear, *precipitate* rebellion," Susan said. "Remember how Elizabeth names herself 'mere English' as if your Spanish blood was some stain. If Lady Elizabeth is involved with the rebels, would they not cry aloud that in imprisoning her you are a tool of the Spanish, that you wish to sacrifice England to them? The whole country might rise against you."

"Oh, they might indeed," Rhoslyn agreed, pressing the hatred of the Spanish as the cause of the rebellion on Mary's mind to the exclusion of Elizabeth.

To Mary, who was certain that nothing better could happen to England than to be guided by Spanish orthodoxy into fervent Catholicism, fear and hatred of the Spanish was incomprehensible. Resistance to her plans to marry Philip thus seemed more and more reformist resistance to the true faith and became in Mary's mind inextricably connected to heresy, treachery, and now, rebellion.

Nor could Rhoslyn relax her vigilance over the following weeks as the rebellion developed. Gardiner tried several times to get Mary to agree to arrest Elizabeth and Mary's growing anxiety was making the notion of Elizabeth in prison attractive. Only the fact that no one could accuse Elizabeth of anything—and the rebels' constant harping on the Spanish threat permitted Rhoslyn's instilled fears to balance Mary's dislike of her sister.

The anti-Spanish rhetoric added to the fact that not once did anyone use her as a figurehead was Elizabeth's protection. Even when Carew escaped from those coming to seize him, when the duke of Norfolk's army defected to the rebels as did the seamen from the ships at Gravesend, when Wyatt started to move his army south, not once was there any mention of Elizabeth as a rival to Mary. Whenever any of the rebels spoke to a crowd or nailed up a proclamation, it was to warn against Spanish oppression and swear their intention was to protect the queen.

Fortunately Renard did not add his conviction about the danger of leaving Elizabeth free to Gardiner's. He was so concerned with the immediate threat that Wyatt posed to himself and his fellow ambassadors, that a distant threat like Elizabeth shrank to insignificance. All Renard's attention and that of the Council during Wyatt's march was on whether Mary should flee London or stay.

Renard's mind had been muddled by Vidal on the subject of Elizabeth, but he was clear enough on political events aside from trying to be rid of her. He knew that if Mary fled and the rebels took London, England would be in a state of civil war and no use to the Empire for many years to come if it were ever of use. Renard was frightened, but he was a brave man; he stayed in London and advised the shaken queen, who distrusted all her English advisors and her dithering Council, to do the same.

He advised another useful tactic—that Mary try to convince the rebels she would listen to their objections to a union with Spain. Mary was transparently honest and protested that to listen to the rebels' objections was ridiculous. They were wrong in their fears. Spain was no threat to England.

Rhoslyn and Mary's other ladies assured her that although they knew Spain was no threat, it would also be true that she would listen to what the rebels had to say rather than fight them. She did not need to follow their advice, but the time spent in conferences with the rebel leaders might well end the rebellion. The common soldiers would likely lose their enthusiasm as time passed and no Spanish threat appeared; they would slip away. Wyatt would have no army and the rebellion would be over.

So Mary agreed to offer a truce to Wyatt, who had reached Blackheath. To show the queen was serious and respected her opponent, no mere herald, but two gentlemen of her household, Sir Edward Hastings and Sir Thomas Cornwallis, carried a carefully noncommittal message: If Wyatt and his friends were in arms only against strangers and in fear of the Spanish marriage, the queen would appoint persons to confer with him.

In this case Renard's advice did not have the anticipated effect. The message seemed only to make Wyatt feel he was already victorious. He sent back with Hastings and Cornwallis an answer that aroused the normally gentle Mary to rage. He would rather be trusted than trust, Wyatt's message read, and for that trust the surety he desired was the dismissal of four councilors to be replaced by others whom he would name and custody of the Tower of London, and Her Grace the queen in the Tower.

Within an hour of that response, Mary had sent a notice to the mayor, the aldermen, and other important merchants that she would speak to them in the Guildhall. She stood before them under a cloth of estate surrounded by her chancellor, her dithering Council, and her trembling but determined ladies. Small but indomitable, she spoke to them in her deep, resonant voice and told them of Wyatt's progress and answer to her offer.

Standing with others of his Company, Denoriel found it within himself to admire Mary's dogged courage. In plain terms, the queen accused Wyatt of threatening a Spanish invasion as a false pretense to cover his opposition to her Catholicism. She reminded them that they knew the conditions of the marriage and that the marriage would give the Spanish no power in English government. And, she added, rather untruthfully, she was not a slave to her lust and her own pleasure; if the nobility, the commons, and the Parliament should deem the marriage not advisable, Mary said, "I will abstain from marriage while I live."

The queen spoke simply and with great sincerity. Rhoslyn, standing with the other women, knew that Mary lied although, perhaps, Mary did not permit herself to know she was lying. What was important was that she had come in her own person and, so to speak, thrown herself on the mercy of her subjects—she asked if they would defend her against these rebels. "For if you do," she said, "I am minded to live and die with you."

The hall erupted in cheering and when Mary had withdrawn

to drink a cup of wine with the lord mayor and then take her barge to return to Westminster, the men in the hall, Denoriel included, went to arm themselves and to gather and arm their dependents.

The next day the streets of London were full of armed men, oddly enough going calmly about their daily tasks. On Miralys, Denoriel was able to visit every part of the city and every part was making ready to defend their queen who sat stubbornly in the palace of Westminster, defying the advice of her fearful Council.

In the afternoon, the guns of the Tower bellowed a warning. The guards there had seen flags moving on the Southwark shore; no long delay proved them to be Wyatt's flags. Joseph came back from the warehouse to tell Lord Denno that word along the Thames was that Lord William Howard had ordered the draw-bridge cut loose so the bridge could not be used to enter the city and sent riders along the river to order that all bridges within fifteen miles be broken down. The next order was for the gates of the city to be shut.

Denoriel went up to his bedchamber and Gated to Llachar Lle where he drew from its chest the silver armor he wore when he rode first in Koronos's Wild Hunt. A gesture darkened the silver to look like iron, another put a simple doublet and cloak over the armor. Thus garbed, he stepped back through the Gate and emerged from behind the cheval glass.

When he came down from his bedchamber, Denoriel found Joseph also armored and with his sword belted on. He nodded approval and asked if there were jacks enough for the men they employed. Assured that all their employees would be properly armored, Denoriel told Joseph that he did not believe it neces-sary to join any other troop in the city unless they were asked for help.

"Remain in the vicinity of the warehouse and watch the river. With the drawbridge down and no other nearby bridges available, Wyatt may try to get his men across in small boats."

"That would be mad," Joseph said and then snorted. "But this whole venture has been mad and here Wyatt is, besieging London. Very well, we will guard our section of the river and I will talk to our neighbors so they set watches on their wharfs also. And you, my lord?"

"I think I will go make my bow to Lord Clinton, who knows me. His first wife was Harry FitzRoy's mother. She learned, perhaps from Norfolk, that I saw the boy often and she invited me to her home to ask about him. Clinton was then very young himself, hardly more than a boy. He knew that the marriage was made to advance him with Henry VIII and was interested in Harry. We met occasionally thereafter and he is aware of my connection with Elizabeth. That I am willing to fight for Mary can only help. Clinton, I believe, has charge of the horse. It is possible he can use my sword."

However, when Denoriel was received by Clinton, he found he had come to the wrong man. Pembroke, young and full of confidence in his personal prowess, was the leader of the mounted defense of the city. Clinton looked at Denoriel's white hair and lined face.

"You will not be warmly received," he said wryly. "I have a far better use for you, Adjoran. I know you hold no office in the Companies of the city, but you know most of the guildmasters and even the lord mayor. Do me the favor, if you will, of speaking to them and of going around the gates and making sure there are no traitors there ready to open to Wyatt if he finds a way across the river."

"Very well, my lord, if that is the way I will be of most use, I will be happy to do it."

"Yet would not Lady Elizabeth be glad to see Queen Mary in Wyatt's hands?"

Denoriel was delighted that Clinton had come out and mentioned his doubts about Lord Denno's own loyalty. He shook his head vigorously.

"Oh, no, my lord. Lady Elizabeth is no fool. Even setting aside the fact that Lady Elizabeth is a loving and loyal sister and remembers the queen's kindness and generosity to her when she had little herself, for purely selfish reasons she wants no part of Wyatt's rebellion. The last thing she desires is to have any harm at all come to Queen Mary. That would incriminate her—no matter that she is totally innocent—and be a cause of endless civil war."

"I am glad to hear that Lady Elizabeth is so sensible."

"She is, and I will do all in my power to see that this stupid rebellion is put down."

There was, however, little to do. Seeing the drawbridge down so the bridge was impassable, Wyatt made no attempt to cross the river. He settled down in Southwark, exerting a tight control over the army that was with him, paying for the supplies his men needed and preventing looting. He was waiting, it seemed, for the Londoners to take the queen prisoner and invite him into the city.

For that, he was a few hours too late. If Mary had tried to flee or had not come in person to appeal to the people of the city, Wyatt's friends in London might have had a more receptive audience. As it was, fired by Mary's courage and steadfastness and perhaps given hope that she would take warning and draw back from the Spanish marriage, London watched the invader on the south shore of the Thames armed and ready to resist.

Nonetheless, Wyatt did have friends. At Ludgate, to which Denoriel had come after dark—he had stopped at the northern gates and eastern gates first—he saw the gate properly closed but a huddle of men standing together. To the mortals, it was full dark and they felt themselves to be invisible to anyone beyond the faint light of their dark lantern. To Denoriel, the dark lantern made it near as bright as daylight.

Responsive as always to his desire, Miralys made no sound and moved into the deeper shadow at the side of the small guardhouse. Denoriel cocked his long ears forward.

"Yes, she is a brave lady," one voice said, "and no one, most of all Sir Thomas Wyatt, wishes her any harm. It is to save her that he has come, to protect her from the evil counsel that has led her to offer herself—and England—to the Spaniards."

"It is true," another voice answered, "that I do not want to see our sweet queen married to that sour Spaniard. I have heard that he wreaked dreadful havoc in the Low Countries, burning men and women and children, too, for defying the pope's rule."

"And if he is Queen Mary's husband," the first voice said, "will he not force the pope upon us and burn us if we resist?"

"The queen is Catholic," a third voice said. "But she has not forced the Catholic rite upon us."

"Not yet," a fourth man said. "But the priest in my church is asking for money to buy chasubles and chalices and thuribles in which to burn incense. I do not like it. I do not wish to see our good, plain worship bedecked in a Catholic harlot's robes."

"And it must be stopped," the first voice said. "The queen must have councilors who will tell her that she may have her Mass but that she may not force it upon us. When Sir Thomas is in control of the city, he will see the right kind of councilors appointed. They will reject this marriage to Spain. If he comes to the gate, will you not allow him entry to achieve this good?"

There was a tight silence. Break it up now, Denoriel thought, before any of the men commit themselves and, with a clatter of seemingly shod hooves, Miralys appeared as if he had come out of an alley onto the main road. The group by the gate fragmented immediately, one man snatching up the dark lantern and darting away along the base of the wall, another hurrying toward the guard house and two coming a few steps toward Denoriel.

"The gate is closed for the night," the man who had spoken against the Catholic rite said. "We are ordered not to open it without an order from Lord William Howard."

"I do not want it opened," Denoriel said. "I am Lord Denno Adjoran, mercer, come from Lord Clinton to be sure the guards at the gates are doing their duty. Has there been any trouble here? I thought I saw someone skulking away down the wall."

"There was one—" the man who had spoken third and defended Queen Mary began.

But the man who had gone into the guardhouse had come out with a torch. Denoriel recognized him as a merchant tailor who had a shop on Watling Street and had bought cloth from Adjoran.

"He was . . . ah . . . asking for news," he interrupted, and Denoriel recognized the voice as the one who had spoken second.

"Very well, Master Harris," Denoriel said. "I bid you and your fellow guards remember that the queen said if the people and the Parliament were against the marriage she would not make it. Now see the gate stays closed no matter who knocks on it."

But no one knocked on it. Wyatt wasted two more days sitting in Southwark and waiting for the Londoners to overpower the queen's guard and invite him to take Mary under his control. Lord William Howard begged the queen for permission to use the guns of the Tower against his encampment, but she would not allow it.

"Think," she said, "of the many innocents in the houses of Southwark who would be killed or injured and the loss of their shelter in this bitter weather."

Word of the queen's mercy was carried from the palace and some who had wondered if they should take the chance to be rid of the Catholic queen were reassured of her goodness. No one urged any welcome to Wyatt. Meanwhile over those three days, all the towns along the river that had bridges showed their loyalty to the queen by obeying Lord William Howard's order and broke them down so Wyatt could not cross.

Wyatt reached Kingston at four o'clock in the afternoon. Only thirty feet of the bridge had been torn away, and the pilings remained. The bridge was repairable. It was then that the seamen who had joined the rebellion saved the situation. The sailors volunteered to swim across the river if Wyatt could disperse the guard set to protect the other end of the bridge.

The guns that the seamen had brought from their ships drove away the guard. That news and the tale of Wyatt's progress came back to London with a man from that guard. Another came hours later, long after dark to say that Wyatt was across the river. The sailors who had swum across came back in barges and Wyatt returned with enough men to drive the remainder of the guard away and to protect the workers on the bridge.

Denno had the news of Wyatt's progress from Lord Clinton to whom he had gone to report that Ludgate and Newgate were not safe and that one John Harris should be watched or warned that if Wyatt entered by Ludgate he would be held accountable. Clinton thanked him, assured him that the warning would be passed to Lord William Howard, and told him that all horse and foot were summoned to be outside the walls of St. James Palace by six the next morning. Denoriel promised he and his men would be there.

He returned at once to Bucklersbury, then Gated to Ashridge and sent the air spirit he had bound to Elizabeth to bring her to her bedchamber. The air spirit could not speak to her or set a message into her mind, but it danced and gyrated and fluttered toward the bedchamber door repeating its performance when she did not respond. Elizabeth just sat, staring into the air over Eleanor Gage's head with as little expression as she could manage.

Air spirits were not clever. Elizabeth feared its movements would brush someone. She wished she could shout, "I understand," but her ladies, and Mary's spies, would think she had run mad. The idea drew a brief hysterical gasp of a giggle from her; she felt as if she *were* going mad. What would she do if Wyatt won? All eyes turned to her and she shivered and then took advantage of the strangled giggle to bend over with a hand on her belly.

"Are you ill, my lady?" Dorothy Stafford asked.

"My stomach roils," Elizabeth gasped. She rose quickly to follow the air spirit and Elizabeth Marberry jumped up to accompany her. "I do not need any audience to watch by my close stool," Elizabeth snapped.

Marberry knew that Lady Elizabeth was supposed to be watched every moment, but she could not disobey a direct order and slowly sat down again. She herself did not like to be watched while she performed her natural functions and even less when those functions were disturbed. Also she was certain that no message had been delivered to Elizabeth. Not even a servant had approached her since they returned to her chambers from the evening meal. And, all alarmed as they were, they had been unnaturally silent. No message had passed to Elizabeth from her ladies.

Possibly Lady Elizabeth was ill, Marberry thought. She was more drawn and pallid each day. She had noticed that the lady merely pushed food around in her plate, hardly eating. Heaven knew there was enough trouble to make Lady Elizabeth's stomach uneasy. And she certainly did not look eagerly excited by the news of Wyatt's rebellion which had come in letters from the Council.

Elizabeth slammed the door of her bedchamber and spelled it locked. She would, of course, have to release the lock the moment she heard someone try the door, but she would at least have warning of an intruder. Then she hurried behind the screen that hid the close stool and with tears streaming down her face threw herself into Denno's arms.

He held her tight and kissed her forehead, her eyes, and more lingeringly her lips. Elizabeth hugged Denoriel back, but did not respond to his kiss. She stiffened and anxiously felt his breast and shoulders.

"You are armored," she whispered. "Will we be attacked?"

"Not Ashridge," he murmured in reply. "London. I came only to tell you that I will not come tonight or perhaps the next few nights. I must be in the city if there is a call to arms."

"Why should you fight for Mary?" Elizabeth hissed angrily. "What if you are hurt? What will become of me? Remember all those mortal soldiers use iron weapons."

"I fight for Mary because too many know I am your favorite. I *must* show myself ardent in the queen's cause. Do not be ridiculous Elizabeth. I do not believe Wyatt can win with the force he has . . . unless the Londoners go over to him."

"If he loses, what will happen to me?" Elizabeth sobbed.

His grip around her shoulders tightened. "No worse than what you endured when they sought evidence against Thomas Seymour. And you have been much more careful this time. I hope—"

The door latch clicked. Elizabeth turned her head and spat "*Ekmochleuo*" over her shoulder, releasing the spell. The latch lifted and the door opened a thread. Someone was looking in to see where she was and what she was doing. Behind the screen around the close stool, she was invisible. "Stickfoot," she hissed, and smiled the first smile in several days when she heard a cry as someone tried to take a step and fell on her face. When she turned back, Denno was gone.

Tears ran down her cheeks again as she straightened her gown of the slight crumpling his embrace had caused. She dropped the top of the stool and sat down on it, taking her head in her hands. How she longed to be queen, to wrest the government from Mary's unsteady hands, to play the treacherous French against the greedy Spanish so that both would grant advantages in trade and policy to England. She could stabilize the currency, pay off much of the debt left by Somerset and Northumberland. England would blossom . . .

"Lady Elizabeth." The anxious voice coming from the still-closed door was that of Agnes Fitzalan. "Are you ill? Do you need help?"

"Ill . . . yes," Elizabeth answered; it being the best excuse for the swollen eyes and reddened nose. "My belly gripes. Come in, Agnes. Find Blanche. Where is Blanche? I need to go to bed."

Chapter 25

Denoriel looked in on Joseph after he Gated to Bucklersbury. Two men and a runner to bring a message to the house if there should be trouble remained at the warehouse. Five of the other men were lounging in the kitchen, with Cropper to keep an eye on them and Cropper's wife to feed them and dole out the ale. Since they were due to meet in front of St. James Palace at six of the morning, they would bed down on the kitchen floor.

Joseph handed him a note from Lord William Howard saying he had left men at Newgate and made sure that gate would not open for Wyatt. He added that he, himself, would be at Ludgate because that faced the most direct road from Kingston. Denoriel was only a little surprised by Lord William's personal response. Lord William was great-uncle to Elizabeth—and very fond of her. Doubtless he had made note that Elizabeth's favorite was doing his best to ensure Wyatt's defeat.

By ten of the clock the house was dark and silent, Mistress Cropper having locked the door to the pantry where the ale was kept and gone home. On the streets the watch called the hours, although instead of "All is well," the watchmen cried "Look to your defenses." Denoriel thought over the plans Clinton had laid out for the leaders of the various groups he comanded. Denoriel freely admitted that he knew nothing of battle strategy being of those commanded rather than commanding, but the plans sounded reasonable to him.

Except that these plans did not even last until the first engagement. At four in the morning drums sounded throughout the city. A messenger had come with the news that Wyatt was already at Brentford and marching on. All defenders were to rise and arm.

Denoriel brought his men to Charing Cross and left them under Joseph's care to join with some other groups of the lord mayor's militia. One of the other captains told him that Lord Pembroke and his mounted troops were on the hill above the new bridge near St. James'. They did not want Wyatt's men breaking up and running loose in the city so the lord mayor had set troops at each road intersection to hold them.

"I am known to Lords Pembroke and Clinton," Denoriel said. "Shall I go and see what news I can pick up?"

He wondered if the lord mayor's man thought he was seeking escape from the coming battle. He could see the man glance at Joseph and his burly and well-armed men, who had settled to the fore of the group. That seemed to reassure the lord mayor's man, and he nodded and agreed that obtaining news was good.

However there was little information available. Pembroke and Clinton had no later news than what occasioned the early summons. Wyatt was still some distance out on the road. On his way back Denoriel arranged with the town tavern to bring bread and cheese and ale to the waiting men. There was no need, he said laughing, for them to face the rebels with empty bellies.

After he had eaten with the men, Denoriel rode out again; he returned a little after nine. Now Clinton had news. Wyatt was still advancing on the city but would not be near them until nearly noon. By then the lord mayor's man was comfortable with Denoriel's coming and going and it was he, who hearing noise in the distance about eleven of the clock, asked Denoriel to go see what it was.

Before the half hour, Denoriel was back, his cloak awry and his hat lost. "Wyatt is in the city," he said, dismounting. He called "Wait" to the lord mayor's man, who had started toward him and pretended to lead his horse into the Temple grounds. When he returned on foot he continued, loud enough for all to hear. "They came up Fleet Street and Lord Pembroke let them pass."

"Is he turned traitor?" the lord mayor's man asked drawing a hard breath.

"No, no, not at all," Denoriel assured him. "It was only a device so that most of Wyatt's army would fall into a trap. When the troops had advanced too far to scatter, Lord Clinton and Lord Pembroke charged from both sides. They broke the force in two. All the officers were in the forepart with only a few hundred men. The rest, without leaders, will be easy to disperse and drive away."

"You rode with them?" the lord mayor's man asked, smiling slightly at Denoriel's disheveled appearance.

"Wyatt was seen marching along the Fleet Road just as I was about to take my leave of Lord Clinton. I could not very well ride away from that immediate threat."

The lord mayor's man smiled as he shook his head. "I am very glad you were not in London when your hair was not white and your face lined with years. I cannot imagine what trouble you would have caused as a riotous youngster. What brought you back here to our quiet waiting?"

Denoriel opened his eyes wide. "But this is my duty." Then he grinned. "Wyatt, his officers, and the mounted are gone for now. They will try Ludgate, where I think they had friends who had promised to open to them. They had no siege engines with them, so they cannot try to force the gate. When they are turned away, they will retreat. We will catch them then."

"You are sure there will be no treachery at Ludgate?"

"I am sure," Denoriel replied with a tight smile. "Lord William Howard himself is at Ludgate."

"But the rest of the army is still in Fleet Street?"

Denoriel snorted gently. "The rest is no army. They are no more than farmers and apprentices stirred up with fear of the Spanish. Now their officers are gone, they will yield readily." He paused and then added, "I do not think the entire army was with Wyatt."

"Why not?"

"Because I heard Lord Clinton ask his lieutenant where Knevett and his brother and Lord Cobham were. Those are Wyatt's chief supporters."

The lord mayor's man stiffened and came alert. "You mean there is a force coming by another road? Where?"

"I have no real knowledge of it, but why not the road that

becomes Holborne?" Denoriel suggested. "That road leads to New
Gate. When I rode round the gates for Lord Clinton on the first
of February, it seemed to me that the guards at New Gate were
much opposed to the queen's religion."

"I am not too fond of the queen's religion myself," the lord
mayor's man said, "but she is the queen, anointed to rule us. She
came to us for protection and we swore to succor her. Beside
that, so far there is no reason to rebel against her."

It was a very lukewarm statement of support, but Denoriel
made no comment. He settled down with the others to wait.
Not long after, two of the men went off and returned with sacks
of bread and cheese and a small barrel of beer for an evening
meal. He ate with the group, but under their illusion of human
contour, his long ears twitched and twisted and it was not very
long after they had packed away the remains of the food that he
came slowly to his feet.

"Something is coming," he said to the lord mayor's man, looking north.

"Don't hear nothing," one of the troop said, "and I've good
ears, I have."

"Not as good as Lord Denno's, I warrant," Joseph Clayborne
said. "I live with him, and I swear from my office he can hear
beetles walking in the garden."

"I—" Denoriel began, but the man who had spoken of his keen
hearing suddenly stiffened and also stood up.

"Hear something now," he said, and looked to the lord mayor's
man. "We should—"

"Archers," the lord mayor's man ordered. "Stand ready." He
turned his head toward Denoriel. "Where?"

"North," he said.

He waved toward the trees and brush that with some small
houses bordered the wide spot in the road where the Eleanor
Cross had been raised in Charing. The archers turned in that
direction and strung their bows. By now everyone could hear
the sound of many men moving, and the whole troop began to
ready their weapons. They were not quite quick enough for the
first assault.

A tight group of about twelve or fifteen men burst from between
the two closest houses. Even with the warning Denoriel and the
trooper had given, the long wait had taken the edge off the lord

mayor's troop and, of course, they were mostly tradesmen, not soldiers. Many had no weapon in hand when the first group reached them. A few were bowled over; a few were simply pushed aside by the attackers who were in too much of a hurry to stay and exchange blows. Denoriel got in a slash and a thrust, but although the slash drew a curse the thrust missed altogether.

Meanwhile the lord mayor's man was shouting to his archers to loose their arrows and to his men to stand fast and not pursue the small fleeing party. Denoriel considered disobeying; as soon as he was out of sight of his own party, he could call for Miralys and overtake those who fled. But the noise from behind the shuttered houses swelled suddenly into bellows of challenge and, moments later, shrieks of pain as the archers finally shot.

In the next moment Denoriel was fully employed. Although many of the attackers simply turned back the way they had come and fled when their fellows were struck by arrows and they saw the men of the lord mayor's troop ready to oppose them, some more determined charged forward. Denoriel was able to disarm the first man to reach him with a thrust to the sword arm. He shrieked "Cursed pope lover," but Denoriel stepped on the very old-fashioned sword lying on the ground and when the man stooped to try to drag it away, Denoriel struck him on the head with his sword hilt.

Aware of movement behind, he swung around without any chance to see the effect of his blow. The noise of conflict swelled. A second man hacked at him clumsily. Cropper disarmed him with a sharp blow of his truncheon. The man shrieked and ran back toward the houses. Cropper charged at another oncoming attacker while Denoriel swung back to face a movement he could not see clearly, slashing with his sword. He struck, wringing a cry from his victim. Then he saw that the boy, for it was no more than a boy, had no weapon in hand. He raised his sword point, but the act of mercy was too late. A second sword thrust past his side and struck the boy, who fell backward, crying out as the sword pulled free of his body.

Denoriel cursed fluently. That child was no threat to Queen Mary or anyone else. What he was doing on a battlefield, Denoriel could not imagine. Likely he had followed an older brother or a father. But the sounds of combat were swelling even higher and Denoriel could not stop fighting to see what happened to the boy.

He was engaged against two men for a few moments. Both were clumsy, but they were on opposite sides and one thrust past a parry that was not wide enough. The sword only struck his elven armor and did not pierce him, but the pang induced by the touch of iron against his silver armor stopped his breath for a moment. Engaged in driving off the other man, Denoriel braced for another blow but Joseph struck the sword away just as Denoriel's weapon twisted that of the second man out of his hand.

He heard the clang when that sword hit a stone and realized that the shouts and shrieks and the ring of metal against metal was falling away. A glance around showed only backs retreating rapidly away from the road that led to London. A few of the men of the troop started in pursuit but were recalled by the lord mayor's man who reminded them that their task was to guard the road and prevent any reinforcements from reaching Wyatt.

"If the city is true and the gates stay shut," he said with grim satisfaction, "we will take Wyatt."

Denoriel nodded agreement, deliberately showing obvious satisfaction. He wanted the lord mayor's man to remember that Lady Elizabeth's favorite had fought against Wyatt.

This battle was over. He wiped and sheathed his sword as he looked around and called to Joseph to discover whether any of their men were hurt. Cropper said one had a minor wound on his shoulder but that his companions had already stopped the bleeding and bandaged him. Denoriel said to send the man home as the action seemed to be ended.

His responsibilities fulfilled, Denoriel returned to where he had been fighting and knelt to examine the boy who had been struck. Too late. Whoever had stabbed him had been too successful. The sword that had come past Denoriel's side had pierced some large vein in the young body. The child was lying in a pool of blood.

Denoriel rose from beside the body, his cloak edge soaked in blood, and signaled for two of his men to carry the body away to the churchyard. There the few dead were laid nearest the graveyard and the others, some wounded, some yielded, were led into the church where they were guarded by a few of the lightly wounded from the lord mayor's troop.

Another hour passed. Joseph, acting as clerk for the lord mayor's man, was listing the names and villages of the dead and captured.

No one was quite sure who would be responsible for notifying the relatives of the dead (or even for prosecuting them because of associated guilt) but the lord mayor's man was sure that lists were necessary. Denoriel sat alone, huddled in his blood-stained cloak, saddened by the waste of a young life that had no chance to bloom even as briefly as was common for mortals.

On the eighth of February, before the sun had broken through the gray clouds of a nasty morning, Lord Denno rode in through the main gate of Ashridge. The guards asked what news, and he said, "The rebellion is over. Long live Queen Mary." But his face was drawn with worry, and one guard murmured to another that there was blood all over the bottom of his cloak.

Sir Edward, still tying his points, met him at the door and asked, low-voiced, "Do we stay or go?"

"It is too late to go," Denoriel replied. "The rebellion is over. Wyatt and his army are taken prisoner. No defense can or should be made against any order of the queen. Is it possible for me to speak to Lady Elizabeth?"

"I do not know," Sir Edward said, his brow furrowed and his lips downturned with worry. "The last two weeks have shattered her peace entirely. She took to her bed on the twenty-sixth of January and has not risen from it. Let me fetch Mistress Ashley."

Denoriel waited patiently in the receiving room to which Sir Edward had escorted him. He was not worried about Elizabeth's health. He had spoken to her often since she received a letter from the queen requesting that she come to London. He had advised her to take to her bed and keep to it. The illness was largely part of a plan, first to avoid coming before the queen at all and if that failed, to delay as long as possible. Mary might give hard orders in a rush of passion that would change and soften—with Rhoslyn's help.

Kat came in in a little while, wringing her hands. "She says she will see you, Lord Denno, but please do not tell her anything that will upset her. She is ill with terror already."

"I am afraid she must know the news I bring." He paused and added significantly, "I am sure she will be glad of it."

Denoriel was not nearly so skilled as Rhoslyn or Aleneil in inserting thoughts into a mortal's mind, but he pushed the idea that Elizabeth *was* glad the rebellion was over at Kat. That Kat should hint Elizabeth was sorry the rebels had been defeated would likely be enough to condemn her. Kat loved Elizabeth. She would not willingly or knowingly do anything to harm the little girl she had raised, but she was gullible and too easily led.

"Oh," Kat cried, raising her hand to her temple. "There, the pain is gone." She looked at him frowning. "What is the news?"

"That Queen Mary is a heroine and so inspired the people of London and her guards, that Wyatt is defeated and taken prisoner."

Kat's face cleared. "Oh, wonderful. Elizabeth will be glad and relieved, too. She was so afraid of being captured by the rebels. Come, tell her. Perhaps it will calm her."

She led him through the parlor and then through a private reception room that at last opened into Elizabeth's bedchamber. Kat left him in the doorway and hurried to the large bed. The thick velvet curtains were partly drawn back. Denno looked around curiously as if he were not familiar with the chamber.

"See who has come to wait upon you, my love," Kat said. "Lord Denno has brought very good news from London."

"What news?" Elizabeth called out, leaning forward from the pillows that propped her up. "Oh, Denno. Come here. Come here to me and tell me the news."

"The rebellion is over," Denno said, striding across the room and around the end of the bed to stand beside Elizabeth.

"And Mary has the victory?" Elizabeth asked breathlessly.

All of Elizabeth's ladies hurried over to stand around Denoriel.

"Completely," he replied. "Wyatt is taken prisoner and the most part of the army that came with him."

"Wonderful," Elizabeth breathed, allowing herself to sink back toward the pillows, but then she jerked upright again. "Denno! There is blood on your cloak. Are you hurt?"

Everyone looked at the dark brown stain that discolored the hem of the cloak. Even the gently reared ladies all knew dried blood when they saw it. Kat came forward and touched Lord Denno's hand. He smiled at her and then at Elizabeth.

"No, my lady, not hurt at all. It is another man's blood." He shook his head and sighed. "Not even a man, only a boy. He should not have died."

"Did you . . ." Elizabeth let her voice drift away.

"No, it was an accident, really. I do not know who killed the child. He had no weapon and I had just drawn my sword away from him. Someone behind me thrust forward. Likely he did not even see whom it was he struck."

Elizabeth stared at him, taking in the real sorrow in his large green eyes. *He has been too long among mortals; most Sidhe would not care about the butterfly life of a mortal.* She gestured to someone behind him and ordered, "Bring a chair." When it was carried to her bedside, she said, "Sit. If a boy was needlessly killed right beside you, you were in a battle. Tell me."

"I need to go a little further back than the battle itself so you will understand. What was your last news about the rebellion?"

"I did not even know a rebellion was brewing until Sir James Croft told me of it and said I should move to Donnington. But then on the twenty-seventh of January I received a letter from the queen, asking me to come to her in London for the better safety of my person. But I had fallen ill and I was afraid also to travel if the country was unquiet. I told her messenger, who was brought to my bedside, that I would come as soon as I felt well enough, and the officers of my household wrote that I would come as soon as my health was amended."

"I am no physician," Denoriel said, "but from how pale you are and how your voice wavers, it seems to me, my lady, that you should not essay to travel in this harsh winter weather."

Elizabeth lay back on her pillows, her eyes almost black with anxiety. "The battle . . ." she whispered.

So Denoriel made a tale for her and the listening ladies of Wyatt's progress from Maidstone to Rochester to Gravesend and so on to Southwark and Kingston. He spoke of how Queen Mary had roused the Londoners to resist and of her stubborn bravery no matter how her cowardly Council and uncertain defenders cried of defeat and retreat.

"But Lord Clinton knew his business and Lord Pembroke and his men were gallant. They cut off and drove away the most of the army who, without leaders, and somewhat dispirited by the labor they had undertaken and the foul weather slipped away. Then the troop of the lord mayor's men holding Charing Cross and the Temple Bar, with whom I had cast my lot, drove off the reinforcements that the Knevett brothers and Lord Cobham were bringing to assist Wyatt."

"That was well done," Elizabeth said.

"Wyatt had only sixty or so men altogether. Perhaps he could have found others to join him in the city itself, as he had found the sailors in Gravesend and most of Norfolk's troops, but Lord William Howard had come to Ludgate and it was far beyond Wyatt's power to force it open. He knew then that his hopes were over."

"Did he then yield?" Dorothy Stafford asked.

"No. I am heartily sorry for Wyatt's foolishness in thinking he could force the queen to marry as *he* chose. He is a brave man and honest. He tried to retreat to where he was separated from most of his men, but Pembroke and Clinton held him. They sent a messenger to the lord mayor's men, and we marched down to join them, but we had barely joined the fray when the Norroy Herald called to Wyatt to yield rather than cause so many deaths of his men. And so he did, sacrificing himself to save his supporters."

Elizabeth shook her head wearily against the pillows. "Whatever reason he believed he had, he was wrong to raise arms against his queen."

The pious sentiment was approved heartily by the ladies, who withdrew from the bedside, beckoning Denoriel to come with them. He did rise from his chair, but he took one of Elizabeth's limp hands in his and kissed it as the ladies' backs were turned. Their eyes met; he mouthed "Tonight," and Elizabeth's head nodded weakly as she fell back, seemingly fainting, against her pillows.

Blanche surged forward with restoratives, and Kat gently shooed Denoriel away from the bed. However, she also cut short the many questions the ladies had for Denoriel by pointing out that he must be exhausted. Clearly he had ridden straight from the battlefield to give Elizabeth the news. Kat was concerned enough to offer him lodging at Ashridge, although lodging was generally not proffered to any except officers of the Court.

Denoriel shook his head. "I thank you, Mistress Ashley, but no. My own lodge is no more than a quarter-hour's ride from here. And there I will be able to change my garments so I am less offensive. Only tell me whether there is anything I can get or send for that will help my poor lady. She is terribly unwell."

"I do not know," Kat said, her eyes filling with tears. "I fear it is her spirits more than her body that is failing. She is so oppressed. She fears . . . she fears her sister will blame her for this trouble."

✧   ✧   ✧

Harry FitzRoy confirmed Elizabeth's fears that night as he sat with her and Denoriel in Denoriel's parlor. His face was bleak, his lips downturned and thin with concern.

"Suffolk will die," he said. "He is stupid enough to deserve it. Imagine joining the rebels after Queen Mary pardoned him for his part in Northumberland's conspiracy." Then he sighed. "I fear Jane and Guildford will die, too."

"Why?" Denoriel asked sharply. "They had no part in this rebellion and Wyatt never said he wished to restore Jane to the throne."

Harry sighed again. "But Jane was once crowned and could well be a focal point for another rising—one with the open purpose of driving out the Catholic queen and the Catholic rite. Wyatt was careful never to raise the question of religion, since many of his supporters were Catholic and only wished to prevent the Spanish marriage. And just now, Rhoslyn says, the queen is very angry. She will finally agree that Jane and her husband must die."

Elizabeth's eyes did not shift to him. She was looking beyond the large glass window that walled the rear of Denoriel's parlor. In the illusionary manor's garden, roses were blooming—a cheerful sight to Elizabeth, who was growing very tired of winter in the mortal world. But even the roses and the brightly sparkling brook that meandered through the garden could not lift her spirits.

She was less frightened Underhill, and she needed the respite from fear. But she knew that in the mortal world her danger was only growing more acute. Both Eleanor Gage and Elizabeth Marberry were lying in a spelled sleep in her bedchamber. She had kept Mary's spies close since Croft's visit so they could give evidence of her behavior, but she needed so desperately to talk to her Da that she had taken the chance of bespelling them.

Her absence would not be noted by her own household. Blanche had locked her own door into the servant's corridor so no one could enter that way and was on guard by the bedchamber door. And Denno would twist time close enough to when she Gated with him that she might have left her bed to use her close stool. But Da was not offering comfort. His expression made clear that he was gravely worried.

"And me?" Elizabeth asked. "Will she order me executed?"

"You must delay coming to her as long as possible," Harry said.

"Mary does not have great steadiness of mind. She will soon be sickened by the executions and so will the Londoners, who did fight to protect her but have little sympathy for her purposes. Most do not wish to see the Catholic rite restored and all are opposed to her marrying Philip."

"There is no danger of your execution," Denoriel growled. "No matter what Mary orders. Be sure always to have with you the tokens that can give me a place to build a Gate. I will fetch you away before any harm can come to you."

Harry saw the despair in Elizabeth's expression. He could not understand how she could prefer the crude, dull, mortal world to the beauties and joys of Underhill, but he knew she did and he loved her enough to put her preference above his own.

"I do not think it will be necessary to bring Elizabeth Underhill," Harry said. "Even a few weeks' delay will be enough to cool Mary's rage. She is only fixed beyond reason and beyond sympathy on the need to restore Catholicism. Even marriage to Prince Philip—although Rhoslyn believes her to be deeply in love with the prince—is part of that purpose."

"But I have conformed," Elizabeth said bitterly. "I have Mass said in Ashfield. I even attend. Mary does not believe me sincere."

"Elizabeth—" Denoriel moved closer to her on the sofa and put his arm around her. "Just because you escape Mary by coming Underhill does not mean that you are exiled from England forever. Harry needed to remain Underhill because Mwynwen had to drain the elfshot poison from him and because Richey died in his place and was buried so the mortal world thought him to be dead. We can arrange an 'escape' for you and then bring you back—"

"That can only be a last resort," Harry said. "Only if they are ready to lead her to the block."

Elizabeth shuddered and Denoriel took her completely into his arms. She kissed him, then shook her head and said to him, "Da, tell him. If I seem to leave the country or merely remain hidden, my chance to inherit from Mary will be greatly diminished. She will have opportunity to name an heir and establish him."

"Too true," Harry said, but suddenly he looked more cheerful. "No need for you to disappear, at least not yet. We can make it seem as if you really are very sick. When Denno said 'Mwynwen,' I realized we could ask her to bespell Elizabeth to look *terrible*.

As I said, Bess only needs to stay out of Mary's hands for a few weeks. Mwynwen can make you look too sick to travel."

"Now that is a good idea," Denoriel said.

"Will she do it?" Elizabeth asked anxiously; she knew that Mwynwen hated to come to the mortal world.

"Yes," Denoriel and Harry said together, and then Denoriel continued alone, "Titania will speak to her if our request is not sufficient."

Chapter 26

Unfortunately despite the confusion and other business involved in rounding up and imprisoning stray rebels, Mary and her Council had not forgotten Elizabeth. Only two days later, on the tenth of February, Dr. Thomas Wendy and Dr. George Owen arrived with a letter from the queen insisting on her coming to London to explain her relations with Wyatt and the French ambassador.

The doctors arrived late in the afternoon. Kat shook her head when they asked to see Elizabeth.

"She is asleep, poor child. I beg you not to disturb her."

Dr. Owen looked coldly at Mistress Ashley. He and his companion had been told that she was entirely devoted to Lady Elizabeth, and he and Dr. Wendy had strict instructions. Unless Lady Elizabeth were truly at death's door and would not survive being carried from her bed, she was to be judged well enough to travel. But when Blanche was summoned to wake her mistress and make her ready for the doctors, they met their match in determination and more than their match in outspokenness.

Blanche looked into their faces with eyes brilliant with rage and said, "No! If you were the queen herself I would not wake her. She did not sleep at all last night and has barely drifted off. If you want to pass that door, you will need to walk over my dead body. Doctors! Assassins more likely, to wake a sick child and frighten her to death."

Both Wendy and Owen were much taken aback by the maid's vehemence and even more taken aback when Blanche turned her back on them, stamped into Elizabeth's bedchamber, and, a moment later, they heard the key turn in the lock.

"You must forgive her," Kat said. "Blanche has been with Lady Elizabeth since she was born and she is deeply worried about this illness. I am also. It is rare for Lady Elizabeth to be so weak she is bedridden for so long."

The doctors consulted each other in swift glances. Orders or no orders, actually they could accomplish nothing by insisting on examining Elizabeth immediately. Both of them were tired and it was near dark. Even if they found her in excellent health, it would be impossible to start for London at once. Tomorrow morning would be soon enough to examine her. Agreed, they allowed Mistress Ashley to lead them from Elizabeth's reception room and to the guest chambers prepared for them.

The air spirit Elizabeth dispatched to bring Denoriel to her was in so great a ferment, reflecting her terror, that it could not make clear what emergency was toward. Frantic with anxiety, Denoriel Gated to Ashridge, learned of the arrival of Doctors Owen and Wendy carrying Mary's letter demanding Elizabeth come to London from Blanche, and Gated Underhill to find Mwynwen. Although she frowned and shuddered when he asked her to come to the mortal world to make Elizabeth look ill, and she asked if he could not bring Elizabeth to her, eventually Mwynwen consented to Gate with him to Ashridge.

By three of the clock past midnight, a profound silence lay over Elizabeth's apartment. Tonight no lady slept in the truckle bed. All had heard Blanche lock the door and no one was prepared to scratch on it to ask admittance. Silent and tense, Blanche sat beside Elizabeth on the edge of her big bed where they had been waiting for hours. Both sighed in relief as a black spot formed on the wall and slowly enlarged to show the cool greens and blues of Mwynwyn's entrance hall. Denoriel stepped through with Mwynwen on his heels, but he whirled to point at the door and the wall that separated the bedchamber from the reception room. It should be empty, but Denoriel would take no chance on being overheard, though spellcasting drained him.

"*Prizivati cutanje,*" he murmured, invoking silence. No sound made in Elizabeth's bedchamber would pass out of it.

Elizabeth slipped off her bed, stepped down two steps, and curtsied to the Sidhe healer. "I am so grateful to you, Lady Mwynwyn for coming to me. I was afraid to go to you. If I were found to be missing from my chamber, I would be accounted guilty of heaven alone knows what crime."

Mwynwyn's expression softened slightly. "Why do you need to appear ill, and for how long?"

So Elizabeth explained about the rebellion and Mary's rage and the fact that her rages did not last long. "If I am brought before her now, she will cry 'Off with her head,' and then later her ministers and the ambassador from the land that nourishes the Inquisition will hold her to that word and I will die. If I can—"

"Those lunatics who destroyed Alhambra?" Mwynwen interrupted angrily.

"Yes, Lady Mwynwen. The priests of the Inquisition seeing the impossible beauty of that wonderful place cursed it and 'exorcised' it, staining it with Evil."

Denoriel looked at Elizabeth with a mixture of admiration and exasperation. He had no doubt that she was really terrified, but her fear did not paralyze her. Her mind moved just as swiftly, just as subtly. She had remembered something Harry told her about Mwynwen and had used that knowledge to build sympathy for herself.

"We must not let that happen here!" Mwynwen said.

"No, indeed," Elizabeth replied. "And if I come to the throne, I assure you there will be no Inquisition in England and no witch hunts against—" she glanced at Denoriel, unable to say the word Sidhe "—my special friends. But to come to the throne, I must survive and, alas, my sister believes she has reason to distrust me. She has sent two physicians to examine me because she believes I am lying to avoid her and I am not really ill."

"And so you are not," Mwynwen said, smiling faintly. "But you will be—and for all the world to see. By tomorrow you will be slightly, only slightly, fevered and have a cough and your heart will beat too fast. By midmorning, you will begin to swell—"

"Not my belly," Elizabeth interrupted anxiously. "If my belly is swollen, everyone will say I am with child by some common lover. Mary says always that I am a whore."

"Ah . . ." Mwynwen thought a moment and then murmured and began to run her fingers over Elizabeth's face and arms and legs. "Your belly will be flat as a charger, but your face and limbs will be swollen—tomorrow noticeably and the next day badly. The swelling will last, oh, two mortal weeks or so and then will diminish."

"Thank you, my lady," Elizabeth said, curtsying again.

Mwynwen nodded, stared at her penetratingly, nodded again, and turned toward the Gate without a word of farewell. Denoriel stepped closer, gestured at it, and Mwynwen stepped through. The Gate closed behind her. Denoriel stepped back, reaching out with one hand, and drew Elizabeth into his arms. Blanche slipped out of the chamber into her own room and closed the door.

"You are warm already," Denoriel said clutching her tighter. "Do not allow those idiot doctors to bleed you. And do not take their potions and remedies. They will surely poison you."

Elizabeth laughed shakily. "That is not why I am warm, beloved. I . . . You had better not come to me in the palace. I may be held there long . . ."

She slid her arms up and around his neck, pulled his head down and kissed him. "God knows when I will see you again . . . not that I wish to see you while I am all swollen and horrible. Do not you dare come near me when I look a fright."

"You never look a fright to me," he murmured against her lips. "Now and forever you are my red-haired witch with a soul that is pure enchantment."

No matter that Elizabeth truly appeared sick, when Doctors Wendy and Owen came at midmorning to examine her, they both remembered vividly their interview with Chancellor Gardiner. Their lucrative positions as Court physicians depended on finding Elizabeth well enough to travel. But both knew she was too warm to the touch, with a nasty, dry cough, and signs of swelling in the thickness of her fingers. Everyone knew Elizabeth's beautiful hands with their long, thin, graceful fingers.

Nonetheless both agreed aloud, speaking to each other, that Lady Elizabeth's heart was strong and the fever insignificant. Neither recommended bleeding; she could not lift her head from her pillows and bleeding would only make her weaker. Both, feeling decidedly uneasy, stated that she was strong enough to travel without serious danger to her health.

"Murderers!" Blanche spat, loud enough for all the ladies in the chamber to hear. "You are not doctors. You are assassins! Who sent you to kill my lady? Not her sister. Not the queen. Queen Mary loves Lady Elizabeth, that I know."

"Be silent!" Dr. Owen roared, the force of his voice increased by his sense of guilt. After all, it was not the queen but the chancellor who had given them their instructions.

A long thin knife suddenly appeared in Blanche's hand. The honed steel flashed, but by their positions, Owen realized he was the only one who saw the threat. He backed away as Blanche moved closer to him and said softly, "You will kill my lady. I will not outlive her . . . But if you try to move her from that bed, *neither will you!*"

"Blanche," Elizabeth whispered. "I am willing to go, really I am." She made a feeble, abortive effort to lift herself from the pillows that supported her but fell back, her breathing loud and rasping.

All the women in the chamber were weeping loudly. The two guardsmen by the door both had their hands on their swords. The doctors looked around uneasily and again consulted each other silently. Even Mary's woman, Eleanor Gage, looked horrified.

"This is a ridiculous and hysterical assertion by an ignorant maid," Dr. Wendy said, trying to make his voice firm and confident. "Lady Elizabeth is only distressed by the terrible events. I have with me a most excellent strengthening restorative. I am sure that Lady Elizabeth will be much recovered by tomorrow. Perhaps our examination tired her today, but we *must* leave for London tomorrow."

He opened the bag he had closed after Elizabeth's examination and removed from it a stoppered flask, which he handed to Blanche. The knife had disappeared and Blanche dropped a stiff curtsey as he told her how to administer the restorative.

The contents of the flask, harmful or helpful, joined the contents of Elizabeth's close stool very soon after the doctors and the ladies who were their witnesses—and how Owen and Wendy wished there had been none—left Elizabeth's chamber. The flask itself, tucked into the bosom of Blanche's gown, was refilled with some good wine mixed with a little brandy and the "restorative" was administered just as Dr. Wendy had recommended.

It had no effect on Elizabeth. The next day both doctors were visibly alarmed over her swollen limbs, but both agreed that what troubled her was merely an excess of watery humors and that moving in the very luxurious litter that Queen Mary had sent would not be dangerous. Her kidneys would right themselves whether she lay in bed or was carried carefully in the litter.

Moreover that evening a delegation from the queen herself arrived. Blanche, who was beginning to worry about Elizabeth's weakness even though she had been present when Mwynwen bespelled her, wondered if she should have used the true restorative. However, when Elizabeth learned who had come from her sister, her eyes brightened. All of the men, Lord William Howard (a hero in the fight against Wyatt and Elizabeth's maternal great uncle), Sir Edward Hastings, and Sir Thomas Cornwallis, were fond of her.

They were all horrified by her appearance; the swelling had distorted her long, thin face out of all proportion, turning her eyes to mere slits, and her arms and legs were so distended that they were hard to bend. Nonetheless, as Lord William whispered to her while bent over her bed, holding her dropsical hand, she must be prepared to start for London the next day. It would be far safer to be seen to be making an effort to obey the queen than to lie abed. She would not be pressed to travel farther than was comfortable for her each day.

The queen's commissioners redeemed that promise. The cortege took a full twelve days to travel the short distance from Ashridge to London. Most of the time, Elizabeth lay still, seeming scarcely to breathe, but on the last day of the journey she bade Blanche dress her in a simple white silk gown. There were no ruches, no pleats, no gathers to conceal any part of her figure. The gown barely swelled over her small, high breasts and lay flat as a game board over her sunken belly.

When they started out, Elizabeth ordered that the curtains of the litter be pulled back so that she would be completely exposed. She was not disappointed. Sir Edward's men had announced her coming in every ale house and tavern and cookshop and the people of London rushed out to see the "mere-English" heir to the throne. Elizabeth did not wave and smile as was her custom; she let the people see that she was ill but still an obedient subject, rising from a sickbed to obey her queen.

Several times her escort urged her to cover herself, fearing the effect of the February cold on her fevered body, but she would not. She only shook her head and set her teeth, as if determined to endure, but actually Denoriel had given her a charm that kept a cozy warmth around her body under the shield that she had called. Nonetheless, she shivered convulsively—not from the cold but from the sight of so many, many gallows, heads displayed on the great gates and dismembered corpses hanging from the walls.

Elizabeth did not weep for them. They were fools and had deserved their fate. A far greater sin to her than which rite was used to worship Christ was rebellion against the anointed queen. She shivered because she knew Mary was a bad queen and a fool and that she had caused the rebellion by her stubborn stupidity; she shivered because she wished her sister dead so that she could heal her country's wounds and make the people cheerfully obedient.

As well as she could Elizabeth had ensured that every soul in London and its environs who took the trouble to come was able to see that she was alive, if not well, and certainly not carrying any child. That was some comfort to Elizabeth and she needed comfort that day.

Perhaps the only reason Mary did not shout "off with her head" at Elizabeth was because she refused to see her. That she was already convicted in Mary's mind was made all too plain. Most of her household was separated from her, her faithful guards and her own ladies, and she was carried to an area in Whitehall palace she had never seen before. She was clearly more prisoner than guest. Nonetheless Elizabeth begged her escort to present a humble plea to be received by the queen, only to be told that Mary had been angered by her presumption in asking for an audience.

Wearily, rehearsing in her mind what she could say to convince any questioner of her innocence, Elizabeth told Blanche to make her ready for bed. But she was not to be left in peace to seek that haven. Before her diminished household could even settle themselves into the cold and empty chambers that had been assigned to them, Chancellor Gardiner and half a dozen clerks entered her inner chamber without announcement or ceremony. The clerks hung back, but Gardiner himself strode up to the chair in which Elizabeth was sitting by the struggling fire.

Without greeting, he said, "You will be received by the queen and judged most mercifully if you freely confess your guilt."

Kat, who had hurried to Elizabeth's side when she saw Gardiner enter, gasped. The chancellor stared at her and said, "Please allow Her Grace to answer for herself, Mistress Ashley."

Elizabeth looked up at him. Although her heart leapt and stuttered within her breast and chills of fear ran icily over her skin, her expression showed only a proud disdain.

"When I was a little girl," she said, faintly but clearly, "I stole some comfits from my elder sister's pocket." A small smile now trembled on Elizabeth's lips. "A little later, Mary reached into her pocket and I, conscious of the evil I had done and fearing my sister, who had always been so kind and loving, would be angry and withdraw her love from me, rushed to her and, embracing her knees, confessed my crime. And Mary, though she told me stealing was very wrong and hoped I would do so no more, lifted me in her arms and kissed me and forgave me. Thus, I know what you say is true, that if I confessed to the queen she would be merciful. Only, I have stolen no comfits, nor have I, since my sister became queen, done any wrong worth confessing."

"You do not consider encouraging an armed rebellion worth confessing?"

"My lord!" Kat protested.

Gardiner gestured one of the clerks forward. "Lead Mistress Ashley away as she will not be silent."

"No!" Elizabeth exclaimed, trying to struggle to her feet and falling back weakly. "I will not be alone in a chamber with all of you men. I have been accused of immorality too often when I was totally innocent. Kat, do not leave me!"

As soon as she understood what Elizabeth wanted, Kat slapped the young clerk's face sharply, wrenched herself free, and ran back to Elizabeth's side where she gripped the chair firmly so it would take considerable force to remove her.

"I will not leave my lady," she cried, "and I still have a few friends in this Court. Somehow, some way, the queen will hear of how you tried to expose her sister to shame."

Gardiner first gaped with astonishment and then choked on a horrified protest. His face turned a deep and ugly red. Although he was sure the queen would not suspect him of impropriety with Lady Elizabeth, she would be very angry if Kat Ashley complained to the Court that he had forced her out so he could be alone with Elizabeth. The queen was already angry with him because he had vehemently opposed the Spanish marriage, trying to convince Mary to marry Courtenay. He needed no more irritation.

"I am a bishop," he snarled, "chaste and celibate by the laws of the Church. How dare you suggest such a thing! Lady Elizabeth, I am shocked that you should think so ill of me."

"And I am shocked," Elizabeth said, even more faintly, seeming to hold herself upright by will alone, "that you should come without invitation into my private chamber and accuse me of horrible crimes when I am sick and dizzy, exhausted from being forced to travel while I am ill, fevered and swollen."

There was a moment of charged silence. Gardiner was furious. Of course it had been his intention to catch Elizabeth while she was weak and confused. He had intended to frighten her with assertions that others had confessed her guilt, but he had not expected her boldly to state that purpose aloud. The red which had faded somewhat from his complexion darkened again. Elizabeth sagged pitiably in her chair and Kat let go of the chair with one hand to help her support herself.

"I am a very busy man," Gardiner said, speaking more gently now. "I came when I had time. I wished only to make all easy for you. A confession of your knowledge and approval of Wyatt's act is all that is necessary to relieve you of all further importunity."

A small gasp of laughter shook Elizabeth and she said, "And of my head, too." Before Gardiner could utter a protest, she obviously made an enormous effort, straightened herself, and said loudly, "No! I never spoke a word to Sir Thomas Wyatt in my life. I never wrote to him. I never sent him any message. I knew *nothing* of his mad and heinous plan and no inducement, not the certainty of heaven, could have made me approve it. I deny any knowledge of it. I repudiate Wyatt and all he stands for. I am now and always have been Queen Mary's most loving and loyal subject."

Behind Gardiner Elizabeth caught a glimpse of the clerks stirring uneasily. She knew Gardiner had brought them to write down what she said, to take down any confession she made so that if she later wished to deny it there would be evidence. They were not sure what to do now, she thought, and not too eager to be in her chamber any longer. If the rebellion had succeeded, after all, it was this lady who would be queen.

Gardiner's face showed his chagrin over Elizabeth's strong denial for a moment, and then he said, "A most bold statement and one, of course, that I wish were true, but we have evidence it is a lie. Wyatt himself says that he wrote twice to you."

"Under torture," Elizabeth sneered, although her voice was fading, "a man will say whatever he thinks the torturer desires to hear." Her eyes closed. "It may even be that Sir Thomas told the truth and such letters were sent." She forced her eyes open. "If so, I did not receive them. Since I moved to Ashridge, I have accepted only letters from Her Majesty and from the Council."

"The truth of that statement can be easily determined," Gardiner said, his tone threatening.

Elizabeth nodded feebly, her eyes closing again. "By all means," she whispered. "You are free to question all of my people. Indeed, my lord, I have nothing to hide and the more you ask the more my innocence will be apparent."

One of the clerks came forward and whispered in Gardiner's ear. He shook his head, but it was apparent that he would get nothing from Elizabeth, who had resisted his attempt at surprise. His own clerks were growing uneasy at his seeming cruelty to her. Gardiner himself suspected that she was not nearly so ill or weak as she pretended; however, since his surprise attack had failed, he would need to try again in other ways.

Mary had refused to see Elizabeth, and Rhoslyn whispered into her mind that was a wise decision. She hinted silently that leaving Elizabeth alone, ignoring her, would make her more and more uneasy. With that notion she included a sense of loneliness and a very brief flash of Mary's own loneliness in the past which had been somewhat assuaged by Elizabeth's joy in her company. But she did not push those memories.

Harry had warned her that in Mary's present mood what the memories of Elizabeth's childhood could call up was a resentment of how the loving child had changed. Rhoslyn greatly admired Harry's ability to read the queen at second hand through her descriptions. In fact, she admired Harry for many things. True, he was only a mortal, but living Underhill would preserve him for many years. True, he was not at all beautiful, as were all Sidhe. But that was all to the good.

He was *different*. She did not feel as if he were her brother when he took her hand. His common mortal face was so open, so bright with thought and interest. He was soft and gentle and loving, but he was also courageous, a most deadly fighter. And he knew the intricacies and deceptions of the human Court as she, who had lived with Mary for so many mortal years did not.

Poor Mary, Rhoslyn thought sadly, she did not understand the Court either. She was blown this way and that by one opinion and then another, only trusting in the one opinion, that of the Imperial ambassador, whom all England hated. She was far too ready to grant her ladies favors, and they were taking bribes to appeal to her. Mary did suspect that. Rhoslyn's importance had been enhanced because she never asked a favor. Rhoslyn sighed. There was no favor Mary could grant her. What Rhoslyn wanted was a home of her own, a place she could invite Harry to share with her, and that could not be in the mortal world.

At least what she had to slide into Mary's mind now was a thought the queen would welcome with joy. Harry had advised her that Elizabeth faced a danger almost as dreadful as execution. Some of the councilors, those most strongly of the Catholic persuasion, had suggested Elizabeth be removed as a focal point of reformist rebellion by marrying her to a Catholic nonentity. Rhoslyn had understood the danger and now she followed Harry's suggestion that Mary's thought should be directed to her own forthcoming happiness as a married woman and that Elizabeth should be punished by being deprived of that happy state.

Rhoslyn's silent reminder of the joy coming to Mary soothed her. Still, Elizabeth was to Mary like a sore tooth. She did not want to think about her, but she could not help it and after a week of pretending Elizabeth was not in Whitehall with her, she summoned Eleanor Gage.

To her horror Mary found that Eleanor, who had been so devoted and dutiful a lady, had fallen under Elizabeth's spell. Mary thought briefly, angrily because no one would believe her, that Elizabeth *was* a witch. Eleanor was surely enchanted. She had only praise to speak of Mary's sister. Elizabeth was such an amusing lady to serve—oh, sharp tongued at times, but all the more interesting for all that. And never, Eleanor assured the queen, never had Elizabeth said a disrespectful word about Mary.

Mary dismissed Eleanor rather coldly, reminding herself that Eleanor Gage must not serve her sister again. Elizabeth Marberry was a relief. She came the day after Eleanor Gage and although she agreed with Eleanor about Elizabeth's general behavior, she confessed with a sigh that she could not truly like Lady Elizabeth.

"You think she had some secret dealings with the rebels?" Mary asked eagerly.

Rhoslyn, sitting beyond the fire with a book of hours open on her lap, tensed. Had Elizabeth slipped so badly that the queen's spy had real evidence against her?

"No, not that," Marberry said slowly. "I do not know what to believe about that. It seems impossible that she should not have conspired with the rebels, and yet, I would swear until Sir James Croft came she had no idea that Wyatt was raising an army."

"James Croft was one of the chief conspirators," Mary said, leaning forward. "He is in prison being questioned. You say Elizabeth received him?"

"She did, your highness, but it seemed to be under a misapprehension that he was your messenger. She said she recalled his father, Sir Edward Croft, was in your household years ago."

Mary's lips thinned. "Sir Edward was placed in my household by my father, when he was pressing me to agree to his setting my mother aside."

Slowly Marberry shook her head. "Lady Elizabeth did not know that, I am sure. Even so, she would not go aside with him. I must admit that. For so high-spirited a lady she lives very retired and permits few visitors. Only your messengers and members of the Council—oh, and that old merchant, who comes now and again."

"A merchant would be likely to bring news," Mary said.

"Not of politics. Not Lord Denno." Marberry smiled slightly. "Sometimes he talks of business, but never of politics or the Court. Mostly though, when he is a guest at dinner, he talks of his voyages. Of far places. He is interesting and amusing. Often when he sits a little apart with Lady Elizabeth, he talks to her of her studies in Greek and Latin. I can see, aside from the presents he brings her—furs and silk and even jewels—why she is so fond of him. But he always brings something for the ladies too."

"You remember, madam," Rhoslyn said, lifting her head from the book in her lap, "that lovely shawl I brought for you some years ago. The black silk lace. I purchased that from Adjoran, Mercer. Not from Lord Denno himself, of course. He seldom makes sales or takes orders. I had the shawl from his man of business, Joseph Clayborne."

"Of course I remember that shawl." Mary looked over her shoulder and smiled at Rhoslyn. "I remember what a sacrifice it was for you to give it up—but you did give it up, for me. It is lovely. I have it still." Then she frowned. "Those 'studies' of my sister, are they not what led her into her false belief?"

There was a silence and then Elizabeth Marberry said, "I do not know, but I . . . I do not think Lady Elizabeth believes in . . . anything."

Witch, Mary thought, but what she said was, "She denies God?"

"Oh no, no. She . . . I do not know how to explain. She believes with her head, but not with her heart."

"She lies when she says she is a Catholic?"

Elizabeth Marberry knew she was disappointing her mistress when she shook her head. "No. At least no one could ever prove that she lied. She goes to Mass. She does not whisper to her neighbors or fall asleep during the service. She pays strict attention to the Mass and to everything the priest says and does. And when the priest speaks of religion among us she is . . . is truly interested. But . . . but I do not think she *loves* God."

Rhoslyn did not like what Elizabeth Marberry was saying. Not to love God was no crime that could be proven in Court against Elizabeth, but it was something that might make Mary think of her sister as less than human . . . and thus one who could be killed as one would kill a vicious dog or horse. Fortunately Marberry had made a point of Elizabeth's ability to think, which made Elizabeth more than an animal. Add pity. Rhoslyn sighed silently. Mary must pity Elizabeth. Part of Mary's dislike of her sister was envy of Elizabeth's charm and cleverness.

"I am not at all sure that Lady Elizabeth has the capacity to love God or anyone else," Rhoslyn said. "It is very sad. She would never be a good wife or mother. You are quite right, Mistress Marberry, to Lady Elizabeth religion is an intellectual exercise."

"She has no faith." Mary's voice was filled with an odd mixture of distaste and satisfaction.

"Perhaps not," Rhoslyn said, "but once she has been convinced of the logic and truth of the Catholic rite, she will support it and be faithful to it. It is very sad about lack of faith. Lady Elizabeth has no support in time of trouble. She can never feel God's hand holding her up. Your Majesty, who has felt God's hand uphold her, should pity Lady Elizabeth for her incapacity."

Chapter 27

Rhoslyn's influence with the queen was further enhanced by the effectiveness of her advice on dealing with Elizabeth. Gardiner wished to question Elizabeth every day, to wear her down, to have other councilors question her about her true conversion to the Catholic faith, to have those in charge of interrogating Wyatt and Croft tell her that the men had confessed her involvement. But Rhoslyn reminded Mary of how resistant Elizabeth had been when she was hard pressed at the time of the Seymour scandal.

"She is always active, always doing," Rhoslyn pointed out. "To leave her with nothing to do, no way to discover what others have said of her, no way to defend herself against accusations is more likely to shake her spirit than harsh questioning."

Mary did remember Elizabeth's sturdy denial of any desire to marry Thomas Seymour, although her own people admitted that he had courted her, unwisely and immorally while he was still married. And Elizabeth had escaped all punishment. The Council at the time had even issued a proclamation stating that she was innocent of all stain. Mary advised isolation. Gardiner obeyed.

He was moderately satisfied with the result. The lack of attention seemed to disturb Elizabeth more than confrontation. She was almost eager to talk with him when he came to question her after two weeks. This time he had sent notice of his arrival;

Elizabeth actually stood to greet him and seemed distraught. And then she made what seemed to be a serious mistake.

When Gardiner accused her of planning to move to Donnington so she could resist the queen's commands, she lied and said she did not even know where or what Donnington was. Gardiner stared her down and told her he had evidence, Sir James Croft's deposition, that would prove she was lying. With knitted brows she first insisted she spoke the truth and then said slowly that she did not know Sir James Croft.

Gardiner smiled and abandoned that line of inquiry; he had caught her in an outright lie. He had Sir James Croft's testimony and that of her ladies to prove the lie. Blandly he asked several easy questions and then sharply asked why the captain of her household guard had bought a great quantity of arms and supplies to feed many men. Elizabeth said somewhat absently that he would need to ask Sir Edward to explain that, but she was frowning and not seeing what she stared at. And then, much to Gardiner's fury—because so far where he had no proof she could not be frightened into changing any tale she had told—she clapped a hand to her forehead.

"Donnington!" she cried. "I knew the name was familiar. Of course, Donnington is one of my properties although I am not quite sure where it is. But now I remember, and I remember Sir James Croft, too. He was the one who told me of unrest in the country. He advised me to go to Donnington. My ladies can tell you of his visit. We spoke in my reception room. At first I thought he was a messenger from the queen or Council, but he was not, and I would not go apart with him."

"So you did agree to go to Donnington!"

"Oh no," Elizabeth replied, blinking as if surprised by the remark. "The queen had bid me live in Ashridge and without her word I would not leave it. But Sir James was so insistent. To make it easier to be rid of him, I told him I would consider it."

"Why would you consider following the advice of a man who told you rebellion was being raised against the queen?"

Elizabeth opened her eyes wide. "Why for that very reason. You must know, Bishop Gardiner, that I was terrified of being taken prisoner by the rebels and made into some kind of a figurehead for them. I was thinking of writing to Her Majesty and asking for her decision about what I should do, but I was afraid to trouble her when she must be so very busy. And then it was too late. Lord Denno told me that Wyatt was advancing on London."

"But you did not write to the queen. You sent out summons to your dependents to gather arms and supplies and meet you at Donnington."

"I never did!" Elizabeth protested indignantly.

"Sir Edward has confessed that he sent warning to your principal vassals to arm themselves."

Elizabeth caught her breath but then shook her head. "But not to meet me at Donnington nor to gather anywhere. Ask where you will and who you will. I am sure you have sent out men to those who owe me fealty. Has even one of them moved off his own land?"

"They have all hired men and brought in supplies. We have proof of that."

"I should hope so," Elizabeth said sharply. "After Sir James told me of the unrest in Kent and Sir Edward sent my people warning. I should hate to think that those who hold lands of me were idiots. *I* did not know until Sir James came that a rebellion was possible—" she pulled herself even more upright and her face showed indignation "—and I tell you now that I think it unkind and unsafe that the Council did not send to warn me of that."

Gardiner's lips twisted. "We were all sure you already knew and needed no warning from us."

"But you were wrong," Elizabeth riposted passionately. "I did not know. And I did need the Council's warning."

Eventually Gardiner gave up. Elizabeth was immovable on two points: that she had nothing to do with the rebellion and that her captain's purchase of arms and supplies was solely defensive, designed to protect Ashridge from attack by the rebels. Gardiner managed to reduce her to tears by insisting that his questioning of Sir Edward might become physical if she did not confess. She begged him to spare her man, offering to plead for him on her knees, but she insisted that all the arms and supplies were still at Ashridge. They had not been used to arm rebels.

"Because there was no rising in Hertfordshire," Gardiner roared. "Had there been you would have been with the rebels."

"Never. Never." Elizabeth sobbed. "I love my sister. I am her most loyal and devoted subject. Why are you so cruel? Why will you not believe me? Should not a Catholic bishop be merciful?"

On that note, several of the councilors who had accompanied him and earlier asked Elizabeth sharp questions, began to remonstrate with him. Gardiner recognized the shifting sympathies and, remarking his cruelty was meant as a kindness, to bring her to confession and then pardon, he took his leave.

After another week of silence—not literal, of course, the women the queen had appointed to take the place of Elizabeth's ladies talked constantly and always of how merciful the queen was to those who confessed their guilt or other subjects to make Elizabeth uneasy—Gardiner tried again with no greater success. He sent others to question Elizabeth; Arundel ended up on his knees begging pardon for troubling her with unfounded accusations.

Nonetheless, although she had confessed nothing and Gardiner could never bring her a signed confession from anyone implicating her in the rebellion, on the twenty-fourth of March the marquis of Winchester and the earl of Sussex came to tell Elizabeth that she was to go at once to the Tower. The utter panic that seized Elizabeth at the thought of being immured where her mother had waited for death, sent the air spirit Underhill on an immediate search for Denoriel.

For one instant Elizabeth's spirit leapt with hope. Then it came crashing down into despair. Denno could not help her. He could save her life, but what life would she have left if she were confined Underhill? What would Mary do to poor England? Who would follow Mary on the throne to heal the wounds?

Frantic, Elizabeth sought for any delay, any hope of escape in what she thought was an immediate summons to death. She begged to be allowed to see the queen, and when that was most emphatically refused, to be allowed to write to Her Majesty.

The marquis and the earl disagreed about allowing it, but Sussex prevailed; he always had a soft spot for Elizabeth—and a sharp eye to the future in which this girl might rule. Elizabeth wrote her letter, taking so long over it that the tide had turned and the barge that would take her to the Tower could not shoot the Bridge. For one day more she would remain safe in Whitehall.

The queen refused to look at the letter and blamed Sussex sharply for allowing Elizabeth to write it. Elizabeth was to be allowed no more excuses. She was to be delivered to the Tower the next day without fail, Mary said—and put a hand to her head as a terrible pain stabbed through her temple and a feeling as if she had swallowed a cup full of ice settled in her stomach. She had promised Renard that Elizabeth would be sent to the Tower and she had done it. Whether she could do more... The pain in her head intensified and the cold was spreading so that her entire body began to shake.

Elizabeth, however, had benefited from writing the letter, although not in the way she hoped. She had time to think that Denno's token could not only bring him to her but also her Da. Da would know what to do. Her mindless panic abated somewhat as she forced herself to consider keeping a visit from Underhill secret.

Denno and Da would have to come to her. She could not dare be missing for a moment in case Mary did relent and agree to speak to her. Mary would send a messenger, who would pass the queen's order to one of her attendants. The attendant would enter her room without any warning. Elizabeth swallowed a sob. They had all been doing that with lame excuses since she had arrived in Whitehall.

No, she could not chance that. No doubt Da and Denno would become invisible if anyone intruded, but that would mean they might not be able to finish talking. She needed to know what they thought was best and safest. Tears ran down her face and she wiped them away. She needed to feel Denno's arms around her, to be assured by Da's strong good sense. She could not bear to miss a moment of the comfort they could give her. She needed to immobilize all her attendants but the guards outside the doors.

Elizabeth worked out how to arrange that, but the thought of the Tower hung over all. Her little hope could not warm away the cold of terror and Elizabeth found herself panting with fear as she waited for an answer from the queen. No answer came.

Slowly the light of the day dimmed. It was time for bed, but Elizabeth could not bear to consider lying in the dark through the passing hours. She would not allow her attendants to acknowledge, no matter what her new ladies insisted, that Queen Mary had long ago retired to her virtuous couch and was sweetly asleep.

Sharply Elizabeth bade the women to hold their tongues. There was still time, she insisted, for her sister to summon her. She could not imagine that her dear sister would not be troubled by committing her, innocent as she was, to the Tower. The queen's sleep would be disturbed. A summons would come.

One by one the attendants nodded off and slept on the sofa or the chairs Elizabeth had graciously offered since she was keeping them up so late. Elizabeth bit her lip and blinked back tears.

"*Bod cyfgadur,*" she whispered, pointing to each attendant (or possibly gaoler) in turn.

Then she drew from her pocket, where she had been clutching it all day, the token that would permit Denoriel to build a Gate to her chamber. Within moments of her laying it down on the floor near a blank wall, the black point formed and began to spread. Denoriel had been waiting for the signal and the Gate was barely large enough to allow him to pass when he sprang through.

"Elizabeth, what—" His voice checked as he saw the attendants asleep.

"They are bespelled," Elizabeth whispered, flinging herself into his open arms. "I could think of no other way to keep them from intruding on me. Denno—" she sniffed and her tears ran over "—Mary has sent orders committing me to the Tower."

But it was Harry FitzRoy's voice that answered. "I'm sorry, love, I know you are frightened, but it was to be expected."

"But I am innocent!" Elizabeth wept. "I know Gardiner has no proof against me. I had no part in the accursed rebellion. I did not even want it to happen."

Denno clutched her closer and Harry patted her shoulder. "I hoped it would not happen," he said. "Rhoslyn has been working on Mary so that she will be miserable all the time you are in the Tower—"

"So she will order me to be executed more quickly!" Elizabeth's voice rose hysterically.

"No," Harry said calmly. "She thinks that if you die she will die also. She tries to believe that you are not her sister, but within she knows it is not true. Too much of you is from our father—the hands, the hair, the manner. To order your execution would make her a kin-slayer. She remembers what happened to Somerset when he ordered his brother's execution."

"But she wants me dead. I know she wants me dead. When I am in the Tower the temptation may become too great for her."

"Mary will never sign an order for your execution," Harry said. "If she could get Parliament to vote an act of attainder for high treason and have you executed without a trial, she might have taken that path—although to speak the truth I doubt it. But Parliament will not vote against you, love. They will not even vote to disinherit you. Even Renard knows that. Gardiner tried it once and was shouted down."

"Perhaps I am to die of an illness or . . . or an 'unforeseen' attack in the Tower. Such things happen there."

"Not to you, Elizabeth," Denno said. "You will not die in any case, no matter what Mary orders. Wear your shields if you fear attack, and if you fall ill, send the air spirit and I will come and take you away."

Elizabeth turned a little in Denno's arms so she could see Harry's face. "But then I will be trapped Underhill . . ."

"No. Mary is only attempting to quiet Renard and Gardiner. You may be questioned further, but I doubt that too. Poor Mary," Harry sighed, "she is sick at heart over all the executions." He came a little closer and patted Elizabeth's cheek. "Last week she pardoned eight of the Kentish gentlemen that actually fought for Wyatt, and only yesterday pardoned Lord Cobham who was one of the chief conspirators. No, love, you will be bored and uncomfortable, but I do not think you need fear more than that."

"But to go to the Tower," Elizabeth said, her voice shaking. "Likely you are right, Da, but . . . but my heart fails me. I am afraid." She began to sob again.

"I will come with you," Denno said. I will wear the Don't-see-me spell and I will walk beside you and hold your hand. You will know you are safe."

Elizabeth turned her head to welcome the offer and saw the lines around Denno's eyes and mouth. He looked gaunt and gray, exhausted by the effort of building the Gate. She remembered now that the Bright Court was starved of power because of the misery of the country. Denno would not be able to renew himself and the Don't-see-me spell would drain him further.

"No," she said, "you mustn't. You are worn thin already, and . . . and you must be strong enough to build another Gate if . . . if that is all that will save me."

"I am not so worried about your needing to build another Gate Denno," Harry said. "But I think Elizabeth must do this herself. She will be too closely watched for even the smallest expression or gesture not to be noted. Whatever she does, however she acts, must come from her own heart, without support." He leaned closer and put his hand on Elizabeth's head, pulling her toward him to kiss her forehead.

"I am so sorry, my love," he went on. "I am so sorry that you will be frightened and miserable, and you know I would not advise it if there were any other way. But I truly think this is best."

In the Dark Court, Vidal looked out over his subjects with solid satisfaction. The throne room glistened with dark splendor and vibrated with power. The benches were full. Some of the ogres and trolls were only half grown but their stony bodies looked fat and polished. The witches snapped and sniped at each other; they had energy to spare. The boggles and banshees muttered and wailed softly, watching their prince, eagerly waiting Vidal's command.

In the forepart of the chamber, the Dark Sidhe sat in their chairs. Each one was sleek and satisfied looking. Vidal nodded.

"Two hunts," he said, his lips drawing back from his sharp-pointed teeth. "One near St. Boniface, which has just changed to the Catholic rite. Let us see if we can kill near the church. The other, in the purlieu of the Holy Redeemer, which is stubbornly reformist. Enjoy yourselves. Rend well the victims, but leave enough to show what died there."

All the Dark Sidhe laughed, their faces eager. "And can we take one or two for some entertainment here?"

The Sidhe who spoke was neither dark, in imitation of Vidal, nor blond and green-eyed. His eyes, less bright than the normal green, were light brown with greenish flecks and his hair was also a medium brown. Vidal stared at him. He knew Cretchar, but why did he feel Cretchar reminded him of someone else? Someone important.

"I think one extra should be allowed to each hunt," Aurilia said, breaking Vidal's uneasy thought.

The interruption did not irritate him unduly. Vidal glanced sidelong at her. Aurilia was as sleek and polished as all the other courtiers. Her hair was brilliant, curling luxuriantly; her eyes glowed with health and energy; a delicate flush of rose gave life to her white complexion.

Vidal smiled at her and nodded agreement. The interruption had been timely. Vidal was aware that something about a Sidhe with nondescript coloring had escaped his memory. He hated those lapses and accepted eagerly the reminder that everything was going exactly as he wished.

The horrible deaths and abductions would add to the anger

and discontent Mary had generated by her choice of a husband. That was the city. The country should be roused too; having several flocks ravaged, especially in those counties that had not rebelled, would do it. Vidal instructed several parties of witches and were creatures to take young ogres and trolls up to the mortal world.

The older ogres and trolls took exception to their exclusion. Some of them turned on the chosen young ones. Vidal laughed and let them fight. The substantial inflow of energy from rage and misery had allowed him to replenish the numbers of monsters in his court. He noticed with satisfaction that the young were giving a good account of themselves. He had created well. The Dark Sidhe cheered and laughed, urging on their favorites.

Screams and groans and the meaty sound of flesh striking flesh soon echoed around the chamber. The odor of blood and feces permeated the air. At first Aurilia sat forward eagerly, sipping at the pain. After a short while, she snorted in disgust and leaned back in her chair. The acrid energy that came off the fighting trolls was weak and flat. It had none of the delicious pungency that mortals emitted when they were hurt and terrified.

"Stop them and send them away, my lord," Aurilia said to Vidal, gripping his arm with her hand so that her long, sharp nails pricked through his silken sleeve. "They are dull creatures and their conflict gives little pleasure. Let them all go to the mortal world. Let the people of England think a plague has descended on them with their new queen. They are too suspicious of each other and too disorganized to come after us. And in the chaos we can choose our own prey."

Vidal laughed. "Perhaps you are right, Aurilia. Perhaps you are right."

He waved a hand and the fighting stopped, although howls of frustration now echoed through the chamber from the creatures that were being magically restrained. Then he ordered silence and told them their battle had won his admiration so they could all go. However they must choose different places of egress so they would be spread out all over the country. Another wave started them all on their way. A third cleaned away the blood and gobbets of flesh, although there were not many of those, the lesser creatures having snatched them up to eat.

When the room was clear, he stood and held out his arm to

Aurilia in a courtly gesture. A brief, almost effortless, exertion of his will brought them into his private parlor. This was so magnificently decorated that it was hardly ominous. Vidal looked around and sniffed discontentedly, thinking that he had not yet achieved the proper mixture of grandeur and darkness. He dismissed the dissatisfaction; he would find some horrors to add to the decor to increase the somberness of the chamber.

"We must have a little celebration," he said to Aurilia as he waved her to her chair by his own. "At last Mary has taken the first step to ridding the realm of Elizabeth. Yesterday in the early morning, Elizabeth was taken to the Tower."

Aurilia pursed her lips. "Do not get your hopes up too high for Elizabeth's execution. At first I thought as you did, that as soon as Mary had any excuse, she would order Elizabeth's head removed, but it seems we were wrong. Albertus tells me that Mary will not do it. In spite of all Renard and Gardiner can do she did not even want to send Elizabeth to the Tower. She has been asking the more powerful members of the Council and any of the courtiers she feels is truly devoted to her to take her sister into house arrest. So far, none is willing."

Vidal looked startled and angry. "Albertus! How can he know?"

"He is one of Mary's physicians. She has told them that she cannot bear to harm her sister, that the moment she thinks of taking any revenge on her, her head nearly splits with pain and her belly feels like she swallowed a bucket of ice."

"Why is Rhoslyn not supporting Mary's spirits?"

Aurilia made a moue of distaste. She did not like Rhoslyn. "Ask her, not me. It may be that we will need to find another way to deal with Elizabeth."

"I can make sure that none of the nobility will agree to take charge of Elizabeth. Some visit Otstargi for advice. I will spread the word that so onerous a charge will bring disaster, reminding them of Elizabeth's 'enchanting' nature and predict that she will seduce their servants and involve them in a new rebellion."

"The hint of witchcraft will not help." Aurilia shrugged. "Mary has been burnt too often and too deeply to accuse Elizabeth of being a witch. What you need to do, my lord, is somehow get Philip here to marry Mary."

Vidal cocked his head inquisitively. "I have apurpose not meddled with his reluctance to take his most willing bride. It seems to me that once Philip arrives and they marry, Mary will forget all about Elizabeth."

"She might," Aurilia agreed, "but so long as Philip gets a child on her Elizabeth will no longer be of any account."

"Will Mary get with child?" Vidal's lips twisted. "She is a scrawny old bitch for enticing much virile play from a man."

"Philip will do his duty," Aurilia said. "Mary may be old and scrawny, but he knows the great benefits a child will bring to Spain and the Empire. He will couple with her and *I* will see that the coupling bears fruit."

Vidal narrowed his eyes. "That is no easy thing."

"No, but I have been studying. I think I know the way."

"Where did they go?" Ilar asked furiously, looking around the outer perimeter of the Goblin's Market.

Aleneil sighed, unable to offer any further help. Of the many Gates that dotted the area outside the market itself, five had been used. Three of those likely had delivered their passengers to Dark Domains, but Aleneil did not have the skill to read the exact destination.

"We need Pasgen," she said. "But by the time I find him, the traces will be overlaid by many other Gatings. The market Gates are heavily used."

"We almost had him this time," Ilar said, through tight set jaws. "I did not realize he had set a lookout to warn him. That was stupid of me."

"Not so stupid," Aleneil soothed. "Neither of us thought he would dare use a confederate who could betray him."

"Not after what was done to Chenga," Ilar said with grim satisfaction. "At least we saved the mortal he was trying to seize, and we saw him and the Sidhe who was assisting him."

Aleneil's lips folded to a thin line. "That Sidhe. He was of the Dark Court I believe, but he was not so deeply stained with their power of pain and misery as are those long Vidal's servants. He must have gone to the Dark Court from the Bright Court not long ago. And the power he held was—" She hesitated and then said distastefully "—from life force."

Ilar gasped and his hand went to the sword at his hip.

"Not mortal," Aleneil said hastily. "Small things and the creatures of the Dark Court, though they have little life force."

"But you said our mortals live and are not injured."

"So says my scrying." Aleneil nodded. "They are held safe, but where I cannot tell."

"We must rescue them."

"Yes. I do not know how much longer they will be safe. That Sidhe . . . he hungers."

"I will try the three Gates that were used," Ilar said desperately. "I will think Dark Court and recent use. Perhaps—"

Aleneil frowned with concern. "Be careful, Ilar. The Dark ones will sense you. I cannot come with you. I would only bring you greater danger."

Ilar nodded and patted the sword at his side. "I will be careful, but we of Cymry do not divide Dark from Light so sharply as Avalon or Logres does. I may pass without challenge."

"Still," Aleneil touched his cheek, "have a care. Meanwhile I will go back to Avalon and try to discover who recently abandoned the Bright Court for the Dark . . . or was driven out. If I get his name, perhaps I can set a calling on him."

"The other was drawing power from Cymry without asking, without even a courtesy call on Idres Gawr," Ilar said indignantly. "As if he had a right to take anything he wanted."

Aleneil laughed briefly and shook her head. "You could not expect him to ask permission to draw power from Idres Gawr if he intended to abduct your mortals. No, he did not wish to be known."

"I am sure of that." Ilar snorted.

"And he was not of any elfhame I could recognize," Aleneil said slowly. "And fat. It is not common for Sidhe to be fat. I will return as soon as I may, and I will scry and try to set a calling."

Pasgen threw up a shield around himself and Hafwen just before the thrown hand ax reached them. It struck the shield and clattered to the stone floor. The ax-thrower had taken shelter behind an earthen redoubt. Pasgen stepped off the Gate platform holding up empty hands.

"Please," Hafwen called, peeping around Pasgen's shoulder. "We mean no harm. Indeed, we seek to bind or destroy the thing that harmed you."

"Who are you?" The voice was not friendly.

"My name is Hafwen and I am from the Bright Court, from Elfhame Avalon."

"What brings you to this rookery from the fine heights of Avalon?"

"Hafwen is a senser of evil," Pasgen put in before Hafwen could answer. "I know Gates and can read their past. We followed whatever it was you are now armed against to this hame. It did much damage to places I value. I am most eager to destroy it so it can do no more harm."

Slowly about midway back from the front of the earthen dike, a small squat figure rose. Its normally brown face was white and waxy, the eyes small black pits; one ear was missing. Hafwen drew in a trembling breath.

"You cannot destroy it," the damaged gnome said. "Pure Evil it was. That will always be with us."

"I am sorry for the trouble it caused you," Pasgen said. "But if it roosted somewhere in this hame perhaps I can drive it out."

Before the damaged gnome could answer, something multilegged and black, glistening with slime, leapt from a fold of the earth about midway between the fortification and the Gate. Pasgen drew breath and drew his sword at the same time. The slimy horror, not at all afraid of the sword, if it saw it, leapt up as if to strike on Pasgen's face but it, too, rebounded from Pasgen's shield and fell back. Hafwen uttered a thin cry of disgust which blended with and distorted a shout of warning from the gnome.

The warning came too late. Pasgen had already stabbed the thing. It made a high, shrilling sound and then simply fell apart. But it was not dead. The many pieces twitched and writhed and then began to grow again; legs formed, legs tipped with claws. And the multitude of tiny creatures oriented themselves and all began to crawl up or try to get under Pasgen's shield.

Hafwen screamed. Pasgen let out an oath, pulled her tight against him, and spread thin the kind of energy that made a levin bolt over the surface of his shield. Most of the creatures were fried and Pasgen, gritting his teeth to keep them from chattering with cold and horror, pointed at any that still moved and burned them one at a time. The effort drained him dangerously. By the time nothing more moved, he was as much clinging to Hafwen for support as keeping her close to protect her.

A ragged cheer came from the gnomes as the last of the slimy wrigglers went to ash. "We tried to warn you," the damaged gnome called.

Pasgen shuddered. "I heard you, but it was too late for me to stop my stroke. What *was* that?"

"We know no more than you." The damaged gnome came forward and climbed to the top of the redoubt. "That Evil brought the creatures or spilled them out of its body."

"When?" Hafwen asked urgently, coming around Pasgen to face the gnomes.

"It would have been two sleeps ago—if any of us dared sleep since that evil thing came through the Gate. It was Sidhe! We thought it had work for us. We welcomed it into our village."

"Sidhe!" Pasgen exclaimed.

This was the first being that had actually seen the Evil. Until Gnome Hold, Pasgen and Hafwen had been following a trail of senseless destruction, mostly Unformed lands turned into vicious Chaos, the mists inimical and treacherous. In one Dark hold of boggles they had found only the dead; seemingly the creatures had turned on each other and killed until none were left.

"Like us?" Hafwen asked. "Or Dark? What did it look like?"

"Not Bright Court looks, but not Dark either," the gnome replied.

"It was . . ." Another gnome popped up beside the injured one. "I keep accounts for this hold and I noticed because I almost did not notice," the second gnome said. "We look carefully at those we work for. They are not above trying to escape payment, especially for a difficult task. I almost did not look at this one. He—"

"Male?" Pasgen asked. "Are you sure?"

"No," the gnome replied. "The Sidhe . . . creature . . . whatever it was sort of faded in and out. Sometimes it was hard and bold, sometimes it was not more than a shadow. Mostly it looked male, but when it faded it could have been anything . . . except it *was* Sidhe. It was always Sidhe. It did not shift form."

"When you could see it how did it look?" Hafwen glanced up at Pasgen. "If it was neither Bright Court nor Dark it will be easy to make a picture in my mind. Perhaps the ladies of the lens could scry for it."

The gnome who had been answering shrugged. "It looked as if it could not make up its mind how to look. Hair neither dark nor light, like mud, the skin like lighter mud. The eyes also were the color of mud, but not dull, bright."

"That I saw also," the injured gnome said. "The eyes were too bright. Brown but with a red underlay. I did not like the eyes. Sidhe with such bright looks are still tasting guilty pleasures and looking for innocent victims." He looked uneasily at Pasgen and went on hurriedly, "Not evil. Mostly Bright Court Sidhe are not evil, but they are careless and indifferent. What does not seem harmful to them causes us to lose face among our own people. No. I did not like those eyes at all. I was telling the Sidhe to go away, that we did not want its work—but it began to laugh and it let loose a small swarm of those black things."

"Rumgunter died," the first gnome said, eyes filled with tears and an unbelieving sound to his voice. "One of those things leapt on him and seized his ear. I thought little of it. I leaned down to brush it off his ear and he was cold and white—drained. I should have been quicker."

"You were quick enough to save me," the gnome who was missing an ear said. "I saw what happened, but I did not understand. When another leapt on me and seized my ear, I tried to pull it off. I was half dead before Hardgrumble drew his knife and cut off my ear."

A third gnome now climbed up on the earthwork. Pasgen noticed that he was careful where he set his feet. "The thing that killed Rumgunter had grown very large," he said. "I made the mistake of striking it with my hammer. I thought it would squash like a spider. But you saw what happened."

"You could not know," Hardgrumble said. "But iron kills them. When I cut off Gosfarri's ear, I cut the sucking thing too and it folded up like an emptied bladder. Only they are so fast that I only struck one other. The others rushed away in all directions."

"Sweet Mother," Hafwen breathed. "Are you overrun by the things? Shall I go back to Avalon and try to gather up a troop to come here and use levin bolts to clear your hold?"

"A kind thought lady, but we are managing on our own very well." The gnome that had first thrown his ax at Pasgen turned to Hafwen and made a little bow; he did not look particularly pleased with the idea of Bright Court Sidhe throwing levin bolts around. "I am headman here; my name is Tomtreadle. There is a black oil that gathers in deep seams of rock in the mortal world. It burns. It burns most fiercely. When the things try to reach us—" he showed his teeth "—they burn. Only a few are left. One you lured out and killed. When you are gone, we will deal with the few that still lie in wait."

"But . . . but the one who loosed this curse? Where is he?" Pasgen asked.

He was not at all sure what answer he wanted. If the Evil he and Hafwen were chasing was still here and there was no other Gate they might have trapped it. But if it could loose more of those monstrosities, Pasgen was not at all sure he could defeat it.

"Gone." Tomtreadle shook his head. "I struck the Evil Sidhe on the feet with my stone hammer and it screamed and reached for me. I fell back and suddenly there was a rush of light. I was blinded."

"As were all of us," the redoubtable Hardgrumble said. "Those things could have killed us, but none leached onto us while we were helpless. It was as if they were frozen by whatever caused the light. And they did not come out from where they had hidden at once, so we were able to learn that fire destroys them as well as iron."

"We never saw more than that one flash of light. When we had vision again, the Evil was gone," Gosfari said.

"May I walk through your village?" Hafwen asked. "I will come alone and I am unarmed, except for my knife." She touched the hilt of a thin blade in an elaborate sheathe. "I wish to make sure that the Evil is not hidden somewhere."

There was a tense silence. The three gnomes who had been on the redoubt dropped down behind it. Pasgen's lips thinned, but all he did was to sit down on the Gate platform. In a few moments, the gnome called Tomtreadle climbed over the barrier. He did not cross the area between the redoubt and the Gate but stood waiting. Hafwen drew a short breath, exchanged a glance with Pasgen, and set out toward him. A very faint blue light glimmered on her fingers, but nothing attacked her and she reached Tomtreadle without trouble.

He made a brief bow to Hafwen and said, "I will lead you, but I warn you that there is iron on the way."

There was, indeed, iron of every sort—pots, pans, griddles, flatirons, knives, and spearheads—lying on the ground between the earth barrier and the first small houses of the village. Hafwen shivered as she made her way through what was clearly meant to be a barrier to the evil spawn. Indeed she saw a number of what looked like very ugly black bags with fringed bottoms lying here and there and a multitude of dead black spiders.

She had to set her teeth against the ache the iron waked in her, but she was not sensitive to iron as she was to evil. Picking her way carefully, she followed Tomtreadle through every street and then around the outer fields and through a small wood. There was, to her intense relief, nothing inimical in the entire hold. Once in the village she hesitated outside a cottage, but after a moment she recognized what she sensed was no more than a curdled nature and a will to do evil; it was nothing like the dreadful malevolence in a Chaos Land that Pasgen had nearly wept over.

Returned to the Gate by her escort, Hafwen said, "Gone. There is nothing evil in the village, not even the disgusting aura those black things cast. And this is a small hold. Only the village, the surrounding fields and that very small woods. I have been through all of them."

"Are you sure?" Pasgen asked, frowning as he watched Tomtreadle climb over the redoubt wall and disappear. "I have been working on this Gate, and it does not seem as if that Thing we are chasing left through here."

"But the gnome, Tomtreadle says this is the only Gate to this hold. They like to keep a close watch on who comes here."

Pasgen shook his head. "Yet it seems as if no one left through this Gate for any time that the gnomes would have called two or even three sleeps. I do not even have the thread of that Evil coming here. If the Gate we started from had not sent us here and the gnomes confirmed the Evil's arrival I would have found no trace of it here. The Gate shows no use until our coming."

"Nonetheless, it is not in this hold," Hafwen assured him. "Have we lost it altogether?"

"I think so," Pasgen said. "Something powerful created that flash the gnomes spoke of and wiped out all signs of our quarry."

"Apurpose?"

He sighed heavily. "I fear so. I fear the flash-maker has in some way joined forces with the Evil Thing. Why else should the traces of memory in the Gate have been destroyed?"

"Joined forces?" Hafwen repeated unbelievingly. "How can anyone join forces with such indiscriminate evil? Surely anyone so strong in magic should realize that it is untrustworthy."

Pasgen shrugged. "The desire for power sometimes wipes out common sense and there is power in that Evil. But we do not need to worry about losing the trail for long. It will burst out again."

He bit his lip. "Unfortunately without us on its heels, it will have time for a more complete destruction of its next target."

Hafwen put a hand on his wrist. "Let us go back to Avalon. I will speak to the ladies of the lens. Perhaps one of them can scry for such a Sidhe as the gnomes have described."

"Will the guards at Avalon pass me?" Pasgen asked.

Hafwen tightened her grip on his wrist and smiled. "I am sure they will . . . now."

Chapter 28

Inexorably in the early morning of March twenty-fourth, Elizabeth was removed to the Tower. To her relief the tide was too low for her to be brought in at Traitor's Gate. The barge that carried Elizabeth to the Tower landed at Tower Wharf. She was helped from the barge by Sir John Gage's men and crossed the drawbridge to the west of the fortress. There were dozens of guards lining the route and Elizabeth paused midway.

"Are all these harnessed men for me?" she asked tensely.

"No, madam," Gage replied, his lips twisting as in contempt.

"Yes," Elizabeth insisted. "I know it is so." Her eyes met his and her head turned slowly so she could see up and down the ranks of men.

"God save Your Grace," one voice called and then another.

Gage flung up his head, but before he could roar for order, about half the men were on their knees with their caps in their hands. Elizabeth shook her head and found a tremulous smile, just as Gage snarled at the men, who came to their feet in haste. Elizabeth allowed one hand to creep through the edge of her cloak and twitched her fingers in acknowledgment, looking back over her shoulder as Gage led her in through Coldharbour Gate.

Within, although she was not led to any dank dungeon, there was less comfort for her. The four commodious rooms assigned to her in the palace portion of the Tower were those in which her mother had waited to die, and the councilors who had accompanied her were planning to lock her in. Gage and Winchester wanted to turn the great keys in the heavy locks but Sussex would not agree.

Tears marking his cheeks, he said, "What will you do, my lords? She was a king's daughter and is the queen's sister. You have no sufficient commission so to do. Therefore go no further than your commission." And after a significant pause, he added, "Let us use such dealing that we may answer it hereafter."

Gage still wished to insist on treating Elizabeth like a common prisoner, but Winchester glanced at Elizabeth's white face and dark eyes and then urged Gage out of the door, Sussex following. Elizabeth listened tensely, but there was no sound of the great tumblers sliding home.

She then turned away from the door toward the three women waiting to serve her. Her heart sank and cold filled her belly. Kat was not there, nor even sweet, silly Alice Finch. She had been sure Dorothy Stafford and Frances Dodd would not be allowed; they were too clever, but even Eleanor Gage had been removed . . . no doubt because she had become fond. Elizabeth knew only one of the faces—Elizabeth Marberry.

She would not weep; she would not. She stared at them for a moment stiff with cold and terror. Was she to be all alone with not one kind face? Without a word, Elizabeth passed what she knew to be her female warders and sought sanctuary in the farthest room, the bedchamber. Eventually they would follow her, but her step was swift, her stride long. At least she would have time to wipe the tears from her eyes.

But then Blanche was there, lifting her cloak from her shoulders. Elizabeth had left all the doors open as she passed. She did not dare utter a word, but Blanche's little smile told the tale. The councilors were male fools; they had not thought to change her servants.

For now, no matter how loyal, the servants could do little beyond offer small comforts, foot-warmers and lap robes and warmed wine. All day on Palm Sunday, as if the heavens wept for her, it rained. The next day was clear, but the servants had whispered that, although the door had not been locked, there were guards just beyond it. Dutifully, Elizabeth sent one of her ladies to ask permission to take exercise; the permission was refused.

The days passed heavily. Elizabeth was not allowed either books or writing materials. She did needlework, but more often the shining needle lay still as her eyes, dark with disquiet, stared out into nothing. On March thirtieth, Good Friday, the Council came in force to question Elizabeth again. Likely they should have known better. They pressed her hard on how a copy of her letter to the queen excusing herself from coming to London because she was ill found its way into the possession of the French ambassador.

Elizabeth looked from one face to another, brows raised, as if she could not believe her ears at such stupidity. "Do you think me an idiot?" she retorted. "Why should *I* provide a copy of such a letter to the French? If one of my servants so betrayed me, you have my leave to punish him or her in any way you see fit. But, my lords, I would suggest you look first among your own people. They would profit far more from selling so empty a letter from me to the French than my people would."

Her near contemptuous indifference and the simple logic of her reply made too much sense. Her women and menservants had already been questioned; every one denied vehemently that Elizabeth had ever suggested giving a copy of her letter to the French. If the copy was made without her permission, she was not guilty of anything. Moreover the copy could have been as easily made when it was in the queen's possession or any member of the Council's. The line of questioning was soon abandoned.

Much more straitly she was accused of planning to go to Donnington and summoning to her support the retainers she had warned to arm themselves. She replied she never, neither by word of mouth nor word on paper, ordered a removal to Donnington.

From that avowal she could not be moved, even when Croft was brought to confront her. She acknowledged that he had suggested she go to Donnington and that she had said she would consider his advice—because it was the easiest way to quiet him and be rid of him. And then added, "But what is this to the purpose, my lords? May I not go to mine own houses at all times?"

Upon which Croft knelt and declared that he was very sorry to be brought as a witness against her, but that he had been tortured and threatened again and again touching what she had said to him.

And the earl of Arundel also begged her pardon for troubling her about nothing. But others asked what she had replied to the letters Sir Thomas Wyatt confessed he sent to her.

"I never had a letter from Sir Thomas," she replied. "If Lord Russell says he delivered one to my house, ask him if he put it into my hand. Whoever he delivered the message to had more sense than to pass it to me."

Despite Arundel's apology, they returned again and again to her planned removal to Donnington. It would have been a sensible move if Elizabeth had been part of the rebellion and if she confessed to having planned to go, incriminating.

Donnington was a castle and was defensible and it commanded the valley of the River Kennet which linked the Thames valley to the main road to Marlborough and the west. But Elizabeth could not be tricked or overawed into any confession. To every question about her plans, the stocking of the castle, and when she planned to go, Elizabeth stubbornly replied in the negative.

"I did not go to Donnington. I did not plan to go to Donnington. I did not order any man of mine to go to Donnington. I will say the same no matter how often you ask. And as I told Bishop Gardiner when he first questioned me, the captain of my guards did order extra food and weapons after Sir James Croft told me of the unrest in the country. It was for our own use in Ashridge. None was sent to Donnington nor anywhere else. I spoke the truth to Bishop Gardiner then. I have spoken the truth to you now. I did not and would not rebel against my sister, my queen. I am Queen Mary's most loving and loyal subject, now and to the end."

But Elizabeth's steady resistance to pressure to confess was not the final hurdle in the race for her life, and she had no power at all over that last test because it was not hers. She could only wait in agonizing anxiety to learn what Sir Thomas Wyatt might be forced to confess. After a month of torment both physical and mental, Wyatt was brought to the scaffold on April eleventh. The tale of the letters sent to Elizabeth had been wrung out of him, but Wyatt was a fine, brave gentleman and whatever temptations had been offered to incriminate Elizabeth faded to nothing when he stood on the scaffold.

Denoriel was in the crowd that had come to see Wyatt die. He was not there willingly; he had never before attended an execution. Bright Court Sidhe killed, although not often; however they did not indulge in public beheading. But Denoriel had to know what Wyatt would say in his last speech. If he implicated Elizabeth, Denoriel would somehow build a Gate to the Tower and bring her out.

Physically shaken, trembling with weakness, Wyatt still spoke clearly to the watching crowd. He confessed he had rebelled, but did not say he was sorry. "And whereas it is said and whistled abroad that I should accuse my Lady Elizabeth's Grace and my Lord Courtenay; it is not so, good people. For I assure you neither they nor any other now in yonder hold or durance was privy of my rising or commotion before I began. As I have declared no less to the queen's Council. And this is most true."

Denoriel uttered a gasp and tears of relief came to his eyes. Beside him, a burly man smelling strongly of onions said, "Good for him. They have used him hardly, I can see, but still he speaks the truth for Lady Elizabeth. And no man would lie when his soul will be facing God's justice in moments."

"Indeed he speaks the truth," Denoriel said fervently. "Lady Elizabeth is no rebel, and all should hear Wyatt's words."

The queen's men on the scaffold with Wyatt were not in agreement with Denoriel—or most of the watchers, many of whom had cheered Wyatt's exoneration of their beloved Lady Elizabeth. The priest who was supposed to minister to him tried to speak over his voice and say his words denied a written confession.

But there was no written confession, Denoriel knew; had there been Elizabeth would have mounted the scaffold also. He saw that Wyatt would have said more, but another of Mary's men pulled at his sleeve to turn him away from the listening crowd. It was too late; they had heard. Elizabeth was a great favorite with the people of London. Word of her exoneration spread, not least to Elizabeth herself in low and hasty whispers from Blanche, who had heard of Wyatt's speech from the other servants.

That night, Elizabeth prayed fervently for Wyatt's soul and then slept better than she had since the day she had arrived. The next day, perhaps hoping she did not know that Wyatt had cleared her moments before he died, Gardiner and some of the Council confronted Elizabeth again. They sought any hint of guilt, so little as a paling or blushing, any admission at all to save their faces and present to the people of England. They got nothing beyond steady denial and avowals of loyalty from her.

Elizabeth's popularity grew as word of Wyatt's exoneration spread. Denoriel did his bit among the merchants of the city. They were already disgruntled by the queen's favoring everything Spanish, and the common folk murmured against so innocent a lady being kept in the grim environs of the Tower. The Council ordered that the "false report" of Wyatt's speech not be repeated, but it was useless. Hundreds of people had come to see the rebel die and had heard him clear Elizabeth of compliance.

The next day, two young men were sent to the pillory for spreading the word that Wyatt had cleared Lady Elizabeth of any part in the rebellion. But they were most gently treated by the crowd; a few folk even cheered them. Moreover, Wyatt's head, which had been exhibited on a gibbet, was daringly stolen on the seventeenth, no doubt to be given an honorable burial. Rhoslyn watched Mary forbid any search for the thief; Mary was sick of death.

Without intruding on their minds—Rhoslyn was afraid that if she touched Renard Vidal would sense her interference—she also saw that Renard and Gardiner were coming to realize Elizabeth would not go to the block. Mary had abandoned that idea altogether, and as soon as she made up her mind to find a different way to deal with her sister, Rhoslyn saw to it that her headaches and stomach cramps all but disappeared. Mary now thought more and more of her coming marriage and less and less of the late unpleasantness, including Elizabeth.

Rhoslyn was sewing nearby when in a last ditch effort to get her to condemn Elizabeth, Renard told Mary that considering all the rebels she had pardoned and the fact that Elizabeth and Courtenay were still alive, he did not think Philip would be safe in England. But even that, Renard's sharpest arrow, this time did not penetrate. With tears in her eyes, Mary assured him that she would rather never have been born than that any harm should come to Philip. But she did not order Elizabeth be put on trial.

A week later, a warrant for Elizabeth's immediate execution was delivered to Sir John Brydges, Lieutenant of the Tower. Had it been delivered to Gage, Elizabeth might have died or been forced to go Underhill, but Brydges, although a firm Catholic, was an honest and careful man.

The warrant had not been delivered by a high Court functionary nor with the ceremony he would have expected to surround the condemnation of the queen's sister. Brydges examined the warrant very carefully. A number of passionately Catholic Council members had signed it, but the *queen's* signature was missing. Brydges did not officially report the matter, but he did tell Lord William Howard, who thanked him with great warmth.

Mary heard of the forged death warrant through a whisper from the marchioness of Exeter, who could not make up her mind whether she was more horrified by the attempt or by Elizabeth's escape from it. And Mary was stricken by the worst headache she had had since she had first decided to send Elizabeth to the Tower—a decision she regretted more each time she thought of it.

She was so ill, she had to cancel a meeting with Renard and go to bed. Rhoslyn sat beside her, reading softly from a book of meditations. In the evening, Mary sent an order to the Tower, which she signed prominently, forbidding any act against Elizabeth unless it was confirmed by herself in person. After that, Mary felt much better and was able to attend her evening Court.

Brydges, seeking to cheer his prisoner, who was bored and tired of her confinement, told Elizabeth about Mary's care for her. Elizabeth spoke promptly and gratefully about her sister's kindness, but slid from that subject to questions about why such an order was needed. Not averse to displaying his cleverness to his enchanting ward, Brydges confessed his detection of the false warrant.

Elizabeth paled noticeably; she resolved at that moment to sleep with her shields up, but only thanked Brydges so warmly that he colored and assured her that her safety and well-being were among the most important of his duties. But only three nights later, a young man with a forged permission from Brydges to deliver a bottle of fine wine to Lady Elizabeth was passed by the indifferent and bored Tower guards into Elizabeth's chambers.

The ladies had gone to bed as soon as it grew dark; there was very little to occupy them since Elizabeth had no books for study, no writing paper for letters, and no confidence in the women. Having learned in her previous confinement that it was dangerous to be unpleasant to her assigned attendants, she spoke to them pleasantly enough, but only on the most mundane of subjects—about the dishes at dinner or their needlework.

The young man made his way through the darkened rooms without difficulty; on Renard's recommendation he had been appointed one of Elizabeth's gentlemen grooms. A little to his surprise he was stopped by the guard at the bedchamber door.

He showed the bottle of wine, and when the man bent down to examine the forged pass, in one swift motion he struck the guard with the bottle.

Softly he opened the door, slipped in, and stood a moment to accustom his eyes to the even dimmer light. It did not take long for him to make his way to the great bed and most silently draw the bedcurtain aside. God's will to forward his purpose seemed clear; Elizabeth was fast asleep on the side of the bed he had approached. Silently he drew the long, thin poniard from its sheathe at his waist, raised it, and struck!

Elizabeth woke with a shriek. The young man cried out almost as loudly because his knife had simply rebounded from the lady's body. Not believing what had happened, assuming the knife had turned in his hand so it did not strike true, he struck again. The poniard still would not bite. It slid down Elizabeth's side into the bedclothes, and was torn from his hand as she twisted away.

When his victim first screamed, he reached out to close her mouth to silence her . . . and his hand simply would not touch her face. He did not believe that either, and could only account it a miracle of God's to protect her. She screamed again and again. The young man turned to flee; then he yelled as a white figure, also shrieking, rose up from the foot of the bed and clutched at him.

He shook off the hands and heard screaming, "Catch him! Catch him! Do not let him escape. Oh, Elizabeth, call the guard. Where is the guard?"

The guard was unconscious, in a pool of wine. The assassin easily evaded the pursuing women, barefoot and clad only in their night rails. He burst through the door past the outer guards and careened away down the stair. The delay of the guards to listen to the shrieking women and try to understand what they said, merely guaranteed the escape of the would-be assassin.

As soon as the women were gone, although she was panting with fear Elizabeth dismissed her shield, found the knife the assassin had tried to use, and added several large rents to the sheets. When the ladies came back, they found Blanche with a stout cudgel in her hand, standing over her weeping mistress. Mary's ladies they may have been, but the terrible shock had awakened a strong sympathy for Elizabeth and they spent the rest of the night huddled around her on her bed.

Morning brought Brydges to Elizabeth's chamber, to ask angrily why Elizabeth's women were telling so mad a tale.

"Mad?" Elizabeth shrieked, and threw a knife at him. "Look at my bed. Just look at it. Do you think I spend my nights stabbing a dagger into my bedclothes for amusement? I admit that my days here are sorely tedious, but I have not yet come to ruining my sheets and coverlets."

"Madam," Brydges said, staring at the knife, which had cut his hand slightly when he caught it, "forgive me. You were well guarded. How . . . how could this happen?"

"Well guarded . . . Yes, by God's mercy, which alone protected me so that the assassin's knife strokes went awry. Not by the men you set to watch. They are keen to prevent me from escape, but not to protect me from harm. They do not care for me. They did not even stop to question whether I was awake and wished to receive a bottle of wine, they just let a murderer into my chamber."

She burst into tears. Brydges did too, but that was little comfort to Elizabeth. She would not listen to his offers of doubled or tripled guards. A hundred men lined up who did not care a pin for her would not protect her, she shouted. She wailed for her own guardsmen, men who loved her, men who had fought for her and kept her safe since she was three years old.

Soon after noon, Gerrit, Nyle, Shaylor, and Dickson were summoned to watch over Elizabeth's inner chambers. In fact, though they were either bald or greying and thickening around the waists, Brydges was rather impressed with the well-used and well-cared-for arms and armor. He was impressed, also, with how they dealt with their trembling mistress and with the Tower guards who would watch the outer door.

Having pacified Elizabeth, who agreed not to complain to the Council, Brydges had every intention of keeping news of the attack on Elizabeth a secret. However, although Elizabeth was confined to the Tower, her maids of honor were not. They were faithful servants of the queen and carried no gossip or rumor that could comfort Elizabeth back to the Tower, but the tale of the would-be assassin was something else entirely. Such excitement, such an adventure slipped out despite Brydges's warning.

Rumor passed from lip to lip. More unkind glances were cast at Renard. Mary did not believe what those looks said, would not believe that the Imperial ambassador had attempted murder because she would not execute her sister. Nonetheless the excuse that keeping Elizabeth in the Tower was for her own safety grew thinner and more tattered with every new rumor.

The people were tired of bloodletting and opposed to any further punishment of the rebels. Mary was tired of the bloody punishments also, and Gardiner realized that even if he found evidence of Elizabeth's involvement now, to attempt to bring her to trial or to induce Parliament to disinherit her was impossible.

Only a few days after Wyatt's death Sir Nicholas Throckmorton, who was actually guilty of having taken part in the rebellion, was acquitted at his trial. And only eight jurors were willing to condemn Sir James Croft even though he had confessed his guilt. The court dismissed those jurors and found other jurors more compliant, but it was clear that to try Elizabeth would waken a tornado of protest. And the queen was unwilling to go further. Despite Sir James's conviction, he was not executed. Mary pardoned him; she wanted to forget the whole horrible episode.

By the end of April Renard had given up any hope of having Elizabeth killed either by law or by stealth. No matter how the yellow diamond on his finger sparkled and tingled, he could find no path to that goal. As he spoke to Queen Mary, still urging some solution to the problem Elizabeth posed, he often pulled at the ring and twisted it on his finger. One day he pulled it off and dropped it. Then Rhoslyn was able to touch his mind when he was not actually in contact with Vidal's amulet. Swiftly she stabbed into his mind a distaste for the yellow diamond.

He never put the ring back on and for once he slept well without a single dream about Elizabeth. He did think about her, but without any roiling hate, without feeling sick because she still lived. The next morning before Rhoslyn's strike could wear off, he dropped the ring into his small chest of jewels. He never associated the yellow diamond with his hatred of Elizabeth, but suddenly he was able to think about other fates for her than death.

He wrote several of his suggestions to his master. By the beginning of the second week in May he had Emperor Charles's approval and he presented his ideas to Queen Mary. For now, he suggested, since the people were growing angry at Elizabeth's detention in the Tower, she should be sent to house arrest in the country.

"I have tried to do that already," Mary replied through stiff lips. "The great lords who could afford to keep her have refused to do me that particular service."

"Madam, I do not blame them," Renard said, smiling. "It would be an onerous burden. But why should the lords pay? Let Lady Elizabeth support herself. She will then have less money available for assisting rebels. If the pecuniary burden is removed, you can find a man totally loyal to yourself. He need not be a great lord, so long as he is a gentleman."

Mary looked at him for a moment with a kind of wondering disbelief and then with dawning joy. "Of course. Of course. My dear Ambassador. You are always of the greatest help. Why did I never think of that myself? And I know just the man. He was the very first to come to support me after Northumberland crowned poor Jane. And he is a man who will follow an order exactly, regardless of clever reasons or enchanting pleas—" Mary's lips twisted in distaste "—why he should not."

Rhoslyn was sitting at a tactful distance, supposedly out of hearing, with Mary's other ladies. She kept her eyes on the book of sermons she was seemingly reading, but if anyone could have seen them, they would have noted her ears were perked sharply forward. Most of the "smell" of Vidal's presence was gone from Renard, but enough remained to make Rhoslyn uneasy. She listened more intently than ever for every mention of Elizabeth's name and within days learned that Elizabeth was to be moved to Woodstock, an ancient and unvisited royal manor, on the nineteenth of May.

Soon the plans were approved by the Council. Gardiner was content because Woodstock was a royal manor, an honorable residence Elizabeth's supporters would accept. Renard was content because the place was old and run down. Elizabeth might fall ill and die there or become resentful enough to try to escape. When all was settled, Rhoslyn asked leave to visit Adjoran, Mercer.

"He has such fabrics as no one has ever seen before," she said, smiling hopefully up at Mary from her curtsey. "You remember the lace shawl. And with the arrival of the prince so soon . . . I wish to be sure my gowns are fine enough. I must choose the fabrics now so that the dressmakers have time to do their best."

Mary smiled indulgently, but a small frown creased her brow. "Yes, the shawl is beautiful, but to honor the prince perhaps you might first examine what the Spanish merchants have brought."

If she went to the Spaniards, she would have to buy from them and would lose her excuse to talk to Denoriel. "I have always bought from Adjoran," Rhoslyn said sadly. "Would it not be unkind to take my custom from him when so many others have gone to the Spaniards?" Then she smiled again, adding, "But I will have all my new gowns in the Spanish style. I find it most pleasing."

Mary put out her hand for Rhoslyn to kiss. "You are a most faithful friend, Rosamund. I do not forget that you rode with me when I escaped from Northumberland's men and stood by my side when many ladies fled Wyatt's attack. Indeed, you shall go to your own favorite merchant."

"You are always so kind, madam," Rhoslyn said, kissing the hand and then backing away as she sent the air spirit to Denoriel.

Mary was kind, but Rhoslyn was very tired of the queen's Spanish obsession. And when Elizabeth had been sent to the Tower, Denoriel, almost out of his mind with fear, had begged her to watch for the smallest hint of execution or assassination, and he had bound an air spirit to her to give him warning if she perceived a threat. Rhoslyn did not think Mary would condone assassination, but Denoriel was in such a state that his anxiety and suspicion caught her and would not let her rest.

Rhoslyn had managed to escape the mortal world almost every night, but it had not done her much good. The domains of the Bright Court were thin of power so her renewal was not complete. And Rhoslyn had discovered a few mortal months past, just before Wyatt's rebellion, that she was debarred from truly living among the Unseleighe ever again.

So far none of the Bright Court had been overtly unpleasant to Rhoslyn. Mostly they scarcely noticed her, but as the anger and dissatisfaction with Queen Mary's choice of husband diminished the general joy in England, power diminished in the Bright Court. Rhoslyn had heard complaints while walking in the public places of Elfhame Logres. The complaints were not directed at her, but Rhoslyn felt guilty about absorbing power that she felt was not rightfully hers.

To avoid taking from the limited supply of power for the Bright Court Sidhe, Rhoslyn had Gated to Caer Mordwyn. There she found power in plenty; the atmosphere was rich with fear as well as pain, anger and misery. Biting her lip in miserable expectation of the discomfort and distaste the sour/bitter power would cause her but needing the strength so freely available, Rhoslyn drew on it.

Her hand flew to her throat. She would have screamed, but she could not make a sound, could not breathe; her whole body was torn and pierced by the pain that had leaked from the mortal world. It was fortunate she had not moved far from the Gate and was able to fling herself onto the Gate platform although vision and sensation were fading.

Harry—

It was not a destination but a mental cry for help. And the Gate at Caer Mordwyn was capable of responding to a desperate need. That was a new ability Vidal had incorporated into his Gates since he realized what his past carelessness had cost him in subjects. He had decided that any creature he had punished so severely it could not think of a destination but still managed to get to the Gate was strong enough to deserve to live.

Darkness and falling . . . Rhoslyn did not know whether it was her failing senses or the operation of the Gate, but in the next instant, when her lungs filled with clean air and her eyes opened, she saw the sparkling bright moss and twinkling sky of Elfhame Elder-Elf.

She could breathe now, but was so weak that she could not stand up. She barely managed to creep to the edge of the platform. Harry must be here, she thought, with Elidir or Mechain or one of the others who had helped him rid Alhambra of evil, but the small, pretty dwellings seemed to be miles away across the flower-starred moss. And she did not know whether she would be welcome in this elfhame. Usually she met Harry at the Inn of Kindly Laughter and he took her to other domains in the Bright Court.

Tears burned in her eyes and she closed them, only to be startled by the pressure of a soft nose and a sharp nip. Her eyes snapped open and she sat rigid, wide-eyed and openmouthed with shock.

"Talog?" she whispered.

For a long time Rhoslyn had done her best not to think about the not-horses. Every time they crossed her mind she had become sick with worry. She had no idea what to do about Talog and

Torgen. They were dangerous and certainly would not be welcome in any Seleighe domain. She knew they should be destroyed, but she could not!

Vicious as they were, the not-horses were faithful to her and to Pasgen. They had fought for them and saved them from attacks by the creatures of the Dark Court. Some would say they were only made things, but over time they had become more and more real. Now, knowing she could never live in the Unseleighe domains again, how could she arrange their care?

One red eye was fixed on her (no horse could look at anything close with both eyes), the red mouth was open showing the gleaming white teeth, one clawed foot impatiently raked the ground. But the foot did not strike out to disembowel her, the teeth had nipped very gently rather than tearing a gobbet of flesh from her arm.

"Talog?"

Tears ran over her lower lids and down her cheeks. Had her need for help to get to Harry been powerful enough to somehow summon the not-horse? But it was impossible! How could a construct have found her? How could a construct have directed a Gate to bring it to Elfhame Elder-Elf?

Rhoslyn struggled to her feet, reaching out for the arched and shining black neck . . . and found herself somehow mounted. Only there were no reins in her hands, no spurs on her heels. Before she could scream with terror . . . What would an uncontrolled Talog do in the peaceful elfhame? They were at the door of a large cottage . . . At least, *she* was at the door of the cottage. Of Talog, there was no sign at all.

The door opened and Harry came rushing out. "Rhoslyn!" he exclaimed. And put an arm around her asking, "My dear, what has happened? What is wrong?"

"I am no longer Unseleighe," she whispered.

Harry pulled her closer in a warm hug and laughed softly. "If that is a surprise to you, Rhoslyn, let me tell you that you are the only one who could be surprised."

"But I could not draw power in Caer Mordwyn!" she said, swallowing hard as tears began to run down her cheeks again. "Oh, Harry, what am I to do? I have no home, no place to go. And it is wrong for me to take power from Seleighe domains when there is so little."

"What do you mean you have no place to go?" Harry asked, raising a hand to wipe her tears away. "Rhoslyn, don't cry. I'll make it right for you, I promise."

"Dear Harry . . . But I don't see how you can make this right. I have not liked Unseleighe power for a long time, but this time when I tried to draw . . . I strangled! I felt as if I had been stabbed and torn with knives and swords. If I cannot draw power . . . I . . . will die."

"No you will not." A second voice, a little thin with age but not at all uncertain drew Rhoslyn's eyes.

On the step before the door of the cottage stood the oldest Sidhe Rhoslyn had ever seen. Her hair was so white and so thin it was like a silver mist; her face was actually graven with lines like an aged mortal. But her eyes, though their green was faded with time, were bright and her expression was more alive than many of the bored ladies of the Bright Court.

"But is it not wrong for me to draw power here when there may not be enough for those whose place this is?"

Mechain wrinkled her nose. "You have as much right to what there is as any other Sidhe . . . and more right than some, I would say. You are at least trying to protect dear Elizabeth, who will bring joy back to England and make the Bright Court rich again. All those others do is complain. Come in, my dear, and I will explain to you."

Harry urged Rhoslyn toward the three steps up to the small entryway. She was trembling and he supported her, asking "How did you get here, Rhoslyn? Did you walk from the Gate?"

Her eyes went wide. "No. Oh, the strangest thing happened to me. I cannot believe it, and yet if it was not Talog who carried me, how *did* I get here?"

"Talog?"

"My not-horse." Rhoslyn smiled slightly at Harry's puzzled expression. When he had helped her to a soft chair and settled her into it, she went on, "Pasgen and I . . ." Then her voice faltered. How did it come about that in her extremity she called for Harry instead of her brother? The obvious answer made her blush and continue hastily, "We desired elvensteeds, but you know that elvensteeds will not live in the Dark domains. And there is no way to compel an elvensteed."

"So you made not-horses?" Mechain, who had come in quietly

from another room, handed her a beautiful goblet. "Drink this. It will make you feel better."

Rhoslyn sipped. "We were young and I was—" she shrugged "—I was so proud of my newly mastered ability as a maker. I made Talog and Torgen—Pasgen's steed. They were a terrible mixture of beauty and horror . . . Vicious, dangerous, but faithful to Pasgen and me and for constructs, quite intelligent." Her voice shook on the last words. "I don't know what to do about them now."

Mechain cocked her head like an inquisitive bird. "You say this Talog brought you here from the Gate?"

Rhoslyn nodded and described what had happened. Mechain smiled and a mischievous glint lit her faded eyes. "Don't worry about them any more. I promise you the problem will resolve itself." Then she frowned. "Now, your problem with using Dark Court power is lack of practice. You used to enjoy the bite of the pain and rage it carries. You have just become unaccustomed and, because you don't like it any more, you tried to draw too much all at once to get it over with quickly. Go someplace—"

"Where did you wish to go, Mistress Rosamund? Do you want a horse or a litter or an escort?"

The sharp impatience in the voice jerked Rhoslyn out of her memories and she realized the gentleman usher of the outer chamber must have asked her the question more than once. Probably he had asked separately about each form of transport and she had just stared at him.

"I am so sorry," she said. "I have been trying to think what would be best. A horse, I suppose. The horse will not mind waiting no matter how long it takes me to choose the fabrics and if I must go on to the warehouse . . . Yes, a horse."

And a horse is not likely to mention how long I stayed or if Lord Denno acted as if we were old friends. There were a number of ladies new to Mary's service and of high rank who would be glad to be rid of Mistress Rosamund Scott. Mary was too fond of her.

Rosamund's place had not been envied in the past, when Mary was always in disgrace because of her religion; now that Mary was queen, almost anything that could be used to lessen Mary's affection for the nobody Rosamund Scott was used.

That was why Rhoslyn had told Mary about buying from Adjoran.

If she had not, someone would surely have reported that Mistress Rosamund rejected the Spanish and clung to her old connections. These days that was enough to erode Mary's trust. So many still urged her to abandon the Spanish marriage.

Rhoslyn hurried to her chamber to change into riding dress. By the time she reached the side entrance of the palace closest to the stable, the horse was waiting. Rhoslyn mounted and set off without delay. She hoped that Denoriel would be at the house on Bucklersbury, that he had not panicked and Gated to the Tower because of the air spirit's message. She was not skilled in dealing with air spirits. They were not clever and she had not dared to try to tell it more than that she needed to speak to Denoriel.

In fact, she was barely in time to stop Denoriel, with his pockets and his purse full of golden angels and gems for trying to bribe his way to Elizabeth. When he saw her, he almost dragged her off the horse, mumbling, "What? Where is she? Is she hurt? What happened?" as he dragged her into the house.

"Everything is fine, fine," Rhoslyn said three times over until she had closed the door of Denoriel's study behind her.

"Denoriel, stop acting like a lunatic. Elizabeth is well. She is about to be removed from the Tower—"

"Removed! What do you mean removed?" His eyes bulged.

"I mean moved to a new dwelling, and that is all I mean. I told you some time ago that Mary had completely given up any idea of execution."

"Yes, I remember," Denoriel said bitterly, "and the next I heard someone had forged an order for instant execution and when that failed sent an assassin."

Rhoslyn sighed. She had not passed the whispered rumors about the attacks on Elizabeth to Denoriel because she was afraid he would do something foolish. Apparently he had heard anyway, likely through William Cecil who was, although not restored to office because of his reformist ideas, quietly working for Lord Paget.

"I remember too, which is why I sent the air spirit for you, but there *is no immediate danger*. Elizabeth has her own guardsmen about her now. You know Gerrit, Shaylor, Nyle and Dickson will not allow any assassin to pass. And Brydges has been sharply alerted."

"Then what *did* make you send the air spirit for me?"

"I do not really know." Rhoslyn frowned uneasily. "But with Elizabeth's well-being at risk, I prefer to be careful. And the Council is being so secretive about releasing Elizabeth from the Tower that I have begun to suspect . . . I know not what."

"That she is to have an accident on the way?" Denoriel's voice rose. "That she is to be murdered in . . . Where are they sending her?"

"To an ancient manor called Woodstock. It was built by Henry II, but Henry VII liked it and restored it. Since he died, it has fallen out of favor and has been long neglected." Rhoslyn shook her head. "And no, I do not believe Mary has any part in any plan to harm Elizabeth . . . I just . . . do not like the secrecy."

"You think others have not protested Elizabeth's release because they hope she will be more vulnerable beyond Brydges's careful wardenship?"

Rhoslyn shrugged. "I finally managed to get Vidal's ring off Renard's hand. I am almost sure the attempts on Elizabeth were urged or engineered by him, but he is more flexible now. Still, I do not like the secrecy with which the Council is trying to act. I know something of the man Queen Mary has chosen as Elizabeth's gaoler. He is solid, he is honorable, he is also stubborn and not too clever. He will do exactly as Queen Mary orders—and the last order she gave was that no harm should be done to Elizabeth unless she, in person, gives the order."

Denoriel drew a long breath and shuddered, like a dog trying to rid his coat of something unpleasant. Then he looked around the room vaguely. "Sorry," he said. "I am half out of my mind."

Rhoslyn smiled. "More than half," she agreed dryly. "There is no immediate danger, as I said, but I think London should know that Elizabeth has been released. That she is set free would be a mark of her innocence. And I think her route and where she is settled should be known also. She should not be buried in a countryside away from her own people so she can be forgotten."

"I see." Denoriel looked around and gestured toward a large leather chair. "Sit down, Rhoslyn. Would you like something to eat? To drink?"

Rhoslyn took the offer of the chair and shook her head at the others. "I'm sorry about sending the air spirit when I could not explain to it why, but the time is rather short. Elizabeth will start her journey on the nineteenth of May."

"Three days?" Denoriel's voice again rose, in protest this time.

"I think the short time was deliberate. I think the Council hoped to spirit her out of London without anyone knowing. She would still be believed to be in the Tower and thus still marked as suspect of being a traitor."

For a long moment Denoriel sat and stared into space. Then, slowly, his lips curved upward. "I will go to the Hanse," he said. "I will set someone to watch the Tower, and tell the Steelyard when Elizabeth's barge starts." He was now grinning broadly. "The Hanse is not pleased with Queen Mary. They will fire their guns, a full salute when Elizabeth's barge passes the Steelyard. And when people rush to discover what occasioned the firing, the merchants will tell them that the salute was to celebrate the release of Lady Elizabeth. The news will be in every shop and merchant's stall in London within hours. I will see that news of her route to Woodstock is spread also."

"Good." Rhoslyn sighed with relief. "And now to fulfill my reason for coming here. I need fabric for gowns in which to welcome Philip. And I need one special length of exceptional quality to present to the queen."

Chapter 29

Thus it came about that Elizabeth's departure from the Tower became an exasperation—the first of myriad and growing exasperations—to her new gaoler, Sir Henry Bedingfield. Instead of a surreptitious and guilty prisonerlike removal from one gaol to another, Elizabeth's release became sort of a triumphal progress.

Queen Mary was not pleased, but she did not, as her father might well have done, take out her irritation on Sir Henry. It was Elizabeth she blamed, even though no one could guess how Elizabeth could have sent news of her release out of the Tower.

Poor Mary was all too aware of the growing dislike of her subjects. There were things that could not be totally hidden from her: scurrilous ballads and broadsheets, tales of a mysterious voice from a wall that said "Amen" to "God save Lady Elizabeth" but was silent for Mary's name, even disgusting representations of the pope thrown into the palace grounds. All the signs of public anger and distrust had multiplied since the rebellion.

Elizabeth knew. Her anxiety had increased steadily since Bedingfield had taken over from Brydges as her gaoler. Seeing her goods packed brought her near panic, and all the strangers coming and going to carry parcels were a danger. She did not dare wear her shields. If someone tried to touch her and could not, the secret of her shield might have been exposed. How could she explain? All she could think of to protect herself was to make everyone aware that she thought she might be furtively killed.

As long as they were still in the Tower she feared a swift and secret execution and demanded to know whether the scaffold on which Lady Jane had been executed was still erected. Elizabeth stopped in the great hall, looked around at clerks and visitors, men and women who had business in the tower and begged to be told whether she was to be dragged to that block.

Assured the scaffold and block were gone and she was only to be taken to a more comfortable dwelling, she cried aloud that the hundred men Bedingfield had assembled were to prevent any from saving her from assassination. Poor Bedingfield was appalled and pleaded with her not to accuse him of such a horrible crime. She only wept aloud and begged everyone to see that her guards, her faithful protectors, had been reft from her.

Bedingfield was a simple man. He was bewildered by the tears and tantrums. He had been ordered to keep Elizabeth securely but that she be treated "as may be agreeable to her [the queen's] honor and her [Elizabeth's] estate and degree." Bedingfield had intended only to provide his charge with guards he felt were younger and more capable. Unaware that these particular guards had been with her since childhood and were unlikely to obey his order that she not be allowed to speak to or send letters to those she desired to see, Bedingfield recalled Gerrit, Nyle, Shaylor, and Dickson. Elizabeth thanked him and went docilely down into the waiting barge.

She did ask to go on deck, but Bedingfield had been warned that Elizabeth was very popular in London and that he must not allow her to show herself lest she provoke a demonstration. Her request was refused, and she accepted that rebuff quietly. But a small, secret smile curved Elizabeth's lips as the demonstrations took place anyhow. Somehow news of her progress upriver was spread; people came to the bankside to cheer the unmarked barge and the great guns of the Steelyard crashed and crashed and crashed in salute as the barge moved slowly ahead.

The roaring of the guns of the Hanse brought out more people, who cheered and waved from the bank as the old and undecorated barge moved upriver from the Tower. There was their hope. Sweet Lady Elizabeth, who proudly said she was "mere" English, unlike Mary's flaunted pride in her half Spanish ancestry.

Their English favorite, they muttered to one another, would not bring Spaniards to rule over them. Although Elizabeth was not allowed to show herself, the crowds increased as word of the release spread. All Bedingfield could do was not allow the barge to stop until they came to Richmond.

However, at Richmond Elizabeth at first refused to set foot on the dock. Shrinking behind her four armed guards, she claimed that she had been warned that Imperial envoys were waiting to marry her by proxy to an unwelcome bridegroom. All the servants waiting on the wharf to welcome her heard her swear, in a high, clear voice, that she would not marry anyone and that she feared her refusal would mean that this night, "I think to die."

If envoys had been waiting in Richmond, they certainly were not presented to Elizabeth. Nor did she die.

The next day, her party crossed the river. Her own servants, first Thomas Parry then Dunstan, Ladbroke, and Tolliver, were waiting on the north bank to greet her. To them she sent Dickson, who was to say, loud and clear, *"Tamquam ovis."* Even Bedingfield's schoolboy Latin knew the phrase meant "as a sheep" and he protested aloud, before Elizabeth could say another word, that she was *not* being led like a sheep to the slaughter.

Elizabeth said nothing at all, and allowed him to lead her away from her people. She had seen Master Parry's smile and slight nod. Bedingfield might interpret the phrase as it touched him most nearly, but Elizabeth knew that Parry had understood the two words quite differently.

Thomas Parry might make mistakes in his accounts, but he made no mistake about his lady. He recognized her reference was to a favorite text she had had reason to quote in the past. "Behold," Saint Matthew's words went, "I send you forth as sheep in the midst of wolves; be ye therefore wise as serpents, harmless as doves."

Latin words and brief communication with her servants were the very least of Bedingfield's worries. Just what Mary had tried to prevent was taking place. The whole country seemed to turn out to greet Elizabeth. The Dormer family were intensely Catholic and it was in the Catholic Dean's house that Elizabeth was lodged that first night on the road to Woodstock. The people, however, were mostly of Protestant persuasion and they gathered by the road and on every rise of ground to catch a glimpse of and to cheer Elizabeth. Men rang the church bells as Elizabeth passed; four were put in prison for it, but not for long.

And no matter what Bedingfield did or threatened, the progress grew more and more triumphant. Every road they traveled was lined with cheering people who proffered flowers, cakes, and other little gifts in such profusion that Elizabeth had to beg them to stop when her litter was swamped. Loyal good wishes rang out and every hillside was dense with folk who came to catch a glimpse of their *English* princess.

On the last night of the journey they were guests at Lord William Howard's mansion. There Elizabeth was greeted and served with such great ceremony that Bedingfield warned her host that he was overdoing his hospitality to "one who was, after all, the queen's prisoner and no otherwise." To which Lord William remarked sharply that he was well advised of what he did and that in his house Her Grace should be merry.

In Oxfordshire, dominated by the very conservative university, which was strongly Catholic, Bedingfield hoped that Elizabeth would be ignored or even taunted. He was disappointed. At Wheatly, Stanton St. John, Islip, and Gosford, the whole population turned out to cry "God save Your Grace." Short of sending his men to disperse the people by force, which, although he was not clever, he knew would be a disaster, there was nothing Bedingfield could do. He was enormously relieved when they arrived at Woodstock.

The relief was short lived. The old manor was in serious disrepair. Windows were broken, slates missing from the roof, and the lead work was defective. Far worse from Bedingfield's point of view was that the manor was very large, and nearly impossible to secure. The outer court was some two hundred feet square, the inner court only a third less, and doors in plenty opened onto the inner court of which Bedingfield could find only three with locks and bars.

That was nerve-wracking enough, almost an open invitation to violate Bedingfield's prime directive, which was to prevent Elizabeth from speaking to any suspected person or to receive or send out any message. Bedingfield knew he could establish guards to watch the courts, but he doubted how effective they could be when there were so many ways to come and go and no way to light the areas sufficiently at night.

Far worse was that Bedingfield could see—and he was not the most perceptive of men—that Elizabeth was clearly as anxious or more anxious than he. Her face was white, her eyes burning bright, her mouth set so hard that her lips had disappeared into a thin line. She quivered with tension and barely touched the meal her servants had struggled to make ready for her. Poor Bedingfield felt certain that she was involved in some desperate plan to escape.

If Elizabeth had been enough aware of any external tensions, she could have—and would have—set his mind at ease. However she was completely absorbed in her own inner hopes and expectations. For the first time since she had been immured in the Tower, where she was closely watched at all hours of the day and night, she could hope to be unobserved. She had no desire at all to escape, at least not in any way for which Bedingfield could be held accountable.

Having examined Woodstock manor carefully while Elizabeth was held securely in the principal reception room, Bedingfield came to the unhappy conclusion that there was no apartment in the manor he could assign to her. Some were too decrepit, with leaking ceilings and ill-fitting windows; some, free of water stains because they were on lower floors, had so many doors and windows that they were open invitations for assault or escape.

Bedingfield raised his eyes to heaven in silent prayer. He felt he needed all the support the saints could give him. He had already been well stung by Lady Elizabeth's displeasure, and was not looking forward to her reaction when he announced that no rooms in the manor itself were livable on such short notice, and that he had no choice but to settle her in the gatehouse until repairs and renovations could be undertaken.

Elizabeth stared at him as if he were speaking a foreign tongue and finally repeated, "The gatehouse? You will lodge me in the gatehouse?"

"It is a temporary measure, Your Grace," Bedingfield said hastily, hoping to ward off Elizabeth's furious complaints. "The manor is old and has been long uninhabited. I fear that the surveyors were not completely honest in their reports to the queen of the condition of the building. Since the gatehouse has been in use, it is in far better repair and can be made comfortable for you in a few hours."

"The gatehouse," Elizabeth muttered.

She looked furious, but her frown was of concentration; she was trying to remember what she had seen of the building as they passed. Two stories, of that she was sure, and surely she had seen a goodly window in that second story. That meant there were decent chambers on the second floor, not only low-roofed cubbies for servants.

"I am sorry if you do not like it, madam," Bedingfield said, speaking firmly, "but I have no choice and it must be so. It will do no good for you to remonstrate with me. I have my orders from the queen and I must obey them."

Elizabeth drew a deep breath. Her eyes fixed on him for one moment, almost yellow as gold in the early afternoon light. Then she bit her lips hard and looked down.

It was very fortunate indeed that none of Elizabeth's long-time maids of honor were with her or some murmur or expression of warning might have been surprised out of one of them. They knew when their lady was bent on mischief. However, the unholy joy that brightened Elizabeth's eyes and made her swallow and swallow to choke down laughter were expressions that were not familiar even to Elizabeth Marberry, who had been considered loyal enough to the queen to remain as Elizabeth's attendant. The ladies that had been assigned to serve her in the Tower and to follow her into house arrest were more acquainted with rage than joy.

There was really no way for Bedingfield to realize that locking Elizabeth firmly into the gatehouse was exactly what she wanted. On first sight of the large, sprawling manor, Elizabeth's heart had sunk. She had never been in Woodstock and had no idea how the lodgings were arranged. She hoped that Bedingfield would be able to close off her apartment in such a way as to preclude his overanxious orders that someone check on her at all hours.

Elizabeth had been afraid that there would be multiple ways to enter any apartment he chose for her, and that would make it much, much harder for her to be sure no one would discover her absence. It was possible in a neglected building for one door to stick; for two or three to do so must cause suspicion. Elizabeth's lips thinned to nothing. No matter what the danger, she *would* escape to Underhill and sleep in Denoriel's arms that night. For her to lodge in the gatehouse might be her salvation.

Her joy increased upon entering the building. There was a substantial stair rising to the second story, which confirmed her hope that there were decent rooms above. She looked at the stair deliberately before passing through the door to the principal chamber which Bedingfield was holding open for her.

Elizabeth sniffed loudly and looked around the room. It was in some disarray since it had been home for some years only to the servants of the official in charge of the empty manor. Although she frowned and wrinkled her nose, actually Elizabeth thought it would be a pleasant place to sit of a morning or afternoon.

Warned by her expression, Bedingfield quickly passed through to another well-proportioned room without speaking. A fire was burning in the fireplace, but the chamber had a definite odor of unwashed inhabitants.

"I cannot sleep here," Elizabeth protested, her voice shrill. "It stinks. And even with the fire it is damp."

There were windows through which a guard might peer and another door in the back wall. Elizabeth suspected the back door would open either to the back garden or to a corridor leading to the kitchen. To lock that as well as the door to the front chamber by magic would not be safe. Elizabeth remembered vividly the consternation she had caused by sealing one door to her bedchamber so that she and Denno could rest in her bed in Chelsea.

"The chambers will be cleaned, Your Grace, and aired. They will be made fit for you," Bedingfield pleaded.

"No!" Elizabeth shouted. "I will not stay here in the servants' filth. I will sooner lie in an open field."

She ran past Bedingfield, who gasped with shock and followed as quickly as he could. She was so quick and light footed that she went past her maids of honor, who had been looking around their probable quarters, through the front room, and out into the entry before any of them could move. Bedingfield could not catch her and was terrified of ordering the guards to stop her physically, but by the time he had come to the door to shout an order, Elizabeth had already stopped and was looking at the stair.

"There are chambers above?" she asked, and, pretending not to see the sudden light of hope in Bedingfield's expression, added thoughtfully, "They would not be damp."

"No, madam," Bedingfield assured her, heartily. "If you would but ignore the disorder in the rooms now and consider that they can be cleaned, thoroughly cleaned, and have scented woods and pastiles burned to remove any odor . . ."

He followed again as Elizabeth climbed the stair, which rose into the front chamber. This had obviously been used as a bedroom by those who had been in charge of the manor. Elizabeth shook her head. It would be impossible to find any privacy in a room into which the stair opened. But there was a door in the farther wall. She walked to it swiftly and flung it open.

Beyond was a somewhat smaller room that was obviously being used for storage. Just visible through the clutter was a fireplace. Beyond the fireplace was a small door, almost invisible in the paneling. Elizabeth threaded her way through the broken furniture and the old chests.

"Lady Elizabeth!" Bedingfield cried, attempting to follow her. "Do not—"

But she paid no attention and opened the door. Since she did not step through it, Bedingfield was able to hurry to her side. Elizabeth bit her lip to conceal a smile. Her gaoler seemed to think she had been seeking a way out. *Fool. Where could she go on foot in an area with which she was not personally familiar, although she did own some lands in Oxfordshire.*

The little door opened only into a still smaller chamber, just large enough for a servant. Perfect for Blanche, Elizabeth thought, turning away from the little room and staring out over the odds and ends that littered the floor. Seeing no way out from the small chamber, Bedingfield had moved to one window and then to the other.

"This can all be cleared, Your Grace," Beedingfield said, coming back from his hasty glances out of each of the chamber's windows. "Your bed would fit on the back wall. With a carpet or two and a good fire, you will not recognize the place."

He spoke cheerfully, brightly, trying to urge an image of intimate comfort on her. In the way his eyes roved the room what he was seeing was two windows too high to invite jumping or climbing, a single door before which a guard could be stationed, and no other way for his prisoner to find freedom or conspirators.

Elizabeth had to go to the windows herself and look out to find time to control her expression. When she turned back, she had bent her brows into an angry scowl.

"How long will it take to ready an apartment for me in the manor?" she asked. "It is not fitting nor will it conform to my sister's command that I be treated as is fit for my estate and degree to lodge me in the house of servants."

"Your Grace," Bedingfield pleaded. "To lodge you here is not of my will, but it would suit you worse to have a bedchamber and sitting room into which the spring rains poured and where the windows rattled like iron wheels on a stone road. Everything that can be done to make this house suitable for Your Grace will be done at once. But for the manor, funds must be found to make repairs . . ." he mumbled unhappily.

Oh good. That will take forever. I can just see the Council agreeing to spend money to make Woodstock manor sound while they have no funds to pay those who fought Wyatt or for any other important purpose.

Elizabeth sighed like one martyred and began to make her way toward the stair. She moved slowly now, seeming discouraged. "The back chamber is not damp or musty," she allowed grudgingly, "for all it has been used only for storage. Well, I hope you will press the Council smartly to have the manor refurbished for me, and since it cannot be helped, I will take that back chamber for my bed. My ladies can use the forward chamber for their beds. The rooms down below—if they can be made fit—will do as parlor and private reception room."

"I will set the servants to work at once," Bedingfield agreed, escorting Elizabeth out the front door.

He gave no particular sign of satisfaction, but he was warm and contented inside. Those last words repaid him for the sharp-tongued complaints and criticisms. Lady Elizabeth could talk all she wanted about private reception rooms, but she would be receiving no one he did not approve, and no one at all in private. He had been directed not to allow any visitors he did not trust completely and even with those he did trust to allow no conversation he did not overhear.

The thought gave him so much pleasure that he agreed to Elizabeth walking in the inner courtyard with her maids of honor while the gatehouse was readied for her. Out of Bedingfield's sight and hearing, Elizabeth forgot to maintain the attitude of despondency. Bit by bit her stride lengthened and her eyes began to dance with glee. She could already see the brilliant twilight of Underhill, the soft moss starred with white flowers, the great brass doors of Lachar Lle.

She wondered about the illusion on Denno's door and beyond the great window in his parlor. In the long months she had been held at Court and imprisoned in the Tower, had he tried to divert himself by making the illusion, which he knew she loved, more elaborate, more beautiful? Were there new flowers? Was the manor house repainted? Had a hedge grown? Elizabeth bit her lips to hide her delighted smile of anticipation.

The queen's ladies, now Elizabeth's minders, glanced from one to another. All were uneasy about Elizabeth's lifted spirits. She had been planning some outrage—they all agreed there could be no other explanation for her excitement when they first reached Woodstock. Something about the place had spoiled her expectation. She had been really shocked when Bedingfield told her she would have to lodge in the gatehouse.

Now, suddenly, her mood had changed from disappointment to satisfaction. She seemed so self-absorbed that the two ladies walking behind were not afraid to consult each other in low voices. They had no idea how keen Elizabeth's hearing was nor how well terror had trained her to understand half-heard words.

"She has some new plan," Mary Dacre whispered.

"Yes," Susanna Norton agreed, biting her lower lip. "From near tears to near dancing. Whatever her disappointment was, she has found some way to amend it."

"But what can we do? The queen will be furious with us if she manages to escape or to make herself the reason for another rebellion." Mary Dacre began to wring her hands and then forced them behind her back lest Elizabeth look around.

"Elizabeth knows her best," Susanna said. "We must talk it over with her."

Elizabeth waited the result of that discussion with some anxiety, wondering how difficult the ladies would make it for her to ensure none would intrude on her during the night. It was possible, of course, for Denno to twist time so that she seemed to be absent for only a few minutes, but she suspected that power was low and thin in the Bright domains because of the unhappiness and unrest caused by the rebellion and the general dissatisfaction with the Spanish marriage. If he only needed to give her some hours for sleep, the twist would be more like a soft curve and take less power.

Since Elizabeth had hardly touched the dinner prepared soon after they arrived at Woodstock, she ate very well at the evening meal, which was served in a still-habitable dining parlor in the manor. When the final sweets and savouries were pushed away, Bedingfield rose and bowed.

"If Your Grace will come with me, I will show you how the quarters in the gatehouse have been prepared and try to amend tomorrow any insufficiencies you find therein."

"I do hope those insufficiencies are not such as will prevent me from soon going to bed," Elizabeth said. "I am sad and tired and I fear I will find little rest in this strange ruinous place."

They set out for the gatehouse without delay, Elizabeth waving away the worn and warped litter in which she had traveled. The walk was chilly, and Elizabeth pulled her cloak tightly around her. She was cold now and her excitement and high hopes dimmed as she worried about what her ladies planned. But arrival at the gatehouse provided a pleasant surprise.

The outer room, which had been littered and dirty, was now warmed by a bright fire; to one side was a cushioned chair, opposite was an old but sturdy bench and several stools. Velvet drapes shrouded the windows and on the floor was a Turkey carpet, also old, showing worn spots, but clean and of a handsome design.

Elizabeth sniffed. The air had a smoky odor of apples; seemingly the wood burning in the fireplace was apple wood. "Very fit, Sir Henry," she said. "I can still feel some damp from the floor, but not impossible to endure until you can arrange to have the manor restored. Let me see my withdrawing room."

Bedingfield looked surprised. His relationship with Elizabeth had been one of complaints on her part and attempted explanations or sometimes exasperated commands on his. He had not expected her to show the smallest thanks for his effort. But before he could respond she had set off for the inner chamber. Here she had to walk into the room before she could see the fireplace, which shared wall and chimney with the fireplace in the front chamber.

Bedingfield braced himself for an outburst, as there was almost no furniture at all, except for a large, carved settle near the fireplace. "There seemed little sense to furnishing this chamber, as you will have few visitors and no occasion to be private with anyone."

Elizabeth blinked. "Do you mean to bury me here in this wilderness?"

"Your Grace, I pray you not to insult me again by accusing me of allowing any harm to come to you. You will only live quietly—"

"Quietly, yes, but surely there will be messages from the queen, and members of the Council will wish to speak with me."

"I do not know, madam," Bedingfield replied stolidly.

But Elizabeth could see in his face that no message would come from the queen and that the Council would be glad, indeed, if it never heard of her again. She could not let that happen, she resolved; she would not let it happen. But first she must secure the private bedchamber that would save her sanity, which would surely be endangered by being locked into a prison with only Sir Henry Bedingfield as companion.

"But *I* do," she said spitefully. "Even a common prisoner in the Fleet or Newgate is allowed communication with the authorities that have imprisoned him. I shall not be less than a common felon when I am innocent of any crime at all."

Bedingfield opened his mouth to say that all but certain proof was held against her and that if she would only confess and throw herself on the queen's mercy, she would hear better news than being held in an old, unused manor. He never got the chance. Elizabeth had whirled about so quickly that the hem of her skirt flicked at his ankles.

"You may take me above to the bedchambers," she said.

In the outer room into which the stairs rose were now three small beds, well garnished with sheets, pillows, and bedcoverings. On the inner wall a fire burned; this one smelled of cedar or pine. There was no carpet, but small fleeces lay beside each bed. Without comment, Elizabeth passed through. If Mary's spies were not satisfied they could complain on their own.

The inner chamber brought from her a sigh of relief. This room too smelled pleasantly of cedar. The fire, again sharing a wall and a chimney with that of the outer room, gave enough light for her to see her bed—not the great, wide bed that she carried from Hatfield to Ashridge or to any of her other manors but the smaller bed, not really wide enough for two, that she had been allowed while a near-prisoner in Whitehall and an acknowledged prisoner in the Tower.

Still it was her bed and was not large enough to share. Perhaps that was meant as a kind of punishment, to deprive her of the comfort of a lady sleeping with her. But since Denno had become her lover more than five years past, she had rarely availed herself of that comfort. In this case it was all to the good; a suspicious lady beside her in her bed might wake if she heard Elizabeth whispering or felt her moving. Half awake, that lady might become suspicious of her sudden, sound sleep.

There was a low cot on the far wall. No doubt one of Mary's spies would sleep there, which was no problem as Elizabeth could bespell her to sleep without moving and so seem asleep herself.

Elizabeth nodded to Bedingfield, who had come behind her into the room. "It is not what I am used to," she said petulantly, "but I suppose you can do no better. There needs a decent carpet and a chair for me to sit by the fire, and a lamp to read by."

Again before Bedingfield could find an answer, she had swept by him, through the adjoining room, and started down the stair. He hurried behind her in case she should try to leave, but she turned right into the parlor where "her" ladies were waiting uneasily.

"That will do, Sir Henry," Elizabeth said, waving him away. "You may go. God give you a good night. I will do no more than speak a few words to my ladies and then find my bed."

What she said was true, she thought, smiling a little. She had not said she would go to sleep. She would certainly find her bed, even lie down in it, so she had not told a lie.

The small, secret smile sparked even greater anxiety in the ladies, who had been infecting each other with all sorts of wild fantasies of Elizabeth somehow convincing the guard to let her by. Elizabeth guessed that fear and it increased her impulse to laugh. It was not so fantastic, since it was Shaylor holding the front door and Nyle the rear; all she would have had to do was say she wished to leave. Neither Shaylor nor Nyle would say her nay, no matter what orders had been given them by others.

Susanna Norton, tired by Elizabeth's swift and athletic pace in walking even suggested she might climb out of the window into the arms of a noble supporter with an army at his heels. All three agreed that Elizabeth was sly enough to conceal herself from them so that they would run about seeking her while she drew a shawl over her red hair and walked out of the gates.

Elizabeth Marberry curtsied and said, "This is an eerie place, Your Grace. That huge, empty manor . . . I feel it looming over us even though the curtains are drawn. Would it be possible for us to be all together?"

"You mean you all wish to sleep in the same chamber? Well . . ." Elizabeth looked doubtfully from one face to another and could not understand the mixed emotions she saw there. "I suppose Blanche could sleep in my room—"

"Oh no, Your Grace!" Mary Dacre exclaimed. "No. We would never leave you all alone with no one but a common maidservant to support you. We would all three like to sleep in *your* chamber together."

"All three of you?" Elizabeth's eyes opened wide.

She looked terribly shocked. She was terribly shocked, but with pleasure. She gazed at them, speechless with delight, furthering their impression that she was appalled. All of them together, she thought. One single sleep spell and they would all be helpless. She would not even need to bespell the door not to open. Blanche could sit by it and answer anyone who came.

"But . . ." she sputtered, "but there is only one bed."

"We will make do," Elizabeth Marberry said, trying not to sound like a martyr. "Unless there is some reason why you do not want us in your bedchamber."

"No," Elizabeth murmured, biting her lip hard to keep from laughing. "No, of course you are welcome to sleep in my chamber. Let me just tell my maid to provide drink and suitable tidbits for all of us."

Looks flashed from one pair of eyes to another. Elizabeth had to turn away from their anxious faces. She went and stared into the fire, as one sorely disappointed might do. She was consumed by a desire to kiss them all and giggle.

The innocents! They cannot decide whether to let me speak to Blanche alone or not. They think I want to tell Blanche to warn away any who planned to free me or conspire with me. If Blanche warned them, those dangerous rebels would not come and the silly hens are afraid to try to trap me with dangerous, perhaps desperate, men. On the other hand they know it wrong to let rebels be warned and escape and lose a chance to prove me guilty.

"Oh, Your Grace," Susanna Norton said, clearly screwing her courage to the sticking point. "Please do not disturb yourself. I will go and speak with your maid."

"As you wish," Elizabeth said, turning from the fire and seating herself in her chair with an ill-natured thump.

She was still struggling with laughter. She did not care a bit what Susanna said to Blanche, since she would have plenty of time to discuss what Blanche should do after the women were all bespelled asleep. She turned her eyes to the fire again. Now she only had to find the strength to act in a manner they would consider natural until they went to bed. And then she would have to be strong enough not to claw with impatience at the wall in Blanche's room where her token would call Denno's Gate.

The Gate opened so slowly that Elizabeth clapped her hands to her mouth to keep from crying out. Mary was destroying the joy of her people and was destroying the Bright Court with it. More than ever Elizabeth regretted Wyatt's failure. She knew that his success would have made her coming to the throne far more difficult, perhaps would have caused a civil war . . . which would have been just as harmful to the power the Bright Court used.

When Denno forced his way through the narrow Gate, Elizabeth clutched him to her, sobbing softly with mingled joy and fear. He still wore the somewhat ravaged face of Lord Denno Adjoran instead of that of the young Denoriel he usually wore for her visits Underhill. That told her how great an effort he had expended to open a new Gate to the mortal world.

"Beloved, beloved," he murmured, resting his cheek against her bright hair. "It has seemed like a thousand years to me. I feared for you. I think I would have gone mad, except for Rhoslyn, who kept assuring me that Mary would not let harm come to you."

Elizabeth raised her head to kiss his lips, and urged him back toward the Gate. With the women who watched her so fearful about what she would do, she was not certain the spell would hold them if they heard the sound of her voice and a man's.

She and Denno went through the Gate still linked, and it was not an easy passage. Usually Elizabeth found herself securely at the arrival Gate just as she became aware of the sensation of darkness and falling. This time she had a long moment to be terrified. Her lips had parted to scream, although no sound ever penetrated the Otherness of Gating. However, they did arrive safely at the Gate to Llachar Lle and Miralys was waiting.

Elizabeth examined the elvensteed carefully, fearing the creature would be less solid or show signs of ageing, and Miralys turned his head to look at her. "I feel I should do *something*," Elizabeth said anxiously to the steed, "although I have not the smallest notion of what I could do. She will not listen to me."

Miralys snorted loudly, then touched Elizabeth gently with his muzzle. Denoriel hugged her tighter.

"It is nothing to do with you, beloved," he said, as he lifted her to the second saddle. "Your one duty for now is to stay alive without being sent out of the country or married off to someone who will be repugnant to your people. If you can manage that, we have hope to cling to."

Llachar Lle, to Elizabeth's relief seemed no less solid or magnificent. Perhaps the white flowers in the moss were not as bright and the palace did not shine with so silvery a light . . . but perhaps that was only her fear darkening her eyes. The slight chill of the spell that acknowledged her as she passed through the small entry portal to the side of Llachar Lle's giant brass doors seemed no more or less than she remembered, and the huge hallway and silver doors were unchanged. But the illusion that masked Denno's doorway seemed dull and flat.

What was Oberon's, Elizabeth realized as she and Denno went into his apartment, had not been affected by the loss of the power of joy. Where Oberon's power came from . . . Elizabeth's lips parted to ask and then closed without a sound. Likely Denno would not tell her; likely he did not know. But if he did, Elizabeth decided, she did not want to hear. She had enough trouble with religion without adding a pagan god to her belief.

"Do you want to eat? Something to drink?" Denno asked.

The odd wavering in the air that signified Denno's servants were present was slow to form. Elizabeth shook her head and turned to face Denno, to put her arms around his neck and press her body against his.

"I want nothing except to touch you, to be with you. To make myself sure that I have really found a breath of freedom."

He nodded, smiling, and walked toward the stair that led to the second story (which could not possibly exist) drawing Elizabeth with him. She could not help being a little frightened that he had not, as was usual for him, swept her off her feet and carried her up the stair. As they came through the door of his bedchamber, Elizabeth pulled off her night rail and cast it away, then ran to him and began to undo the fastenings of his doublet. He raised a hand to gesture, but she shook her head vehemently.

"I need to peel you, stitch by stitch," she said, kissing him again.

Her Denno's eyes brightened so that he looked less worn. He

had taken what she said as a ploy to heighten sexual anticipation. Elizabeth was glad of it, but the truth was that she was trying to save him even the minuscule outlay of power that it would have cost to remove their clothing by magic.

However as this and that garment was cast away, Denoriel's skin was bared and Elizabeth's mouth found his neck, his shoulder, his broad breast, his small man's nipple. He groaned and caught her to him, his own mouth hot against her neck. She thrust him away a little, enough to open his points and the tie of his slops. And as she nudged the garments off his hips, her hands slid along his flesh.

Denoriel raised one foot and pushed slops and stockings down on his other leg. Elizabeth's hands wandered from his hips to his groin. Denoriel groaned again, and they were lying on the bed. He was not aware of the power he used to raise them both. It did not seem to cost him any effort. A warmth seemed to flow from Elizabeth into him that filled his empty channels for magic.

With that warmth came a rush of passion so rich, so raw that he lost awareness of any refinement he had intended to use to please her. He rid himself of the remains of his clothing with two frantic shoves with his feet, rolled over so that he was above her, and thrust.

Perhaps he used magic again without thinking of it or willing it. Without positioning, his shaft slid home. Elizabeth shrieked and surged up against him. He seized her hips so he could draw, but he did not get far; her legs came up and locked around him, and she ground herself against him, crying out again.

It was enough. It was too much. His climax drained him and drained him again. He could feel her body pulsing around him. Bliss mingled with pain when he had no more to give. But by then Elizabeth was still also, only her lips touching his chin gently and then falling away.

Sidhe do not sleep, but a vast lassitude enwrapped Denoriel so that it was an enormous effort to lift himself off Elizabeth and slide to the side. It was true, he thought slowly—even his thoughts moving languidly—that mortals were not healthy for elven-kind. He had had Sidhe lovers and enjoyed them, but he had never been so wrenched, so burnt, so *consumed* by pleasure. Nothing would ever match his Elizabeth and when he lost her he would go through his long, long life aching for what he would never find again.

Chapter 30

After the months of tension and terror, the nights full of night-mares of execution, Elizabeth slept like one bludgeoned. She woke remarkably refreshed. Denno looked better too, the lines of worry smoothed from his face.

His first words, delivered smiling, were "It is Tuesday. Shall we go and meet the others at the Inn of Kindly Laughter?"

"Tuesday?" Elizabeth replied. "Oh, so it is, for we set out from London on Saturday. I hope Alana will come. It is so long since I have seen her."

"I think everyone will be there. I left messages that I hoped you would be Underhill today. What do you want to wear?"

"I will choose something from my wardrobe, I think," Elizabeth said, popping out of bed. Denoriel, stimulated by the sight of her naked body, made a grab for her. Laughing, she skipped away toward the door. "I would not want Lady Alana to feel that I do not appreciate the lovely gowns she prepared for me." She smiled impishly over her shoulder as she went out. "And you know how often she has warned me about your taste."

It was the best she could do to save him the power he would have expended to form a gown and clothe her. And when she opened the garderobe door she felt well-rewarded for her small sacrifice. The gowns were lovely. She chose silken undergarments from a small chest at the foot of the bed she almost never used and then chose a relatively simple creation in shades of green.

The gown was simple enough, but the long chain of emeralds set in gold, which she wound twice around her neck, the large pendant emerald she added to hang between the top and bottom of the long chain, would have been priceless in the mortal world. Elizabeth gave no thought to carrying them with her, knowing they would turn to dross as she passed through the Gate. She busied herself rooting through the jewel chest and came up with a tiara of emeralds she set into her hair, several rings, another long gold chain to tie around her waist, and bright buckles for her shoes. Here she could indulge her taste for jewelry, without having to pay for it or fearing the envy of the Court.

Elizabeth did not actually remember when Denno had given her the emeralds, but she thanked him for them when she went down to the parlor and found him there. He laughed. "Easy enough to make—" he broke off and sighed "—or used to be." Then he smiled. "I am glad you still had them. They look well with your hair."

"Thank you, but I am starving. Can we go?"

Miralys was at the foot of the steps as usual, but instead of taking them to the Llachar Lle Gate, to Elizabeth's surprise he carried them directly to the Bazaar of the Bizarre. How he did so was very strange even for Underhill, she thought, as Denno lifted her down from the saddle. She remembered mounting and looking across the white-starred moss toward the Gate. And then . . . no darkness, no falling, nothing at all except Miralys walking down the broad avenue to the market.

It was useless to ask Denno. He would only shake his head and admit that the Sidhe knew very little about the elvensteeds although they had been closely bound to them for as long as the Sidhe existed. And then they were at the door of the Inn of Kindly Laughter, as usual no more than a short walk from the Gate into the market—no matter by which Gate they entered—and Lady Alana was jumping to her feet and rushing to embrace her. It was a touching sign of affection, Sidhe being mostly unwilling to touch others.

"Elizabeth! Dear Elizabeth! I am so sorry not to have been with you when you needed me—"

Elizabeth shook her head. "It is just as well that you were not among my ladies, Lady Alana. You would not have been allowed to serve me anyway when I was imprisoned. All my ladies, even Kat, have been sent away and replaced with Mary's creatures. But since you were not with me at the time of Wyatt's rebellion, it is possible that when the Council's stupid suspicions about me have faded, you will be allowed to serve me again."

Aleniel sighed heavily and drew Elizabeth toward the table, where two more chairs had appeared. "Very gladly, if Ilar and I can lay our hands on this monster who is snatching mortals from Cymry. We know who he is now—well, Ilar and I caught a glimpse of him with a dear little child in his arms. Ilar could not reach him and dared not cast a levin bolt at him for fear of hurting the child. And he disappeared—Gated, where no Gate was."

"Where no Gate was?" Denoriel repeated, sitting down in the chair next to Harry's.

Harry was already on his feet and had seized Elizabeth in a tight hug and kissed her on the forehead. "We were all worried about you, love. I wanted to bring you here, but Denno said you would not be happy."

Elizabeth returned the hug and kiss, planting hers on Harry's cheek, but she passed his empty chair without speaking to him to hold out her hand to Rhoslyn. "Thank you," she said. "Thank you so much for all you have done for me. If not for you, I might not have survived."

"I did not really do so much," Rhoslyn said, taking Elizabeth's hand and smiling shyly. "I only made sure that Mary did not speak out in a fit of rage or despair. She might then have said what she would later, and always, regret. Although she fights the knowledge, she *does* know you are her sister and though she might well wish you would *drop* dead, she cannot make herself the instrument of that death. The chancellor and her most trusted advisor have both urged her strongly to be rid of you. But she cannot."

"Perhaps," Elizabeth said, "but I still feel that it is your effort that has kept me safe. And I know how hard it must be for you to work for Mary's heir. You are fond of her."

"Yes." Rhoslyn sighed. "But she is hurting Logres and the Bright Court, and my friends—" she looked around the table "—are all suffering for her fixation on this Spanish connection."

Harry had sat down again and he reached out and covered Rhoslyn's hand with his, but he looked up at Elizabeth. "England is small and not powerful. Its salvation is to play France against Spain, not to marry Spain and be drawn into her wars."

Rhoslyn sighed again. "I am sure you are right, Harry, but it is hard to blame Mary. Much is the result of the cruelty of her father and her contrary fixation on her mother. That caused her dependence on Emperor Charles. Her Council is so divided she knows not whom to trust and so she leans on the Imperial ambassador."

"I do understand," Elizabeth said, "and I want to assure you—here, Underhill, where there could be no purpose to any lie—that I had no part in the rebellion against my sister and never tried to hurt her. It would not serve my purpose."

"We all know that to conspire against Mary would damage your future reign," Denoriel said with a cynical twist to his lips; he loved Elizabeth but also understood how ruthless she could be. "Come here and sit down. You said you were hungry. We will never get the attention of that server if you do not sit down." He looked at his sister, across the table. "Now what were you saying about a Gate where none was? With the lack of power that is plaguing the Bright Court, random Gates are not easy or likely."

"Cymry is not so short of power as most of the Bright Court," Aleneil replied, "but the power did not come from Cymry."

"How can you know that?" Pasgen asked, always interested in any aspect of power.

Aleneil smiled. "The Sidhe of Cymry use very little magic; their mortals do most tasks for them for which we use magic. A spell is noticeable in Cymry and it is not overlaid with dozens of other spells, so it is easy to feel what kind of power created it. That was how Ilar and I discovered that this Sidhe who steals mortals is being aided and abetted by a Dark Sidhe. The Gate by which the mortal-stealer fled was built with Dark power."

"Did you touch that Gate yourself?" a soft, pleasant voice asked, eager but anxious.

Elizabeth did not recognize the Sidhe who had spoken, but she was sitting close to Pasgen so Elizabeth assumed it was the Hafwen she had heard Pasgen was working with. The she-Sidhe was quite beautiful . . . well, all Sidhe were beautiful . . . but Hafwen was soft and lovely, not brilliant as many Bright Sidhe were.

Most Bright Sidhe had hair that really looked as if it were metallic gold and glowing emerald eyes. Nor was Hafwen as pale as Aleneil, with her silver-gilt hair and almost blue eyes. Hafwen's hair was a little darker than gold, a little less bright, like warm honey; her eyes were a softer color too, not silvered or faded as the elder Sidhe were, but barely misted with translucent gray.

"For the briefest moment," Aleneil replied to Hafwen's question as to whether she had touched the Dark Gate. "I was closer than Ilar. I had felt the Gate first and gone toward it. The Sidhe who had the child was too large for me to stop, and like Ilar, I could not attack him because of the child, but I hoped to catch hold of the child. I thought perhaps I could tear it from his arms."

"Too bad you failed," a voice full of clicks and whirrs said.

Everyone at the table looked with considerable interest at the server who had arrived. Tonight it was a shiny metal creature— Elizabeth thought the metal was steel but had no idea steel could be worked in such an intricate fashion. Whatever it was had six double-jointed legs and a long, oval body with short wings, slightly raised around a broad, flat area on its back. The head was broad at the top, with huge many-faceted eyes, and narrowed drastically to a pair of slicing jaws with serrated edges but no teeth.

"Grasshopper!" Elizabeth said triumphantly when she had made a mental adjustment for the size.

"Cricket," the server said crossly. "No fair, you are human so you have seen them. No one else knew it was not my own idea."

"Oh, I beg your pardon," Elizabeth said. "I did not know the forms were supposed to be your invention. I have never recognized any of the others—even the barber pole, which you said came from the mortal world."

"Long after your time," the server said, but the voice, clicks and whirrs and all, sounded mollified. "So, what do you all want?"

When they had ordered and the creature clanked away, they all sat looking after it for a moment.

"What is it, really?" Hafwen asked.

"Only the Great Mother knows," Pasgen replied, "I have no idea." But he was grinning. "I suspect it would be a life's work to find out." Then his grin faded. "And I think I have a life's work, and a much less pleasant one, in hand already."

Rhoslyn bit her lip and Harry patted her hand, but it was Hafwen who looked at Aleneil and asked, "You are a FarSeer. Did you sense any evil in the Sidhe who stole mortals or the magic that made the Gate?"

"Evil?" Recalled to their interrupted conversation, Aleneil frowned. "The Sidhe? He was overflowing with pride and selfishness but not real evil. And it was Dark power that built the Gate, full of misery and pain, but no, not evil, just ugly and sad. Surely you do not mean that the Dark power is evil."

"No, she means evil, real evil," Pasgen said. "It seems as if Underhill has gone mad since Mary took the throne." He nodded toward Aleneil. "There is a Sidhe abducting mortals Underhill. That is mad. There is a whole world full of mortals of whom many would not be missed. And then Hafwen and I stumbled on real evil."

"It was the same as I felt in Alhambra that hurt me so much I fell unconscious," Hafwen said, flushing slightly over her weakness.

Harry, who had been looking at Rhoslyn, turned sharply toward Hafwen. "The evil you said was gone from Alhambra when you were last there?" His voice was a little too loud. "God help us! Is it loose Underhill?"

"I don't know," Pasgen said. "I know it *was* loose."

He went on to tell Harry of the tainted Chaos Land, the small domains that had been ravished and destroyed, and of the damage to Gnome Hold. In the midst of his tale, the server came back with the food and drink they had ordered, passing plates with its legs by some miracle of dexterity from the flat surface on its back. It did not speak, however, but hurried away, presumably to serve other patrons.

All ate while listening intently to Pasgen. Now and then when he paused to address his own meal, the others exclaimed with horror; however, none of the evil had touched the Bright domains, so much of what Pasgen said was new to them. Denoriel asked anxiously how they had lost track of the evil, after having followed it for so long.

Pasgen shrugged. "The gnomes told us there was this flash of light, which blinded them, and when they could see again, the Sidhe that spawned the black things which drained life force was gone. What was even stranger and more disturbing was that all trace of it was gone from the Gate and from the hold, nor was there any trace of what had created that flash of light."

"We have been seeking and listening for news, Pasgen and I," Hafwen put in, her face troubled, "but there has been no more damage done—at least not to any Unformed land we have visited or to any hold. *Something* removed that evil from Underhill." She hesitated and then asked, "Could Oberon have sensed it and caught it?"

Harry pushed his empty plate away and his lips twisted wryly. "Not without flaying the Bright Court alive for permitting such a thing to happen without telling him. He would have skinned me first, because I started the trouble by wanting to drive the evil out of Alhambra and El Dorado."

Aleneil shook her head. "I do not believe Oberon knows anything about the evil. Eirianell told me that he is not now Underhill, nor has he been for some time. He has been gone, she said, since the last Great Ball."

"Then who or what—" Harry began. He looked anxiously from Pasgen to Hafwen. "I didn't think," he began again, guiltily. "I suppose it *is* my fault, but we had it bound into the altar stone and surrounded by sigils of silver and iron. The elder Sidhe and I were working on a way to move the altar stone to the Void without letting it loose."

"Since Oberon was gone, you could not have gone to him anyway," Denoriel said, giving Harry a quick hug. Then, clearly to divert Harry from self-blame, he said to Aleneil, "What made you ask Eirianell about Oberon?"

"I didn't. That was only a bit of gossip she dropped. I had come to her because I could not see clearly in my scrying mirror who was seizing the mortals from Cymry. Eirianell laughed and said the only thing she has never been able to See clearly is where Oberon goes when he leaves Underhill."

"Thank the Great Mother for that!" Denoriel said, laughing. "The last thing we need is to see Oberon more clearly than we do. I am not sure I want to know where he goes." He rolled his eyes. "Just think what would happen if Titania discovered Eirianell could See him."

Aleneil laughed and shuddered at the same time, then clearly dismissing Oberon and Titania and their world-shaking clashes, she said, "More important to me, Eirianell *could* See through the magic the mortal-stealer used to disguise himself or that the Dark Sidhe used to disguise him. She told me the Sidhe was not from any elfhame with which we are familiar, that he was somewhat different from the Sidhe of the western realms. For one thing, he is fat."

"Fat? Eirianell said the Sidhe was *fat*?" Elizabeth dropped her knife and looked up at Denoriel. "Denno, the Sidhe that tried to seize me in Fur Hold was fat. Could it have been the same Sidhe?"

"I suppose," Denoriel said slowly. "But what if it was?"

"He wanted me," Elizabeth said, eyes bright as gold coins. "He wanted me enough to try to seize me again after I had Pushed him."

"Likely he wanted to murder you," Denoriel said acidly.

"Yes." Elizabeth laughed. "Particularly since his gaudy clothes were all besmattered with the urso's nuncheon." Then she sobered. "But that does not matter. What matters is that he will remember me, I think, and I can be bait for a trap for him."

"Bess!" Harry protested. "Have you not just come through enough danger?"

"No!" Denoriel's voice mingled with Harry's. "You idiot! He is likely working with or for Vidal, and Vidal does not wish you well."

Having waited patiently for her two protectors to finish with her eyes raised to heaven—or, at least, what she thought was the sky above Underhill—Elizabeth replied with ostentatious patience, "I did not plan to rush out to seek this mortal-snatching lunatic all alone or in any place where he might trap me. I assumed that you would come with me and guard me."

"And we will guard her too," Aleneil put in. "Me and Ilar and as many of those from Cymry as you desire." She turned to Denoriel eagerly. "Do not forbid her, Denoriel. Please. You have no idea how much pain this monster has caused, snatching away fathers and mothers and children, breaking families."

Elizabeth saw that Aleneil was deeply distressed and was rather surprised because Aleneil had spent so much time in the mortal world. Then she realized that Aleneil's time in the mortal world was spent with her ... and she had no family, not anymore.

Kat was dear to her and some of her ladies, but they were not family, not as her brother had been. She felt a pang of regret for the animosity Mary bore her—or, really, bore her mother. Elizabeth pushed that thought away and the knowledge that she was waiting for her sister to die. She thought about the Sidhe, who rarely had families either. No wonder those of Cymry were fascinated by the bonds of affection that held families together. Elizabeth sighed, thinking of Mary again and the daggers of hate that could develop in families too.

"And we never know where or at whom he will strike."

Aleneil's anxious voice broke Elizabeth's thought but before she could speak Denoriel said repressively, "Aleneil, have you forgotten that Elizabeth was snatched out of Cymry by Vidal himself. She is too important to be risked. She must come to the throne of Logres. Do you want the Bright Court diminished to nothing?"

"But if we knew this mortal-stealers's target—"

"No!"

"I don't think we should lay the trap in Cymry," Elizabeth said thoughtfully, ignoring Denoriel's explosive denial. "I am sorry to say that I suspect he must have . . . if not confederates at least informers in Cymry."

Aleneil cried out in protest, but Elizabeth shook her head at her and pointed out that Cymry was a well-run, happy elfhame but not heaven, and that disaffected persons existed everywhere.

"Mortals are well treated, but some must be dissatisfied. Perhaps they believe their lot would be better in the mortal world—poor fools. Perhaps they simply wished to be rid of an enemy. And likely there are Sidhe who are envious or spiteful. One or another might have been lured into talk and been offered the satisfaction of wants or a desired prize. And you know, having helped a criminal once, whoever did so is now in his power and can be forced to help again."

Everyone stopped eating to look at Elizabeth. Denoriel's face was grim, Harry's was sad. Aleneil looked very surprised, Pasgen mildly interested, and Rhoslyn rather relieved. This was not the wild child or the happy reveler they were accustomed to seeing. The face was still very young . . . but the eyes were old.

"My little girl is growing up," Harry said.

Elizabeth smiled at him, but she spoke to Aleneil. "It should be easy enough to spread word throughout Cymry that the red-haired mortal is visiting Underhill again." And then she turned to Denoriel, leaning against his shoulder and kissing his cheek. "My love, you know sooner or later that fat Sidhe would hear I was Underhill and would begin to hunt me."

"Then I will not bring you Underhill!"

Elizabeth laughed and shook her head at him. "You must let me come Underhill. That stupid gaoler Mary assigned to me will otherwise drive me mad. Can you imagine having no one but Bedingfield to talk to for however long Mary decides to keep me imprisoned in Woodstock?"

Denoriel groaned and dropped his head into his hands. Elizabeth kissed the tip of his ear which peeped above his fingers.

"I will be careful, beloved. I will wear my shields whenever we are out of your own rooms and I am sure Da will bring Mechain and Elidir to me or me to them. When we tell them what danger is involved, I would not be at all surprised if they knew some spells that would permit you to trace me . . ." Her voice faded.

"No!"

The roar came from both Harry and Denoriel. Aleneil and Rhoslyn jumped. Pasgen raised his eyebrows.

"No, what?" Pasgen asked, very surprised.

"She intends to let herself be abducted," Denoriel roared.

Everyone looked at her again.

"But it would be the easiest way to find out where he takes the mortals," Elizabeth said in a coaxing tone. "I will have my shields up at their strongest. You know they even stood up to Oberon's command . . . Well, it was not aimed at me, of course. I doubt the shields could have resisted a direct attack from Oberon, but I am sure this fat Sidhe cannot be so powerful. Remember, whatever he intended to launch at me—"

"Elizabeth, *no!*"

This time it was three voices. Aleneil had added her protest to that of Denoriel and Harry.

"No. No." Aleneil pleaded. "If anything should happen to you, I swear by the Mother I would die of guilt and grief. Please, Elizabeth, do not endanger yourself to that degree."

Elizabeth sighed. "I do not see that I would be that much in danger if I go with that fat fool—"

"I think that would be unwise," Pasgen said. His voice and expression were neutral. He was by no means devoted to Elizabeth as were the others, but he did not like the heavy flow of power that was going to the Dark Court and sometimes tainting the Unformed lands; he wanted Elizabeth to come to the throne. "There are places Underhill that are really secret and spell-warded so that perhaps your call spell would not reach anyone outside."

After a brief contemplation of Pasgen, Elizabeth sighed and nodded. "Very well. I suppose if we capture him you will be able to convince him to show you where he has taken his captives."

"Yes!"

Again it was three voices with varying degrees of anger and determination. Pasgen laughed and Rhoslyn said, "And if sweet persuasion does not work, I will just go into his mind and rip the answer out."

The server came to collect the mostly empty plates. Several of the party ordered sweets and dessert wine. The argument about trapping the mortal-stealer continued but mostly it was now concerned with practical matters such as bringing the news of Elizabeth's return Underhill to their prey in a way that would not make him suspicious and where to arrange the confrontation. One of the great markets seemed the best place as almost any number of guardians could be concealed in the crowds.

When the topic ran out, the party began to disperse. Aleneil said she was off to Cymry to start the rumor that Elizabeth was Underhill again and plan with Idres Gawr and Ilar how to protect her. Rhoslyn sighed and said she had better return to Whitehall since Mary rose early and she was on duty. Pasgen and Hafwen went off together. As they rose from their seats, Denoriel asked Elizabeth if she would like to have him look for a ball to attend.

"Not this time, love," she said, raising her face for a kiss. "I don't want you to need to twist time too much. And I think I would like to go back to Woodstock to be sure that all is well."

She yawned and cuddled to Denoriel's side as they passed out of the market gate and found Miralys within two steps. Nor did Elizabeth linger when they reached Llachar Lle, although Denoriel would have drawn her into his bedchamber. She laughed and shook her head at him and went into her own room to shed her Underhill finery and slip on her night rail. Then she stood for a moment contemplating the joy of being able to say to Denoriel, "And you will come for me this mortal night, will you not?"

Blanche was asleep in her own bed when Elizabeth and Denoriel Gated to Woodstock, so Elizabeth knew that no trouble had arisen. She kissed Denoriel silently and watched with a smile as the Gate closed behind him. Then she hurried to her bed, snuggled under the covers and lifted the sleep spell from her ladies. They went right on sleeping, and Elizabeth smiled as she closed her own eyes.

Most of the day was spent in unpacking and putting away the clothing Elizabeth had brought with her. She did not have much jewelry. Most of what she had was locked carefully away in Hatfield and Ashridge, but in the bottom of the one strongbox she had carried with her throughout her imprisonment was a mirror in a magnificent silver frame.

Elizabeth had not touched that mirror, except to move it from one strongbox to another so it would always be with her, since she had traded the winged kitten for it so many years ago. It was not a mirror she cared to look into for her face had grown harder and more strained, her eyes older, when she caught a glimpse as she moved the mirror. Now she took it out and laid it on the dressing table beside her. She let it lie face up, but turned slightly on her stool so she did not need to look into it.

Blanche came to bring her a handkerchief and glanced down. "Why there's that old mirror, Your Grace," she said. "Does it still have that funny twist in it?"

"Yes," Elizabeth answered, mouthing "thank you" at Blanche, who had provided an explanation for what her maids of honor would see. "I'd forgotten I had it, but there it was on the bottom of the box. She looked beyond Blanche and smiled at Elizabeth Marberry. "Do come and look, Elizabeth." And she held the mirror so that she could see her maid of honor's face.

What the mirror showed was not so terrible, only greed and worry and dissatisfaction.

Elizabeth Marberry snorted. "It certainly is not a very good mirror. Something . . . Mary, come here and look."

She gestured to Mary Dacre, who obligingly came over and peered into the mirror, which Elizabeth still held so she could see the reflection. Dacre's was even less threatening. It was simply dull and bored. Whatever expectations she had when she was ordered into Elizabeth's service had not been fulfilled, Elizabeth guessed.

Marberry frowned slightly. "It doesn't seem to have any imperfection. I mean my face is clear, not too long or too wide, but somehow, it doesn't look like me . . . exactly. It does and it doesn't." She turned her head toward the door to the parlor and called, "Susanna, come here."

Susanna Norton was the eldest of the ladies sent by Mary to serve Elizabeth. She glanced only briefly into the mirror when Elizabeth held it toward her, but long enough for Elizabeth to see that here was the danger from her women attendants. Susanna's face showed real animosity. *If she could find a way to do me harm,* Elizabeth thought, *she will. Maybe Da will know why. He might have known her when he was at Court.* Norton was also a very passionate Catholic, Elizabeth remembered. Likely, like Mary, she felt Elizabeth's conversion insincere.

Although she gave no sign, Elizabeth sighed inwardly. Norton would be actively watching her for any sign of resistance to the Catholic rite. No doubt she would report any inattention to Mass, any flicker of expression that implied disapproval of the full Catholic rite. Norton, Elizabeth thought, would not hesitate to lie to please the queen, if she could get away with it. Elizabeth resolved never to be alone with her if she could avoid it.

As if absently, Elizabeth carried the mirror downstairs. No breakfast was set in the parlor, nor was Bedingfield waiting to escort her to the ruinous manor to eat. The door to the inner room was open, however. Elizabeth walked over to see if more furniture had been obtained—and stopped dead.

There was more furniture. It was in this room that a table had been set up for breakfast.

Bedingfield was standing behind a short bench set at the foot of the table. He turned when he heard Elizabeth coming, an expression that mingled stubbornness and apprehension on his face. Elizabeth stood and stared. She understood he had arranged the inner room as a dining parlor to make clear to her that she would not be receiving any visitors. So Bedingfield was not quite as stupid as his face looked.

Furnishing a dining parlor to make a point without words was a clever ploy, but at this moment Elizabeth had a more important question to be answered. Was Bedingfield an honest if dull-witted gaoler or a clever assassin?

Elizabeth looked at the table, looked at Bedingfield, raised a hand as if to gesture as she expostulated—and then looked with pretended surprise at the mirror in her hand.

"Oh," she said, and laughed. "My mind is truly elsewhere this morning. Just look at what I have carried down from my bed-chamber without thinking."

Bedingfield had turned fully to face her and bowed. Elizabeth thrust the mirror at him, again angled so it showed his face without catching hers. He looked into it briefly. Elizabeth looked into it. Bedingfield turned his head toward Elizabeth, but only to look at her while he spoke. He was not making an attempt to avoid the image in the mirror and Elizabeth had a long look at his face.

She started to smile and then bit her lip, recalling that she was supposed to be angry about being deprived of a private receiving room. Truly, however, she knew there would be no one to receive and she was so relieved at what the mirror showed that she did not really feel like quarreling with her warden just now.

Bedingfield's image in the mirror was plainly and simply Bedingfield. Like Blanche's image, nothing at all had changed. What showed in the mirror was exactly what Elizabeth saw when she looked at him directly: dull stubbornness, a transparent honesty, kindliness but overlaid with stern dedication. Elizabeth sighed gently with relief. Bedingfield would be no part of any attempt to assassinate her. He would both keep her confined and keep her safe with equal dedication.

"There is something very strange about that mirror," Elizabeth Marberry said before either Elizabeth or Bedingfield could speak. "No one looks exactly right, and yet the image is bright and the glass does not seem to be uneven or ill made."

Bedingfield looked slightly relieved when Marberry opened a neutral topic of conversation. He took the mirror from Elizabeth's hand with a slight bow, raised brows for permission, and stared into it intently. Elizabeth got another long look at what the mirror portrayed.

"There does not seem to be anything wrong with it, Mistress Marberry," he said, bowing slightly again as he handed the mirror back to Elizabeth.

"It is very old. Perhaps the glass has somehow been distorted over the years, and that only shows in certain light," Elizabeth said, walking to the head of the table where her chair was placed.

She laid the mirror face down on the table beside her place. Dunstan appeared suddenly from some shadowed recess of the room and pulled the chair out. As she seated herself, and Dunstan pushed the chair to the table, Elizabeth gestured for her companions to sit also.

"And now, Sir Henry," she said, staring down the length of the table at him, "how is it that this chamber, which I thought would be suitable for private meetings, is fitted out as a dining parlor?"

"Because there is nowhere else to eat," Bedingfield said, "unless you wish to walk to the manor every day through good weather or ill. And let me remind you, Your Grace, that my orders from the queen are that you have no visitors and certainly no private meetings."

Chapter 31

A lbertus had been almost completely at ease when he brought
Aurilia the news that Elizabeth had been sent to the Tower.
Almost at ease because the prince of the Dark Court and his
consort were never predictable. However, ever since Mary had
decided on the Spanish marriage, dissatisfaction and distrust had
sent more and more power to the Unseleighe, and Vidal and
Aurilia had been mostly very good tempered. Albertus had never
mentioned that he was sure Mary would never order Elizabeth
executed; had he done so, he was afraid that Vidal would somehow arrange Elizabeth's "accidental" death and Albertus was still
determined to save her to spite his master.

Now Albertus was bringing what Vidal would consider very bad
news and he was tense with fear. Elizabeth was not to be executed;
she was to be released to house arrest. He tried to concentrate
on that fear, on the sense of disappointment for being unable to
please his master. He tried to bury deep, very deep, his desire to
see Elizabeth come to rule.

Actually Albertus rather liked Queen Mary; she was a gentle soul,
but her dithering about everything except the one thing she should
abandon irritated him. And being at Court for the first few months of
Mary's reign had allowed him to meet Elizabeth, who suffered from
headaches. Like so many others and rather against his will because
the feeling was dangerous to him, Albertus had been charmed.

He confessed Elizabeth's emancipation to Aurilia, on his knees, filling his thoughts with helplessness and frustration at failure. Aurilia shrugged.

"It is not your failure, Albertus," she said lazily, looking into a mirror. "I do not blame you. It is Vidal's creatures that are at fault."

She was more beautiful than ever, Albertus thought; she glowed with power. In the past, from time to time, he had been aware that there were scars on her forehead and her complexion was somewhat raddled and realized that the spells that disguised those imperfections were weak. Now no one, no matter how familiar with the truth, would have been able to find any hint of those blemishes.

"I did what I could, my lady. When the queen complained to me of indigestion or headache, I told her that if she rid herself of her anxiety about Lady Elizabeth, those symptoms would soon disappear."

What Albertus said was perfectly true. That, indeed, was the advice he had given Mary. What he carefully kept in his mind was that if Elizabeth were dead, Mary's doubts would be over; he did not dare think that he had given what subtle hints he could that sending Elizabeth away would be equally effective.

"A doctor is not a great mover or shaker," Aurilia agreed with mild contempt. "You have prepared more of the headache potion?"

"Indeed I have, my lady, and your servant—the one who heals any physical hurt—has the large flasks. She can refill your bottles whenever necessary."

"And you are keeping Queen Mary in good health?"

"Yes, my lady, as good as possible. She is only mortal and not young. But she should live many years yet."

"As many as possible. She is a great asset to the Dark Court."

As she spoke, Aurilia gestured at Albertus. He felt himself wrapped in something, although there was nothing he could see. Reflexively, his body jerked and he thrust out his arms to push away the invisible blanket.

"Nothing to fear," Aurilia said with a trill of laughter. "I've merely raised a shield around you so that if Vidal is annoyed by your news he will not blast you to nothing before he stops to think."

Albertus should have been grateful. In a way he was grateful but he was also annoyed. Aurilia could have told him she was going to shield him and saved him the spurt of fear that still had his heart pounding. He had thought she was going to smother him; he had seen her reduce several servants to unconsciousness . . . and kill one.

However, the precaution had not been necessary. Vidal, who looked wonderful—sleek and polished, his dark hair shining and his eyes showing a spark instead of looking like unpolished black stones—flung no spells at him. When Albertus knelt and delivered his news, Vidal only stared into the distance with pursed lips.

"Who is interfering with my orders?" he asked; his voice was strong but not roaring.

"My lord, no one that I can tell," Albertus faltered. "The common gossip is that the queen only really listens to the Imperial ambassador and he is known to have advised her again and again to have Lady Elizabeth executed. And I, myself, heard the chancellor, Bishop Gardiner, say that Lady Elizabeth was guilty of treason even if it could not be proven in a court of law and that the queen should order her death. Nor have I heard any rumor about any strong support for the queen's sister . . . but you know I cannot sense spells or those from Underhill."

"Do you know all of Mary's women?"

"Well," Albertus said hesitantly, not knowing where this question was leading, "I know their names and sometimes how they won their places, but I am only a common physician and they are noble ladies . . ."

"One among them, her name is Rhoslyn . . . No, her name as the queen's lady is Rosamund Scott—" Vidal hesitated and then nodded and continued, "Ah. I see you know Rhoslyn."

"Yes, my lord. She is a most trusted lady and often brings messages from the queen."

Vidal smiled slightly. "Good. If she asks your help for any reason, be sure to do anything you can to assist her." He paused, thought. "So you say Elizabeth has been set free."

"Not free, my lord. She has been sent deep into the country under the control of a devoted servant of the queen. It is a kind of imprisonment, but far from London where she is, in the queen's opinion, too popular."

"Is the place secret?"

"It was supposed to be, I think, but somehow word was sent out from the Tower about Lady Elizabeth's release, and all of London exploded in celebration of their favorite's freedom. And I mean exploded. The Steelyard fired all its guns in salute as Lady Elizabeth's barge went by. Bankside was lined with people, waving and cheering. And news came back to the queen that Lady Elizabeth had been greeted and cheered all along her route."

"You seem to be enjoying that," Vidal snarled.

Albertus shrank in on himself. "I beg your pardon, my lord. I was just remembering all the excitement in the city when it was known that Lady Elizabeth had been released. But because she was hailed all along her route, it is known now where Lady Elizabeth was sent. It was to an old, ruined manor in Oxfordshire. Woodstock."

Vidal brightened. "A ruined manor, you say."

"That is what I heard it called, my lord. I was never there myself. Never in Oxfordshire at all. I studied at Cambridge."

"Hmmm." Vidal frowned, but it was in thought; actually he looked pleased and interested. With the plentitude of power available, he had lost much of his irritability. "I think this is work for your mortal servant."

"My mortal servant?" Albertus repeated. "But my lord—"

"He who gathered a troop to help Mary escape her pursuers."

"Ah, Francis Howard. Yes, my lord, but . . . but . . ."

But Albertus had dismissed Howard as soon as Mary was firmly in power and kept the last payment that was supposed to ensure Howard's regular attendance at a meeting place. Albertus did not dare say that. He cast a frightened glance at Aurilia who might have looked into his mind and seen the truth, but she had lost interest in what Vidal was planning and was frowning critically at a grouping of chairs under a black and gold hanging across the room.

"But?" Vidal snapped.

"But I have not used him in so long, my lord. I am not sure he will still be coming to the place where I used to meet him."

Vidal just looked down at Albertus as if he had gibbered like an ape. His lip lifted in a sneer. "Then you will find him. Tell Howard to gather his men and test the defenses of Woodstock. If he needs more men he should hire them. He is to seize Elizabeth. You will then bring her here . . . alive or dead."

Albertus's mouth opened to protest. Vidal waved his hand, and Albertus crashed to the floor of the bedchamber he used in Otstargi's house. He sat up, cursing and rubbing the places that had been bruised.

Bedingfield won the contest over whether the inner chamber was to be a dining parlor or a receiving room. Privately Elizabeth knew that there was no other place for a dining hall so unless she wanted the servants to need to set up a table and seats for each meal, she would need to accept Bedingfield's arrangement. Moreover, it was highly unlikely she would be allowed to receive visitors; she would not need a private receiving room. Still, she picked at him and whined at him for two days before she conceded. It was the first of endless clashes of will.

According the Mary's instructions, Elizabeth was to be allowed to walk in the upper and nether gardens. After a few days Elizabeth complained that was not sufficient for proper exercise; she demanded to be allowed to walk in the orchard also. Bedingfield, who adhered strictly to the letter of his instruction, insisted on the gardens only; Elizabeth nagged unmercifully; Bedingfield wrote to the Council for permission. Elizabeth won that one; in Bedingfield's company she was to be allowed to walk in the orchard.

After a month, Elizabeth asked to be allowed to write to the queen. Bedingfield said he had no order that permitted her to write to anyone. Elizabeth said bitterly that even the most common criminal in Newgate prison was allowed to write to the queen. Bedingfield consulted the Council, his letter carrying Elizabeth's bitter words. The Council consulted each other; Elizabeth was allowed to write. It did no good. Mary was angry and said she wanted no more "colorable" letters, but the Council was reminded, as the arrival of Philip of Spain drew closer and closer, that the "mere English" heir to the throne was alive and kicking.

By Mary's order, Elizabeth was to be allowed any books within reason. Within weeks, Elizabeth had been through every book available. John Fortesque, who was Thomas Parry's stepson and a student at Oxford, promptly sent three books. There was a cover letter for each, which made Bedingfield very suspicious. He sent the books to the Council. They found one of the cover letters suspicious, but Fortesque, wide-eyed and bland-faced, explained the words. Elizabeth got her books.

Next she asked for an English Bible. Bedingfield felt that was an heretical article. Without prodding he appealed to the Council to decide whether he could supply what she asked for. Bedingfield won that one.

When he could not convince Mary to execute her sister and was told that Elizabeth would be released from the Tower and held in a royal manor, Renard had made a new clever plan to which Mary tentatively agreed. He proposed when Elizabeth had been secluded and forgotten, she would be quietly sent abroad to Brussels, to the Court of the emperor's sister, where she could be married to some good Catholic nonentity and forever forgotten.

Only Elizabeth's triumphant progress to Woodstock and her constant petitions to the Council—which somehow often were known throughout the Court despite the queen's displeasure at any mention of her sister—precluded any chance of forgetting her. Between the complaints of her friends that she was too straitly constrained and the protests of the Marians on the Council that she had never confessed her crimes and should be tried and executed, Elizabeth was frequently a subject of discussion and certainly present in the thoughts of the Court.

To Mary's even greater displeasure Elizabeth agreed completely with the suggestion of a trial. When she was accused by some member of the Council of treason, she herself roundly demanded to be brought to London and tried. She was innocent, she declared in a ringing voice, and a jury would surely proclaim her so.

No one would take the challenge. The Marian faction was too aware that English juries had declared several known leaders of the late rebellion innocent of any crime, and those who secretly supported Elizabeth felt it would be too dangerous; juries had been known to be rigged. Nonetheless word of Elizabeth's willingness to be tried spread and some who had doubted her now felt she was innocent.

And so it went as the weeks passed. Bedingfield won many of the contests, but not until Elizabeth had forced him to write to the Council for instructions. Elizabeth might be held, theoretically without the ability to communicate with anyone, in a decaying manor in Oxfordshire, but few in the government had any chance to forget her.

Besides, as June passed into July the preoccupation of the Court turned away from the past rebellion toward future problems. At last Philip was coming to claim his bride. Compared to their concern with reaction of the public to the arrival of the Spanish prince, Elizabeth was a distant complication they could deal with in the future . . . or possibly Philip would deal with her and they would not bear the blame.

As the date of Philip's arrival neared, Elizabeth began to hope she would be summoned to Court to meet Philip. Before she could begin to urge Bedingfield to allow her to write to the Council on that subject, she was dissuaded from even mentioning the idea. In the Inn of Kindly Laughter one Tuesday, Harry and Rhoslyn both cried out in protest at such a meeting.

Elizabeth had been Underhill five nights out of seven during her so-called captivity at Woodstock. There was far less danger of discovery than there had been even in her own manors at Hatfield or Ashridge. Bedingfield never intruded on her after she was abed, as Kat had sometimes done, and Mary's spies had put themselves all together into her power by begging to sleep in her chamber. That permitted the use of one sleep spell to hold them all.

On two different nights each week, Elizabeth slept in her own bed and did not bespell the women. That permitted them to wake naturally during the night and see her blamelessly asleep. It also gave Denoriel some rest—not so much from lovemaking as from the use of power in taking her through the Gate and twisting time to bring her back before dawn. Elizabeth was worried about the lack of power in the Bright Court, but there was nothing she could do to help them . . . except manage to stay alive until she inherited the throne from Mary.

As they came through the Gate from Blanche's chamber to Logres, Elizabeth remembered her second night of freedom, when she was delightedly assuring Denoriel there was no danger Mary's spies would discover her absence.

"They all begged to sleep in my room, so I bespelled them all together."

"But why do they wish to sleep in your chamber?" Denoriel asked as he lifted her to Miralys's saddle.

"They think they are foiling some plan I had to escape from Woodstock. Do not ask me why they think I would want to escape. Where would I go? What would I do? Lead another rebellion or flee to France to lead a French invasion?" Scorn dripped from her words. "Fools. Even were I so stupid as to involve myself in rebellion at all, it is far too soon after the last debacle."

"A successful rebellion that set you on the throne could not come too soon for the Bright Court," Denoriel said, sighing as he dismounted at the wide portico of Llachar Lle and lifted her down.

Elizabeth reached up to touch his face, aware again that he had not donned his "young" appearance. "Denno," she said, "is it too hard for you to come for me every night? Does it take too much power to open the Gate and bring me through? Perhaps—"

"No, beloved, no," Denoriel said, crushing her against him. "There is little power involved in opening a Gate already built. It is just . . . We are all uneasy as well as starved for power. Titania is also gone so far as we can determine."

"Where?" Elizabeth had whispered.

Denoriel shook his head, and released her so that they could go inside. Elizabeth looked back over her shoulder, but Miralys had already disappeared. The elvensteed had looked and felt just as solid as usual, but where elvensteeds got their power was a total mystery to the Sidhe.

Elizabeth's eyes widened as Denoriel warned her to stay close to him if they went to the market, not for fear of the mortal-stealing Sidhe, but of others of the Dark Court. The Bright Court had new problems connected to the lack of power. With the increasing strength of the Dark Court and the absence of Oberon and Titania, there had been sly invasions of Bright domains, a few actual armed clashes.

Fortunately there were few Dark Sidhe and the knights of the Bright Court were far superior to any of the lesser creatures of the Dark, but there was less visiting and fewer parties and balls. The Bright Court was no longer so carefree and careless in its use of power.

Each time she came Elizabeth looked anxiously at the magical palace before they passed through the human-sized portal near the great brass gates. She could see no change in Llachar Lle, and the chill of the recognition spell seemed the same as usual. Nor had the illusion that made Denoriel's door look like an opening into an open lawn with a manor house in the distance faded. It was perhaps flatter, not as vibrant, and there had been no change in it since Mary had come to the throne. Before that, Denoriel had added small details because he knew finding them amused Elizabeth.

Denoriel noticed her anxiety and laughed at her. The Bright Court had seen hard times before, he assured her. Not in his life-time, that was true, but in the past Oberon and Titania had left the Sidhe to look after themselves. There had been real pitched battles between Dark Court and Bright and the Dark had always been beaten back. It was some comfort to hear that, but Elizabeth still felt as if *she* should be doing something.

Elizabeth had spent Monday night at Woodstock; tonight she would go Underhill. It was Tuesday, and although Denoriel put her up on Miralys they did not go to Llachar Lle. Without direc-tion Miralys brought them to the great signposts just outside of the overhead, which to Elizabeth read Bazaar of the Bizarre. She did not smile as she passed the first warning.

NO SPELLS, NO DRAWN WEAPONS, NO VIOLENCE on one line and below that ON PAIN OF PERMANENT REMOVAL.

That was no joke and no false warning. Elizabeth knew of cases of permanent removal; it was not only permanent but no one, not even the most highly skilled FarSeers, had ever discovered to where the perpetrators had been *REMOVED*.

The second sign, which Elizabeth read as CAVEAT EMPTOR but she knew appeared in Elven to Denoriel and any other language any who entered the market could read, did make her smile. It was as serious as the threat of *REMOVAL*, but the consequences, if the buyer was not sufficiently aware, were usually less drastic. It was said of the Bazaar of the Bizarre that everyone who came could find their heart's desire there but the cost to obtain it ensured utter disaster. Elizabeth could only be thankful that the crown of England was not on offer.

Harry and Rhoslyn were already seated at the usual table in the Inn of Kindly Laughter talking to Aleneil and, somewhat to Elizabeth's surprise, Ilar. Pasgen and Hafwen were missing. Eliza-beth rushed to embrace Aleneil.

"I am so glad to see you," she said. "I miss my Lady Alana so much, even though, buried as I am in the depths of Oxfordshire, fine clothing is not necessary." She sighed. "If my ladies had a thought or two devoted to anything other than the correct rite with which to worship God perhaps I would miss you less." Two more chairs had appeared at the round table. Denoriel sat down next to Harry. "But," Elizabeth continued as she slid into the chair next to him, "I have had an idea about how to get back to Court. When Prince Philip comes, I will beg to meet him."

"No!" Harry exclaimed.

"No. No." Rhoslyn cried, reaching toward Elizabeth. "Oh, Lady Elizabeth you must not."

Elizabeth blinked, then looked from one to the other. "But surely enough time has passed. All the prisoners from Wyatt's forces have been released, even his chief henchmen—"

"It is nothing to do with the rebellion," Rhoslyn said earnestly, "but if Prince Philip should look on you with real favor, Mary would swiftly find a reason to have you dead. I swear, I think she would kill you with her own hands if necessary."

"Elizabeth," Aleneil said, "remember how jealous she was when you were at Court together and all the young men found you so attractive. That was when she began to give Lady Margaret Douglas and the duchess of Suffolk precedence over you."

"The queen has convinced herself that she is madly in love with Prince Philip," Rhoslyn said. "She goes ten times a day to look at his portrait. That some callow young men had a preference for you she could force herself to overlook; that Prince Philip should find you more to his taste than she would be a disaster."

"And whatever lies she tells herself," Harry put in, "she has good reason to fear that Philip is not overjoyed about the marriage. He has not written once to her in all the months of negotiations over the contract. He wrote to Renard, saying he was pleased by the proposal; he wrote to the Council, saying he was happy to accept the terms of the agreement; but not one word did he write to Mary herself."

Elizabeth drew herself up with offended pride. Elizabeth did not like Mary, but an offense to her sister was an offense to Elizabeth on family terms.

"You mean," she said in a voice that could have cooled the whole room, "that that Spanish codswollop still has not addressed my sister—"

"No, no," Harry said hastily. "It was not meant as any personal insult. Philip has made himself hated in every country he has visited not by personal cruelty but by his utter ineptness in dealing with people. He wrote to Renard and the Council because there was business he had to do; he had to agree or disagree before they could move further in their negotiations. Since Mary was not involved, he did not feel it necessary to address her."

"Not address his prospective bride?" Elizabeth's eyes were wide with disbelief. "You mean my sister is marrying an idiot?"

"Not at all," Harry said. "Do not make that mistake. He is not at all perceptive about what people feel, but he is very clever about politics and how greed will buy compliance even from those who dislike him. I think it very unwise for you to meet him before everyone else has taken his measure . . . and offended him in some way. I will get information on what he likes and does not like and on whom he likes and dislikes. When you finally get to meet him, you will charm him so completely—and without any looks or words to which Mary could object—that he will protect you from her."

Elizabeth sighed with resignation and remarked a little bitterly that if Rhoslyn and Da felt it needful, she would remain buried at Woodstock. Just then the kitsune server came to take their orders. He was much less interesting than the usual server, but less distracting too when there were serious matters to discus.

Philip's arrival out of the way, Aleneil and Ilar reported while the meal arrived and they ate, that the hunt for the mortal-stealer had stalled. He had not managed to snatch anyone else, but that was because the mortals were being virtually imprisoned by their owners. No one was happy with the arrangement.

Elizabeth promptly offered herself again as bait. Ilar smiled at her but shook his head. "As you know, my lady, Prince Idres Gawr is most grateful for your offer to help. However he feels as your half-brother and guardian do that you are too precious to the Sidhe as a whole to risk for the good of ordinary mortals, no matter how much beloved. In fact, I asked Aleneil to bring me specially to ask you to take extra care."

Denoriel and Harry both came sharply erect and pushed away the remains of their meals.

Ilar sighed. "What you said to Aleneil about Sidhe not being perfect is alas too true. We did our best to keep knowledge of your return Underhill a secret, but it is all over Cymry. And we have kept our mortals safe from him for several weeks." His voice shook slightly when he spoke again. "I fear it may be time that he must have another."

"I will wear my shields," Elizabeth said calmly. "They are very good shields. I do not believe anything he can launch against me could penetrate them. Then too, I have some defenses of my own, and Denno will be with me."

"Not in the market Elizabeth," Denno said. "The shields are fine, but no spells. Remember what the market does to spell-casters."

"Yes," Harry said and then looked at Denoriel. "And for heaven's sake, do not draw your weapon."

Denoriel grinned at Harry, but before he could speak, Ilar put in anxiously, "No, please. I mean even if you are not in the market, please do not kill the monster. If he has not . . ." He hesitated and when he spoke again his voice trembled. "If he has not used our people, we must be able to question him as to where they are hidden."

Elizabeth nodded sympathetically. "I will only use Stickfoot or *Bod oer geulo* which will freeze him. Then Denno will be able to secure him and I will release the spell. No harm should be done him and you may have him to question. But what of the Dark Sidhe who built the Gate for him? Is there no way you could trap him?"

Rhoslyn had been looking at Harry, but she turned her head suddenly and asked, "Have you asked Pasgen to examine the Gate? He can read things in Gates that no one else can find."

"I would," Ilar sighed, "if we knew when or where a Gate would appear."

"Of course," Rhoslyn said, blushing slightly. "How foolish of me. Like my mistress, my mind seems to be fixed on one subject. But for another reason. When Mary is married, I will ask for a long leave. I have been almost constantly in the mortal world for near two mortal years. I need to *live* Underhill for a time."

"Speaking of living Underhill," Harry said, "Don't you need a domain, Rhoslyn?"

"Yes, but with the power so thin in the Bright domains . . ." She hesitated, blushed again, and went on. "I . . . really it makes me sick to think of using Dark power. I can live in the empty house if I must, or Pasgen will guest me in Gorphwys Fwydd." She sighed slightly. "But it is all right angles and black and white."

Harry had been chewing his lower lip gently while she spoke. Now he smiled and said, "Maybe you will not need to be a guest. Gaenor told me something interesting—and Pasgen was involved too, so he may be able to tell you more. Do you remember the Unformed land where the mist seemed almost intelligent?"

"You mean the place that made the lion and the winged kitten for me and the two dolls, and hid me from Vidal?" Elizabeth asked eagerly. "You promised not to tell Oberon about it. Remember we thought the baby should be allowed to grow."

Harry nodded. "I do remember, and it has not made anything dangerous or threatening, but it made a house."

"A house?" Almost everyone echoed at once.

"Gaenor was afraid that the house was an invitation to be swallowed up or something, but Pasgen went into it."

Rhoslyn gasped. Harry shook his head at her.

"It didn't do him any harm at all," Harry continued, "but the house was ill made, empty on the inside and crude and sagging."

"It lacked power?" Rhoslyn asked.

"No, at least Gaenor said nothing about power. She thinks the mist doesn't know how to make a proper house. It . . ." Now Harry hesitated as if he was not sure whether to go on or not, but finally he said, "It asked Pasgen for Elizabeth."

"No," Denoriel said.

"How?" Elizabeth asked, eyes suddenly bright gold.

"Gaenor said Pasgen didn't know how, he just had a mental image of Elizabeth and knew the mist wanted her."

Elizabeth stood up. Denoriel caught her hand; she squeezed his in response, but she was grinning as she looked at Rhoslyn. "Come, Rhoslyn, let us go now. I cannot spend enough time Underhill to teach the mist anything—at least anything more complicated than a kitten, but you are a maker. If you think at it, likely it will prefer you to me."

Rhoslyn stared at Elizabeth. For a moment she was suspicious of what she thought of as generosity. Then she nearly laughed aloud. *Elizabeth was mortal, not Sidhe. She was not being generous because she wanted no domain of her own . . . she would have all Logres when she was queen. For her, the Unformed land had been an idle amusement or a place of refuge. It was safe to trust her. She did not want to make that Unformed land her own.*

"Oh, imagine making in a place where the mist cooperated instead of fighting me," she sighed and started to get up.

Harry seized her arm. "Rhoslyn!" he exclaimed. "Do not encourage that mad child of mine."

"Can we not just *look* at the Unformed land and see what the mist has done?" Rhoslyn asked Harry. "I am sure I can control it. I have subdued quite inimical Chaos Lands, and you say no one has ever been hurt in this one."

"I didn't say that at all," Harry protested. "It wrapped Vidal up in ... well, in something, and kept him prisoner for years."

"Yes, but Vidal had killed the red-haired doll," Elizabeth pointed out. "It never hurt anyone—actually it didn't even hurt Vidal—and it let Pasgen kill the lion instead of letting the lion hurt him." She looked at Denoriel. "Please, Denno," she pleaded. "We can fetch Gaenor before we go and Pasgen too, if Rhoslyn knows where to reach him."

To Denoriel, who had been watching Elizabeth while Ilar spoke and suspected that she was planning to try to play bait for the mortal-stealer, the responsive mist seemed a lesser danger. Unlike the Sidhe themselves, Elizabeth was not content to play games, play at love, and go from one ball to another. She had been coming Underhill for two months. She needed more challenging occupation.

Moreover Elizabeth had been in the mist of that Unformed land alone several times and it had never harmed her; indeed it seemed as if it tried to help. Denoriel did not completely trust Rhoslyn, but he was reasonably sure that she would do nothing treacherous while Harry was there. And Gaenor knew that mist. Denoriel sighed, smiled, and stood up.

"Very well," he said. "Let us collect Gaenor and Pasgen if we can find him, and look at that Unformed land."

Chapter 32

To his mingled surprise, disappointment, and relief, Albertus in the guise of John Smith found Frances Howard at the second ale-house he visited. It was a darker, smokier place than their usual meeting place. The ale was weaker and sourer, the rough table stained and slopped with spilled drink, and the bench he sat on edged with splinters. Albertus was disappointed because he did not really want to instruct the man to abduct Elizabeth from Woodstock and bring her to Vidal, dead or alive. On the other hand, it was a relief to be able to obey Vidal promptly.

Another surprise came when Howard did not eagerly snatch up the purse Albertus offered with his instructions. Considering the poor quality of the ale-house, Vidal had assumed that Howard was short of money and would jump at a well-paid task.

Instead, Howard said "I am not thrilled with the queen's desire to make a Spanish marriage nor with her outspoken pride in her Spanish heritage. I am beginning to wonder if the "mere English" Elizabeth would not be a better queen, despite being of the reformist persuasion. And I do not like that "alive or dead" provision of bringing her to you," Howard added, remembering the sweetness of Elizabeth's smile and her willingness to name him "cousin" the one time he had met her. "I would not be the cause of the death of a daughter of Great Harry."

"You do not even know if you can get to her," Albertus said, actually well pleased although he managed an angry frown. "So you can leave that worry for the future. Sir Henry Bedingfield took a hundred men with him. First find out whether an attack on the manor is possible. If it will mean hiring an army, I must go to my principal and discover what he wishes to do."

Howard laughed without humor. "You need not bother asking your master. I would not hire enough men to attack Bedingfield's force. I tell you that right now. Do you think I wish to find parts of myself on gibbets all over London?"

The purse still lay on the table between them. Albertus stared at it. Would Aurilia or Vidal know if he kept it? He shuddered and pushed the purse toward Howard. "Take it and find out just what the situation at Woodstock is. Discover whether the guards can be bribed, how many entrances there are. Exactly where Lady Elizabeth is lodged and how many attendants are with her. When I have that information, I will be able to tell my principal and he can decide whether he wants to go forward or not."

Howard picked up the purse and weighed it in his hand. He and his men had fought Wyatt's force at the Temple Bar. They had got nothing for their effort; the old duke had been disgraced when his force was routed. Howard himself had no more hope of appointment to some office in the queen's government, and three men were dead, a dozen others still recovering from their wounds.

Even the open rebellion had not proved to Queen Mary how unpopular her choice of husband was. Howard had hoped she would try to propitiate the people and remain unmarried—specially as she was likely too old to bear a child. But he had heard the rumors that she was acting like a lovesick girl, staring at Spanish Philip's portrait and blushing when the marriage was mentioned by her courtiers. English merchants were suffering while Spanish goods and Spanish people were preferred.

After a moment he nodded curtly and tucked the purse away in his doublet. He would take two or three men and go himself to see what was to be seen in Woodstock.

A week later, Howard was drinking at the Bull in the town where Thomas Parry, Lady Elizabeth's controller, was living. No secret at all was made about the conditions of Elizabeth's house arrest. She was allowed no visitors at all. Bedingfield was adamant on that, and the armed force guarding the gatehouse in which she lived was alert and well-trained. Howard himself spoke to the captain and determined attack would be useless.

Abduction remained a possibility. Elizabeth might not resist as it was also no secret that she was not happy with her imprisonment and repeatedly complained to the Council. How to reach her and get her agreement or arrange for her to be taken was the basic problem.

The three men and three women allowed to serve Elizabeth could not be corrupted and used for Howard's purpose. The men could be reached since they were not restricted to the gatehouse and actually came out to the Bull often because Parry arranged for the household expenses. However, they were all absolutely devoted to their mistress and could be neither bribed nor threatened. Howard lost one of his men who made the mistake of trying to bribe and threaten Sir Edward Paulet. He was found dead about midway between The Bull and Woodstock manor. A second man was severely beaten when he approached the major domo, who was enthusiastically supported by Lady Elizabeth's two grooms.

The women, who might have been glad to help because, Howard learned, they were really Mary's servants, were unapproachable. They were never out of the gatehouse except in the company of Elizabeth and Bedingfield. They walked in the gardens, Howard learned, and in the orchard—but only with a strong escort.

However, information about Elizabeth's lodging and habits was easy enough to come by. There was resentment among her people about her being lodged without sufficient honor in the gatehouse while repairs were made to the manor. One angry gentleman indignantly pointed out the windows of her bedchamber on the second floor of the gatehouse.

Howard himself, rather relieved, felt he had done all he could to earn the fee paid him. He was ready to return to London when the third man he had brought along, who was devotedly Catholic and feared that Elizabeth would become Mary's heir and revert to her reformist preferences, said he had looked at the gatehouse through a ship's glass and seen that it would be no great difficulty to climb to the bedchamber window.

"And carry the lady out?" Howard said sarcastically. "Do not be a fool, her maid will be there and likely also one of her ladies shares her bed or her room. Even if you should be able to open her window, there will be a passel of screaming women to call the guards at her doors."

The man shrugged. "I can look in and see how the room is arranged. Elizabeth must be got rid of. Queen Mary . . . if she should get with child and die . . . we would have the devils from Geneva destroying our Church."

Howard shrugged. He was less worried about the devils from Geneva than the masters from Spain, but he did not wish to expose himself to a henchman who might betray him. "If you will," he said. "But do not let yourself be caught. We do not want to give any warning to Bedingfield, who is as careful to keep danger away from his charge as to keep her controlled."

Her three watchdogs soundly asleep, Elizabeth stepped through the Gate to Underhill without a second thought. Blanche went to bed after seeing her mistress off. She trusted Shaylor, who was guarding the door, to make enough noise to wake her if anyone should try to intrude. No one had in the two months they had been at Woodstock and she was not really worried about that. However, she was not sure how many more nights of good sleep she would get.

Blanche sighed. Although Elizabeth picked and nagged at Sir Henry, she was actually in good spirits and did not always hide it. The ladies now seemed to feel that Elizabeth was resigned to being held at Woodstock and did not need to be watched so closely. They had been requesting leave to move their cots back into the outer chamber.

So far Elizabeth had held them by saying she had got accustomed to their presence and would feel abandoned and insecure without it. Soon, however, Blanche thought, yawning, they would think of leaving one at a time, accustoming Elizabeth to their absence little by little. Probably Elizabeth would not be able to find an excuse to prevent that. Blanche yawned again and sighed. Then she would have to sit at the door while Elizabeth was away to keep them out.

The thud that woke her at first mingled with that last thought and brought her out of bed more than half asleep; she knew only she had to get to the door and prevent entry into Elizabeth's room. She snatched up her candle, lit it at the night candle, and hurried into the bedchamber. In the doorway she paused, realizing there had been no second knock, and began to scan the room. Had a lady fallen off her cot?

They were all there, still bespelled. Instinctively Blanche looked to see if Elizabeth had returned. She saw the shadow holding back the curtain of Elizabeth's empty bed. There was an intruder in the room!

Blanche's mouth opened to scream for Shaylor and snapped shut. She dared not allow anyone, not even Shaylor, into the bedchamber. He would ask why Elizabeth's ladies did not stir even for the noise of a fight and why Elizabeth's bed was empty.

At the same moment her mouth closed against raising any alarm, Blanche wondered who could have gained entry into Elizabeth's bedchamber with no more noise than one thud. If the intruder had fought Shaylor, surely there would have been cries and the sound of metal clashing against metal.

Sidhe! It could only be one of the Sidhe and no friend to Elizabeth!

Blanche's free hand wrenched at the necklace of crosses, twisting the largest and heaviest iron cross from the chain. She shifted the candle to her left hand and raised her right to throw the cross, but the intruder was no longer beside the bed. She pursued the shadow, wanting to be sure the iron cross would strike the bare skin of the face to burn and poison. The intruder gasped.

Howard's man had found it much easier than he expected to elude the bored and sleepy night guard. It was also easier than he expected to clamber up the side of the gatehouse to one of the windows of Elizabeth's room. There were protruding stones and beams and a thick vine. However, when he reached the window, he was sorely disappointed. It was closed, despite the balmy end-of-June air, and the curtains were drawn across it.

He paused only a moment and then tried if the window was locked. It was, but he could feel that the whole frame was badly warped. A gentle application of his knife undid the latch. Carefully, wary of squeaks and screeches, he opened the window, leaned forward over the low sill to pull the drape aside, leaned forward just a little too much . . . and tumbled into the room pushing the drape open as he fell.

Springing to his feet, he was half out of the window again before he realized there were none of the screams he expected. Only the sound of deep-sleep breathing and his own half-strangled gasps disturbed the chamber. Carefully, one hand still on the open window he looked around. The night-candle gave enough light to see three beds holding three humped bodies. Another long moment assured Howard's man that the sleepers had not stirred.

He paused, staring, but nothing moved. His shoulders squared from their defensive hunch. *What could make all the women sleep so sound? Were they all addicted to laudanum?*

A wide grin spread his lips. If the ladies and Lady Elizabeth always slept so soundly it would not be impossible to gag and bind the lady and carry her away without anyone being the wiser. He could ask any price for such a prize.

He came away from the window to peep through the bedcurtain to make sure his prize slept as soundly as the other women. For a moment he was frozen with shock. The bed was empty! *By the mercy of God, what had he discovered?*

Before he could give any consideration to the many aspects of what the empty bed could mean, a new light and a soft gasp made him spin around. Holding a candle that showed her clearly was a stout middle-aged woman, her mouth open to scream.

Howard's man flinched then froze. But she did not scream. To his amazement, the woman's mouth shut hard, she shifted her candle from one hand to the other and reached toward her breast. Shaking off his astonishment, Howard's man let go of the bedcurtain and ran toward the window. The woman pursued him!

With one hand on the window frame and one leg over the low sill, his foot feeling for the vine that had supported him on the way up, the intruder saw the woman raise a hand to throw something at him. By instinct, without thought, Howard's man ducked and leaned away from the missile. He was aware of something heavy hitting his shoulder and bouncing off. His last thought, as his foot slipped and he pitched out of the window was relief that she had not thrown a knife.

Howard had not slept well that last night in the Bull. He had shared the room with his three fellows and now was alone. He felt heavy and guilty, not so much about the men but because of the way each had been disposed of. All three gone, one by one, seemed a bad sign, a warning. Each time he wakened and found his man had not returned, the warning became clearer.

He was breaking his fast in a quiet corner of the tap room when the excitement from Woodstock manor finally boiled over into the Bull.

"A dead man?"

Howard heard Thomas Parry's voice loud with shock.

The controller was looking up into the face of one of the men-at-arms who guarded Lady Elizabeth. Howard always wondered about those men and how they had held their posts so long. Lady Elizabeth seemed very loyal to her servants. This one, although still straight-backed and hard looking, had taken off his helmet in respect and was almost bald.

"Yes, Master Parry," he said earnestly. "Right under Lady Elizabeth's bedchamber window, he was. Body wasn't seen until the morning when the sun got up over the wall. He was right near the building where it's dark and half covered by the bottom of that big vine. Sir Henry was in a taking, he was. He'll peel the skin off the night watch for letting him get in."

"Grace of God," Parry breathed, but the room was now so quiet that Howard had no trouble hearing him, "was Lady Elizabeth in danger? What did he intend to do?"

"God alone knows what the fool thought he would do," the man-at-arms replied, lips twisting with scorn. "He wasn't armed. If one of the ladies or Lady Elizabeth yelled, I'd of been in there and spitted him. I've spitted worse things than one man. And there's three ladies and Mistress Blanche sleeping in that room as well as Lady Elizabeth. No way was any one going to make it from the window to the bed without waking someone."

Howard could see Master Parry's hand tremble when he lifted his tankard of ale. Parry knew, if Shaylor in his overconfidence did not, that if the man had managed to climb up and get in, he could have stabbed Elizabeth before anyone could come to her aid.

An unpleasant chill spread from Howard's belly up through his chest. Some of the men he had hired were fanatics. The one that insisted on climbing to Lady Elizabeth's bedchamber might just have been crazy enough to have killed the lady so that Queen Mary could leave her crown to a good Catholic heir. Howard didn't care two pins for which rite was used to worship God, but he suddenly felt quite sure that Jesus Christ would not approve the murder of so gracious a lady—gracious enough to call him "cousin"—over whether or not candles and incense were used in church.

His hand went to the place under his full doublet where the purse that was to hire a troop of men to take Elizabeth "alive or dead" lay undisturbed. He had promised to pay the three who accompanied him when they started back to London, but no one except he himself was going back to London.

Howard stared down into the tankard still half full of ale. Why should he return to London? Any hope he had of advancement was dying with the old duke of Norfolk in Kenninghall. Might it be that he would advance farther under the rule of a lady willing to call him cousin even if she preferred the reformist rite?

But London was not the place to wait for that. This fool of a queen with her Spanish marriage was sure to breed more rebellion. The man who called himself John Smith would doubtless want him to help fight the rebels, as he had helped fight poor Wyatt. Nor could he hide himself from John Smith in London. Too many people knew too much about him in London.

Slowly Howard lifted his tankard and drank. He had a heavy purse and four horses. He was already well north and the weather was promising to be fine. He began to smile as he drew his breakfast platter toward him, clapped the thick slice of meat onto one slice of bread, wiped his greasy fingers on the second slice, and clapped that over the meat. He had lost his appetite for breakfast, but the bread and meat would serve for an afternoon bite along the road. It was a good day to ride for Scotland.

No one noticed or cared when Howard left. Master Parry was still intent on the dead man, whose death had decided Francis Howard to have no more to do with those who intrigued to remove Lady Elizabeth from the succession.

"Are you sure Lady Elizabeth was not hurt?" Parry prodded at Shaylor, who was not the brightest of the guards.

"Sure as sure. I saw her when she came down to break her fast. Such a good lady. She was concerned that help should be offered to the man if he was not dead. But he was. And Blanche says he never got through the window, that it was still closed when she opened it this morning. And the ladies swear they would have waked and called me if they heard the window opening."

Parry was not so sure of that as Shaylor was. Those ladies, he thought, could barely be trusted not to knife Lady Elizabeth on their own.

He ground his teeth with frustration because that blockhead

Bedingfield would not allow him to speak to his lady—as if he could do any real business without her approval. And as if he would plot treason with Bedingfield listening to every word they said. It was fortunate indeed that Dunstan was so clever.

Sighing, Parry looked up at Shaylor. "Thank God Lady Elizabeth is safe." He sighed again. "Tell Master Dunstan that I wish to speak with him as soon as you can, Shaylor."

Elizabeth heard the true tale of the intruder as soon as Denoriel brought her through the Gate not long before dawn.

"One of the Fair Folk?" Denoriel breathed, his hand going to his sword.

"Now I don't think so," Blanche said, her voice hardly above a murmur although the door between her room and the bedchamber was shut. "Even if I hit him with the cross, would one of the Fair Folk have fallen out of the window and been so clumsy as to land on his head and break his neck? I saw him lying on the ground. You can look. He's still there. I'm pretty sure he's dead."

"What did he want? Was he going to kill me?" Elizabeth whispered tremulously.

"I don't think so, my lady," Blanche said. "He had no weapon in his hand and he was just peeping through the bedcurtain, like to be sure you were there."

"Did he see that the bed was empty?" Elizabeth gasped.

"Don't matter, does it love?" Blanche replied, smiling. "He won't be telling anyone, now will he?"

"But if one man could get in, who is to say another will not?" Denoriel asked, his mouth grim.

"Don't think you need to worry about that none either," Blanche said, giving Elizabeth who was shivering a hug. "When Sir Henry finds that dead man right by your window with every sign he died of a fall, isn't he going to stick bars on your windows and guards below? What we need to worry about is that he'll seal up the whole place with iron shutters, not that he won't make sure no one else tries to get in your windows."

"That's true," Elizabeth said with a wan smile. "And, of course, since he never got through the window—I think I will speculate to Sir Henry that he fell when trying to open it—I will know nothing about him until the body is found." Her voice grew stronger as she spoke and the smile grew broader. "And this will be the perfect reason to insist that my ladies continue to sleep in my bedchamber. Three of them to give the alarm if there should be another intruder."

Denoriel was not smiling in response. "It wasn't one of us this time, dearling, but I would not swear the mortal was not hired by some agent of the Dark Court. And since this attempt failed, and Vidal must know Oberon is gone, he might try a direct attack. They have power enough for anything now and . . . Who knows where Oberon is and when he will return?" He pulled Elizabeth into his arms and kissed her. "I need to find Pasgen. He knows Gates. Perhaps he can tell me a way to make your lodging resistant to Gate magic."

"But then you will not be able to come for me!"

"I do not know where you will be in more danger," Denoriel said, crushing her against him and kissing her again. "I want you to be safe."

"Then do not take my freedom from me. If I am locked in here with Bedingfield, I will go mad." She hung around his neck, kissing his chin and throat." Come tomorrow," she begged. "Promise you will come tomorrow."

"Tomorrow is the night you do not bespell your ladies. I am sure Bedingfield will set a guard right below your window from now on, so I do not need to worry about mortal intrusion. Let me look for Pasgen and hear what he has to say. I will promise not to close my Gate or do anything else until I speak to you about it."

With that, Elizabeth had to be content. Since she truly was reassured about any threat posed by mortal assassins and felt she had her own defenses against the Sidhe, she let her lover go. Perhaps Pasgen could reassure Denno; in any case once dearling Denno was over the shock of hearing about the possible attack, he would understand her need to go Underhill.

Meanwhile she slipped into bed, released the sleep spell on her ladies, and while she waited for them to wake naturally concentrated on how she should react when she was told about the dead man.

Her deception was successful and she polished it by attacking Bedingfield for his carelessness with her safety. On his knees with tears in his eyes, he apologized most sincerely and promised that she should have bars on her windows and men patrolling the building at night. Spitefully, she threatened nonetheless to complain to the Council of his lax care for her.

For a long moment, he stared at her and then said, "If you will do that, and ask them to beg the queen to appoint another warden for you, I will be forever grateful, Your Grace. You could not do me a greater kindness."

For another long moment Elizabeth stared back, mouth a little open in surprise at the subtle attack. Then she laughed heartily and shook her head. "Well, I will not complain," she admitted, pouting. "I only wished to hear what you would say. I may be cross and a fool, but I am not such a fool as to cast out the honest devil I know and welcome one who might be much worse."

Elizabeth believed Bedingfield had merely made a shrewd riposte. Later she discovered he was not as clever as she then thought and had spoken only the plain truth. She did remind herself that Bedingfield, though slow and stolid, was not really a fool. She would have liked a more intellectual and more flexible guardian, but Sir Henry was at least honest and as earnest to protect her as he was to keep her under control.

She paid more attention to studying her keeper for the next few weeks, which was just as well because she had little else to occupy her. Denoriel came the day after, but he would not take her Underhill. As compensation they made love in Elizabeth's bed. It was not much of a compensation. Both were uneasy and constrained, fearing the sleep spell would fail. Denoriel could disappear; there was no real danger of discovery but neither could find a complete release. Then, frustrated, they quarreled bitterly.

Another night passed. Denoriel did not come and Elizabeth did not bespell her women. Mary Dacre complained that the guards who walked their rounds disturbed her sleep. She had slept much better before they were so carefully guarded. Susanna Norton agreed. No harm had come to Elizabeth, she said; bars had been set over the bedchamber windows. Why did they need a herd of flat-footed men tramping round and round and saluting each other as they passed?

Elizabeth was concerned. She would not be able to bespell them for several days, at least. After that if they commented on sudden sound sleep, she could say they had grown accustomed to the noise of the guards. Then Elizabeth Marberry commented thoughtfully on how soundly they usually slept.

Elizabeth hurried to say it was likely because they were all comforted by being together. She, in particular, felt she would not be able to sleep at all if they were not with her. And it was doubly important now, if there should be another intruder, that at least one of the three would surely wake and give warning.

On the next night Elizabeth bespelled her ladies but only for a brief time. When Denno came she told him she would not be able to go Underhill for at least a week. He shook his head, laughing ruefully, and admitted he had decided just the opposite, that she would be safer in Llachar Lle. As to proofing the gatehouse against Sidhe Gates, he had found Pasgen, he said, and Pasgen was delighted to look into the problem since he and Hafwen had still discovered no sign of the Evil and had no idea where else to look.

They kissed fondly and Denoriel returned Underhill while Elizabeth released the sleep spell and went to her own bed. She slept very ill indeed. As a result, she drove poor Bedingfield to tears over her demand always to have ink, pens, and writing paper, which were specifically forbidden. He would write to the Council, he conceded at last, but he would receive no answer since Prince Philip was due to land in England in three days. Through gritted teeth, Elizabeth said she was glad to hear it, but she still wanted her writing materials.

No one was happy when Elizabeth was not. Sharp with frustration, Elizabeth kept all three ladies very busy all day long. She wanted this, she wanted that; having what she asked for, she sent it away, demanded to be entertained. She needed distraction, she cried, after nearly being murdered in her bed. All the ladies prayed for night; at least Lady Elizabeth never asked for any service after she had gone to bed.

Fuming, but grimly cautious, Elizabeth waited four days, then bespelled only Susanna Norton. The other two ladies envied Susanna her ability to sleep through the noise the guards made. On the sixth day, Elizabeth bespelled both Norton and Elizabeth Marberry. Only Mary Dacre was restless, bemoaning her more sensitive senses for keeping her awake. On the eighth day all three slept soundly.

Chapter 33

Elizabeth did not recover the full freedom of Underhill as soon as her ladies were safely under control. Denoriel was sure she was safe in Llachar Lle, but not yet willing to expose her to less secure places Underhill. Her disposition still jangled from taking out her frustrations on Bedingfield and her ladies, Elizabeth agreed to remain in Denoriel's apartment.

She was well-rewarded for her meekness because Elidir and Mechain came and taught her two new spells, and Da played at primero with her. She sighed over the exquisite cards, which she knew she could not bring into the mortal world. There was a little silence while everyone else remembered that for safety's sake Elizabeth had been told she could bring nothing from Underhill to the mortal world.

It was Titania's command, and everyone agreed very wise. Likely no ordinary mortal could escape Underhill on his own and even if he managed to escape and carry back some of its wonders, it would not matter. Either that person would be assumed to be lying to protect his source or would be deemed mad. A queen was very different. Elizabeth would not willingly harm Underhill, but if her last hope for the survival of England rested on tearing the wealth from Underhill . . . she would lead an army there and do it. She had to believe Underhill's wealth useless.

Before the silence could be noticeable, Denno offered to get a pack bespelled to survive in the mortal world, but Elizabeth only shook her head.

"Everyone will ask from where they came. What could I tell them?"

He laughed. "Why that you got them from Adjoran, Mercer, of course." And then his eyes widened and he looked horrified. "No. On no account. I could get a good price for them and Joseph will want to take orders, but it is too hard to ken anything now."

Everyone fell silent again and looked anxious. The lack of power in the Bright Court was growing dangerous. There had been word of an attack by Dark Sidhe and their servants on a Bright Court domain. The knights of Avalon had come and driven them off, but not before one of the liosalfar of that domain had been mauled and two of the mortal servants stolen.

It was another reason for Denoriel to resist taking Elizabeth out of the heavily guarded and fortified summer palace, but the entertainments could not keep her satisfied for long. On the third week, when Tuesday came along, Elizabeth insisted on being taken to the Inn of Kindly Laughter.

"No one could touch me when you and I are on Miralys," Elizabeth said testily, "and the Markets are safe, even from the Dark Sidhe. What can they do? Both weapons and spells are forbidden and the markets have their own strange form of security."

"You were taken from a market once already." Denoriel snapped.

"That was arranged by Pasgen, who has a brain. That fat Sidhe seems only to have arrogance." She shrugged. "We are forewarned. I will be careful. I *will* go, even if I must walk to the Gate."

Most mortals could not make a Gate work, but Denoriel knew that Elizabeth had done so several times when she was frightened or angry—and she was rapidly growing angry enough. Sighing, Denoriel yielded. He could not keep her imprisoned forever, not in both worlds. Her temper was worn very thin; she might do or say something disastrous if she had no relief.

When they arrived, Rhoslyn and Pasgen were waiting, both all smiles. "I am free," Rhoslyn cried, starting up and holding out her hands, which Elizabeth took. "Mary is in a happy dream in which she hardly knows her ladies are there. I think she was glad to be rid of me so there would be fewer watching when she meets Philip."

"What is he like?" Elizabeth asked.

Rhoslyn blinked and her smile faded. "Correct. Polite. He is trying very hard to be agreeable. He was very disappointed when he saw Mary. Well, not *very* disappointed. In the back of his mind was a memory of having written to one of his friends that he had been ordered by his father to marry his maiden aunt . . . and there she was."

"But you said Mary was in a happy dream?"

"She, thank the Great Mother, cannot look into his mind as I can, and his manner to her is . . . gentle." Rhoslyn hunched her shoulders. "To her it speaks of love. Also they cannot really understand each other, so it is impossible for him to say anything wrong. He speaks Castilian Spanish, which she thinks she understands, but she only understands Aragonese, which is different. And it is many years since she used that language often. She speaks French to him, which he does not understand too well but is too proud to admit."

Elizabeth bit her lip and wrinkled her nose. "More important, does he lie with her?"

"That, yes," Rhoslyn said. "He is doing his duty. He knows he must get her with child for the Empire to hold onto England."

"I had hoped so young a man would not be so dutiful," Elizabeth said dryly. "Mary is no sweet and tender morsel."

Rhoslyn shook her head. "From what goes on in his head, I do not think Philip ever was a young man." she said. "He seems to think only of politics and power."

"Well," Elizabeth said, sighing, "I can only hope that Mary is too old to conceive."

That hope, however, was doomed to disappointment. By the end of September Master Parry had received news from the Court. The queen's physicians believed her pregnant. The news was passed to Elizabeth in the gentlest way possible by Master Dunstan. Because she was forbidden to receive any news, Elizabeth was able for a time to pretend she did not know of Mary's pregnancy. She was able to attribute her bursts of fury and weeping to some small cause.

For the Bright Court Underhill there was a fortunate aspect to the queen's pregnancy. As the news spread, the persistent dissatisfaction with the Spanish presence in England was allayed. A wary acceptance of Philip's servants and supporters spread, and the black pall of resentment that lay over the country lifted. In late November Cardinal Pole's long exile was ended by Queen Mary's invitation to him to return to England. He came bearing a commission to reunite England with the Catholic Church.

The rosy flush of joy the nation felt over the conception of a true and unarguably legitimate heir made the reunion welcome, particularly since Pole confirmed the permanent transfer of what had been Church lands to those to whom Henry VIII had given them. A spirit of relief that everything was now settled swept over the nation. Celebrations small and large took place all over the country. The power of contentment and in some cases of joy sifted down into the Bright Court.

The attenuation of the power of misery very soon disquieted Vidal, who had gladly dismissed the doings of the mortal world as long as his Court was well fed on pain and fear. By mid-December he was alert and angry. He could not afford to be starved of power. The number of Dark Sidhe who filled the seats before his throne had increased and the dark forces of witch and were, ogre and troll, and all the evil creatures of the night had multiplied most satisfactorily. He would have to act to reestablish the correct flow of power.

Act how? He seemed somehow to have lost his tight grip on Renard and he could not deal with him until he knew the true situation. Who at Court . . . Of course, Aurilia's servant was a only a lowly physician, but he was physician to the queen. That was an ideal position from which to gather gossip.

Vidal appeared in Otstargi's parlor shortly before Albertus came in for the night. An imp caught at Albertus's hair and dragged him into the room. The door shut with a slam behind him.

"You have accomplished nothing," Vidal snarled. "Elizabeth is safe and well and power drains from the Dark Court to the Bright."

"Only for a very short time, Your Highness," Albertus gasped, falling to his knees. "Believe me, soon there will be anger and grief in plenty. Now is only a small time of celebration, of joy because the queen has conceived—"

"Mary is with child," Vidal said, the words trailing off. A memory of something dim but very evil flickered in his mind.

"Yes. Yes," Albertus cried, his voice louder, sharper than normal. "That she has conceived is a near miracle, and this further demonstration of what she believes is God's favor has emboldened her to invite Cardinal Pole back into England and to sue for reconciliation with the pope. Parliament has passed strong laws about the punishment of heresy, and Pole, I have heard, speaks softly but is a fanatic eager to bring in the Inquisition. He is determined to root out all the reformists in the country."

Albertus poured out his news in a rush of eager words. He was trying to distract his master from the failure of the attempt to abduct or kill Elizabeth. The tool he had used with considerable success to help Mary gain the throne had not only failed but broken. The men Francis Howard had taken to Woodstock were dead and Howard himself had disappeared.

He succeeded better than he knew. Vidal stared at Albertus as the half memory that had tickled his mind when the physician said Mary was pregnant slipped away. The mention of the Inquisition had fixed his attention. Once the Inquisition got a grip on a country, it was very difficult to be rid of it. It had held Spain for several hundred mortal years.

"The Inquisition? Are you sure?"

"My lord, I am no intimate of Cardinal Pole. I will try to get Mary to recommend me to him as a physician; then I will be more sure. But rumor in the Court is very strong that it is Pole's intention to bring in the Inquisition."

Albertus did not say that the rumor was mostly spread by those of hidden reformist tendencies in a vain attempt to arouse fear and weaken Pole's influence on Mary. Albertus knew it was useless. Mary was utterly tenacious in her conviction that only Cardinal Pole and the Imperial ambassador were to be trusted.

Vidal stared unnervingly at Albertus who dropped his head and began to pray that the rumors of the Inquisition were true. His earnest sincerity came across to Vidal, who barely touched the surface of the man's mind. Vidal felt his fear, fed off it for a pleasant moment. Then it occurred to him that if what Albertus said did come to pass and the power shift to the Bright Court did not last long, there would be no need for him to exert himself in this disgusting mortal world that made his bones ache.

"Very well," Vidal said. "If there is any change, come to Caer Mordwyn and tell me. Now, I want to know when this unnatural spate of mortal happiness will end."

"Very soon, I think," Albertus said eagerly, holding back a sigh of relief. "Only a few mortal months. By the bill passed in Parliament, heresy will be punished by death. Pole has been advising Mary to make a strong example of some outspoken Protestants. I was near the queen and heard this myself. Pole spoke of it with sorrow and regret but said he believes a single burning or perhaps two will curb and frighten the heretics and that will save many souls."

Vidal frowned. "Will it be necessary to turn the queen's mind away from this device? I do not desire quiet acquiescence."

"No, no." Albertus shook his head vehemently. "It is far more likely that burning an outspoken Protestant will turn the popular feeling against the Catholic reunion. It will cause more resistance and will generate more burnings..."

Albertus spoke more out of hope than out of knowledge, but the events turned out just as he foretold. On the ninth of February, 1555, he went himself to watch the first burning so he could report to Vidal and Aurilia. John Hooper, bishop of Worcester, had been condemned to the stake. A large crowd had come to witness the spectacle although it was a bitter cold day and threatening rain.

The burning was terrible. The faggots used were green and would barely burn. Twice the fire went out completely and had to be renewed. The third time more faggots and kindling were brought there were murmurs through the crowd that God did not want His people burned, no matter how they worshiped Him. And the victim did not scream for forgiveness or recant his heresy. He died, as those near enough saw and could spread abroad, impervious to the torment of being burnt a slow inch at a time for near an hour, still firm in his conviction that his rite was the true one and that Lord Jesus would receive his spirit.

Only a few days before Vidal spoke to Albertus and decided not to trouble himself for the present about matters in the mortal world, Elizabeth was informed officially that her sister was with child. There had been a ceremony of thanksgiving for her conception in St. Paul's on November twenty-eighth and Bedingfield assumed correctly, if two months late, that despite the prohibition against giving the prisoner any news she would be told.

Those two months, however, had been crucial. Over that time Elizabeth had—if not reconciled herself to Mary bearing an heir to the throne—at least decided how to receive the news when she was told. Moreover in the two months, she had recovered some hope of succeeding her sister. It was very dangerous for a woman near forty to deliver a first child. Mary might die and the child with her; even if the child survived delivery, it might die. Elizabeth knew that the primary reason her father had set aside his first wife was that all her children except Mary were stillborn or died within weeks of birth. But to inherit, Elizabeth knew she must be alive. She must give no shred of an excuse to be accused of treason and executed.

Bedingfield was not looking forward to delivering the news of Queen Mary's pregnancy. He was braced for fury, for disbelief, for tears and tantrums. What he got was almost the broadest smile he had ever seen on Elizabeth's face, and warm thanks for the wonderful news he had brought her. For once there was no cutting edge to Elizabeth's voice.

She convinced Bedingfield of her joy in her sister's success. Bedingfield was not acute, but even the most suspicious of Mary's spies was ready to swear that Elizabeth was truly overjoyed. And when they came to prayer, Susanna Norton heard Elizabeth pray loud and strong for the queen's safe delivery and the child's health.

Elizabeth's performance was seemingly heartfelt, but it had taken two full months of rehearsals—and a very small self-ensorcellment spell—to produce the effect. Back in September when she first came Underhill after hearing of Mary's pregnancy she had not been so calm and accepting of her fate. She wept in Mechain's arms and hiccuped out her fury and disappointment to Elidir.

"Silly child," Elidir had said with a small, knowing smile. "It must be a lie or a mistake. Had your image disappeared from the great lens or a new image appeared, someone would have sent word to Denoriel. So?" He looked around at Denoriel, who was standing near, his face twisted with misery. "Have the FarSeers bespoke you?"

"No. No they have not," Denoriel admitted, blinking at the revelation but glad it had come from Elidir so Elizabeth could not think *he* was saying it just to make her feel better.

That was the beginning of Elizabeth's ability to pretend joy over Mary's pregnancy. She still wavered into doubt and fear, particularly each time some bit of rumor about how Mary was in blooming health and needing to have her gowns let out was whispered in her ear by Blanche or passed into her hand by Dunstan in a note from Parry. But as often as she doubted, she reminded herself that the FarSeers had been correct about Edward's short reign, about poor Jane Grey, and about Mary's unlikely but successful bid for the throne. Through all that, the image of the red-haired queen and the joy of her reign had been constant.

It was still hard perpetually to wear a mask of calm and delight. The expectation, the determination, to mount the throne of England had been a central core of Elizabeth's life since her brother's death. Now one moment her succession was in doubt altogether and the next moment it seemed the throne would be hers in a few short months . . . if Mary and the child died.

What kind of monster am I to pray for the death of my sister and my sister's unborn child?

Elizabeth could not forget for a moment in the mortal world. The very fact of her imprisonment kept her position as unwelcome heir presumptive constantly in her mind's eye. Underhill, where she could express her alternate unease and elation, she went wild. There was little Denoriel could do to steady her. He could only enlist what extra protection he could find and give her her head.

Most often Harry and Rhoslyn joined in Elizabeth's adventures because Denoriel thought the land of the self-willed mist might be safer than exposing her to the mortal-stealer in the markets. When they had first spoken of that Unformed land the previous July, they had done very little, only looked out from the Gate platform.

There had been nothing to see, only the coiling and roiling of the mist. Elizabeth had wanted to go down and speak to the mist, but Denoriel held her back when he saw that Rhoslyn was pallid and breathing hard with shock. Gaenor, who had come with them at their request, had looked puzzled and a little distressed too.

Later, when Elizabeth asked Rhoslyn what was wrong, she had shaken her head and said, "It is waiting."

And Gaenor had nodded agreement. "It has wiped itself clean. Before there were . . . I don't know . . . faint echoes. Now there is nothing. And yes, I, too, caught the feeling of waiting." She looked at Elizabeth. "What did you feel?"

"Nothing," Elizabeth replied, a little puzzled, a little hurt and resentful. "The mist never 'spoke,' if that is the right word, to me.

I spoke to it. I asked it to do things . . . politely. And it did. And I thanked it, but I never felt anything, except perhaps welcome."

"Politely . . ." Rhoslyn murmured. "Yes. That will be a problem. I have always forced my will in making."

But Rhoslyn had been in no position to work on that problem for the next mortal month. The preparations for Mary's wedding to Philip consumed July, and the after-wedding celebrations filled the beginning of August; Rhoslyn hardly came Underhill at all. And after she finally obtained leave from the queen at the end of August, she disappeared for nearly a mortal month. Harry seemed concerned when the others asked for her, but not anguished.

Then in October, just when Elizabeth was over the worst throes of adjusting to the idea of Mary's pregnancy, Rhoslyn appeared with Harry at the Tuesday meeting in the Inn of Kindly Laughter. Rhoslyn was as shocked as Elizabeth could have desired to learn of Mary's condition and just as displeased. Later Elizabeth learned it was because Rhoslyn was afraid Mary would recall her to duty, but at the time she was soothed by Rhoslyn's sympathy and seeking to say something that would interest Rhoslyn, asked whether she had again visited the seemingly sentient mist.

"No, and I have come here to ask you to come with me for just that purpose," Rhoslyn said. "I have been putting my servants in stasis." Her eyes shone with tears for a moment. "Poor things. They are all greatly weakened and I simply cannot bear to destroy them or take in the horrible power the Dark Sidhe use to renew them. I thought if you would . . . would *ask* the mist . . ."

"Rhoslyn," Elizabeth said eagerly as Rhoslyn's voice faded doubtfully, "you don't need me. I'll go with you of course, but you should ask the mist first to make you a house . . . and tell it how."

"What? But that is a much greater use of its substance than to renew my poor servants."

"Yes, but Gaenor said it was trying to make a house. Mist doesn't need a house. If it was making a house it was for someone to live in. Now, perhaps it was for the dolls, but I don't think so. The dolls seem to have disappeared. I think it wanted *me* to live in the house and tell it to make things. But Pasgen told it I cannot live Underhill and now it has made nothing and we all felt it was waiting. I think it is waiting for . . . for you."

"No. It was you it wanted."

"But it cannot have me. I will be—" Her voice cut off abruptly as she remembered the baby in her sister's belly.

"You will be queen some day," Rhoslyn said. "When Vidal was away from Caer Mordwyn, I went to the Tower and I looked in the pool. The image of the red-haired queen is still there, and there are flickering images of two or three other women, one stronger and steadier than the others, but there is no image of a small child. Yet your image was there before you were born."

Elizabeth's face lit in response to Rhoslyn's reassurance and she smiled. "So, as I said, the mist cannot have me, but I think the only reason that it 'wanted' me was because I was the only one who told it to do anything. It needs someone with an ability to make vivid images and a strong will—a maker."

Rhoslyn looked hopeful but uncertain. "But Gaenor was a maker, a great one. Why did the mist not respond to her?"

"That's easy to answer," Harry said, grinning. "Gaenor went to that Unformed land with the single purpose of keeping the mist from doing anything. When she exerted her will, she told the mist to rest, to be quiet."

Elizabeth looked enlightened, but before she could respond Aleneil and Ilar came in, closely followed by Pasgen with Hafwen. Aleneil was looking very pleased with herself. A moment later, when the table had rounded and provided enough chairs, she sobered.

"Sometimes a FarSeer doesn't need a lens," she said. "I knew Rhoslyn was ready to try the mist and I sent an air spirit to Hafwen. I didn't foresee any trouble, but I wanted Hafwen to smell around in case something has slipped into the mist. It has changed since she was last there."

"And that Evil is still missing," Pasgen said somewhat grimly.

Hafwen touched his hand.

"You are all in a hurry," the server said disapprovingly. "The Inn of Kindly Laughter is not a place to eat and run. But I will excuse you this time."

Today it was huge and hairy, its features and body a mingling of human and ape. And it had absolutely enormous feet, the toes long and agile for grasping.

Looking at the feet, Elizabeth said, "Where did you see it?"

"Not in your time." The server laughed. "But your ships will sow what later generations will harvest. So. Food?"

They ordered and the meals came quickly, but the server did not speak again. Denoriel looked after him—very obviously a him because he was naked and the hair on his hide did not completely conceal his genitals.

"What is it?" he asked softly.

Pasgen shook his head. He knew Denoriel was not asking about the creature the server now wore. Rhoslyn said, "Beyond me. His shields are impenetrable. Looking brings you only to a solid wall that isn't even a wall. Just . . . you can't go any farther."

There was little more conversation. All of them applied themselves to their food and when they were finished with the main course all agreed to forgo dessert.

At the Gate, Harry paused and said, "I told Gaenor to meet us there. I asked her to come to the Inn, but she said she wanted some quiet time to feel the mist. It has been so quiet recently that she fears some core of resentment that could burst when it perceived a large number of possible victims."

But Gaenor, unharmed, was waiting on the Gate. The platform, which had been a small one, obligingly enlarged so the whole party was not crowded together. Again, there was nothing to be seen in the mist beyond what was normal for an Unformed land.

Suddenly, with the recklessness that filled her every time she remembered her sister might bear a living heir to the throne, Elizabeth seized Rhoslyn's hand and jumped down from the platform. Denoriel cried "No" and reached for her, but he was too late, and the mist had withdrawn slightly.

"Stop," Rhoslyn said, holding up her free hand in a "halt" gesture to the others. Then looking out into the mist again, "I will have to go deeper in," she said. "The empty house is in view of the Gates because it invited visitors, even enemies. My old domain was hidden by many Gate transfers so it was visible from the final transfer. I do not wish to hide this domain. I hope friends will Gate here, yet I desire some protection from the curious and mispatterned arrivals. And there are those in the Dark Court who might wish me harm . . ."

The words trailed away as a stone wall formed and stretched away into the distance. At Elizabeth's and Rhoslyn's feet a wide gravel path had appeared, leading to a pair of beautifully wrought gates. They looked like black iron, but Rhoslyn felt no pain and guessed they were of the elven metal alloy that made the Sidhe's silver swords as strong as steel. The gates stood open.

"Oh my," Elizabeth said, walking toward the gates. "Mist, you have outdone yourself. How perfect. How beautiful. The walls are finer than those that protect a palace. Thank you. Thank you. Those walls will be my gift to this lady—" She pushed Rhoslyn forward and murmured to her. "Think that you need a house. You need a place to live. Quick."

Rhoslyn started. She had worked in many Unformed lands but never seen such a response. She swallowed hard and her voice quavered when she said, "Mist, my name is Rhoslyn and I . . . I need you. I need a house. I have no place to live. I wish my house to be out of view of the gates—"

Her voice caught on a gasp as a wide meadow of grass extended out on both sides of the path, which curved into a seeming endless distance. But just beyond the open gate were five elvensteeds and with them, black and gleaming with glowing red eyes and long, white teeth . . . the not-horses.

"Torgen!" Pasgen bellowed, and leapt off the Gate platform. "Don't you dare—"

He was through the gates and among the elvensteeds while Rhoslyn stared at Talog as if frozen. Within a single step of Torgen, Pasgen raised a hand, whether to strike at Torgen or grasp him by the nose was impossible to say because he did neither.

Pasgen knew magic, knew its feel, its smell, the texture of things created by magic. This *was* Torgen; he knew Rhoslyn's making, and yet . . . A glowing red eye winked at him. He stood for a moment, staring at the not not-horse; his throat worked and he leaned forward, put his arms around the creature's strong neck, and buried his face in its gleaming hide. Down the neck, now curved so that Torgen's soft muzzle could touch Pasgen, ran a single shining drop.

Horses do not laugh, Elizabeth thought. *It is a generally accepted truth that only humans laugh and it is one of the things that sets humans apart from animals.* Yet as Elizabeth approached the elvensteeds in Denoriel's wake, she was quite certain they were all laughing. Even the second black not-horse, which had stepped a little aside from the rest of the elvensteeds and was watching Rhoslyn approach.

"Talog?" Rhoslyn whispered, a hand stretched toward the waiting creature. "You *are* Talog but now—" her eyes were huge and shining "—now you are real. What I hoped for. What I dreamed of. What I could not make while I was full of hate and envy and using the power of pain."

She sighed in a totally satisfied way and leaned against what was no longer her making. "Talog and Torgen are gone now?" she asked, looking up into the one red eye she could see. "Oh, thank you. Thank you. I could not bear to destroy them and I could not bear to abandon them. Thank you. I will do anything you want—"

She then reared back with a stunned look on her face and said, half laughing half doubtful, "Of course. You and Torgen will have the finest stables in the entire worlds both mortal and Sidhe. Show me a picture and I will make it."

She got no direct response, but Talog gave her a firm shove with her nose and Rhoslyn turned sharply to face the sound of hooves approaching.

"You don't want to live in a flat plain like this," Pasgen said.

He came up to her with one arm over Torgen's withers, just as one male Sidhe might throw his arm over the shoulders of another Sidhe who was his friend, and the other arm around Hafwen's waist. Rhoslyn had never seen her brother touch Hafwen in public. Now his firm grip had a faintly proprietary air.

Rhoslyn's lips parted, but nothing came out. The new Torgen, like the new Talog, was an elvensteed who had somehow absorbed her making. Elvensteeds chose where they willed, but Rhoslyn knew from bitter experience they only chose liosalfar. Surely that meant Pasgen, and she also, must be acceptable to the Bright Court.

Rhoslyn knew that individual Sidhe might reject them, but the Court convened would not. There was a suspicious streak on one of her brother's cheeks, but Rhoslyn did not stare at it and his voice was very normal, slightly disapproving as he looked right and left.

"You had better tell the mist—"

Rhoslyn laughed, interrupting him. "Ask the mist, Pasgen. Ask. I do not think it wise or safe to *tell* this mist anything."

"Yes, yes," he said impatiently. "Ask. Fine. Ask for some trees along the road."

Rhoslyn also looked right and left. Some indistinct forms

wavered along the road. Elizabeth came past Talog, giving the creature an absentminded pat on the croup. It was a fearsome looking beast with those red eyes, carnivore's teeth, and heavy, clawed feet instead of hooves, but Elizabeth was not afraid. Nothing mingling with elvensteeds would harm her.

"You have to show it with a picture in your mind what the trees you want look like, Rhoslyn," Elizabeth said. "I had a picture in my mind when I asked for the lion and for the kitten. And, of course Pasgen is right that you will want trees and maybe a few low hills, but you had better pick the place you want for your house and the kind of house before you begin to change the land."

Suddenly Rhoslyn put her arms around Talog and rested her head against the black hide. "It is too much," she said faintly. "I am so happy I feel I will burst with joy, but I can't *think*."

"Come home with me," Harry said, coming up beside her and gently rubbing her back. "Denno has to take Elizabeth back to the mortal world and I think he wants to stop at Bucklersbury to talk to Clayborne. We'll have his rooms to ourselves."

"But the mist," Rhoslyn said doubtfully, "will it accept me another time? Will it grow impatient? Will I need to begin anew?"

"It always knew me each time I came," Elizabeth replied slowly, "but I don't know how much of what is here now it will retain. It did keep the lion, but . . ."

"Tell it," Gaenor said, passing between Pasgen and Harry and putting a steady hand on Rhoslyn's shoulder. "Tell it that you are only Sidhe and now must rest. That you will soon come again to look for a place to build your house and that you hope the walls and the meadow will be here when you come again."

So Rhoslyn turned her back on the company and looked out into the long distance where mist rolled over the meadow and she thought to the mist. Almost at once she felt a sense of relief and she saw a tiny image of the wall and the meadow, saw the image covered with mist and then the mist rolling back to show the image unchanged.

She turned to Gaenor tears of relief filling her eyes. "You are right and not only about Sidhe tiring." She laughed faintly. "I think the mist is tired too. And I think it showed me that it would keep the wall and the meadow but cover them with mist."

"Oh good," Elizabeth said with a deep sigh. "That means we can do the house and the furniture and the garden a bit at a time. I was wondering how we could ever build a whole domain in one day. I couldn't imagine, even though there were two of you, how you and Pasgen made the empty house all at once."

"We didn't," Pasgen said. "Mostly we did one room at a time and then a stasis spell to hold it."

Rhoslyn started as if prodded and then shivered. "No. No stasis spells. The mist doesn't like stasis spells."

Chapter 34

Wise in making, Rhoslyn never expected to build her domain in a few days. Actually it took all the remainder of 1554 and into the spring of 1555 to complete the place. The wall and entry gates remained unchanged. From the gates, the wide graveled path now wound through a gently undulant landscape, well-treed and with an underwood of flowering shrubs. There were also occasional open areas in which from time to time the alarming Talog and Torgen could be glimpsed. They made Rhoslyn comfortable, at home.

Unlike the classical empty house and the fantastic faerylike castle she had lived in with her mother, when the dwelling came into view it was a plaster and beam English country manor. The patterns of the dark beams against the white plaster were complex and elegant, and the red tile roof gleamed in the Underhill glow.

From the moment the manor appeared, Harry was at ease in it, and long before it was completed he had taken an affectionate leave of Denno, made one room habitable, and moved in with Rhoslyn. Together they planned the layout of the chambers, Harry telling Rhoslyn how his favorite lodging was arranged and Rhoslyn picturing the chambers to the mist.

Elizabeth imaged much of the furniture for the mist. She had good taste and a strong desire to be comfortable. Grateful for keeping Elizabeth busy and safe Denoriel did the gardens. Harry

laughed, remembering that poor Denno had pretended a passionate interest in gardens to disguise his visits to the child he had
been assigned to protect.

Over the years, the interest in gardens had become genuine;
the illusion one saw through Denoriel's parlor windows had a
well-defined garden. Now he was the one who was best able to
visualize the garden down to the individual stalks and the blooms
upon them.

To amuse himself and astonish visitors, Denoriel did not simply
choose the flowers he wanted and bespell them to bloom all the
time. He worked out when each species would blossom in the
mortal world and arranged for his bespelled plants to do the same.
Thus Rhoslyn's gardens were unique Underhill, changing from the
sere of cold-killed annuals and the dark green of evergreens to
the bobbing, colorful beauty of narcissus, daffodil, and hyacynth.
Before those were gone, the richer blooms of summer came, to
be capped by the brilliant foliage and ripened fruits of autumn.

Harry was enchanted. "I'd almost forgot what it was like," he
muttered as Denoriel ran the whole cycle through for him. "It was
nice," he said, with the first touch of wistfulness for his lost life
that Denoriel had ever heard, "to feel the seasons come and go."
He came and hugged Denoriel. "And now I'll even have that."

Elizabeth hardly gave the garden a glance. Gardens that changed
with the season were an everyday experience of a life mostly lived
in the mortal world. However, as her work in the house neared
completion and Mary came closer to the day of her delivery,
Elizabeth was becoming more and more restless.

She had begged permission to write to congratulate Mary as
soon as the pregnancy was officially related to her. Permission was
denied, but when Bedingfield reported to the queen and Council,
he described what he thought honestly how cheerfully Elizabeth
had received the news and mentioned that she had willingly joined
in his prayer for the progeny of the queen's excellent person.

Elizabeth was undecided about what to do and for once Harry
was equally undecided. One thing he assured Elizabeth of was
that she was not forgotten. Stephen Gardiner was again agitating
for a Bill in Parliament that would disinherit Elizabeth once and
for all. To say there was no enthusiasm for his proposal was a
vast understatement. No one would listen to him at all and the
idea was quietly dropped.

The queen was soon to bear a child and neither she nor the child might survive. No one dared even hint at such doubts, but it was at the back of everyone's mind and right there with the death of Mary and her child was Elizabeth, clearly named in the Act of Succession, heir presumptive for years, young and healthy.

Harry's sources were servants, ubiquitous and ignored. It was from them he learned that Elizabeth had a new and very powerful friend. Philip, who cared nothing for Mary's old hurts and hatreds, was all too aware that his wife, frail and not young, might not survive childbearing. If the child lived, Philip had been heard to confide in an intimate, all would be well because he would be Regent; but if the child did not survive, he might be torn to bits by a population that hated him and all his kind.

In that case, the servant confided to another servant who whispered Philip's thoughts to a third, who had an odd wizened and dwarfed friend who traded him small, exquisite things in exchange for Court news. In that case, Philip had said, it would be most useful to have Elizabeth near him in the palace as a hostage.

Naturally he could not hold her hostage long, but if he had already made her his friend and made her grateful to him for his support against her enemies, like Gardiner, who knew what he might accomplish. If he could get her married to a good Catholic prince subservient to Spain, he could secure the English alliance.

Elizabeth said very unladylike things when Harry reported what Philip planned among his own friends, but Harry did not laugh as he usually did when she waxed obscene.

"Do not you dare offend him!" he exclaimed.

"I fear I will never be allowed near him," Elizabeth snapped.

"That you will, and in no long time. He has already convinced Mary to bring you to Court. It is necessary, he told her, that you publicly acknowledge the child. The queen is expected to be brought to bed in the first week of May. I warrant you will be sent for in a few weeks, certainly before the end of April."

To Elizabeth's mingled delight and terror, Harry was right to within a few days. On the seventeenth of April Bedingfield received a letter from Mary bidding him bring Elizabeth immediately to Hampton Court for the lying in. Bedingfield was beyond delight, he was ecstatic with joy to learn that his long purgatory as Elizabeth's keeper was to be ended.

Elizabeth was equally happy but afraid, too. "What if, with the imminent birth of an undisputed heir, Mary decides to be rid of me," Elizabeth said looking from face to face as she, Denoriel, Harry, and Rhoslyn sat together in the parlor of Rhoslyn's new house. "Bedingfield was honest and truly tried to protect me. In Hampton Court . . . who knows? I might not be allowed to keep my own men about me. I could fall victim to an accident."

"You have your tokens?" Denoriel asked anxiously. "I will set an air spirit to watch also. Your shields will protect you until I can make a Gate."

Harry was shaking his head. "I am not worried about your physical safety. I am worried about what impression you will make on Philip. Bessie, listen. It is really important that he believe you a fool." As the words passed his lips, he shook his head sharply and bit his lip. "No, that will not do. Too many know you to be clever and, in any case, you would surely say or do something that would expose you."

"Why should I act the fool?" Elizabeth asked resentfully. "This will be the first time many in the Court have seen me for almost a year. I do not want to seem to have lost my wits."

"No, not a fool," Harry said, obviously not having paid the smallest attention to Elizabeth's angry protest. "Innocent. Yes. You must be innocent and ignorant of politics—more than ignorant, uninterested."

"That I could do," Elizabeth said grudgingly. "I always pretended not to care about politics. But why, Da? Would Philip not be more interested in an ally who could help him?"

"Philip does want protection from the populace of England. You know the people blame him for the burnings—"

Elizabeth shuddered and Denoriel put an arm around her and hugged her. She leaned her head against his briefly. The cruelty of the death did not trouble her so much as the political disaster Mary was creating.

"But more even than his own safety," Harry continued, "Philip wants the assurance of England's steady and unwavering alliance with the Empire. It was for that he married Mary. He wants to win your trust and confidence so that when you are queen you will lean on him as Mary leaned on his father."

Elizabeth made a disgusted snort, and Harry looked at her with reproof.

"No more cynical sniffs. For Philip to believe he has achieved that goal, you must play the admiring innocent. As long as you do, no harm will come to you while the life of Mary's babe is in doubt. Philip will be very tender of you, I am sure."

"There is no babe," Rhoslyn said very softly, lifting her head from Harry's shoulder. "I looked in the black pool of ForeSeeing again—"

"Rhoslyn!" Harry protested. "It is dangerous for you to go to Caer Mordwyn. What if Vidal should seize you? You must smell of the Bright Court now. You might be set upon and hurt."

She shook her head. "Talog took me. She does not like the Dark domains, but she knew what was in my mind and would not let me go alone. *I* was safe." Her large, dark eyes glistened with tears. "There is no babe, nothing at all . . . nothing but Mary's so-passionate desire for a child that her body responded to it."

Three pairs of eyes fixed on her in horrified disbelief. For a long moment no one spoke or moved.

Then Elizabeth said, "Thank God." But as she spoke, her eyes also filled with tears."Oh, but poor Mary. My poor sister. Better there had been a babe and both died."

Rhoslyn nodded sadly. "The shame will be terrible. I will need to go back to my service with her. I will be able to soothe her spirit a little, give her a little ease."

"That is very good of you, Rhoslyn," Harry said. "It will not be a happy Court."

"No, it will not."

Vidal Dhu learned that Queen Mary would not bear a child almost at the same moment that Rhoslyn told Elizabeth, Denoriel, and Harry. While they sat in stunned amazement, Vidal erupted in rage. He sent an imp to drag Albertus Underhill, roaring loudly enough about what he would do to that false mortal that Aurilia heard him. She listened until the roaring of uncontrolled fury died into a peevish hissing, and then she slouched into Vidal's chamber.

"I heard you," she said, smiling at him and sliding a hand down his arm as she seated herself on a stool by his side. "What has put you out of temper?"

"Mary is barren!" he snarled. "I thought we were all set for an eon of rich misery from the mortal world. "The babe—"

He stopped speaking abruptly, his mouth still formed for the following words, and then he said them, slowly, almost tasting each word.

"The babe was to be invested with Evil."

"Evil?" Aurilia repeated. "Where . . ."

"Alhambra," Vidal said, almost absently.

He now remembered fully the ruined domains, the mutilated and senselessly destroyed Dark creatures, and the carrier of that Evil, in whose feeble body It had stupidly imprisoned Itself. Now he remembered how he had trapped Dakari and his inhabitor. He remembered, too, how he had planned to use the Evil.

Vidal caught his lower lip between his pointed teeth. How could he have forgotten? Surely his memory was not as faulty as it had been before enforced contemplation in the Unformed land of the silken bands had restored him? No, his memory was not at fault! It must have been that Evil, lashing out to muddle his thoughts before it was fully contained. Half-laughing, half-snarling Vidal felt the Thing had got what it deserved for meddling with him. It had been imprisoned for almost two years.

Aurilia watched the expressions chase each other over Vidal's face in puzzled disbelief. "Alhambra," she repeated. "You sent Dakari with a witch and werewolf to clear Alhambra of the devices of the Bright Court. Are you telling me that Dakari was successful? That that pallid nothing captured the Evil?"

Much calmed, and not about to admit to Aurilia that the Evil had muddled his mind, Vidal laughed. "It is a moot point who captured whom, but yes, Dakari and the Evil are now inextricably bound together. But it was I who captured them and held them."

"How very wise," Aurilia said, looking admiring. "We do not need to loose the Evil now. Your chosen queen has provided enough misery to make us rich all on her own." Then she frowned. "Although there has been altogether too much good feeling since she got with child—"

"Curse the woman, she is not with child!" Vidal bellowed, his good humor disappearing. "It was my intention that the Evil be transferred into the child Mary was about to bear. It was to breed widely so that the Evil could be spread abroad and infect the entire country. We could have had an eon of hatred, murder, war . . . and that stupid bitch convinced herself and all around her that she was increasing so that my plan came to nothing. Wait. Wait until I get my hands on that lazy, stupid physician . . ."

From the moment Vidal told her Mary's pregnancy was not real, Aurilia guessed Vidal intended to kill Albertus in the most prolonged and painful way he could. She did not intend to allow it. Albertus was hers. Not only did he make that blue, cloudy potion that soothed her so well, but he was so deliciously frustrated and terrified in her presence. She was not going to permit Vidal to destroy *her* toy. And when Albertus's usefulness was ended, she would drink the power that flowed from his dying. She tried to think of something soothing to say.

But Vidal's voice had drifted away. His brows were knitted in thought, not rage. Aurilia held her tongue. Then Vidal spoke again, slowly. "London is full of newborn babes. I will give that lazy fool one more chance. He *is* one of Mary's physicians and can come to her without needing elaborate arrangements. Why should not a babe seem to be born from the queen's body?"

"What?" Aurilia said. "How can that be done?"

Vidal laughed. "Easily enough. You want to keep your little pet who brews you potions? Then help him deliver a babe from Mary."

Aurilia's mouth opened, but nothing came out for a moment. Then she said, "The queen is attended by many people. Do you think anyone will believe Albertus if he says he delivered the queen alone and no one else in the room noticed. Not to mention how he would bring the child in or that it would not look like one just taken from between a woman's legs."

"You and your Albertus will arrange all that." Vidal waved a negligent hand. "You have done nothing but suck in power and preen since Mary came to the throne. It is time to use that power to ensure our future."

"The future is ensured," Aurilia snapped. "Mary is growing madder and madder in her desire to make Logres Catholic."

"Stupid grimalkin," Vidal said silkily, "you think like a cat, intent on this moment and your own body and nothing else. Mary is mortal and frail. This swelling of her body, like as not it is a disease. She will not live long. She needs an heir or Elizabeth will come to the throne and we will starve for power."

Aurilia's fair skin flushed and blue light played along her fingers at the insult. Vidal sneered and laughed. She did not loose the bolt of power that had formed although retaining it seemed to burn her insides; it was clear enough to her that Vidal was shielded and confident that she could not hurt him.

Part of her raged worse and part cringed in recognition of his strength. She could leave him, she thought, but atop that came second thoughts, that she would need to make a domain and care for it or find another who would provide for her. And no one else was so strong. No one. He had gained more than any other from the flow of power to the Dark Court.

"So what do you want me to do?" She tried to keep her fury and resentment out of her tone.

Vidal nodded, smiling again with satisfaction. "First bid your Albertus catch a woman about to bear and hold her. When she begins her labor, you can gather a few of Mary's women and some of the Council. All you need do then is to bend the minds of those attending the queen to believe they witnessed her bearing the child and fix in the minds of those waiting word of her bedding that a healthy child was born."

"And how will Albertus bring the newborn into the palace?"

"In the bag in which he carries his instruments and medicines," Vidal said sweetly. "He always carries that, I am sure, and no guard would bother to look into it."

"And what will you be doing while Albertus and I perform this miracle?"

The sly taunting disappeared from Vidal's expression. He looked wary and determined. "I will be convincing the Evil that It must bind Itself into the newborn and wait some time to come to full power. It will not be easy." He stood up, contemptuous now, and waved a dismissive hand at her. "Go fetch your pet. He must have arrived already. I have serious work to do. It is time that I went to speak to that Evil and to Dakari."

On the words, Vidal disappeared. Aurilia shrieked a curse into the empty room, started forward to break or besmirch something and came up hard against a force field that shielded every part of the chamber except a narrow path to and from the door. She stood a moment, trembling and gasping for breath, thinking of ways to revenge herself.

Her first thought was of foiling his plans for the false birth. But enraged as she was, she realized that would be stupid. She would benefit more than Vidal if Mary bore an Evil child. When power was thin, Vidal always got the greatest share. Only when power was plentiful did she get filled to repletion. So her frustration grew. She would do it, but someone would suffer for it.

Because the imp Vidal sent could not actually drag Albertus Underhill, he had to use the token Aurilia had given him to operate the Gate in Otstargi's house. Thus Albertus arrived in Aurilia's apartment rather than Vidal's. She was not there so he knew it was truly Vidal who had sent for him. He clutched his medical bag to his chest and tried to breathe.

Albertus had not believed he could be more afraid, but when Aurilia told him what Vidal had demanded she and he do to repair Mary's barrenness, he very nearly fainted. Despite his terror he whimpered, "Impossible. Impossible. There are doctors and midwives and all sorts of nurses and attendants. How are they to be convinced they saw the queen delivered?"

"I will attend to that," Aurilia said.

It occurred to her as she spoke the words that likely Albertus was more right than she. It would be impossible to gather up all those who would attend the birth, impossible to convince everyone that the queen had actually given birth to the baby. But then she realized that was all to the good. Aurilia's eyes brightened as she thought of the charges and countercharges, of the rumors that the child was not the true heir. Like as not there would be more rebellion, battles in which men would suffer and die. More rich fare for the Dark Court.

"My lady, my lady, there are so many who should be present. How will you reach them all? How can I bring in a child? And the guards on the queen's rooms . . ."

At which point Aurilia said, "Then you would rather go and explain why this is impossible to Prince Vidal?"

All Albertus's original terror returned. The thought of facing Vidal with a refusal to accomplish what he ordered jolted Albertus's brain out of its paralysis. "Very well," he said, "but I cannot be in two places at once. Either I can take you to those who are to attend the queen so you can bespell them, or I can carry the child into the palace. Which do you want me to do?"

Aurilia grimaced. "You will have to gather together those who are to be bespelled. You know who they are."

"My lady," Albertus went down on his knees. "I am the least of the queen's physicians. The others will not listen to me if I bid them come with me. And if the woman has not come to term, someone must cut the child out of her."

Aurilia grimaced again, and reminded herself that it did not really matter if some of the queen's attendants or high Court officials were not included in the mind bending. They would accuse those who had been bespelled of complicity in a deception. Doubt would be cast on the legitimacy of the child, which would provide meat for conflict for many years.

"Very well. You are stupid beyond belief. I will tell you in the simplest words I can find what you must do. On the last day of the mortal month of April, you will take the Sidhe you will meet here to the palace. He will assume the appearance of one of the queen's servants and you will tell him who to summon and where to take them. They will be bespelled to wait where he sets them until I come."

"Otstargi's house is some way from the palace. Should I have ready a chair to carry you from Otstargi's house to the palace? My lady, what will I tell the chairmen? How will I bring you in past the guards?"

Aurilia was growing more and more annoyed with Albertus. He should know without being told that she could bespell the guards and the chairmen. He was only trying to find more sources for doubt and alarm. Maybe he was not really devoted to her, not worth more than the pungent flow of power that could be wrung from his death.

"No chair. No guards," she snarled. "This is too important for your silly doubts." And she told him what Vidal was planning to do with the baby Mary would seem to bear.

Albertus stared with starting eyes. Even more annoyed with the horror she saw in his face—was he not hers? Should not his first joy be what pleased her? And to loose a horror on England *did* please her. With a gesture Aurilia cast a little spell at Albertus, who gasped with a wrenching pain in his gut and began to weep.

The ooze of pain and fear that came from him soothed her and cleared her mind. She knew she needed a Gate direct into the palace and she muttered a curse on Pasgen for having disappeared. A moment later her scowl smoothed away. There was another who could build Gates, a Sidhe whose power, aside from bare life, blossomed only from death. He had come not long since from the Bright Court . . . ah. Cretchar.

"There is a Sidhe who can build Gates," she said to Albertus, who tried to straighten up lest she do worse to him. Aurilia made a short impatient gesture and he succeeded. "You will leave a token in the room to which you bring the queen's attendants. I will give Cretchar someone to kill and he will build a Gate for me."

Aurilia then gave orders on the details of how to get the baby to Mary and how to collect all the necessary people. Albertus knew many were ridiculous but buried that knowledge under thoughts that she had given him a real hope the plan might work. He was finally released and he left with several amulets for emergencies, all of which looked innocently like brass keys on a chain.

He kept her plan in the forefront of his mind until he passed the Gate and was free of Underhill. Then he stood in Otstargi's bedchamber and ground his teeth in helpless hate and rage. Horror grew in him. Vidal intended to set a Devil on the throne. A real Devil, not some churchman's fancy.

Albertus would never have thought of himself a patriot or said that he loved England, but he knew he hated Vidal. And when he turned away from the Gate to go to his own room, his muscles shrieked in protest . . . and he hated Aurilia too. She hurt him not to punish him but for her own pleasure. But what could he do?

He sat in glum thought in his own room, planning, because he dared not disobey, how to abduct a woman heavy with child. It must be a woman whom no one would miss, was his first thought. And almost as soon as that thought became clear, a slow smile twisted his lips. He need only pick a whore out of the gutter, too poor even to pay to rid herself of the babe. She would be unlikely to survive the bearing, and the child would be half dead already. Softly, Albertus began to chuckle.

If the babe did not live, perhaps the Devil would die with it. In any case It would not rule England.

Invigorated by his determination to foil Vidal's plans, Albertus picked up the amulet that disguised him as John Smith. Since the disappearance of Francis Howard, no one would know that face. Possibly no one would recognize him as Albertus, the queen's physician, in the worst slums in London, but he did not want to take even that small chance. Nor did he want to take the chance that the groom in the stable where he hired a horse would connect him with the doctor who lived in Otstargi's house.

He was successful at his third destination. The first two places had no pregnant women. In the third street, which housed three low taverns, he found a woman with a protruding belly that looked huge in comparison with her starved body; she was quite literally lying in a gutter. Albertus dismounted, cast a quick glance around the street and saw only a staggering drunk. He threw his cloak over the filthy form and hoisted her over the saddle.

There was no need to keep anything he did secret from the near-mindless servant. If Vidal looked into the poor creature's mind he would see Albertus following the plan Aurilia had devised. Thus, he instructed the servant to carry the woman up and lay her on the floor of the guest room. There he cut away her filthy, tattered clothing and told the servant to burn it, then bring food. He washed her, noticing with satisfaction that the stretched skin of her belly showed movement. The child inside her lived.

Aurilia had set the last day of April for the false delivery. Albertus was sure the babe would not be born before then. On the thirtieth he would cut out the child. The woman would die, but that did not matter.

He spent a few hours in the morning making sure the woman would neither die nor waken and then set out for the palace. When he came to make his bow to the queen, to his surprise he saw among her women Rosamund Scot, who had been on leave since the queen's wedding. He knew Mistress Rosamund was actually Sidhe and assumed that Vidal or Aurilia had sent her to spy on him.

At first he suffered a moment of panic, but he did not believe that Rhoslyn could read his mind as Vidal did, and outwardly he was doing exactly what he had been ordered to do. Having made his bow to the queen, been recognized and graciously dismissed, he went to speak to the cluster of physicians and midwives, who were as usual discussing whether there were any signs yet of the queen being brought to bed.

Mostly heads were shaken; Albertus noticed that the chief midwife looked very unhappy and one of the physicians cleared his throat uneasily. Having looked over his shoulder to be sure they were well away from the royal party, he muttered softly that the queen's belly was less raised than it had been.

"Is that not common near term?" Albertus put in quickly. He could not afford to have substance added to the uneasy rumor that Mary looked less and less pregnant and the midwives in particular were having doubts about the likelihood of a baby being born. "It has been my experience that when the child drops before birthing the belly looks flatter."

Two of the doctors agreed with him, citing this and that case with which they were familiar. Albertus bowed acknowledgement, turning as he did so, which permitted him to exclaim as if he had just seen Rhoslyn.

"If you will excuse me, gentlemen and ladies. I have just seen Mistress Rosamund among the queen's ladies and I wish to greet her. She has been most helpful to me in calming the queen in the weeks before Philip's arrival."

He did not wait to respond to any of the questions about Rhoslyn, everyone being most eager to meet a lady who could calm the queen, but sidled away. Coming up behind her, he touched her gently on the shoulder.

"Mistress Rosamund," he murmured. "Let me welcome you back to Court. I am very glad to see you, and I would be grateful if you could spare me a few moments of your time."

Rhoslyn was startled. She knew Albertus, of course, for he had often given her calming potions for the queen and she had already realized that Mary was no longer in her fool's paradise. Whether she knew but would not acknowledge what was whispered among the women—that she was not pregnant—or whether she was upset because she could not convince her husband to remain in England more than a few weeks longer, Rhoslyn was not sure. But if Albertus had something of importance to tell her, she needed to hear it.

With a soft murmur of excuse, Rhoslyn closed her book, laid it on her stool, and slipped out of the half-circle of women. Albertus had already left the room. She followed him out and was not surprised to have him touch her arm just a few steps from the door. She walked with him until he opened the door of a small, empty chamber and stepped inside.

"If Lady Aurilia sent you, I am very grateful," he said. "I realized after I left her that I will need help."

He had already put one hand up to his throat, the fingers under the gold chain. It tightened at the use of Aurilia's name but not enough to choke him . . . yet.

"I will be glad to help," Rhoslyn said, "but the lady was in a hurry for me to take up my duties with the queen and did not tell me exactly what you plan to do."

"Give Mary the child she desires, of course," Albertus said.

For a moment Rhoslyn simply stared at him, utterly blank. "But—" she began. Stared again and when he grinned from ear to ear, said "But—" again without any idea of how to go on.

"But there is no baby in her belly?" Albertus murmured in her ear. "What matter? There are babes in plenty born every day in London."

Rhoslyn simply gaped, wide eyed, and Albertus explained the plan to her, except about the Evil, chortling now and again with good humor. He was so taken up with his cleverness and with relief that he would have help in dealing with Mary's attendants and the palace guards, he did not notice how Rhoslyn paled and shuddered.

Later she drew back so he no longer touched her and asked, "When?"

He shrugged. "On the last day of April. That is the date Aurilia set, and I dare not argue with Aurilia."

"You will kill the woman?" Rhoslyn breathed.

Albertus shrugged. "Yes, I must. We do not need any tales of missing newborns on the day the heir to the throne is born."

"I see," Rhoslyn said calmly, trying to swallow the sickness rising in her. "Be sure to tell me what I must do and when. Tell me in good time and clearly. I do not want to make any mistake."

Chapter 35

When Elizabeth arrived at Hampton Court on April twenty-fourth there was still eager expectation of an heir, although that covered some doubts disguised as a tense anxiety about the coming lying in. Elizabeth's heart fell somewhat when she was taken secretly to a back entrance to the palace, but her spirits rose again when she was led to the prince of Wales's lodging. The rooms had been built for Edward when he was heir. Elizabeth sighed as she looked about, recalling those happy days when she and Edward and poor Jane Grey had all been schooled together under Catherine Parr's kindly eye. She was the only one still alive.

The thought sent a nasty chill down her spine, and though she pushed away immediate fear, she found herself grieving again for those she had loved and lost.

The mood did not last long. On April twenty-fifth she was given something else to think about. She received a curt message from Mary bidding her wear her very best clothes on the next day because Philip would visit her. Elizabeth stared at the messenger, none other than Mary's favorite lady and long-time confidant, Susan Clarencieux; she curtsied deeply.

"I beg you to thank Her Majesty for me for her great kindness in sending me this warning. I will do my best to obey her as I always have and always will."

She thought Clarencieux's expression showed a flash of dissatisfaction over her answer and wondered whether she should have tried to look awed or delighted, but dismissed the doubt. She was thinking too intently about the reason for Mary's warning. The most obvious possibility was the simplest: an affectionate urge to be sure her baby sister made a good impression.

Absently Elizabeth thanked Clarencieux personally for carrying the message and politely dismissed her. Far more likely, Elizabeth thought, Mary had a double purpose: first to make her dress inappropriately so that Philip would dismiss or discount her and second to give her time to work on prepared speeches that would raise doubts in Philip's mind of her sincerity.

Her ladies, of course, had heard Clarencieux's message and began to babble. Elizabeth Marberry at once described one of Mary's most ornate gowns, a red velvet over a gold-brocaded underdress with huge fur sleeves. Elizabeth smiled at Marberry; Susan Norton said she thought Philip was very fond of cloth-of-gold. Elizabeth sighed and said she had none.

At last she said she would lie down and desired quiet. The ladies remained in the parlor of the suite while Elizabeth went into the bedchamber. There, Blanche settled herself beside the bed and described what Philip and Mary had worn for several days.

"So much black," Elizabeth sighed. "I have read that Spain is a country with fine weather and much sunshine. Why are they so gloomy?"

Blanche laughed softly. "It is fortunate that you look well in black. There is that pale blue satin undergown with only a very little silver embroidery. You can wear that with the black velvet kirtle. His highness will like the black velvet."

"And perhaps the simple undergown will make him think I am simpleminded," Elizabeth growled under her breath.

It had been a long time since Elizabeth had any excuse to wear her most magnificent gowns and the priceless jewels that Denoriel had given her. But Blanche had told her the tale of how Philip would not wear the surcoat Mary had sent him to the wedding banquet. The robe was of cloth of gold, embroidered with the roses of England and the pomegranates of Spain intertwined in gold beads and pearls and had eighteen huge buttons, made from table diamonds. Philip said it was too ostentatious, and left it behind in his lodgings. Elizabeth growled again, but chose a relatively simple, although large, blue sapphire hung on a long gold chain that could be wound several times around her long, slender neck.

"Hush," Blanche said, patting her arm. "Be glad he is so curious about you that he comes only two days after your arrival. I suspect that did not entirely please the queen."

"Hmmm. No. You are right about that, Blanche." Then she sighed. "I almost wish Da had not made it clear that Philip is so important to me. Now I am so anxious that I am sure I will say or do something that will turn him totally against me."

"No you won't, love," Blanche murmured. "You always know just what to say to people." She paused and grimaced. "Unless, of course, you want to cut their livers out with your tongue—but I warrant after the talking to His Grace gave you, you won't do that to King Philip no matter how you feel."

"King Philip?" Elizabeth snarled softly. "Not yet, he isn't."

"Oh yes he is," Blanch insisted. "The emperor abdicated the throne of Naples and gave it to Philip. It was announced the day before the wedding so that Queen Mary could marry a king."

"Oh," Elizabeth said flatly.

She had been indulging herself with the pleasure of giving Philip a nod of the head instead of the full reverence due a king of England. She thought she could get away with that as she was playing the role of young, innocent, and ignorant.

"Yes," Blanche said. "And you keep in mind what His Grace of Richmond told you. He said not to annoy King Philip and warned you not to be too smart."

So it was when Philip was announced and entered Elizabeth's private parlor that she sank all the way to the ground, head bent. She told herself as Philip graciously took her hand and raised her up, that she would have done as much for any visiting royal personage to whom her father or brother introduced her. The man was only her sister's husband, not the king of England.

He said something and Elizabeth raised her head, offering a tentative smile. She cocked her head as if she were trying to understand, but used the few moments to examine him closely. Had she not held in her arms the exquisite beauty of a Sidhe, she would have found Philip pleasing to look at. She did not at all wonder that Mary, who had likely never even thought of a man as a man, was wholly enamored.

Philip had pleasant, regular features, a broad brow above large, blue eyes. His thick eyebrows, hair, and beard were probably called golden; to Elizabeth who was familiar with truly golden hair, Philip's was merely yellow. His nose was straight and his mouth wide, normally something that Elizabeth liked, but Philip's lower lip was thick and pendulous. She thought of being kissed by that mouth and had to stiffen her shoulders against a shudder.

She turned the incipient motion into a shake of the head, denoting incomprehension, and replied to what Philip had said in French, speaking slowly in the hope he would understand. "I am so sorry," she said. "If only my sister, the queen, had given me a few weeks to make ready, I would gladly have learned Castillian Spanish. I am very good with languages. I also speak Latin and Italian, if either of those would be easier for you than French."

"What a learned young woman you are," Philip said in Latin, a language in which he was fluent from his constant association with churchmen; he thought briefly it was a shame Mary's Latin was rudimentary, only phrases from the Mass.

Elizabeth smiled again. "My father was most insistent that his children be well educated," she replied in easy Latin, proving she had not been boasting. "And since I was a daughter what I was taught was mostly languages. I know some Greek too, but I am not fluent enough truly to converse in that language."

"No history, no art, no music?"

"Oh yes, all of those, but we each have our own special abilities. Mine were for books. In music, yes. I can play the Virginals, but, Your Majesty, my ability is nothing compared with that of the queen. Queen Mary loves music. She is truly an accomplished performer."

From his expression, Elizabeth thought, music was not what Philip wanted to talk about.

"Surely you learned history."

"Surely I did." Elizabeth laughed and gave him a sidelong glance. "What I remember is another matter entirely."

"You do not find history interesting?"

She could not divert him; he would talk politics. Elizabeth sighed. "It does not seem very pertinent to my life. I have even been forbidden to hear any news, except, to my great joy, that of the queen's increasing."

"Your sister is very sorry for the restrictions she was forced to put on you, but she is afraid that you will again be involved in treason—"

"I never was!" Elizabeth interrupted rudely and loudly. "I never would be! I am Queen Mary's most loyal and loving subject."

Philip looked taken aback by her violence, but would not abandon the subject. He said, "Then how did your letter get into the French ambassador's mail pouch?"

Elizabeth widened her eyes and shrugged, indifferent now that he had no new information, only that old chestnut. "How should I know? I had nothing to do with the French ambassador, nor had any person in my household. God knows they were questioned closely enough. Not a hint of guilt was discovered. And I was in Ashridge while the ambassador was here in London. It would be stupid to send such a thing by messenger. Is it not more likely that someone in the queen's own household—it is much larger than mine and not every person in it as close or well known—copied the letter and sold it? The copy was not even writ on paper common in my supplies."

"No one is blaming you now," Philip said, raising a placatory hand. "The rebels have been punished or pardoned. Just to ease your sister's heart you should be willing to beg pardon for a fault and allow her to grant you the mercy of pardon."

Mercy of pardon, Elizabeth thought. *More likely the mercy of the axe.*

"Not that fault!" she said, loud and indignant again. "I never would. Never! I have never been disloyal in word or deed to the queen."

Now Philip laughed, waved the subject away, and with his last words transferred the guilt for raising it to Mary. "Well, I said I would try to convince you. Before she is brought to bed, the queen wished to have a clean slate."

Elizabeth shook her head, speaking more gently, almost regretfully. "I cannot confess to something of which I am not guilty. That is a lie before God. Let the queen ask me to confess to pride, to vanity . . . Oh, there are so many faults of which I *am* guilty."

Philip laughed again. "If God will forgive you, Queen Mary will also."

It was almost a promise, Elizabeth thought, and set her hand on his when he offered it. He was smiling and led her toward a pair of chairs, one a little more elaborate than the other. As they approached, Elizabeth curtsied again, though not so deeply, and seated herself on the lower chair. Philip did not seem to notice, but he was still smiling and Elizabeth was sure he had noticed. He was, she had heard long before she started for London, very aware of his dignity.

The next subject he raised was totally unexceptional—English gardens and the English landscape. His own country was in many places too hot and arid for such lush greenery, he said. Elizabeth thanked him for his compliments and said she was sure there were great beauties in Spain that did not depend on grass. There was a momentary pause in which Philip's eyes looked into the distance, seeing some picture. And when he spoke Elizabeth thought she heard a lonely echo in his voice.

It must be hard, she thought, *to be exiled for political purposes to a place where you are hated.* So when she answered him, Elizabeth's voice was softer and her smile enchanting. Philip, aware without being aware of the more genuine welcome, stayed longer than he had expected, and spoke with animation of several neutral topics, particularly of the difference in Spanish customs and English customs.

Elizabeth listened with real interest, commenting frankly and intelligently on which of the Spanish customs she thought sensible and more elegant than those of England. But she was quick to point out that she herself was "mere English" and never wished to leave the land of her birth. Nonetheless when he finally rose to take his leave of her, Philip seemed almost reluctant to go.

After Philip's visit, Elizabeth hoped that she would be invited to dine or that other members of the Court would come and call on her. However, no other sign that she was known to be in Hampton Court appeared. Five days passed slowly, until soon after dark on April thirtieth. Discouraged and downhearted, Elizabeth was in her bedchamber, reading by the light of a branch of candles with her ladies seated on cushions around her chair, when Blanche sidled in and touched her arm.

Elizabeth was startled. Not only was Blanche returned too early from visiting (and collecting gossip from) a friend who served one of the queen's ladies, but her eyes were wide with distress and her face pale. Susanna Norton looked up with a disdainful frown; she had told Elizabeth outright several times that Blanche was far too free in her manner.

Heart leaping in her throat because she understood something terrible had happened, Elizabeth made three swift jabs with her forefinger, and muttered, *"Bod oer geulo!"*

All three women froze, Susanna with her mouth still open to reprimand Blanche.

"What?" Elizabeth asked barely above a whisper, not because the women would hear but because she did not really want to know.

Blanche seized Elizabeth's hand and pressed it. "The maid told me in confidence that her mistress had been called away because the queen is in labor."

Elizabeth pressed her free hand to her mouth as if to suppress a cry, then breathed, "I have been living in a false dream of hope because Rhoslyn saw no babe. "Oh, God help me. I must release these women and act as if I were overjoyed."

"Release them, but say nothing about the queen, say nothing about any excitement. The maid said she should not have told me. Mayhap something is wrong. Meanwhile, say the reading has given you a fierce headache and I should bring you a tisane. Then you will be able to go to bed. I do not think many know yet that the queen is brought to bed. And remember if Rhoslyn saw no babe, like as not this one will not live. You can settle your mind to what has happened over the night."

Shying away from the horrible hope that her sister's child would die, Elizabeth said only, "I do not think I will ever settle my mind to it. With an heir to follow her, Mary will destroy this realm and I will be unable to save it."

"Certainly you will not if you are dead," Blanche said dryly. "First save yourself, then worry about the realm."

As the hour advanced toward midnight, Rhoslyn became more and more tense. Earlier the queen had withdrawn to her bedchamber. Soon after, other courtiers left for their own beds. When the door opened inward, however, Rhoslyn started violently and the book she had been reading slipped from her hands. Sidhe! She sensed Sidhe. She blessed her reaction as she bent to pick up the book, which let her watch the servant who had just come in. She could not see through his illusion of humanity, but she knew him to be Sidhe.

He moved quickly, bent as if to whisper into the ear of the countess of Arundel. She rose rather stiffly and walked right out of the room; the servant bent over Lady Rochester who swiftly followed the countess of Arundel. The duchess of Norfolk looked mortally offended, staring after the women who had left.

Now everyone was looking at the servant. Rhoslyn did so too, her heart pounding in her breast. The lindys fastened to her bodice began to quiver. Yes, he was Sidhe; she was sure of it. Albertus's plan to provide a child for the barren queen was under way. Rhoslyn was now supposed to go to the garden entrance of Hampton Court to escort another Sidhe, wearing the face and body of Albertus and carrying his medical bag, into the queen's bedchamber. No one would question her; the doctors came and went with increasing frequency.

The women remaining in the chamber were moving around talking to each other in uneasy whispers. Rhoslyn rose, put her book down on the stool on which she had been sitting, and hurried out. To her relief, the lindys was now almost leaping off the bodice of her gown to which it was fastened. She knew Pasgen was waiting in the empty house for his lindys to signal the alarm. He would Gate to Otstargi's house, follow the false Albertus, and rescue the newborn . . . if it had survived its cruel birthing.

Meanwhile Rhoslyn had to stop the flow of attendants and Court officials in whose minds Aurilia was planting the false images of the queen's delivery. She scuttled through the corridors to the chamber Albertus had shown her but stopped well away from it, catching her breath. Even at a distance and through the walls and closed door she could sense Aurilia's power. Shivering, she pressed herself into a shadowed doorway.

There was too much power in the Dark Court. The burnings for heresy, which had started in February, had continued and increased. Not only the agony of the victims, but the fear and hatred of those who shared the victims' belief had overwhelmed the joy and good feeling engendered by the queen's announcement of her pregnancy; strength poured into the Dark Court. Aurilia had power to spare and Rhoslyn was afraid to confront her.

The Sidhe acting as a servant was leading two blank-eyed courtiers down the corridor. Rhoslyn recognized one of them as a member of Mary's Council. She could not recall his name but that a member of the Council had been snared was dangerous. If an officer of the Court announced the birth of an heir, he would be believed.

The Sidhe looked toward her—likely he sensed the presence of another Sidhe—but did not stop. Rhoslyn hoped he still had others to gather up. If Bishop Gardiner and Lord Paget were already in that room she would be too late. No, he hadn't enough time to get to them. If she could bind him, too few would announce the false birth. Pasgen would make sure the child did not arrive.

Rhoslyn backed down the corridor until she could slip around a corner. She could still see the door but she wished to put as much distance between her spell and Aurilia as possible. When the Sidhe dressed as a servant came out, she gathered her strength, and as he passed the side corridor, she stepped out, caught his sleeve and drew him back around the corner.

He sensed her as Sidhe as he had sensed her earlier; that made him compliant in responding to her pull. His lips parted to ask what she wanted—and Rhoslyn thrust a violent "Obey" command into his mind. His face blanked; his eyes looked without seeing. Rhoslyn breathed a long sigh of relief.

When the lindys shook, Pasgen assumed mortal disguise, leapt to his feet, and rushed to the door of the empty house. Torgen was waiting, and Pasgen drew in his breath with pleasure. The Gate was not far; he had planned to walk to it, not to trouble Torgen. But Torgen frequently knew what he needed before he did. In fact, Pasgen thought as he reached toward the elvensteed, he would need a horse in the mortal world, unless he was fortunate enough to catch the false-Albertus before he left Otstargi's house.

Pasgen hugged his elvensteed fondly just before he mounted. "But you don't look anything like a mortal horse," he pointed out.

He was also going to explain that his Gate opened into a human bedchamber where there was no room for a horse; however, he found himself stepping out of the Gate into Otstargi's room.

"Torg—" he began, and swallowed the words as he hurried out. He could not get used to the way elvensteeds knew more than their riders. Torgen would be where and when he was needed.

First Pasgen glanced into Albertus's bedchamber; it was only slightly disordered and empty. In the other chamber, however, the servant was washing the floor. Beside him was a rolled pallet almost soaked in blood. Pasgen's lips thinned. Albertus had torn the babe from the mother's body.

He turned away without speaking to the servant, who would clean as well as he could without further instruction, ran down the stair, and out the door into an empty street. Torgen was waiting.

"Can you follow where he went? He was carrying a newborn, who would smell of blood . . . and likely of death."

By then Pasgen was mounted and Torgen, who now looked like an ordinary if beautiful black horse, took off at a fast trot down the street toward Hampton Court Palace. One curiosity; no sound of horse's hooves disturbed the quiet of the night.

Pasgen was prepared to stun any guard at the garden gate, but it was not necessary. He overtook Albertus—and to Pasgen's initial surprise it was Albertus himself, no disguised Sidhe—in the side lane leading to the garden gate. Thus there was no need for stunning; they were all still well out of sight of the guard.

Lips parted in a vicious grin, Pasgen simply leapt down from Torgen's saddle and froze the physician. He had realized that Albertus could not allow a Sidhe—and likely one of those who took too much pleasure in mortal pain—to cut the baby from the mother. Doubtless the Sidhe would have taken so long about it, that the child would not have survived.

The thought struck Pasgen painfully. Deprived of them, most Sidhe loved children. Hastily now, he took the bag from Albertus's hand and opened it. His eyes widened and his grin hardened into a pained rictus. Tears sprang to his eyes as he knelt, put down the bag, and carefully lifted the tiny body out. The babe was so pale and still he thought it dead, but it was chilled, not stone cold and clammy and where his hands cupped it, he felt a slight warmth . . . and then it twitched.

Pasgen gasped and tore off his doublet to wrap around the bloodstained rag covering the child. The night air was too cold; it would chill his fragile burden. Clutching the baby to his breast, he closed Albertus's bag and replaced it in his hand. He turned to Torgen, about to ask for help in mounting, but the elvensteed had already knelt. When he was in the saddle, he whispered the Don't-see-me spell, released Albertus from stasis, and watched him continue toward the gate to the garden without the smallest sign of awareness that he had been relieved of the fruit of his crime.

"Hafwen," Pasgen said, holding the infant with great care.

Hafwen would know to whom to bring the child if she could not save it herself.

The street that led to the garden gate seemed unusually long to Albertus, but he put that down to being tired. He had not dreamed that the skinny bitch would have so much blood in her or that the baby would be so small. He almost could not find it for all the blood. He should have cut her throat before he cut out the child, but he wanted the babe alive.

All he needed was for it to live until all the notables had seen it and it could not be exchanged for something more healthy. He did not think this babe would survive more than a few days. No one would think that strange or suspicious. The death of the infant would be part of the queen's family history. All of Mary's mother's children, except her, had died within minutes or at most a few weeks of being born.

He frowned as he came to the gate. Rhoslyn was supposed to be there, to have told the guard he had been summoned to the queen. Thank God he had his physician's letter. The guard was suspicious because it was nearly midnight, but the queen's seal on the letter together with Albertus's indignant claim it was an emergency passed him through. He had a moment of panic when he thought the guard pointed to his medical bag, but it was a gesture of recognition of the physician's case and he was waved ahead.

No doubt the guard thought he would turn right and enter into the lower apartments where he would need to pass several more guards before he came to the queen. He turned left instead.

Albertus was accustomed to uncovering interesting information and he had learned the queen had her own private stair by which she could slip down into the garden. He had showed it to Rhoslyn, told her to make certain that the door was unlocked. If she had failed in this second task . . .

He found the stair and hurried up it. At the top he paused to listen at the door; he heard nothing. Carefully, he twisted the knob, breathed a sigh of relief as it turned, and opened the door a bare crack. With an even greater sigh, he pushed the door open, entered, and closed it behind him.

Before him was what seemed a room full of statues. Mary was kneeling at her *prie-dieu*. Albertus frowned briefly. It would have been better if she were already in bed. Now Aurilia, not as careful about details as she should be, would have to implant memories of her going to bed as well as feeling her pains start.

To each side of the queen knelt Susan Clarencieux and Jane Dormer. Jane Russell and Mistress Shirley were frozen mid act in examining one of Mary's gowns at the back of the room. Another maid was closer, lifting a pitcher but had fortunately not begun to pour.

Movement drew his eyes. Albertus sucked air nervously. Rhoslyn was still missing, but Aurilia was already in the chamber. If Aurilia had sent Rhoslyn away she would have to call her back, Albertus thought, quivering on the edge of hysteria. Rhoslyn would know the routines followed when the queen went to bed. Aurilia would need to insert into everyone's minds that they had . . . No, if the queen's pains started there would have been excitement and confusion. They would have sent for the midwives and the doctors.

He turned eagerly to Aurilia and began to tell her what she must implant in the mind of each person in the room. As he spoke, he knelt down to open his case, shaking with excitement. Just before he reached inside, he became aware of the ominous silence above him and looked up.

Aurilia should have looked pleased; instead she looked furious. "That will take all night," she snarled. "And most of the plan is already thrown into disorder."

Albertus drew a sharp, frightened breath. "Why? What is wrong? I had no trouble entering . . ." He started to pull back the flap of his satchel. "And I have here—"

"Everything is amiss," Aurilia hissed, raising a hand to make him suffer for her frustration. "You did not give me the right directions for the important Court officials. The Sidhe I sent for them has lost himself somewhere in the palace. There are only a few I have been able to bespell to believe the queen has borne a child."

While she spoke, Albertus had reached into his case to snatch out the body of the baby. He knew protest that he had not given the wrong directions, that the uncaring Sidhe had not listened, was useless. He thought if she saw the child, she would realize it was more important to make those in the room believe the queen had given birth than to punish him.

But his hand did not touch the yielding flesh of the new-born.

"Where?" he gasped, looking down, in seeming indifference to Aurilia who was talking to him; she snarled, outraged, but he only opened the satchel wider.

There was no baby!

Trying to believe that the little body had rolled to the side and down among the instruments, Albertus pulled the steel tools from the case and flung them away.

A screech that nearly split his ears rang out. Albertus looked up from his frenzied search inside his medical bag just in time to see Aurilia pull her foot from under one of his scalpels. The foot was already swelling and a tiny thread of blood trickled from where the point of the instrument had touched her.

"Iron. You struck me with iron!" Aurilia shrieked.

"No!" Albertus screamed.

His head was seized and wrenched backward. He struggled, twisting in the grip that was sinking Aurilia's long nails into his skull, feeling his neck about to break. That was a mistake. Blood ran down Aurilia's fingers, sliming them. It was the last insult. Snarling with fury, Aurilia's free hand smacked down on Albertus's chest. He had no time to cry out again.

Aurilia sucked in his life force, using it to dull the pain and counter the poison of the iron that had touched her. Using it to transport her from the queen's bedchamber into the room where she did not even notice the half dozen mortals who stood vacant-eyed. Using the last remnants to thrust her through the fading Gate to her chambers in Caer Mordwyn.

Chapter 36

Aurilia's shriek had penetrated through the door of the queen's bedchamber into the private retiring room where her ladies waited on her pleasure. Few were there now. The duchess of Norfolk remained, grimly waiting for her friends and rivals for Mary's attention, the countess of Arundel and Lady Rochester, to return. She was furious that they had been summoned and she had not.

Mistress Rosamund had come into the chamber a few moments earlier, seemingly to retrieve the book she had left, but she was pale and breathing hard. Ordinarily the duchess of Norfolk did not concern herself with Mistress Rosamund. The queen was very fond of Rosamund because she had been one of her ladies from before her father died and all through the years Mary had been in disgrace. True, but Mistress Rosamund was nobody, a mere esquire's daughter.

Still, the duchess of Norfolk noticed that Mistress Rosamund was looking at the queen's door with wide eyes that looked very frightened. Could it be that she knew what was going on behind that door? The duchess of Norfolk got slowly to her feet, intending to ask Mistress Rosamund what she knew with all the power of her exalted position.

She was just about to call out to Rosamund to wait for her, when a shriek rang out so dreadful that for a moment she was paralyzed. That moment was enough for Rosamund to leap across the room and fling open the door to the queen's bedchamber just as a second scream tore the air.

Outraged that Mistress Nobody had dared to run ahead of a duchess and also dared to open the door to the queen's bedchamber without invitation, the duchess of Norfolk pushed Rosamund aside. She heard Rosamund cry out but her eyes were fixed on an enormously tall, exquisitely beautiful woman with so vicious an expression on her face the duchess cringed away. But then the woman vanished! Vanished! And behind her Rosamund was softly keening gibberish.

"Who is that?" the duchess cried.

"Albertus," Rosamund answered. "He is one of the queen's physicians. Oh, God have mercy, I think he is dead!"

Caught by the word "dead," the duchess of Norfolk finally noticed the body on the floor. Her lips parted to ask again about the giant woman who had disappeared, but the words stuck in her throat. There was no woman standing above the body. Surely that vision had been some kind of reflection or false image. All else—except the dead man—looked perfectly ordinary.

The queen, kneeling at her *prie-dieu*, was just turning her head. She looked faintly annoyed at being interrupted at her prayers, but not at all startled. As if neither of those dreadful shrieks had sounded. Then Queen Mary saw Albertus on the floor, his case open, his instruments strewn about, and blood streaking his face.

"What is this?" Mary asked, eyes wide with shock.

The question was addressed to the duchess of Norfolk, who was standing in the doorway. The duchess turned to push Rosamund forward to answer. But Rosamund was not there. Everyone except Rosamund was staring at her, mouths and eyes open with shock. Rosamund's book was lying on the chair where she had left it. Had she imagined that beautiful, vicious woman, the duchess wondered? Had she imagined Rosamund? Had she imagined the screams?

"Did you not hear the terrible cries?" the duchess of Norfolk asked in a failing voice.

Rhoslyn had released the spell holding Mary and her women in stasis as soon as she saw Aurilia disappear. She had no time to try to wipe what the duchess of Norfolk had seen out of her mind nor to do anything about Albertus dead on the floor. She had to get to the room where Albertus had told her the courtiers would be kept until Aurilia had fixed the knowledge of Mary's delivery into their minds. If a servant entered or anyone else saw them with blank faces and empty minds a terrible outcry, likely an outcry of witchcraft, would be raised. The last thing needed in Hampton Court when the queen was about to bear a child was a witch hunt.

She found the room, closed the door behind her, opened her mouth to release the half dozen men and two women—and clapped her hand firmly over her lips. She dared not simply release them. If Aurilia had already fixed in their minds the conviction that Queen Mary had borne a child, they would rush out and spread the news to the world. Even if no one conceived the notion of making that the truth by bringing in a babe as Albertus had intended, much trouble for Queen Mary could ensue.

Near her stood Lady Rochester. Rhoslyn placed her hands on each temple and sought within. Yes, the thought was there. Lady Rochester was sure that the queen had been brought to bed of a fair boy, large and healthy. Rhoslyn first tried simply to remove that memory, but it was not a surface overlay on the woman's thoughts. It was a conviction, deeply implanted.

Aware of the passing of time, aware of the duchess of Norfolk having seen Aurilia, aware there was an unexplained dead body on the floor of the queen's bedchamber, Rhoslyn was tempted to carve out the memory of the queen's delivery and leave the hole in Lady Rochester's mind. She would fill it with something, Rhoslyn told herself, and then shuddered as she thought she might fill it with the duchess of Norfolk's tale. It would be easy to convince herself that the terrible events that caused Albertus's death and loud screams had been lost to her memory by shock.

But the queen and the five women with her in her bedchamber would not have heard any cries. What would they say to each other? How would they explain Albertus's dead body on the floor? Would they believe the duchess of Norfolk's claim that she had seen Aurilia and that the woman had disappeared?

Rhoslyn sought the root of the thought Aurilia had planted and slowly, carefully, dug it out. Tears of impatience blurred her sight. Usually when she implanted or removed a thought, the result was almost as swift as the thought itself had been. This was far different, and no matter her care, she scored the memories around the idea that the queen had given birth. Something would remain, a shadow of a doubt, a feeling of uneasiness.

She heard a sound in the corridor and knew she had no more time to spend. Rhoslyn released Lady Rochester to stand like an automaton and whirled toward the door, but the steps went by and she rushed to the countess of Arundel and seized her temples. She was less careful, pulling roughly at the memory of a quick, easy birth, pushing in the thought that whoever gave the news was too glib, not trustworthy.

There was more noise in the corridor. Rhoslyn could not make out any words, but the voices were high and excited. Desperately, she rushed from one man to another, muddling the memory of news of a successful delivery, overlaying that thought with the memory of a second announcement that no child had been born, the first news was from an overexcited maid who had misunderstood something she had overheard.

Then the latch of the door clicked. Rhoslyn whirled about, bespelled the latch to stick for a moment, spoke the words of release of the stasis that had held the ladies and gentlemen in the chamber, and cast the Don't-see-me spell on herself. She was so drained, so empty, that she was barely able to stagger out of the way of the people in the chamber and sink down on the floor. Ladies and gentlemen were now looking about in astonishment and asking each other how they came there.

The short spell on the door ended and the door burst open. Lord Paget stood in the doorway, his clothing showing the haste with which he had donned it. "What are you all doing here?" he asked.

A burst of answers made all of them unintelligible. Both ladies cried almost together that they must go back at once to the queen. Something was wrong; they knew something was wrong. They had been summoned to hear news but . . .

One of the men said, "The queen is brought to bed. Surely she is already delivered. It was barely dark when I was called here. Why have we had no further news?"

"Brought to bed?" Paget repeated like a man stunned. "I have had no message that Her Majesty had begun her labor."

He turned and went out of the room; those who had been

there hurried after him. On the floor, Rhoslyn sobbed softly with weakness and released the Don't-see-me spell. Her keen hearing told her that not all the men had turned in the direction of the queen's chambers. At least two, and she feared the two she had least time to work on, had set off in the direction opposite that Paget took.

The news that Queen Mary had given birth to a beautiful and healthy male child was all over the palace in less than an hour; from the palace the news ran out into the streets of London. Church bells rang, happy citizens brought firewood for bonfires. People hugged each other and wept with relief. Even though many of them did not like the Spanish connection and liked the renewal of Catholicism less, an undisputed legitimate heir secured the future.

No immediate contradiction of the rumor came from the queen's apartment. There utter confusion reigned. The servants and the few ladies who had been in the outer reception room had all heard the terrible screams from the queen's bedchamber. They crowded the doorway behind the duchess of Norfolk and supported her contention that she had opened the queen's door uninvited because the cries made her fear ill had come to the queen.

Moreover, there was the dead body of the physician lying on the floor, blood staining his scalp and cheeks, his medical instruments flung hither and yon. That could not have happened in silence. Yet the queen and her five ladies had heard nothing. Mary looked from one to the other and saw no answer in their frightened faces. She strained for an answer, any answer, to screams that had been heard through a closed door that she and her women, in the same chamber as the screamer, had not heard.

At which point Lord Paget pushed his way through the crowd at the door and said, "Madam, I was told that you had been brought to bed. What has been going forward here?" And he saw Albertus's body. His hand fell to his sword hilt. "What is that? Who is that?"

Everyone began to explain at once, voices mingling and over-riding each other, producing a cacophony that was no more than noise. Twice the queen tried to speak but could not be heard. Anger with others who would not listen caused raised voices which only led to more noise. Eventually Lord Paget bellowed, "Quiet!" and the room fell still.

Paget pushed his way into the room and bowed deeply to the queen. "Madam, I beg your pardon for intruding, and for raising my voice in your chamber . . . but how did this dead man come here?"

Queen Mary and Lord Paget did not always get along. From time to time Paget had been accused of corruption and Mary suspected him of gathering around him supporters of less than pure Catholic conviction apurpose to interfere with her policies. She dared not say to him that she did not know how a man died in her bedchamber, that she did not even know how he had come into her bedchamber.

"My lord—"

The voice, high and thin and trembling, was nonetheless pitched so that Paget looked down, every eye in Queen Mary's bedchamber, and all those still in the reception room strained to see the speaker. Mistress Rosamund stood, white faced, clinging to the door frame, seeming barely able to stand.

"I saw," she said. "I saw what I can hardly believe, but I did see it. The duchess of Norfolk saw too. There were two terrible shrieks. We ran together to the queen's door and pulled it open. The queen was kneeling at her *prie-dieu* with her ladies behind her. She was rapt in prayer, entranced in prayer. It was plain that she had not heard the cries that drew me and Her Grace of Norfolk to the door."

"So it was," the duchess of Norfolk agreed faintly.

She waited uneasily for Rosamund to describe the fearsome woman who had vanished; she could not decide whether to admit she had seen the woman and also had seen her vanish. But Rosamund said nothing of that terrible female figure. The duchess let out a relieved breath. Perhaps she had seen some twisted reflection in a window. There had never been a vanishing woman.

Rosamund was speaking again, her voice a little stronger. "The man was already lying on the floor with blood spurting from his head, as if something with claws had held him and then discarded him. I can only believe that some great evil threatened our queen and God protected her and all those with her because of the sanctity of her life and the sincerity of her prayers."

"It is true that I did not hear the cries," the queen said. "Nor did the ladies who were with me."

Mary looked around at the women who had been in the room

with her. All murmured agreement that they had not heard the screams, that none of them had seen the man enter the room. All were wide-eyed and breathless with wonder. All gazed at her with awe. Even Paget who was not a credulous man, was convinced that the ladies with Mary were telling the truth as they knew it. Whether or not God had actually shielded them all from evil . . . that was not so easy for a rational man to believe as it was for a superstitious woman.

It was not, however, a subject on which Paget was about to argue. There had been so many "miracles" on Mary's behalf since Edward had died: that she had been crowned and Northumberland's plot defeated; that she had triumphed over Wyatt's revolt when the rebel was entering the city; that she was with child at her age . . . if she was with child . . .

"Let us all thank God for his mercies," Paget said, just as Mistress Rosamund slumped to the floor.

The queen ran to her and knelt beside her. The other ladies ran, too. As he was forced away from the woman, Paget briefly wondered if Mistress Rosamund was somehow involved with the death of the queen's physician. Had she told the tale of the depth of the queen's prayers to cover her crime? But he could not see how that was possible. The duchess of Norfolk had heard what Mistress Rosamund heard and had seen what she saw. A quick question to the duchess of Norfolk confirmed that Rosamund had never entered the queen's bedchamber.

Paget then turned his attention to having the dead man removed from the queen's bedchamber. The ladies were all occupied with Mistress Rosamund, who was revived from her faint. Her maid was summoned and she and Susan Clarencieux supported Rosamund to her bed.

Meanwhile various alarms had been transmitted to the chancellor and to King Philip. Both had heard that the queen had been brought to bed and that the queen had been attacked. Both tales were obviously untrue; Mary was unharmed, calm, even exalted, and quite clearly had not borne a child. However, long and elaborate explanations were necessary before the two most powerful men in the country could understand everything that had happened.

It was well into morning before anyone got to bed and most of the men involved were in foul moods. Their servants hesitated to wake them again to inform them that the entire city was celebrating the birth of an heir. When each learned, he felt a flicker of hope that a babe could be procured to confirm the false rumor. It was no more than a flicker. Each man knew in an instant that Queen Mary could never be convinced to agree to such a deception.

For one thing, Mary still expected to bear her own child. For another, she was a person of such transparent honesty that she could never sustain the pretense.

Some effort was made to discover how the false rumor of the birth of an heir came about, but no one who confessed to passing word of the queen's delivery could remember how they knew of it. They were sure. Someone of great authority and close to the queen had told them, but who, which of the queen's ladies, could not be identified. Late on the first of May proclamations went forth denying a prince had been born. Such a joy was still a matter of expectation.

Elizabeth had missed all the excitement. Stricken by a violent headache, she had taken a dose of opiate and slept heavily all night on the thirtieth of April and well into the morning on May first. By the time she woke, Blanche had the true story and told it aloud with embellishments to her mistress and the other ladies. All exclaimed equally in wonder and horror. By no flicker of an eyelid or tone of voice did Elizabeth betray any emotion not completely shared by the ladies who served her on Mary's orders.

After such thrilling events, the week that followed was exceedingly dull. No one came to visit Elizabeth; her ladies did go out—to report to the queen, Elizabeth thought—but she made no comment and no complaint. She merely listened more keenly while her eyes were bent on the pages of a book; she learned that uneasiness was growing among Mary's attendants about the possibility of her bearing any child.

A kind of affirmation of that doubt came in the middle of the next week in the arrival of Chancellor Gardiner and several members of the Council. They came to ask if Elizabeth was yet ready to submit herself to the queen's mercy, to which she answered sharply that she had no reason to do so having never by word or deed ever willingly offended Her Majesty. Rather than mercy, Elizabeth said, she wished for the law. Let her be tried in public where these sly accusations could be exposed and shown to have no substance.

Gardiner and the Council members left without the smallest satisfaction, and some of the Council members looked very thoughtful. If Queen Mary did not soon deliver a child, the lady with whom they were crossing swords might be the next queen.

The next day Gardiner returned carrying a message from Queen Mary herself. She marveled, Gardiner reported the queen as saying, that Elizabeth should so stoutly refuse to confess that she had offended. It seemed, Mary added, that Elizabeth thought she had been wrongfully imprisoned.

Elizabeth smiled thinly. "No, not at all. It is the queen's right to deal with me, her subject, as she pleases."

"Well," Gardiner returned angrily because she had said nothing rebellious, "Her Majesty wants me to tell you that you must tell another tale before you can be set at liberty."

Liberty from my life and my chance at the throne, Elizabeth thought, and said, "Then I would rather remain in prison with honesty and truth, than to go free under a cloud. This I have said and I will stand thereto, for I will never belittle myself."

Suddenly Gardiner dropped to his knees, "If this be true, then Your Grace hath the advantage of me and the other lords, for your wrong and long imprisonment."

But Elizabeth did not fall into that trap and assure him that she did not blame him. She smiled very slightly and said, "What vantage I have, you know. Taking God to record, I seek no vantage for your so dealing with me. But God forgive you . . . and me also."

Elizabeth's voice was even, her smile unchanged, but two of the Council members who had come with Gardiner began to edge their way toward the door hoping she had not noticed them. What would God have to forgive her for if not for what she would do to them when she came to power.

The others made deeper bows as they said quiet fare wells than they had on arriving. They doubted Elizabeth had failed to notice every person who came in Gardiner's train. Gardiner met Elizabeth's eyes; they were dark, not blue, but the look reminded him painfully of Henry VIII, who had not dealt with him gently when crossed.

Gardiner reported to the queen and to Philip, making it clear

that he was certain Elizabeth would never confess any connection
with the rebellion or even ask a general forgiveness. Philip had
to suppress a smile when he remembered how roundly Elizabeth
had defended herself from his accusation. He did not admit how
much Elizabeth interested him, nor did he protest when Gardiner
again said that Elizabeth was the worst threat to Mary's reign and
to ensure its safety must be removed.

When Gardiner was gone, however, Philip asked, as if mildly
curious, how Elizabeth was to be removed.

"Declared bastard, which she is," Mary hissed, "and debarred
from the throne."

"And how likely is this to happen?" Philip asked gravely.

Mary bit her lip. Gardiner had tried many times to push
through a bill with those provisions. He had never even succeeded
in bringing it to a first reading, let alone a vote. Parliament was
not in the least interested in having the heir presumptive declared
ineligible and having civil war or total anarchy in the country.

"When the child is born," Mary said, placing her hand on her
still-swollen but rather flabby belly. "Then they will vote to set
her aside."

Philip made no direct answer to that assertion. He remembered
the taut distension of his first wife's belly when she was carrying
Don Carlos, and he thought it less and less likely that Mary was
going to bear a child. To remove Elizabeth would make Mary of
Scots, the French dauphin's wife, heir presumptive; whatever Mary
felt about Elizabeth, Mary of Scots on the throne of England
could not be tolerated by the Empire.

"Perhaps you have gone about this in a fashion ill-suited to
such a headstrong chit," Philip said slowly, as if thinking of something new. "As she believes she has been harshly treated for no
real cause, Lady Elizabeth must have little faith in your mercy.
Perhaps if you see her and bespeak her kindly and release her
from confinement—she can be watched from afar—she would be
more willing to confess her fault."

"You do not know Elizabeth," Mary snapped.

Philip shrugged, the indifferent gesture a lie like the words. "No,
nor do I wish to know her, but I know when certain measures
must be acknowledged a failure and new measures tried."

A week later, when her belly was even softer, Mary sent for
Elizabeth. She did not invite her to dinner, nor to attend any

Court function; she would not give her the satisfaction of being publicly acknowledged. Mary even waited until after dark, when no one would see Elizabeth brought to her rooms. Philip, curious, concealed himself behind a curtain in the bedchamber, not far from the garden stair which Albertus had climbed.

Now when the door opened, Elizabeth entered, straight and slender and lithe. She did not wait for Mary to speak; as soon as she was well into the room, Elizabeth fell to her knees and declared in a clear but not aggressive voice that she was a true subject in word and deed and begged the queen to so judge her.

Frustrated and infuriated, Mary forgot all about appearing to be kind and forgiving and said, "You will not confess your offense but stand stoutly to your truth. I pray God it may so fall out."

"If it does not," Elizabeth returned steadily, "I request neither favor nor pardon at Your Majesty's hands."

"Well, so you stiffly persevere in your truth. Likely you also believe you have been wrongfully punished."

There was a tiny pause. Peering out of a crack in the curtain Philip saw that Elizabeth was fighting to control a quivering lip. "I must not say so, if it please Your Majesty, to you," she got out in a slightly unsteady voice.

"No, but doubtless you will quickly enough say so to others."

Elizabeth raised a perfectly solemn face and said, most soberly, even sadly, "No I would not, if it please Your Majesty, I have borne the burden and must bear it. I may only humbly beseech Your Majesty to have a good opinion of me and to think me to be your true subject, not only from the beginning but for ever, as long as life lasts."

There was a slight sound behind the curtain. Elizabeth's eyes flicked in that direction. She lowered her head and bit her lip as Mary looked over her shoulder and murmured an apologetic-sounding sentence in Spanish. *So Philip was there. How very interesting.* Her mind flashed back over what she had said and how she had looked, and she was satisfied enough to need to suppress a smile.

"I can hope if I take your word it will be so," Mary said, ungraciously, obviously suppressing emotions other than laughter.

She gestured for Elizabeth to rise and gave her leave to go. Elizabeth backed cautiously away, until the hand held behind her touched the door. She curtsied, went out, and wondered, as she went down the stair into the garden to join Bedingfield and the escort he had brought, what Mary had thought the meeting would produce.

She did not need to wonder for long. Five days later, soon after breakfast, Bedingfield asked for audience, and when Elizabeth agreed, he came in bringing Sir Edward Paulet with him. Behind Bedingfield's back, Sir Edward was grinning to split his face. Elizabeth did not acknowledge his expression with so much as a blink, merely asking, "What would you have of me so early, Sir Henry? I hope you have no order to travel. I am not ready."

"May Christ, his Merciful Mother and all the saints be praised, I desire nothing of you, Your Grace, except to bid you farewell. The queen has lifted the burden of your care from me. I return it, with joy and gratitude to Her Majesty, to Sir Edward."

For a long moment Elizabeth was silent, then she held out her hand to be kissed. "Most faithfully, if often not to my liking, have you fulfilled your charge, Sir Henry. I cannot say I am sorry to bid you God speed, but you are an honest and faithful man and free of you, I wish you well."

Taking that as a dismissal, Bedingfield almost ran out of the room. Sir Edward stood looking after him, his grin even wider. "I think, my lady, that Sir Henry did not fully appreciate the honor of your care."

Again Elizabeth was silent for a moment, although her lips twitched. She was aware of the expressions of surprise and dismay on the faces of Elizabeth Marberry, Mary Dacre, and Susanna Norton. They expected as immediate a dismissal as she had given Bedingfield but Elizabeth was far too clever to do that.

"You will replace Bedingfield's guards with my four," she said.

"Done, Your Grace. Gerrit is at the door of the apartment and Nyle at the back entry. But, Your Grace, if you have any suspicion of trouble, I beg you give me warning so that I can add a younger man to watch with each of them. They are devoted, but . . ."

"Are there younger men you think could be trained by my four? They know without needing long lists—" which Elizabeth had no intention of supplying so Mary would have written evidence of whom she regarded as friends "—who I would wish to see, whom to announce, and who to turn away with an excuse. But I know they are not getting any younger. Only make clear that they will be welcome to me as long as they wish to serve."

Sir Edward nodded, his grin changing to an ordinary smile. "They know." He bowed. "Your orders, Your Grace?"

Elizabeth thought he was looking at her with purpose, as if he wanted her to draw him aside as if to give orders so that he could tell her something privately. She would not give Mary's spies such a piece of evidence against her. What she did was shake her head and hold out her hand.

"No orders other than what you know to do better than I can tell you, to find whatever men will be needed to replace Bedingfield's guard. Oh, and in the hour before dinner—" she smiled at him "—you can take Sir Henry's place and walk in the garden with me. It is the only exercise I am allowed." She noticed Sir Edward's lips part slightly when she said that and shook her head at him infinitesimally to stop him from saying he had no orders to confine her and would not in any case. She went on smoothly, "I do hope, however, you will have more conversation than Sir Henry."

Sir Edward caught the tiny head shake and the following glance toward the attendant ladies. He sighed gustily. "Oh, yes, my lady, but I fear my conversation will be no more entertaining than Sir Henry's. His departure was very sudden. I had no warning. I am now burdened with a dozen household decisions upon which I need to hear your preference."

"We can talk of that as we walk," Elizabeth said.

He took that as dismissal, which it was, bowed over her hand and went away. Before her ladies could ask about their status with her, she engaged them in their ordinary morning activities, acting as if she had not been given a clear signal that she was no longer to be considered a prisoner.

Eventually Susanna Norton said, "Will you be leaving Hampton Court, Your Grace?"

Elizabeth turned on her a wide-eyed shocked gaze. "Leave Hampton Court?" she repeated. "When my sister has not yet been brought to bed? No, indeed. Nor would I consider departing until the queen gives me leave to go and tells me where she prefers that I take up residence."

"How very obedient you are," Susanna said.

Elizabeth smiled. "I have always been and always will be Queen Mary's most loyal and obedient servant."

That was the end of that kind of question. Elizabeth had made

it clear, both by words and by not dismissing them that the seeming opening of the gates of her prison would not induce in her
any wild or careless behavior. There would be nothing, her ladies
realized, to report to the queen, not for some time . . . if ever.

Perhaps that conviction allowed the ladies to listen a little less
closely, particularly as Elizabeth and Sir Edward did talk of who
would stand guard and who would run messages. Only later did
Sir Edward talk of replacing the men-at-arms who had left with
Bedingfield.

While asking whether to bring men from Elizabeth's estates or
hire men from the city, Sir Edward managed to impart to Elizabeth
that Bedingfield had seeded the small troop Sir Edward had been
allowed with his own men. "He recommended them most highly,
and they are good enough men," Sir Edward said, his eyes filled
with amusement and his voice not completely steady.

"Sir Henry is a very honest man," Elizabeth replied, shaking
her head and swallowing down a choke of laughter—imagine
the idiocy of recommending men to Sir Edward and expecting
they would not be known as spies—and then added, in a soft
murmur, "if not the most clever. By all means," she went on in
a more normal voice, "you should keep and carefully consider
the advice of all the men Sir Henry recommended to you. I am
glad to give them employment."

For a week the hour's walk before dinner was as constant as
the walk with Bedingfield had been. On the eighth day, however,
when the door opened at the usual time, Sir William Cecil came
in in Sir Edward's stead. He bowed generally and with indifference to the ladies, then came forward and bowed more deeply to
Elizabeth. Now that her business had been replaced in her own
hands, he said, he was come to inform her as his employer—he
was surveyor of Elizabeth's properties—that he would be out of
England for some weeks. He had been assigned to go with Cardinal Pole to try to reconcile France and the Empire.

"Journeys abroad are always perilous," Elizabeth said. "I would
be grieved to lose your services. Do take care."

Cecil bowed, knowing Elizabeth was not concerned about the
physical journey but about his close involvement with Cardinal
Pole who was fiercely Catholic. Cecil was of the reformist persuasion, but, like Elizabeth, not at all inclined to martyrdom. He
promised to be careful and vigilant.

Sir Edward arrived before Master Cecil had time to say more and Elizabeth suggested that they continue their visit in the gardens. She needed her exercise she said; without it she could not eat. Whereupon Sir Edward smiled and said she would soon have occasion for more vigorous exercise. He had sent for her horses, and Ladbroke and Tolliver were already on their way.

Under the talk of horses, Master Cecil named a code they had used in the past and the name of the tenant who would, as soon as Cecil returned to England, begin a correspondence about a piece of property he rented from her. The rest of his conversation mentioned that his wife had come back to the house on Cannon Row in London and would like permission to call on Lady Elizabeth while Cecil was abroad. Elizabeth assured him she would be delighted to see Mildred, turning to tell the ladies who followed that Mildred Cecil was a very old friend, indeed; that they had been schoolmates at this very Hampton Court years ago.

A few days later Elizabeth's great uncle Lord William Howard came to call on her, greatly enlivening the quiet of her rooms with his jokes and his booming voice. Elizabeth encouraged him. That very afternoon the marquess of Winchester paid a call and asked about her future plans. She had none, Elizabeth replied, until she heard what Her Majesty the queen intended her to do.

This time she said nothing about remaining until Mary's child was born, and Paulet did not speak of it either. He did mention that he hoped Cardinal Pole could ease the tension between France and the Empire. The king's feeling against France was very strong, Paulet remarked—Elizabeth knew he was warning her against any contact or communication with the French ambassador—and if the war came to actual fighting, Philip might need to go abroad and supervise the Imperial forces.

May ended and the days of June rolled by. That month was notable, as was July, for several times encountering in the garden a slender, upright figure in somber black. Sir Edward stopped as soon as it became clear their paths would intersect and Elizabeth went forward alone to drop a deep curtsey. King Philip lifted her at once and said always that he hoped his company would not be distasteful. Invariably Elizabeth laughed and begged him, in fluent, fluid Latin to walk with her. During those meetings, Philip learned personally what Renard had reported, that Lady Elizabeth had a spirit full of enchantment.

Their pleasure in each other's company was not reflected in the country at large. Sentiment against the Spanish grew more and more bitter. England never recovered any of the good spirits founded on the hope of an heir. The crowning disappointment was the false rumor of Queen Mary's delivery. The weather was terrible, cold and wet; crops drowned and rotted in the fields and the temper of the country grew worse and worse. Constant broadsides blaming the queen and her Spanish husband for all the troubles of England were published daily.

Agitators carrying the bones of those burned for heresy as if they were holy relics encouraged more heresy and so there were more burnings. The mood of the people grew uglier and uglier. There were riots not only in London but all over the country that the earl of Pembroke needed an army to suppress. And still the queen did not give birth. No one except herself alone and one or two sycophantic physicians now spoke of the possibility that a child would be born.

By the end of July even Queen Mary had to admit she had never been pregnant. Quietly, without fanfare and using the excuse that the Hampton Court needed cleansing, which it certainly did, being dirty and stinking from overuse, Mary left the palace in London for her country house of Oatlands. Oatlands was a small, unpretentious estate; it would not accommodate any except the queen, her husband, a few of her dearest ladies and Philip's most essential servants. The Court, most of them with sighs of relief, dispersed.

Possibly room could have been made for Elizabeth, but Mary was tired of hearing who and how often those of her Court were now making their peace with Elizabeth. Mary gave her sister leave to move to a house of her own, only three miles from Oatlands. She knew quite well that many would pay calls at the new house, but she would not need to hear about it.

Chapter 37

Underhill, the misery of England was received with rejoicing by the Dark Court. Vidal decreed orgies where mortals and beasts snatched from the world above were torn apart and their raw and dripping flesh consumed. And he made all punishments public spectacles of torture; those occurred frequently since plenty made the denizens of the Dark Court wilder and more vicious rather than better behaved.

Vidal was so content that he had forgiven Aurilia for the failure of his plan to provide a babe for Mary almost without a word of anger. The truth was that he had been unable to get the Evil to agree to transfer itself to a newborn. He had a new and better plan now. He would disguise Dakari as King Philip; Dakari would couple with the queen and the Evil would root itself in Mary's womb. The seed that Dakari would carry would not be his own—Sidhe could not breed with mortal—but a packet drawn from a mortal prisoner and held in stasis by Vidal's spell and the power of the Evil. Vidal had won agreement to that plan because he had convinced the Evil It could influence Mary herself from the womb, and Mary was queen of England.

By the time he had the agreement—it was not easy to communicate with the Evil, who knew no words—it was too late to implement the plan. At the end of August, Philip had left England to be invested with the most important of Emperor

Charles's domains. Had times been happier in England and power less available to the Dark Court, Vidal might have made some effort to reach Philip in Flanders and induce him to return to his wife's bed; however, with the terrible harvest and increase in prices adding to the religious unrest in England, he was satisfied to relax and enjoy the merrymaking of his Court.

During the time between Mary's move to Oatlands and Philip's departure, Elizabeth had three weeks of relative freedom. She was living in her own manor with her own trusted guards at her doors. She still had Mary's women watching her, but the guards would not pass those ladies once Elizabeth was said to be asleep and they did not have the authority that Kat once had to pass the guards by. The one woman in her chamber Elizabeth could bespell to sleep, and she welcomed her Denno back into her arms with the enthusiasm of a three-months' absence.

The Bright Court was thin and faded as joy was drowned with the rotting harvest, starved with higher and higher prices of food, and scorched with the agony of the burning martyrs. Little sweet miasma of pleasure sifted down from the mortal world, only the sour strength of sorrow, the bitter of hatred, the burning of rage. These most of the Bright Court Sidhe could not or would not touch.

Few balls or parties were held in the Bright elfhames or private domains of the Seleighe Sidhe. That did not trouble Elizabeth, who was particularly at peace and lighthearted in those three weeks, and for good cause. Sometimes she and Denoriel simply stayed in his own rooms, played silly games and made love. Rhoslyn and Harry would often join them; the first time they did so, Rhoslyn told Elizabeth that Philip had virtually ordered Mary to remain on good terms with her sister no matter what happened.

Rhoslyn had all the news about the queen—not that there was much. Mary was desperately trying to stop Philip from leaving her; he was gentle, but adamant. He must go in person to be invested with the lands his father was abdicating in his right. Mary was devastated; not only had she just gone through the most humiliating experience of her life, but she was about to lose the man she truly loved.

In her grief, Mary clung even closer to the women who had supported her in her past miseries. Rhoslyn was very high in Mary's regard since her mortal alter ego Rosamund had proclaimed the miracle that had kept Mary safe from the evil that had slain her physician Albertus. And Rhoslyn, who truly pitied Mary, did all she could to hold the queen's regard. She knew what had really happened that night and knew she must be alert for some other device by the Dark Court to give the queen an unholy heir.

Not all was gloom in the Seleighe domains. The great markets seemed to have their own mysterious sources of power. They were as lively and more crowded than ever; indeed it seemed as if most of the Bright Court came to the markets for amusement when they were denied the mortal power of gaiety and mirth. It was to the markets that Denoriel took Elizabeth and in the markets they were forever meeting Sidhe who knew Denoriel but did not know Elizabeth. She was delighted to leave matters that way. She was very tired of being watched.

The three weeks was all that Elizabeth had, however. Philip's favor had its disadvantages. He did not permit Mary simply to appoint another "governor" for Elizabeth and leave her behind when he started for Dover. No, despite Mary's distaste for Elizabeth's company during the last few days she would have with her beloved husband, Elizabeth was invited to join them.

Not knowing how long she would be deprived of her Denno and Underhill, Elizabeth wanted a last entertainment. But the Bright Domains were faded. No brilliantly colored flames leapt about the crystal logs in Denoriel's fireplace; the illusion of the manor house was gone, the window itself was gone, from Denoriel's parlor. Denoriel knew he would not be able to create a ball; instead he arranged a come-one-come-all party at the Inn of Kindly Laughter.

It seemed as if all the liosalfar Underhill and a great many of the neutral oddities, like kitsune and urso, accepted the invitation. To accommodate the guests, the Inn of Kindly Laughter stretched to impossible dimensions and at least five of the strange forms the server took were present. Elizabeth only shook her head, resigned to not understanding and not caring much right now. She was being handed like a refreshment from one partner to another and having the unusual pleasure of being of no importance at all, only Prince Denoriel's favorite human.

She danced with a great many Sidhe and other beings. One made her laugh by his repeated attempts to dance with her; ursos were very clumsy. Finally, in pity, she allowed him to take her in his arms and stump away among the other twirling dancers . . . only to discover she had made a mistake.

The urso kept urging her toward a dark corner of the inn and telling her what delights he had prepared for mortals who would come with him. She laughed and said she could not, that she was bound by duty to the mortal world. He only increased his offers of riches and pleasure. He was very strong and less gentle than was usual for an urso, but before Elizabeth could become really frightened or call for help, the strange server, wearing the form of the tall stick with bristles, came between her and the urso. The bristles bent forward and touched the urso; he cried out in an odd voice and let her go.

Had the being drawing her into the dark been Sidhe or mortal, Elizabeth would have been more cautious, but an urso must have been joking. They were known for liking a jest, and what could an urso want with a mortal? They did not keep mortal slaves. She laughed as she saw the bristle part of the server sweep the urso toward the door. Apparently the server did not appreciate that urso's humor. Then Denno was there and she slipped into his embrace, as natural to her as breathing; she thought no more of the matter.

Later, in a hidden pocket in a Dark domain that had fallen into ruin when its maker challenged Vidal some hundreds of mortal years before, Paschenka said angrily to Cretchar, "I almost had her. Like all mortals she is stupid and greedy. I would have had her through that Gate you made if not for that strange creature."

Cretchar shuddered slightly. He did not admit that Paschenka would never have got Elizabeth though the Gate which had already faded. Paschenka had brought him only two gnomes and a goblin to slaughter, and the creatures of Underhill did not contain the same rich life force as mortals. And the server had returned after it thrust Paschenka out and . . . eaten . . . what was left of the Gate. Cretchar had fled before it caught him, but what flowed from it made him swear he would never again attempt a Gate in the inn.

"That was the server of the Inn of Kindly Laughter," Cretchar said ominously. "It rarely looks the same twice and has powers that no one understands. But if it has an interest in the red-haired girl, you will not be able to take her from there. You will need to seize her in the fair itself."

"How will I find her?" Paschenka snarled. "The Bazaar of the Bizarre is rather large."

"Not the Bazaar. The Elves' Faire. I still know Sidhe in the Bright Court. Prince Denoriel will hear of otherwhen jewelry there. She is known to love jewelry. Denoriel is besotted and will take her to see it. He does not oversee her choice of jewelry. It should not be difficult simply to pull her between two stalls and hold her quiet. I will bring a rug and wrap her in it. The market would not register that as violence, and we could carry her to a gate."

Paschenka wrinkled his nose. "It would be better if you made a Gate right where I seized her."

"For a Gate formed inside the market, I will need to kill two of the mortals you have taken. I would need that much life force to open and close the Gate."

"I do not believe you," Paschenka snarled. "You are lazy and stupid. There is so much power here that I am full to repletion. You cannot have any of my humans. I have other purposes for them. I am not even sure I want that red-haired girl. I have done well enough. I will put my mortals into stasis and bring them home."

Cretchar laughed. "Try," he said. "You go nowhere without the redhead. We agreed you would take her and I wish her gone. Just try to leave here without me. A Gate from nothing in a place so full of coercive magics as a great market needs life force, but I can deal with a Gate in a half dead domain. This Gate will not open for you. I helped get you those mortals. Some are mine."

"No." Paschenka's hands began to glow.

Cretchar backed away, then suddenly was gone. He was not completely helpless without life force; there was so much Dark power available even in the dying domain that he could increase the distance a step would take him and pull over himself the Don't-see-me spell. Paschenka roared with rage as a net of light flew from his hands. It fell uselessly where Cretchar had been.

The very day after the party in the Inn of Kindly Laughter, Mary and Philip, with Elizabeth discreetly in the background, took a barge down the Thames to London. Mary was supposed to continue by water to Greenwich, but she could not bear to be separated from Philip for even the short time it took to traverse

London. She was not well enough to ride, so Philip rode and Mary was carried in an open litter through the city.

She was greeted with considerable joy, largely owing to the rumors that she was dead and they would be ruled by the Spaniards. Elizabeth was not put on show; she went by barge all the way from Hampton Court to Greenwich Palace. She was not sure how she felt about that. She always loved the way the people cheered her and cried "God save the Lady Elizabeth," but she was not sure whether she wanted Philip to be made too aware of her popularity.

On the twenty-ninth of August, Philip set sail for Flanders. Elizabeth, to her consternation, learned that her sister planned to remain in Greenwich until his return . . . which Elizabeth suspected would be never. All she could do was lie with a sympathetic face, bite her tongue when Cardinal Pole lectured her on the great need to remake England as a Catholic nation, and meekly attend Mary as she sought the consolation of religion for her husband's absence.

September brought Elizabeth one great advantage. Renard, an inveterate enemy despite Philip's favor, was relieved of his duty as the Imperial ambassador. Mary was utterly dismayed; she had relied on his advice for so long. Elizabeth could not help but wonder whether Philip, having recognized Renard's fixed animosity toward her, had arranged the recall. Whatever the reason, Renard was gone and the new Imperial ambassador was scrupulously polite.

Elizabeth's good fortune was not mirrored in England. There was no improvement in the weather; there would be famine, Elizabeth thought when the twenty-ninth of the month brought what was written into the chronicles as the greatest rain and flood that ever was seen in England. Mary only said it was proper weather for the one-month anniversary of the day Philip left her.

Another joy came to Elizabeth in September: Roger Ascham returned to England from a diplomatic mission. He was Latin secretary to the queen and thus was able, without rousing any suspicion, to resume his sessions with his old pupil. Elizabeth joyously seized the opportunity to stretch her mind, to escape the company of her lachrymose sister. She and Ascham were reading together the orations on ruling by Aeschines and Demosthenes and discussing the ideas . . . but in Greek, which no one else at Court could understand.

In October Parliament was about to convene and Mary finally had to give up the pretense that if she waited at Greenwich Philip would return. Periodically bathed in tears, Mary sailed up river to settle into St. James' Palace. As an anodyne for her constant ache of longing, Mary threw herself into the business of state. She did not wish to forget Philip, not for a moment; she wished to serve him.

Elizabeth did not dare show any interest in any political matter nor hold any serious discussion with any member of the Court. She had nothing to do except attend on Mary, and the attendance was deadly dull. Mary spent every morning in prayer, which Elizabeth had to attend; in the afternoon the queen met with the Council, to which meetings Elizabeth was certainly not invited. By the end of a week Elizabeth was beginning to feel as if she would almost prefer to be sent to the Tower again as to be locked into Mary's company any longer. By the middle of the month she felt as if she were going mad.

A fortnight into October, Elizabeth took her courage in both hands and with suitable humility begged the queen to allow her leave the Court and retire to Hatfield. The city air did not agree with her, she said. Mary had started the letter to Philip that occupied her in the afternoon and often well into the evening. She hardly glanced at Elizabeth and waved her away without reply.

Fortunately for Elizabeth Mary finished her letter quite early and the Council had not been as difficult as usual. Susan Clarencieux suggested a game of cards and the other ladies urged the amusement; Jane Dormer asked whether she should send to Elizabeth and discover whether she wished to join them.

"I do not think we should trouble her," Rosamund Scot said. "She looks very pale and thin . . . well, she is always pale, but this last week she has a yellowish look to her skin, and her hands are like claws."

Mary said "Elizabeth?" rather absently.

Susan Clarencieux frowned. "She asked for leave to go into the country, to her manor at Hatfield. She said the air of the city does not agree with her."

"She does look ill," Jane Dormer agreed.

Mary looked down at the letter she had just finished. She remembered Philip's lectures on why it was necessary to win Elizabeth's trust and regard. He spoke of her only as a political pawn, of seeing her married to a good Catholic prince so she could be sent out of the country if necessary without creating chaos and so that she could have good Catholic children—*to inherit the throne*. He did not say that aloud, but Mary understood.

For a moment she considered denying Elizabeth's request to go to Hatfield where doubtless she would sow more seeds of rebellion. But if Elizabeth were truly ill, perhaps she would die. How convenient. Then Mary shuddered. How angry Philip would be. How wrong she would be to disobey her husband. She reached for her quill and added a postscript, saying that Elizabeth wished to retire to the country; should she agree?

Philip, released from the prison of a land he hated and a wife who did not appeal to him, was having the time of his all-too-sober life. He was masking, dancing, drinking, gambling, fawned over by favor seekers, and he had found the lovely, *young*, complaisant Mme. d'Aler. He remembered Elizabeth's witty conversation, the charm of her smile. "Let her go into the country," he wrote.

On the eighteenth of October, Elizabeth left London for Hatfield. Five days later Kat Ashley was established as the first lady of the household. Three days after that Dorothy Stafford and Eleanor Gage rode in to be greeted with tears and kisses. Alice Finch followed and last came Agnes Fitzalan. The ladies Mary had sent to replace Elizabeth's trusted friends now realized they would see and hear nothing Elizabeth did not intend them to see and hear. They wrote to Queen Mary, but she made no reply; indeed, what could she write? She knew they would report any sign of treason without instructions.

Of a truth, however, there did not seem to be anything of note to see or hear. Thomas Parry took up his accustomed duties. He and Elizabeth did their business quite openly, discussing this and that tenants' troubles well within the hearing of Mary's ladies. Indeed, it was not until the thirteenth of November that there was any break in the routine that was so dull to them. That day Dunstan stepped soft-footed to Elizabeth's side and murmured in her ear. Mary's spies all became alert. Elizabeth Marberry turned to look at the doorway; Susanna Norton looked fixedly at the book she held; Mary Dacre turned half away and spoke to Alice Finch.

They need not have bothered to pretend not to care what Dunstan said because Elizabeth clapped her hands and cried aloud,

"Lady Alana? You say Lady Alana is here? Oh, bring her to me at once." She stood upright with impatience, dropping the book cover she was embroidering without even fixing the needle.

Everyone was looking at the doorway, Kat Ashley with a big smile on her face and all the ladies with some expression of pleasure. Thus it was permissible for the ladies assigned by Mary to stare with curiosity. Each felt only more curiosity when Lady Alana came through the doorway. She was nothing to look at; indeed later when they discussed with each other why Lady Alana was so eagerly welcomed, they found that none of them could remember anything about her except her enchanting dress. And none of them could say just why what she wore was so perfect; it just was! Elegant and lavish and yet neither precious nor ostentatious.

Elizabeth had walked forward to meet Alana who was taken in an embrace before she could bow. "And are those family problems that have kept you from me so long at last settled?"

"In one way, not at all, and I fear Your Grace will need to have a hand in the solution, although you know I hoped I would not need to trouble you. However, the main cause of my absence, the great aunt who could not abide you, that problem is settled at last, and finally. My great-aunt died two days since, on November twelfth. She will never trouble you again."

"I did not wish her *dead*," Elizabeth said, frowning.

Lady Alana shrugged. "I do not believe her death was anything to do with you, my lady, no particular measure that she took or planned to take. Unless her general spitefulness and hatred burned her up from within. In any case, you need feel no guilt."

"No, not about her." Elizabeth grinned. "It seems that it is either unhealthy or unprofitable to work to my discredit," she said for the sake of Mary's spies. "I need do nothing but sit meek and quiet and my enemies confound themselves. But my dear—" she took Alana's hand "—you must be tired and travel worn. Go now to your chamber. When you are rested and wish to tell me of the trouble you think I can solve, I will be waiting."

So, Elizabeth thought, she was needed for some business Underhill, perhaps something only a mortal could do in the current weakened state of the Bright Court. She was eager to help. She knew *her* power was not diminished in any way, but she was afraid Denno would forbid her and be angry with Alana . . . and she could not ask.

Despite her words, Mary's spies were watching her brightened eyes with interest, but then Parry came in with a pack of letters. Most he laid aside for Elizabeth to glance over when she had time or simply to hand back to him, but one he laid on the table.

"From your surveyor," he said, knowing not to say William Cecil's name. "Usually he is perfectly clear, but this time I do not at all understand what he is saying. Here—" Parry pointed to a passage in the letter "—he says George Orwell's flax field—" Parry frowned and said with marked irritation that he did not remember the tenant's name "—is . . . gone."

"Gone?" Elizabeth repeated. "The field is gone? For good?"

George Orwell was the code name that meant what followed was important Court news. The field of flax was the code name for Bishop Gardiner, the chancellor. Usually Cecil's message was about stones (Elizabeth was a stone and the trouble was the attempt to dig out the stones) and briars (Gardiner's enemies, who might or might not be Elizabeth's friends). That the field was gone, was confirmation of Alana's news that her great-aunt was dead.

"Yesterday, he says, he had the news that the field would trouble him no more," Parry said, wrinkling his brow over the odd phrasing. "He said the field was to be taken in hand by a higher authority than yours."

"I cannot think what he means by that," Elizabeth said, most untruthfully; Cecil was remarking that God would judge Gardiner. "Just leave the letter. I will give it some thought later. Lady Alana has at last returned to us and I am setting aside business. She says there is a problem in her family that I may be able to settle. I am sure it is over the estate her great-aunt left her. The woman insisted she leave my service to inherit."

With the great-aunt's estate as an excuse, Elizabeth invited Alana to share her bedchamber. Mary's spies were not happy at being excluded, but they knew better by now than to try to get by one of the four old guards who stood by the door. No excuse would work.

Inside, Aleneil was saying, "The snatcher is back." She covered her face for a moment with her hands. "It has been so long since we nearly caught him that we thought we had frightened him away. But he took four children . . . four! Now Ilar and Idres Gawr are beside themselves. Ilar thinks that mortal-stealer has . . . has used up the mortals he took earlier. But children. Why children?"

Elizabeth shook her head. "You know I do not understand how and why power is used by you and yours. But that changes nothing. I told you when this first began that I would be glad to be bait for a trap. Only Denno will be so angry with me . . ."

"It's us he's angry with. Idres Gawr spoke to him and made it a matter of his duty, so he agreed to let you do it but—" Aleneil shivered. "Be careful, Elizabeth, I beg you to be very careful. Do not let the snatcher take *you*. I will lose my brother if anything happens to you. He will declare blood feud on all of us."

Indeed, it looked as if the blood feud had already been declared when, after midnight, Denoriel stepped through the Gate. His eyes were black with anger and his lips drawn into a thin line. Elizabeth, having given considerable thought to how her lifelong protector might feel about her being bait had decided how to deal with him; she bounced to her feet and ran to embrace him.

"I think the good Lord is supporting me," she said, with a light laugh. "Cecil wrote that Gardiner is dead."

"I told you the word in London was that he was very ill."

"You also told me his opening speech to Parliament was as strong as ever."

Elizabeth drew his head down so she could kiss his lips; meanwhile Alana slipped past them and through the Gate. Elizabeth felt Denno stiffen and knew her diversion had not fully succeeded, but she did not let him pull away from her kiss to which he was responding.

"That is two bitter enemies gone in two months." She said when she lifted her lips. "God's grace shines around me."

Denno would not be diverted to talk of Elizabeth's good fortune. He said, his voice hard, "That was Alana, I suppose."

"Don't be angry with her," Elizabeth pleaded.

Denoriel took a deep breath. "No. She is not happy about endangering you. But what if *you* are taken? Aside from what I feel for you, you are more important than a whole town full of mortals."

"I will not be taken," she said. "I think the whole of Elfhame Cymry will be watching me, and my shields will protect me. I do not know why, but my power is not diminished at all."

For a moment Denoriel was diverted from his fears. "Pasgen thinks that you may draw directly on the power that is so plentiful in the mortal world. He has been working on how Sidhe might use it, but without success. It is too strong even for him to handle."

Then he put his arm around Elizabeth and walked to the Gate. She drew in an anxious breath. The Gate looked . . . different. The edges were ragged and the image of the exit was pale, almost misty. Nonetheless Elizabeth stepped forward without hesitation . . . and wished she had not. The usual black of passage was lit by strange rents of pearly light, as if the Gate would dissolve, and it was not gone between one breath and another but clung for several long moments as if it were sucking at her.

Denoriel held her tight for another long moment when their feet were firmly on the beautiful image of the Gate platform at Logres. Elizabeth bit her lip. Denno's hair was white, plain flat white, and the lines of pain and anxiety carved into his face seemed deeper.

"I do not like Alana's plan," he said, stepping down from the platform but not moving away from it. "A gnome came to me just as I left Llachar Lle. He said he knew that I was interested in strange and wonderful jewels . . . How would a gnome know that?"

"Well, gnomes do cut gems." Elizabeth smiled and stood tiptoe to kiss his cheek. "And you have been known to buy gems for me." He shook his head, and Elizabeth stopped trying to soothe him. "More likely because that stupid Sidhe who tried to seize me is trying to set a trap in some jeweler's stall. Love, don't worry so much."

"I have just realized how I might save myself any worry at all," Denoriel said, smiling down at her. "I will take on an illusion to look like you." He uttered a bark of laughter. "Then let that mortal-stealer try to seize you."

Elizabeth pulled down his head and kissed him again. "Can you?" she asked sadly. "Look." She gestured out toward Llachar Lle. The area between, usually carpeted by the vivid, dark green moss starred with white flowers, lay dull and yellowish, dying. "And even if you can build the illusion and speak and carry yourself like me, if I appear without you in close attendance our prey will know we have divined his purpose and wait for another time. That means you would need to cover me with an illusion of you." Elizabeth giggled. "I could never carry that off. No, love, let us go and finish this. He last stole children . . . four children."

"Aleneil told me." Denoriel closed his eyes. "The Great Mother alone knows what he will do with them."

Elizabeth put an arm confidently around his waist. "Let us go to the Elves' Faire now, Denno. I think the folk of Cymry will have had time enough to spread throughout the market. I do not wish to be reminded of how thin the Bright Court grows. I will make it up to you all when I am queen, I swear it, but until then I can do nothing and it makes me so sad to see the fireplace empty and the window gone."

Gating from one place Underhill to another was not as difficult as Gating to and from the mortal world so the passage to the Elves' Faire was only infinitesimally longer than usual. Still, Elizabeth was very happy to see the great signs warning against magic or violence and urging the buyer to beware.

Although she had not come to buy anything, Elizabeth looked about her with unfeigned interest. She had a ready and easy source of payment in mortal goods. The Sidhe could ken almost anything, but they did not seem able to create things on their own. If they wanted a copper pitcher or a glass bowl, they had to have one first in order to copy it.

"Jeweler's Row is that way," Denoriel said, and gestured. He did not touch Elizabeth because he knew her shields would ward his hand away.

"Oh, let me look at the other booths. We always go to the Bazaar of the Bizarre. It is long since I have been at the Elves' Faire. I know you said a gnome promised you some special gems, but gems do not spoil like fruit. They will be there another day."

Cretchar, who had been hidden behind the sign that said "NO SPELLS, NO DRAWN WEAPONS, NO VIOLENCE" on one line and below that "ON PAIN OF PERMANENT REMOVAL," drew a breath of satisfaction. He had been afraid that the gnome had made Denoriel suspicious and that Elizabeth would not come at all. He still doubted she could be taken in the trap, and if she were not that Paschenka could be induced to try for her again. But that did not matter. Since she was here, he would use another plan he had been hatching.

That plan had formed itself after he thought he recognized several Sidhe from Elfhame Cymry drifting one by one into the market. He had seen two of them deliberately ignore each other. Of course it was possible that those two were enemies, but it was more likely Elizabeth had been enlisted as bait to catch Paschenka, and the Sidhe from Cymry were the teeth of the trap.

He had warned Paschenka not to seize the children, that the Sidhe of Cymry were even more devoted to the mortal children than to the adult mortals. Paschenka would not listen. He was far too strong for Cretchar to control; Cretchar's only choice was to flee and he liked the ruined domain. He would like to make it his own. He watched Elizabeth turn away from the direction Denoriel had pointed and slipped out of his hiding place to follow.

If Paschenka tried to take Elizabeth, and Cretchar provided a Gate he might succeed. But did he want Paschenka to succeed? How much better to be rid of Paschenka. Really, that was all that was necessary. Elizabeth was no danger to *him*.

Once Paschenka was gone, he would have all those mortals. With their life force he could restore much of the ruinous domain. He would not need to bring himself to Vidal's notice by asking favors for having Elizabeth abducted. He could not be sure Vidal would be grateful. He had almost been blasted by Aurilia and his Gate had not failed, only faded so that she had been disoriented when she had to leave the mortal world in a hurry.

Cretchar was not sure whether Elizabeth and Denoriel did not notice he was following or did not care. He wished they would settle into a place so he could fetch Paschenka. But there were more than goods available at the Elves' Faire: mortal and Sidhe entertainers—musicians, acrobats, declaimers of poetry—eating places and drinking places, games of chance and skill.

Denoriel and Elizabeth wandered the broad central avenue, stopping here and there to watch and listen, Elizabeth or Denoriel putting down a coin in appreciation or laughing whether they won or lost a game. They stopped to eat at a cookshop, not nearly as elegant as the Inn of Kindly Laughter, but with a most satisfactory hearty stew, and then, attracted by the sing-song voice of a vendor selling goods at auction, walked farther down the side lane to where mortals, animals, and some seemingly animate things of metal were being sold.

Elizabeth was far more interested in the metal creatures than in the humans. Slaves were known in England, but they did not provide a good return for what was paid and she remembered all the Latin essays she had read about the trouble slaves caused.

Anyway mortal servants or slaves could be easily enough obtained in England. The metal things, however . . .

Denoriel was fascinated too. He crouched down to examine one of the devices while Elizabeth went to the back of the stall where the vendor stood on a dais. It was a queer creature he was selling, seemingly a mortal but covered with hair—an ape, she would have guessed, but it was much too large. The vendor called for bids but Elizabeth stepped aside and spoke to one of the assistants to the vendor.

The assistant passed her to another over at the side of the stall. He was speaking to some very small, slender creatures who had blue skin and yellow hair and eyes. They had small wings too, which made Elizabeth wonder if they were fay, but they were much too large. Eventually one of them removed a circular object from a belt pouch which the vendor's assistant placed into a flat black box. They all nodded at each other; the round disk was returned, and the assistant turned toward Elizabeth and bowed.

She asked if he were prepared to answer questions about the metal oddities and he said he was. Elizabeth shook her head. The sounds he made did not seem to fit with the words that came into her head, but that had happened to her before in the market. She spoke in English, knowing the assistant could not understand, but of course he did understand. Elizabeth made sure that the things were not Sidhe made and invested with magic.

"Magic?" the assistant repeated, and laughed as if he did not believe in magic. But he was not so rude as to say that. He said, "No, indeed. It will work anywhere its battery can be recharged."

Elizabeth saw Denoriel touch the squat metal object he had been examining, shake his head at the person in charge of it or watching that he did not steal it, and start in her direction.

What the vendor's assistant had said made little sense, but Elizabeth thought she could get a further explanation later. What she needed to know was, "What does it do?"

"So there you are," a loud voice said almost in her ear.

"Who are you?" Elizabeth asked, drawing back.

"Your master, mortal," the fat Sidhe said.

The assistant to the vendor frowned and stepped away, raising a hand with two fingers up, one down between them and two down on each side, to summon those who dealt with slaves.

"You are no master of mine," Elizabeth said sharply, now recognizing the Sidhe that had tried to buy her from Denno and whom she had Pushed into the urso's al fresco. "My friend, Prince Denoriel, told you that I was a free mortal, allowed by Queen Titania's gracious permission to come and go as I will Underhill."

"And I am Sidhe. There are no free mortals. My word is worth more than yours. I say you are a runaway slave! Ho, slavemaster, come and put irons on this impudent creature."

"Oh, go away, you fat nuisance," Elizabeth said, turning away to look for Denoriel, who was pushing aside two burly, blank-faced creatures that Elizabeth thought must be constructs.

The fat Sidhe tried to seize her arm, but his hand slipped away off her shield. "Seize her!" he roared at the constructs.

One of them also tried to grab Elizabeth; the other stepped between her and Denoriel. Elizabeth hissed with irritation and spun to face the fat Sidhe. He was reaching for her again, laughing with satisfaction because she was hemmed in by those the vendor used to control recalcitrant goods. About to Push the nuisance again, this time hard enough to send him to the Void, Elizabeth remembered where she was.

The frustration made her utterly furious. And the knowledge that she dared not even slap his face lest the market consider that a form of violence, made her angrier still. Then she saw Denno struggling in the grip of one of the constructs, while the other reached for her again.

"Let me alone," she ordered the construct in a voice of command. It stopped, confused by two orders equally powerful. Elizabeth called to the vendor, "I am no slave of his!" and she stepped forward and spit directly into Paschenka's face.

The vendor, who controlled the constructs, ordered them to stand. He recognized the gesture of contempt and knew from long experience that she who made it had never been the Sidhe's slave.

"Pest!" Elizabeth snarled, and began to turn away toward Denoriel.

The word was swallowed up in Paschenka's howl of fury. His hand came up, blue light flickering around each finger.

Elizabeth backed up, eyes wide. "No!" she cried. "No! Don't!"

The fat Sidhe laughed at her, sure she was afraid of his power. The blue light arced in her direction.

"Don't!" Elizabeth shrieked. "You will be REMOVED."

She was too late. The last words were not nearly as loud as she expected. They echoed as if coming back from a long distance.

Several other exclamations of horror came from the crowd around the vendor. Tall and commanding, Idres Gawr came forward with Ilar and Aleneil just behind him. Denoriel pushed past the unmoving constructs and put an arm around her.

"I am so sorry," Elizabeth said to Idres Gawr. "It never occurred to me that he would try to use a spell against me and be REMOVED. Now how will you find the children he stole?"

"No, no. You have done all that is necessary. We have his partner, who says our mortals are safe and will take us to them." Idres Gawr bowed to her and gestured toward a knot of broad-shouldered mortals.

"I am so glad I did not spoil everything," Elizabeth said contritely. "I lost my temper with that fat fool."

"We are very grateful to you," Idres Gawr went on, then turned his head toward Denoriel, who still looked grim and angry. "And I wish you to know, Prince Denoriel, that Lady Elizabeth was never in any danger. I know this vendor of old, and he would take my word that Lady Elizabeth was a free mortal. Not to mention the word of Princess Aleneil and half my Court—all of whom do some business here. We expected Paschenka to have her brought to the vendor to mark her as a slave."

Denoriel was trembling with reaction from his fear. "And what if that creature had built one of his Gates and the other pulled her through? That was how he seized your people, was it not?"

Idres Gawr shook his head. "Gates are not easy to build in a market. I am sorry you were anxious. We were busy taking the Gate-builder, the creature that calls himself Cretchar, prisoner, which is why we were slow to go to Lady Elizabeth's aid. I swear to you, Prince Denoriel, there was no danger."

Elizabeth hardly listened. She had not been afraid, except for the one moment when she nearly forgot she was in a market and was about to Push. She was giving most of her attention to the grim-looking mortals. In their midst was a weeping Sidhe and around them was an empty space the other Sidhe avoided. Each mortal held a thick silk bag that Elizabeth realized could be opened with a swift pull of a drawstring.

"They carry Cold Iron," Aleneil said softly in Elizabeth's ear.

"They are of the earliest families to join the Sidhe of Cymry. I have been told that they were neither captured nor bought but came with the Sidhe of their own will. They are utterly faithful to Cymry and are the peacekeepers. Cretchar will cause no trouble to anyone, at least for eons, at most, never again."

Chapter 38

That was the last visit Elizabeth made Underhill for some time. In compensation she had Lady Alana's presence in her household over the dull days of winter. Christmas was celebrated quietly. The ugly news of new and more frequent burnings for heresy made Elizabeth more reluctant than ever to display a passionate Catholicism and too fearful to refuse Mass or confession.

Only one lighter note appeared during the somber season. The old merchant, Lord Denno came to spend the twelve days in his house near Hatfield and visited Elizabeth every day. He came laden with twelve days' worth of gifts, exotic dried fruit and sweetmeats for the early days, furs and lace for middle days, and twinkling chains of beads (and real jewels for Elizabeth) on the twelfth day. Elizabeth cheered up during his visits and what Lady Alana was able to do with the furs and trimmings he brought put all the ladies, including Mary's spies, into good humors.

Whatever pleasure and celebrations could be scraped together in the bitter weather after Christmas were very welcome. Denno continued to visit often; that was because Elizabeth was not going Underhill, not for any fear of detection but because the Gate was harder and harder to power and to stabilize. He was very welcome, although they could do no more than steal a kiss now and again, but at the end of February he brought bad news.

Denno was not political, but he was a merchant and merchants are acutely opposed to violence and unrest. He spoke for everyone, including Mary's spies, to hear. The burning of heretics was more and more unpopular; the queen was more and more unpopular. There were rumors of a new rebellion.

In March the whole plot dissolved when one of the conspirators confessed to Cardinal Pole. The first arrests were made on the eighteenth of March and questioning led to other arrests. And when examination was made of the confessions and depositions the names of Elizabeth's friends and, worse, members of her household began to appear as actually involved in the plot.

True, no conspirator had spoken or written to *Elizabeth* about the rebellion or about the plan (again) to marry her to Edward Courtenay. Had any done so, he would have been less ready to call her a "jolly liberal dame" as she had been known among them. Elizabeth wanted no part of Courtenay, who was spendthrift and weak, and would have burnt the ears off any man who proposed such a marriage to her.

No one did ask Elizabeth, not even Kat Ashley, who (again) nearly dragged Elizabeth to the executioner's block. For in Kat Ashley's coffer in Somerset House, Elizabeth's London residence, was discovered a huge cache of seditious anti-Catholic broadsheets and pamphlets. There was no direct evidence against Elizabeth herself . . . yet. Mary, facing her husband's ever-extended absence and her own barrenness, again had a chance to rid herself of her unwelcome heir. But she had sworn to obey her husband and she wrote to Philip about Elizabeth's apparent guilt.

Philip's friendship held firm—or, at least, his violent distaste for the notion of Mary of Scotland, the French dauphin's betrothed bride, as heir to the English throne. When he received Mary's accusation of Elizabeth's involvement in this new conspiracy to overthrow her reign, Philip replied without the smallest hesitation. All investigation into Elizabeth's personal connection with the conspiracy should be ended at once and Elizabeth should be assured of Mary's trust and love.

Kat was briefly imprisoned, then dismissed from Elizabeth's service; other members of the household were examined, one cleared, one convicted and under threat of execution, although later pardoned. But Elizabeth herself received a kind letter from Mary stating that she understood that Elizabeth's name had been taken in vain by her servants and that she would not be neglected nor hated but loved and esteemed.

What that letter cost Mary, Elizabeth could not guess. All she could do was write back. She did not even need to think long; Mary would not believe her no matter what she said and she penned a letter of fulsome and high-flown assurances of duty and loyalty.

Mary did have some small revenge. She kept Kat Ashley in the Fleet prison for three months and gave herself the satisfaction of reorganizing the household at Hatfield. A new "governess" was appointed in Kat's place, to whom Elizabeth was painstakingly polite, and Sir Thomas Pope was installed as governor. Since Sir Thomas was an old friend, a witty, cultivated man, the founder of Trinity College, Oxford, Elizabeth did not mind at all. That he was much taken with Lady Alana and polite but uninterested in Susanna Norton, Mary Dacre, and Elizabeth Marberry added to the pleasant atmosphere.

After the failure of Vidal's plan to provide an infant to Mary, he occupied himself with learning how to communicate with the Evil and then convincing It to grow in Mary's womb. He could not feel any great sense of urgency as one trouble after another made the people angrier and more miserable. Burnings now needed armed men to prevent the people from attacking the executioners and freeing the heretics, and executions followed as rebellion failed and those guilty went to the gibbet. Power was so rich and of so strong a flavor in the Dark Court, that Vidal took until August of 1556 to consider using his now clear communication with the Evil.

Understanding sealed, the new plan of giving Dakari the illusion of Philip and thus transferring the Evil to Mary became possible. If, of course, Vidal was able to get Dakari, even wearing an illusion of Philip, into Mary's bed. Faced with action Vidal realized he did not even know which palace Mary was likely to be in. And shortly after that occurred to him, he admitted that he no longer could draw on the intimate information about the Court available to him in the past. And he would need even more intimate information about Mary to implement his plan.

Vidal snarled softly and caught a passing imp, which he impaled on one long claw. The screeches and writhings cast no helpful light on his problem. He had, at present, no bound minions in Mary's Court. Wriothesley was dead, Rich had no place in Mary's government and was almost never at Court, Renard had been replaced as ambassador, and that stupid bitch Aurilia had killed Albertus, who now could have truly been useful as Mary's physician. Vidal rent the imp in squirming pieces and threw those on the floor.

Little as he liked it, Vidal realized, he would need to become Otstargi again to fix his talons into someone who could tell him when Philip had returned and when he was likely to share the queen's bed. Vidal pulled at the lobe of one long ear as he thought.

Not one of the courtiers; the men might know when Philip was expected in England, but were unlikely to know when he might bed the queen. He would need to own one of Mary's women. That was harder. They were all devoted Catholics who believed looking into the future was a sin. So he would not look into the future; surely he could find some other way to bind Mary's woman.

Having reestablished himself in Otstargi's house, Vidal sent notes to those of the Court who had visited him in the past. A surprising number came; Mary's Court was an uneasy, unhappy place. Many complained of his lengthy absence and said he was no good to them if he was so unreliable. Vidal made no defense. Actually the fewer clients he had the better off he would be.

Those clients who wanted advice from him gave him most unpalatable news in return. Philip was having the time of his life in the Netherlands and showed no signs of wishing to return to England. Mary had sent messengers and special ambassadors to plead with him to come back, but she had not been able to obtain from Parliament what Philip demanded, a vote to set the crown of England on his head. He had the name of king; Parliament would not give him the legal right to rule the nation. His influence in England rested on Mary's life. And her failure to give him independent rule was making Mary sick.

Vidal's latest visitor, Sir Francis Engelfield, confirmed that information. Engelfield was close to the queen and had been her servant for many years. He was uneasy—only a year previously he had sat as one of a commission to examine persons who used unlawful arts of conjuring and witchcraft. But Engelfield knew Otstargi's name from Ambassador Renard, a good and pious Catholic, and utterly trusted by the queen. Renard was no longer in England, but Engelfield remembered he had consulted Otstargi.

Moreover Otstargi made no claim to look into the future. There were no arcane tools on Otstargi's table or in his chamber and he made no mysterious gestures beyond closing his eyes when he considered a question. In any case Engelfield was so torn with worry that he decided to try the man Renard had trusted.

He spoke first about the latest failed attempt to induce Philip to return to England and admitted that Mary had been overset anew when Philip sent for the last of his suite still in England, his seventy-year old physician, who was in no condition to travel. The queen was losing hope, Engelfield said, and her attendants feared that her health was breaking up.

That last information was whispered with nervous glances around the room. To discuss the queen's health was treason. The speaker wrung his hands. He was not asking for his own sake. He cared nothing for that. If there were something Otstargi had learned in his travels that might give the queen hope her husband would come back to her . . . He meant no treason; he truly loved the queen and the words were wrung from him out of his genuine concern.

That was the worst news Vidal had yet. If the queen's health should fail, his entire hope for generations of strife and misery in England would come to nothing. Otstargi pursed his lips. But bad as the news of the failure of the queen's health was, it had given him the opening he needed to snare one of the queen's women.

"It is possible that I could be of some help," he said, slipping a ring from his finger and rolling it from one hand to the other.

"Are you a physician also?" Engelfield asked hopefully, his eyes following the bright glitter of the ruby in the ring.

"No, not at all. However, for my own health, I have long taken a tonic designed for me by a wise woman of Seville." He smiled. "It does not promise life eternal or any such foolishness, but it does offer a stronger vitality and a sense of well-being."

With his eyes caught by the intermittent gleam of red under Otstargi's fingers, Engelfield said, "Oh, I would not dare offer the queen any draught. How could I explain from whom I had it?"

"No, nor would I suggest that. The queen is far too precious to take a chance on strange potions. And to speak the truth, I do not know if the draught is suitable for a woman. Perhaps there is a lady of Queen Mary's household who would take the chance and try it? I know there is no harm in the potion. I drink it myself, but if it would make a woman's stomach uneasy... No worse effect would come of the trial, I promise."

Three days later Engelfield was back and Vidal gave him a small flask. It contained a slightly sweet/tart liquid that did, indeed, over the next week make Engelfield feel more cheerful. By early September Engelfield was sure the potion was safe. Then, in Croydon in an apartment reserved for her by Cardinal Pole, where Mary should have been perfectly safe, a new calumny struck her in person. Someone with free access to her rooms strewed her apartment with the most disgusting image yet. It showed Mary as a wrinkled hag, mostly naked, suckling at her shriveled bosom a host of Spaniards. Around the drawing were the words "*Maria Ruina Angliae.*"

The effect on Mary was devastating and ended all Engelfield's doubts. He told Susan Clarencieux his tale of consulting Renard's favorite advisor and of Otstargi's potion.

Susan was not quite the favorite that she had been before Mary's false pregnancy. She had been one of those who clung longest to the fiction that Mary was pregnant. When Jane Dormer had long been silent on the subject, except to follow Mary's prayers, Susan had offered hope. Now Mary could hardly look at her. If Engelfield had a potion to improve Mary's health and spirits, Susan would gladly try it to make sure it did no ill—and if it did good, offer it to the queen. Perhaps it would redeem the queen's trust.

Engelfield had no more of the draught and made an appointment for Susan to speak to Otstargi herself. She was reluctant at first, but Engelfield assured her that Renard trusted Otstargi, who did not tell fortunes or practice witchcraft. Susan came away from her meeting with him deeply impressed with his candor and sobriety and wearing a handsome ruby ring that she smiled at, remembering that she had it from her grandmother when she was too young to wear it.

She also carried two small flasks of the sweet/tart potion, which Otstargi had sampled before her eyes. If it did her no harm and the queen liked it, he said as he saw her out of the house, he would give her more. Unfortunately it did not keep well, he said, so he could not give her a large amount. She would have to come back to his house, or send a messenger, to obtain more.

❖   ❖   ❖

Elizabeth had spent an extraordinarily peaceful summer. She was not really bored. She had her estates to administer—under Sir Thomas Pope's watchful eye. But for all he watched, he did not interfere and in other ways he was a most indulgent governor. He rode hunting with her and he did not at all object to Lord Denno's company either, talking eagerly of merchant ventures.

Nonetheless, Elizabeth was not content. The fact that Pope had been assigned her governor and Kat and others of her household dismissed, marked her as guilty or untrustworthy. As Mary looked less and less healthy, Elizabeth wished to keep herself—young, healthy, and unsullied—in the eyes of the Council and the people. That was difficult, hidden away in Hatfield as she was. In August, Elizabeth wrote to Mary and begged permission to come to London.

She did not ask to join the Court, but even the more general request received no answer. That did not really surprise her. Mary was not eager for her unwelcome heir to be too visible and possibly make herself more popular. Elizabeth thought of writing again, and then thought better of it; her letters seemed to annoy Mary. She spent the next few weeks mulling over various expedients: whether to ask Sir Thomas to make the request for her or write directly to the Council or to dare to come to London on her own.

She was still trying to decide when, on the twenty-fifth of September, Lord Denno rode into Hatfield in haste bearing news that must soon alter the situation. Uncharacteristically, he blurted out the news in front of Sir Thomas, and then apologized for his carelessness.

"I do beg your pardon, Sir Thomas. One of my ships newly in from Italy carried the word. Perhaps I should not have told Lady Elizabeth that Edward Courtenay is dead, but her name has so often been linked to his—"

"Not by *my* will, I assure you," Elizabeth said, wrinkling her nose. "I suppose I should be sorry to hear of his death, and in a way I am; he was young. It is sad when someone you know dies young. But to speak the truth, I am more relieved than sorry. Edward Courtenay was a weak fool, and it gave me the green grue to hear him called my beloved bedfellow."

"Lady Elizabeth!" Lord Denno exclaimed in a shocked voice, although he was more tempted to laugh than be shocked.

Thomas Pope was the one who laughed. "That does not altogether surprise me."

"I will never marry," Elizabeth said, looking at her clasped hands lest her eyes wander to her Denno. "My experience has not given marriage a good odor."

But Courtenay's death solved Elizabeth's problem about showing herself. Only a few days after the news was confirmed by the Council, in October of 1556, Elizabeth was relieved of Sir Thomas's supervision. She said a fond fare well to him, almost sorry to see him go for he was good company. But less than a month later, in mid-November, Elizabeth received an invitation to join Mary's Court.

She was delighted, but she was not going to arrive like a penitent. She rode through Smithfield and the old Bailey, along Fleet Street, accompanied by two hundred armsmen and gentlemen all in scarlet velvet coats slashed with black. Greeted by the usual tumultuous welcome from the Londoners, Elizabeth rode to Somerset House. She was a little disappointed that none of the courtiers had ridden out to greet her, but over the next three days many came to pay calls at Somerset House. Cautious herself, Elizabeth did not blame them for not wishing to be obvious.

On the third day an invitation came from the queen. Elizabeth was pleased, expecting to be received openly by Mary and thus, in a sense, recognized as sister and heir. To Elizabeth's surprise and disappointment, she was escorted to Cardinal Pole. He was seated and did not rise. Elizabeth curtsied and kissed the ring he held out toward her, exasperatedly running over in her mind how many Masses she had heard recently and how ambiguous she dared make her professions of adherence to the Catholic faith.

Only the cardinal did not question her conversion. He said, "You have often been accused of disloyalty and of ambitions to seize your sister's throne."

"I have been unjustly accused," Elizabeth said firmly. "I have never by word or deed been disloyal to Queen Mary."

"That may well be true," Pole replied, "but you could easily avoid all such suspicions in the future if you had a husband to manage your affairs and shield you from public censure."

Like Mary's husband shields her? Elizabeth did not voice her thought, only shook her head. "I will never marry," she said. "I will never give my body and my soul into some strange man's keeping. Better by far I keep them myself."

"That is not a natural state for a woman." Pole frowned.

Elizabeth's voice had become more and more vehement as she spoke.

Elizabeth did not like Cardinal Pole. She knew he was said to be saintly by many, but she thought common sense in a government minister was of more value than saintliness. She also blamed him for the continued persecution of heretics when it was obvious that the burnings were inflaming heresy rather than suppressing it. She had heard Pole expressed fanatical opinions on the need to root out all heretics. On the other hand Elizabeth had much evidence of Mary's kind and forgiving nature. It seemed unlike her sister to cling to so cruel and useless a policy without outside urging.

"Nonsense!" she snapped. "The Bible tells us over and over that chastity is the highest state for any person. Saint Paul only accepts marriage as the lesser evil if a person must satisfy carnal desires. I assure you, Lord Cardinal, that I have no problem at all with carnal desires." *Not while Denno satisfies them so well.* "I have never found a mortal man—" she said with a tight smile "—who awoke in me the smallest inclination to abandon my chaste state."

Cardinal Pole's pale, ascetic face had flushed. He was offended by Elizabeth's tone and by her free mention of carnal desires. He said it was a woman's duty to bear children, with Latin citations to prove it. He was shocked when Elizabeth, who clearly understood what he had said, gave back chapter and verse from the Bible and citations from Saint Paul and Saint Augustine that held other duties higher than childbearing. Elizabeth's scholarship might be no real match for Pole's, but her Latin was fluent and her knowledge of the Fathers and the Bible itself extensive.

Never before had Cardinal Pole confronted such a woman. Even the queen was overawed and docile to his authority. However he was no fool and saw that Elizabeth was actually enjoying herself. If she were not a woman and not a heretic—he was sure of it; no good Catholic would have so argued with a cardinal of the Church—he would have enjoyed the disputation. As it was, he left her with the last word—that she would *not* marry—certain he would never be able to seize it, and sent her on to the queen.

Owing to her interview with the cardinal, Elizabeth was not as shocked and frightened as she might have been when Mary said she had tidings of great joy for her. Elizabeth was about to say that it was sufficient joy to be received so affectionately by her sister, that she desired nothing more. But before she could get the words out, Mary announced in her deep harsh voice that it was her pleasure to offer to Elizabeth a noble prince, Emmanuel Philibert, prince of Piedmont and duke of Savoy, as a husband.

"No!" Elizabeth exclaimed, loud enough for every person in the chamber to hear. "I will never marry, and certainly not a foreign prince of nothing but empty titles."

Mary gaped at her, shocked by the crude truth; then without answering it, said, "Is this the obedience you always claim? As my loyal subject you are duty bound to marry as I direct."

"No!" Elizabeth cried, and burst into tears. "I will obey you in anything else, madam, but I do not wish to marry. I cannot bear the thought of committing my body and my soul to any mortal man."

Seeing Elizabeth in tears, Mary became softer and cajoling, relating to Elizabeth all the joys of marriage. She would no longer need to carry the heavy responsibilities of managing her people and her property, all questions of conscience would be made clear and decided by her husband's strong mind. Mary described, in fact, every worst nightmare of helplessness and impotence Elizabeth had ever had and assured her her husband would make it come true.

The more Mary tried to convince her, the more vehement became Elizabeth denials. Never, never, she screamed between sobs. She would never marry. She would! Mary shouted back, exasperated. If she would not marry, Mary would order Parliament to remove Elizabeth from the succession and name a new heir.

"Well?" the queen demanded, surprising Elizabeth by her ferocity. "Now will you accept Emmanuel Philibert?"

"Never," Elizabeth shouted, raising her tear wet face. "I will never marry. I will never, of my own will, leave England."

Mary's face turned nearly black on those words, proving what had been her intention. "Then you will be no one," she screamed. "You will be buried in obscurity. No sister of mine. Parliament will repudiate you."

Although those were the last words Mary spoke to her before an angry dismissal, Elizabeth was not much worried about what Parliament would do. Mary had less and less influence with the Commons and the bills she urgently supported were not passed.

To get Parliament to vote the subsidy needed for the government's expenses, Gardiner had had to promise not even to raise the question of Philip being crowned. No, Elizabeth was certain, Mary could never convince Parliament to disinherit her.

Even the Council was unlikely to agree to disinherit her or order her to marry, Elizabeth was sure. Gardiner, who had been able to rally some of them to apply pressure to Elizabeth, was now dead. There was no powerful, single leader. And Mary was ageing fast; she was thinner and had been ill the past autumn. Very few were about to declare themselves enemies of the next queen.

What Elizabeth did fear, what paled her cheeks and made her breath draw in fast, was fear of being abducted, carried overseas, and married by force. As soon as she had returned to Somerset house she summoned Sir Edward and told him what had happened.

"I will send messengers out to gather your men," he said grimly.

They were on the road by December third and reached Hatfield without hindrance. Elizabeth made no secret of the fact that she had hired more men and that the manor house was defended like a fortress. And Elizabeth finally dismissed the women Mary had forced on her when she was first accused of being embroiled with rebels. She dismissed them kindly with gifts and many thanks for their long service, but she made it plain enough that considering the threat to her freedom, she would no longer tolerate information about her or about the routine of her household being passed to the queen.

If the queen sent informers to judge Elizabeth's defenses, they must have reported that Hatfield would not be taken without great noise and bloodshed. One attempt that a small party could find entry and abduct Lady Elizabeth failed; none of the would-be invaders survived. Two attempts at bribery of her guards were uncovered by Elizabeth's faithful four, who knew armsmen and "smelled" when guards were dishonest.

One who had entry at any time at all without question was Lord Denno. Several of the more dedicatedly Catholic councilors knew that and asked to see him by appointment. Acknowledging that he had known Elizabeth for many years, he answered without hesitation that Lady Elizabeth had always affirmed she would never marry—from the time she was a child. Moreover—he admitted this last in confidence—she had expressed contempt for Emmanuel Philibert the first time he was proposed to her as a husband and her opinion had only grown more fixed as the "so-called," she said, prince of Piedmont became more and more dependent on Spain.

However, interest in marrying off Elizabeth was declining—a subject to be considered in more quiet times—as renewed war between France and Spain became more imminent. France had hesitated to engage Spain while Philip, at his wife's side, could easily draw England into the conflict. Now France had a new and powerful ally: in 1555 a new pope had been elected and Paul IV was ready to add the might of Rome to that of France.

This alliance made essential Philip's rapprochement with his wife. Now he wrote to her of his sorrow at being unable to return to her, that the defiance of the pope and the threats of France were keeping him on the Continent. He urged her to bring England to his assistance.

Mary did her best. She forced loans in the amount of 150,000 ducats and she bedeviled her councilors into agreeing to send the six thousand foot and six hundred horse soldiers agreed in the 1546 treaty to defend the Netherlands. What she accomplished, however, was little more than a drop in Philip's very large bucket of trouble and Mary could do no more. She wrote in February that if he came to England, his presence would sway the councilors who only argued with her.

Chapter 39

Susan Clarencieux told her chairmen to stop on the Fleet where it met the Strand. She walked down the Strand past the Imperial ambassador's residence and to a modest house beyond. The door opened for her as she reached the top step and the servant, who always made her shudder because he looked like a dead man walking, opened the inner door of Master Otstargi's parlor. She went in smiling and sat down in the comfortable chair opposite Otstargi's.

"I am so glad that you were able to supply me with an extra flask of the potion," she said, after the customary greetings were exchanged. "My lady has had word that her husband, King Philip, will soon return to England and she is *that* overjoyed and overset she cannot eat or sleep. I asked if she would again wish to share my calming potion and she was most eager to have it."

"So the king is to return," Master Otstargi said. "I suppose there will be great entertainments. When is this to be?"

"Oh, I must not say. There are some lunatics who blame poor King Philip for all . . ."

The woman's voice faded and her eyes fixed on Otstargi's. Vidal was careful as he entered her mind. He gleaned the facts he needed from it gently; it was easy because Philip was all she was thinking about. No one in the queen's service had thought or talked about anything else for days. When she left, Susan carried with her the flasks of calming potion and a clear memory of a pleasant but unimportant conversation.

She made two more visits to Otstargi, only one of which she remembered. With Philip's arrival at Greenwich on the eighteenth of March, Mary's need for calming potions was no longer necessary and Vidal had to set into Susan's mind a compulsion to visit Otstargi every second week. At first she had no news to interest Vidal. Mary was not well, suffering a bad cold and toothache. Philip too was ill, possibly lingering effects of the passage or simply roiled guts from knowing he needed to couple with his unappetizing wife.

Still, by mid-April they were settled in Westminster and Philip had been several times in Mary's bed. Susan had reported, resentment coloring her thoughts, that Philip was growing more attentive as resistance stiffened to his intention of drawing England into his war with France. He had discovered that pillow talk was more convincing to Mary than any other argument, and the day after he coupled with her she became almost as fierce as old Henry VIII in her treatment of her Council.

Now Vidal became less gentle, ruthlessly extracting from Susan's mind everything she knew about the arrangement of the king's and queen's apartments and about who and how many would be on duty and the mortal hours when the royals made ready for bed. Susan became a little vague and forgetful, a little quieter. Twice during April Rhoslyn asked if Susan were ill or worried, but Susan laughed and shook her head.

Then in early in May, Vidal decided to act. Routines were well set and Vidal felt he should wait no longer. He did not like Rhoslyn's questioning Susan; he did not trust Rhoslyn, and would take no chance on her discovering he had meddled with Susan's mind or interfering in what she thought might hurt Mary. Thus when Susan last visited in the first week in May, he probed deeper into her mind than before. He gave Susan an amulet that would mask her into a cloudy shadow and a compulsion to place the ruby ring she wore by the back door of Philip's set of rooms.

Susan went back to Westminster and went on with her life. On the night of May seventeenth Susan believed she went to bed and to sleep when the queen had retired. What she actually did was steal into the servants' passages and make her way to the door of Philip's valet. There she laid her ruby ring on the floor and stood back against the wall.

A black point formed in the air. Susan stared into nothing. She did not see the point widen and widen again until within was a large room hung in black velvet with trimmings of dark crimson flecked with gold. She did not see Vidal in his own form, taller and broader than a mortal man, with dead black eyes and dead black hair, step from that black velvet room into the corridor, towing behind him another.

Brimming with power, Vidal had no trouble building a Gate from Underhill to the mortal world with the ruby ring as a guide. With Vidal came Dakari, bespelled in a reflective cocoon from without and controlled by the Evil within. As long as Dakari was docile, Vidal knew the Evil would follow his plan. Vidal's long ears tilted forward as he listened. Someone was in the room, a single person doing something quiet. Vidal smiled and opened the back door to Philip's valet's room.

The valet froze in the act of preparing to lay away Philip's shirt. Vidal, towing Dakari by a line of force, opened the door to Philip's bedchamber slightly but did not enter. There were five men in the room: Philip, the duke of Feria, two secretaries, and a groom. Philip was already dressed for bed, the secretaries were turned toward the door on their way out, the groom had gathered up gloves, Philip's sword and belt and several other small articles. He, too, was turned toward the outer door. Feria looked over his shoulder and then at Philip; he was waiting for the others to leave before he spoke. Vidal waited too.

As soon as the door shut behind the groom, Vidal struck at both Feria and Philip. Both men simply stopped. Vidal drew Dakari forward and swiftly painted onto and into him Philip of Spain's appearance. Then he directed Philip to lie down in his bed and pull the covers over himself right over his head so he was completely covered. Feria, whom he had recognized as a nobleman, not a servant, he directed to close the bedcurtains and to sit in a chair in the shadow, close by and concealed by the bedcurtains.

Susan then led Vidal, now wearing the illusion of the duke of Feria, and Dakari/Philip to the short corridor that connected the apartments of the king and queen. At the entrance, Susan stopped; Vidal and Dakari went on alone.

As soon as Philip appeared at the end of the corridor in Mary's chamber, Mary dismissed her ladies. When they had made their curtsies and gone, Vidal froze the queen, but only momentarily. Only until he negotiated the most dangerous part of this whole enterprise.

Vidal now needed to release Dakari and the Evil that invested him from the prison that had held them so long. He *thought* the Evil intended to impregnate Mary with itself and the mortal seed and grow in Mary's womb. However, if the Evil had deliberately deceived him—a thing as likely as not, considering the Evil's nature—It might try to seize him instead of following the plan.

Dropping the illusion of Feria, Vidal drew up his most impervious shields and layered them one atop another. He did not think even the Evil at Its greatest power could penetrate those shields, and the Evil's power had diminished greatly while in Dakari's body. There was no other living thing in the chamber but Mary; Vidal hoped the Evil would invest the child because that would mean many years of misery for those of Logres, but if It took Mary instead It could likely prolong her life and still keep the Dark Court rich with power.

"Couple!" Vidal thrust the thought into Dakari with all the power he had left from his shields. "Couple with the woman!"

As the command left his mind and seared into Dakari's, Vidal broke the paralysis on Mary and thrust Dakari/Philip forward toward her bed.

Mary was considerably surprised by the rapidity and intensity with which Philip seized her and coupled with her. She was also greatly surprised by his silence. Usually as he caressed her, Philip spoke to her about what to say to her councilors, what promises and what threats to make to induce them to declare war on France. Tonight, for once, he seemed totally immersed in what he was doing.

After his long isolation in Vidal's cocoon of force, Dakari's own desire was simply to flee away before Vidal seized him again. He did not have that choice. Vidal's compulsion, even now that the shell around him was dissipated, was stronger than his own will. He had a brief moment of doubt whether the woman in the bed would resist him, but she was obviously welcoming and he climbed into the bed, took her in his arms, and pushed her down.

She looked surprised and mouthed mortal words at him, but she did not push him away. He made no attempt to understand or to answer her, searching urgently with his hands for her nether mouth. She was speaking more intensely, saying the same word over and over. Dakari simply muffled her words with his lips and pushed himself inside her.

Pleasure flooded him. Instinct bade him withdraw slightly and then press forward again. An increase in the pleasure made him hasten his withdrawal and his thrust and then repeat the movements even quicker.

Something stirred inside him. Dakari knew that thing was dangerous and had an unbreakable grip on his life force. But the pleasure, mounting with each stroke higher and higher until it was coming to a crescendo nearly pain, would not let him stop. He drew and thrust, groaning and writhing, until the dam that had held in the pleasure burst. More pain/pleasure as all that Dakari was seemed to flow out of him. He felt the pleasure ebb and groaned softly; he tried to stop, to swallow back the last few pulses of his life, but he could not.

"Philip!" Mary cried.

And Vidal froze her again. He had felt Dakari die and knew the illusion had died with him. It was imperative that he remove the Sidhe's body, but first it was imperative that he discover whether or not his plan had worked. Was the Evil set in Mary's womb? Was it loose in the chamber? His shields were so dense that he could not sense it.

Little by little Vidal reabsorbed the power of the shields. He felt nothing, no attack, no sense of imminent doom. He drew more of the shields back into himself. Still nothing. Smiling he went forward to the bed.

Mary lay under Dakari's body, but she did not look crushed. Dakari, who had never been much, was now barely a shell. Vidal grasped the body by the shoulder, pulled it from under the cover, and dropped it on the floor. Then he turned his attention to Mary.

There was no evil in her mind. Vidal paused, drew up a memory of the time before this that Philip had coupled with his wife. Adding only a slightly greater intensity and the reason for it that Philip had to leave early to finish some work, Vidal had the memory replayed for that night. Slowly, and very, very carefully—he did not want the Evil to seize his probe and ride it back into him—he extended his scrutiny along Mary's body.

There! Vidal had to press his lips tight together to keep back a shriek of satisfaction. There to the back and upper part of her belly there was a little spot of blackish red within a tiny, sick yellow, flaccid sack. It was an angry thing, a greedy thing. Even as Vidal let his sense rest there, the blackish red pulled something into itself and expanded. Vidal sighed with pleasure. Years, maybe eons, of Evil would be loosed on Logres.

Reminding himself severely that he must not spoil his success by slipshod work that would warn anyone there was something wrong with Mary, he scooped up Dakari's body. It took no time at all to go back through the passage, out into the corridor where Susan still stood, and thrust Dakari through the Gate.

Last Vidal returned to Philip's bedchamber and inserted into Philip's mind that he had done his duty and begged off from lying with Mary longer by saying he had work to do. In Feria's mind he inserted only the thought that everything was as usual. Then grinning with satisfaction Vidal freed the valet as he went out the door, scooped up the ruby ring, set it back on Susan's finger, and sent Susan back to her bed with the knowledge that she had slept very well, undisturbed.

When Vidal stepped through the Gate and closed it behind him, he was still replete with power. He hardly needed to suck in more but did so for the pure pleasure of touching so much fear and misery. In fact, his sense of satisfaction was so strong that it seeped through to Aurilia, who always kept a tendril of watchfulness aware of Vidal.

A quick check in the full-length cheval glass to be sure she looked her best, and Aurilia slipped out of her suite and along the corridor to Vidal's. She opened the door with modest caution and shields ready. It was not unknown for Vidal to set a trap for the unwary with signs that he was unusually benign. But this time the signs were true.

Vidal greeted her with a broad smile and when she asked what had given him so much satisfaction replied that, unlike her, he had completed a complex and delicate operation in the mortal world without a single problem. "Forethought and careful planning are necessary," he taunted her, smiling with half-lowered eyelids, and described how he had begun planning three months earlier and brought the plan to fruition just this mortal night.

"Oh, excellent," Aurilia praised sycophantically. "That was indeed a flawless working."

Delighted with the flash of rage she had failed to conceal completely under her praise, Vidal felt magnanimous; he would ask her for advice. Let her feel superior about her knowledge as a female.

"And when may I expect to see results from it?" Vidal asked.

Aurilia could not resist trying to rub the shine off his satisfaction. "Assuming Mary will carry the infant to term—"

"Why should she not?"

Now Aurilia smiled sweetly as she knew how, lips covering her sharp-pointed teeth. "Because her mother failed to do so many times. The Spanish women were not good breeders."

Vidal frowned, but then the expression of anxiety cleared. "No, I do not think I need to worry about that. The Evil is bound into the child growing in Mary's womb and I think it will take good care that that child not be expelled too soon. But how long will it take for the young to be birthed?"

Aurilia uttered a giggle. "Three-quarters of a mortal year."

"What?" Vidal was indignant; even ogres did not take so long.

"A Sidhe takes longer."

Vidal thought back, but he could not remember a breeding in the Dark Court. "There has been no Sidhe born since Llanelli invoked death magic to make her lover Kefni fertile."

"He was not her lover," Aurilia put in. "That was how the two sets of twins were conceived. Kefni broke Llanelli's compulsion and rushed back to his life mate, who also conceived."

"Bearing those accursed protectors of Elizabeth, Denoriel and Aleneil."

"And Rhoslyn and Pasgen too," Aurilia said thoughtlessly. Pasgen had been on her mind since she had killed Albertus. It had been Pasgen who had brought her Albertus, and she missed her cringing and sometimes useful pet.

Vidal made an ugly sound deep in his throat. Kefni's blood was very strong. Despite all his effort to make Llanelli's twins true members of the Dark Court, Pasgen had broken away completely and, though Rhoslyn gave him lip service, he had never trusted her. She had not been to his Court for a long time, most of her constructs were gone from the empty house, and he suspected that she had dissolved her true domain. Where she had gone, he had no idea ... Let her go. She was near useless. He had many new adherents since the Bright Court had begun to fade.

Aurilia was sorry now that she had distracted Vidal from his satisfaction. She had intended to ask him to arrange for her to have a new mortal physician—since he was so skilled in dealing with the mortal world. Now was not the time.

"Oh well, it is not so long, really. Mary's Evil will be born in a mere nine mortal months. Scarcely more than an eyeblink for us. Are you planning to bring It Underhill for teaching or go to the mortal world yourself?"

"I am not sure yet," Vidal said. "It depends on how much It can influence Mary without teaching. Likely it will not be needful for me to do anything." He laughed briefly. "After all, Mary has managed to do enough evil without prompting."

"Hmmm, yes. Perhaps it would be unwise to make her reign worse. The rebellions provide us with much rich power, but we do not want so great a dissatisfaction that she is overthrown and executed."

"True enough. True. And I have some work in hand in Caer Mordwyn. Let Logres go its own way until the Evil is of an age for me to direct and instruct."

Early in February Roy Gomez, Philip's closest friend, had arrived in England to say that Philip would soon follow. After a few days of Mary's excited concentration only on what she would do and say when Philip came, Rhoslyn decided that she could more profitably spend the next few mortal months playing with the self-willed mist and developing the domain she already loved. Harry would be there too.

The more Mary talked about Philip, excusing his infidelities and worrying about his needs for war, the more Rhoslyn thought of Harry, of his goodness and honesty, of his eager lovemaking and solid fidelity. She had not seen much of him recently. When the Bright Court was strong, she had Gated back Underhill almost every night. Now she did not dare make the transit often.

Poor Harry. When she came he complained of how much he missed her—and proved it with his ardent caresses—and then begged her not to come because the Gates to the mortal world were unstable and might be unsafe. *But,* Rhoslyn thought, *if Philip is coming, Mary will not need or want my support. I can ask for a long leave—three months or even six—so I will only use the Gate once to reach Underhill and once to return here.*

A week later—Philip was expected in March—Rhoslyn did ask for leave. But she made the mistake of saying Mary would be so happy and so occupied in her husband's presence that she would not want too many ladies taking up her time. To her surprise, Mary's face clouded.

"You do not like Philip. You, too, hate the Spanish."

"Oh no, madam!" Rhoslyn exclaimed. She was horrified at how Mary had managed to read the truth; Rhoslyn did not like Philip. She knew his unfailing politeness covered a strong distaste for his adoring wife—a distaste that grew stronger as Mary's love grew more intense. "How could anyone dislike so kind and courteous a king? I only want to be out of your way."

"You are never in my way Rosamund," Mary said fondly. "And you . . . you . . . somehow talking with you makes me feel calm, even better than that elixir Susan Clarencieux uses. You know I will give you leave if you really need to see to your brother's lands and people, but if you were thinking you would oblige me by going away . . . No. I would rather . . ." she hesitated and a look of anguish briefly twisted her face. "If there is war. If Philip must leave . . . I would rather you were here."

"Of course, Your Majesty. Of course I will be here."

The effect of that talk at the end of February was stronger than Rhoslyn had expected. Mary more frequently asked Rosamund to read to her, to pray with her. And even after Philip was back in England, Rosamund and Jane Dormer were the two ladies most often gestured to accompany the queen when she walked and talked with her husband.

It was hard on poor Rhoslyn, who could "hear" Philip's disdainful thoughts about Mary as a sort of undercurrent to what he said aloud. Not that most of his thoughts were a secret. There were times when he openly threatened Mary that if she did not bring her Council to heel and make them declare war, he would have no purpose in England and would leave.

Those times it took all of Rhoslyn's self-control not to reach out and just squeeze Philip's innards so he would suffer as he was making his poor wife suffer. By mid-April, however, external circumstances had come to Mary's aid. A new revolt was brewing, its purpose to prevent Mary from drawing England into a Spanish war. But the rebels landed in Scotland and were threatening to invade England with French and Scottish troops.

That was enough to raise the north country—not in support of the rebellion but to resist any French or Scottish army. The rebels were captured without the smallest difficulty and executed, but the people had been roused to indignation against the French. As reluctant as the Council was to be drawn into the Spanish war, the French insult must be avenged.

More money and more men were offered to Philip, but all through May the Council still resisted making an open declaration of war. By the end of May, Mary grew more strident, acting very much as her father would have done. She talked loudly of dismissing all but a few Council members, keeping only those who would obey her. Then she had them summoned one by one and she threatened them with the loss of their goods and estates if they would not consent to the will of her husband.

Rhoslyn was troubled by Mary's new vehemence, but she put it down to Philip's insistence. And, indeed, once the Council yielded and declared war against France on June seventh, Mary ceased to threaten them. Her thoughts and attention were taken up completely by the plans for war. Mary gave orders for securing the Scots border, for outfitting the fleet—and, to raise additional money, because she could force no more loans nor, Parliament not being in session, raise more taxes, she began to sell crown lands.

But nothing Mary had done or promised to do would keep her husband in England, and as soon as he received the news that Roy Gomez had brought the Spanish fleet carrying more troops and more gold, into the channel, Philip prepared to leave. All he could get had been wrung out of Mary and England; he offered no assurances of his return. When the war was over, he said vaguely; when he had settled the unrest that a war caused; perhaps some day . . .

Finally, on July seventh, Philip set sail from Calais. Mary retained her dignity until he was gone and then retreated to what privacy she could find and wept. Now she wanted no human comfort; for days she drank Susan Clarencieux's potion and slept. By the end of the month, good news from France seemed to bring her back to the world. St. Quentin was taken from the French with the capture of thousands of common soldiers, dozens of the most distinguished nobles, and the constable of France, Montmorency himself.

The good news buoyed Mary's spirits all through August and made her ladies cheerful and hopeful—all except Rhoslyn. She was more and more and unhappy. Something about Mary was making her uneasy. There was something just beyond her ability to sense clearly, as if a perfectly clean surface somehow gave a sense of being greasy. Perhaps, Rhoslyn told herself, she was, without realizing it, resenting the fact that the queen had grown less and less fond of Rosamund's company. During the last month of Philip's presence in England, Mary often sent her on errands or maneuvered so that Rosamund was seated well away from Mary's inner circle.

Rhoslyn was beginning to think longingly of asking again for permission to leave the Court, but some uneasy presentiment made her need to watch Mary, who was behaving in uncharacteristic ways. For one thing, all the doubts the kindhearted queen had begun to feel about the burning of heretics seemed gone. Some months earlier her doubts had driven her to write to Emperor Charles to ask if she should continue the policy, since it seemed to be encouraging rather than destroying heresy. Recently Mary had been eagerly reading the reports of the executions and even writing to her bishops to be expeditious in their questioning and punishment.

In September Rhoslyn's long ears caught Mary praying for the hope that had been rising in her to be true—that this time she truly be with child. As unlikely as that might be, it *was* possible. During the time Philip had been trying to make Mary force England into the war, he had slept with her most nights. Rhoslyn had not been Underhill for some time and had had no opportunity to consult the FarSeers. What if the Visions had changed?

There was no easy way for Rhoslyn to go Underhill. She surely was not about to try to build a Gate just to consult the Black Pool or the Bright Court's lens. However, if Mary was truly with child, it might be worth the effort, and it would be easy enough to find out. Last time she had known there was no pregnancy merely by touching Mary.

This time Rhoslyn had to find an excuse, since Mary no longer offered her hand to Rosamund to be kissed. Not such a difficult problem; Rhoslyn found a solution that very same afternoon. Mary had given Rosamund a book of prayers to be said in times of hope. Now Rosamund would ask Mary which prayers she felt were specially appropriate—not mentioning the pregnancy, of course, perhaps hope for victory in the war.

Shockingly, touching Mary was not so easy as Rhoslyn had thought. She found in herself the greatest reluctance to approach the queen. And when she did start toward Mary in spite of her reluctance, she felt as if she were thrusting her body through resisting water. Mary eyed her with definite wariness, which puzzled Rhoslyn. Mary might shift her favorites now and again, but why should she be wary of Rosamund, who had been her faithful servant for near twenty years?

Perhaps in an attempt to warn Rosamund off, Mary turned her head away. Doggedly, Rhoslyn continued to advance, one step, two . . . holding out the book of prayers, which was suddenly heavy as iron. Then she felt as if her foot was sticking to the carpet.

"Madam—" she said, thrusting herself forward against the pressure, just as Mary rose from her seat and took a step sideways.

"I cannot—" Mary began.

And they collided.

Rhoslyn screamed, fell to the floor, and burst into tears. Mary stood over her for a moment, eyes wide and mouth open. Then she bent down and put her hand on Rhoslyn's shoulder. Rhoslyn cried out again and shrank away.

"What is it? My dear Rosamund, what is wrong?"

Curled in on herself, Rhoslyn fought her sense of horror, forced herself to lie still under Mary's touch, to sob aloud only, "A pain, madam. Oh, I beg your pardon. I beg your pardon."

Mary turned and gestured to two of her women. "Help Rosamund to her chamber and send someone for her servant." Then she bent over Rhoslyn again and stroked her arm. "Shall I send my physician to you, Rosamund my dear?"

"No, I thank you, madam," Rhoslyn said, fighting her desire to shudder and pushing herself upright. "I am better already. This is only an attack of the illness I used to suffer from when I was anxious about my brother. I have not had an attack in so long, I had almost forgotten the symptoms. But I do have a medicine for it. Only the pain recurs at unexpected times. I am afraid I will need to be away from the Court for a week or two."

"Of course, Rosamund," Mary said, not smiling but exuding a sense of relief and satisfaction as her women helped Rhoslyn to her feet. "Take as long as you need."

And yet that relief seemed apart from Mary herself, who also was filled with concern—as if Mary's heart warred with . . . something else.

Rhoslyn would have fled the palace at once, on foot if no better way was possible, but the queen had already given orders for a litter to take her to her accustomed lodging in London and for attendants to see she was well received and well cared for.

The next day, having rid herself of the people Mary had sent with her, Rhoslyn came down from her chambers in the Golden Bull. She walked slowly, holding to the stair rail, aware of a desperate need to reach Denoriel and a choking panic because she could not think of how to reach him. The air spirit that had once attended her to carry messages was gone, too feeble and faded to withstand the inimical conditions of the mortal world. All she could decide was to go to his house in Bucklersbury. It was unlikely he would be there, but perhaps Joseph Clayborne would know where he was.

How to get to Bucklersbury? Order a chair?

"Madam," the landlord's voice was deferential but uncertain.

Rhoslyn realized she had reached the foot of the stairs and stopped there, still clutching the end of the stair rail. She looked toward the man, who was holding out his arm for her to take, as if he thought she needed help to walk.

"Are you sure you wish to ride, madam?" he asked anxiously. "The horse—" he looked over his shoulder out the open door.

Past the landlord's bulk, Rhoslyn caught a glimpse of a shining black hide, an irritably stamping hoof. She barely bit back a cry of joy and relief.

"—looks to be . . . ah . . . rather spirited." The landlord went on. "It bit the hostler and kicked at anyone else who approached."

Smiling brilliantly although she felt more like staring with her mouth hanging open, Rhoslyn said, "I am accustomed to Talog's ways." And she directed all the power she had to invisibly changing her skirt into a divided form for riding.

"But are you well enough, madam?" the landlord asked more directly. "You were coming down the stairs so slowly . . ."

Rhoslyn had been a very welcome guest for many years, taking and promptly paying for the most expensive lodgings in the inn. He did not want to see her dashed to the ground and injured or killed.

"Only because I was thinking so deeply, good host," Rhoslyn

replied. "Hold my rooms although I am not sure I will return for dinner or even to spend the night. I have a visit to make and business to do in the country."

Then she was out of the inn and had flung her arms around Talog's neck. "How did you come here?" She whispered. "How did you know I needed you when I did not even know it myself?"

The ostlers were standing well back and Rhoslyn wondered how she was to mount. Underhill, she was just suddenly in the saddle but that would be a disaster in the mortal world. Talog nudged her firmly, prodding her toward the mounting block, and Rhoslyn could only shake her head at her own bemusement. And when she was ahorse, Talog set out at a gentle pace for the main road on which the inn was sited.

They soon came to the edge of the West Chepe, where Talog turned aside into a narrow lane. Then the world seemed to blur around her. Rhoslyn was sure the elvensteed had not Gated because there was no darkness, no vertiginous drop. Instead she felt wind brushing her face and lifting her hair. Then they were on the grounds of a small but elegant manor house. And Miralys was grazing in a field bordered by a high stone wall.

Rhoslyn was deposited at the door—without any idea of how she dismounted—which opened to reveal Denoriel. "What is it?" he asked, drawing her inside and closing the door. "What is wrong? Can Mary be dead?"

"Worse," Rhoslyn said. "She is possessed."

Chapter 40

Having led Rhoslyn into a small parlor, seated her, and asked whether she wanted food or drink, Denoriel listened carefully to the tale she told. She described her slow growing uneasiness, Mary's slight but significant change in character, her reluctance to approach the queen and the horror that had seized her when they touched by accident.

"There is an Evil growing within her. It is still weak, but it is growing stronger day by day," Rhoslyn finished. "We must do *something*, but what? What *can* we do?"

"First we need Hafwen," Denoriel said. "Not that I do not trust you, Rhoslyn, but she is an expert in judging evil." He hesitated, then shook his head impatiently. "No, first we need to get one of the tokens I made for Elizabeth. If you have that and can lay it by an outer wall in Mary's bedchamber, I can build a Gate right into the room. Then I can freeze everyone there, and bring Hafwen and whoever else we need through the Gate."

Tears rose to Rhoslyn's eyes. "But Denoriel, is there power enough to build a Gate from Underhill to Mary's chamber? And will the Gate be firm enough to let us all come through?"

"Yes," Denoriel said, his expression rather grim. "There is more than enough power in the mortal world. And for this purpose I can use it."

"Don't," Rhoslyn said. "Elizabeth will kill me—and do not tell me that she will not be able to reach me. If harm comes to you through me, Elizabeth will somehow tap the power she has within her, drive a path through to Underhill, and harrow Underhill until I am butchered meat."

The grimness went out of Denoriel's expression as he grinned. That was his Elizabeth! A moment later he was sober again. "You are sure?" he asked Rhoslyn. "This is not some evil growing in the queen's heart because she knows she has lost her husband for good?"

"No." The color drained from Rhoslyn's face. "When I touched her... It was horrible...horrible. This was nothing of human hate or rage. This...it was like what had been in Alhambra before Harry and the elder Sidhe..."

Her voice drifted away and Denoriel watched fear and anguish chase each other in her expression. She clutched her arms around herself and began to shiver.

"Can it be that?" she whispered. "Harry told me that the evil disappeared from Alhambra altogether. They had bound it into that strange altar stone with magic sigils of iron and silver. They were going to try to send the stone into the Void, but one day when they came to check all was well, all the sigils were missing and the Evil was gone also. Could it have got loose? Wait... wait. Remember Pasgen and Hafwen were pursuing some mad thing that was killing and destroying without reason..." She looked up into Denoriel's face.

"I do not know," he said. "I have given more attention to the mortal world than to Underhill for some time. I remember Harry saying something about going to Oberon with the tale of the missing Evil. But then Oberon left us and Elizabeth was suspected of treason." He stared at Rhoslyn for a moment and then said slowly, "But if *that* Evil has somehow found its way into the queen of England..."

Rhoslyn swallowed hard. "I cannot be sure, but I think it must be. It was...it was as if all the prayers Mary said were twisted awry, as if her God was twisted awry. Was that not what destroyed Alhambra and El Dorado? Priests from the mortal world who cursed those domains because they did not conform to their ideas?"

"But how did it come to Mary?"

"Vidal..." Rhoslyn breathed. "Remember that Pasgen told us

what had happened in the gnome's domain, how the Evil had come and killed and destroyed and then suddenly was gone. Remember Pasgen said he had traced it through the Gate *to* the gnome's domain but it had not gone out through the Gate. He and Hafwen searched, but it was truly gone."

"You mean that Vidal somehow bound the Evil and removed it? Why? How?"

"How? He has been different since he was held by the mist. He often thinks and plans before he acts now, and he has more than enough power." Rhoslyn shivered. "The Dark Court is awash with unhappiness and pain and fear. Why? That I cannot even guess, unless his FarSeers saw Mary's life ending; she is frail. So perhaps he seized the Evil for the purpose he used it? To ensure . . . Oh, merciful Mother . . . to give Mary a child, an evil child, who would ensure the misery of Logres for . . . for eternity."

Denoriel did not answer her. He looked past her, a little to the side and a moment later his face twisted and a low exclamation of pain forced itself past his lips. He closed his eyes. Rhoslyn started out of her chair.

Before she could reach Denoriel, he had reopened his eyes. They were what they should have been, except for the dearth of power in the Bright Court, the deep, brilliant green of a young Sidhe at the height of his power. His hair was still white, but it shone silver and almost lifted as if it would throw off sparks. The lines in his face were gone and his body no longer slumped or was held erect by effort. Smooth muscle that hinted of easy strength and energy filled his clothing.

"Are you all right?" Rhoslyn asked.

"Yes." Denoriel sounded surprised. "I am. I do not know whether I can do that again, but this time all is well. Come. We need to talk to Pasgen and Hafwen about your suspicions. I know I said we would go to Elizabeth first, but during the day that is difficult and there is a safe Gate in Hatfield that I can open to reach her at night. I will just send the gardener's boy with a note to ask her to have Lady Alana attend her tonight."

The Gate Denoriel opened from his bedchamber to Underhill was bright and quick, but the Bright Court should better have been called the Dim Court. The moss, which ordinarily sprang erect almost as one lifted a foot, lay limp after Miralys and Talog had passed. Llachar Lle still stood, but the glow was gone; the blue-veined white marble of the steps and portico was dull and worn.

Denoriel and Rhoslyn did not stay long; there was a strange feel to his apartment, almost as if it were damp and musty. Thus Denoriel bade the air spirits he dispatched to find Pasgen and Hafwen to bring them to Rhoslyn's English manor house in the domain that had once held the self-willed mist. But even the restless mists of Rhoslyn's domain, which usually devised some new detail in her house or lands to surprise and please her, lay quiet.

Harry met them at the door, at once thrilled to see them and alarmed about the weakness of the Gates. He was torn between relief and concern when he learned how Denoriel had found the strength to make the Gates work, and led the way to Rhoslyn's cozy private parlor before he enquired what drove Denoriel to that expedient. But he was utterly horrified, beyond horrified, devastated, when Rhoslyn told him of Mary's possession.

"My fault," he breathed. "Human mischief. Why did I not leave the Evil alone? It seemed content in Alhambra. Now it is about to spread to England." His lips thinned to a narrow line. "No. I will not permit it to destroy my country. My fault, my duty to correct it." He looked at Denoriel. "You'll have to Gate me to wherever Mary is. I'll—" he swallowed and shuddered, his eyes glittering with tears. "I'll kill her."

"Grace of God, no!" Denoriel exclaimed. He did not believe in the mortal God, but so many years of living in the mortal world had fixed his expressions. "We will find a way to separate the Evil from Mary and be rid of one without harming the other."

"Yes, of course," Harry agreed, drawing a deep breath. He hesitated and sucked his lower lip for a moment, then said, "I would not be surprised if Mwynwen would know how. She cannot cure human illness, but she can heal human wounds, and this Evil is no true part of Mary. Surely it can be drawn out of her."

"Yes," Denoriel agreed eagerly. "And do not think the Evil would have been forever easily contained. If you had not diminished it and driven it out, Harry, in our present weakness, it might well have flooded over into the Bright Court."

"Or into the Dark," Rhoslyn said, moving closer to Harry on the sofa on which they both sat and taking Harry's hand. "At full strength it might even have possessed Vidal. He is bad enough as he is. Filled with senseless, unreasoning Evil . . ."

"But my sister," Harry said, pulling Rhoslyn closer against him. "My poor sister. What are we to do with her? She never wanted to be queen. She has no skill for the role and no common sense. She has turned a whole people that loved her into enemies of the crown. England is bankrupt by her idiotic return of Church property and her selling of lands to pay for Spain's war. She cannot be allowed to hold the crown, even without that Evil within her. Elizabeth must rule."

"Not by our doing," Denoriel said firmly. "I know it hurts you to see the realm mismanaged. Elizabeth is half mad with rage and frustration. And her state is worse than yours because she dare not let a word of criticism pass her lips."

"Poor Bessie—" Harry started to say, but did not finish as one of Rhoslyn's girls slid into the room.

"Two Sidhe," she murmured, "Pasgen and Hafwen."

"Invite them in and see we have mead and nectar. And some cakes and nuts," Rhoslyn said.

"And wine for me, Crinlys," Harry said, smiling. "Mead and nectar are too sweet."

"Wine for me, also," Denoriel said, and to Harry, "And how do you know that girl is Crinlys? They all look alike to me."

"Violet ribbon around the neck," Harry said. "Rhoslyn might be able to tell them apart, but I can't."

Crinlys slipped out but the door opened again almost immediately, held for Hafwen and Pasgen by an identical girl with a yellow ribbon around her neck.

"Thank you, Elyn," Pasgen said, and the construct closed the door behind him.

"Yellow ribbon," Harry muttered to Denoriel.

But Hafwen was looking around the room, her face creased with worry. "What is wrong?" she asked. "Pasgen, I told you something was wrong."

"And I believed you," he replied, "since I powered the Gate to get us here safely." He led Hafwen to a chair and then went and took Rhoslyn's free hand. "What has overset you so much, sister?"

When the tale of the Evil that had rooted itself in Mary was told, Hafwen was weeping softly and Pasgen's face was twisted into a hard mask of mixed fear and determination.

"No matter the cost, it must be destroyed," he said. "You did not see what that Evil did among the Dark, the Bright, and the totally innocent. Hafwen and I—" he moved to her side and put a gentle hand on her shoulder "—we followed its trail. It was—" he closed his eyes, cleared his throat, and began again, "It *is* unthinkable that that should be loose, should rule, in the mortal world. There will be nothing but grief. The Bright Court will fade to nothing."

They talked for a few minutes about Rhoslyn's notion that the Evil had somehow shifted into Dakari, perhaps when he had come to spy out Alhambra, that Vidal had captured Dakari and removed him and the Evil from the gnome domain. Pasgen merely nodded when Denoriel asked if he thought Vidal would have seeded Mary with the Evil.

"That may have been his purpose from the beginning and why he stopped Dakari from running amok, but it doesn't matter who did it or why. The Evil must be removed."

Everyone agreed to that; there was less agreement on how. Harry suggested that Mwynwyn could draw the Evil out of Mary, but Hafwen thought it would be near impossible to win Mwynwyn's consent to go to the mortal world in the first place and then destroy an unborn child.

It was not as difficult as they expected. The idea was at first rejected with the near fury Hafwen had predicted, but Mwynwyn was a sensitive and the universal horror clawing at every one of them made her reconsider her impulse to throw them out.

"Why should I commit such an abomination?" she cried.

"We do not wish to harm Queen Mary," Rhoslyn said. "This is a separate thing we believe was implanted in her by Vidal Dhu."

"To keep power flowing to the Dark Court," Mwynwyn sighed.

Then she listened to what Rhoslyn had felt in Mary's touch, and to Harry with tears streaking his cheeks say that if she would not remove the tainted unborn, he would have to kill Mary, his own sister. *Harry?* Mwynwyn thought, *kill his sister?* What was in Mary's womb must be truly terrible, and to birth it would be worse than the deliberate death of an unborn child. In the end Mwynyen placed her hands on Hafwen's temples and asked her to think of what she had seen while she and Pasgen pursued the Evil.

White-faced and shivering when she had read Hafwen's memory, Mwynwen agreed to go with them the next mortal night and remove the Evil from Mary's womb.

A far more serious problem became apparent when Denoriel and Rhoslyn Gated from Underhill to Hatfield not long after midnight to get the token for setting a Gate from Elizabeth. When they told her for what they needed it, Elizabeth's eyes went wide with shock, with grief for her sister for whom she still held a thread of affection, but mostly with horror of the married state, which to her mind had created all of Mary's problems.

"See what comes of marrying," she cried. "I will never marry, never. Even to have a child is only a deadly trap."

However, once she was calmed and dried her tears, she became intensely practical. First Elizabeth pointed out that the token Denoriel had given her was bespelled to act when *she* set it somewhere (a protection for Denoriel who did not want to be frantically trying to build a Gate because one of Elizabeth's ladies somehow found a token and dropped it on the floor).

And after Denoriel thanked her for reminding him and, sighing over the cost in power, said he would make a new token, Elizabeth asked what they planned to do with the Evil once it was extracted from Mary's womb.

"You cannot destroy it," Elizabeth said, looking from one to the other. "Da and I talked about that when he was trying to free Alhambra. He and the elder Sidhe were thinking about sending the whole altar to the Void, but Sawel had not got the spell right."

There was a dead silence while Denoriel, Rhoslyn, and Aleneil stared at her.

"It will get loose from the—" she searched for an unfamiliar Latin word "—fetus when the fetus dies," Elizabeth pointed out. "Where will it go? You told me that Pasgen and Hafwen think from the gnomes' description that it was using a Dark Sidhe called Dakari. If it got into Dakari, can it get into someone else?"

"I don't know how it got into Dakari," Denoriel said, "but if what we think is true, Vidal held Dakari and the Evil in him captive for some time. The Evil could not escape from Dakari. Vidal must have had some kind of shield around the Sidhe that prevented the Evil from escaping or striking at him."

"Mirror shield," Rhoslyn said. She and Pasgen had tried many different shields to protect themselves when they were still part of the Dark Court. "Turned inside out. Mirror on the inside."

"Can you cast one?" Denoriel asked her.

"I know how," Rhoslyn told him, "but with my strength at so

low an ebb, I cannot think it would be proof against the Evil's power."

"Can you teach me?" Denoriel asked then. "I can get the power if I must."

Elizabeth made a wordless sound of protest, but Denoriel, face grim, shook his head at her.

"I can try," Rhoslyn said. "A mirror shield inside out is a rather complicated spell. But Pasgen will be with us and he knows the spell too."

"He won't have much more power than you because he will be holding the Gate," Aleneil pointed out.

"Perhaps if we all three cast it at once," Rhoslyn suggested. "I do not know whether the three spells will blend—likely Pasgen will know that or how to do it—but even if they do not blend there will be three layers, which is better than one."

"Then you will have at least a few moments to do something final with the Evil before it gets loose," Elizabeth said. "What will you do with it?"

Another long silence. They had all hoped that the Evil would die when the fetus died. Elizabeth's reminder that Evil could not be completely destroyed brought them forcibly to face a problem they had not, with typically Sidhe disinclination to plan ahead, wished to address.

"I will come with you," Elizabeth said in a small voice. She sounded very frightened. "I do not think the Evil will be able to break my shields and seize me." She shivered slightly. "It must be me. There is so little power in the Bright Court, I think the shields will be all you can do. I will Push it. I will Push it very hard . . . I hope into the Void. I have done that before."

All three looked at her.

"It is my realm," she said, her voice growing stronger, surer. "It owns my life, my heart, my mind, my body." She swallowed. "I am afraid," she admitted, "but afraid or not, it is my duty to save England from any threat."

The next night soon after full dark Elizabeth left Blanche on guard by the door of her bedchamber and escaped with Lady Alana, both hidden by the Don't-see-me spell. Aleneil was trembling with weakness from holding the spell over both of them just for the time it took to reach the court where Ystwyth waited. The elvensteed carried them swiftly to the park behind Westminster Palace where they found Rhoslyn, who had ridden Talog from the Golden Bull.

If either of the Sidhe had been at full strength, she could have used the Don't-see-me spell to bring Elizabeth into Mary's bedchamber. But Aleneil was already exhausted and Rhoslyn did not dare expend the power, which she would later need for the mirror spell. However, Rhoslyn knew the palace and Mary's routine.

She led Elizabeth, dressed simply as a maid, in through the side entrance Mary's ladies always used. The guards there would recognize Rhoslyn and let her pass; there was no reason for them to know she was not supposed to be at the palace. Except among the servants, none would know her maid, who was safely waiting at the Golden Bull. Elizabeth too was passed without question.

Only once during their progress through the corridors, did they need to slip into an empty room while a party went past, coming from some business with the queen. Rhoslyn thought she recognized some of the voices—councilors. By bad luck, one might want to speak to her because he thought her a favorite; by the worst luck one of them might recognize Elizabeth.

When the group passed, Rhoslyn sighed with relief. "Good," she muttered. "That means the queen is still at work. Now she will probably go to her closet to write in her journal or to Philip. If our good fortune holds, the bedroom and dressing room will be totally empty."

They did not have that much good fortune. Elizabeth stunned the guard, and they slipped through the door. Two of the queen's chamberers were in the dressing room when Rhoslyn opened the door, but Elizabeth was quick with her freezing spell. Rhoslyn closed the door, Elizabeth releasing the guard just as the latch clicked.

Then they were through the dressing room and out into the bedchamber—which was empty. As Rhoslyn shut the door behind them, Elizabeth said, "*Deffro*," and the women came to life, never aware that they had lost a little time.

Elizabeth then jammed the lock on the door so that she could examine the walls and the furniture in peace. If she heard someone trying to get in, she would release the spell on the lock and Rhoslyn would hide them with Don't-see-me, but that would be a last resort.

The maids, however, remained in the dressing room talking

in low tones. Elizabeth settled at last on a short stretch of wall between two paintings, one of Philip and the other of Philip and Mary together. She did not have much choice as much of the wall was covered by furniture or tapestries.

Satisfied that the space was large enough and that those who came through first could move aside quickly to allow others to enter, Elizabeth laid down her token. Now it was only necessary for them to find a place to hide until Mary went to bed. If they should be discovered, Rhoslyn would conceal them with the Don't-see-me but both hoped that would not be necessary. With luck, they would not need to conceal themselves for long.

As soon as Mary had dismissed all her attendants except the lady who slept with her and perhaps a maid to bring anything the queen wanted during the night, Elizabeth would set a sleep spell on them all. Once they were ensorcelled she would invoke the token and the others would come through the Gate from Avalon.

Then the luck turned toward them. Having little to do Rhoslyn had been listening to the chamberers' conversation. Most of it was concerned with the clothing they were working on, but while Elizabeth was looking for a place to hide, Rhoslyn's keen ears detected the maids' decision to go to their own small parlor and take some refreshment before the queen sent for them to undress her.

When Rhoslyn heard the click of the outer door closing, she and Elizabeth hurried into the dressing room. Here they hoped to find a safe place. The room was crowded with many gowns, undergowns, sleeves, stomachers, sets of shelves that held gloves and stockings and such small articles of dress.

"Well," Rhoslyn murmured, "how thoughtful of them to lay out her night rail. We need not worry about which shelf they will approach. I think . . . there—" She pointed to a rack that held Mary's very richest gowns. "She will not be wearing any of those early tomorrow, so we need not fear the chamberers will come to that rack to lay out tomorrow's garments."

After a small struggle to slide behind the garments without disarranging them, Elizabeth and Rhoslyn sat quietly on the floor. They did not speak; there was nothing more to say and Rhoslyn was concentrating on gathering her strength. Elizabeth prayed. She seldom mixed Christian religion with her Underhill experiences, but this time she felt that although God might try the faithful, He could not really want a Devil Incarnate to rule England.

Time passed slowly, but it did pass; then Rhoslyn heard the chamberers returning, exchanging pleasantries with the guard. Both she and Elizabeth stood, hoping their shoes would be hidden by the long skirts of the fine gowns. Now Elizabeth began to grow anxious, not about being found—the maids moved to the bedchamber without looking around the dressing room—but because she was apprehensive about Mwynwyn's task and about whether she could Push the Evil far enough.

Mercifully there were no setbacks to make her more anxious. Rhoslyn could hear the conversations in Mary's bedchamber while her ladies disrobed her, removed and put away her jewels, and brushed out her hair. She pressed Elizabeth's arm when the queen gave her ladies leave to go, warning her it was almost time to act.

A few softer murmurs marked Mary and her companion climbing into bed and the chamberers smoothing the bedclothes over them and pulling the bedcurtains closed. Only one of the women returned to the dressing room carrying Mary's dress. She spent a few moments laying it away and then went out, wishing the guard a good and quiet night.

Now Rhoslyn and Elizabeth extracted themselves from behind the clothing. Rhoslyn listened for a moment at the door and heard nothing. That meant that probably no one was sitting up in bed and chatting. She did not think everyone was asleep; she knew Mary slept very badly—Elizabeth's spell would take care of that—but she did not want anyone's last memory to be of falling asleep in the middle of a sentence.

They heard someone shift in her bed when Rhoslyn opened the door, but Elizabeth's spell took that person before she could speak or remember waiting for an answer. They could hope that she would think whatever had disturbed her had been unimportant and she had then fallen asleep. They went in, closing the door behind them.

Because she had been standing in the dark behind the clothes, Elizabeth was able to see well enough by the night candle. She went directly to the token, touched it, and said, "Come." She thought again as she invoked the token that as soon as there was even a small amount of power to waste, Denno had better change the word of invocation to something her women were unlikely to say. She had had the thought many times and as many times it had slipped her mind; when she was with Denno, they had much better things to do.

Dark as the room was, the spot that formed on the wall was still blacker, or perhaps it was that the black glowed that made it visible. Elizabeth stepped out of the way as Pasgen came through. He looked less strained than she expected and she felt the power of his shields as he, too, stepped out of the way to give room to Denno, also well shielded. He was followed by Hafwen and Mwynwen, naked of protection, as they needed to be to use their Gifts.

Hafwen gasped as soon as she entered the room, and Pasgen hurried to her side to take her arm and steady her. "There." Her head turned toward Mary's bed. "It is there."

"Can you mark it for me exactly, Hafwen?" Mwynwen asked. "It would be a tragedy if I killed an unborn and we later discovered the evil was in an amulet or some other artifact Vidal had planted in this chamber."

Rhoslyn hurried to the bed and drew back the curtain on the side where she knew Mary always slept. Hafwen took a step, then another toward the bed. It was not far to go, but Elizabeth could see she was shaking and that Pasgen was supporting her. However, he was not holding her back or trying to shield her in any way. Denno, Elizabeth thought, could take a lesson from Pasgen; then she bit her lip to curb a smile. This was no time for smiling, but Denno often still thought of her as the three-year-old he had dandled on his knee.

"Yes, there," Hafwen said, pointing to Mary's belly.

She had run her shaking hand down Mary, from the top of her head, where she actually rested her fingers on the queen's forehead to be sure the Evil was not in Mary's mind, down her body, down her legs, to her feet. Then with her eyes closed, she seemed to let her hand drift. It wavered slightly and then came to rest on the queen's abdomen.

"Thank you," Mwynwen said, but her tone was bitter. She had hoped to the last they would find some other site for the Evil.

Nonetheless, she came to Hafwen's side and ran her fingers over the lips Hafwen had bitten bloody; the lips healed. Then she slid her hand under Hafwen's and looked down at Mary.

"If you need strength," Denoriel said, moving beside her, "you can draw on me."

After a moment of silence, Mwynwen gasped. "I may need to," she said, her voice thin and choked. "I have touched it." She shuddered. "It is evil, indeed. And now it is aware of me."

She bent forward over the bed, one hand on Mary's belly, the other stretched out. Denoriel took it between both of his. He looked away from his fellow Sidhe, looked once at Elizabeth. Her eyes were huge and brilliant with tears but she made no sign, no gesture, to stop him from what he was about to do. She loved her Denno with all her heart, but England was at stake . . . and in the end, Elizabeth knew her realm came first.

She saw the pain in his face, the way Mwynwyn's hand jerked in his as the jolt of power ran through his body like flame. She saw Mwynwyn's other hand lift a sliver from Mary's body, an ugly yellowish . . . something . . . following her hand. In the next moment her hand slammed down on Mary's belly so hard the queen's body bounced.

Mwynwen uttered a pained cry and clutched Denoriel's hand tighter. Elizabeth could see a sheen of moisture on his face, which was graying under his sun-darkened skin as Mwynwen drew power from him.

"Oh, poor thing. Poor thing," Mwynwen sobbed.

Tears ran down her face as she drew her hand up again, twisting her body to give herself leverage. The yellowish stuff rose higher and Mwynwen seemed to fix her fingers in it. She backed a step away from the bed, drawing the thing with her.

Inside it Elizabeth could see something red, a tiny, not quite human form with a head as large as the rest of the twisted and deformed body. It twitched. Elizabeth caught her breath and sent more power into her shields. Mwynwen gripped the yellow stuff tighter and pulled harder.

Suddenly the little red thing, which had seemed limp and quiet, straightened from its coiled position and reached arms? tentacles? thorns? toward the yellow stuff, piercing it, rising toward Mwynwen's hand. Elizabeth cried out, wanting to run away, but she was the only one with power to spare. Swallowing, she cast a shield over Mwynwen. At the same moment the trail of yellow goo still attached to Mary's stomach snapped, and the puslike clot that enveloped the tiny red monster was jerked free of Mwynwyn's grip and flew through the air right at Hafwen.

She threw up her own shields, but they were gossamer veils

designed for playing games among the Bright Sidhe, not really meant for protection. Pasgen shouted and something black and dense formed around the clot of goo. It struck Hafwen, who recoiled with a cry, stumbling backward. The black mass jerked and bulged, the creature within now showing its power and threatening to split the dark mirror spell. But if not strong, Hafwen's shields were slick; the Evil slid down those shields without piercing them.

Rhoslyn had come forward and was repeating Pasgen's words, pointing at the black mass rolling crazily around the floor. The black grew denser, but what it enclosed only became more violently agitated.

Denoriel, so drained by Mwynwen's need that he felt as if his body would fall in on itself, grasped at the first thread of power he saw. It was thicker than he wanted, but he dared not take the time to look for a less potent line. He dreaded the consequences; he had drunk lightning twice before in these terrible two days. But the encased thing was not subdued. Twitching and rolling, it then convulsed violently and leapt up at him, forcing a thread-thin hook through the two not-dense-enough mirror spells. Denoriel drew in the undiluted mortal power, crying out with pain as it burned through his power channels.

Elizabeth cried out too. If Denno burned himself so badly he could not use magic, she would lose him. She was badly frightened and on the edge of vomiting from the disgusting sensation that had oozed through her shield when she tore a clot of the yellow goo from Mwynwyn's hand.

Now that thing was attacking her Denno! She watched with starting eyes as a thin red hook, somehow pushed itself through the dark envelope and scraped for a purchase while it slid down Denno's shield. Elizabeth shook with the desire to rush over to him and pull the thing off. Her shields were stronger than his now and it might get its claws into him because he could not say the spell as fast as Pasgen and Rhoslyn.

They could not help; Rhoslyn was drained and Pasgen still had to hold the Gate. And she could do nothing either! Elizabeth knew the danger to a spell-caster if the spell failed. She dared not interrupt or distract Denno while he was casting.

Another convulsion within the surrounding black of the mirror spells sent the Evil from Denoriel's hip right up to his face. The red hook caught. Denoriel spat out the last word of the spell. With a shriek, Elizabeth leapt forward, seized the writhing black ball, yanking loose its grip on her Denno, and flung it away.

Rage and fear and sickness roiled together. Heat rose from her belly to her breast. She opened her mouth and felt flames pour out with her breath.

"*Begone!*" she shouted, her eyes fixed on the black ovoid that swelled and sank in furious pulses. "Begone to that empty place from which nothing ever returns."

And it was gone.

The room was silent. Everyone stood as if struck to stone for a moment, then Elizabeth flung herself around to clutch at Denoriel, drop her shield, and run her hands over his face. "Are you hurt, Denno? I saw it catch at you. Are you burned?"

"That was some Push!" he sighed. "I could feel the power lines all around me tremble." He fended off her hands, dropped his shield, and drew her close to kiss. "It's all right, love. If I could feel what you did to the lines of power, I still have magic. And the thing, whatever it was, didn't take hold, only caught for a moment where the shield bulges over my nose."

"I am very glad we did not need to depend on the mirror spells," Pasgen said with a sigh. "That thing was incredibly strong and it understood mirror spells. It did not try to use magic, only force. We should have considered that. After all, we did suspect that Vidal had held it prisoner with a mirror spell." He smiled faintly. "That was a good Push indeed, Lady Elizabeth. I will do some checking, but I am sure you sent it to the Void."

He looked at Elizabeth, remembering when she had nearly sent *him* into the Void. Well, he had been trying to kill her, so perhaps it was justified. He turned his head, saw Hafwen, and moved to stand beside her. He surely did not envy Denoriel, who had to deal with that temper and that kind of power.

"I do not know what the physical thing was," Hafwen said, nervously clutching Pasgen's hand, "but what was in it was pure Evil." She closed her eyes. "I have never felt anything like that before."

"The form was that of a very young unborn," Mwynwen said. "Only it was malformed. I do not think it could have lived, even if it had been birthed."

"Poor Mary," Elizabeth said. "My father was very wrong to see her only as a political pawn. She wished so much to be a wife. She loved children. He should have found her a good husband so she could have been happy . . . instead of ruining England."

"She will not harm Logres for long," Mwynwen said sadly. She leaned over Mary again, touching her belly and then shook her head. "Poor woman. She cannot live long. There is something growing in her womb. Not a magical thing, a human illness about which I can do nothing."

Elizabeth's heart leapt within her when Mwynwen said that Mary could not live long. In the next moment she felt a flush of shame at her callousness toward her sister and she bit her lip and buried her face in Denoriel's breast.

Rhoslyn was looking around the bedchamber. For all the frantic activity, nothing had been disturbed. She pulled up the light coverlet and smoothed it over the queen's still form; her eyes stung with tears. Mary was a good woman, truly kind and loving. Elizabeth was right. It was Henry VIII's desperate need for a son to follow him that had twisted Mary all awry. Tenderly she smoothed Mary's hair. She suspected now that the Evil was gone, Rosamund would be a favorite again.

Mwynwen had already passed through the Gate, Elizabeth was waiting near it to release the sleep spell, Denoriel right behind her. Then Hafwen went through. Pasgen came and slid an arm around Rhoslyn's waist.

"This is hard for you, Rhoslyn. I am sorry."

Although she was surprised by her brother's attention and gentleness, she was glad of it and leaned her head on his shoulder. Torgen and Hafwen had drawn him into Bright Court ways. The Bright Court Sidhe might still be careless and inconstant, but they liked playing with the softer emotions and readily displayed them.

"I have been her handmaid for over twenty years. It is very strange to think that she will be gone. She is a good person. It is unfair that she should know only sorrow."

Pasgen, like almost every other living being, had no answer to that. They stepped back so Rhoslyn could close the bedcurtain. Elizabeth released the sleep spell and they went through the Gate which, with a sigh of relief, Pasgen allowed to close.

When they came through, there was quite a crowd near the Gate platform. No one wanted to carry away for private consideration the disgust and terror the Evil had wakened in them. Harry and Lady Aeron were waiting with Talog, Hafwen stood between Talfan and Torgen, who was all decked out in red eyes, carnivore teeth, and claws. Miralys had made a double saddle to take Elizabeth and Denoriel.

All, however, were looking after a single drooping figure mounted on an elvensteed that was moving very slowly toward the cottages beyond Avalon.

"Mwynwen would not stay," Hafwen said. "Healer that she is it cut her to the heart to have to send to death even so evil a thing. And to feel death creeping close to Mary and be unable to ward it away . . ." She sighed and shook her head.

They watched Mwynwen move away through a darkling gloom. In the vault of the "sky" the stars were either gone or dim. The shining twilight was shading into black night. Elizabeth shivered as she looked at the sad, wilted moss and the dull, lusterless palace in the distance. No flag flew bravely, due to the fact that there was no breeze from the dark staff on the tallest spire.

Where were Oberon and Titania? After eons, was Underhill dying?

Elizabeth swallowed hard and glanced around at her friends, her lover. "God willing," she said, making her voice firm, "I will give it all back to you when I rule. I swear I will stint no effort to make a happy realm." She blinked away tears and added in a determinedly cheerful voice. "At least we have warded off the worst threat today. Evil will not rule Logres forever."

"Let us put this aside," Denoriel urged. "Aleneil and Ilar are waiting at the Inn of Kindly Laughter to hear whether we succeeded. For this one mortal night let us account ourselves victors."

Chapter 41

At first Elizabeth did not think waiting for Mary to die would be very difficult. The queen seemed to have given up on either suspecting her of rebellion or trying to get her married and out of the country. Although Sir Edward kept a tight guard and had messengers ready to ride and rouse Elizabeth's liegemen, nothing disturbed the quiet of Hatfield. Mary was totally concentrated on supplying men and money for Philip's war.

And in the beginning that went very well. The English fleet drove French ships back to their harbors and from time to time did even better and took a prize. Sometimes they even raided the French coast. Pembroke, at the head of his five thousand foot and five hundred horse, accompanied Philip to a share in a striking victory, besieging and taking St. Quentin.

Mary sent Elizabeth a smug letter to announce the victory and to report that *Te Deum* Masses were being sung throughout London and the country. Elizabeth promptly ordered that all her estates have Masses sung, light bonfires and serve a feast to all who could come. That was in August. By September there was more good news. The pope and King Philip came to terms and a peace was made. But then the tide that had rushed in began to draw back.

Through the autumn, October and November, there were strong signs that the king of France was not beaten and intended to revenge his losses by the greatest coup he could deal to England. He meant to take back Calais, which had been ruled by the English since Edward III captured it in 1347.

Elizabeth was as aware of the threat as Mary and her Council. No one doubted any longer that the queen was failing, and a trickle of courtiers—those who believed Mary would die soon—came to seek favor with Elizabeth and brought news. Elizabeth welcomed them all graciously, but was very careful never to ask a question or say a word of criticism against the queen. She heard enough without asking to chill her blood.

For once, despite the desperate situation, Elizabeth could not fault Mary's intentions. She was aware of the danger. She ordered the defenses of Calais to be renewed and sent three hundred more men. But Mary was nearly bankrupt. Her government had never been rich and she had poured out money to Philip. The work to protect Calais was never finished, the five hundred more men that Pembroke said were necessary never sent. Rumor was that the best general France had was advancing on Calais.

Mary did what she could with no money but she was distracted. Although this time she made no public announcements, she was aware of the change in her body. Her belly swelled and her fluxes, never very regular, stopped altogether. In December, Mary wrote to Philip, that this time she was certain that she was with child.

She begged her husband to come to her. Philip, pleading the duties and anxieties heaped on him by the war, sent Count Feria, who had three missions. The first was to determine whether it was actually possible that Mary was pregnant. Philip had done his marital duty regularly during the four months he had been in England, so it was barely possible. Feria's second commission was to convince Mary to make her will as childbirth was always dangerous. The last was to promise Elizabeth that Mary would publicly name her heir to the throne if she would accept Emmanuel Philibert as a husband.

The first mission was easy to discharge. Mary's women were sure she was not with child despite the swelling of her belly. It was clear from their looks, from tear-filled eyes, that the cause for the swelling belly was far darker than a coming child. None said in plain words that Mary was dying, but Feria's betrothed wife, Jane Dormer, wept every time the subject arose.

Jane was the closest of all the women to Mary now, although Rosamund Scot was well enough loved to give Jane some relief from attendance. For that Feria was grateful, although there was something he could not like about Mistress Rosamund; he suspected she was like too many English and hated him because he was Spanish.

As to the will, Mary agreed without any difficulty. When she had thought out the provisions and taken advice from Cardinal Pole and the few other councilors she trusted, she would make her will. About agreeing to name Elizabeth her heir, she was far less complaisant. A flush rose under her graying pallor and she did not lower her loud, harsh voice as she said that Elizabeth was *not* her sister. Ann Boleyn had been a whore, and Elizabeth had no right to the throne.

Feria wrote to Philip that he would broach the topic with Elizabeth first. If he could get her to agree to maintain the Catholic religion in England, possibly Mary would put aside her doubts about Elizabeth's parentage. Instead Feria came away from that meeting with a firm conviction that Elizabeth would never marry Philip's choice and would always do as she pleased. He left Hatfield with a permanent and violent dislike of her.

Elizabeth, who had totally lost patience with the efforts to have her marry the powerless and subservient Emmanuel Philibert, for once spoke her mind. "What kind of a fool do you think me after seeing how this nation responded to my sister's marriage to take a foreign husband? Why, I would sooner marry my dear old Denno." She gestured to the white-haired common merchant talking to Lady Alana near an open window.

Feria flushed with rage at the insult and descended to a threat. "Then perhaps King Philip will use his influence to prefer some other claimant to the throne."

Elizabeth smiled very faintly. "The king is a very clever man, I doubt he will act the fool. I am Great Harry's daughter and both his will and an act of Parliament place me next in the succession. Recall what happened when Northumberland tried to set Queen Mary aside. England will brook no other claimant." Now her eyes pinned Feria as a butterfly is pinned to a board. "And my sister is alive and well and queen. Surely there is no need to talk about such matters."

It was hopeless, Feria wrote to Philip. "She is a very vain and clever woman and has been thoroughly schooled in the way her father ruled. I am afraid she will not be well-disposed in matters of religion, for the men she has around her I suspect are at heart heretics and I know the women to be. Beside that, it is clear to me that she is highly indignant about how she has been treated during the queen's lifetime."

Although Feria did not know that when he spoke to her, any accommodation with Elizabeth was already hopeless. On January tenth news came to England of a disaster that Elizabeth credited entirely to Philip's war and Philip's pernicious influence on Mary.

In mid-December Calais had been lost.

Mary sent no letter to Elizabeth to announce the disaster, but there was no need. Regular reports of all rumor and most Court business now came from William Cecil, and all the news the courtiers who visited Hatfield brought was bad.

Even before the loss of Calais, events in England were driving Elizabeth to angry, if concealed, impatience for Mary's death. The burnings continued and the people were more and more enraged. It was often necessary to call out the men of the nearest armed post to protect the executioner and more particularly the priest who accompanied the victim. Twice the small troop had been rushed and a woman and child rescued. Soon, Elizabeth feared, riot would become a common habit in the people, making them impossible to govern.

Robert Dudley, returned from serving with the army at St. Quentin, gave his opinion between his teeth—Elizabeth's ladies were out of earshot. Money went to build churches; money went to Philip. The crown was so poor that armed troops had to be small.

"Sixty thousand pounds in revenue she has handed to Cardinal Pole to restore the Church." Robert Dudley's fine dark eyes blazed; Elizabeth thought him a very pretty man. "There will soon be no kingdom in which to raise churches."

Elizabeth said calmly, in a normal voice, "Mary is queen. She must do what she thinks best."

But inwardly she was furious with Mary's stupidity. To worship God was good and right. To beggar the kingdom to raise churches was wrong. If the people wanted churches, they could tithe and raise them on their own. It was no business of the crown.

From the beginning Mary had made one mistake after another in governing. She had not thought about who would be best to help her rule, but let gratitude and affection create the overlarge Council that only fought each other, sought advantage, and accomplished nothing. And to allow her fixed love of everything Spanish to select a husband her people hated was utter idiocy. The love of the people was a sovereign's best security. Finally, Mary's blind devotion to her husband's demands had cost England Calais.

When the news of Calais' fall came on the tenth of January, 1558, Elizabeth did not try for public restraint. Even her long-time attendants were shocked by her language. And then she wept bitterly, groaning "Lost. Lost." That was all she said aloud, but she was sure if she had been queen, Calais would still be English; England would never have been involved in the Spanish war.

She might as well have said the words aloud. Mary would not have cared. She seemed to be slipping into a world that was not quite real. At the end of February she invited Elizabeth to come to Court. Terrified anew that an effort might be made to abduct her, Elizabeth arrived with a huge attendance of noblemen and their wives and daughters.

Whether Mary had intended abduction or simply wanted her sister's company, remembering the red-haired child who had run to greet her with love, no one ever knew but Elizabeth. She did not say—not even to Denno, who on this visit to London attended her openly. Whatever Mary's reason, Elizabeth's visit did not serve the purpose. She returned to Hatfield within a week.

In March Mary completed the will Philip had asked her to write—a document based solidly on delusion. She wrote it as if she would certainly bear a living child. No mention at all was made of Elizabeth.

April brought a proposal of marriage to Elizabeth from the king of Sweden. He offered his son and heir. Mary wakened from her languid indifference to be furious; she thought Elizabeth would snatch at the proposal, which certainly did not favor Spain. And Mary could not bear the thought of Elizabeth married, able to hold her husband with her "spirit of enchantment," young enough to bear children.

Mary sent Thomas Pope to sound Elizabeth out. Elizabeth said what she always said, that she did not know what she would do in the future, but for the present she did not intend to marry.

Pope did not believe her; neither did Mary but no more could be got from Elizabeth, not a wink, not a flicker of expression.

Over the summer, Mary grew weaker, losing interest even in the possibility that Elizabeth would become a happy wife. In August the queen was very ill with a raging fever. Courtiers now arrived at Hatfield with greater frequency. Some said the queen was already dead and had named Elizabeth as her heir. Elizabeth said that could not be true, Mary still ruled, and said no more.

Elizabeth waited a sure sign lest she commit treason. She knew such a sign would come. She had charged Sir Nicholas Throckmorton to bring to her the black enameled betrothal ring that Philip had sent to Mary. That, Elizabeth knew, would never leave her sister's hand while she was alive.

Mary recovered somewhat during September, but not completely. Through October she lay for hours in a melancholic stupor; she was alive but had ceased to rule. Her own Council gave her up for dead; if not today then very soon. On the sixth of November the Privy Council, warned by Mistress Rosamund Scot that the queen was awake and lucid, came to her bedside to persuade her to make a declaration in favor of Lady Elizabeth concerning the succession.

Mary no longer cared; wearily she agreed the girl she insisted was a bastard should rule. She knew Elizabeth would be queen no matter whom she named as heir. All her further refusal could accomplish was to start a civil war—and by now Mary sadly acknowledged she had done her country enough harm.

Elizabeth woke on the eighth of November, 1558, with no notion the day was special. She did ask immediately whether there had been any news; she could not help it, although she knew it was silly. If the news she waited for—that Mary was dead—had arrived in the night someone would have wakened her. No news, Kat said, and Elizabeth prepared to go about her ordinary business.

But it was no ordinary day. Just after Elizabeth finished dressing, Blanche, who was about to hand her a fan, froze. Elizabeth instinctively drew up her shields as she whirled around, spells trembling on her lips. She drew a breath to speak one. Everyone in her chamber was still as marble—everyone except one tall, exquisitely beautiful Sidhe.

"Lord Ffrancon," Elizabeth breathed, dropping a curtsey.

Oberon's chief factotum merited a curtsey, but the truth was the bow owed more to the sudden weakness of Elizabeth's knees than to respect. Elizabeth had not been Underhill for more than a year, not since she and the others had torn the Evil from Mary's womb. She did not go because she could not bear to see what she thought of as the unfading land of dreams slowly die. In the beginning she had not altogether approved of Underhill where she felt life was a too-easy lie. Now she loved it dearly and desperately desired to save it . . . but all she could do was wait for Mary to die.

The powerful Sidhe gestured for her to rise. "No need for that any more," he said with a smile. "You are summoned by High King Oberon and High Queen Titania to attend a Great Court Underhill. At mortal midnight a portal will open. Do not fail."

And he was gone.

The fan Blanche had been about to hand her dropped to the floor. Automatically Elizabeth turned back to take it as Blanche bent to pick it up. She heard one of her ladies finish a sentence she had started but could make no reply and just shook her head. *Summoned? By Oberon? Summoned where? Had Oberon returned Underhill?*

She spent most of the morning reliving Lord Ffrancon's brief visit, seeking in her mind for signs of age, of decay, of the ruin that was overtaking Underhill. Hope made her breath come quickly. There were no such signs. Lord Ffrancon's face was unlined, its perfect features sharp and clear; his long silver hair glowed with life, his green eyes were bright with vitality. Of course, Denno looked as strong and lively as ever too. Could Lord Ffrancon also be able to drink lightning?

After dinner Elizabeth received another shock. When she heard that two members of the Privy Council had come to speak with her, her heart stopped and then leapt. Mary was dead!

Elizabeth stood tall and still, her hands clasped at her waist, her breath held . . . but the bows the Privy Councilors made were not deep enough. Elizabeth allowed her breath to sigh out and drew it in evenly.

"My lords?" she asked quietly. "What can I do for you?"

They told her that her sister had at last acknowledged her as heir apparent. Few conditions were being placed on her elevation, only that Mary desired Elizabeth to promise to maintain the Catholic religion and pay Mary's debts.

Elizabeth had no more intention of continuing Mary's mad attempt to force England into Catholicism than she had of trying to fly. She made no response to that, instead hurrying to promise to do her best to pay Mary's debts—after all, she would need the goodwill of those creditors in the future. She knew she should make a graceful, ambiguous speech about religion, but could not.

Had Oberon known that Mary was dying and would name her heir? How could he have known? Where had he been? All Elizabeth could do was thank the councilors for coming to her, ask after her sister's welfare, and hope that the officials would believe she was so strongly moved she could not make sense.

To appear cooperative was the habit of many bitter years but Elizabeth's mind was in total turmoil and she fumbled for the equivocal phrases about her faith. She was shocked and confused that the promise of what she had dreamed of and hoped for from the moment of her brother's death could be so overshadowed by a message from King Oberon.

Finally Mary's comptroller and master of the rolls took their leave. Elizabeth's mind jumped from what Oberon's summons meant to the fact that she was now the undisputed heir to the throne; that jump prodded her to send a messenger to Brocket Hall where William Cecil was staying. Since the Hall was no more than two and a half miles from Hatfield, Cecil returned within half an hour, his face faintly flushed, his eyes bright with satisfaction.

Cecil had always been aware of Mary's determination to ruin Elizabeth and set God knew who on the throne. He thanked God, he said to Elizabeth, that the Council had that much common sense. Between Henry VIII's will, the Act of Succession, and Mary's final acknowledgment there was no longer any danger of civil war. Elizabeth was the accredited, recognized heir.

Cecil's disciplined, logical mind moved on to the next problem. The ugly subject of Cardinal Pole. Elizabeth did not like the cardinal; he returned the compliment in no uncertain terms. But Mary had made Pole archbishop of Canterbury.

"Do you think he will refuse to crown you or try to wring some oath of subservience to the pope from you?" William Cecil asked. "He is as obsessed as Mary with bringing England under the pope's rule again."

"He is very ill," Elizabeth said. One of the secretly Protestant courtiers had brought the news. "Some kind of fever. Surely it would be possible for me to excuse him from the coronation on the grounds of his health?"

"That would be best," Cecil agreed, "but then who will you get to crown you?"

Crown. Elizabeth could not remember Oberon ever wearing a crown. Not that it mattered. Everything about Oberon declared him High King. Cecil said her name, gently questioning her lack of immediate response.

"I have no idea," Elizabeth admitted, not willing to say to Cecil that she could not really think about it.

Her eyes followed the servants who were lighting candles throughout the room. She pulled herself together, knowing that the Catholic bishops Mary had appointed would all try to wrench some promise from her, or would be unwilling to crown her, claiming she was at heart a heretic, or insisting on some Catholic service she wished to avoid.

"You had better begin a canvass of the bishops who might be willing," she suggested finally, and then admitted. "I am all heels over head. Mary must have known since this pregnancy was also false that I would come to the throne, but I was afraid she would die before she conceded or name someone else just for spite. I need time to swallow this down and digest it."

"Yes." Cecil bowed, then took the hand she held out to him and kissed it. "And it is growing dark. I had better get back to Brocket Hall. There is much to do now, and it will be easier as I can do it more openly."

Elizabeth watched him go without really seeing it. Mention of the coronation had sent her mind back Underhill. Her father had been the greatest mortal ruler Elizabeth would acknowledge (Charles V was probably greater, but the rack could not have dragged that admission out of Elizabeth) but Oberon was in no competition with Great Harry; he was Other.

There was no air spirit to send for Denno. He was in London, his informants at Court listening for the first word of Mary's death. And Alana was away too, probably at Cymry, which was less affected by the loss of power because the Sidhe there used less magic. Elizabeth had no one to talk to. She said she was cold and would change to a warmer gown, which gave her an excuse to tell Blanche, but the maid was no help. She was frightened. She could not imagine why King Oberon should want to summon Elizabeth.

How could I have offended him? Elizabeth wondered. *I have not been Underhill in so long.* But what if he did know that Mary was dying and he wanted her to find him a place in the mortal world? Elizabeth shuddered. Perhaps Oberon had abandoned Underhill. The last she had seen of it, the mortal world was richer.

Elizabeth's mind leapt back and forth between the ultimately authoritarian Oberon as she had seen him last, massive and utterly magical, and the horrible possibility of an Oberon small and shrunken pleading with her to make him a duke or send the power of joy to his dying realm.

That could not be, she told herself. Lord Ffrancon had said Oberon would open a Gate for her. That meant Oberon had power. Elizabeth clung to that thought. At an hour before midnight she dismissed her ladies, saying she wished to be alone to pray and consider the great news the men of the Privy Council had brought her. The two who remained in her bedchamber she bespelled to sleep.

Now Blanche helped her into her very finest gown, a cloth-of-gold kirtle heavily embroidered with roses and thistles with an overgown of black velvet embroidered with gold thread. The very wide sleeves of the overgown were turned back so fitted sleeves of the cloth-of-gold kirtle showed. A high collar of pleated lawn was fastened around her neck and the long chains of jewel-set gold that Denno had given her hung over her breast. Around her waist she wore another gift from Denno, square links of gold, each holding a precious stone.

Promptly at midnight the wall where the Gate had always opened yawned widely. This time there was no luminous black spot that grew into a Gate; the Gate was simply there. But this time Elizabeth could not make out what was on the other side. Surely Oberon had not decided he would make her step into oblivion. Surely she was too valuable, heir apparent to the throne. Oberon always played games of power. He only wanted to frighten her.

Elizabeth took a deep breath, lifted her chin and stepped forward. She did not feel as if she were falling, nor did her vision go black. She simply was standing with her back to the huge double doors of an enormous chamber. The roof soared above her into unseeable dimness, twice or thrice the height of St. Paul's, yet silver light shone from it and the whole chamber was nearly bright.

A weird combination of relief and rage made Elizabeth's teeth snap together. She had no doubt that Oberon had created this hall, possibly a whole great building and a landscape to go with it, possibly for this occasion alone. There was no lack of power in Oberon—or in Titania either; she glowed light beside his radiant darkness. How dare they? How dare they abandon their kingdom to sorrow and decay?

She stood at the head of a long aisle, which ended at a dais on which was a huge, magnificent double throne. One throne that glowed with a pearly light and on it she saw Oberon and Titania, seated together.

Elizabeth started down the aisle and saw it was bordered on each side by seats, which looked to her countless. The seats were filled with Sidhe—to her left, which would be the right of the throne, a mass of golden hair and bright green eyes; to her right, the left of the throne, a more mixed group, dark and light but nearly all with glowing dark eyes. And all those glowing eyes were fixed on her with open hostility.

Elizabeth's shields rose, thick, impenetrable, and her lips tightened into a thin line. She grew angrier and angrier with each step she took down the aisle. One move, one insult, one hiss of "Silly weak mortal" and she would Push them all right through the walls of the building, and the throne and its occupants, too. Heat built in her belly and spread up over her chest and arms. She slowed, turning slightly toward the hostile Sidhe.

A huge laugh, surprisingly warm and companionable despite its volume, broke her intensifying rage. And Elizabeth found herself clear of the hostile Sidhe, standing right before the throne.

"Gently, gently, Lady Elizabeth," Oberon said. "This is a Great Court to make peace—"

"Whose peace?" Elizabeth snapped. "I will have no peace dictated to me. I have lost no battles. I have not yet begun to fight."

Titania's thrilling musical laugh cut off whatever Oberon had been about to say. "Peace, my sweet Elizabeth. You know I have ever been your friend. I promise no one, not even my dear dictatorial lord, will force any measure on you. That is not our purpose here."

The placatory tone soothed, at least enough for Elizabeth to come to her senses and realize that she could not win a contest with Oberon and Titania no matter how contemptuous she was over their abandonment of their subjects. She drew a breath and dropped a deep curtsey to Titania.

When she raised her head, Elizabeth was startled again by a beauty so great it could not be remembered. The golden hair, the green eyes, the translucent flesh that seemed lit from within . . . one could tell over what one saw, could bring up a memory of the High Queen, but the reality was always so far greater than the memory it was a shock.

"And will you not give some sign of respect to my lord also?" Titania asked, laughing again.

Her knowing eyes glanced sidelong at Oberon. Elizabeth saw Titania clearly remembered that every time Elizabeth and Oberon met there was a greater or lesser clash of wills. And Elizabeth suddenly realized she was alone—for the first time she was Underhill with no Denno beside her.

"Where is—" about to say my Denno, Elizabeth also recalled Oberon's violent objection in the past to her claim of possession of his subject and decided on a little diplomacy "—Lord Denoriel?" she asked.

A black eyebrow, as black and cleanly marked as if drawn in ink by a master hand, lifted. Elizabeth had a moment, her rage abated, to marvel again at Oberon's beauty, as great as that of Titania's if completely opposite. At the hair, so black it shone with blue and green and purple lights, waving back from the widow's peak on the high, white brow; at the eyes, so luminous one could swear they were light, although they were as black as the hair. A perfect nose, straight and strong, and a mouth so beautifully curved that for all her resentment, Elizabeth was much tempted to kiss it.

"Behind you," Oberon said, lips quirking with amusement.

Elizabeth turned, blinking, and saw that her friends were all seated in the first row of right-hand chairs. Angry because Oberon had brought her to the dais without giving her a chance to see even Da and Denno—and thus made her look foolish—she opened her mouth to snap.

In that moment she remembered Oberon's way of testing people. A queen should not allow herself to be annoyed into doing things that were stupid and dangerous—at least not where she had no power to enforce her will. In a little while, Elizabeth told herself, she would be a queen. She smiled sweetly at Oberon and sank into another deep curtsey.

"Thank you, Your Majesty," she murmured dulcetly.

"Very good," Oberon exclaimed, laughing that warm, intimate laugh that made one sure one was laughed with, not laughed at. "Very well recovered," he praised. "Now, do be seated among your companions."

He gestured her up and toward the seats. Now she saw there was an empty place between Da and Denno and she went and sat down. Aleneil was on the other side of Denno, who frowned and shook his head slightly at her in remonstrance for her behavior, and Mwynwen, head down, shoulders slumped, beyond. Rhoslyn, looking very wide-eyed and anxious, sat next to Da with Pasgen at the end of the row.

"I have come to look into several problems I had no time to solve before I left Underhill," Oberon said.

His voice was mild, his face nearly expressionless, but he glanced over toward the left and a wave of movement, almost a shrinking away, passed through the Sidhe there. Two seats were separated from the rest, set at right angles into the space before the dais. Elizabeth caught a glimpse of very gold hair worn in a low fringe on the forehead; she had seen that Sidhe before, she thought, but could not remember where or when. Beside her was a male who, had Oberon not been there might have been impressive. He also had very black hair and eyes but he looked faded and tawdry compared to the High King. Elizabeth was sure that was Vidal Dhu, who had tried so long and hard to kill her.

"There was an Evil set loose Underhill and that Evil was trapped and then transferred to the mortal world. Such acts are forbidden." Oberon's head turned. "Harry FitzRoy, you began this enterprise."

Elizabeth gasped with fear and was about to leap to her feet to stand with her Da. Denno caught her arm and held her still. She knew how Denno loved her Da and knew if Denno expected Oberon to strike at her Da, Denno would be standing in front of him to take the blow. She sat quiet. A moment later she saw Denno was right and was soon fascinated by how Oberon extracted the truth of what had happened from each being who had had any part in the affair from the escape of the Evil from Alhambra to Its expulsion into the Void by Elizabeth's Push.

When the tale was told, each having given evidence of his or her part, Oberon nodded. Then he held out his hand.

"Come here, Mwynwen."

She was still weeping over her inability to separate the Evil from the unborn or to help Mary. Elizabeth, seeing her clearly when she rose to go to Oberon, was shocked at how ill she looked and how tired. The High King gestured for her to step up on the dais and took her hand.

"That Evil touched you," Oberon said. "It could not take hold on you but it has tainted your life."

Mwynwen shuddered and her hand tightened on his. Then a long sigh lifted Mwynwen's breast; slowly her slumped shoulders rose. In a moment more, she looked up into Oberon's face, smiling now.

He let go of her hand and patted her cheek. "It is gone now. Take up your work again, Healer."

"Thank you, my lord." Mwynwen lifted his hand and kissed it. "Yes, my lord."

And she came down from the dais with a light step, smiled at them all, and sat easily.

"Pasgen and Rhoslyn Silverhair." They both stood and clasped hands nervously. "I knew your father, Kefni. He was one of my knights. I grieved for his death. If you wish to join the Bright Court, you are welcome." He swept the right-hand seats with a hard glance that quelled a murmur of protest. Suddenly he grinned, looking young and full of mischief for a moment. "Your elvensteeds are . . . a refreshment."

Then he was serious again and said, "Harry FitzRoy . . ."

Harry jumped to his feet and bowed jerkily. "My lord? I am certainly at fault for not attending more closely to the Evil." He sighed. "If there is some way for me to atone for that, I will do it gladly. It was surely my responsibility to see that thing did no harm. And I failed. It did do harm. Lord Pasgen told me."

Oberon nodded soberly. "In the future, you must be more careful. But I think I have a fitting punishment in mind for you." Harry braced his shoulders and Elizabeth jumped to her feet, Denoriel's grab at her missing. Then quite suddenly with never a glance at her, the High King grinned again. "Yes, most fitting. You are to go and take the elder Sidhe you have so thoroughly wakened to new mischief and clean out El Dorado . . . and be quick about it. There will be tenants for the place soon."

Relieved of any fear for her Da, Elizabeth was about to sink quietly into her seat when her eye was caught by movement in the chairs to the left of the dais. The golden-haired woman shifted sharply and leaned over to hiss into Vidal Dhu's ear.

Meanwhile Oberon had continued speaking to Harry, "You will find that Alhambra is now occupied. Go and visit the domain with the elder Sidhe if you are so minded, but those who live there now are a strange people." His glance flashed toward Vidal Dhu and his companion, returned to Harry. "Be careful."

Suddenly he was staring at Elizabeth a mixture of amusement and exasperation on his face. "You will very soon have your own kingdom to rule. I would appreciate it if you left mine to me."

Elizabeth blushed. "Forgive me, my lord. I . . . I only wish to defend those dear to me, sometimes unwisely and when it is not necessary, but my heart bids me—"

"You must become more discriminating," Titania said, her clear voice holding a note of severity. "A queen must not think first who is dear to her but what is best for all."

"That is true my very dear," Oberon remarked, chuckling. "Now if only you would follow your own wise rule . . ."

Titania laughed again and put a hand on Oberon's shoulder. "You would not be where you are," she finished sharply.

Oberon sighed but made no attempt to wrest the last word from Titania. He looked at Elizabeth. "In ten days your sister will be dead and you will be queen of Logres."

Elizabeth caught her breath. Sick as she often was, Mary had already lingered over a year. Since the summer she had been given up for dead three times . . . and yet lived. Elizabeth had not been sure whether she would have to wait another year or even longer while her sister's misgovernment continued to damage England.

"Ten days," Elizabeth breathed.

"No!"

A chair crashed to the floor. A blue bolt, spreading as it moved, sparkling and crackling and leaving dead black motes in the air where it caught some happily dancing air spirits, roared away from where Vidal Dhu had been sitting. A shining white wall met it. Thunder crashed. Wind howled. Elizabeth would have been knocked from her feet had not Denoriel and Aleneil both leapt up, Denoriel in front of her, shields up, blue light limning his fingers, Aleneil to steady and support her.

A Gate had already started to form just behind Vidal. It winked out.

"That is enough!" Oberon roared. "I am king here, not you."

Vidal, shields useless against Oberon's power, was frozen where he stood, one hand still raised, his face twisted with hate and rage. Aurilia shrank away from him as far as her seat would permit, her hands over her face.

"Elizabeth *will* be queen of Logres and will reign long and successfully. Not you, Vidal Dhu, nor you Aurilia, nor any minion of yours will attack her. That is my will and I will enforce it."

The occupants of the whole of the right-hand set of chairs rose to their feet. "Elizabeth and a happy Logres," a clear voice called and a roar of cheers agreed. Swords began to be drawn, energy crackled. The Sidhe in the left-hand seats began to rise.

"Sit!" Oberon bellowed. "I will have no battle at a Great Court." He lowered his voice to its normal penetrating volume. "I am king of all—Bright Court and Dark. I have no desire to see the Dark Court diminished to nothing while the Bright Court thrives. I have arranged for a source of power to be fed to the Dark Court. You will not be quite as rich during Elizabeth's reign as you have been during Mary's, but there will be power enough to make your dark creatures, to build domains, and to—" his lips quirked "—to fight each other."

At that point he released Vidal Dhu, who sank into the chair that had righted itself. Vidal was still glaring across the chamber at Elizabeth, and he was trembling violently. Elizabeth wondered whether it was with fear or rage.

"We must be able to defend ourselves against the mortal world," Vidal cried.

"That is not unreasonable," Oberon said. "Elizabeth?"

"And the mortal world must be able to defend itself against you," Elizabeth snapped back, staring boldly at Vidal. "I will not exhort my people to make sacrifice to you, nor to let your creatures run amok, killing herds of cattle and sheep, nor fail to carry Cold Iron to fend off your Wild Hunt."

"To that I agree," Oberon said, "but what of your Church? It was the Church that corrupted Alhambra and El Dorado."

Elizabeth was silent, staring angrily at Vidal but then she glanced at her Denno, still on guard to protect her, and at Alana, less aggressive but always supportive. The Church—Catholic or Protestant—would burn Denno or Aleneil for being Other, not caring what good they had done. Slowly, her eyes which had been dark and troubled lightened. As a solution came to her that would satisfy Oberon and incidentally be of the greatest benefit to her—Elizabeth did not fancy a powerful Church with tentacles deep into her Council—her eyes glowed gold.

"I may not always be able to control the princes of the Church, but I will try—that I promise. However, what I will swear to you, by my God and by your Great Mother, is that I will never have any powerful churchman as one of my high government officials. I will have no bishops for chancellor or comptroller or on my Privy Council or my great Council." And thinking of Cardinal Pole, she added, "I will have no religious fanatics for advisors no matter how saintly."

"Done!" Oberon roared. "Done, my lady."

"Done, sweet Elizabeth," Titania echoed. "And be sure that Underhill will always be open for you and—" she cast a flashing glance at Oberon and laughed "—your Denno and your Lady Alana will still protect you."

Oberon uttered a kind of exasperated growl, but again allowed Titania to have the last word. He looked now at Vidal. "Vidal Dhu, I have promised that your Court will not be straightened for power. But you must pay for that flow of power. The Bright Court must flourish also."

Vidal made no reply. His face was flushed, his nostrils pinched with temper, but an uninterrupted flow of power was not something he would throw away. There would be ways of adding to what he received, he was sure.

Smiling broadly and showing, to Elizabeth's faint distress, teeth as sharp as Vidal's and a good deal longer and stronger, Oberon named his price. "Queen Elizabeth—and Lady Elizabeth until she becomes queen—is sacrosanct. The moment she dies, or is in danger of death from whatever cause, be you innocent or guilty, all power to the Dark Court will be choked off until she is in good health and safe again." His voice rose to a bellow again. "Hear me! Elizabeth's person is sacred to me."

"And to me also," Titania echoed. "And I will do a great deal worse to you than cut off your power if Elizabeth's rule does not fulfill completely the promise our FarSeers have Visioned."

"Thank you." Elizabeth sank down in a curtsey right to the floor. "This may be the last time I may do you a reverence with bent knee, for as queen it would not be seemly for me to bow, but in my heart there will always be reverence for King Oberon and Queen Titania and for all of Underhill, which has been my salvation in my times of trial. While I reign, all of you who do no harm and wish no ill to my people will be welcome in England."

Oberon's word held the Sidhe of the Bright Court in their seats, and prevented any demonstration—but it seemed to Elizabeth that she could *feel* the joy, the good will, and the relief coming from them. It felt like a tide, buoying her up, so that as Denno stepped to her side, she hardly needed his hand on her elbow to rise to her feet again.

"So let it be written!" Oberon said, his voice filling the Hall.

"So let it be done!" caroled Titania, turning the words into a song.

But Elizabeth had ears only for one voice; for Denno, who whispered with all of his old strength and gaiety, and yet with a new respect she had never expected to hear from him—

"And very well spoken, too, my gracious Faery Queen."